LITTLE HEROES

GLORIANNA O'TOOLE is the Crazy Old Lady of Rock and Roll. She remembers Woodstock and Altamont and Springsteen. Technology put her out to pasture . . . until she's hired to create the first computer-generated rock star.

BOBBY RUBIN, second-generation computer nerd, is a master of the visual synthesizer. Assigned to Glorianna's project, he holds the destiny of a generation in his sweaty little hands.

SALLY GENARO, pudgy, pimply, music synthesizer wizard with the secret heart of the rock star she can never be . . . until via her electronic alter ego, she gets to live her dreams in ways she never imagined.

PACO MONACO is just another hardened streetie punk until he joins the Reality Liberation Front, where he confronts the reality of revolution—and ultimately, himself.

KAREN GOLD is on the run from nouveau poor Poughkeepsie and never looking back. She's rescued from the streets by the Reality Liberation Front. But when she falls for Paco, she gets a bigger dose of reality than she ever thought possible.

MORE RAVES FOR LITTLE HEROES

"Intelligent, well-crafted and gutsy . . . An absorbing and provocative work."

—*LOS ANGELES TIMES BOOK REVIEW*

"An excellent, extrapolative science fiction adventure . . . One of the best books ever written about the soul, or lack thereof, of the music and its merchandisers. . . . Spinrad's heavily stylized rendition of rock in the future is as caustic, cynical and on target as his early gonzo success, *Bug Jack Barron*."

—*THE HOUSTON POST*

"[A] cyber-punk classic." —*THE DETROIT FREE PRESS*

"One of the best books ever about rock and roll."

—*RAVE REVIEWS*

"*Little Heroes* is written with wisdom, human warmth, astonishing insight, sophistication and the master touch. Norman Spinrad is a major literary figure of our time. It's a rare pleasure to read this engaging mind."

—Timothy Leary

"Vintage Spinrad. A novel which mourns the death of rock and roll—and celebrates its rebirth."

—Michael Moorcock

"*Little Heroes* is a magnificent book, and I recommend it highly. . . . Spinrad is trying hard to become the crazy old man of science fiction. And, brother, can he boogie!"

—*Analog*

"*Little Heroes* is a funny, irreverent, sexy and more than slightly off-the-wall novel. It is a welcome return to the blend of science fiction and bizarre social criticism that Norman Spinrad does best."

—*UPI*

OTHER WORKS BY NORMAN SPINRAD

NOVELS
THE SOLARIANS
THE MEN IN THE JUNGLE
AGENT OF CHAOS
BUG JACK BARRON
THE IRON DREAM
RIDING THE TORCH
PASSING THROUGH THE FLAME
THE MIND GAME
A WORLD BETWEEN
SONGS FROM THE STARS
THE VOID CAPTAIN'S TALE
CHILD OF FORTUNE

SHORT STORY COLLECTIONS
THE LAST HURRAH OF THE GOLDEN HORDE
NO DIRECTION HOME
THE STAR SPANGLED FUTURE
OTHER AMERICAS

NON-FICTION
FRAGMENTS OF AMERICA
STAYING ALIVE: A WRITERS' GUIDE

ANTHOLOGIES (EDITOR)
THE NEW TOMORROWS
MODERN SCIENCE FICTION

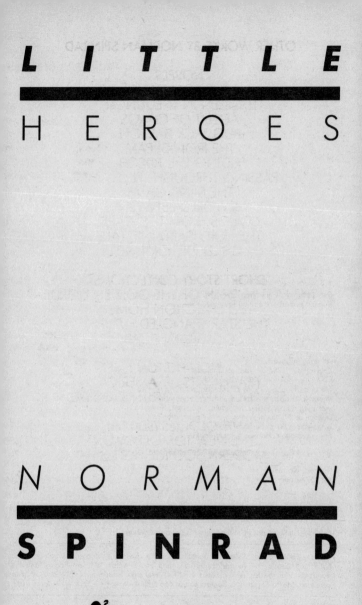

LITTLE HEROES

NORMAN SPINRAD

BANTAM BOOKS TORONTO NEW YORK LONDON SYDNEY AUCKLAND

LITTLE HEROES

A Bantam Spectra Book

Bantam hardcover edition / July 1987
Bantam paperback edition / August 1988

Library of Congress Cataloging-in-Publication Data

Spinrad, Norman.
Little heroes.

I. Title.
PS3569.P55L5 1987 813'.54 86-47911
ISBN 0-553-27033-8

Published simultaneously in the United States and Canada

Bantam Books are published by Bantam Books, a division of Bantam Doubleday Dell Publishing Group, Inc. Its trademark, consisting of the words "Bantam Books" and the portrayal of a rooster, is Registered in U.S. Patent and Trademark Office and in other countries. Marca Registrada. Bantam Books, 666 Fifth Avenue, New York, New York 10103.

PRINTED IN THE UNITED STATES OF AMERICA

O 0 9 8 7 6 5 4 3 2 1

FOR
RICHARD
PINHAS

Transcendentalism is all very fine, but how do you relate all that to what you see on the Subway?

—Dona Sadock

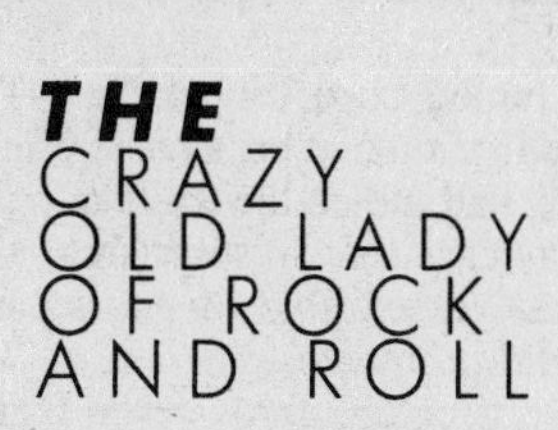

THE CRAZY OLD LADY OF ROCK AND ROLL

Glorianna O'Toole had seen better times and worse.

At the occasional peaks of her long career, she had opened for the likes of Pearl and the Airplane and Springsteen, and had even gotten out two solo albums of her own, though neither had come within a light year of ever shipping gold.

At various karmic nadirs, she had been reduced to dealing acid in the Haight, suffered through a two-year amphetamine jones, and been forced to sing voice-overs in cheap tv commercials.

In between the heights and depths, which is to say most of her forty years as a rock and roll singer, she had done more back-up work on other people's albums than she cared to remember now, had taken an endless succession of tank-town tours of the universe, and while it had taken her a very long time to stop hoping for better, who could say that it had not been one long blast?

Certainly not the self-styled Crazy Old Lady of Rock and Roll as she tooled along the freeway in her monstrous old Rolls-Royce convertible.

She had lucked into a deal on the car as the buyout of his debt on a fucked-up coke deal by a rock star who need be nameless, her sometime lover and never again partner, who had laid it on her as a basket case. Over the years, with this and that score, she had used her charms to have it lovingly restored at cut-rate prices by the best in the business. It hadn't even started out as a convertible. That had been done as a surprise birthday present by Sam Perry to get her over her case of the over-thirty-five blues. Replacing all the metalwork with solid brass she had done slowly over the years at her own expense. The free paint job must have cost her thousands in retouching over the past ten years, but who could slap a new coat of lacquer over such a work of art?

One mad afternoon, she had turned on a trio of New York graffiti artists to mescaline for the first time at her Laurel Canyon tree house. Within two hours, they had turned the Rolls into their pièce de résistance with their spray cans, not so surprising, since in those days one of those dudes was capable of putting up a throw on a whole subway car in thirty minutes.

But Glorianna's Rolls had been a unique throw even then, a fitting memorial to the lost art, for there, under the shade of the eucalyptus, looking out over Los Angeles to the Pacific on a clear mescaline-blue day, these three refugees from Manhattan had been moved to create what may have been the world's only example of graffiti pastorale, a phantasmagorical stylized arabesque rendering of mountains, and sea, and sunset, of the jeweled cityscape of night and the night city of the stars, all done up in brilliant blues, and forest greens, and neon swirls, and of course with the Hollywood sign rendered in psychedelic gold across both front door panels.

The stereo system, on the other hand, was a much more recent manifestation of her current ectoplasmic means of support. This she had suggested Tod Benjamin lay on her back when he was still president of Muzik, Inc., in return for procuring certain necessary substances for obstreperously sensitive talent.

Glorianna had her scruples about actually dealing dope. Long experience had taught her that the paranoia of dealing was terminally bad for the psyche, and morality insisted that participating in the obscene profiteering that had been going on for the last twenty-five years was karmic poison to the soul. But if she could assist the needy without becoming one of the greedy, well that was her good deed for the day, and it certainly was worth a present from the Factory's A&R budget.

Glorianna had been luscious jailbait when she hit the Haight in sixty-six, a sexy rock and roll queen in her long youth, a red hot mama in the flower of her maturity, and now, with her pipes long since honorably retired, and her looks gone to gray hair and wrinkles, the Crazy Old Lady of Rock and Roll got by on her chutzpah and her connections.

And north of forty years in rock and roll had cushioned her shaky retirement as a singer with plenty of both. Though part of the karmic contract seemed to be that none of them had held her full interest for more than a year or two, a red hot mama of a sometime lead singer who really knew how to boogie had had her pick of lovers well through her fourth decade, and while none of them had stuck as her one and only, more of them than not were still her friends.

And inevitably, since she had met so many of them through the music business, and since all of them had long since reached their mature years, a good many of them were placed where they could assist her in her survival enterprises.

So if Glorianna's golden years were not exactly financially sound, at least she was well set up to boogie through them. The mortgage on the house had long since been paid off, the Rolls she owned outright, she made sure she had more dinner invitations than she could ever accept, she hadn't had to pay for getting loaded in twenty years, she had instant imperious access to the freebie list of every club and concert in the known universe, and so all she really needed money for was gas, clothes, utilities, and metabolic enhancers.

It was by way of obtaining a fresh supply of same that she had deigned to take a meeting with Billy Beldock at the Muzik Factory. For while she loathed just about everything that Muzik, Inc., had done to rock and roll, even the Crazy Old Lady thereof could hardly afford to turn down an offer to talk business from the latest president to pass through the revolving door of the conglomerate monstrosity that had come to so utterly dominate the music business.

Glorianna took the Wilshire exit off the 405, and sailed through the traffic east on Wilshire amid the usual bug-eyed stares a couple of blocks beyond Westwood Boulevard to the Muzik Factory.

This was a twenty-story tower of mirror glass the color of a motorcycle cop's shades. Rainbow glass pillars ran up the four corners to form a false deco pagoda roof at the top supporting the Factory logo—"Muzik" lettered in gold like notes beneath a tie-line. At night, they ran laser beams through the whole thing, so that it reminded Glorianna of some ancient Mafia jukebox in a sleazy Valley bar.

An appropriate corporate image for Muzik, Inc., as far as Glorianna was concerned.

For while no one could accuse Muzik, Inc., of being owned by some petty mob of gangsters from Sicily or yaks from Yokohama, the yaks and the maf could certainly learn something about big league sleaze from the Muzik Factory.

Muzik, Inc., pressed forty-five percent of the videodiscs sold in the United States, and moved the lion's share of them through their own nationally franchised chain of Muzik Stores. They had Muzik clubs in New York, Los Angeles, New Orleans, Chicago, and San Francisco. They had a string of twenty-four-hour music tv stations all across the country hyping their own product. They were to the music business what IBM was to the computer industry or McDonald's still was to greaseburgers, and somehow there was nothing that what was left of the antitrust division of the Justice Department cared to do about it. They were employing people, weren't they?

Glorianna showed her permanent pass, parked in the underground garage, and took the express elevator to the twentieth floor. Even here there was a screen and quad speakers subjecting her to the national satellite feed from MUZIK, some dead-ass plastic max metal thing with a ton of swagger and rubber underwear and a spec sheet for a soul.

Oh yes, Muzik, Inc., had by far the biggest payroll in the music business, for sure they employed more people than they would like. They employed techs to program the production robots in their disc factories, and they employed bartenders, bouncers, waitresses, and assorted flunkies in their clubs, and they employed five vjs and a small team of workers to beam the MUZIK feed to their satellite and maybe a hundred or so others to handle it at the tv stations at the other end.

But mostly they employed the people who turned out this shit.

They didn't employ drummers or keyboard players or guitarists or any other kind of sessions musicians. They employed instead VoxBox wizards who could replace bands, orchestras, and even back-up vocalists, with a keyboard, a vocoder, and a black box full of wizardware.

They employed platoons of shrinks and unemployed former Pentagon psy-war spooks to think up best-selling scenarios for their songhacks and VoxBox mercenaries to turn into lyrics and music, and they employed producers and sound crews to record the audio, and once in a while they even still hired cameramen to shoot some footage their image organ hacks couldn't quite conjure up from raw bits and bytes or stock footage.

And of course Muzik, Inc., was an endless gravy train for pr people, market experts, demographic analysts, disc pluggers, and the "consultants" who were the beneficiaries of their freebies, among them, admittedly, Glorianna herself.

The ubiquitous Muzik motto assaulted her eyes as the elevator doors opened onto the twentieth floor. Even here at the top, the golden letters were emblazoned on the wall directly across from the elevator bank, as if nobody in the Muzik Factory, and especially the head honcho of the moment, had better forget it:

"MUZIK *is* Music!"

Maybe, Glorianna thought sourly, but it sure ain't Rock and Roll!

The head honcho of the current moment, Billy Beldock, sat in the familiar black leather throne in the big corner office with the frazzled look of a man who expected to have it yanked out from under him at any moment.

Glorianna, over the years, had seen many asses perched in the black leather chair behind the big polished gunmetal desk, and over the years they had changed the president's office little.

There were two picture-window walls—one gazing up at the eternal dream of Hollywood, at the houses and condos and villas glitzing and glittering up the hills, the other looking out from on high over the vast smog-shrouded barrio of lowland Los Angeles, where most of the city's people struggled for survival, an endless genteel faevela in full sight of the city on the hill. As if to say to all who entered here, there but for show biz, go *you,* kiddo, no matter how far you've managed to climb, your plug can always be pulled.

There was a wall-sized video screen with the current state-of-the-art decks, and there was a whole wall of miniature yellow videodiscs to remind the current occupant of the gold shipped by his predecessors, just in case he missed the point.

The only possible personal touches were changes of incidental furniture and bric-a-brac, since the sadist who had designed the president's office had cleverly seen to it that there was no blank wall upon which to hang personal artwork.

Billy had filled the place with the sort of horrendous mismatched collection of antique French couches and chairs that decorators used to embellish the waiting rooms of superstar transplant surgeons.

Poor Billy certainly looked uncomfortable in this ultimate motel room of music industry power as he sat there in a two-thousand-dollar powder-blue suit smiling peculiarly at her with his shoulders hunched slightly, as if to say with some embarrassment, "What a long strange trip it's been."

He had been a drummer back in the early seventies when they

were lovers, not a great one, but a real rock and roller, and good enough to keep himself riding around in a Porsche. When sophisticated Drumulators and percussion synthesizers enlisted drummers in the great army of the unemployed, Billy had read the writing on the video screen wall well enough to go with the wizardware rather than go out rockin' with his drum kit. He got hold of one of the early primitive VoxBoxes, went with the enemy, became the producer of some early VoxBox hits, and gained entry to the business end, and now, here he was, at the top of the corporate pyramid, about to have his heart ripped out and sacrificed to the Great God of the Sacred Bottom Line, by the look of him.

"You look as sexy as ever, Glorianna," he said by way of greeting.

"You look like an old man, Billy," Glorianna replied, resting her bones as best she could on the uncomfortable chair in front of the desk.

Actually, as a physical specimen of mature manhood, Billy still really wasn't so bad. He kept his body trim with the best metabolic enhancers, he gardened his luxuriant crop of long silver-gray hair with expensive German scalp fertilizer, and he had the perfect leathery tan of endless weekends in Hawaii and Mexico.

But as John Lennon once observed, one thing you can't hide is when you're crippled inside.

Billy shrugged, and grimaced owlishly at her. From the Crazy Old Lady of Rock and Roll, the president of Muzik, Inc., would take this shit; indeed, he craved it, as Glorianna knew full well. Her attitude was her major stock-in-trade in these dim days with all these poor old rockers who had become the people they had long ago warned themselves about. Oh, yes, they could feel like winners feeling sorry for this poor old broken-down anachronism from their musical prehistory, but some sad part of them needed to know that Glorianna O'Toole still felt sorry for *them*.

"Yeah, well, I'm not going to get very much older in this chair unless I start shipping some AP gold," Billy said frankly. "The stuff just isn't making it big enough, and our stock is down seven points from its fifty-two-week high."

"Maybe there is a God, after all, and maybe he knows how to boogie."

"Aw, come on, Glorianna, you *know* that APs have to be the

future of the industry," Billy whined. "It's too cost-effective not to be inevitable."

"What do you want from me, Billy?" Glorianna asked. "You know how I feel about AP rock stars. It'll never work."

"But it *does* work!" Billy insisted. "I got here proving it, didn't I? We're shipping respectable numbers on Lady Leather and Gay Bruce and the Velvet Cat and even Mucho Muchacho, and nobody outside the industry even believes the rumors that they're APs. I just haven't been able to come up with a big hit, is all. You just don't *want* to believe we can synthesize a major league rock star."

Having long since replaced sessions musicians and back-up singers with VoxBox cyberwizards, Muzik, Inc., had turned their cost-cutting attention to automating out rock stars themselves. They collected big royalties, didn't they? They were egotistical pains in the ass who frequently showed up at recording sessions stoned or not at all. They didn't want to listen to the demographic experts or the marketing department; they wanted the songhacks to turn out material to their own specs. Fuck 'em! Who needed 'em? Let's replace them with Artificial Personalities who we don't have to pay royalties to and who won't give us any prima-donna shit!

The wizardware was certainly there. Journeyman VoxBox players had been synthesizing back-up vocals out of voice programs for years, syncing them to the bass or counterpoint line, so in theory all you had to do was play the synthetic voice track with the instrumental lead, and you had yourself a lead singer. As for the visual persona, APs starred in half the tv commercials made, and you couldn't tell the footage from something shot with a live actor. You gave your image organ player a still photo and he danced it through the bits and bytes, or even created an AP visual out of pure specs if the little nerd insisted on being a cyberpurist.

What was more, Muzik, Inc., had turned hit-making into a *science,* hadn't it? The psychological profiles of the total mass audience had been broken down into fine demographic slices, and the boys in the research department had a trillion kilobytes of words, images, rhythms, chord progressions, and inaudibles keyed into their inner mythic structure. And the marketing department, making full use of the Muzik clubs, and the Muzik Stores, and MUZIK was for sure the Big Green Machine.

So why had Lady Leather and Mucho Muchacho and the

Velvet Cat and the rest of Muzik, Inc.'s, stable of well-crafted AP software never shipped gold or cracked the charts with a megahit?

If this was an arcane mystery to poor Billy and everyone else who had forgotten the obvious, it was crystal-clear to Glorianna O'Toole, and anyone who had to ask was never going to find out.

"That soulless crap is to the real thing as white bread is to pumpernickel," she declared from the bottom of her heart. "It's—"

"I know, I know," Billy sighed, joining her on the chorus.

"It's just not Rock and Roll."

Billy laughed; he reached into a drawer and came out with a dust kit, a silver mirror, a golden straw, a tiny golden switch-blade that he snicked open with a flourish, and a crystal vial of the blue powder. And for a moment he was forty years younger, laying out lines for her in one of the hundreds of motel rooms they had once shared together.

"I haven't become quite that much of an asshole, Glorianna," he said as he cut a pile of the synthetic into hits. "I know what's missing. That's why you're here today."

"It is?" Glorianna said with a sinking feeling, grabbing for the mirror. "Give me some of that designer dust, will you? I've got the feeling somehow that I'm really gonna need it."

She tooted up a line of the tailored blow, so much better than the crude Peruvian extract of her youth and middle years that an old doper like her needn't worry about overtaxing her cheaply enhanced metabolism or developing a jones again in her dotage. Soft on the nose, sweet to the taste, nonaddictive, and a blast of energy to the brain. Just what the geriatrician ordered.

"Look, Glorianna, we've got one of the best young VoxBox players in the business, Sally Genaro. And we got Bobby Rubin, who's the absolute state of the art on the image organ. They've both worked on AP discs before, so we know the wizardware is there, and we know that these kids can make it do anything. . . ."

"Except boogie."

Billy shrugged. He did a line of dust. "So she's a little fat girl from the Valley and he's a second-generation computer nerd," he admitted. He beamed at her falsely. "That's why we want *you*."

"To do what?" Glorianna demanded dubiously, declining another hit with an imperiously upraised palm.

"To *make* them boogie."

"Huh?"

Billy leaned back in his chair and played presidential. "For old times' sake, I'm about to give you the chance of a lifetime," he declared expansively.

"I'll bet you are, Billy," Glorianna said with dripping sarcasm.

"I kid you not, Glorianna, I'm offering you a chance to be a producer. Ten grand a month. Four-month trial period. All you have to do is get these kids to come up with one AP rock star that ships gold two discs in a row and I'll give you a three-year contract."

"Fuck you, Billy," Glorianna said genially.

"Aw, come on, don't bullshit a bullshitter, I know you need the money, but okay, okay, twelve grand a month, that's really as far as I'm going to go."

"You want *me* to produce an AP rock star?" Glorianna said with angry passion. "You want me to take the bullshit cranked out by your songhacks and your marketing department's specs and somehow get two dead-ass cyberwizards to spin it into gold? You want me to collaborate in the creation of a best-selling rock star who exists only as software?"

"You got it," Billy said approvingly. "You'll be in charge. We'll give you sets of specs, and you choose which ones to go with. You can order up whatever you like from whichever songhacks you choose. Do it your way. Give me a viable AP rock star, I don't care how."

"Why me?" Glorianna said, and she found herself up and pacing before she could think about it. "You *know* how I feel about APs, you know how much I hate the whole idea, you know as well as I do that a disc with no soul will never be real rock and roll!"

"Two out of three ain't bad," Billy said.

"What's that supposed to mean?"

Billy Beldock leaned across his desk, pushing the dust kit toward her, and practically purred at her, the way he had the very first night that the sexy young drummer had coaxed her into bed. He even gave her what was left of his bedroom eyes.

"Why you, Glorianna?" he said slyly. "Because you're the Crazy Old Lady of Rock and Roll. Because inside that, ah, mature body, there still beats the heart of a rock and roll queen. Your voice is gone, and you hardly ever wrote your own material, and you can't play the VoxBox or the image organ, but what you've got left is all that we need to complete the equation, the soul without which, as you say, no disc can ever really be rock and roll."

"What a line of bullshit," Glorianna scoffed. But she sat down and tooted another line of free dust as Billy Beldock spun out his temptation.

"Look at it this way, Glorianna, you'd be falling all over me in gratitude if I was offering to let you take a band and some songwriters and a raw lead singer with technical virtuosity and try to turn them into the Beatles or the Rolling Stones at our expense even if I wasn't paying you twelve thou a month for the privilege; can you deny that with a straight face?"

Before she could answer, he had snorted another line, and was off and running again. "So what's the difference? Like the man says, it's not the singer, it's the song, right, so if a disc needs soul to ship gold, then if it ships gold, it's real rock and roll, and what's the difference between a live lead singer and a wizard piece of software when you pop it in your disc deck? Either way, all you really see or hear is a digital playback."

"Even if it were possible, even if I could really do it, it would be wrong, Billy," Glorianna said quite earnestly.

"Would you mind explaining why?" Billy said smugly.

"Because . . . because . . ." She threw up her hands. "Because you fucking can't make real music without a single real musician! Jesus H. Christ, Billy!"

"For sure!" Billy Beldock agreed. "But don't you see—that's you!"

"Me? I don't write lyrics, I don't write music, I can't play anything, and my voice is shot! I don't have any way to make music anymore, goddammit!"

"Wouldn't you like to?"

"Wouldn't I like to *what*?"

"If we conjure up Mucho Muchacho or the Velvet Cat out of nothing but chips, programming, and data base, we can sure as shit do *you,* Glorianna," Billy cooed. "Think of it, your cyborged comeback at the age of sixty-three! We could take your cracked old voice and run it through vocoders that will make it better than young again, better than you or anyone else ever was back when you were never quite good enough to have a real career as a recording artist. We could lay down visual tracks in which you'll be what you were in the sixties, young and beautiful, and solarized forever. You just do the best you can and our wizards will cyborg you into a superstar. Wouldn't *that* be real rock and roll?''

''Fuck a duck. . . .'' Glorianna whispered softly. ''You really could do that, couldn't you?''

The president of Muzik, Inc., just smiled a shit-eating smile. ''You squeeze an AP rock star that ships gold two discs in a row out of my little cyberwizards, and we do you next,'' he said.

Glorianna snorted a line up her left nostril. ''Do I have to sign a contract in blood?'' she asked, and took another up the right.

''I gather I've made you an offer you can't refuse?'' Billy Beldock said.

Glorianna's brain was working in overdrive now. Sure, giving Muzik, Inc., what they thought they wanted would seem to be treason to the spirit of everything she had ever been or believed in.

Nevertheless, she felt that long-remembered spirit moving through her now like the music of a braver and grander age waiting to be reborn through her frail and age-drained body and wizardware circuitry.

Because if by some miracle she succeeded, if she could somehow fulfill her end of the bargain with the corporate powers, why then the assholes would get far more than they had ever bargained for. They would get themselves the Glorianna O'Toole that had never existed except in her heart of hearts.

For forty years and more, her one great dream had been to become, if only for one shining hour, the great voice of that spirit which had now all but vanished from the world. And if it was given to her to become at this late date, through the machineries of the enemy, the reigning queen of rock and roll she had never in her youth quite been, why then real rock and roll might yet be reborn, and with a vengeance that the powers that be would not like at all.

Because real rock and roll was music that kicked their kind of ass.

And for the chance to do that great deed this close to the end of her road, she would indeed have signed on the dotted line with Satan.

''Billy, my love,'' she told the president of Muzik, Inc., almost gaily, ''you've made me an offer that you can't understand.''

PACO MONACO, MUCHO MUCHACHO

Nada, man, zip! Paco Monaco had scored nothing in the past eight days—no dinero, no chocha, no wire, and now the wan October sun was oozing down the flinty gray sky over East Fourteenth Street, and it was La Hora Frontera of another wasted day.

You're getting too old for this shit, muchacho, Paco told himself once more. La Hora Frontera did this to him lately, he hated this twilight time between day and night in his bones, even as the gordos feared it in their tight white culos, if not for quite the same reason.

One by one the lights behind the windows of the Stuyvesant Town co-op towers on the north side of the street were coming on as the hordes of the gainfully employed sidled nervously past him into the safety of their nighttime holes. The zonies guarding the open gate in the high electrified barbed-wire fence paced in paranoid little circles stroking their Uzis, and then the mercury vapor spots snapped on, searing the cracked gray pavement with cruel television-blue light.

Without conscious thought, Paco found himself dashing reflexively across the gutter to the sombre side of the street like a roach scuttling into the shadowland beneath the sink after the kitchen light came on.

He stood there with an empty street-bag in the shadows by the stoop of a burnt-out building staring across the Line at the ancient redbrick apartment houses and cursed himself for the pettiness of his longings.

For he was still haunted by the faded early childhood memories of a life inside the walls of a project not that much unlike this one, over on Avenue D, when he, and his mother, and his two sisters, and two teenaged uncles had lived in the two-bedroom apartment of his abuelos. Memories of hot stuffy steam-heated winters and sweaty stinking summers, of rancid cooking odors, and farts, and toilet sounds, and the cries and grunts of fucking.

There had been real food daily in those long-lost days; chicken hearts with spicy rice, cuchifritos, eggs, Coca-Cola, bread, and cheese, and even the occasional ice cream.

Hijito, those were the days, his mother had never stopped telling him, after Abuelo Gutierrez had lost his job in the garment center, after the Devaluation, after the welfare checks dwindled away to a daily ration of kibble, when she staggered back, stinking of wine and cum, to whatever shithole they happened to be squatting in after a long night of hooking.

And then one morning when he was maybe fourteen, she just never came back, ODed, knifed in an alley, busted, quien sabe, and chingada, here he was seven years later, wishing he were what, some pale white gordo with a shit-ass job pushing a rack in the garment district or sweeping the floor of Macy's, with a quarter share in one of these two-bedroom co-ops, and a fat momacita he was too tired to fuck?

"Chingada, man, you just need some wire," he muttered aloud to himself as he turned on his heel, kicking a paper Coke cup to vent his ire, and headed west along the sombre side of Fourteenth.

But the thing of it was that wire required dinero, and he had been Ciudad Nada for eight days now, and there were only two ways he knew to score.

He could head over to West Street or someplace even worse and sell his dick or his culo to some disgusting old maricón, which he had not had the stomach to do since he turned sixteen, or he could cruise Round the Corner and hope to catch some stupid gordo too stoned to know when he crossed over the Line.

Of course that was just what he had been doing for these past eight days, but mostly up in midtown, where the Line between sombre and sol was clearly drawn by the city cops, and the gordos scurried around in hordes for safety like cucarachas, and Round every Corner lurked little gangs of streeties with a muy malo attitude about solos poaching their turf.

Verdad, during the nine-to-five, the gordos ruled Ciudad Trabajo, the world of gleaming glass canyons in mirror shades, of crumbling loft-factory buildings watched over by hard-eyed zonies, and natch at night, the vecino was deserted by prey and predators alike. When the sun went down, the plushie-tushies retreated in cabs and limos to the Zones—Upper West, Sutton, Lincoln Center, Park Plaza, Soho, 'Beca—where it was all town houses, glitz palaces, fancy restaurants, floodlights, and whole armies of zonies with a license to blow you away just for showing your brown-skinned face.

And the gordos, by their sweaty little millions, stuffed themselves into the subway for the ride home to their half-a-room share in a co-op; even now Paco felt the rumble of an IRT in the soles of his feet, and oh, yes, it was tempting to think of all those assholes with money in their pockets passing right beneath him in the subterraneo!

But no one with the street smarts to survive in N'York for ten minutes was dumb enough to try a crash and grab in El Sub. If the transit cops didn't frag your ass—or write you a long ticket to Rikers if they were feeling mellow—fifty-seven vigilantes would fill you full of holes. Even ancient abuelas packed .357s in El Sub. Or streeties themselves would carve you into cuchifritos, for the same reason you wouldn't win any popularity contest by *shitting* where they slept, either.

Between Halloween and Easter, a million streeties would probably freeze to death if the city chose to clear El Sub at night by pumping through tear gas, which they did now and again when it threatened to become too much of a combat zone for the gordos to ride to Ciudad Trabajo. Every streetie knew that the plushie-tushies were more than willing to watch a million of them turn to corpsicles in the gray winter slush before they would let it come to that.

The sun was just about down by the time Paco reached the corner of Fourteenth and Avenue A, and, as it usually did, his black funk began to dissolve as La Hora Frontera faded into Noche Nuestra. For as surely as the day belonged to the gordos and the plushie-tushies, with their nine-to-fives, and their dinero, and their zonies, so did the night belong to el pueblo sombre, to the people of the streets, to fist and knife, to shadow and cojones, at least here, just Round the Corner from both Boho and Tompkins Square Park.

The park itself was an oasis of grass and benches well-lit by the golden globes of phony antique streetlamps and patrolled by plainclothes zonies. There were town houses along its Tenth Street side and fancy co-ops along Avenue A and Sixth. Farther west, up and down First and Second Avenues, were the main-drag midways of Boho, aka the East Village, chockablock with bars, restaurants, galleries, boutiques, and gourmet bodegas. The glitz promenaded eastward to Tompkins Square across St. Marks and Sixth Street, but half the turf bordered by Second Avenue and Avenue C, by Fourteenth and Houston, had been left Round the Corner on the sombre side of the street.

Because the gordos and the plushie-tushies who favored this turf were assholes who actually *wanted it* that way; pervos and dopers, artsy-farts and wire-chippers, who *got off* on skirting the sombre, on slumming it in luxury, on the adrenaline rush of knowing what lurked in the shadows for the unstreetwise, on being able to score wire and meat just Round the Corner from their well-armored front doors.

They didn't want any city cops here, oh no, muchacho, and they had the dinero to grease them away, and the zonies they hired were wireheads and junkies, sometimes even streeties with ambition, and they dealt wire and dope and meat on the side. They let you wander up and down the midways as long as you didn't look like you were ready to crash and grab or deal on their turf, and Tompkins Square Park was a primo mercado, where the gordos and plushie-tushies could bump bellies with tu putamadre, and score cheap snorts and overpriced wire likely as not to fry their brains.

Paco despised these cabrones with a brainburning hard-on of contempt and envy, and yet he was drawn to this vecino as he was to the wire, and indeed, the charge that he got on these streets and the flash of plugging in to the Prong were from a certain angle one and the same.

Plugged in to the Prong, with his dick hard and hot as an electrified switchblade, and every muscle of his body as taut and twanging as oiled spring steel, and a primo Mucho Muchacho disc blasting max metal into his ears, and Mucho himself leering and dancing and singing to the hunger of his soul, ah, he was no longer Hernan Gutierrez, the cockroach son of his putamadre, but Paco Monaco, muy macho muchacho, ready, able, and more than willing to fuck the world of the gordos up its tight white culo!

So too, out here just Round the Corner from the cockteasing world of look but don't touch, from these chocharicas in their slick silver leather jeans wiggling past him with their little noses in the air, from these pasty white maricónes with their pockets full of dinero and their pants full of shriveled cojones, did he feel his street-hard muscles taut against his skin, his cock bulging against the zipper of his dirty pants, his brain burning with the streetwise knowledge that one wrong move, one false step Round the wrong Corner, and any one of these soft creatures would find themselves on the sombre side for real, would meet the bruising for which they were cruising, Paco Monaco, the true machó man.

Bouncing on the balls of feet now, flashing challenging sneers at the men and lip-sucking kisses at their women, both of which were studiously ignored, Paco turned west off crowded Avenue A onto Ninth Street, a narrow shadowy block of renovated five-story tenements with few shops and many garbage can storage areas below street level under the stoops. Seeing that the block was for the moment deserted, he ducked into the nearest of these alcoves and hunkered there in the dark, with his back against a garbage can and his eyes level with the pavement, and waited.

The buildings on this block had for the most part been converted into the sort of co-op apartments inhabited by young wage-slave migrants from Cleveland or Long Island who were willing to fork over two-thirds of their salaries to cram themselves three or four to a two-bedroom for the privilege of living where the action was. Meaning, first, that the gordos on this block couldn't afford their own zonies, and second, that they sometimes staggered home alone and loaded from some meatrack or singles bar over on First or Second after striking out with the muchachas.

Paco squatted there in the darkness below the sidewalk for what began to seem like several hours as gordos drifted by in groups of three or four or five, jabbering to each other, entering buildings across the street, passing joints, sniffing dust from aluminum bullets, out of reach, and indifferently unaware of who crouched impatiently waiting to pounce just Round the Corner beneath their feet.

His ankles were getting numb, his patience was getting mighty thin, and he was thinking of packing it in and trying elsewhere, when the sound of a single set of footfalls coming up the sidewalk toward him on his side of the street gave hope that his long streak of mala suerte might be about to change.

He rose to a standing crouch, wriggling the numbness out of his feet, as he saw his prey approaching, lookin' good! A young dude in fancy blue leather pants, trendy gunmetal boots, and a white linen jacket, long curly black hair, slimly built, and at about five eight, giving away about three inches to Paco. Though the gordo's face was hidden from this angle, he was walking a little loose around the knees, seemed a little loaded.

Buena suerte! Paco thought as the dull metallic boots of his victim came even with his eyes. This maricón for sure I can handle!

Still crouched in shadow, Paco tiptoed to the front of the garbage can pit and grabbed hold of both ankles. Before the asshole even had time to scream, he yanked with all of his strength, pulled him down into the darkness, let go, socked him in the kidneys, flipped him around by the left arm as he fell to the concrete, came down on the dude's chest with one knee, got him in the cojones with the other, clamped his left hand around his Adam's apple, choking off his wind, and cocked his right fist back about two feet from his face.

"One sound, motherfucker, and I break your motherfucking face!" he snarled, pressuring his knee into the gordo's cojones for emphasis.

"Q-q-qué pasa . . . ?"

Paco looked down at the bug-eyed, choking face of his terrified victim. And instead of some pasty-faced gordo, he saw a brown-skinned, dark-eyed muchacho not that much older than himself, with a pencil-line moustache and a thin little puberda goatee.

He froze for a moment as he locked eyes with this unsettling mirror-image of himself as he might have been, wearing a thousand dollars' worth of clothes, and playing macho man with the rica gorda chochas in the fancy make-out bars on Second Avenue. He hated this slick little Blankriqueno would-be gordo with a sudden blood-burning passion. But he also envied this motherfucker with a sickening longing, and what was worse, he couldn't keep himself from knowing it. Nor could he keep down the shameful feeling that he was betraying something he could not quite fathom.

"Tu dinero, puberda shithead, what the fuck you think I want, chingar tu culo?" he hissed.

"Hey, amigo—"

"No amigo me, maricón motherfucker!" Paco said, squeezing the throat harder in stomach-twisting fury. "Ponga tu dinero, or I rip your prick off, hijo de gorda puta!"

A look passed between them then, a wounded yet superior contempt behind the very real fear in the eyes of his victim, a guilty acknowledgment of that truth in the eyes of Paco. Then, without looking away, without breaking that accusatory stare, the arrogant little son of a bitch reached into his pocket and pulled out his wallet.

Paco snatched it up with his free hand and fumbled free a thin sheaf of bills.

"That's all you got, man?" he complained.

"No soy gordo rico, hermano. Por favor, let me keep mi plastico, you can't use it, and it'll be a motherfucker convincing the man I'm not running no number. Tu sabes que pasa, amigo?"

Paco's grip loosened. "I don't want your fuckin' credit cards!" he said, flinging the wallet as far as he could across the street, where it would take this . . . this Blankriqueno scumbag a good long time to find it.

"You fucking well stay right here until I turn the corner . . . *amigo*," he said. "Tu sabes what's good for you?"

Then he leapt up and let go the dude's throat in one motion, dashed up onto the sidewalk, broke into a run, and didn't look back or pause to count the money until he had rounded the corner of Avenue A, crossed over, and faded into the street traffic, Round the Corner in plain sight, just one more faceless streetie who none of the gordos among whom he now ambled would care to even lock eyes with.

Only then did he read the score and get the malticia.

A twenty, a ten, and two fives! Chingada!

That cheapo little motherfucker with his three-hundred-dollar boots and his wallet of plastico had only forty bucks of real money in his pocket! No wonder all the sincojones son of a bitch was worried about was his credit cards! No wonder he had been such a pussy when it came to coughing up his cash!

"You're getting too old for this shit, muchacho!" Paco muttered loudly as a gordo couple who had been walking up the street past him took a sudden jog into the gutter and looked away.

In his own ears, his complaint had levels of meaning whose complexities were far beyond his ability to fathom, but whose streetwise gut feelings did a switchblade stompada in the pit of his stomach. Somehow, his anger at the slim proceeds was only a two-step around the incomprehensible pain of a far deeper and more elusive fury.

Somehow he had been made to feel like a cockroach on a shitpile, yet somehow he also felt a contemptuous superiority to the Blankriquenos of the world in his heart of hearts. But what was worse, he also somehow felt deeply ashamed, for he knew not what, and that incomprehensible feeling of self-loathing was what filled him with such a passionate hatred for an enemy who seemed nonexistent.

Paco stared with curled lip at the slim sheaf of bills between his fingers and rubbed them disdainfully, as if they were smeared with old snot. For a wild moment he almost tossed them into the gutter.

But the sheer shock of such an asshole thought moving through his mind brought him to his senses. Eight days of nada, and you have to hit on some stupid spick like yourself with ninguno dinero! You got a right to be pissed off at yourself, muchacho, he told himself, but that don't mean you gotta throw away enough money to buy half an hour of the Prong!

Chingada, man, you felt like this before, and this time you've got what it takes to buy the cure. Look on the sol side, hombre, you got enough money off the maricón to plug into some wire and feel like Mucho Muchacho!

Dojo was on the door at Slimy Mary's when Paco arrived, and appeared less than overjoyed to see him. "I thought I told you I didn't want to see your face unless you had the yen to imitate a paying customer, my man," Dojo said by way of greeting, folding his big arms across his chest and barring the door with his war-machine body. "You plannin' to do anything inside except cruise for free pussy?"

Paco liked Dojo, despite the fact that the big black bastard generally treated him like cockroach shit. He knew it was nothing personal. Dojo treated everyone like cockroach shit, as befitted his exalted position and the necessity of his role as jefe of a meatrack where crash and grabbers, street meat, and burned-out wireheads came to score perv and wire. It took mucho macho, muchacho, to work the door at Slimy Mary's!

"Gonna plug into the Prong, Dojo," Paco said proudly, pulling the sheaf of bills out of his pocket and waving it under the doorman's nose. "Got enough for half an hour on the wire."

"What you do, suck some cheap faggot's cock?" Dojo said with a narrow-eyed sneer and easy attitude which was as close as he ever came to granting approval.

"Naw, all I had to do was let this cheap black nigger suck mine," Paco told him, grabbing his crotch and leering.

Dojo laughed. "Got to admit you got balls, boy," he said. "Too bad they're located where your brains are supposed to be."

He stepped aside, shaking his head. "Go on in and fry what little you got left with that wirehead shit," he said.

Although he made mucho dinero off all the wire action inside, Dojo loftily disdained wire himself. Nothing but classic coke or designer dust for him; it was part of his mystique.

As Paco marched by him, Dojo caught him by the elbow, leaned close, and spoke to him in confidential tones. "How much balls you really got, my man, I mean seeing as how you mean to plug in anyway, how'd you like a special deal on something real wizard . . . ?"

"Real wizard . . . ? What's the flash?"

"Well, that's the thing of it, son, no one here's ever seen the Zap before, it's the latest thing from Silicon City, they say it's made by the same dudes that make the red boxes the video pirates use to take over broadcast satellites. Makes the Prong and that shit seem like sticking your dick in a light socket."

Paco eyed Dojo dubiously. "What you're talking about is some piece of shit from out of town that no one you know has plugged into before, motherfucker," he said. "Something could fry me to cuchifritos."

Dojo beamed at him. "You're not as stupid as you look, bo. That's the only reason I'm willing to let you have half an hour on the Zap for the same thirty bucks as half an hour on the Prong. Two weeks from now, the price triples."

"Unless it turns out to be another brainburner and you can't give it away."

Dojo shrugged. "If you don't have the balls to try it . . ."

"Who's dealing this Zap for you?" Paco shot back.

"Monkey Girl. Just tell her Dojo sent you."

Slimy Mary's occupied the basement of what appeared to be an abandoned formerly renovated tenement on Third just off Avenue D. The word on the floor was that Dojo and his yak compadres had captive wire wizards up there in the dark behind the boarded-up windows, permanently plugged in to their own products, and turning out merchandise just for the juice. Up

There was where old wireheads went to Florida, muchacho, and anyone who got too curious was likely to end up the same.

The meatrack itself was typical of such streetie oases, burrowed into basements beneath ruined buildings without obvious full-time squats visible from the street, and running on juice from jumpers that the Con Ed cops were greased to ignore.

Down a dark flight of metal stairs, and Paco was suddenly in another world, the closest thing he knew to home turf.

Only the dance floor was lit, and that by dim red, white, and blue bulbs set in the aluminum-foil-covered ceiling, and flashing on and off in a cheaply randomized sequence. On three sides the dance floor was surrounded by a twilight zone of dirty old cushions, orange crates, and spavined stuffing-burst couches, where the clientele sprawled—plugged in, burnt-out, hustling each other's meat, or taking care of light business. The walls of the big basement were out there somewhere in the musty darkness beyond the clearing, where the fucking and the heavy dealing took place, where those who could not bear the light shared the shadows with the roaches and ratones.

There were about a dozen people on the floor at this hour, all dancing to the tune of their own fading flash, but all of them moving to the max metal beat of the Lady Leather disc playing on the big screen behind them.

Eat my big black whip
You dirty little dip
Shove it up your hole
Suck my leather soul
The whip! The whip!
Trip to the whip!

Up on the videowall, Lady Leather, wearing gunmetal jackboots and skin-tight black leather from neck to knees, cracked her two long whips to the beat, snarling and spitting and strutting like a crazed stormtrooper on a carpet of writhing pink bodies, while behind her was a big close-up of her own face, lip-syncing the lyric in the innocent bliss of an endless orgasm.

Paco couldn't see why anyone would pay to play this shit, and, in fact, he saw, no one was; el Lizardo's disc deck was idle, this was just the usual caga being broadcast by MUZIK, which el Lizardo tortured the meatrack with when he had no paying customers.

Paco wanted some Mucho Muchacho, but it cost ten dollars a pop to have el Lizardo play your disc, so he knew he had better save it for later, since by the time he bought himself half an hour of wire, he would have only enough dinero left for one five-minute number.

So he hung back in the sombre zone until his eyes adjusted to the murk and he spotted Monkey Girl hunkered on a cushion deep in the shadowy darkness.

Monkey Girl wore an IBM T-shirt and a formless skirt of crud-smeared burlap. Her hair was a greasy black mess. Her face, skeletal, lined, and leather-dry, might have been that of some souvenir shrunken head were it not for the perpetual grin of happiness on her cracked lips, and the monkey-bright eyes, which stared right through you out of those deep and blackened sockets.

She wore a crown of wire, a crude helmet of sheet-steel strips studded with chips and bits of breadboard. A long umbilical of power cord trailed away to some hidden wall socket from the stepdown transformer on the top of her head.

Monkey Girl's flash was the Blue Max. Contact electrodes pumped amplified alpha waves into her cerebrum, and by now only bits and pieces were at home. You didn't last too long permanently plugged in to the Blue Max, but no one could say you didn't go out with a smile.

"Dojo sent me," Paco said, squatting down on the floor in front of her. "Made me a deal on the Zap. Thirty for media hora."

"Wanna tap the Zap . . ." Monkey Girl babbled in a skittery-skattery voice, fixing her big dark eyes right at him, but giving Paco the feeling she was seeing something else. She reached down and came up with a piece of wire unlike anything Paco had ever seen.

There was hardly anything to it, just a crumpled spiderweb of very thin flexible metal threads attached to a flat and concavely curved round breadbox about the diameter of a beer can bottom.

"Qué pasa?" he demanded dubiously as Monkey Girl held the thing under his nose with one hand and held out her palm for the dinero with the other. "Where the fuck's the power cord? This some nojuice piece of shit?"

Any piece of wire worth anything, let alone thirty dollars a half hour, had to plug into a wall socket. Every low current battery-powered piece he had ever tried had been a bullshit ripoff that failed to flash, shit gordo kiddos conned each other with outside fancy schoolyards. Every real wirehead knew that nojuice pieces were for asshole wirechippers who didn't know the difference because they didn't even know what a real flash was.

"The Zap don't flash, you get back the cash," Monkey Girl burbled. "Science flashes pretty out of Silicon City!"

Well chingada, muchacho, if that was the deal, there was nothing to lose, he had never heard of anyone offering money back for a no flash before, and if the likes of *Dojo* were willing to back this new piece with his own dinero, he *must really believe* that this was real wizard from some Silicon City spook shop, not cabezacaga wired together by the brainburned zombies upstairs.

He handed over the thirty dollars and took the strange piece of wire. Shaking it out, he saw that it was a wirework helmet shaped to the head, a form-fitting hairnet, really. The breadbox had a single green touchpoint, and a sliding battery compartment lid, aside from which it was a featureless sealed can. When he put the thing on, he couldn't even feel the wire mesh; all he could feel was how the bottom curve of the breadbox fitted comfortably to the curve of the upper back of his head. Something about all this was beginning to convince him that he really was about to score a real wizard flash.

Pero primero, let's have some Mucho Muchacho instead of this gordo pervo shit MUZIK keeps playing. He snake-danced through the dancers on the floor to the table at the side of the screen, behind which el Lizardo sat, ensconced behind his disc decks, and surrounded by untidy mounds of videodiscs piled waist-high around him on the floor.

El Lizardo was a sallow-skinned stony figure in black denim jeans and a McDonald's T-shirt he wore backward with a crude green tyrannosaur head painted onto it. The teeth were bits of old razor blades epoxied to the cloth. His hair was lacquered into a green ridge of dinosaur scales up over his shaved head. No one had ever seen the eyes behind those gleaming black mirror shades.

"Hey Lizardo, why you playing this shit?" Paco demanded. It was everyone's standard greeting to el Lizardo.

MUZIK went to a commercial now. Foxy Lady, a black momacita wearing a well-torn tie-dyed T-shirt and clean white jockey shorts, was shaking her thing in front of a huge concert audience which moaned like it was coming, and blasting out

"Down and Dirty Tonight," while the title of the disc flashed a pink neon strobe over her, and a sexy voice just at the edge of audibility sighed "Buy, buy, buy."

"Because pinheads like you are too cheap to put their money where their mouth is," el Lizardo said in his flat voice. It was his standard comeback.

"Let's have 'Tu Madre También.' "

El Lizardo began rummaging through his discs. "I can stand it if you can," he said, favoring Paco with his horrid grin as he snatched his money, peeling open his thick rubbery lips to reveal a mouthful of teeth that had been filed to points and painted black.

Paco faded away across the dance floor into the twilight zone as el Lizardo popped "Tu Madre También" into the videodisc deck. "Saludo amigo," he whispered into the dark as Mucho Muchacho exploded onto the screen to a rhythmic blare of air horns and a heavy beat of drums and stomping feet, screaming out the beat line with the multiplexed voice of an angry army.

Tu ma-dre TAMBIÉN
Tu ma-dre TAMBIÉN
Tu ma-dre TAMBIÉN

Mucho Muchacho, naked to the waist, had the leanly muscular body of a martial arts fanatic, and his bronzed hairless upper torso was filmed with oil and smudged here and there with black ash. He wore clean white and skin-tight cut-off jeans that outlined the bulge of a superhuman cock and were belted by a gunmetal chain. His feet were bare, and the only adornment of his true nobility was his great crown of hair, a central red mohawk serpent arising out of a jet black helmet of close-cropped fuzz.

Beneath this culebra de machismo, Mucho Muchacho's big brown bedroom eyes were almost angelic, but his nose and the chiseled angles of his dark brown face were mercilessly Aztec, and his mouth writhed its defiance around his perfect white teeth as he proclaimed the lyric over the insistent beat line.

Somos cholos in the night
(Tu ma-dre TAMBIÉN)
Con color and you are white
(Tu ma-dre TAMBIÉN)

So besa me pica
(Tu ma-dre TAMBIÉN)
And ponga me your sister
(Tu ma-dre TAMBIÉN)
Better call me Mister
Y TU MADRE TAMBIÉN!

Paco's feet danced in place in the darkness to the razor-sharp rhythm, the bones of his body thrummed to unheard subsonics as he leaned slightly forward like a warrior on a stalk. His dick began to throb, and all the shit of the world outside seemed to slough off his skin as Mucho Muchacho sung him the secret marching music of his soul.

Mucho danced, pelvis outthrust, through a vast suburban shopping mall, up Fifth Avenue, in front of the White House, through a crowded restaurant filled with old men in black tuxedos and beautiful blond women in evening gowns, jewels, and furs, and through an endless suite of offices where tight-bodied bitches in skin-tight gray business suits sat chained to computer consoles. Behind him paraded a vast tide of rag-clad muchachos just like Paco, roaring the mighty chorus with Mucho Muchacho's multiplexed voice as the chochas went wild in their wake, tearing off their clothes, shaking their tits, and breaking into a sweaty mating dance.

Nosotros somos gigantes
(Tu ma-dre TAMBIÉN)
Cojones de elefantes
(Tu ma-dre TAMBIÉN)
So pull down all your panties
Y TU MADRE TAMBIÉN!

As Mucho Muchacho's face snapped into full close-up, eyes peering straight into his soul as two subsonic vocodor vocals doubled on the lyric and beat line and the guitar tracks screamed toward redline, Paco's hand went to the breadbox on the back of his head and hit the touchpoint.

At first, there seemed to be no flash at all, not even the generalized greasy tingling of juice going through his head. Mucho Muchacho danced a stompada at the head of his army of streeties now, pumping his fisted right arm up and down to the beat like a throbbing hard-on, and sang more insinuatingly, his voice furred into an enormous lubricious lion purr.

Your sisters and your aunties
(Tu ma-dre TAMBIÉN)
Chocharicas elegantes
(Tu ma-dre TAMBIÉN)
Don't want no gay romantics
(Tu ma-dre TAMBIÉN)

And then, somehow, Paco suddenly seemed to have melted, dreamlike, out of his body and into the screen, or somehow Mucho Muchacho had emerged from the screen to don his body like a skinsuit, for it was Paco Monaco, Mucho Muchacho, who found the song pouring forth from his lips, who found his taut, muscular, well-fed body prancing and preening in an endless adoring mob of beautiful women of all ages, dripping with fur, and jewels, and silk, and throwing money at him as they danced around him, legs a-spraddle.

They all want macho mucho
(Tu ma-dre TAMBIÉN)
Mucho Muchacho
(Tu ma-dre TAMBIÉN)
So get out there and hustle
(Tu ma-dre TAMBIÉN)

He knew himself to be Paco Monaco, hijo de puta, existing on the meager ration of people kibble doled out at the dispensaries, crashing in subways or burnt-out buildings, sneered at by the fucking chocharicas on the streets and their rich gordo maricónes, who hadn't gotten laid in two weeks. And yet just as surely, he knew himself to be Mucho Muchacho, the max in streetwise macho, who had the chocharicas of the world which despised him on their knees before him in the puberda truth between their sleek sweaty legs.

Use your mojo muscle
(Tu ma-dre TAMBIÉN)
Get it while you can
(Tu ma-dre TAMBIÉN)
From a red hot macho man

(Tu ma-dre TAMBIÉN)
We all remember when
Y TU MADRE TAMBIÉN!

He had come home to the Mucho Muchacho he had always known himself to be, as if every Mucho Muchacho cut he had ever heard had just been his own secret macho man talking to him in his sleep. And now he had awakened to his full unfettered glory.

He might have spent his life scrabbling around for survival on a shitpile, he might be nothing but a streetscum little spick in the blind eyes of the patrónes cabrónes of Ciudad Trabajo, but he was the cocko de la calle between the legs of their virgin sisters and esposas putaricas, y tu madre también!

And when the disc ended, he was *still* Mucho Muchacho, moving out into the blinking multicolored lights of the dance floor with animal grace and the sure steel certainty that he had the world by the chocha, and all he had to do was fuck it.

Verdad, the garden of flesh had melted into the dance floor of Slimy Mary's, but a Slimy Mary's transformed and a Paco transformed, for the flickering waves of multicolored light were flashing from his skin, and there before him moving to the throbbing beat of the blood in his loins was the woman of his wettest dreams.

Somewhere in his dreamtime, he had known her all his life. She was elegantly slim through the legs and waist, with the ass of a jogger, and tits like soft ripe guavas, the nipples hard and brown as walnuts through the sheer fabric of her tight white evening gown. Her long blond hair fell over the silvery fur stole flung around her pale bare shoulders. Her hands were encrusted with diamond rings, and her long neck was draped with a dozen thin gold chains. Her eyes were icy blue with the arrogance of a thousand years of steel-snatched transactions with the limp-dick patrónes of Ciudad Trabajo, but the serpentine tongue licking her moist red lips told him that she would turn into a mindless sex-crazed animal just for him.

He strutted across the dance floor toward her to the jungle rhythm of some afrometal shit MUZIK was playing, but somehow that didn't matter, somehow it segued into "Tu Madre También" in his ears after a few bars, and somehow he wasn't in Slimy Mary's anymore.

Instead, he was dancing in some fantastic plushie-tushie disco high atop the towers of Ciudad Trabajo, with invisible glass walls open to a brilliant starry night and to the jeweled city spread before him far beneath his feet. Men in black tuxedos and tall elegantly dressed blond women were gliding in languorous boredom around the floor to a dead-ass black dance band in evening clothes.

But Mucho Muchacho moved to his own music, and as he danced his chingada stompada, the patrónes quivered and cowered and seemed to age ten years into white-haired balding old men as their cool blond women began to shake their things to *Paco's* beat, began to writhe, and grimace, and blow kisses at him holding their crotches, in their mad lust for the superhuman machismo of his perfect body.

He ignored these begging bitches with lordly disdain, and danced up to the perfect creature of his dreams, pelvis outthrust, his gigantic hard cock literally bursting from his tight white pants, engorged with outrageous certainty.

"You," he said, clutching his cojones and beaming at her. "I want to fuck your brains out."

Her ice-blue eyes snapped wide open in disbelief of her fantastic good fortune. "Me?" she exclaimed. "You want to fuck *me*?"

"You want my big hard dick up your chocharica," he told her evenly, hypnotizing her with his pitiless Mucho Muchacho stare. "You want to know what it's like to have a real macho man giving you what you know you need."

"You *really* want to fuck *me*?" she said, dancing closer to him, wriggling her chocha inches from his pelvis.

"Best you'll ever get, momacita," he told her with a proud lion grin.

"Well then let's cut the bullshit and get on down to it before you change your mind!" she declared, grabbing him by the hand and dragging him off the dance floor, into a mirrored elevator, through the streets in a block-long white limo, and into an immense luxury apartment, whose endless gilded and carpeted rooms and parlors stuffed with antique furniture, overflowing chests of jewels, silver bowls heaped with dust, and tables brimming with money seemed to go on forever.

Into a huge bedroom with a smoke-glass mirrored ceiling lit by a fireplace glow and papered in lip-red velvet, where she tore off her white gown, rending it to gauzy rags, grabbed him by the cock, and pulled him down onto a big round bed whose golden satin sheets were warmed to blood heat.

He pinned her wrists to the pillow with his hands and entered her with a triumphant long thrust that seemed to never end, as if years of nada had become a mighty battle ram, capable of opening up the innermost depths of the tight white cunt of look-but-don't-touch and at last gaining him entry.

He went on and on and on, for weeks, for centuries, for a thousand years, and somehow he was also on the ceiling watching himself, watching a bronzed Mucho Muchacho moving to the beat of "Tu Madre También" astride the perfect blond bitch at the center of the world.

As she moaned and cried in grudging ecstasy, she clung naked to his side as he promenaded up Fifth Avenue in his black tuxedo; as he watched his dark and perfect body master her pale white flesh, he snorted teaspoons of dust from a silver mirror, and it seemed that he had become the Cocko del Mundo when his brain and his dick went off in a simultaneous explosion of shattering glass towers.

And he went sailing out like his own private helicopter through the aerial canyons high above the shitpile streets of Manhattan, soaring free as a bird and rich as a plushie-tushie up out of the sombre and into the sol, cruising lazily around the deco pinnacle of the Chrysler Building in the golden afternoon sunshine—

"Some people just got no class."

Paco blinked into a dark cave of odorous gloom, where max metal music smashed and tangled, where shadowy figures sprawled on heaps of rubbish, where something scuttled across the unseen floor, and where he lay with his pants around his ankles across a soft, sweaty, sour-smelling body.

"—what the fuck—"

"Quit your bitchin', Paco, I waited for you to come, didn't I, even though it meant giving you three free minutes."

Paco squinted up at Dojo, who stood above him, curling his lip, shaking his head in disapproval, and holding the limp wire mesh of the Zap in his meaty hand.

"Must have really been quite a flash to have you humpin' away at Miss Piggy there," Dojo said. "My eyes seen it, but my stomach still don't believe it."

Paco rolled off the fat smelly body, pulling up his pants in the same motion, and popped up onto his feet, looking down on the perfect blond dream creature he had been fucking.

What he saw made his gut drop and his manhood shrivel into a sticky pimple of shame. The girl in the grungy nest of cushions had her raggy blue dress hiked halfway up her torso to reveal a gross heaving belly, huge thighs wadded with folds of grimy flesh, and the bottoms of squishy pendulous breasts. Her hair was a greasy black halo around her fat, acne-reddened face.

She looked up adoringly at him through heavily lidded puppy dog eyes and beamed him a smile of perfect contented bliss.

"Thank you," she sighed. "That was wonderful."

Paco stumbled off toward the exit through the twilight zone around the dance floor, the flickering pattern of colored lights mercifully fragmenting the stream of his thoughts into rainbow confetti. Dojo caught up with him at the foot of the exit stairs, catching him by the elbow.

"Come on, my man, what was the flash?" he demanded. "You think I let a wormy mother like you try a piece of wizard wire like this just because I think you're pretty?" He held up the Zap in front of him as if he were flourishing a wad of bills. "I wanna know whether you wirehead assholes are going to plug in to these things. My supplier wants three hundred apiece, and I don't wanna tie up any heavy capital in some nojuice bullshit."

Caught in the big doorman's firm but gentle grip, Paco found his scattered wits drifting back down to street level like crystal snowflakes melting into dirty gray slush in the gutter.

"The fucking thing is real wizard all right, Dojo," he said. "It makes you feel . . . it lets you . . . I was . . ." He threw up his hands in frustration.

"Well, shit, man, would you do it again?"

"Would I do it again?" Paco repeated dreamily.

He remembered what lay blissfully back there in the shadows with his cum inside her, and he remembered the perfect woman of his wet dreams on gold satin sheets, and he remembered being Mucho Muchacho fucking the queen of Ciudad Trabajo forever in her penthouse bedroom, and he remembered what it had felt like to fly like a plushie-tushie helicopter as the king of the city.

"Quién sabe?" he said distractedly. Then, snapping back into some semblance of focus: "Why don't you try it yourself, Dojo, and see if you've got the cojones to handle it?"

Dojo smiled at him knowingly. "You know I don't truck with no wirehead shit," he said, rubbing the piece of wizard wire thoughtfully between his fingers. "But lookin' at you, I got the feeling I've got my hands on something primo."

* * *

Out on Third Street again, Paco found himself walking south through the dark ruined buildings toward Houston, and then turning west toward the border of Soho. What the fuck happened to me? he wondered.

If he hadn't come out of the flash atop that fucking fat puerca, he would have thought that the whole flash had just been some wirehead dream inside his head. For now that he thought about it, he realized that he had dreamt bits and pieces of it for years, curled up in some subway station or shitty hole in the ruins. Oh yeah, he had known that stuck-up chocharica bitch all his life, and for sure he had dreamed of fucking her brains out!

Reaching West Broadway, and peering longingly south along the brightly lit avenue lined with galleries, and fancy restaurants, and fabulous plushie-tushie meatracks, it seemed as if he were staring straight up the dress of the queen of the city. In the distance, between the forbidden thighs of Chocharica City, he watched rich bitches promenading along West Broadway, guarded from the likes of Mucho Muchacho by pale white patrónes and Uzi-toting zonies. Up there at the vanishing point beckoned the secret key to everything.

"Tu eres muy loco, muchacho!" Paco told himself. "It's just some fucking piece of wire!"

But out here in the sombre, just Round the Corner in sight of the city of his dreamtime, Paco knew that he would do just about anything to go there again.

ELECTRIC DREAMS

Bobby Rubin pulled his Cadillac Samurai into the parking garage of the Muzik Factory on Monday morning in a bubbling good humor. Not only had he wormed his way into a wild Bel Air party Saturday night, he had actually scored there after a fashion, and today he was finally going to be given the chance to show the pinheads upstairs what he could *really* do if only they would let him.

He had gotten to the party at Davy Stone's by the happy fluke of running into Stone's manager, Marty Beckman, as he had emerged from Billy Beldock's office after getting the big news from the president of Muzik, Inc., himself. Bobby had worked on one of Stone's discs a couple years ago, the last one that shipped gold, in point of fact, and Beckman, upon seeing him emerge from a private séance with Beldock himself, had deigned to remember him.

"Bobby . . . ah . . ."

"Rubin."

"Right, you played the image organ on . . ."

" 'Streets of Strangers.' "

"Yeah, hey, that was good stuff. . . ."

"Last disc of Davy Stone's to ship gold."

Beckman's ebullience narrowed a bit, and he eyed Bobby speculatively. "Yeah, well just between you and me, the songs they've been giving Davy lately suck, and the visuals have been amateur night. So what have *you* been up to . . . ?" He nodded significantly in the direction of Beldock's office.

"Billy has sworn me to secrecy," Bobby said airily. "We're working together on a whole new concept."

Technically speaking, it was all true. Project Superstar certainly was a whole new concept, and Beldock had certainly made it crystal-clear that he would never work in this town again if he went around shooting his mouth off about it.

Still, he had to resist the strong temptation to tell Beckman that it would not be long before smart-ass pretty boys like his meal ticket Stone were out on the streets eating kibble, and cyberwizards like himself were the new lords of the industry jungle.

For while a glamorous prince of rock and roll like Davy Stone was precisely what he had wet-dreamed of becoming as a horny kid from Long Island fresh to the High Life of Hollywood, he had soon learned that here, as in high school, he was just another faceless nerd to the tantalizing prime pussy who hung all over the preening hunks and charismatic rockers.

But he kept his mouth shut and contented himself with projecting silent mysterioso as he entered the elevator with Beckman, and his virtue was rewarded before it reached the garage by an invitation to the party at Stone's house that weekend.

The party was filled with starlets, would-be starlets, once-were starlets, high-class hookers, and hordes of groupies chosen for their beauty and star-fucking ambitions. It would have been pussy paradise for Bobby, had not the party also been filled with handsome out-of-work actors and musicians, middle-aged cunt-hustlers who called themselves producers, and dust dealers dispensing their wares gratis to promising partygoers of the feminine gender.

These, of course, were getting all of the action that Bobby didn't even know how to begin to come on to, and so he counted himself lucky to be able to latch onto a secretary from CBS who had gotten there by the grace of a girlfriend who did bit parts in porno discs.

She hadn't been so bad, really, a head full of show-bizzy babble, and a bit big-assed and flat-faced, but once he had fed her the dust with the promise of which he had lured her to his Franklin Avenue apartment, she had looked a lot better, especially after he snorted about a half-dozen lines himself and allowed her to fuck his brains out.

So all in all, he had to count it a successful weekend, and it felt like anything but Blue Monday as he took the elevator to the eighth floor, to Studio Four, one of the Factory's best, where his gear had been moved from the monkey block down below on five.

The studio was empty when Bobby arrived, and he had time to savor the luxury of his new playpen alone for a while, and contemplate how wrong his father had been to call him a bum when he turned down the long-sought MIT scholarship to open his own basement operation.

Daddy had done okay as a computer programmer until the advent of language interface chips reduced him to a precarious living repairing hardware, so in order to preserve his son from such an economic fate, he had pointed Bobby toward a career as a software designer and a life as a computer nerd virtually from birth.

He had bought him a Commodore when he was just five, taught him programming by the time he was seven, and so Bobby had spent his childhood happily zoned into his VDTs and controllers, creating and playing computer games, doodling for hours with his light-pen and mouse, and babbling contentedly to himself about algorithms and pixels.

Daddy had certainly been right about the dire state of the job market he would confront in his young manhood, but he had been dead wrong about the path to a sure meal ticket, for the simple reason that millions of other daddies had also foreseen the obvious.

Now there were millions of desperate little computer nerds with degrees in software design fighting each other to the death for some boring job writing programs for assembly line robots.

And indeed he would no doubt now be one of them had it not been for rock and roll and his horny longing to be something sexier than a stoop-shouldered hacker. For while it was all very well to get off playing with bits and bytes in the nursery, in high school he became all too painfully aware of his nerdishness in the form of his inability to get laid.

The early home vidconsoles were coming onto the market, little more than two read-write disc decks, a monitor, a sound camera, and a modem, interfaced with a personal computer and packaged in wood-grained plastic for about $6000. But the disc decks did handle bits and bytes for the computer as well as video and sound, so with the right software, it would serve as controller and mixer for the stereo video equipment.

It had certainly been a far cry from the toys they had now given him to play with in Studio Four, or even what he had had to work with in the monkey block, but since it *would* download broadcasts, videodiscs, and library footage onto disc, and allow you to mix it with the camera feed, it was enough to let you produce some pretty fancy visual tracks for garage discs by the dubious standards of the local high school bands.

That is, if, like Bobby, you were enough of a computer nerd to master the bits and bytes of this novel new medium. For while anyone in theory could now become his own videodisc producer for about $6000, making this early cheap stuff fulfill your visions, genius or otherwise, required far more software smarts than was generally contained within the cranium of your average teenaged rocker.

Videodiscs having long since replaced audio records and cassettes, and MUZIK having long since steamrollered most music radio, any kid band dreaming of a recording contract or even local airplay had to at the very least have a demo disc with a visual track that would hold the attention.

And while established acts might have the budget of a major tv commercial to work with, the stuff that the poor boys and girls trying to boogie out of their basements disced on their home vidconsoles was of necessity cut together to the music out of what they could shoot themselves and bits and pieces of old stock footage, and unless there was some mad cyberwizard to blow an inspired riff through the bits and bytes with these secondhand images, it looked it.

Thus was it given to Bobby to boogie after his own nerdish fashion into the life fantastic of Long Island rock and roll.

For he was just the sort of computer nerd who knew how to make a vidconsole sing. Shamelessly scamming his father for the equipment, and writing his own software like a fiend, he put together the local state of the art. Couple extra monitors. Three recording decks instead of two. ROM upgrades. Animation chips. Ten-track video dubber.

He could work cut-rate magic. He wrote his own visual emulator program which would synthesize simple images out of pure algorithm and which let him do rude kinestatic pseudo-animation with images off the air and old tapes and discs. He could even make dead rock stars caper and dance jerkily with the local talent.

So to his father's horror, when he graduated from high school, instead of going off to MIT, he stayed home, built a shed in the backyard, and turned it into a studio. Despite his softhearted mom, Daddy would have kicked him out as the bum he kept calling him had not he himself gone through a prolonged period of severe underemployment while Bobby was at least bringing in a few bucks doing visuals for shoestring local tv commercials and playing high school dances.

Bobby endured over two years of this tense life en famille as the grudgingly tolerated black sheep thereof before two local groups got Muzik, Inc., contracts largely on the strength of his visual tracks for their demos.

Then he was offered a five-year work-for-hire contract muy pronto and was swept up into his present life in Hollywood before he really understood what he was signing. "Come to work for us, kid," they told him over a fancy lunch in Le Pavilion. "We're making you an offer you can't refuse. Mucho dinero. Porsches. Designer dust. Groupies. State-of-the-art equipment. The chance to work with big stars instead of the kiddie corps. When it comes to rock and roll, compadre, Muzik is where it's at!

"Just sign right here," they told him back at the New York office, shoving a contract under his nose as they shoved dust up it.

Only a good deal later, when he found himself churning out crap to order in the monkey block alongside whole platoons of young cyberwizards who had been conned into the same contract by the same line of bullshit, did he learn the reason for Muzik, Inc.'s, beneficence to backyard cyberwizards in terms of their own Bottom Line.

These goddamn kids are too good; they're putting together out of junk image organs almost as good as the ones Moog and Mitsubishi are soaking us an arm and a leg for! Such talent we always need if we can sign it to work-for-hire contracts, and what we sure as shit *don't* need is a plague of pimply little genius nerds turning out bargain-basement videodiscs as good as ours for a hundredth of the cost. We better get control of this technology before it becomes too unprofitably democratic!

And by the time Bobby's five-year contract was up, he had the fancy apartment on Franklin, and four years left on the seven-year note on the Cadillac Samurai, and a taste for the Hollywood high life that far exceeded his grasp, and besides, they were willing to give him a good raise to sign him up for another five-year hitch.

So what if he was handed specs dreamed up by the cynics in market research and told to turn them into visuals for discs that amounted to commercials for themselves? So what if he never got a cut of the royalties? So what if he was a musical mercenary?

Who wasn't? By that time, you worked for Muzik, Inc., or one of its lesser clones, or you developed a taste for people kibble.

And if somewhere buried deep within the heart of hearts that he pretended to himself he didn't have, Bobby harbored a gnawing yearning to flow with his own creative impulses instead of reaming out crap to the specifications of the pinheads on the top floor, well, here he was in Studio Four, wasn't he, with a mandate direct from Billy Beldock himself, and a real rock and roller as the producer.

Bobby, of course, knew all about Glorianna O'Toole, the Crazy Old Lady of Rock and Roll; who in the industry didn't? She had known everyone who was anyone back in the fabulous Golden Age of Sex, Drugs, and Rock and Roll, and these days she was famous for taking shit from no one, including the pinheads upstairs, for whom she expressed open contempt and somehow made them love it. She went to all the best parties, and just working with her was bound to upgrade his social life if he could make her like him. And since Beldock had told him flat out that she was completely in charge, as a producer, she would be no mere messenger girl carrying specs down from the assholes up in research and marketing.

Bobby checked and rechecked the equipment, impatient for Glorianna O'Toole to show up so they could get started. He had not felt like this on a Monday morning since his early months in the Factory. Then, as now, he had felt he was about to embark on a grand boogie into rock and roll adventure. Then, as now, he had practically gotten a hard-on from the upgrade in equipment.

Jeez, with *this* wizardware, he could do just about anything! Four decks and a mixer with infinite tracking capability. A macrobyte of RAM memory that would enable him to random-access a whole cut in virtual disc for editing and processing. An infinite color palette that could vary hues angstrom by angstrom and intensity photon by photon. Direct modem access to every image library in the United States and state of the art animation programs already in ROM. Microsensitive joyglove image controllers. Ten independent image sequencers per track with infinite overdubbing. Automatic lip-syncing.

If I can't synthesize a solid gold AP rock star with *this* wizard gear, Bobby told himself, then it fucking well just can't be done by anyone short of the Pentagon!

Then he heard a woman's footsteps outside the door and his excitement rose to a peak.

"Hi, Bobby!"

A pudgy girl in a loose yellow and silver Muzik, Inc., T-shirt and electric-blue velour pants that made her ass seem enormous stepped into the room and beamed at him happily. Her bleached blond hair was frizzed into some weird afro frosted with ratty black swirls, and a smattering of zits was not quite concealed by her heavy suntan makeup.

It was Sally Genaro, the VoxBox player assigned to the project, and upon sight of her, Bobby suddenly remembered why the name had sounded vaguely familiar.

He had worked with her once before, on "Long Gone Skyway," a Long Jim disc for the shitkicker market that had shipped gold. She had been real wizard, one of the best VoxBox artists he had ever worked with, and his intellect had to admit that Beldock had made a shrewd choice. Musically speaking, he knew he should be pleased.

Nevertheless, his stomach sank.

For little Sally from the Valley had made it all too clear that she found him "cute," "wizard," and even "snaky," and she had never stopped coming on to him the whole time, sidling up to him in the studio, sticking her face in his ostensibly to discuss the material, inviting him to her apartment for extracurricular consultation, and constantly rubbing her flabby tits against him "by accident."

And the whole time she had this enormous inflamed acne pimple just off center on the tip of her nose. Yech! The memory of it still made his flesh crawl.

He had gotten through it only by staying obtusely professional, by adamantly refusing to acknowledge that he ever knew what was really on her mind no matter how blatant her come-ons got, by being cool, and icily civil, and all business, and telling himself that if he told her to fuck off, it would only screw up the sessions and prolong the agony. He had done his work, and she had done hers, and they had zipped through "Long Gone Skyway" in a week, after which he had been able to heave a great sigh of relief, knowing it was over, and he would never have to sit in the studio with the Pimple again.

And now here she was, and he was going to have to go

through the whole damn thing over again, and on the most important assignment of his career.

Well, if I got through it once, I can get through it again, Bobby told himself. There's just too much at stake here. I just *can't* let her get to me. Maybe she's found herself a boyfriend. Maybe she's forgotten all about me.

"Hi, Sally," he said neutrally, "I guess we'll be working together on this thing."

"For sure!" Sally said all too eagerly in a rough, slightly nasal purr that she probably thought was sexy. "We had a bitchin' time working together on 'Long Gone Skyway,' remember?"

Bobby forced a bland smile. "How could I ever forget it?" he said dryly, choking back any ironic inflection.

"I see you two know each other."

Glorianna O'Toole had entered through the open door, a robust-looking old lady in a bizarre loose-fitting pajama suit of soft thin white flannel, tie-dyed in neon red, green, and yellow, and belted with a black silk obi. Her long thick gray hair fell in carefully groomed waves over her shoulders. Her tanned face, softly lined like fine old parchment, was devoid of concealing makeup, but she wore subtle silvery-red lipstick, and her black eyebrows, over deep emerald eyes, made even more dramatic by heavy black mascara, were frosted with metallic speckles.

On a much younger woman Bobby would have found the whole effect quite sexy, and he had to admit that for an old lady, Glorianna O'Toole still cut a dashing figure. Wrinkles and gray hair or no, it was hard to think of her as grandma.

"We worked on 'Long Gone Skyway,' " Sally said brightly. "We did some real wizard tracks together." She inclined her body subtly in the direction of Bobby. "It was like . . . chemistry."

Glorianna O'Toole looked the Pimple up and down apprais-ingly. She regarded Bobby in like manner, then cocked an eyebrow at him subtly.

Certainly not! Bobby telepathed at her indignantly. "You got some specs for us?" he said, determined to get this onto a neutral professional level immediately.

Glorianna sat down on the nearest of the director's chairs scattered about the studio and pulled a thick sheaf of readouts from the snakeskin briefcase she was carrying. Bobby waited till Sally had pulled up a chair and sat down to her left before placing his own chair at Glorianna's right, as far away from Sally as he could discreetly place himself.

"You mean these?" Glorianna O'Toole said, waving the papers under their noses. "These demographic breakdowns from the marketing department? These character sketches from dead-ass shrinks?"

She smiled sweetly. "Fuck 'em," she said just as sweetly, tossing the specs over her shoulder and into a heap on the floor with an imperious flourish.

Bobby stared at her in open amazement. "You don't even want me to *read* the psych profiles or the demographic targets?" he exclaimed. He had dreamed of such a moment for seven years, but now that it had come, he suddenly found himself feeling strangely lost. "How am I supposed to start without them?"

Glorianna O'Toole rolled her eyes toward the ceiling in theatrical anguish. "Fuck a duck!" she groaned. "Look," she said, regarding him with contained exasperation, "if the pinheads upstairs knew jack shit about what makes a real rock star, would they be paying a crazy old lady like me to play Svengali to you two cyberkiddies?"

"What about, like, the songs?" said Sally from the Valley.

"You're the VoxBox player, aren't you?" Glorianna O'Toole said, nodding her head toward the VoxBox rig across the room from the image organ equipment. "You're supposed to be able to make that junk play like the rock and roll symphony orchestra and sing like the Mormon Tabernacle Choir on wire, aren't you?"

"Well, yeah . . ." the Pimple whined uncomfortably. "But I need at least a voice spec and some lyrics, I mean, I just do the *music*. . . . Someone has to give me, you know, like words and parameters. . . ."

Glorianna O'Toole sprang to her feet and paced before them in small circles, wagging a finger at them as she spoke like some hardnosed high school teacher giving two unprepared pupils what for. But no high school teacher had ever read Bobby the riot act like this.

"Demographic breakdowns! Psych profiles! Voice specs! Parameters! You two sound like refugees from Silicon City, not rockers! Let's get one thing straight, kiddies, you're not here to ream out Muzik to specs, you're not working for the pinheads upstairs now, you're working for me, and I'm here to tell you that you're here to prove to the world that out of all this fucking wizardware you two little geniuses can make some real rock and roll!''

Glorianna's ire swiftly subsided. ''Look what you've done,'' she said with a rueful grin. ''You've got me ranting and raving like a corporate fascist.''

''Come on, come on,'' she said, shooing them toward their equipment like errant chickens. ''Boot up and boogie, let me just see some random jamming.''

She winked at Bobby as he sat down before his console and began throwing switches. ''Loosen up, man,'' she said. ''All I'm asking you to do is have some fun. It's only rock and roll.''

Sally Genaro booted up her VoxBox with a queasy void in her belly that the jelly doughnut she was munching did little to fill. Glorianna O'Toole sat on a high stool behind her, the better to look over Sally's shoulder and make her even more uptight than she already was.

A week into Project Superstar, and she already had the hollow feeling that she was blowing it.

In a way, these sessions were like the old days with the Razor Dogs in Cliff Jones's garage, jamming together to come up with a new song or two for the weekend's gig.

But the Razor Dogs, however lame, had at least been a *band*. Cliff mostly wrote the words and did *all* the lead vocals, so there was none of this stuff about making up voices without analog input or specs and trying to fit them to some silly AP on an image organ screen.

The Razor Dogs hadn't even *had* an image organist. Cliff's image fronted the band, and he had made it up all by himself. A skin-tight silver body suit with these tacky hairy-clawed animal feet out of some costume shop, and a long bushy tail. His shaved skull was grease-painted black, and the mohawk crest of hair that he had left down the middle was dyed steel-blue and gunked into a hard knife edge with waveset before each performance. He actually performed with a set of phony plastic fangs in his mouth which tended to fall out when he was really wailing.

The only processing he ever let Sally put the vocals through were a limited range of occasional special effects, mainly the blood-curdling wolf wailing and harsh metal-grinding robot grunting that were the Razor Dogs' signature.

The Razor Dogs might have been the pits and Cliff and Karl

might have treated her like a human being only when they wanted her to give them blow-jobs, and she certainly hadn't thought twice when Muzik, Inc., offered her a contract without them, but at least they were a *band* and Sally knew her place in it.

And in a way, working in the Factory had not been all that different from playing with the Razor Dogs until now, except that mercifully she did not have to face a live audience.

Sally loved playing the VoxBox, but she had always hated live performance, hiding behind her VoxBox in the background shadows while Cliff and Karl danced in the spotlight, assuming the bar they were playing in had one that worked. They wouldn't even throw a spot on her for a few bars when she was doing a vocoder chorus, and it was one of the thousand indignities which the guys inflicted upon her about which she never dared complain.

So Sally actually *liked* her job as a studio VoxBox wizard at the Muzik Factory. The producers gave her lyrics from the songhacks, and voice specs, beat-patterns, style-parameters, and sometimes even melody lines from the research department, and all she had to do was make it into songs, one track at a time. Most of the time she had a live recording of a real singer to play with, and when they let her do vocals from scratch, they had these real wizard *scientists* to tell her what they wanted in the way of voiceprint parameters.

For sure, sometimes when she was making some foxy lady with a voice like a telephone operator and like a total inability to even keep in key or follow the beat sing like a superstar, Sally wished she had the bod to stand up there and belt it out herself.

After all, any voice was just analog input for the vocoder circuitry, so why not her own? So what if her raw voice was harsh and squeaky? She could sing a lead line into the mike as well as any of the beautiful dips they used as fronts for their discs, and once she had an analog input, she could turn it into anything she liked. She could filter it, enhance it, raise or lower it, multiplex it, fuzz it, sharpen it, add overtones, sync it to the lead instrumental, and it would come out the other end of the VoxBox singing like an electric angel or demon precisely on the beat and in perfect pitch.

And in fact, they had let her do it on two AP discs. The voices they used on Lady Leather and the Velvet Cat might have used detailed voiceprint parameters from research, but the raw analog voice input had been Sally's own.

But of course no one was about to use *her* bod even as rotoscope input for a vid track! Los Angeles was full of luscious airheads who could shake their Ts and As far better than she could, and needless to say, they had a lot better stuff to shake!

That was why she had liked doing Lady Leather and the Velvet Cat better than processing live input. If it wasn't Sally Genaro up there on the vid track as a wet dream for all the world, and if their voices owed as much to the parameters and specs of the research department as they did to her raw lead-line input, well, it wasn't any *other* real girl they saw dancing either, and if Sally wasn't really doing the singing, then who else was, smart guy. Sally was all in favor of having Artificial Personalities replace stuck-up hot-stuff rock stars. If *she* couldn't be a real live rock star, why should anyone else?

So she had really been pleased when they assigned her to Project Superstar, first because she wanted the idea to succeed, second because it sure beat processing live singers as far as she was concerned, and third because Bobby Rubin had been assigned to the project too.

Bobby certainly had no bitchin' surfer bod, being somewhat slouch-shouldered and skinny, and his nose was too big, and his hair was a black mop, but he dressed real well, and he had these big dark brown eyes, and a snaky little smile, and he was a level to which she might reasonably aspire.

It had really been a turn-on working with him on "Long Gone Skyway," it had like *inspired* her, given her tracks soul, but somehow they had never quite gotten it on.

Every time she had invited him back to her place, he had begged off, and whenever she tried to give him messages with body language, he had been too shy to respond.

That turned her on too; she could tell that this somewhat wimpy little guy wasn't exactly a successful make-out artist, you could tell how horny he was by how he pretended to ignore sex vibes, he was probably afraid he wasn't a good lay, and so once she finally got to give him the terrific blow-job she had perfected in the shopping malls and car seats of the Valley, his cute little cock would be hers to command.

Alas, they had finished the "Long Gone Skyway" gig before she could figure out how to break through his shyness, but Project Superstar had sounded like something that would last a lot longer than one week, and surely she could get her hands in his pants during the process.

Or so she had thought when they began the gig last Monday.

But just as these sessions in the studio had failed to ignite any musical chemistry thus far, so, too, was any personal chemistry missing between her and Bobby Rubin. Every time she even tried to be *friendly,* he retreated into his equipment, or made some smart-ass remark to cover up his nerdy embarrassment.

Sally ran her hands randomly up and down her main keyboard. An electric guitar line came out of the speakers. "Bomp-ba-pa-dupa ba-doom pam-bom," she sang into her mike, inputting it into RAM memory. She ran it up and down a few times between the sub and supersonics. She turned it into a black male bass with a standard soul ROM chip. She multiplexed it into a chorus, then added a female voice singing lead above it in a mighty operatic contralto. She stored a lead guitar line, drum, tambourine, bass, rhythm guitar, and organ, laid the whole thing out across the keyboard, and then played a few bars of the result.

"Wonderful," Bobby said dryly. "The Bo Diddley Tabernacle Choir meets the Phantom Lady of the Opera."

"*Bobby!*" Sally groaned. "I was just testing the equipment!"

From his image organ rig to her right, Bobby looked at her blandly. "Really?" he said, suddenly giving her that smirky-sexy smile of his. "Gee, I thought maybe we were finally coming up with something. I even did a quick track to it. Wanna see?"

Without waiting for an answer, he swiveled one of his monitors so she could see it and hit a volatile memory playback command.

A chorus line of Bo Diddleys danced across the stage of some opera house, while Lady Leather, with the addition of a white tutu, swung overhead on a vine, and then sailed out over an audience in formal evening clothes.

"Oh, Bobby!" Sally cried somewhere between a giggle and a moan of exasperation.

"Wait a minute, kiddies," Glorianna O'Toole said from her stool behind them. "Maybe we've got something here."

Bobby's eyes met Sally's and rolled upward in a rare moment of personal contact.

"Sally, wipe the female lead, give it to that black male voice, kill the multiplexing, bring it up half an octave, and let me hear it slow and easy, with just a sax and a piano. . . ."

"Are you *serious*?"

"Humor me," Glorianna said. "I think it might remind me of

someone I used to know. . . . We haven't been getting anywhere with songs or images, so maybe we should concentrate on a voice . . ."

Sally shrugged and changed the parameters. Maybe the Crazy Old Lady had a point.

So far, the three of them had just been chasing each other in circles. Without lyrics or a lead singer voice to work off, all Sally had been able to do was complicated arrangements of dumb random tunes running through her head, and without any songs or even voiceprint specs, all the voices she tried seemed to be just mimicking familiar performers. Without music, character specs, or even a voice to work off, Bobby's visuals were just a lot of smart-ass video doodling.

And though Sally *knew* that the songhacks and the research department were passing down *reams* of lyrics and specs to her, Glorianna O'Toole kept them all inside her snakeskin briefcase, refusing to even look at them *herself* until they had "laid down some tracks with soul."

Sally punched up a playback. "Bomp-ba-pa-dupa ba-doom pam-bom," a clear vibrant baritone crooned to languid piano and syrupy sax.

"Way too clean . . ."

"Yeah . . ." Sally agreed, and she furred up the voiceprint a bit, graveling it with subsonics, and lagging an overdub program just behind the high notes, doubling them with exaggerated ghost-peaks just short of breaking.

"Bomp-ba-pa-dupa ba-doom pam-bom. . . ." The voice was more gutsy now, but also slightly shriller, a bit more manic. Almost sexy.

Glorianna bounced off her stool and came up closer behind them. "Bit more up in the nose, maybe . . . ?" she suggested to Sally. "Bobby, give me a quick visual. . . ."

"Like what?"

"Just any old still from the data banks, first thing that comes into your head. . . ."

Bobby shrugged and punched up a stock photo of Albert Einstein's head on his four screens.

"Real wizard . . ." Sally said with a little laugh.

"Let's just lip-sync Albert to the vocal and see if we can teach the old fart to boogie," Glorianna insisted.

Bobby loaded a lip-sync program and Sally got a silly little charge as he plugged his image organ into an output jack of her

VoxBox, so that the lip-sync program would follow her vocal track as its sequencer. Somehow, it made her think of what she'd *really* like him to plug into her 'Box.

"Bomp-ba-pa-dupa ba-doom pam-bom," sang Albert Einstein.

Sally giggled. "Give him a bitchin' bod, Bobby!" she said.

Bobby called up a bodybuilder shot and laid it in under Einstein's white-haired old head.

"Get serious, kiddies, we just finally might be onto something here," Glorianna O'Toole said earnestly, peering intently at the screen. "Blacken his hair. Lean him down to something human. Put him in a white lab coat, tight-fitting."

Einstein's grayish-white fright wig turned black, somehow becoming a sixties rock star aura in the process, Jim Morrison in a lab coat, with the big sad soulful eyes and wise old face of the saintly sage of the atom.

"Hey . . ." Bobby purred to himself, staring at his main screen and punching away madly at his keyboard as if no one else were in the room.

Einstein's wrinkles vanished, his chin tightened up, and his bushy eyebrows turned a bitchin' lustrous black. His great mane of black hair developed frosted red highlights. Only his nose and his warm soulful eyes lookin' right at ya remained the same, as Bobby Rubin reshaped his lips into a visual echo of his own snaky smirk.

Bobby gave Sally the same exact smile as he looked up from his controllers and right into her eyes. "What says the demographic median?" he said. "Does this turn Sally from the Valley on?"

"Don't call me that, Bobby!" Sally snapped.

She *hated* it when Bobby called her Sally from the Valley, for even though she knew it was just like his New York attitude, that he couldn't know what it meant to her, it still never failed to flash her back to her horrible puberty in the San Fernando Valley as a fat pimply daughter of the nouveau poor.

Her father had bought a cheap tract house in Pacoima at a relatively low mortgage rate back in the seventies, when there was still money to be made as an aerospace technician, so at least the family wasn't thrown out onto the sidewalkless streets when he was reduced to working as a cable installer and lucky to have that.

But while her schoolmates in high school arrived in their own cars or at least on *scooters,* Sally was constrained to ride the bus, and while the golden girls were riding to the beach with their boyfriends, she hung around shopping malls with her ugly duckling sidekicks, surrounded by a lost world of goodies she could never touch. Sally from the Valley was everything a California Girl shouldn't be—poor, afoot, overweight, and fighting a constant battle against acne.

"*Please* don't call me that, Bobby," she said plaintively, feeling that she had blown it, that maybe he had finally asked her the question she had been waiting to hear, and all she had been able to do was snap at him for disguising his true feelings behind his usual smart-ass sneer.

For what he had turned Einstein into *did* turn her on, and all the more so because he had given it his own smile, as if to say, behind this sneery grin there's a gentle sensitive guy lookin' right at ya the only way he knows how.

"Let me see if I can give him something to dance to," she said, retreating from her embarrassment into the realm of the VoxBox, her one and only plastic fantastic lover, which, from those first magical moments at Timmy Knight's stupid party, had shown the ugly little duckling her dream self as a secret rock and roll queen.

Timmy was a shitty VoxBox player in a dead-ass high school band, and his 'Box was only a sleazy mass market model, but somehow, ignored by the boys as usual, she had found herself diddling with it. Sometime later she became aware that she was diddling with it for a rapt audience. Later, when the band inflicted themselves on the party, they let her sit in on a number.

By the time the party was over, she knew she had to have one.

What she had to do to get the money was both degrading and exhilarating to a frustrated fat girl who had not remained a virgin by choice. She took to hooking at shopping malls far from home, and since she could hardly do much of a trade on looks, she made herself an expert at giving head.

And while sucking all those faceless cocks for a few dollars made her feel like *cheap and dirty,* she *enjoyed* the way it made her feel raunchy and pure all at once—reduced to a cheap sex object on the one hand, and yet doing it all out of passionate commitment to a higher cause on the other.

Strange to say, she felt a vibe much like that right now as she stared dreamily at the image on Bobby's screens, at the charismatic creature with the soft sad eyes of a saint, and Bobby's own smile, and just let her fingers do the talking for what she felt between her legs. Before she really knew what she was doing, she was laying down multiplex instrumental tracks.

A wailing, distorted, feedback-shrieking guitar line, like some horny guy just begging for it, and a slow, heavy jungle beat on the drums and bass, and then a clear ringing instrumental lead generated by laying a single huge tenor church bell out on the keyboard, bumping it up an octave, and equipping it with vibrato and sustain so she could play it like a horn.

She sang a few slow bars of a moldy oldie that seemed somehow appropriate into her mike for tune and lyric input, then sequenced it to the instrumental lead, ran it through the current voice program, and then played the whole thing out on the keyboard.

"We are star-crossed lovers, we are sisters and brothers, we are star-crossed lovers, we will meet here again . . ." sang a cunt-teasing male baritone while the instrumental lead ringingly proclaimed his pure horny littleboyish desire.

"*All right* . . ." proclaimed Glorianna O'Toole. "Okay now, let's see Albert do a song and dance to it."

"Wait a minute, I've got a few ideas, just let me lay in some background and a little of this and that, give him some wire . . ." Bobby cackled to himself, swiveling Sally's monitor so she couldn't see what he was doing, and clicking away madly for a minute or two at his keyboard.

"Okay," he finally said, sticking his right hand in a joyglove, and letting Sally see a monitor again, "and a one, and a two, and a three. . . ."

Sally played back the previous mix, sequencing the lip-sync program to her love song while Bobby danced the figure on the screen to it with his joyglove.

The snaky young man in the white lab coat with Einstein's eyes and Bobby's smirking mouth now had a rather ridiculous caricature of a wirehead device fitted crazily over his red-frosted crown of shiny black hair, like a headpiece from an antique electric chair, festooned with a random assortment of spark-coils and vacuum tubes. Bobby had laid in a colorized frame from *Bride of Frankenstein* as background, and a long power cord ran from the thing on the head of the figure to the Victorian mad scientist rig, upon the table of which a female body lay, restrained by metal bands, and hooked up to sparking machinery.

"We are star-crossed lovers. . . ."

The young mad scientist did an Elvis number, waggling his

pelvis at the girl on the table as sparks ripped up the gap of her machinery and sizzled around the wirehead piece in his hair.

"We are sisters and brothers. . . ."

The girl on the table twitched in sync with the beat, and the sparky aura around Young Einstein's head flashed and flared with the moaning pitch-breaks of the guitar line.

"We are star-crossed lovers. . . ."

Young Einstein danced over to his electrified beloved, and embraced her in an explosion of sparks and static as she bolted upright and empty-eyed into his arms on the final beat.

"We will meet here again. . . ."

Bobby Rubin laughed uproariously.

"Fuck a duck!" Glorianna O'Toole exclaimed.

Sally's ears tingled, her lower lip trembled, and she felt a flush of heat go through her. "What's *that* supposed to be?" she said in a petulant whine.

Bobby shrugged at her innocently. "Just something off the top of my head," he said. "What's the matter, Sally, don't Valley girls have a sense of humor?"

"Don't nerds from New York think about anything but *playing with themselves*?" she shot back without thinking, and instantly regretted it when she saw him shrivel and cringe.

"Play it again, and back off, you two," said Glorianna, stepping forward to stand between them and study the screen. "It's only rock and roll." She cocked her head speculatively as the sequence ran again. "Or anyway the Disney version . . ."

"What would you call him?" she demanded of Bobby.

He threw up his hands. "Is not my job," he said.

"Willy the Wirehead?" Sally suggested earnestly, trying to make it up to him for putting him down.

"Bad demographics, Sally," Bobby said in what seemed like a somewhat placating tone. "Burnt-out wireheads don't have the money to buy discs."

Both of them looked up at Glorianna O'Toole, who stood between them, peering at the final freeze frame on the screen with a peculiar expression on her face, as if she had eaten something really weird and couldn't tell whether she liked it or not.

"Don't look at me," she finally said. "It may be my job to get you two to turn out this shit, but as far as I'm concerned, one AP is as bad as another. But if I was one of the pinheads upstairs, I do believe I'd think old Albert here has as much potential as, say, Mucho Muchacho or the Velvet Cat. You two have worked on this crap before, what do you say, should we show him to marketing and research?"

"I really do like the voice," Sally admitted somewhat grudgingly. "I think I could lay down good tracks with it with the right lyrics. And he *is* kinda cute. . . ."

"A rockin' mad scientist . . ." Bobby mused. "It's dumb, but then, so are the songhacks and the assholes who buy this crap, aren't they? At least it's something to show to the pinheads upstairs to justify our salaries. . . ."

Glorianna O'Toole shook her head ruefully. "Man, just listen to the three of us!" she said disdainfully. "What spirit, what enthusiasm, what a wonderful attitude toward the audience we have!"

"Yeah," Bobby told her snidely, "then what's a Good Ol' Girl like you doing in a place like this, Glorianna?"

Glorianna O'Toole flared at him for a moment like some mean old gray cat. "Maybe I just like slumming," she snapped.

"And maybe you just need the money like the rest of us?" Bobby suggested.

Glorianna's finely lined face softened. "Maybe," she said. "But just maybe there's a pot of something at the end of this rainbow of dumbness for me that you're too young to understand."

"Try me."

Glorianna O'Toole gave Bobby a long stare from deep down in those big green eyes and shot him a challenging grin that, if she wasn't this decrepit old lady, would have said in words of one syllable, *Maybe I will.*

Bobby's eyes widened for a beat, and then he immediately looked away from her with a weirdly discomforted look on his face that told Sally that he had picked up the vibe too.

Gross! thought Sally. Disgusting! How could this dirty old lady think that Bobby would ever want to make it with *her*?

Surely they must have both imagined it, for Glorianna O'Toole herself acted as if nothing had passed between them in the next beat, and she was all business, picking up a house phone and sitting back down on her stool.

"Hard-copy it to disc," she told them, "and I'll tell Billy Beldock we finally have something for the songhacks and research to play with."

As she dumped her audio track through Bobby's vid recorder

so he could disc the whole thing, she listened to her own electronically transmogrified love song to Bobby sung one more time through the snaky smiling lips he had given to the AP on the monitor screen. Einstein's warm wise old eyes seemed to peer longingly into her own, belying the smart-ass sneer on his young face as he capered like a rejuvenated Mick Jagger around his wirehead zombie bride.

She glanced back over her shoulder at Glorianna O'Toole, frail, and gray, and wrinkled, in a loose red silk shift that hid her decrepit old bod, but with the easy elegant vibe of a woman who had known what it was to be sexy and beautiful for a long time peering unmistakably through those bright green eyes.

Good thing you're an old bag now, Sally thought. For she knew in her heart of hearts that never could she have competed for Bobby's attention for one minute with what this old lady must once have been.

Yet strange to say, in that moment she would have traded places with Glorianna O'Toole without hesitation just to know the memory of having been the beautiful rock and roll queen that poor fat and pimply Sally from the Valley could never get to be.

She snuck a glance at Bobby, who watched his monitor screen with a weird boyish longing on his face that somehow seemed in sync with something inside herself, that for a moment seemed to link them with an emotion that went beyond her lust.

"We are star-crossed lovers. . . ."

For just as she was never going to get to be a sexy rock and roll queen, so nerdy little Bobby, despite his smart-ass put-downs, was never going to get to be the superfox he had conjured up on the screen. The girl Glorianna O'Toole had once been wouldn't have looked at him twice.

"We are sisters and brothers. . . ."

Oh yes we are, Bobby Rubin! she thought. You're another lonely little duckling just like me.

"We are star-crossed lovers. . . ."

But if only you'll let me, I'll show you what it feels like to be someone's beautiful swan.

"We will meet here again. . . ."

RETURN TO THE BIG APPLE

Karen Gold had done everything her parents had told her to do to regain the urban middle class existence they had known and lost, but it was all coming out wrong.

"You don't want to be stuck here in Poughkeepsie for the rest of your life, do you?" her mother had told her when she entered high school.

Indeed she did not!

As far as Karen was concerned, this grungy little city about seventy miles north of Manhattan was Siberia, for she had golden memories of spending the first nine years of her life on Manhattan's Upper West Side, in a five-room apartment looking out across Riverside Park onto the Hudson and the Jersey shore beyond. Two blocks east was Broadway, with its movie houses, and restaurants, and the crazed bustle and wonderful smells of Zabar's, where she would go shopping two or three times a week with her mother.

On weekends, Mommy and Daddy would take her to Central Park, or the Museum of Natural History, with its endless halls of stuffed animals and weird artifacts, or the Hayden Planetarium, or even to an occasional play, and they would eat with chopsticks in a fine Chinese restaurant.

She had friends like herself in the private school she went to. When the weather was good, they would play in the park, frolicking on the grass in the spring and summer, staging snowball fights, riding their sleds, and building snowmen in the winter.

Admittedly the pubescent Karen enduring her exile in the Poughkeepsie gulag knew that her memories of Manhattan were gilded somewhat by the fact that she had never actually set foot outside a Zone. There had been nice zonies with their impressive-looking machinepistols all over the Upper West Side. They had patrolled the park, convoyed her to and from school with her classmates, and kept the dazzling excitement of Broadway off limits to any of the bad streeties her father was always warning her about. The excursions around town had been conducted in cabs, and always to venues where reassuring zonies abounded. Her parents had *never* gone anywhere by subway, and she had never been in one in her life.

But her parents had always promised her that when she entered high school she would be permitted to go anywhere within the Upper West Side Zone all by herself, and even travel with girlfriends and *nice* boys with sufficient funds to all the wonderful movies and restaurants and parks in the other safe Zones of Manhattan, provided, of course, that she *always* traveled by cab and *never* let herself wander out of the sight of the nice zonies.

Instead, Mom had lost her job with the Welfare Department when the vast bureaucracy was dismantled during the post-Devaluation depression, and Dad was laid off a few months later when Simon & Schuster eliminated two-thirds of its legal department as part of its attempt to stay afloat, and they were two months behind in their rent, on the verge of eviction, and actually reduced to eating *kibble,* when Theodore Gold miraculously landed a job as an insurance claims adjuster for Allstate in Poughkeepsie.

So instead of tripping the life fantastic in the cosmopolitan fantasy Manhattan she had been promised for her thirteenth birthday, Karen found herself entering her teenage years as an exile from that golden New York of the mind among these hicks in the boonies.

"No, Mother, I do not want to spend the rest of my life stuck in Poughkeepsie!"

Mom understood. She had grown up in Brooklyn Heights and gone to college at NYU in the Village and taken her graduate degree at Berkeley, and had even been some kind of hippie, taking drugs, and probably going to orgies, before she married Dad and moved to the glamorous Upper West Side. And now, here she was, with a graduate degree, and all those wonderful memories, fated to spend the rest of her life as a housefrau in wonderful suburban Poughkeepsie.

Anything but this for her only child! Study hard, Karen, she told her daughter. Your only way out of here is a college scholarship. Karen dutifully beavered her way through high school. There were few distractions in Poughkeepsie anyway. The girls were all airheads, and the boys were dips; besides, the last thing in the world she wanted was a boyfriend who might even make her *consider* remaining in this burg one minute longer than she had to.

Her grades and SATs were not quite good enough to get her her dream scholarship to NYU in the Village, but she did manage to get a scholarship to Rutgers. And while Rutgers was in *Jersey,* there were boys there with cars, or at least the money for train fare, and Karen, with her thick honey-blond hair and her trim lean body, was a looker when she let herself be, and she made it perfectly clear to one and all that a proper excursion to the Apple was a sure means of getting laid, whereas any date that did not cross the Hudson guaranteed nothing but the certainty of a case of the blue balls.

So Karen at least got to be a frequent day-tripper in Manhattan during her college years. Her dates took her to the theater and expensive restaurants and fancy clubs if they could afford it, and to movies, tours of the Soho art galleries, Chinatown, and Second Avenue meatracks and bars if they couldn't. She smoked dope, snorted designer dust, chipped a little wire, and put out freely with an open heart for just about any presentable boy who would squire her around the night life of the Big City at his own expense. From each according to his ability, to each according to her need.

She loved Manhattan with a far deeper and purer passion than she felt for any of the Rutgers students she day-tripped with. And while she saw things in New York that far exceeded the esthetic bounds of her innocent childhood memories—the blocks of ruined buildings, the savage raggy streeties lying in wait for the unwary, the kibble dispensaries, the garbage, and the filth, and the rats—these were mostly viewed from the safety of cab interiors or at worst under the eyes of watchful zonies or city cops, so none of it reduced the siren call of the city to her spirit.

As for her academic career at Rutgers, this was obsessively focused on the singular goal of securing upon graduation some kind of job, *any* kind of job, that would pay her well enough to let her live in Manhattan.

What this would take would be about $20,000 in cash to buy

into a share in a co-op and about $2000 a month to keep up the payments.

The down payment she began accumulating in her sophomore year by dealing wire. It was neither as dangerous nor as lucrative as it sounded. There were plenty of wirechippers at Rutgers with enough money and sufficient lack of street smarts to pay her a premium of twenty percent or so to score a piece of the latest wizard for them on her excursions to New York, and plenty of fancy meatracks in Manhattan where streetie dealers were admitted on good behavior to conduct just such business. Thus, $100 and $200 at a time, did she slowly accumulate the necessary capital, hoarding it in Swiss gold certificates, and living like a pauper.

Choosing a career that would net her the $2500 a month she estimated she would need just to barely survive as a Manhattanite was, however, a more difficult matter.

Her natural academic inclinations were toward those subjects largely based on verbal skills. She loved to read fiction, and history, and psychology, to expound in class, to write. She aced history, speech, English literature, composition. Science, math, or any subject involving computation, lab work, or problem-solving, were bummers she ground her way through.

In her intellectual heart, she daydreamed about becoming an English teacher, a lawyer, a journalist, even a novelist or poet.

But Daddy had a law degree and look where it had gotten him, teachers were paid peon wages when they were employed at all, journalists, print or media, had to put in years and years slaving away in Peoria or Akron before they could even *dream* about trying to land a job in the Apple, and garrets in which to be a starving writer or poet in Manhattan were called ateliers and went for half a million.

So she gritted her teeth, held her nose, listened to the sage advice of parents and guidance counselors, and sweated her way through four years of a major in computer science, specializing in word-processing, printing, data storage and retrieval, and librarianship, where the math was at least minimized, and verbal skills maximized, hoping to land an entry-level job in something like publishing, from which she might hope to screw her way to executive country.

What she managed to land upon graduation, three months of commuting from Jersey to pound the pavements, and a weekend in bed with the flunky doing the hiring, was a $4500-a-month job translating clothing specs into instructions for production robots in a sleazy Thirty-first Street shirt factory. It was shit work indeed, and after deductions the take-home was only about $3300 a month, but things could have been worse, as they certainly were for so many of her classmates who found themselves subsisting on kibble in Passaic or gunfoddering in Venezuela.

She had an actual job in Manhattan, and she had been able to luck into a third-share in a one bedroom on East Twenty-seventh Street, where her share of the payments was $2200 a month and where she even had the living room as a solo sleeper, seeing as how Bill and Marta, her co-op mates, were sleeping together. She had attained the long-sought status of New Yorker, and the city spread itself like a free smorgasbord before her.

For the first six months she haunted the singles bars and déclassé meatracks on First and Second Avenues, where admission was free to the ladies, looking to score a Mr. Wonderful, or at any rate, a Mr. Rich, who would sweep her away to the real high life, which she could see, but not quite touch. But it slowly dawned on her that the guys she met in places like these were more or less in her shoes, hanging on to some crummy job, living three and four to a co-op, and dreaming their frustrated dreams of somehow becoming a Prince of the City.

So she took to saving up her money and buying admission to fancy meatracks in Soho or the Village like the Temple of Doom or the American Dream, where such New York princes were said to abound. And indeed there were plenty of well-heeled plushie-tushie princes in such venues looking for instant romance. But there were even more guys pissing four to a pot and spending most of their money on fancy clothes and cover charges, with lines of bullshit they were sure would score them a slumming princess or at least a good piece of ass for the night. And of course there were whole platoons and squads of girls every bit as attractive as Karen and then some competing fiercely for the available natural resources.

So while she got some meals at fancy restaurants and free snorts of designer dust every once in a while out of this foraging, after eighteen months in the Big Apple, Karen was still working in the shirt factory, living with Bill and Marta on Twenty-seventh Street, and wondering somewhat forlornly when her life was really going to begin, and indeed beginning to wonder what it was really all about.

Still, she told herself bravely, things could be worse.

She was right.

Bill lost his job writing ad copy and ended up waiting tables in some plushie-tushie joint uptown. He grew more and more depressed and then started chipping cheap wire. He lost interest in Marta, who took to complaining to Karen about his impotence in endless gory detail. They began to fight on a daily basis, and then Marta moved out of the bedroom and onto a trundle bed in the living room, where she kept Karen awake half the night snoring like a horse. Bill's brain was beginning to burn, he spoke little, and bathed less, holding himself together just well enough to keep his job and his share in the co-op.

Still, things could be worse.

Right again.

Marta found herself a new boyfriend named Greg. Greg was a *zonie*! A big swarthy *animal* who took to staying over almost every night and fucking Marta on the trundle bed right beside where Karen tried to sleep.

Karen wanted out of this horrible scene, but under the terms of the standard co-op share contract, she could get her $20,000 back only by selling out to Bill or Marta or to a third party with the consent of both of them. Neither Bill nor Marta had the money, and no outside party would be about to buy into this mess.

Moreover, the nature of Greg's sleazy game was becoming all too apparent. He wanted a share in the co-op, but he didn't have the buyout money. Bill was going downhill fast; it was only a matter of time before he'd be too burned out from all the bad wire to hold any kind of job anymore. According to the terms of the share contract, if one of the three shareholders failed to meet two monthly payments in a row, he had to either find a buyer acceptable to the other two, or his share would revert in another thirty days to his two partners, who would then be legally prevented from reselling it.

In the ordinary course of events, this prevented ripoffs, since unless the other shareholders permitted the defaultee to get his money back by selling his share, they would forevermore be forced to assume his share of the monthlies.

But in this case, the contract clause became a license to steal, since Marta had a veto over any sale of Bill's share, and Greg had the income to assume Bill's share of the monthlies.

It looked as if Karen was going to be stuck with Marta and Greg as roommates forever when Bill finally got fired. It looked good on paper, since she would then own a half share instead of a third, but in reality she could hardly imagine a worse situation.

This time she was wrong.

Bill wasn't the one who lost his job.

She was.

Some son of a bitch had chipped a program that translated simple designer drawings into code for clothing production robots. They told her all about it at the shirt factory the day they canned her. You fed sketches into an optical reader, popped a shirt-specific chip into your computer, specified the sizes and production runs, and out the other end came discs that any moron could feed to the production robots. The software cost less than $3000, the computer mod $2000, and the optical reader $8000, meaning that eliminating Karen's salary would pay for the changeover in less than three months, and after that the factory's profit margin would be $4500 a month greater forevermore.

"Nothing personal, kid, we just need every edge we can get to keep half a step ahead of the chinks."

Karen kept the bad news from everyone for over three weeks while she haunted employment offices and tried not to panic. Surely *someone* would hire her. She had a degree in computer science, didn't she?

But she had forgotten that it had taken her three months and some sleazy sex to land the shirt factory job in the first place, and since then the job market had deteriorated even further. Jobs for computer operators had been all but automated out of existence, and those that remained were filled by overqualified software designers quite willing to take anything they could get at peon wages under the dire circumstances.

As for shit jobs, New York was occupied by a vast army of the unemployed, so even if by some miracle she landed a job as a waitress or a cleaning lady or orderly in a nursing home, the wage scale was so depressed that it would take three months to earn one month's payment on her co-op share.

In desperation, the weekend before she was going to have to tell her co-op mates that she wasn't going to be able to make the monthly, she went home to Poughkeepsie and tried to borrow the money from her parents.

The numbers were hopeless. Dad would have to sell the car to come up with $2200 in cash, he needed it to get to work, and anyway, thirty days later she'd be right back where she started.

When Karen got back to the apartment Sunday evening, there seemed nothing for it but to finally confront the inevitable.

"I lost my job," she admitted as the four of them sat around on the beds in the living room. "I'm not going to be able to make Tuesday's monthly."

Neither Greg nor Marta, holding hands on the trundle bed with thin little smiles, seemed particularly surprised by this revelation. Bill, gaunt and hollow-eyed, had long since passed the point where he was capable of much of a reaction to anything.

"I can cover," Greg told Marta, already regarding Karen in the past tense.

"It's not fair for you to cover, Greg, unless you have a share," Marta said primly. "Bill and I will have to make up the difference. Eleven hundred extra apiece."

This finally roused Bill from his wirehead stupor. "Hey, I don't have that kind of money," he told them.

"Tell ya what," Greg said quickly. "I'll do everyone a favor and buy out Karen's share." He gave Bill a cold hard stare. "Any objections?" Bill glared at him silently, clearly afraid to open his mouth.

"Okay by me," Marta said.

"You two have it all figured out, don't you?" Karen snapped. Greg grinned at her fatuously. If she had had a gun at that moment, she surely would have blown the bastard away.

"Don't you even want to hear Greg's offer?" Marta said sweetly.

Karen just glared at her.

"I'll give you six thousand for your share right now," Greg said.

"You son of a bitch! It's worth—"

"Twenty-two hundred more than it will be in thirty days," Greg said diffidently. "If you wait a month to take me up on it, I'll have to deduct the monthly payment I'll be fronting for you, now, won't I?"

"Forty-four hundred more than it will be worth to Greg in *sixty* days," Marta chimed in.

"And of course in *ninety* days, it won't be worth *anything* to me, since your share will revert to Bill and Marta unless you sell it to someone acceptable to both of them before then," Greg said.

"And you'll veto anyone but Greg, won't you, Marta?" Karen sighed.

"Technically speaking, you'll actually owe Greg six hundred dollars if you wait for your share to revert," Marta said. "But I'm a good guy. I won't even bother to take you to small claims court for it."

Forlornly, Karen looked imploringly at Bill. He shrugged at her. *Better you than me.*

"Asshole!" Karen shouted at him. "If you let them do this to *me,* how long before they pull the same number on *you*?"

"They can't do that, can they . . ." Bill whined. "They wouldn't be able to come up with sixty-six hundred a month just between the two of them."

"Yeah, and as soon as you're too burned out to keep *your* job, they'll find a buyer who'll pay *you* shit and kick back what the share is really worth to *them,* and you won't be able to do a damn thing about it!" Karen pointed out angrily.

Greg and Marta glanced at each other in sudden dim comprehension.

Marta beamed at Karen. "Hey, thanks, Karen," she said brightly. "That's a good one!"

"What do you say, Karen?" Greg asked. "Six thou now, thirty-eight hundred on Wednesday, sixteen hundred thirty days after that, or zip in two months? Doesn't matter to me, I can wait it out if you can."

"Go fuck yourself!" Karen screamed. "I'll get a job! I'll find the money! I'll . . . I'll . . . oh, shit!"

She bolted from the bed, and, turning her back on the three of them to hide her tears of rage and frustration, she fled into the night.

The streets looked a lot different to Karen now that she was forced to contemplate the likelihood that she would soon be thrown out onto them. Indeed, this past week it had almost seemed as if she were a streetie already, since she had returned to the apartment only to sleep, and that for only five or six hours a night, unable to bear the presence of Greg or Marta, or for that matter the cowardly Bill, unless she was quite comatose.

She made the daily rounds of the employment centers without any real hope, just to kill time. She hung out in the singles bars and meatracks along First and Second Avenues until closing time, far too spaced to be viable pick-up material or to care.

And she wandered aimlessly through Manhattan, exploring the city through a new set of eyes, as if she were scouting out the future terrain in which she would soon be constrained to forage for survival.

Now she really noticed all the rag-clad and predatory-looking streeties lurking in alleyways, disappearing down shadowy side streets, ducking into doorways at the sight of city cops and zonies. Like every other New Yorker, she had known that there were something approaching a million indigents subsisting on people kibble and their predatory instincts in Manhattan, but somehow they had always remained emotionally invisible.

But now the street-level reality of the city was intruding upon the forefront of her attention. It was Indian summer now, but where did all these streeties go in the winter? How many of them froze to death? How many succumbed to diseases? Did they prey on *each other*?

She knew that no one had to starve to death, the kibble dispensaries were everywhere on the peripheries of the Zones, holes in the wall guarded by city cops, where you could get a paper bag of the chewy, tasteless gray nuggets anytime you wanted to with no questions asked. There was no need to ration kibble; it supplied all the necessary nutrients, but it had been deliberately designed to taste like wet paper, so that no one would eat any more of it than they had to.

Nevertheless, Karen took to eating a bag of the vile stuff every day or two even though she still had food money, as if training herself for a future that was slowly taking on the solidity of the inevitable.

In point of logical fact, of course, there was nothing inevitable about it; she could go home to Poughkeepsie, she could take Greg's pittance and go to some small city in the West or South, where rents were cheap, and unemployment lower, and where she could survive in a more or less civilized manner on the wages from some shit job until . . .

Until *what*?

Until she met Mr. Wonderful in Poughkeepsie or some other hick town? Until she gave up and married some dumb dip just because he had a job? Until they started hiring computer operators in Manhattan again?

Never!

She would *never* marry some asshole content to live the rest of his life in the sticks! And they would *never* start hiring computer operators at her level again in New York.

Since before she had entered high school in Poughkeepsie, she had had only one dream, to make a life for herself in the lost wonderland of Manhattan, and she had fashioned her whole life into an instrument for achieving it. She had worked so hard in high school, she had sweated through four years of courses she had hated in Rutgers, she had dealt wire, she had even screwed a fat creep to get the job in the shirt factory. She had been diligent, dedicated, motivated, and hard-working in pursuit of the only dream she knew.

She had done everything she was supposed to do right, and now it had all come out wrong.

She had only one thing left to cling to. Come what may, she would stay in Manhattan. Against all reason, against the evidence of her own eyes and nostrils, she knew that her life had no other source of hope.

Greg's first deadline came and went almost beneath her conscious awareness, and by the time she realized that she had procrastinated $2200 down the tubes, it seemed that an inevitable transformation had already taken place.

When she had been a little girl on the Upper West Side, the nice zonies had been her friends and protectors, and when she had been a day-tripping student from Rutgers and a gainfully employed computer operator with a secure share in a co-op, the zonies had been *her* anonymous mercenaries, hired to patrol the borders of an invisible but quite real bubble of security, whose function it was to keep her safe and the dangers of the streeties *out*.

But now she saw that bastard Greg in every zonie's face. Black, white, Puerto Rican, male, female, fat, thin, tall, short, they all seemed to have the same hard, implacable eyes and brutal, self-satisfied mouth. Somehow, her protectors had all become the enemy. Somehow that callous uncaring son of a bitch had turned her world upside down.

She found herself unwilling to meet the cold, appraising stares of the zonies, which she had never even really noticed before, and she found herself occasionally locking gazes with the eyes of streeties, something she had always carefully avoided.

And while these miserable, streetwise, savage creatures regarded Karen with implacable hostility when her eyes chanced to look directly into theirs, knowing her for what she was by her carriage and her clothes, she caught herself wondering what sad stories like her own had formed those bitter masks, what thwarted dreams had died or still might live behind those angry eyes.

Had they, too, done everything right, only to have it all come out wrong? Someday soon, would another girl like Karen Gold look into a streetie's hostile and defeated eyes and see *her* staring back?

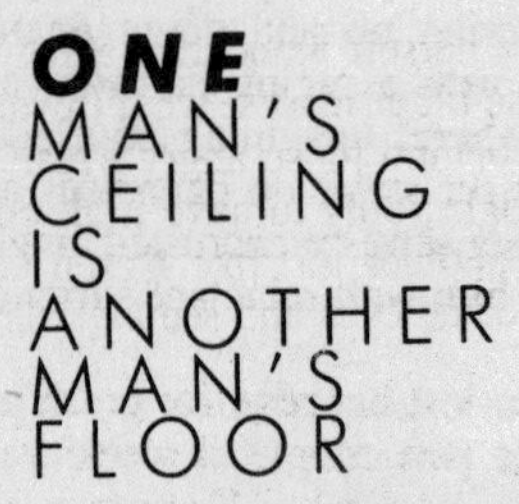

ONE MAN'S CEILING IS ANOTHER MAN'S FLOOR

"Come on, man, I gotta have one, just tell me what I've gotta do,'' Paco Monaco whined.

''I told you a thousand times what you gotta do, my man,'' Dojo told him with a patronizing air of weary patience. ''Slip me four hundred.''

''Chin*ga*da!'' Paco snapped, nuancing the word with just enough singsong irony to take the edge off his frustrated rage, for no matter how red his fury, he wasn't loco enough to really piss off the big black doorman. ''Where the fuck am I going to get *four hundred dollars*?''

Dojo laughed. ''Do I look like your moma?'' he said. ''How should I know? Rob a bank. Mug a plushie-tushie. Suck two hundred faggot cocks. Show a little good old American *enterprise*, my man.''

''Por favor, Dojo, put me onto something.''

Dojo took a half step out of the doorway to Slimy Mary's and peered down at Paco more narrowly now. ''Put you onto something?''

''Yeah, man, anything, I mean, like I *gotta* have my own Zap, I feel like . . . I mean I . . .''

Ever since that night on the Zap in Slimy Mary's, Paco had felt himself to be a changed man, and in ways he couldn't quite understand.

For one thing, he had lost his taste for cheap chocha. Not that he wasn't *horny*, not that he was turning into some kind of fuckin' *maricón*, he just didn't seem to have the energy to bullshit the crummy pussies in Slimy Mary's anymore, let alone do any crash and grab for a few bucks to buy the wire to pry open their pants.

Instead, he found himself wandering up and down Second Avenue eyeing all the chocharicas with a raging hard-on, and then jerking off in the ruins somewhere, imagining an elegant blond woman wearing only a silver fur stole, on her knees and stroking his hot cojones with her long jewelry-encrusted fingers as she sucked him off, staring up at him with reluctant surrender in her icy blue eyes.

And for another thing, he had also lost his edge for crash and grab itself. He had done a few in the past couple of weeks, and what had the poco dinerò bought him, muchacho? He sure as shit had no taste for the Prong anymore! He didn't want any wire that would do nothing but make him hot for the puercas in Slimy Mary's.

And, strangely, after trying it three more times, he didn't want to flash on the Zap again in Slimy Mary's either.

It had been more or less the same each time. He'd pay Monkey Girl her thirty dollars, put on the Zap, grease el Lizardo his ten, then hit the touchpoint on the breadbox as the Mucho Muchacho disc came on.

And the music would start, and his heart would pound, and Mucho would dance across the screen, and he would melt into the reality of wherever it was as Mucho Muchacho donned his flesh, his oiled-steel muscles rippling fluidly beneath his taut bronze skin, his mighty superhuman cock all but bursting from his tight white jeans, "Tu Madre También," or "Hombre de la Sombre," or "Besa mi Macho" pouring like hot lava from his throat as he capered and strutted through elegant nightclubs under the stars, promenaded up Fifth Avenue, paraded through shopping malls, restaurants, aisles of beachside cabanas, around Las Vegas swimming pools, across Hollywood sound stages, with all the look-but-don't-touch chocharicas of the world tearing off their clothes and flinging themselves at his feet.

But the length of the flash, like the length of a dream, was unpredictable. The first time he bought half an hour's worth again, he had stayed inside it until Monkey Girl had hit his touchpoint and told him his time was up, but the second time, and the third, too, he had popped out after fifteen or twenty minutes, and had to hit the touchpoint again to get his full time on the Zap.

And in the moment of cold harsh reality between, there he was, just a spick streetie dancing to a disc on the tacky dance floor of a crummy meatrack in the basement of a boarded-up tenement on Third Street off Avenue D, unable to forget coming out of the flash and back into just that reality lying atop a fat smelly puerca under Dojo's disdainful gaze.

And when he shuddered and hit the touchpoint again, a part of him still knew, even within the dreamtime of the flash, that the woman out of his dreams dancing her cocktease tango before him would turn back into slime from Mary's as soon as his thirty minutes were up.

So he did no more humping on the Zap in Slimy Mary's, and he had no more motivation for el cheapo crash and grab, for the fulfillment of the desire that filled him now, that obsessed his every waking hour, demanded a major score.

Paco had done mucho wire in his day, but never anything like the Zap.

This flash was in many ways like dreaming. On the Zap he became the mucho macho muchacho of his heart of hearts, the object of the adoring lust of all the chocha he surveyed. Scenes and times melted and flowed into each other exactly as they did in a dream. And on the Zap, a woman that he recognized as a creature out of his dreams appeared to him; cool, blond, with icy blue eyes, swathed in fur and dripping with jewels.

But unlike the sweet dreams that came to you curled up at night in the hallway of an abandoned building, on the Zap, what happened was in a certain sense *real*.

You might not be dancing in some fancy nightclub, but you *were* dancing on the floor of Slimy Mary's. You might not be fucking a beautiful blond bitch in a fabulous penthouse apartment, but you sure as shit *did* come out of it on top of some disgusting fat girl on a nest of grimy pillows in the musty darkness.

And the Zap was a *nojuice* piece. If you owned your own, you could put it on, and hit the touchpoint, and *really* march down West Broadway, up Fifth Avenue, down Second and First, past the galleries, and the fancy bodegas, and the bars and saloons, among the gordos and chocharicas, *while you were flashing,* and you would *really be there*!

And not as some nada little streetie, but with all the powers of *Mucho Muchacho*!

If you could go off into the real-life dreamworld of the gordos and the plushie-tushies and the chocharicas on the Zap, might you not awake to find yourself on real golden satin sheets with a rich momacita out of your dreams in thrall to the machismo of Mucho Muchacho?

There was much that Paco did not understand about the Zap.

But one thing he did know—he *had* to have one of his own!

"Por favor, Dojo, put me onto something, I mean, I'll do anything. . . ."

Dojo looked down at him from the unfathomable heights of his exalted position as doorkeeper to the realm of a desire Paco had never before known he could feel.

"*Anything?*" he said with an ironic little grin.

"*Anything,* Dojo."

Dojo shrugged. He seemed to measure Paco's manhood with his eyes. His expression hardened, and when he spoke again, he was all serious business. "Bring me an Uzi."

"Qué?"

Dojo's big brown eyes peered into his, and in them Paco seemed to see his whole life, his soul, his last chance at something he could not even name, hanging in the balance.

"*An Uzi?*"

"Shit man, you know what a fuckin' *Uzi* is, don't you?"

He looked back at Dojo, his stomach sunk down to his knees, or so in that moment it seemed. "An Uzi?" he said.

Dojo smiled at him with lofty indifference. "An Uzi machine-pistol," he said. "The piece they issue to zonies. It's only worth three fifty on the open market, my man, but I'm your friend, Paco; for you, I'm willing to break even. You bring me an Uzi and I'll trade it even up for a Zap. For which I can get four hundred."

"How the fuck am I supposed to get an Uzi?"

Dojo shrugged, holding up his hands. "Do I have to tell you *everything*?"

"Off a *zonie*?"

"Well, if you don't have the balls . . ."

"Who says I don't have the balls, nigger?"

Dojo laughed. "*Quién sabe?*" he said, mimicking Paco's voice with cruel precision.

"Y tu madre también!" Paco snapped back.

Dojo clapped a huge meaty hand on his shoulder, pursed his thick lips, nodded almost imperceptibly. "That's the old American spirit, son," he said in a fatherly tone with hardly any discernible mockery in it. "You show me the color of your cojones, my man, and who knows, I might just start putting you onto things on a regular basis."

Paco locked eyes with the big man. The task Dojo had set for him was, to say the least, the most difficult and dangerous piece of business he had ever even thought of attempting. But the payoff, if he succeeded, would be a transformation of his existence beyond his current capacity to even perceive.

"Thanks, Dojo," he said quite earnestly, and he really meant it. A motherfucker of a job had certainly been laid on him, a task that only un hombre muy macho could hope to perform, and the thought of what he had to do scared the shit out of him. Yet beneath that fear was a strange and complex emotion, a kind of exhilarated calm mixed with cold determination. If he had ever experienced the concept before in his life, he might have told himself that the deal that Dojo had offered him was *just*.

As it was, he did know that the doorman of Slimy Mary's had never before treated him this *seriously*. Never before had Dojo held out the possibility that he might one day acknowledge him as an equal, as a real man.

He set off into the night feeling a bit more like Mucho Muchacho already.

"What do they want, blood?" Bobby Rubin said, snorting up a line of designer dust, then collapsing back onto the paisley velvet couch with a petulant shake of his head, in a foul mood already.

He had finally persuaded Glorianna to take him to one of her A parties. Come on up to my place, and we'll go in my Rolls, she had even told him.

So he had duded himself all up, and driven way up a succession of ever narrower and ever more winding streets to the top of Lookout Mountain with high hopes. What could be better than being driven to a fancy industry party by the Crazy Old Lady of Rock and Roll? Being escorted by *Glorianna O'Toole* would certainly be an entree into the inner circles, and on the other hand, she was far too old for anyone to take him for her *date,* so he would be free to forage among the prize pussy as a man of *importance* instead of just some faceless nerd who had managed to bullshit his way inside.

And Glorianna's legendary tree house had been everything he expected it to be.

Perched in a thicket of eucalyptus high on a ridge road overlooking the jeweled nightscape of the city and constructed of unpainted redwood timber, the house didn't look like much of anything out of the funky ordinary from the street side, except for the geodesic dome that crowned it, and the extravagantly decorated Rolls in the doorless carport.

But the entranceway led directly into the big living room that looked out over the city from on high through the glass doors that opened out onto the deck, and dominating the room, its branches overarching the couches and the redwood stump tables and the big stone fireplace, and forming a leafy subceiling just under the glass dome, was the legendary giant bonsai, the fully mature dwarf eucalyptus that turned the whole room into a forest glen.

But Bobby had scarcely had time to utter a breathless *wow* before he heard another car pull up outside, and a moment later, in waltzed Sally Genaro, flashing him a wink and a warm smile. What a bummer! Glorianna had never bothered to tell him that she intended to drag *the Pimple* along!

"Somehow I get the feeling they'll settle for money," Glorianna said dryly, passing the dust kit across her lap to Sally from the Valley, who had stuffed herself into a sheeny low-cut gunmetal fabric gown that Bobby had to admit would have looked sexy on someone twenty pounds lighter.

She had also frosted her bleached blond hair with black tiger stripes, conked it up into a bluejay crest, and applied a thick layer of fairly subtle two-tone makeup that sharpened the pudge out of her cheekbones and would almost have made it if it had done a little better job of covering the outbreak of acne on her chin.

"But we're like *making* them money, aren't we?" Sally said earnestly, snorting up a line off the obsidian slab.

"They want *gold,* Sally, that's it, isn't it, Glorianna?" Bobby said with as much gentleness as he could muster. Poor Sally from the Valley! She did try so hard, and she *was* real wizard on the VoxBox, and she took all the put-downs he threw at her with a puppy-dog good-naturedness that was almost infuriating, and he *did* feel sorry for her. If only she'd give up coming on to him and just let it be, he might even be able to *like* her.

"Go to the head of the class, Bobby," Glorianna said. "The thing of it is, Billy's job is riding on it, and shit, as they say in show biz, flows downhill."

Bobby nodded in what he hoped was a knowing inside manner. Unlike Sally, he knew how to read the numbers. They had produced three releasable discs so far, starring three different AP rock stars, and while all of them were selling well enough to eventually show a thin line of black ink on the balance sheets, none of them was going to be more than marginally profitable.

"Well, it's not like *our* fault, is it?" Sally said petulantly. "I mean it's the specs and the lyrics they send down that don't make it. I mean, *we're* not screwing up *our* end of it, are we? How can they expect us to be any better than the stuff they give us to work with?"

"Yeah!" Bobby agreed. For once the Pimple was right. "The pinheads upstairs have no one to blame but themselves."

Glorianna looked at Sally. She looked at Bobby. She rolled her eyes toward the ceiling and groaned.

"What's the matter?" Bobby demanded.

"If you have to ask," said Glorianna O'Toole, "you're never gonna know."

"Huh?"

"Never mind, kiddies," Glorianna said, taking the dust kit from Sally and laying it down on the big redwood table. "It's time to boogie. You *do* at least know how to party, don't you?"

It had been a *fabulous* ride along Mulholland in the front passenger seat of the open Rolls, marred only by the fact that Bobby had gallantly *insisted* that she take it while he sat by himself in the back, for of course Sally could have imagined nothing more totally *perfect* than cuddling with Bobby in the backseat while old Glorianna sat up front and drove alone as if this were *their* Rolls and she was like their *chauffeur*.

The party house belonged to some producer of something or other whose name she could not quite remember, and it was situated on just *acres* and *acres* in a secluded private valley just down from the Mulholland ridge road, with a giant swimming pool, tennis courts, and even an actual duck pond.

Inside, the place was just *room* after *room* after *room*—big ones with bright lights, bars, and buffets, smaller ones with muted lighting and all kinds of designer dust just *laid out in bowls,* a dance floor with flashy lighting and a live band, and if that wasn't enough, the whole thing spilled out through a succession of big glass doors onto a lawn and a huge patio surrounding the swimming pool, with its Jacuzzi, and sauna, and hot tub, where yet another bar and buffet had been set up.

And the people—*awesome*!

It was more like walking right into the middle of some movie than any real party Sally had ever seen. She recognized *hundreds* of famous faces, or so it seemed; actors, actresses, rock stars, some senator or something, two talk show hosts, and those she didn't recognize had these clothes and like this *attitude* that seemed to disdainfully proclaim that *they* knew they were more important than the ones she did. The only partygoers who didn't seem to be anyone famous or important were women so staggeringly beautiful she wanted to *kill* them.

It was like some kind of wonderful dream.

But not for very long.

Glorianna O'Toole whisked them inside, took them on a quickie grand tour, stuck some more designer dust up their noses, got them glasses of champagne and piled food on plates for them, introduced them to a dozen actors, actresses, and rock stars, who gave them the big smile and the glad hand and looked right through the two of them, and then, apparently having done her duty to her charges by her own lights, the horrid old lady had somehow contrived to just *disappear*, leaving her and Bobby standing there in a huge room full of people who obviously couldn't care less that they existed, balancing plates of food on one hand and holding champagne glasses in the other.

"Fabulous, isn't it, Bobby?" Sally said, trying to fork a piece of smoked duck crepe into her mouth with the same hand that held her glass, and dribbling champagne onto her overloaded plate in the process.

But Bobby didn't notice. "Uh-huh . . ." he muttered, checking out all the actresses and starlets and high-class hookers with his *tongue* practically hanging down to his *knees*.

"Terrific food. . . ."

"What?" Bobby said distractedly.

"I said the food's great, Bobby, try some of this duck thing."

He finally deigned to look her way, shrugging foolishly as he stood there balancing his plate on one hand and holding his glass in the other like a harried waiter in some diner.

Sally couldn't help giggling. "Come on," she said, "we'd better sit down before someone asks us for a refill on their coffee."

Bobby scowled; he obviously didn't think it was very funny, but he did follow her over to an empty couch in a corner, where he sat beside her silently, picking absently at his food, sucking up champagne, and staring hungrily at all the perfect sexy bitches like a sad little poor boy outside a bakeshop window.

Sally filled the awkward silence with smoked duck crepes, caviar canapés, salmon mousse, cold crab claws, and Black Forest cake, pissed off at him to be sure, but knowing all too well just how he felt, sitting there just like her, forever an outsider looking in.

"I think this caviar is the real Russian stuff," she finally ventured. "I never had any before, have you . . . ?"

"Don't really remember. . . ."

"You tried the crab claws yet?"

"Don't really like crab much. . . ."

"Great cake, huh . . . ?"

"S'okay. . . ."

After a few minutes of this, Sally gave up, and concentrated on her food. It really *was* terrific stuff, she could see that she wasn't going to get anywhere with him right now, so she might as well enjoy what she could.

She had finished the salmon mousse and the caviar canapés and was halfway through her cake by the time Bobby drained the last of his champagne, put his still-laden plate down on the arm of the couch, stood up, and spoke to her again.

"Be right back, gonna get another drink," he said. "Want me to get you one?"

"Yeah, sure, thanks, Bobby," Sally said, smiling at him brightly. Wasn't that sweet?

Apparently not, as it turned out, just a lame excuse for leaving her flat, for that was the last she had seen of him, and now she had been wandering around alone like a fish out of water for what *seemed* like *hours*, trying to find Bobby, or Glorianna, or at least make eye contact with a friendly face.

But Glorianna must have been getting loaded with her fancy friends, and by now Bobby was probably off somewhere *balling* some good-looking airheaded slut, and none of these Beautiful People was about to pay her any heed.

In the worst possible way, this was just like all the parties she had endured as a teenager in the Valley. All the snaky guys just looked right through her. None of them tried to hit on her, and she entirely lacked the courage to try to even start a conversation with them.

Indeed, this was *worse*. At least at those Valley parties there were usually a few of her wallflower girlfriends to pass the time with, and now and again she *would* be hit on by some horny guy who had heard that there would be a blow-job in it for him if he was nice to her. But she didn't know *anyone* here, and these guys were all movie stars, and rock singers, and producers, and directors, and the party was full of beautiful women who had probably come here just to put out.

So all she could do to pass the time was snort up the free designer dust, scarf up the food, get sloshed on champagne, and listen to the band that was playing for the dancers.

They were pretty lame and old-fashioned by her standards. They didn't even have a real VoxBox player, just an electric guitarist, a keyboard player, and of all things an actual *drummer* playing an old acoustic drum kit. These were all old guys who looked at least *forty* in their black leather and moldy eighties spiked mohawks, and they sounded it. They didn't seem to have any original material of their own; all they seemed capable of playing were covers of stuff from the eighties, the seventies, and even the sixties.

Obviously these lames were only getting even lowly party gigs on the basis of their lead singer, a tall, alabaster-skinned redhead poured into a tight black dress slashed down to her navel. She had the face of a fallen angel and the bod of a weight lifter, and she was so sexy that if there had been any dyke at all in Sally, she would have wanted to *go down* on her.

But her voice was thin and nasal, and her phrasing of the moldy oldies was flat as last year's tortillas, and they weren't even processing her through a vocoder.

And Sally hated her with a purple passion. With her VoxBox rig, she could sing this no-talent airhead into the *ground*!

Why her? Sally thought angrily as she stood there fading into the woodwork for what seemed like centuries. Why not *me*? Put a bag over her and she couldn't sing her way out of a pay toilet! Some day . . . somehow . . . Aw shit!

Woozy from all the champagne, slightly stoned from the residue of her last hit of dust, more than a little bloated from all the food she had crammed into her face, and completely pissed off at the cosmic injustice of it all, Sally finally wandered away from the dance floor, through two or three other rooms, and out onto the poolside patio.

About a dozen beautiful people of both sexes were swimming in the pool without benefit of suits, people actually seemed to be balling in the Jacuzzi, and she didn't even want to *think* about what was going on in the sauna. She staggered off across the lawn toward the duck pond, where, she saw, a single solitary figure sat at the edge of the water, curled over, staring at the ground between his feet, and rocking back and forth rhythmically like a Jew in a synagogue.

She looked again, and saw that it was Bobby.

"Hi, Bobby," she said in a flat, depressed voice, hunkering down beside him.

Bobby slowly lifted his head to peer at her blearily, his eyes moist and bloodshot.

"Hello, Sally," he said glumly, then hung his head back between his knees.

Sally sat down beside him. He didn't look at her, but at least he didn't get up and walk away. "Some party, huh?" she ventured. "Having a good time . . . ?"

Bobby made a strange urking gurgly sound. "Just terrific," he muttered sarcastically. "Tha's why I'm sitting out here all by myself. . . ." he said forlornly, and heaved a great sad sigh.

Sally longed for the courage to reach out and throw a comforting arm around his shoulders. She went so far as to lay a hand lightly on his knee. He didn't seem to notice, but then he didn't shy away either.

Emboldened, she leaned a little deeper into his body space. "Yeah," she said softly, "I know just how you feel. . . ."

"Do you, Sally?" Bobby said bitterly.

"For sure!" Sally told him, daring to pat him lightly on the shoulder for emphasis. "I mean, here we finally are at this fabulous party, like we've walked right into this *movie* we've always dreamed of being in, and all the stars and even the *extras* just look right through us like we didn't exist."

A long shudder racked Bobby's body. "Shit . . ." he moaned softly. "Jus' what I need to hear . . ."

"Well, like *who* needs 'em, Bobby," Sally cooed woozily into his ear, letting her arm drape sympathetically over his shoulders. "Buncha no-talent sluts and airhead hunks think they're better than we are just because they got their pretty faces and perfect bods, we'll show 'em, won't we, *we're* gonna be the stars, and *they're* gonna be the ones on the outside looking in!"

"*We?*" Bobby snapped, writhing out of her embrace, and finally turning to look right at her with an angry scowl. "What the hell do you mean, *we*?"

"I mean . . . I mean like, you know, Project Superstar,"

Sally stammered, taken aback. "That's *you and me,* right, Bobby, that's our chance to show them all, I mean, have you *heard* the band they've got playing here?"

"How could I help it?" Bobby said sourly.

"Well what do you think of them?"

"Are you kidding?" Bobby snapped. "They suck!"

"For sure!" Sally agreed brightly. "And if that's like the *competition,* we're gonna rock 'em into the ground!"

Bobby bleared at her narrowly. "Yeah!" he shouted. "Y'know, you may not look like much, ol' Sally from the Valley, but you can really boogie with that VoxBox, I ever tell ya that, and I am the greatest image organ player what ever lived!"

"For sure you are, Bobby!" Sally cried, her spirit soaring.

Bobby rose shakily to his feet. "Ya hear that, you no-talent pricks!" he yelled vehemently, waving his arms as if to encompass the whole party. He rocked back and forth on his heels as if he were having difficulty maintaining his balance. "Ya know what, Sally?" he said rather wildly, his eyes rolling loosely in their sockets.

"What?" she said, suddenly aware that she was looking up straight into his crotch.

"We are gonna *do it,* that's what!" he shouted. "Put all the bastards on the kibble lines where they belong! Lookit all these airheaded sons of bitches think they own the world got all these pussies hangin' all over them think they're such hot shit! You can kiss my ass, you motherfuckers, if you ask real nice, when *we're* the kings of rock and roll!"

Through her own woozy haze of booze and dust, it finally dawned on Sally that Bobby Rubin was roaring shit-faced blitzed. Somehow this perception reminded her that she, too, was a little loaded, and that gave her spirit energy and loosened her tongue, and filled her with joy as she synced into his righteous raving wrath.

"Yeah!" she shouted back. "We'll show 'em, won't we, Bobby, you and me! No-talent bitch! Dead-ass old farts!" Without quite remembering how she got there, she found herself on her feet beside him, holding his hand. And he didn't pull it away.

"Who the fuck do they think they are treating us like shit?"

"Airheads!"

"Pinheads!"

"MOTH-ER-FUCKERS!"

* * *

"We are in somewhat deep shit, babes," Billy Beldock said nervously. "I mean, our stock has dropped another two points this week, and the pressure is really coming down, and if we don't start shipping some AP gold real soon . . ."

"What do you mean *we,* white man?" Glorianna O'Toole cracked with a wry little smile. But Billy was apparently in no mood to be amused. He had come up to her on the dance floor, boogied with her a while for old times' sake, with no heart in it, and then dragged her away from the action and into this murky little room full of little cabals of dealmakers doing their thing over dust, and had spent the last ten minutes snorting up line after line compulsively and bitching and moaning at her. It was hardly Glorianna's idea of how to party. Time was, Billy wouldn't have wasted party time this way either.

"I'm *serious,* Glorianna," Billy told her. "I got where I am by proving to the board that the AP *technology* can work, and the Factory has put significant capital into it on my say-so. And I have been told in words of one syllable that if it doesn't start paying off in gold *real soon now,* my ass is grass."

"You won't be the first president of Muzik, Inc., to get himself canned, and you won't be the last," Glorianna said philosophically. "Look on the bright side. You've already collected that fancy salary longer than most. Haven't you socked any of it away?"

"I thought you were my *friend*!" Billy whined at her petulantly.

"I am, Billy," Glorianna told him. "What do you want from my life?"

"I want an AP rock star that ships gold before they ship *me* off to Miami, goddammit!"

"I'm doing the best I can," Glorianna said softly. "The kids are giving it all they've got."

Billy shoved another line of designer dust up his nose. "Well so far that's been *mediocre shit,* and you know it!" he snapped.

"What do you want, miracles?"

"Yeah! If miracles is what it takes, then miracles is what you gotta come up with!"

"This whole mess wasn't *my* idea, if you'll remember, Billy!" Glorianna shot back, her temper finally flaring. "You knew bloody damn well what I thought about this whole stupid AP rock star bullshit when you sweet-talked me into this crap! It just ain't rock and—"

"Don't say it!" Billy Beldock snarled angrily. "*Please* don't say it, Glorianna," he said much more softly, placing a tender hand on her knee and begging her with those long-remembered bedroom eyes of his. "Take a good look at me. . . ."

Glorianna shrugged. She touched his hand. "Okay, so here's looking at you, kid . . ." she said softly, staring warmly into his eyes and giving him a little smile.

What she saw was a tanned, well-preserved man in his sixties, with a luxuriant mane of silver hair falling to the shoulders of a beautifully tailored black velvet suit that must have set him back $3000. What she saw were uptight bloodshot eyes that seemed a good deal sadder than those of the hot young drummer who had been her lover many long years ago. What she saw was a true rocker she had once loved and admired, somehow grown older into a man of power just trying to hold on, whom she now found it in her heart to pity.

"Lookin' good!" she lied.

"Yeah, sure," Billy said. "What you see is a sixty-five-year-old man who nobody will hire again. What you see is a guy who's a little long in the tooth to go back to his drum kit at this late date, kiddo, even if there were still work for drummers, which, as we both know, there ain't."

"I left my gypsy violin at home," Glorianna said, not all that unkindly.

Billy Beldock smiled wanly. He took yet another hit of dust, and his expression hardened, but it also seemed to go backward in time, to another Billy, to a comrade in the night, to the young spirit that somehow might still live behind those about-to-go-down old eyes.

"I'll tell you what else you see," he said with more of the old passion. "You see the last president the Muzik Factory will ever have who ever even played in a rock and roll band! Maybe I have sold out a little, maybe what I'm asking you to do isn't exactly your idea of real rock and roll. And, okay, okay, so I'll admit that maybe it isn't quite what I'd like to turn out either. But you know as well as I do what's behind me waiting to take over. Cost accountants. Marketers. Motivational researchers. They'll never go with another broken-down old rocker again."

"What do you want me to say, Billy?" Glorianna said tenderly. "That all things pass? Let it be? Keep on truckin'?"

Billy's lower lip trembled. "Don't give me that old hippy-dippy line,'' he said wanly. ''That's not what I'm paying you for, babes. . . .''

''Isn't it, Billy?''

Despite himself, Billy Beldock laughed, a shrugging, ironic laugh, that somehow in that moment touched Glorianna's heart. ''You're a crazy old lady, you know that,'' he said softly.

''You're not so bad yourself.''

They looked at each other for a long silent moment. They shared a little shrug that went back thirty years and more.

''So?''

''So I'll give it my best for you, Billy, I'll stand over your little cyberwizards with a whip, I'll shove acid down their throats, at least we'll go out rockin', I'll—''

''Hey, Glorianna, I think those kids you brought are up past their bedtime!''

Eddie Friedkin, their genial host, had stuck his head into the room with a somewhat distasteful curl on his lip. ''They're out by the duck pond stoned out of their minds and raving.''

''Oh shit,'' Billy groaned. ''Now what?''

Glorianna laughed as she gathered herself to her feet. ''Who knows?'' she said. ''From where they're coming from, that may be progress.''

Bobby Rubin's stomach seemed to be filled with sloshy green foam, his knees refused to lock into a stable position, and the back of his throat tasted like a desert of powdered aspirin. The house, the pool, the trees, and the duck pond all seemed to be revolving in slow circles around his head, and the lights of the party seemed to be shining through a diffracting sheet of glycerin.

He had no idea how much booze he had drunk or in what loathsome combinations, nor did he know how much of what designer dust he had snorted, but both had certainly been a lot more than enough.

''Pathetic!'' he shouted. ''It's all so fuckin' goddamn *pathetic*!''

Oh yes, he had succeeded in escaping from Sally from the Valley into pussy paradise. Everywhere he looked there were beautiful women who made his dick ache with longing. They danced in hordes to the music of the live band, they leaned over tables snorting up dust, they purred into the ears of actors and singers and producers; they even swam naked with rock-hard nipples in the swimming pool.

Bobby had never gained access to a scene like this before. It was like his fifteen-year-old wet dream of nirvana.

But it was pure pathetic nightmare too.

For he didn't even know how to begin to approach any of these unreal creatures, he couldn't even hold eye contact when any of them chanced by accident to gaze in his direction. They were all film and tv actresses or rock stars, or at the very least women who had come here with the intention of glomming onto someone who would turn them into same. And the men were all sleek, tanned, well-muscled Hollywood studs with perfect features from Central Casting, or self-confident make-out artists moving in a musk of money and power, and frequently both.

Here, or so at least it seemed, *everyone but him* was a show-biz glamour boy, and none of the glamour girls would look even once at a below-the-line tech like him. Unless . . . unless . . .

He didn't quite know unless *what,* but somehow it seemed to involve getting so drunk and so stoned that his mind would turn off, and courage would come from someplace magical, and his chemically augmented consciousness would instinctively evolve words of such total savoir-faire that he would be able to catch one of these tantalizing creatures in a brilliant web of conversation. . . .

Instead, of course, the more loaded he became, the more impossible it seemed to venture so much as a word to one of these women. And the more angry and depressed he became, the more dust he snorted and the more foul cocktails he drank, and the more the reality of the party took on the agonizing aspect of something wonderful going on behind a pane of glass with his poor nose pressed against it like a starving little match boy slavering outside a pastry shop.

Finally, all he could do was stagger out into the night to sit by himself at the duck pond, brooding incoherently, and trying to convince himself that *he was not going to vomit.*

And now, here he found himself, howling in the night like a tortured animal and defiantly not caring jack shit that everyone within earshot probably thought he was some kind of *asshole.*

"We'll see who turns out to be the assholes, MOTH-ER-FUCKERS!" he shouted in the general direction of the swimming pool. "You're all *dinosaurs* and I'm gonna kick your asses into the tar pits where they belong!"

"Stuck-up no-talent bitches! Like you couldn't sing your way out of a pay toilet!"

Huh? What . . . ? Did I . . . ? *Oh, shit!*

A bubble of sour gorge erupted from his churning guts to sear the back of his throat, and the effort of choking it back before he barfed all over himself snapped Bobby's barbled brain back into some semblance of mortified self-awareness.

No, he *hadn't* shouted the last; it had been Sally Genaro.

He now remembered, as if it had happened to someone else, that Sally from the Valley had come out here to *sympathize* with him, that she had put her arm around him and whispered into his ear that it was all right, that she understood how he felt, that *she* felt just like *him,* and Jesus, *he had let her,* he hadn't even denied it, and now, here he was, so pissed he could hardly stand, on the queasy edge of throwing up, raving like a maniac, and *holding hands with the Pimple*!

"We'll show you bubbleheads, won't we, Bobby! Bomp-bomp-ba-doo-pa—"

"Sally! Sally!"

She was gibbering drunk out of her mind! Her makeup was smeared all over her face, revealing the zits on her chin; her eyes were bleary and bloodshot, and she was holding on to his hand and swaying vertiginously toward him.

"—pa-doop-bam-PAH!"

Grinning crookedly, she flung her arms around his neck, pursing her lips juicily around the climactic PAH! and planted a hot, sour-tasting wet kiss on his lips, insinuating a thick avid tongue into his mouth, and grinding her pelvis against him.

This was more than Bobby's bilious stomach, besotted equilibrium, and horrified brain could finally endure upright.

He pulled himself away from her, teetering off balance backward in the process, and went down smack on his ass, breaking his fall by planting his hands on the ground behind him. The jolt, the visceral revulsion, the shame of it all, finally combined to trigger the inevitable, and he barely managed to roll over onto his hands and knees to avoid puking all over himself as a huge bolus of bitter vomit exploded from his mouth.

He knelt there on his hands and knees for a good long while, emptying his guts of all the booze and assorted mixers, letting it all pour out without any attempt to hold back, and, though the taste was vile indeed, and his head rang like a hollow gong, there was something almost pleasant about the relief of shutting out the world and just puking it all out with his eyes closed and his mind greened out into the narrow focus of spewing out the night's constricted accumulation of chemical and psychic bile.

When his drained stomach finally subsided in a dampening series of dry heaves, and he collapsed back onto his haunches on the grass, however, his inebriation had cleared to the point where the full mortification of the moment, of the whole evening, slapped him across the face like a cold wet towel.

There he sat on the lawn of a Hollywood mansion in front of a puddle of his own puke. Sally Genaro, the Pimple, hunkered down on the grass beside him with her arm around his shoulder, cooing sympathetically while Glorianna O'Toole peered down at them with her hands on her hips, shaking her head and grinning.

"*Jesus* . . ." Bobby moaned.

"It's all right, Bobby, it's all right . . ." Sally said, tenderly stroking his hair.

He could have killed her.

"You kids!" Glorianna said dryly. "When I was your age, it took me a good twelve hours of partying to reach the barfing point."

Bobby just groaned and looked away, unable to meet her eyes, unable to even find the strength in that horrid moment to pull himself free of the Pimple's loathsome and shameful embrace.

Glorianna laughed good-naturedly. "Don't take it too hard, Bobby," she said. "Take it from one who was there, Jim Morrison didn't look any better after hugging the toilet bowl than you do now. Maybe we'll make a rocker out of you yet!"

REALITY LIBERATION FRONT

With the chilling gray days of November descending upon the city and Greg's next deadline only five days away, Karen Gold finally admitted to herself that she wouldn't let this one go by without taking what she could salvage. For while $2600 might be an insulting pittance to accept from the bastard for a co-op share that had cost her $20,000, from her current street-level perspective it was quite a tidy fortune, and Karen, of necessity, had begun to teach herself to think like a streetie at least when it came to survival economics. As she wandered about the city, she ran the calculations in her head over and over again.

Kibble was free, and she had plenty of clothing back in the apartment, including the luxury of cold weather gear, so that $2600 could be carefully husbanded to keep her above a brute survival level for *years* if need be.

She could do a wash in a Laundromat for about ten dollars twice a month, so it should cost her only $240 a year to dress like a human being instead of a filthy streetie. She had found bath houses where you could get a shower and towel for as little as fifteen dollars, meaning she could keep herself from really stinking by bathing twice a week, at an annual cost of about $360. Meaning, at least in theory, she could avoid looking or smelling like some foul street creature for *nearly five years* if she remained strong and refrained from pissing much of it away on frivolities like real food or new underwear.

There were plenty of singles bars and meatracks where admission would remain free to a girl who kept up her appearance, so she could still cadge free drinks and even occasional meals in exchange for sex, and more importantly maintain her access to respectable social levels, where sooner or later she must surely make a connection, romantic or otherwise, which would rescue her from indigency.

She had managed to convince herself that she could certainly keep things together in this manner until the days began to turn colder and she realized that she had not yet really given much thought to the matter of *shelter*.

When she finally did, she soon relearned what every New Yorker including herself knew all along, namely that $2600 would not buy you very much of *that* in the Big Apple.

The sleaziest hotels extant ran at least $400 a week for a thin cot in a foul little closet, meaning that her money would be gone in less than two months. *Streeties* either slept in the subways or squatted in abandoned buildings, a prospect Karen found terminally unacceptable.

A woman squatting alone in the ruins would face at the very least the prospect of rape on a nightly basis. The subways would provide safe haven from the approaching winter cold during the day, when the trains ran and the transit cops patrolled them, but she could well imagine what jungle law must prevail at night, when the transit cops abandoned the stations and tunnels to the streeties.

So it seemed that the best she could hope for after all was a couple of months in some slimy fleabag hotel in which to somehow find some source of further income, after which she must either risk the death of her body in the ruins or the subway, or, possibly worse, face the death of the only dream she had ever known, and slink back in the terminal defeat of her spirit to Poughkeepsie.

Which she would choose when and if the time came was something she entirely lacked the courage to contemplate.

Brooding upon it in the back reaches of her brain nevertheless, she was walking aimlessly down First Avenue near Third Street on a blustery early evening, when, as if conspiring to add to her misery, the sky opened up on her with a sudden fit of cold driving rain that had her half soaked and shivering before she could even find a doorway to duck into.

The first doorway she did find was that of a sleazy-looking little bar with a green neon sign proclaiming it "The Clearing" hanging in the unadorned plate-glass front window. The doorway was shallow, the wind was whipping the rain into it, and so, without any consideration of economic reality, Karen slipped sloshily inside.

It wasn't much; just an ancient Formica bar with green plastic and rusty chrome stools in front of it and a fat old black bartender with a thoroughly grayed afro behind it, a half-dozen tacky tables and chairs presided over by a gaunt waitress with the hollow eyes and indifferent demeanor of a heavy wirehead, two toilets, and a pay phone. The jukebox was an antique audio-only model that might have been worth a small fortune to a collector if it was cleaned up. Some sort of muttery jazz that Karen didn't recognize was playing at low volume.

Aside from the bartender and the waitress, the only people in the bar were a couple who were obviously wireheads coming down sitting at a table over steins of beer staring into space, a guy in an old peacoat at the table nearest the door nursing a big glass of vodka and drumming his fingers nervously on the table as if waiting for someone who was very late to show up, and a man and a woman seated together at the bar.

The man was a middle-aged uptown type wearing a fancy tan trench coat. The woman was about Karen's age, with short, randomly combed blond hair, nervous blue eyes, and an ironic twist to her mouth. She was wearing old jeans, work boots, a loose-fitting red T-shirt, and a yellow plastic poncho. On the T-shirt, the initials "RLF" had been rather crudely stenciled in jagged electrified yellow script.

There was something weird about this dive. It shouldn't be this empty on this street at this hour, and in fact it appeared as if whoever owned it wasn't really doing much to encourage business at all. The bartender gave her a dirty look as she hesitated in the doorway. What clientele there was—

Then the woman in the red T-shirt handed something in a manila envelope to the man in the tan trench coat, who pocketed it and slipped her a thin wad of bills, and the whole thing clicked.

The spaced-out wireheads at the table. The guy in the peacoat waiting impatiently for someone to show. The moldy old jukebox without even a simple screen. The look the bartender gave her.

This was a *dealer's* bar.

Karen had made connections in joints like this now and again when she was a college student scoring wire for her classmates in Jersey. The house got a piece of the action and did not encourage social drinkers to linger. In fact, if you had no business in a place like this . . .

Karen turned, looked out into the rain, then hesitated, caught in a moment of indecision, and by more than the foul weather outside. Twenty-six hundred viewed as *capital* was certainly a sufficient stake to get her back into this game at the modest level she had played it at in college. She was rusty, she knew no ready customers, she had no connections anymore, and she had never ventured to front her own money in a wire deal, but . . .

While she stood there staring out into the rain, the man in the trench coat, having concluded his business, brushed by her and out the door, sending a wet, cold blast of bad weather into her face. Karen turned away from it, back to the warmth of the bar interior, and found herself virtually nose to nose with the woman in the red T-shirt, who had apparently been on her way out behind him.

Their eyes locked for a moment. The dealer eyed her narrowly. The language began to come back to Karen. She nodded almost imperceptibly. *Yeah, I saw.* A hardness in the other woman's eyes. A little curl of Karen's upper lip. *Shit, no. I'm not a cop.* A little smile.

"Buy you an Irish coffee?" the woman in the red T-shirt said with guarded diffidence. "You look like you need it."

Is she a dyke? Karen wondered. Does she want to make sure I'm not going to make trouble? Just being friendly? Or a chance to get in on something? Who cares!

"For sure," Karen said truthfully.

The dealer led her to a back table, ordering two Irish coffees from the waitress en passant. "Leslie Savanah," she said laconically when they had seated themselves.

"Karen Gold."

"Out of a job? Broke? On the street?"

"More or less," Karen answered cautiously.

"More what? Less which?"

"Out of a job, still have a few days before I'm out on the street," Karen said, avoiding committing herself on the subject of her potential capital stake one way or the other.

Leslie Savanah nodded; she smiled a bit. "Didn't make you for a streetie," she said more warmly.

Karen shrugged. "Not yet anyway," she said with a friendly little edge.

''But you've got streetwise eyes,'' Leslie observed carefully. ''I mean . . .''

Karen hesitated. The hell with it, she decided, we're gonna get down to it sooner or later unless she *is* just a dyke coming on. ''I . . . I dealt a little wire in college.''

Leslie laughed. ''Didn't we all?'' she said rather gaily. ''Where'd you go?''

''Rutgers.''

''Michigan State.''

Now it was Karen's turn to laugh. This was taking an unexpected turn; it was getting almost silly. ''Get your degree?'' she asked.

Leslie nodded. ''Computers.''

''Really?'' Karen exclaimed. ''Me too!''

''And now look at us!''

They both laughed together ruefully. The waitress arrived with the drinks and slapped them down on the table in a somewhat surly manner. Karen took a long sip of the hot Irish coffee and luxuriated in the warmth spreading down her gullet and into her stomach. ''Say,'' she ventured, ''are you, I mean . . .''

Leslie laughed. ''Give me a break, Karen,'' she said good-naturedly. ''I'm not after your bod, if that's what you mean. And you?''

Karen took another long drink of Irish coffee. She felt herself relax. ''That's not the kind of action I'm looking for either,'' she said, and before she knew it, she was telling Leslie an edited version of her sad story, leaving out any mention of the $2600, buying another round with her dwindling supply of pocket money, and listening to Leslie Savanah's not-too-dissimilar tale.

Leslie had taken her Michigan State degree to New York, gotten a job in a data bank, and moved in with her boyfriend, Rex, a law student at NYU, liberally subsidized by his father, a well-heeled commodities trader. Round the bend of the last turn in the downward economic spiral, Rex's daddy went bust, Leslie got canned, they lost their co-op, the relationship quickly soured, Rex dragged his cowardly ass back to Des Moines, where he was now probably flipping greaseburgers in a McDonald's, and Leslie, well . . .

''And now you're making it dealing wire,'' Karen blurted out somewhat woozily.

''*Wire?* Hell no!''

''But I saw—''

"You didn't see what you thought you saw."

"Come on, Leslie, I'm righteous, you don't have to—"

Leslie pointed proudly to the initials on her T-shirt. "Don't you know what this means?" she said in a tone of some small amazement.

Karen shook her head.

"Jeez, Karen, I thought that's what all this was getting to," Leslie said. "I'm in the *Reality Liberation Front*! The RLF would *never* deal *wire*! We deal *bedbugs*. I was slipping that guy a bedbug disc, not some shitty piece of wire!"

Karen certainly knew what bedbugs were; she, like most of her crowd, had fooled around with them often enough in college. She had used a bedbug program to charge all her long distance calls to Poughkeepsie to null credit card numbers. It was common enough to run one through the college computers, if you could access a terminal, to change your grades to something closer to the heart's desire. She had heard stories of people who had managed to bedbug the IRS computers into making their returns invisible. The real hackers bragged about bedbugging their bank account balances and utility company records. There were supposed to be bedbug wizards who played the stock market with phantom margin accounts through their computers. She had even known a guy who claimed to be able to write bedbug programs that generated PIN numbers that would make cash machines cough out bills and charge the debits to nonexistent accounts.

But she had never heard of any Reality Liberation Front. "What's that?" she asked Leslie.

"What's *what*?"

"The Reality Liberation Front."

Leslie eyed her peculiarly. "You don't know what the RLF is?" she said. "I thought you were angling to get in, I mean, having a computer degree, and being broke, and all. . . ."

"I might be if I knew what you were *talking about*. . . ."

Leslie shrugged, ordered another round, and began to declaim in a slightly singsong voice, as if reciting someone else's words more or less from memory.

"The whole damn country is broke, twenty million people are out of work with no prospects, even people with jobs are living worse than people did twenty years ago, and in general it can fairly be said that America is in the toilet."

Karen squinted at her in incomprehension. "So?" she said impatiently.

Leslie smiled at her crookedly. "So how is it *possible* for a country like this to be worse off now than it was twenty years ago?"

"Huh?"

"People haven't actually gotten any *stupider*, have they? We've got more knowledge and better technology than we had in the 1970's and yet the economists tell us that our standard of living peaked in about 1972 and it's been downhill ever since. How the hell can that be possible?"

"Ya got me there . . ." Karen admitted, and she meant it in more ways than one. Leslie hadn't told her anything everyone didn't know; she had just turned it around into a question she hadn't even heard anyone *ask* before. Karen hadn't been sucked into a conversation like this since college, and, weirdly enough, considering her own dire personal circumstances, she found herself feeling an emotion she had all but forgotten she had ever had—intellectual curiosity.

Leslie Savanah smiled somewhat smugly at her, as if reading her mind, or at least the interest in her eyes. "Some people *have* figured out the answer," she said. "And we're trying to do something about it."

"The Reality Liberation Front?"

Leslie Savanah nodded. "Want to meet some people?" she said speculatively. "We've got a loft a few blocks from here if you can handle getting wet again . . ."

"A loft?" Karen's ears pricked up at the mere mention of anything that even sounded like it might lead to the remotest possibility of crash space.

Leslie smiled all too knowingly. "Don't think I don't know exactly where you're coming from, Karen," she said. "I mean, six months ago *I* was standing right in your soggy shoes. To answer the question you're afraid to ask—*maybe*."

Karen eyed her silently and narrowly.

Leslie nodded. "No one in the RLF ever has to sleep in the subways," she said.

Karen laughed. "Say no more," she said quite seriously. "What do I have to do to sign up? I'll do anything. And I do mean *anything*."

Leslie Savanah did not laugh. "Not so fast," she said. "You've got to convince us of your worth to the movement and, just as important, of your *sincerity*.'' Her expression brightened, and now she did laugh a friendly little laugh. ''And since right now you know even less about us than we know about you, it's a little early for you to be swearing your eternal dedication. Shall we take a little walk?''

''Let's go,'' Karen declared, fortifying herself with the remains of her third Irish coffee. ''It's the best offer I've had all month.'' She laughed. ''And about that, believe me, I'm sincere!'' she said. ''It's been the *only* offer.''

The rain had let up to a dense foggy drizzle, and Leslie kept in the lee of buildings as much as possible as she led Karen down to Houston, across the wide main crosstown artery, and three blocks west to Lafayette, where she turned south for half a block, then pressed the doorway intercom button of a crumbly industrial loft building that seemed about half occupied.

''Reality Liberation Front . . .'' said a scratchy voice through the rusty little speaker grid.

''Leslie . . .''

The front door buzzed open, and Leslie led Karen, damp and panting, up five long flights of musty, grimy stairs to an unmarked gray-painted steel door on the fifth-floor landing. She pressed a button in the doorframe, Karen saw someone flip aside the inside cover of the peephole, heard the clickings and clackings of several locks and bolts, and then the door opened, and a tall, stoop-shouldered, reedy black man thirty some-odd years old stood in the doorway, regarding her owlishly through thick wire-rimmed glasses.

''This is Karen Gold,'' Leslie told him. ''Possible recruit. Karen, this is Malcolm McGee, our number one wizard, or so he keeps telling us.''

Malcolm continued to regard Karen dubiously. He wore black jeans and a dirty white T-shirt with the ''RLF'' logo stenciled on it in black.

''Karen's got a degree in computer science from Rutgers.''

Malcolm's expression brightened. ''Well, that's more like it . . . maybe . . .'' he said, standing aside. ''We're the only anarchist cabal that requires a minimum of three years of college.''

Leslie led Karen into a large oblong high-ceilinged loft space as Malcolm went about resecuring two door locks, a chain, a bolt, and a police-lock bar. A big curtain sewn together out of a raggy assortment of tarps, old bedsheets, and blankets hung across about a quarter of the room on a clothesline. One long wall was given over to a series of big windows which looked as if they hadn't been cleaned since the administration of Ronald Reagan. There was an old stove, a big refrigerator, a steel restaurant double sink piled with dirty dishes and pots, and a jury-rigged shower clustered together against one short wall behind a big rude kitchen table.

The rest of the loft looked like some kind of Canal Street used electronic equipment warehouse.

There were at least a half-dozen computer set-ups of various moldy vintages wired together on desks and folding tables; weirdly mismatched keyboards, free-standing disc drives, monitors in naked frames that looked like they had been pulled out of old tv sets, hanging wallscreens, clunky old modems, bits of bread-board circuitry that Karen could not begin to comprehend. There were tottery stacks of videodiscs, ancient floppies, and books piled everywhere—on tables, on dirty old couches, on chairs, in crates, on the unpainted splintery gray wood of the floor. There must have been two dozen telephones scattered about the loft, free-standing or wired into modems. Wires and cables ran from everything to everywhere like an explosion in a spaghetti factory.

The overhead lighting, long fluorescent fixtures, was all but overwhelmed by the green, amber, and black and white glow of assorted monitors and the pools of light cast by the Tensor lamps and artist's lights illuminating the workspaces. Drives whirred, keyboards clacked, and Karen imagined she could even hear circuits sparking and smell the ozone.

"Je-sus . . ." She had no idea what she had expected, but no one could have expected anything like this!

"Welcome to the electronic village," Malcolm said dryly, coming up behind her. "The hardware may be the pathetic crap you see, but the software's got its heart in the right place."

"What are they all *doing*?" Karen asked him.

There were a half-dozen people huddled intently over their keyboards and computers, beavering away, and paying the visitor no mind. Two women and four men, none over thirty by the look of them, five whites and an oriental, intense, rather untidy, half of them sucking on cigarettes. One of the women, a thin mousy-haired girl who couldn't have been twenty-five, and two of the men, the well-built oriental, and a somewhat soft-looking white guy with a black mohawk, wore RLF T-shirts. It looked like a convention of computer nerds to Karen.

"They're doing our thing," Malcolm told her. "Writing bedbugs."

"Hey Markowitz, get your ass over here!" Leslie called out.

A big burly older man who had been peering over one of the female hacker's shoulders looked up, crossed the room, and scowled at Leslie with a resigned expression. He looked like a forty-five-year-old biker, with long wavy black hair, a bushy black beard, and intense blue eyes that seemed to look intently into Karen's without any malice.

"My name's not *Markowitz,*" he said by way of greeting as if he had said it a thousand times before. He held out a meaty hand. "That's just Leslie's idea of humor."

Karen shook his hand uncertainly. "Karen Gold. I'm afraid I—"

"*Gregor* Markowitz."

"Who?"

"*The Theory of Social Entropy . . .?*"

"What?"

The bearded man winked at her peculiarly. He shot a wide-eyed glance at Leslie. "What have you brought us, Leslie, a tender young virgin?"

"In an ideological manner of speaking. But she *does* have a degree in computer science."

"In that case, conditionally pleased to meet you," the bearded man said, shaking her hand again. "I'm Larry Coopersmith, the local commissar, as it were."

Coopersmith led Karen and Leslie over to a dusty couch while Malcolm returned to whatever arcane electronic doings he had been involved with at his work station. He offered Karen a cigarette, shrugged when she declined, lit one up himself to the nose-wrinkled grimace of Leslie.

"Okay, Karen, so you've got a degree in computer science and you're thinking about joining the RLF," he said, leaning back expansively and throwing his arms up wide on the back of the couch. "Why?"

"*Why?*" Karen repeated cautiously as if she didn't understand the question. *Because I desperately need a place to crash,* the simple honest truth, was obviously not what was called for.

"I mean just how much do you know about the Reality Liberation Front?" Coopersmith said.

Karen looked from Larry Coopersmith to Leslie Savanah in

befuddlement, seeking some kind of rescue. What was she supposed to say, *nothing*? But what else *could* she say?

Leslie indeed came to her rescue, but not in any way Karen could have anticipated, and not in any way she could presently fathom. "What we have here, Markowitz," she said, "is a pure example of naive class self-interest."

Karen looked at Leslie. What the hell was that supposed to mean? She looked at Coopersmith. Now he was hunched forward studying her intently with those intelligent blue eyes and positively beaming at her as if Leslie's gibberish had made all the difference in the world to him.

And when he saw her confusion, he laughed warmly, slapped her on the knee, and said: "Let me tell you your story."

"Huh?"

"Middle-class parents, right, but for sure not as middle class *after* the Devaluation as before. Be smart, little Karen, don't get screwed like us, get yourself a degree that'll assure you a real job that will last your lifetime, something nice and high-tech and post-industrial, like . . . *computer science*. So good little Karen keeps her nose to the grindstone like she's told, and she gets her computer science degree, and probably even finds herself some kind of half-assed computer operator job, buys into a co-op, and thinks she's got it made. Then one day not just her job but *the whole class of jobs of which she is capable* gets put on a chip, and she gets canned, and she's got no prospects, soon no place to live, already no hope, and today she runs into Leslie, who tells her about this bunch of loonies who just might let her crash in their loft, and poor little Karen will do just about *anything* for a place to flop that will keep her out of the subway."

Coopersmith leaned back, took a deep drag on his cigarette, coughed out smoke in Karen's direction, eyed her narrowly, and grinned. "As the asshole mayor of this burg used to say when I was a kid," he said, "how am I doing?"

Karen gaped at him in dismay and amazement. This guy had not only seen right through her, he had summed up her entire life in about two minutes.

But Larry Coopersmith laughed heartily, reached out, and lifted her slack jaw back into place with his forefinger. "Don't goggle at me like I'm some kind of psychic," he said. "All I've got is a *dialectic*." He indicated everyone in the loft with a grandiose sweep of his arm. "You think anyone here is any different?" he said. "It's been done to *all of us*! It's the reality that's been imposed on the whole fucking country! It's *official reality*! It's why America is in the shit!''

He subsided into a more human and less declamatory mode. ''But at least in the Reality Liberation Front,'' he said, ''we know that we're not alone, we know that we're all in the same shit together.''

''End of speech, Markowitz, yes?'' Leslie said owlishly.

''You mean . . . you mean you're not pissed off that I'm trying to get into this Reality Liberation Front just to save my own skin?'' Karen said slowly. ''You . . . you don't think I'm a hypocritical self-serving little shit?''

''Maybe you brought us a live one,'' Coopersmith told Leslie Savanah. He winked at Karen. ''Congratulations,'' he said. ''You've just defined class self-interest.''

''I have . . . ?'' Karen muttered. *Class self-interest?* She laughed somewhat nervously. ''You're not gonna tell me I've fallen in with a bunch of Communists . . . ?''

''*Communists!*'' Larry Coopersmith fairly shouted, rolling his eyes toward the ceiling. He groaned. ''Those bug-brained motherfuckers are even worse control-addicts than the schmucks who think they're running things here!''

''Well then, what is all this *about*?'' Karen asked plaintively. ''What are you *doing* here?''

''I thought you'd never ask,'' Coopersmith said sweetly. ''What we're trying to do in the Reality Liberation Front is, of course, liberate reality.''

''*Liberate reality?* That doesn't make any sense.''

Coopersmith beamed at her. He got to his feet and began pacing in small circles. ''Speech number two,'' Leslie groaned good-naturedly.

''Hell no,'' Coopersmith declared, waving his arms, ''this is speech number one! This is the whole raison d'être! Look, Karen, for all practical purposes, this is the most advanced technological civilization the world has ever known, right?''

''Sure.''

He pointed a finger at her like a high school teacher. ''Then why are people's lives more fucked up than they were twenty years ago?'' he demanded.

Karen shrugged. It was the same question Leslie Savanah had asked her in the bar; it seemed even more central now than then, but she still could not even venture a guess.

''Hey there kid, is it something you did?'' Coopersmith went on. "Didn't you do what you were told you were supposed to do? Didn't you play by the rules? Didn't we all? And what have we all gotten by fulfilling our end of the social contract?"

"Fucked . . ." Karen said softly. There was no denying it. In fact, there was a certain exhilarating relief in admitting it.

"Yeah, but by *who*?" Coopersmith said slyly. "By *what*?"

"The . . . the power structure . . . ? The fat cats . . . ?"

"But they're in the shits too!" Coopersmith exclaimed. "The stock market is in the toilet, corporations keep folding, the country only avoided national bankruptcy by devaluating the currency and stiffing its creditors, and that didn't do much either because its creditors were *us*!"

"So . . . ?"

"So if we're all losers, there's only one conclusion, isn't there? The *system* is fucked! Reality obviously doesn't work the way the rules say it's supposed to work! The official map does not describe the territory!"

"And you, I suppose, have your own idea of what kind of rules will really work?" Karen said dubiously.

But Coopersmith beamed at her. "Shit no!" he said. "How the fuck should I know? *Anyone* who tries to lay *any* official reality on you is talking out his asshole! It's the whole stupid idea that there's any such thing as one true vision of reality that's fucked!"

"Huh?"

"*Huh?*" Coopersmith mimicked. He collapsed onto the couch beside her. He shook his head sadly. "You poor kids . . ." He sighed. "Once upon a time a whole generation said *fuck you* to official reality. This is a new age, the age of *multiple realities* created by tv and drugs and telephones and the global village and rock and roll! Let a thousand flowers bloom! Let a thousand new tribes multiply! Let a million versions of reality joyfully contend!"

Coopersmith paused to study Karen. He shook his head again. "You never heard of that, did you?" he said. "It's not in the history books, is it?"

"I'm not as stupid as you seem to think," Karen told him indignantly. "You're talking about the sixties, the dope, and the hippies, and all—"

"And a little minor incident called the Vietnam War," Coopersmith said. "Sex, dope, and rock and roll was one thing, the powers that be could tolerate that, seeing as how times were flush, and they were making big bucks off of it."

Coopersmith paused to light a cigarette, and when he went on, it was in a more coldly ironic tone. "But when they found a whole generation saying fuck you to getting their asses blown off as gunfodder in some crummy jungle and beavering their lives away in nine-to-fivers, well, shit, *that* was over the edge, wasn't it? It was *bad for business*. You couldn't run a modern industrial economy if nobody wanted to grow up to be a wage slave. You couldn't play the good old nation state game with a generation that believed it was *stupid* to go out and die for abstractions. So what do you think they did?"

"They came down hard on all that stuff, didn't they?" Karen said.

Coopersmith nodded. "They came down hard on the mind-altering drugs. They reestablished control of the media. They killed off hundreds of underground newspapers one way or another. They took back control of the colleges and the high schools and the textbooks. They did what they had to do to reestablish an official reality."

Coopersmith leaned back, puffed on his cigarette, and grinned sardonically. "But they ended up imposing a new official reality on *themselves*. They made the fatal mistake of believing their own bullshit. They engineered a monster recession to break unions and create a big permanent pool of unemployment to keep wages down and to keep kids like you toeing the line and doing what you were told for fear of joining it. They listened to asshole economists who told them exactly what they wanted to hear and wrote the biggest rubber check in history and passed it off on *themselves*. They blathered on about a post-industrial economy and how everyone was going to work in service industries for peon wages without realizing that everyone couldn't make a living taking in each other's laundry. They automated out as many workers as they could to increase productivity, but it never dawned on them that they couldn't sell all the shit if people didn't have the money to buy it."

He cocked his head at Karen. "Begins to sound familiar, doesn't it?" he said. "I mean, here we all are today, with enough production robots for thirty million workers to turn out three times as much goods as we can sell anywhere, and twenty-five or thirty million people like you without a pot to piss in and wondering why."

Not since college had Karen subjected herself to anything remotely like an extended historical argument, and never, certainly not in any history course at Rutgers, had she heard *this* version of recent history. And never had she even imagined that such a historical lecture could be delivered with such angry personal passion, or that some recitation of events that had occurred before she was even born could roil her own emotions so.

But Larry Coopersmith had managed to convince her of one thing at least, namely that historical forces did not play themselves out without shafting real people, for she could hardly deny that *she* was personally and precariously perched on the shitty end of this one.

"You're saying we're all the victims of some gigantic con job . . . ?" she said slowly.

"You got it," Coopersmith said, nodding his head. "Including the schmucks that did it to us."

"And the Reality Liberation Front is out to . . . to do *what*?" she asked dubiously. For what could a bunch of hackers in a grungy Lafayette Street loft hope to do to roll back the gigantic steamroller of history?

"To liberate reality as best we can," Coopersmith said. "To throw our little electronic monkey wrenches into the works. To destroy the viability of official reality."

"No bomb-throwing? No riots in the streets? You're talking about bringing down the system with nothing but a bunch of bedbug programs?"

"Precisely," said Larry Coopersmith. "These days, the system *is* really just one great big interconnected web of software, now isn't it? Data banks, the telephone system, IRS computers, bank computers, ATMs, satellite networks, credit card records, utility company records, the stock market, the commodities exchange, electronic bulletin boards! It's all in the bits and bytes. And where there are bits and bytes, there are openings for—"

"*Bedbugs!*" Karen exclaimed.

Coopersmith laughed. "Hundreds of bedbugs, thousands, millions of them, *bedbugs to the people*! All nibbling away at official reality and turning it into a great big electronic Swiss cheese riddled with little liberated holes. And when there are more holes than cheese . . ."

"Reality is liberated!

"Chaos is reborn!"

"And then what?" Karen said.

Coopersmith looked at Leslie. Leslie looked at Coopersmith.

They both put on crazed wild-eyed faces. They laughed maniacally. They chanted in unison. "THEN THE FUN REALLY BEGINS!"

"You people are really crazy!" Karen said.

But she was grinning as she said it, and she said it approvingly. She looked around the great untidy loft, at the endless mounds of electronic jury-rigging, at the people much like her beavering away over their keyboards and monitors, not to program some dumb production robots to put more people out of work and collect a paycheck till they did it to themselves, but in the service of some loony political notion she could barely understand.

Loony or not, however, she could see the energy behind it, she could hear it in the clicking and clacking of the keyboards and drives, she could smell it in the ozone in the air. *Idealism* had never been more than a word in the dictionary to her before, and she would have scoffed had anyone told her it was the possibility she was tasting now, but what the hell, what did she have to lose; at the very least this was a place to crash.

"You people may be crazy," she said, "but I guess I'm not playing with a full deck myself. Count me in."

But Larry Coopersmith eyed her much more coldly now. "Not so fast," he said. "You have to be *voted* in. How good are you? What can you do for us?"

"How good am I?" Karen said in some dismay.

"How good a programmer are you? What kind of bedbugs have you written? Tell me some wizard ideas."

"What is this, a *job interview*?" Karen muttered with a sinking sensation in her stomach. For the truth of it was, as she well knew, that she was no computer wizard at all, she had never written anything but dumb routines, and in fact she didn't even really have any enthusiasm for playing with computers as these people so manifestly did. To her, ironically enough in the present circumstances, computer science had never been more than a means of securing a safe job.

"Come on, Larry," Leslie Savanah said in a somewhat wheedling tone, "don't be—"

Coopersmith cut her off with a raised hand. "Might as well tell us the truth now, Karen," he said not entirely unkindly. "We'll find out quickly enough. . . ."

Karen could only hang her head.

Coopersmith held up his hands and shrugged apologetically.

"Larry! Don't be such a shit!"

Coopersmith looked at Leslie Savanah with a somewhat relenting expression. "If it was up to me . . ." he said. He looked across the room at the electronic beehive of activity. "They won't vote her in as a charity case, and you know it, Leslie," he said.

Leslie regarded Karen forlornly. She mimicked Coopersmith's apologetic shrug. Then suddenly her eyes brightened. "Wait a minute!" she said. "Karen used to be a big-time wire dealer, isn't that right, Karen, isn't that what you told me?"

Coopersmith studied Karen with a certain bemused speculation. Leslie winked at her, telling her to play along.

"Wire dealer . . . ?" Coopersmith said slowly. "What good is that? We don't deal fucking *wire*!"

"But we don't deal many bedbugs in the meatracks where heavy wire dealing goes on either, now do we, Markowitz?" Leslie pointed out. "The RLF may be long on computer wizardry, but when it comes to street smarts . . ."

"Hmmmm . . ." Coopersmith muttered. "You just may have something there. . . ."

"And Karen here is a real wizard wire dealer; she knows her way around—The American Dream, The Temple of Doom, Hog Heaven—you know your way around that circuit real well, don't you, Karen?"

"For sure," Karen said. "No problem." It really wasn't that much of an exaggeration, was it? She had never hung out much in places like that when she was scoring cheap wire for her classmates in Jersey, but she *had* paid her way in trying to meet interesting men in these fancy joints when she had been able to afford it, hadn't she?

Besides, when it came to any wire dealing scene, these people didn't know jack shit by their own admission, did they?

"You'd be willing to deal bedbugs for the RLF in the meatracks?" Coopersmith asked. "You think you can do it?"

"Sure," Karen said. "Why not? From each according to her ability, to each according to her need, right? I need a place to crash, and you need someone with the ability to deal."

"Well, maybe," Coopersmith owned. "Maybe that's enough to convince me. But if I'm going to stand up and vouch for you, I'm going to need something more. . . . Something to convince everyone else that you're not just some sleazy wire dealer angling for a place to crash. . . . something to prove that you're really *sincere*. . . ."

His intelligent blue eyes seemed to stare right through her. They seemed to be looking for something hidden. Something deep inside. Something she did not at all want them to see. But something she knew was there nonetheless.

And all at once she knew what it was.

Twenty-six hundred dollars.

She stared right back at Larry Coopersmith and knew for a certainty that she could buy her way into the Reality Liberation Front. Not because they were cheap-shit mercenaries, but because it would be *just*. Because it would hurt. And because it would hurt, it would be a genuine proof of her sincerity. And because she genuinely believed in *his* sincerity, she believed he would understand. She thought of that bastard Greg. She thought of the wire she had dealt to get the money he was stealing from her. What would the money buy her anyway? A couple of months in a sleazy fleabag hotel. A few score trips to bath houses and Laundromats.

Or a grand gesture.

She had never made a grand gesture in her life.

She had never before even conceived of the concept.

But she understood it now.

And it felt good. It felt right.

"I've got twenty . . . I've got two thousand dollars," she said. "You guys let me in, and I'll donate it to the cause. Is *that* sincere enough for you . . . Markowitz?"

Coopersmith stared at her. He did not smile. "You'd do that?" he said softly. "You'd really do that?"

"Try me," Karen said.

Larry Coopersmith beamed at her. He threw his huge arms around her in a great bear hug. He planted a big wet sexless kiss on her lips. "All *right*!" he exclaimed. "You're in, or *I* walk right out the fucking door!"

Karen Gold looked out across the loft of the Reality Liberation Front. She looked at the sprawl of electronic junk. She looked at the people hunkered over it. She peered out the grimy windows at the implacable and uncaring streets of the city beyond. She looked at Leslie Savanah, giving her the high sign. She looked at Larry Coopersmith looking at her with a respect and affection she had never known before.

And for the first time in her life, she knew what it felt like to be on the inside looking out.

SCORING

Manhattan was crawling with fuckin' zonies, and the Uzi was their weapon of choice, but figuring out how to *crash and grab* one of the putamadres and get away with his piece instead of a skin full of holes seemed about as easy as walking across the Hudson to Hoboken to Paco Monaco as he slunk around the fringes of various Zones for days on end searching for a target of opportunity.

All his street-smart instincts had schooled him to avoid the motherfuckers and do his best to make himself invisible as far as they were concerned. His experience in *stalking* zonies was exactly nada; indeed, he had never heard of anyone even trying to do such an asshole thing.

But while he could feel his bowels loosening in terror every time he so much as looked at one of these mean-eyed malhombres with the fantasy of crash and grab in his head, the fear itself, and the knowledge that he was out to do a deed that no one who wasn't bugfuck bananas had ever even thought about doing before, were like a flash of the Prong.

As he had so often wandered among the look-but-don't-touch chocharicas promenading down Second or First or A with an aching hard-on of unfulfillable desire, so did he now stalk many of the same streets with a frustrated hard-on of another kind for all these putamadre zonies. For just as the dream of fucking some cool blond chocharica bitch into adoring submission had more behind it than just cooling his cojones, so did the thought of scoring an Uzi by beating the shit out of a zonie mean more to him than just scoring himself a Zap.

The way these maricónes tracked him with their eyes as he slunk past them, forcing him to look away like some fucking perro pobre for fear that they just might decide to blow him away for forcing them to notice his lowly existence, the sincojones stance he had automatically fallen into in their presence all of his life, now had a keener edge to it as he contemplated vengeance, and he used that edge to hone his fear into a gut-wrenching rage that he hoped would give him the necessary courage when the moment came.

Pero courage, sí, assholery, no. He had learned more about zonies in these few days of intense and purposeful scrutiny than he had in an entire life lived under their cold and suspicious gazes.

While not all of them were hulking heavyweights, all of them had the look of muchachos who spent hours and hours building up their bodies and practicing some hard martial art. And almost all of them had the streetwise look of malhombres who had fought their way up out of the gutter, no soft down-on-their-luck gordos need apply. And of course, while not all of them packed Uzis, all of them were always conspicuously heeled.

And you never saw one of the putamadres with his back to an alley or doorway or street corner. Even when they were on the move, they seemed somehow to be able to keep a wall to their back. Chingada, they were *good,* they were as streetwise as any crash and grab artist like Paco, not so surprising, really, since half of them had probably started out just that way.

How then to catch one of these wary putamadres off his guard? This was the question that had taunted Paco since the stalk began, and while the answer was something that he had not yet let percolate up into his conscious awareness on the late evening of the eighth day, his feet had finally begun to figure it out, as they took him, without his self-aware decision, west along Houston Street, across Seventh Avenue into the West Village, and onto Bedford, a short side street that ran three blocks northwest to dead-end into Christopher.

Bedford Street was narrow, shadowy, and pretty much devoid of storefronts, but this was not the sombre side, son, this was a street of well-kept apartment houses and even some carefully restored old town houses, definitely a Zone, muchacho, sure to have at least one zonie patrolling it who would not take kindly to the intrusion of such as Paco onto his turf.

Qué pasa, muchacho? he asked himself as he found himself staring up the dark canyon of Bedford Street toward the light and flash of Christopher at the far end. Muy loco, what you think you're doing, walking right into a Zone? He paused, started to turn back east. Better get your ass out of here before—

Just then, two reedy well-dressed gordos turned the corner of Bedford onto Seventh, walking hand-in-hand, and Paco's palms and scrotum broke into a queasy cold sweat as he abruptly realized what foul but streetwise instinct had brought him here.

Verdad, this was a Zone.

Pero una Zona Maricóna.

Oh no, muchacho, chingada man, you're not gonna . . .

Paco had not ventured near this vecino for years and years, not since he was a tight-assed sixteen-year-old willing to do anything for a score, willing to let faggots suck his cock for a few dollars, willing to let them have it up the ass in the ruins on West Street for a few dollars more, willing even once or twice . . .

He hadn't even allowed these old memories to surface, he wasn't about to . . .

Por qué no, muchacho? a dirty bird whispered in his ear.

This was a Zone where rico maricónes lived; Christopher Street was still the main drag of what was left of the faggot meatrack scene. These fuckin' faggots had plenty of dinero for zonies, and they needed them for sure. But not too many real machos were about to work *this* Zone, and besides, las frutas liked to hire their own.

And while Paco knew full well that the kind of faggot who worked as a *zonie* would be no easy sister, how good could anyone be with his pants unzipped and his dick in his hand?

Chingada, it wasn't as if he were about to let any maricón motherfucker *do* anything to him, was it? All he had to do was get the fucker worked up, get him to drop his pants and whip it out, and then . . .

Serve the son of a bitch right!

Paco hesitated for a long moment at the mouth of the dark little street, sweating in his jeans, a hollow bubble of nausea churning in his gut. Chingada, man, don't be such a fuckin' chicken! he told himself. What would Mucho Muchacho do? Shit man, probably nothin' gonna happen anyway. You come all the way over here for nothing?

At least just walk up the street to Christopher and back. Up and down. Just once. Up one side and down the other.

Paco nibbled his lower lip for a moment. Then he took a deep breath, unzipped his fly halfway to flash the top of his pubic hair, and began walking up the right side of Bedford, nervously, rapidly, but with a rolling, ass-waggling, exaggerated maricón mince.

One block. A block and a half. No one on the street, just the dimly lit aisle between the low buildings and the obscene garish lights of Christopher up ahead. You got yourself all worked up for nothing, Paco told himself. Nothing's gonna—

"What the fuck you doing on this street, asshole?"

Madre de Dios!

A great big ugly motherfucker had somehow managed to appear out of nowhere and had the muzzle of an Uzi pointed right at his belly button. Chingada, what a monster! Oh shit!

The zonie must have been six foot four, though from Paco's perspective he might as well have been eight foot six. He wore a tight white T-shirt outlining perversely chiseled wrestler's muscles, and tight black leather pants with a huge chromed zipper that gleamed in the light of a streetlamp. He had closely cropped black hair, little steel earrings up and down both earlobes, a hideously acne-scarred skin, beady black eyes, and a mouthful of rotten teeth behind a vicious scowl that told Paco in no uncertain terms that he was not amused.

"I *said,* what the fuck are you doing on this street, asshole," the zonie repeated.

Paco came as close to shitting in his pants as he ever had in his life; he had to tighten his sphincter by an act of will. Oh man, oh fuck, what am I going to do? But he was committed now, there was no backing out, this fucking faggot son of a bitch had his Uzi pointed right at his gut, and he could see the bastard's finger eagerly stroking the trigger. What would Mucho Muchacho do?

Mucho Muchacho wouldn't be here, asshole! he realized. This isn't some videodisc, this is *real.* And with that realization, he felt a strange energy course through him. He felt a tingling at the base of his spine, a heat behind his breastbone; he felt the blood pounding in his arteries and behind his temples, and, horror of horrors and wonder of wonders, he felt his cock hardening, a hard-on not of lust, oh no, but of rage, and fear, and cornered determination.

"What are *you* doing on this street?" he made himself answer in an insinuating tone.

The zonie looked at him speculatively now. His ratlike eyes ran up and down Paco's body. He smiled thinly. Paco stared openly at the crotch of his tight black leather pants and watched the monster's cock engorge, bulging the shiny chrome zipper outward.

Paco was beyond thinking now. It was far too late for that. He was running on pure instinct. He fixed his gaze on the zonie's crotch, ran his tongue slowly around his lips, and hooked his right thumb into the open top of his own fly, watching the big zonie's gaze follow.

"Hey man, that's sure a big gun you have," he said softly. "You really know how to use it?"

The zonie's eyes seemed to acquire a glistening sheen now. He thrust his pelvis forward and ran his free hand along the short barrel of the Uzi. "Want me to show you?" he said.

Paco wriggled his ass in place. He took a deep breath, reached out, and ran a forefinger very slowly along the barrel of the machinepistol, twirling it around the tip. "Oooh . . ." he purred. "It's so cold and so hard."

"You like something hotter?"

"For sure, man," Paco said, reaching down with his other hand and unzipping his fly the rest of the way loudly. He glanced around him. There was a dark alley between a town house and an adjacent apartment building close by, a line of garbage cans along one wall, plenty of empty space by the bricks of the other.

"In here," he whispered, clasping the barrel of the Uzi in one hand and pumping rhythmically as he pulled the zonie forward, as he undid the top button of his jeans with the other.

Slowly, as if in a trance, the big man followed him into the alley. Paco reached out, caught the tab of the chrome zipper, and yanked it downward. The zonie's huge hard cock popped out. Paco moaned in delight, turned, offered up his ass, placed both hands up against the wall, and writhed seductively.

He peered back over his shoulder as the zonie slung his Uzi onto his back, grabbed his dick with one hand, reached for him with the other.

"Fuck you, maricón!" Paco screamed, pivoting on his right heel, kicking out with his left foot, and catching the zonie square in the cojones.

The big man screamed in agony and amazement. Paco slammed into the back of his neck with the side of his right hand as the zonie folded, clutching his nuts, grabbed the Uzi off his shoulder with his left hand, caught him in the chin with another full-force kick, stuffed the gun into his street bag, and ran.

* * *

It was no surprise to Glorianna O'Toole when they finally gave Billy Beldock the ax. Billy had told her at Eddie Friedkin's party that his days as president of Muzik, Inc., were numbered unless Project Superstar paid off in gold soon, and the kids had accomplished nothing of significance since.

Indeed, whatever had gone on between them before Bobby barfed his guts out all over Eddie's beautifully groomed lawn, far from finally syncing their creative vibes as Glorianna had hoped, only seemed to have poisoned an already testy professional relationship.

Sally was mooning quite openly after Bobby under the apparent delusion that whatever had happened had brought them closer, and Bobby alternated between putting her down and trying to pretend she didn't exist. Under these circumstances, Glorianna hadn't been able to squeeze even marginally marketable dead-ass crap out of them, and for poor Billy's sake, she had certainly tried every trick she knew.

She had brought dust into the studio and let them blow their brains out with it for days at the Factory's considerable expense. She had brought in good old-fashioned grass. She had dragged them to every club in town. She had even spent a small fortune of the Factory's money setting up alternate VoxBox and image organ equipment in her own house in the foredoomed hope that the vibes there would prove more creative.

None of it worked. All she had to show for it was a king-sized pain in the ass, a huge stash of free dust and pot, and a living room now cluttered with electronic junk. These kids were technically brilliant, any idiot could see that. But these kids were out of sync with each other and with the mysterious inner heart of rock and roll, and any real rocker could see that too. The whole damned project was misconceived from the beginning, and she had told Billy that up front.

To hell with the promise that they would do her next if she came up with two AP discs that shipped gold! It was never going to happen anyway, and if it hadn't been for her feelings for poor Billy, she would have already told the Factory to take it and stick it.

Now that he was out, and this Carlo Manning was in, she went into the meeting he had summoned her to with every intention of telling him just that.

Manning was so new to the black leather chair behind the permanent gunmetal desk that, while Billy's French antique furniture was already out of the president's office, his hadn't even been moved in yet, and aside from the desk, the hot-seat, the disc decks, and the screen, the only furnishings in the place were a hideously mismatched collection of temporary director's chairs and folding tables.

Somehow it seemed appropriate. Carlo Manning was maybe a shade under forty. He had short well-barbered black hair, wore a conservative black suit with a white shirt and plain blue and silver striped tie, and he had a bland anonymous face that would fade into the woodwork at any party Glorianna had ever attended. He had gotten to the president's chair through the research department, and as far as she knew, had never sung or played any instrument.

At last a generic Muzik, Inc., president, Glorianna thought dryly as she plopped her bones into an uncomfortable chair and watched Manning pretend to study a sheaf of printouts intently for long moments before he spoke.

"Thirty days," he finally said in a flat even voice by way of greeting.

"What?"

"You have thirty days to bring me a demo disc that marketing estimates will ship one million plus or minus ten percent to a seventy-percent certainty," Manning told her, regarding her with his cool brown eyes as if she were no more than a printout herself. "That's the bottom line."

It was loathing at first sight. Who did this little punk think he was, talking to her like that?

"You don't waste much time on small talk, do you?" Glorianna snapped.

"My salary is a mil a year, sixteen thou a week, about three a day, two hundred sixty an hour," Manning told her. "It is therefore my responsibility to the company to manage it in a cost-effective manner."

Glorianna O'Toole had never heard such horseshit in her whole long life, and she had heard plenty. "Yeah, well I'll lay you even money you don't keep your ass in that chair long enough to collect six months' worth of it, sonny."

If she had managed to piss Manning off, he didn't show it. "It is my intention to be here a good long time," he said evenly. "It's about time the company had stable professional management at the top instead of a succession of broken-down old hippies like Billy Beldock."

"Yeah, well, watch your mouth, kiddo. Billy is a friend of mine, and as a matter of fact, I'm proud to say I'm a broken-down old hippie myself!"

Manning favored her with a sardonic corporate smile. "So I've noticed," he said.

Glorianna glared at him. If I were a man and twenty years younger, I'd punch out this little prick, she thought. Shit, twenty years ago I would've punched him out anyway!

"Go fuck yourself," she told Manning, rising to her feet, "you'll probably meet a better class of people. And if that doesn't get you off, stick your thirty days up your tight little asshole! This broken-down old hippie quits as of now."

"Sit down," Manning said in a voice of cold confident authority. "This meeting is over when *I* say it's over."

"We have nothing to talk about," Glorianna told him.

"Ah, but we do, Ms. O'Toole," Manning said smoothly. "Unless of course you prefer to discuss matters with the district attorney."

"The district attorney?"

"Do sit down, Ms. O'Toole," Manning said. Once more he made a fetishistic pretense of studying his readouts. "We have thus far expended approximately four million dollars on Project Superstar, counting salaries, studio time, production, promotion, and advertising on the discs we've already released, and . . . certain other items. I do not intend to simply write all that off, even if I *can* blame it on Beldock. That would not be fiscally responsible."

"That's not my problem . . ."

"Oh but it is," Manning said, leering at her openly now. "A small but significant portion of your budget contains the rather ambiguous category of 'research materials.' We both know what that really means, now, don't we?"

"You wouldn't . . . You couldn't . . ." Glorianna stammered. She found herself collapsing back into her chair without conscious volition.

"Designer dust, marijuana, and perhaps other illegal substances, procured by you with funds embezzled by you from Muzik, Inc., and resold at a profit to Rubin and Genaro," Manning said. "Several criminal charges would be involved . . .

possession with intent to sell . . . embezzlement of company funds . . . even possible income tax violations. . . ."

"You'd never make any of that bullshit stick, and you know it!"

Manning shrugged diffidently. "Maybe yes, maybe no," he said. "I'd be willing to leave it up to the courts. We have plenty of lawyers we're already paying handsome salaries to to present our side of the case. You, of course, would have to pay counsel to defend yourself against criminal charges of some complexity in several jurisdictions. Can you afford it?"

"You're a cold son of a bitch, aren't you?"

"I'm an expert in human motivation," Manning said. He pointed at the wall of miniature gold discs. "I was responsible for the motivational specs on thirteen of those," he said proudly. "That's why I have this job." He smiled fatuously at Glorianna. "And I do believe I've succeeded in motivating you, now haven't I?"

Glorianna O'Toole studied this corporate monster with utter dismay and loathing. Was this what the industry had finally come to? Am I going to give this creep what he wants just to save my own ass?

Stupid question, Glorianna. A better question would be how do you feature spending your dotage in the joint? Where would you get the money to hire a lawyer?

More horribly to the point, how in hell am I going to do the impossible in the next thirty days?

"And if I try and fail . . . ?" she asked plaintively.

Manning cocked his head at her and drummed his fingers thoughtfully on the desktop. "I'm not an unfeeling man," he finally said. "You do your best and convince me of your sincerity, and I'm willing to leave that question open."

"What does *that* mean?"

Manning picked up his sheaf of readouts and buried his nose in them. "It means," he said, without looking up at her again, "that this meeting is now over."

Glorianna did not go to the studio after her meeting with Carlo Manning. Instead, she drove directly home, went out onto her deck with a gram of dust and a full bottle of Pouilly-Fuissé, lay back on a beach chair staring down from her mountaintop at the thick brown layer of smog over the city, and did her best to get righteously loaded.

Her best, alas, was not quite good enough. The dust merely kept her mind crystal-clear and going round and round the circuit of her dilemma, and the wine merely kept her blood sugar up and supplied her with energy so that she couldn't even blitz herself into oblivion.

What I really need, she thought as the sun began to set in gorgeous smog-born flaming orange into the invisible Pacific, is some acid. Some mescaline. Some peyote.

The thought made her sit bolt upright.

Do I dare feed these nerdy little kids some real psychedelic?

Is there anything else left to do that I haven't tried?

Alas, the younger generation was, generally speaking, scared shitless of psychedelics. They had grown up afraid in a world they hadn't made, and even when it came to getting loaded, they were conditioned to play it safe. They preferred designer dust that was guaranteed to always take you to precisely where you thought you wished to go.

Glorianna O'Toole looked out over the smog-bound city, where a million lights were coming on, transforming the endless impoverished barrio of lowland Los Angeles into an immense shimmering wonderland of living jewels under the smoggy glory of the setting sun. How many times had she experienced such a magic moment of reality transformation from on high as the LSD or the mescaline or the peyote began its rush through her brain, as ordinary earth-bound reality dissolved into the multiverse of the infinite possible, taking her spirit with it?

Rock and roll, after all, as anyone who was there knew full well when they were still willing to admit it, had flowered to its full glory on acid. Leary and Kesey had turned on the world to the music of the Airplane and the Dead and Big Brother. It was the music of transformation, or it just wasn't rock and roll, it was *product,* Muzik—precisely the kind of technically proficient soulless shit Bobby and Sally had been turning out!

Without acid, would rock have ever been anything more than ass-kicking music for greasers? Where would *your* career have been without good old Owsley? Remember what the Dormouse said?

It's not as if I was going to tie them up and force it down their throats, she told herself. I'll just score some good stuff and leave it up to them, see what they're really made of. She laughed. "Lucy in the sky with diamonds . . ." she sang full out with what was left of her pipes into the fragrant Laurel Canyon night, "ah . . . ah . . . AH. . . ."

Cackling merrily to herself, she picked up her phone and began to call connections.

But as it turned out, peyote and magic mushrooms would seem to have all but vanished from the face of the earth, nobody had anything they would even try to palm off as mescaline, and the only LSD available was in the form of tabs.

Glorianna did not trust acid in tabs. Nine times out of ten, the filler was some shitty form of speed, and half the time there wasn't any real LSD in the tablet at all, just some PCP or STP or other brainburner that gave a nasty crude high powerful enough to convince the naive that they had dropped the Mighty Quinn.

It was against her religion to take acid other than blotter or windowpane or the actual pure liquid when you could get it. Since LSD was the only drug she knew that was effective in microgram doses, if all you were taking was a little blot on paper, or a tiny sliver of clear gel, or a single drop of liquid, if you got off at all, it had to be on the real thing.

And if she wouldn't drop a tab herself, she could hardly offer up such questionable goods to two innocent young lysergic virgins.

For a mad moment she actually toyed with the notion of descending from the Hollywood Hills into the flatland barrio and seeing what she could score on the streets.

Forty years ago she had done it all the time, thirty years ago she wouldn't have thought twice, twenty years ago she just might have risked it, but these days it really *was* another world down there.

The Third World begins at Pico, as they said up here in show-biz country, and while Glorianna might nurse a romantic nostalgia for the long-gone days of solidarity with The People, the closest she had gotten to same in the last five years was passing through at sixty on the Harbor Freeway, for the law ended at the off ramp when you drove through North Mexico, and an old lady in a Rolls would be spare parts and dogmeat by the time she hit the first stoplight.

A two-hundred-mile drive up the coast to Big Sur was, from this perspective, a much shorter trip than a suicide run down into the barrio visible from her mountaintop, so if she was desperate enough to even think about scoring on the street, it was long since time to call Ellie Dawson.

Ellie had been around almost as long as she had. She had been a rock journalist on the *Berkeley Barb* when Glorianna first met her, had gotten political and even been a Weather Underground fringie for a while until they actually began blowing things up in earnest, at which point she had segued into the Human Potential Movement, later on dabbled in the think tanks around Palo Alto, had married a computer wizard, and settled down in Silicon City, divorced him, and went back to traveling the upper-class guru farm circuit between Mendicino and Big Sur.

But if her official bio gave the impression that she flitted from this to that somewhat inconsistently, and with no more than ethereal means of support, the fact of it was that Ellie Dawson had been a dealer for almost all of her adult life.

A *connoisseur* dealer. Glorianna had never heard of Ellie dealing in anything as mundane as grass or coke, and she righteously refused to have anything to do with speed, smack, or downers. She specialized in psychedelics, of which acid was the least arcane, she refused on principle to deal anything she hadn't tried herself, and she gave honest reviews to her customers, which had run, during various incarnations, from rock musicians, to science fiction writers, to revolutionaries, to Human Potential devotees, to cyberwizards, and, so she claimed, to politicians whose names would surprise you.

If anyone could get Glorianna some proper acid, it would be Ellie Dawson, and the only reason Glorianna hadn't called her until she got desperate was that Ellie now lived in Big Sur, four hours up the coast.

After the opening pleasantries, Glorianna explained the situation to Ellie, leaving out nothing; not her considered obscene opinion of Carlo Manning, not her analysis of the psychic states of Bobby Rubin and Sally Genaro, not the sad fate of Billy Beldock, not the nature of Project Superstar, and not even the sling her ass was going to be in with the law. With Ellie's Silicon City connections, her phone was more secure than the Washington–Moscow hotline.

There was a long pause at the other end after her tirade had run down. "Jeez, Glorianna, I'd really like to help you," Ellie's voice finally said. "But acid is really rather *tight* just now. . . ."

"Meaning even *you* don't have any . . . ?" Glorianna moaned.

"Nothing I'd care to drop myself, if you know what I mean. . . ."

"Shit. . . ."

Another pause.

"*However . . .*" Ellie said in a slow, cautious, conspiratorial tone.

"However . . . ?"

"There's something rather peculiar going on in Silicon City, I mean, it's so murky that even *I* don't know which stories to believe. . . . You've heard about the underground wizard shops . . . ?"

"Stories," Glorianna said.

Someone was turning out sophisticated devices that somehow enabled pranksters to temporarily commandeer broadcast satellite transponders. Everyone knew that much, since occasionally HBO or NBC or MUZIK feeds were interrupted with clips from grainy old porn movies. There were stories that military and diplomatic satellites had been monkeyed with too, the best of them being that a hotline tête-à-tête between the president and the Soviet chairman had been interrupted by some choice cuts from *Deep Throat,* but such stuff was obviously too hot for even the *National Enquirer* to handle, assuming for the moment that it was actually going on.

"Well the video pirates are real enough and so are the wizard shops," Ellie said. "But no one seems to know who either of them are, or what they're really after, or even if it's the same outfit. But there's a piece of wire starting to turn up that—"

"*Wire?*" Glorianna exclaimed. "I ask you for *acid* and you're trying to peddle me *wirehead* shit?"

"Am I some burnt-out wirehead, Glorianna? Have I ever dealt wire before? Would I deal something I haven't tried myself? Will you at least hear me out?"

"Go ahead," Glorianna said dubiously.

"This is no ordinary piece," Ellie told her. "It's not a mess of breadboards and hand-wired circuitry. It's elegantly made and you can wear it around, and everything's on a single chip, and the story is that it's underground wizard shop product. Face it, Glorianna, this is the electronic age and we're talking state of the art. . . . Want to hear more?"

Glorianna was beginning to become intrigued despite herself. She had to admit that part of her prejudice against wire had to do with what circuitry had done to rock and roll. Then, too, most wire was brainburning garbage for juice junkies. But so were chemical highs like speed and reds and smack. Acid, however . . .

"I'm still listening, Ellie," she finally said.

"It's called the Transcortical Shunt—"

"En inglés, por favor . . ."

"The Transcortical Shunt," Ellie repeated, carefully enunciating the syllables one by one. "It gives the dream centers a transient zap and shunts the output across the cortex to the centers of waking consciousness. It shunts sensory input through the dream centers before it gets to the areas of the brain that process it into sense images. And it keeps the motor control centers active in the bargain too. I had one of the things taken apart by some of my friends up there before I even tried it, you better believe it."

"Terrific," Glorianna said dryly. "But as the wireheads say, what's the flash?"

"A bit like sleepwalking, a bit like a lucid dream in reverse. You've got motor control, you walk, and talk, and even make love, but you're doing it all inside a dream. You're interfaced with external reality as if you were awake, but you're experiencing it imagistically. Like what the Australian aborigines call a Walkabout through the Dreamtime. You wouldn't *believe* what the EKG looks like!"

"Sounds mighty dangerous," Glorianna said. "I mean, what's to keep you from sleepwalking into a wall while you dream you're walking down the beach?"

"That's the real wizard touch! You're getting transformations, sure, but you're still processing real sensory input! You see and hear what's going on around you, but it's glorified into a Dreamtime Walkabout. You may not see that wall as a wall, but your unconscious transforms it into an image that lets you know *something* solid is there. And as for sex . . . Mr. Ugly can be Mr. Wonderful if your karma is clean."

"An electronic acid trip . . ." Glorianna said softly.

"Why do you think I mentioned it?"

"But what's to keep a real Prince Charming from turning into a frog on you? What's to keep the dream from turning into a nightmare?"

"What's to keep an acid trip from turning into a bummer?"

"What's inside of you . . ." Glorianna muttered.

"Exactly," Ellie said. "Only this is safer. Each tap of the touchpoint gives you a flash that lasts something between ten minutes and thirty minutes, not hours and hours. And if the trip turns nasty, another tap pops you right out of it, like a reset button for bummers."

"You've tried it?"

"You know me . . ."

"And what was it like?"

"What's a dream like? What's an acid trip like?"

"It's like . . ." Glorianna laughed. "It's like trying to tell someone about rock and roll."

"Which according to you is precisely your problem."

"So it is. . . ." Glorianna said. "Fuckin'-A!"

The sun had fully set now. She breathed in the sweet eucalyptus and bougainvillea scent of Lookout Mountain and gazed out over the vast nightscape of Los Angeles spread out before her, a fantastic electric starscape that made the stellar display above seem pallid indeed. Who could deny that this was the age of electronic marvels? Who could deny that the future belonged to those who embraced the cybersphere? Who could deny that she who wasn't being born was busy dying?

"You gonna be home tomorrow?" she said into the telephone, itself an instrument of the digitized realm of bits and bytes.

"I'll be waiting," said Ellie Dawson.

"See ya later," Glorianna said, hanging up the phone. What the hell, she thought, I always loved the drive up to Big Sur anyway.

THE KEY TO ANY DOOR

Karen Gold smiled, reached into her capacious purse, withdrew a bedbug disc in a brown manila envelope, handed it over, scooped up the cash, stuffed it away, and took another sip of her white wine. The balding man in the tan suit and red silk shirt seated on the barstool beside her slipped the envelope into a jacket pocket, glancing furtively around the gallery of The Temple of Doom for no particular reason, slugged down the remains of his Jack on the rocks, and then sauntered away from the bar and down the stairs to the dance floor, doing his somewhat ludicrous best to look casual as he completed his part in the time-honored pavanne of dealing choreography.

Eons ago it would have been a nickel bag of grass, later a gram of coke, currently a piece of wire more often than not, and now it was bedbugs. The items of commerce might change, but the moves remained the same.

And now, perched on a barstool sipping white wine, and surveying the gallery of a Soho meatrack over the lip of her glass with a hooded gaze like some desperado in an old gangster movie, Karen felt fully entitled for the first time in her life to the sleazy thrill of dealer's paranoia.

While drug trafficking had always been an unequivocal felony, dealing wire to kibble eaters was winked at by the authorities, for the powers that be couldn't care less if indigents sold to other indigents wirehead devices that would fry their brains beyond employability. Indeed, since wire addiction generally shortened the lifespan, there was something to be said for *encouraging* such street-level commerce, economically speaking.

Peddling wire to the gainfully employed, however, was a

definite no-no, tending as it did over time to convert taxpayers into kibble-eating vegetables. When Karen had scored in New York for her wire-chipping friends at Rutgers, the people she copped from were somewhat desperate characters who were risking three-to-five on the average if they were busted, though a college kid like herself could expect nothing worse than an overnighter in the tank and a pompous lecture in the morning for serving as a connection.

The use of bedbug programs to defraud banks, credit card companies, utilities, or, God help you, the IRS or state tax authorities, was, however, an unequivocal felony under any number of computer crime, tax, fraud, and theft-of-service statutes.

True, it was impossible to prosecute someone for mere possession of something as insubstantial as a program you could keep in your head if you were wizard enough. True too, that as far as even Larry Coopersmith knew, *dealing* bedbugs on disc was a brand-new crime, limited thus far to the Reality Liberation Front, and therefore not yet covered by specific legislation.

But Karen knew damn well that dealing bedbug discs would be treated as a serious crime one way or another if she were busted with the goods in her possession.

The bedbug that she had just sold for $400 was typical. With it, the guy she had sold it to, some kind of advertising executive apparently, could run up a huge balance on his expense account every month, and then cause his company's computer to spread it out in increments of a few cents each over every item of debit in the entire system. Malcolm McGee, who had written the thing, had made it invisible. You loaded it, did the dirty work, then erased the program from memory until you did it again. The accountants would go crazy trying to figure out how every debit on the books could be about seven cents too high, they would blame the software, the programmers would blame the hardware, and the repair techs would find nothing. When the monthly cost of continuing the futile search for the bedbug exceeded the system drain, they'd give up and write it all off to what Coopersmith called "system entropy."

If, however, she should somehow be arrested in the act of dealing such a bedbug, they'd surely nail her for something. Conspiracy to commit computer fraud or embezzlement. Maybe even possession of burglar's tools if they couldn't come up with anything better.

But until the authorities realized that commerce in bedbug

discs existed, the risk of selling one to an undercover cop was nil, and the dealer's paranoia that Karen allowed herself to feel as she sat on her barstool finishing her wine was really just a cheap thrill, even as the part of intrepid streetwise dealer that she played for the benefit of her newfound friends at the RLF loft was a put-on that wouldn't have impressed anyone less naive than these innocents.

And in a very real way, the Reality Liberation Front *was* a cabal of innocents.

Tommy Don, grandson of industrious Vietnamese immigrants. Bill Connally and Iva Cohen, whose parents had sweated and scraped to send their offspring to college in the traditional hope that their whiz-kid children would rise above their own working-class status. Teddy Ribero, the first in his family to even complete high school since his ancestors came to New York from Puerto Rico. Malcolm McGee, scion of the black middle class from Tarrytown. Eddie Polonski and Mary Ferrari, who had won scholarships to New York colleges, and thought they had made their escape from the permanent depression of the midwestern Rust Belt.

What all these cybernaifs had in common was that they had all been computer wizards virtually from birth. They had grown up obsessed with computers, happily lost in the dance of the bits and the bytes. Unlike Karen, they had no childhood memories of a lost New York Eden on the Upper West Side to torment them. Unlike Karen, their degrees in computer science had been the ultima thules of their hearts' desires, not a grimly calculated escape route back to Manhattan from the exile of Poughkeepsie.

Oh yes, they too had been betrayed when their personal economic shit hit the fan, but now, blissfully ensconced behind their keyboards and screens and hacking away at bedbugs for the hell of it, living, eating, and breathing the ozone air of their beloved cybersphere day and night, they had what they wanted. The bedbugs that they wrote, the computer babble that they conversed in, even the revolutionary raison d'être of the Reality Liberation Front, were all like some vast computer game that encompassed their lives. They hardly bothered to leave the loft at all. They didn't even think about money. The uses to which their programs were being put by the customers Karen and Leslie Savanah peddled them to were mere abstractions. And the world of the streets might as well have been another planet as far as they were concerned.

Only Leslie Savanah and "Markowitz" were different.

Leslie reminded Karen of herself. She too had no real passion for the bits and the bytes. She might have grown up in the Midwest instead of the Upper West Side, but she knew what it was to lose a share in a Manhattan co-op and find herself out on the street, broke and desperate, but unwilling to give up and leave the Apple. Her bedbug dealing might have been limited to lowlife bars and she had not spent the weekends of her college years scoring wire in fancy saloons and meatracks, but she *was* a dealer and she *had* picked Karen up in The Clearing. So although Leslie Savanah had preceded her into the RLF by half a year and indeed had recruited her, Karen thought of her affectionately as a kind of country cousin.

Larry Coopersmith, aka Markowitz, was something else again, though no two people in the loft could agree on quite what, and he wasn't telling. Even Leslie, his occasional lover, didn't know his age any closer than somewhere between forty and fifty-five. He looked as if he had been a biker, he had a collection of books like a former college professor, and he spoke as if he had been both, mixing four-letter words and four-hundred-dollar words in the same sentence with impunity. He never spoke of his past. There was no one in the RLF who had been there before he rented the loft. No one knew where the money to do it had come from. No one knew where "Markowitz" had come from.

He seemed to know programming but Karen had never seen him write anything of his own. He insisted he wasn't a Communist or an anarchist and proclaimed his hatred of "anything that ended in *ism.*" Leslie had dubbed him "Markowitz" because Gregor Markowitz, an obscure political theorist Karen had never heard of, was his main intellectual guru. He had piles of old hardcover books by Markowitz with titles like *The Theory of Social Entropy, Chaos and Culture,* and *Order Against Itself,* which he offered to let her read, but somehow Karen had never gotten around to it.

All in all, Larry Coopersmith had more mysterioso than any other man Karen had ever met, and if someone other than Leslie had been what passed for his main lady, she just might have been interested.

And then again maybe not. For while Coopersmith might be a man of no little fascination, and while the RLF loft was a long way from crashing in the subway, and while she considered Leslie her friend, and while the vaguely defined goals of the

Reality Liberation Front tickled her esthetic fancy, the truth of it was that in her heart of hearts she could consider the whole scene as no more than a station on the way, and certainly not a lifestyle to which she planned to become permanently accustomed.

No, it was scenes like The Temple of Doom and the lifestyle they implied that still represented the New York of her aspirations.

While not quite up to, say, The American Dream, The Temple of Doom was typical of the glitzy meatracks where those with the money to live in the fantasy New York of which Karen had only childhood memories gathered to drink and score and make out and find their way to secret insider parties.

The bar at which Karen sat ran completely around the gallery that encircled the dance floor below. The bar itself was a counter of black stone (or anyway a reasonably convincing synthetic replica) carved in vaguely Aztec motifs, and the mirror that ran all the way around the gallery behind it was of rosy red glass. The bartenders, naked to the waist and hunks to a man, wore short trapezoidal Aztec kilts brilliantly painted in subtly obscene abstract patterns and plume-crested brass helmets. The waitresses who served the cocktail tables along the rail of the gallery wore somewhat more flowing skirts in the same vein, similar helmets, and skimpy brass halters. Gas lamps set above each table and simulating torches illumined the gallery with a musky red glow.

The dance floor itself was brilliantly tiled in more pseudo-Aztec motifs, cunningly overglazed here and there with something that gave the appearance of permanent pools of bright red blood. Three large video screens displayed the visual tracks of the discs played by some hidden dj.

From the gallery one could look down upon the solid tangle of bodies dancing on the floor below and pretend to be a Princess of the City surveying the lowly peasantry from on high. The fact that Karen knew full well that most of the people who paid their thirty dollars to get in and drank watered booze at twenty dollars a pop were buying the same illusion was something she tried her unsuccessful best to forget.

She finished her wine, thought of ordering another, looked around the gallery. There was no Prince Charming to be seen, only pretenders like herself, she had dealt her last disc to the same, and had $1600 in her purse, an excellent take for the evening. She might be a nobody here, but at least in the RLF loft she had attained the status of number one dealer.

Time to call it a night.

She descended to the dance floor, snake-danced through the wall of bodies and noise, went down a short corridor to the cloakroom, where she retrieved her parka, then outside past the doorman, bundled into an old raccoon coat and huddled into the doorway against the cold wet wind.

The Temple of Doom was on the Bowery at the eastern fringe of Soho two blocks north of Grand Street and well south of the RLF loft farther west on Lafayette. On a better night than this Karen would have detoured down to Grand anyway in order to walk home across this well-lit main drag.

But the fickle early December weather had taken a turn for the worse while she was inside. The temperature had dropped below thirty, a gusty wind was blowing a thin cold rain in her face, she hadn't any gloves, and this *was* a Zone, after all, so she flipped up the thin hood of her parka, hoisted her purse to her shoulder, stuffed her hands into her pockets, hunched forward against the nasty wet wind, and turned the northwest corner of the block, heading back to the warmth of the loft by the most direct route possible.

It was after midnight, and there were few people on the side street between the looming dark residential loft buildings, but she passed several scurrying for cover on the first block, and even the reassuring figure of a big black zonie pacing back and forth to keep warm and cradling the cold metal of his M-16 in thick greasy brakeman's gloves.

The parka hood cut off a good portion of her peripheral vision and muffled her hearing, the cold rain was dribbling down into her eyebrows and freezing her nose, the sound of her own high heels clacking on the pavement was the loudest thing she heard, and she was thinking of little else but getting out of the weather, so it wasn't until she found herself alone on the next dark block that she began to suspect that someone was stalking her.

It began as just a vague prickling uneasiness at the back of her neck, a cool queasy shadow of seemingly sourceless irrational dread creeping up on her from behind. Then, as her senses sharpened to full paranoid alert, she realized where it was coming from.

She had been hearing a subtle muffled afterbeat to her own footsteps, a mushy padded counterpoint to the sharp clicking of her high heels on the concrete of the sidewalk.

Or was she just being paranoid? Was it just some weird echo?

Something kept her from turning her head to look back.

Instead, she increased her pace slightly, then broke stride with a momentary halt, and just as arhythmically began walking again at a much slower pace.

She clearly heard a series of stumbling, shuffling footfalls behind her for a moment before the sounds smoothed back into an afterbeat to her own sharp footsteps.

Cold claws gripped Karen's guts. There *was* someone following her. Without thinking, still not daring to look back, she began walking faster.

Bad mistake!

The footfalls behind her quickened to an even faster pace than hers without breaking into a run, but getting louder and closer, as if whoever it was had surmised she was onto him and tentatively abandoned stealth, but had not quite yet made up his mind to pounce.

The next corner was at least thirty yards away, thirty yards of empty sidewalk, darkened ground floor windows, shadowy doorways, and the black mouths of ominous alleys. Terror-stricken, Karen slowed her pace again, as if by not reacting to the presence of her oncoming stalker she might by some sympathetic magic make him disappear.

But the footfalls behind her broke into a near trot, and now it sounded like a whole army of muggers.

Ignorance blissful no longer, she *had* to turn and look now.

Oh shit!

There were *two* of them!

A big bulky figure in a filthy and ragged khaki army coat with some kind of raggy padding wrapped around his feet, a long mat of ratty brown hair, a leer full of rotten teeth, and a foul mass of scab on his forehead. An even taller man in an old peacoat, younger, thin almost to the point of emaciation, his face aflame with angry acne, his left hand gripping the crotch of his muck-smeared jeans, his tongue licking his bluish lips lubriciously.

Just a glance, then—

Seeing her turn to look, they broke into a dead run toward her—

Karen began running for her life, stumbling and sliding in her high heels along the wet sidewalk. She slipped, staggered, almost fell, regained her balance momentarily, and then—

Cruel rough hands grabbed her around the padded neck of her parka, hard in the crack of her buttocks, the sounds of grunts and ragged breathing, a heavy press of bodies slamming into her back and shoving her sideways and then forward toward a pile of garbage cans at the shadowy mouth of a dark alley—

From the depth of her loosening bowels, from the pit of her howling stomach, she screamed and screamed and screamed. . . .

A warm fragrant Santa Ana wind blew the sweet and pungent perfumes of bougainvillea and eucalyptus across the deck of Glorianna O'Toole's Lookout Mountain tree house, tossing the crowns of the trees, susurrusing through the foliage, cleansing the air to near desert clarity, so that, for once, the rich sprinkling of pinpoint stars and the bright crescent moon shining down from the pure black sky were a fair mirror of the electrical brilliance of the jeweled cityscape spread from horizon to horizon below.

It was as perfect a night for a trip as Glorianna could have ordered up from the gods of special effects, but Bobby Rubin seemed considerably less than enthusiastic about embarking on this magical mystery tour.

"What is it, a pleasure-center jolter, a temporary-lobe job?" he said, standing against the rail of the deck with his back to the magnificent vista, holding out the limp net of fine wires and sniffing at it dubiously as if it were a dead fish.

"I *told* you, this isn't some crude piece cobbled together by the usual burnt-out wireheads," Glorianna said in a tone of no little exasperation. "This is wizard wire from Silicon City."

"Which you haven't tried yet, right?"

"Come on, Bobby, this could really be *fun,*" Sally Genaro said brightly. She had already put her Shunt on and sat on a redwood deck chair, with the wirework helmet all but invisible in her frizzy hair.

Bobby glared silently at her, and in that sullen stare, Glorianna finally read the true nature of his reluctance. Being afraid of strange wire was not necessarily a sign of assholery or extreme chickenheartedness considering the shit that was floating around, after all, and no doubt his fear of frying his brain was not entirely feigned. But Glorianna would bet her last buck that what Bobby Rubin was *really* afraid of was that the piece would indeed work as advertised, and he would find himself sharing a trip of acidlike profundity with *Sally Genaro.*

Which, of course, was exactly what Ellie Dawson had promised.

Which, of course, was Glorianna's last hope of getting Project Superstar off dead center and saving her own ass.

* * *

Poor Bobby had gotten bitchier and bitchier with her since the gross barfing scene at that awful party, but while it was really starting to get under Sally Genaro's skin, especially since she had blown off seven pounds absolutely *starving* herself on salad and grapefruit to look good for him, she knew she had to be patient.

After all, how would *she* be feeling now if *she* had been the one who had poured her heart out to *him* and then puked her guts out just when things were really starting to get romantic?

So Sally could well understand how he might still be *embarrassed,* and she could even understand how all her best efforts to assure him that it didn't matter to her, that she still thought he was snaky anyway, might need a bit more time to convince him. After all, he *was* a little nerdy to begin with, not exactly heavy on like *savoir-faire.*

But she never expected him to be such a *chicken* about a little piece of wire. What was there to be scared of anyway? It wasn't like some awful psychedelic drug, where, once you swallowed it, you were going to be stoned for *hours* and there was nothing you could do about it if it turned out to be a bummer. All you had to do was hit the touchpoint on the little box on your head, and you came right out of it.

Glorianna O'Toole stepped closer to Bobby. "It wouldn't have been fair for me to try it first without you," she said, putting on her own Shunt and smoothing the breadbox into a comfortable position at the back of her head. "Ellie wanted me to try it with her, but I said no, the three of us are in this together, and we should go into it as equals."

Sally got up off her deck chair, walked over to Bobby, and reached for the wire mesh helmet hanging limply from his fingers. "Come on, Bobby, it's a beautiful night, here, let me—"

Bobby snatched his Shunt away from her angrily, spread out the mesh with both hands, and pulled the net down into his hair in an angry series of impulsive gestures. "I can fry my own brains without your help if I have to!" he snapped.

Sally recoiled, hurt and uncomprehending. "Why do you always have to be such a little *shit* about everything, Bobby Rubin?" she flared, and then instantly regretted it as he shot her a look of poisonous intensity.

"Children, children, *please*!" Glorianna O'Toole moaned, rolling her eyes skyward. "This is not exactly the karma with which to begin a beautiful experience! Look at those stars! Smell that air! Listen to the music of the wind in the trees! Get with it, will you!"

Bobby Rubin knew full well that any further protests on his part would only be postponing the inevitable. There was no way he was going to admit to having less courage than *the Pimple*!

Besides, the truth of it was that he wasn't really all that afraid of this piece of wire in the first place, indeed the supposed effect, as described by Glorianna, had intrigued him from the beginning.

He had never tried any psychedelic drugs, but if he was a naif when it came to psychopharmacology, he certainly was a wizard of the bits and bytes, and as such, this device, unlike other wire, appealed to him.

Most street wire, messily soldered together on breadboards by burnt-out assholes and plugged into powerful 120-volt house current, was crude dangerous stuff that worked by jolting vague areas of the brain with an electrical overload. But the Transcortical Shunt was a low-current device that ran on small batteries, meaning that the effect, whatever it was, could not depend on brute electronic force. And one look at the workmanship of this thing made him believe Glorianna's story about Silicon City wizard shops.

No, if Glorianna O'Toole had taken him up onto a mountaintop into this warm fragrant Santa Ana night, showed him the stars above and the brilliant lights of the city below, and invited him to Shunt with her, he would have had no hesitation.

He locked gazes with Glorianna for a long moment. There was a warmth in those eyes, a wisdom, a spirit of adventure, God help him, a *sexiness,* that made him wish for a time warp, for certainly there was nothing he would have liked more than to embark upon this adventure with the hot young girl this old lady had so manifestly once been.

It was taking this Magical Mystery Tour with *the Pimple* tagging along that filled him with an entirely rational dread.

After all, look what had happened when he had made the mistake of merely getting drunk with her! She, and the booze, and the dust, and the frustration of it all, had somehow tricked him into letting his mouth run out of control, into giving voice to feelings that no man should speak aloud. Worse, without realizing what he was doing, he had let her touch him, put her arm around him, hold his hand, presume so far as to actually *kiss* him. The memory of it made his testicles shrivel and his stomach turn even now.

Worse still, ever since that night, Sally from the Valley had had it in her head that she knew the secrets of his soul; worst of all, he couldn't quite escape the knowledge that, in the most loathsome way possible, she was, in a certain sense, right.

Now she was convinced that this was a psychic bond between them, that it was only a matter of time and persistence before it ripened into . . . yech!

How much worse would it get if he *shunted* with her?

He certainly did not want to find out.

He glanced at Sally's hot eager eyes out of the corner of his own for a moment, and cringed inside.

But he was going to.

He shrugged, lifted his hand, and poised it above the touchpoint of the breadbox snugged against the back of his head. "We who are about to fry salute you," he said.

Sally from the Valley goggled at him uncomprehendingly. But she too positioned her finger above her touchpoint.

Glorianna O'Toole winked at him, pointed the forefinger of her left hand above the back of her head, and waved the forefinger of the other up and down like a bandleader's baton to the downbeat.

"One-two, one-two-THREE!"

"You got in there what that shit-eating grin *says* you got in there, my man?" Dojo said, eyeing Paco Monaco's street bag with a mixture of surprise and approval that warmed the cockles of Paco's manhood.

He beamed at the big doorman. "I'll show you mine if you'll show me yours," he said, reaching into the street bag.

"Are you out of your fucking mind?" Dojo hissed. "Not out here!" He scanned his eyes up and down the dark street.

"Watch the door while I get the Count to take over for me and try not to blow anyone away with that thing while I'm gone," he said, ducking inside, and leaving Paco actually serving as temporary doorman to Slimy Mary's.

Dojo was gone for almost five minutes, while Paco slung his street bag over his shoulder, crossed his arms, stuck his chin imperiously in the air, and imagined for the moment that he was Dojo, master of all he surveyed. He hoped someone, anyone, would try to get in before Dojo got back, because whoever it was, it would be no way, Jose, just to see what it felt like.

But before any such thing could happen, Dojo returned with the Count, scowling and muttering under his breath to himself. Fortunately, it was obviously the Count, rather than Paco, who was the object of his displeasure.

The Count was a tall figure in a ratty black leather jacket and blue jeans with a dirty black blanket wrapped around his shoulders like a cloak. He, or someone, had knocked out all his teeth but two, which he had filed into fangs. His head was shaved bald, except for a high greased crest in back like a vampire's collar. Paco remembered when the Count had been a powerfully built and intimidating figure, but now he was skeletally thin, the taut skin of his face was so sallow it was almost green, and his watery blue eyes looked as if someone had dribbled Tabasco sauce into them.

The Count's steady deterioration toward walking corpsehood was due to the fact that he was a heavy combo wirehead, there wasn't a piece he wouldn't plug into, and Paco had once seen him plugged into three at once. El Lizardo claimed to have seen the Count stick his prick into a light socket and just stand there grinning, and Paco almost believed it.

"Just don't let in anyone whose name you can't remember until I get back, you think you can still handle that much, asshole?" Dojo told the Count, and led Paco down the dark stairway into the meatrack.

"Gotta get rid of that zombie before he really starts to stink," he grumbled to himself as he skirted the twilight zone around the dance floor, sticking to the darkness around the walls, and unlocking the door to a room Paco had never even known existed.

Dojo flicked on a dim ceiling fixture with a wall switch, revealing a cozy little room with an unmade bed which had obviously seen recent heavy action, a disc deck, monitor, and speakers, and three walls piled high with cardboard cartons.

"Let's see what you have, Paco," he said, still standing.

Paco reached into his street bag, pulled out the Uzi, and handed it over. He thought he saw Dojo's eyes widen for a moment, but the big black doorman played it cool as usual, popping the magazine out, working the action, popping it back in, all without uttering a word or looking at Paco.

"Seems okay," he finally grunted. Now he looked up at Paco

and studied him speculatively. "How did you manage to snatch it?" he demanded. "Never thought you really had it in you," he added in a clear tone of approval.

Paco hesitated. Unzipped my pants for a fuckin' maricón would not exactly make it. "Rolled a zonie, nigger, how else?" he said cockily.

Dojo eyed him dubiously. "Sure," he said sneeringly.

"Okay, so I found it in el sub, you wanna believe that one," Paco said in the same vein.

"You *really* did a crash and grab on a zonie?" Dojo said, allowing a certain open admiration into his voice now.

"You're holding the Uzi. . . ."

"How the fuck did you manage that?"

"Yo soy mucho muchacho, you better believe it!"

Dojo laughed dryly, shook his head, went over to a pile of cartons, laid the Uzi down carefully behind them, and fished out a Zap, neatly sealed in a clear plastic bag. "Here, killer," he said, tossing it to Paco, "have fun."

Paco struggled for a moment with the plastic bag, trying to unseal it, quickly lost patience, and tore the wrapper to shreds with his fingernails. He shook out the wire mesh, then fitted the net over his head, the sleek little breadbox with its magic touchpoint cool and snug and promising against the back of his skull, the whole piece completely hidden from casual sight in his bushy hair.

His whole body trembled with a wonderful anticipation. All he needed now was ten dollars to slip el Lizardo for five minutes of Mucho Muchacho, maybe Dojo would—

But before he could begin to try to hit up the doorman for ten, Dojo fixed him with a cold businesslike stare that drove any such asshole thought from his mind. "Just maybe you can handle it," he said.

"Handle what, Dojo?"

"The fuckin' Count has fried his brains to vegetable tempura, I mean they're leakin' out his ears. I've had just about enough of that creep. I just decided I need a new relief doorman. . . ."

"*Me?*" Paco exclaimed, hardly able to believe his ears.

"I figure any dude can roll a zonie just might be able to hold his own with the brainburn cases here," Dojo said. "Thursday through Monday, just when I need relief. Ten bucks a night and I don't care what you deal at the door, but I better not catch you collecting money to let anyone in. You got the balls to give it a try? Or were you just bullshitting me about being such a red-hot bad-ass, Paco?''

''I'm your man, Dojo!'' Paco declared without having to think about it for an instant, hardly believing his good fortune, but pouncing on it instinctively like a bird on a turd, you better believe it, muchacho. ''For sure!''

Dojo smiled. ''We'll see about that, my man. Starting next week.''

He opened the door, ushered Paco out of the room, turned off the light, locked the door behind him. ''Just one thing,'' he said. ''It's not my business if you fry your brains on your own time, but I *don't* want to see you wearing wire on the door. Let the Count be a lesson to you, my son.''

''Uh . . . what *about* the Count?'' Paco said hesitantly. ''Do I have to . . . ?'' He suddenly remembered that while the Count might be in terrible shape, he had a rep as a kung-fu killer or something.

Dojo laughed. ''Don't you worry about the Count,'' he said, favoring Paco with a suddenly chilling leer, and nodding significantly toward the ceiling, toward the legendary upstairs rooms, where Dojo supposedly kept burnt-out wireheads turning out pieces. ''The Count just won himself a free one-way ticket to Florida.''

Paco shuddered a bit, and he hung back away from the dance floor deep in the dark shadows at the rear of Slimy Mary's as Dojo went back to the door to relieve the Count, for no way did he want the Count to notice him when he came back in. When the Count did come down the stairs a few minutes later, he marched straight to his customary pile of cushions in the twilight zone near the dance floor, picked out a piece from the assorted pile of wire, jammed it on his head, plugged in, and flashed out, staring up into the flicker pattern of the colored bulbs on the dance floor ceiling as if nothing had happened.

Maybe nothing *had* happened yet. Maybe Dojo hadn't told the Count anything. Maybe he'd just wait until the Count passed out, and when the mother woke up, he'd find himself plugged in upstairs in Florida. Maybe the Count was already so fried he wouldn't even notice it.

Paco laughed hollowly. No reason not to go on in and flash, he realized. The Count wasn't going to give him no shit. But still he hung back in the shadows.

Some stupid gordo thing with a lot of sparks and flashing

lights and wailing weirdos was playing, about a dozen of the usual Slimy Mary's regulars were dancing to it, he didn't have the money to get el Lizardo to play a Mucho Muchacho disc, and besides, he remembered, the whole reason he had risked his sweet culo to get himself his own Zap in the first place was so he wouldn't have to flash on it with the puercas and puberdas in a shithole like this.

Paco grinned to himself. Chingada, qué noche loca! Nearly cocked in the culo by a fuckin' maricón, kicked the fuckin' faggot zonie in the cojones, snatched an Uzi, hired by Dojo, and now I got me my own Zap, and I'm gonna take me a little trip to Chocharica City! Qué noche grande, muchacho!

And this magic night, he had a feeling, was only just beginning.

Paco loped south to Houston, then west to the corner of Houston and West Broadway, not even noticing the chill that was blowing in on the rising breeze or the thin mist slicking his face as he felt the delicious tension building in his body like a slow-rising hard-on from his toes to the cool sleek pressure of the Zap's breadbox snug against the back of his head.

He stood there for a moment looking south through the bright lights of West Broadway, the main drag of Soho, the golden avenue of restaurants, galleries, plushie-tushie meatracks, saloons, fabulous bodegas, flash and neon glitter that opened up before him like a tantalizing peek straight up the skirt of Chocharica City.

He remembered that night, a few short weeks and a long lifetime ago, when he had stood more or less on this very spot and thought that very thought, staring forlornly up between the forbidden thighs of the queen of the city, and swearing to himself that one day soon he would return, not as Paco Monaco, dirty little streetie spick who dared not set foot in this forbidden Zone, but as Mucho Muchacho, Prince of the City, to ram his mighty machismo straight up its fuckin' chocha.

It had been warmer then, and West Broadway had been thronged with chocharicas and their putamadre maricón boyfriends, and the zonies had been out in full force. It was colder now, and it was beginning to rain, and there were fewer people on West Broadway, and they were scurrying back and forth between the brightly lit buildings, and the zonies were huddled in doorways.

But here he was, verdad, standing in the sombre, looking into the sol, poised on the edge of his own personal Hora Frontera, and the magic key to crossing over, the key he had won by his own courage and daring, lay just a touch of his finger away.

Paco reached up to the breadbox on the back of his head, singing softly to himself, but hearing the music pounding out to a max metal beat in the ears of his mind—

Nosotros somos gigantes
(Tu ma-dre TAMBIÉN)
Cojones de elefantes
(Tu ma-dre TAMBIÉN)
So pull down all your panties
Y TU MADRE TAMBIÉN!

—and hit the touchpoint.

Nothing seemed to change as he snake-danced effortlessly across the sparse traffic against the light to the stompada rhythm, his keening muscles bulging deliciously under his taut skin like the mighty hard-on chafing expectantly against his tight white cut-off jeans.

And then he seemed to have stepped through an invisible doorway from the sombre into the sol. The rain no longer fell in dead gray sheets but hung between the buildings like a warm shimmering summer fog, casting rainbow auras around the streetlamps and transforming West Broadway into a long glowing corridor of golden light.

Neon signs writhed sinuously like brilliant electric culebras in the pearly mist. The darkened windows of galleries and clothing stores and bodegas tantalized with heaps of shadowy treasures piled high within. The illumined windows of restaurants opened into dream vistas of endless dining room tables set with snowy linen, gleaming silver, shining china, where rock stars, old men in tuxedos, bemedaled generals, verdad, kings and princes of the city in gold-braided silken uniforms, gorged themselves on turkeys and hams and whole roast pigs and lambs, washing it all down with great goblets of wine, while elegant women in long gowns and festooned with jewels hung on their shoulders and laid out huge lines of dust.

Muttery musky music and the sound of nervous female laughter oozed out into the street from bars and fancy meatracks, and within, through smoky plate glass and walls through which he somehow peered with Superman's x-ray vision, were hundreds, thousands, millions of beautiful bejeweled and befurred chocharicas, rubbing their silken thighs together in desperate horniness for a *real* macho man, while pale fat gordos, hairy old maricónes, pimply creeps in silk suits, drooled and slavered over their guava-ripe tits, and hopelessly tried to get their feeble trembling hands up their skirts.

Your sisters and your aunties
Chocharicas elegantes
Don't want no gay romantics . . .

A mighty max metal band marched behind him, buoying him forward on a wall of music as the lyric poured up and out of him, and his huge hard cock throbbed in time to the drumbeat and the bassline chanted by an unseen rough-voiced chorus.

Tu ma-dre TAMBIÉN
Tu ma-dre TAMBIÉN
Tu ma-dre TAMBIÉN

A tall blond woman, her bare shoulders draped with a silver fur stole, her huge tits bursting from her low-cut white gown, her misty blue eyes staring hungrily at his bulging tight white crotch, came up the avenue toward him on the arm of a grotesquely fat hump-backed dwarf with terrified red eyes and a huge pimply beak of a nose.

Mucho Muchacho laughed, winked, cupped his huge throbbing cock, smacked his lips, and sang straight at her.

Get it while you can
From a red-hot macho man
We all remember when . . .

The fat ugly dwarf rolled his eyes in terror and dragged his chocharica toward the nearest meatrack door as she sighed and moaned and came in her panties as Mucho Muchacho roared out the beatline climax with the mighty voice of his streetwise army. "Y TU MADRE TAMBIÉN!"

He laughed, not deigning to follow, and danced off up through the golden spreading thighs of the glowing canyon of light opening up before him toward the throbbing cunt of the city itself just begging for it at the vanishing point, for there were other chocharicas on both sides of the street, busty redheads in skin-tight jeans, luscious pale-skinned putas with coal-black hair, brunettes in furs, willowy ice-eyed blondes with great bulging tits and hard pink nipples revealed against the sheer white fabric of their gowns, and every one of them bent over with unbearable horniness, all of them licking their lips and drooling for his huge hard cock.

Verdad, there were gordos and plushie-tushies trying to hoard most of this treasure-trove of sweet chocharica flesh for themselves; walking beside them, scowling, tugging at their arms, snarling, scuttling, trying to shield them with their pale soft bodies, but hola, they were all putamadre maricón weaklings, fat little overfed cabrónes sin cojones and he was Paco Monaco, Mucho Muchacho, karate-killer rock star, and he was the Prince of Chocharica City, general of the avenging army of the night, macho master of all the chocha he surveyed, and tonight was his night to pierce the tight white cunt of the queen of the city with his mighty blade of vengeance.

Chingada, here came the perfect woman of his dreams floating up the street toward him; tall, and blond, and blue-eyed, and cool, hugging her mink coat around her, eyeing him hungrily, her high-heeled feet not really touching the ground, sí, *ella,* this one, this one I fuck till her teeth fall out!

Mucho Muchacho danced his stompada up to the queen of Chocharica City, singing his love song.

Nosotros somos gigantes
Cojones de elefantes . . .

He unzipped the fly of his cut-off shorts with one hand, reached for the quick of her with the other.

So pull down all your panties . . .

"What the fuck?" The skinny old putamadre cabrón who had been hanging on her arm stepped in front of her, the sincojones motherfucker actually was trying to shove aside *Mucho Muchacho*! Paco laughed and sang in his face.

Besa me pica!
And ponga me your sister!

And caught him square on the jaw with a roundhouse right—

Better call me Mister!

—and flipped him backward on his ass as he started to go down with a karate kick to the guts.

Y TU MADRE TAMBIÉN!

Shrieks and screams pierced the glowing golden mist, turning to gut-wrenching prowl-car sirens. The blonde was staggering and stumbling down the street. The air seemed to shatter into a million razor-sharp shards. The temperature took a sudden bone-chilling drop and a hard wet rain began to fall.

And out of a nearby doorway stepped a motherfucking *gorilla* with an M-16!

It was the most horrible fuckin' zonie the world had ever seen. An actual gigantic *ape* covered with thick ropy black hair and about nine feet tall stuffed into a white T-shirt bursting at the seams and tight black leather pants with a huge gleaming chrome zipper halfway open to reveal the leathery black head of an enormous gorilla dick. It had little steel earrings up and down both earlobes, beady black eyes, and a mouthful of big sharp rotten fangs slavering blood. It was about three feet from him and pointing the muzzle of the M-16 right at his belly button.

Time seemed to stop. Everything was frozen.

Except the music.

TU MADRE TAMBIÉN! TU MADRE TAMBIÉN! TU MADRE TAMBIÉN!

A mighty max metal band belted it out behind him and a great army of rough voices chanted out the bassline. And Mucho Muchacho remembered who he was and smiled.

"Hey man, that's sure a big gun you have," he sneered at the huge blood-drooling monster.

The beady black animal eyes of the gorilla thing widened for an instant, the mouthful of horrid teeth dropped, and then—

"TU MADRE TAMBIÉN, PUBERDA!" roared Mucho Muchacho, his lithely muscled body already leaping forward with its left foot as it went into a spin-kick with its right, neatly catching the M-16 and flipping it high into the air out of the zonie monster's grasp. Mucho came down still whirling, and threw a counterspin kick with his left foot that got the fuckin' thing right in the cojones with his full weight expertly behind it. Mucho brought up his knee as the ape screamed and folded, bringing down the heel of his right hand at the same time, getting the motherfucker on the point of the jaw and the back of the neck.

The nightmare zonie shriveled away to nothingness, as if he had never been, like a burst balloon collapsing at his feet, filled, like all gordos and plushie-tushies and their goons, with nothing more than hot air, muchacho, when it came to standing up to a real man.

But dozens of giant rats were pouring out of bars and restaurants, evil red-eyed putamadres with needle-sharp teeth, dressed up like gordos and plushie-tushies in suits and jeans and sheepskin coats, dozens of ratones the size of *dogs*, man, cowardly sincojones motherfuckers in a one-on-one, verdad, but circling him in a mob, working up their courage, twitching their ugly naked pink tails like cats getting ready to pounce, and chittering to each other like ten million enraged cucarachas.

''Getta zonies! Calla cops! Spickmothafucka bastard!''

Mucho Muchacho pivoted slowly in the center of the circle, crouched over, flicking out karate punches and kicks, keeping the gordo rats at bay, sneering his contempt, flicking them the finger, daring any individual to step forward and try to be a man.

Far away, a siren began to wail, like someone stomping again and again on the same fuckin' cat, and even Mucho Muchacho knew it was time to run.

''Fuck you, assholes!'' he screamed at the top of his lungs, lunging straight at the nearest bunch of rats in gordo clothing, windmilling his hands in mighty blows, brushing them aside like cockroaches, breaking through.

And then he was off and running south down West Broadway, soaring, leaping, his feet barely touching the ground, past bars and meatracks and restaurants, red and blue snakes snapping at him from neon signs, rats and roaches, cur dogs and feral cats, pouring out of buildings to nip at his heels as he ran for his sweet life down a long gauntlet corridor alive with pitiless and piercing actinic light—

—Paco Monaco was running through a bone-chilling rain down West Broadway a few blocks north of Grand, where the midway faded out into dark empty blocks of looming residential loft buildings. Glancing back over his shoulder, he froze for a long moment.

Chingada! What the fuck?

There was no horde of giant rats in gordo clothing chasing him down a corridor lit with eye-killing white light, no snakes snapping at his heels from neon signs. But there sure as shit *were* half a dozen fuckin' gordos comin' down West Broadway toward him and for sure there were a couple of zonies waving their pieces, too, and chingada, the fuckin' siren was for real, 'cause that *was* a cop car turning the corner about six blocks up!

Near to shitting in his pants, Paco dashed to the next intersection, turned east on the side street. He ran forward about a block and a half and then stopped, panting, and terrified. Chingada, he finally had time to realize, what a time to pop out of the fuckin' flash, what am I gonna do?

Quién sabé? He didn't know.

But he knew someone who did.

He reached up and gave himself another tap of the Zap.

Mucho Muchacho turned, looked, smiled, and disappeared into the sombre that waited for him just around every corner from the sol, slowly, deliberately, his head held high. West Broadway, Chocharica City, the forbidden Zone of the sol, was just a distant muzzy blur of light from this perspective, fading from sight and memory like a bad dream.

It was a different world in here in the sombre, *his* turf, a world as forbidden to his pursuers as their turf was to him. Blocks and blocks of narrow side streets lined with dark and looming buildings stretched out before him in the falling rain, rising around him like the trees of an urban rain forest, *his* jungle, verdad, where he knew all the secret paths, where every alley and doorway was his refuge, where the dripping rain, and the far-off echoes of unseen traffic, and his own knowing and padded footfalls were the music of *his* night.

Mucho Muchacho, Lord of the Concrete Jungle, sauntered easily eastward, inhaling the cool night air, oblivious to the cold, his ears attuned to the subdued chitterings and mumblings of the night sounds, sliding along the sides of the buildings like a shadow, shielded from the worst of the rain by the canopy of their eaves high overhead, verdad, it was another world in here, with the sidewalks glistening with moisture and rivulets of water gurgling softly down the edges of the gutters and foaming and rushing down the drop into the sewer catchpockets, and nothing to disturb the velvety tranquility of the jungle night except—

A woman's screams!

They were coming from an alleyway halfway up the next block, shrill piercing cries of terror and pain, and behind them, like a loathsome bassline, guttural grunts and wordless male cursing.

He was running toward the alley before he had time for thought, without knowing why, and when he got there, what he saw filled him with a roil of conflicting emotions he did not pause to understand.

Two big filthy putamadres had a woman pinned against a pile of overturned garbage cans. Her long blond hair was soaked with rain, her coat was unzipped, her skirt was down around her knees, a big fat slob in an army coat with his dick hanging out was trying to pull down her panties while a thinner creep in a peacoat held her arms above her head, spread-eagling her backward over the garbage cans, and her blouse had been ripped open, revealing perfect upthrust white breasts, hard pink nipples glistening with moisture.

His mighty cock grew rock-hard, chafing cruelly against the zipper of his pants. At the same time, he was filled with red-hot outrage. Who did these motherfuckers think they were? How dare these dirty sons of bitches fuck *his* chocha?

Mucho Muchacho took three long running steps forward and on the third one kicked the man in the army coat in the base of the spine with all his might. He screamed horribly, bolting upright, and then falling backward into a straight-armed fisted punch to the back of the head. He went down and lay still like the sack of shit he was.

The other putamadre whirled around just in time to catch a kick in the throat which slammed his head into the wall with a sickening thud. He slowly slid down the wall into a heap with the rest of the garbage, smearing a long trail of blood on the brick.

Mucho Muchacho stood there with his hands triumphantly on his hips, gazing down on his prize, her panties halfway down her thighs, her wet blond hair fanned out behind her, rivulets of water running down the soft white flesh of her breasts, her full red lips open and panting, her ice-blue eyes slowly coming around to look up at him.

He smiled. He stepped forward to tower, erect and proud, over her. She slowly began to rise up off the heap of garbage cans. He licked his lips and his right hand went to his fly.

Sobbing, she threw herself into his arms, clutched him tightly, and buried her head between his neck and chin, her mouth pressed below his ear, her bare breasts heaving against his chest.

"Thank you, oh thank you, thank you, thank you. . . ." she sighed, her warm moist breath pouring into his earhole like musky perfume.

He felt his hard cock pressed against her stomach. He felt a warm, hollow, and not at all unpleasant feeling in the pit of his guts. He felt a strange itchy tingling in his eyeballs. He felt her trembling body nestled in his arms. He felt something he could not put a name to, something he had never felt before.

He put his arms around her, then started to drop one hand to feel the cleft of her ass.

"Oh God, it was . . . it was . . ." She started to sob uncontrollably.

He felt the hand that had been grabbing for her ass reach out to gently smooth her rain-soaked hair. He felt his other hand just as gently lift her chin so that her tear-filled eyes were looking into his, inches away.

"Hey, girl," he found himself saying, "you're with *Mucho Muchacho.* Nothing can hurt you now."

She smiled at him, choking back her tears. She planted a soft, closed-mouth kiss on his lips. He held her out at arm's length, and then gently pulled up her panties, smoothed down her skirt, wrapped her in her parka, and zipped it shut.

"Will you . . . will you take me home?" she asked imploringly.

He smiled at her. He put a protective arm around her shoulder. "For sure," he said.

"It's not far . . ." She hoisted her bag to her shoulder, wrapped an arm around his waist, kissed him on the cheek, and snuggled close against his strong hard body.

And he walked westward with her through a city transformed. The wet gray loft buildings sparkled and glistened in an impossible silvery moonlight like the shining glass towers of Ciudad Trabajo, and the grungy Soho side street had somehow become Fifth Avenue under a golden glowing sunset as he promenaded past the great department stores and the jewelry shops with the blond-haired, blue-eyed, fur-clad woman out of his long-remembered dreams clinging tremulously to his side.

Like his dreams, and yet not like his dreams, for while he floated through the Ciudad Trabajo of his dreamtime with the blond chocharica of his wettest dreams, no avenging army of streeties marched behind him, and what he felt in this moment was nothing like the fiery lust to fuck the queen of the city into animal-eyed frenzy and slavering submission.

She led him to the entrance to a gleaming white town house and opened the great oaken door with a golden key. Inside, a long spiral staircase of black marble led upward, glistening under crystal chandeliers.

She paused outside the door, slipped out from under his arm, placed both hands on his shoulders, and looked deeply into his eyes. "I . . . I . . . don't even know your name," she said, her blue eyes shining.

"Mucho . . . *Paco,*" he said. "Paco Monaco. Y tu . . . ?"

"Karen . . . Karen Gold," she said, smiling at him uncertainly. Actual tears came to her eyes. "I . . . don't quite know what to say. . . . I mean, I've never met a knight in shining armor before."

A delicious yet somehow embarrassing warmth poured through him, a warmth that made his eyes water and his feet shuffle in place, and his whole body seem to pulse with a radiant glow.

"Hey. . . ."

They stood there silently gazing into each other's eyes for a long, long moment, hardly even breathing. Then she hesitantly leaned forward and touched his lips in a short, chaste kiss.

"You gonna be okay now, momacita?" he said.

She nodded; she turned to look up the long marble staircase, but when she looked back at him, she was frowning, and her lower lip was trembling. "This . . . I know this is silly of me, but would you mind walking me upstairs, I mean . . ."

"Hey, no problem," he said softly, and hooking her arm in his, gallantly escorted her up the long staircase to a golden doorway at the top.

She withdrew a ring of keys from her purse, undid what seemed like a hundred locks, opened the door, peered inside, stood there on the threshold of the darkened interior for a moment, looking into his eyes. "Would you . . . would you mind coming inside for a bit?" she finally said. "Everyone's asleep, and right now . . . right now I really don't know if I can handle being alone. . . ."

He nodded silently, and let her take his hand, and she led him across a huge dark room lit only by the wan light leaking in from two great walls of tall pearl-frosted windows, a vast magician's palace unlike anything he had seen or dreamed before, velvet couches and elegantly carved and gilded tables, sí, but endless mysterious devices as well, a vision of the marvels of some incomprehensible future, reeking of wealth and power.

She parted the folds of a gigantic embroidered tapestry that hung across the room and took him by the hand into a fairyland corridor of tented chambers. Down the endless corridor, where she lifted up a golden velvet flap, and took him into a huge bedroom with a smoked-glass mirrored ceiling lit by a fireplace glow and papered in lip-red velvet.

She took off her long silvery fur coat, tossed it aside, kissed him, and sat down on the edge of a big round bed covered with golden satin sheets, looking up at him uncertainly.

"Want me to go now?" he said, not moving, knowing for sure that she didn't.

Karen Gold hunkered on her cot, looking up at her rescuer, at this dark-skinned, starved-looking stranger, at this streetie dressed in rags, wondering why she didn't say yes, wondering why she had brought this creature of the streets up here in the first place.

She was safe now, one scream and Larry and Malcolm and the others would come a-running, safe from his rough hands grabbing at her ass, ripping open her blouse, slamming her down across a pile of garbage cans, kneading and pulling and poking—

She blinked. She flushed with shame at what was running through her head as she looked at Paco Monaco. This wasn't one of her attackers, this was her savior. If he had wanted to harm her, if he had any thought at all of raping her, he would have done it right out there on the streets, when she was helpless, with her breasts naked to the freezing rain, and her panties down around her knees. . . .

But he hadn't. He had been fearless and strong, then tender and gentle, he had been everything she had needed a man to be in the worst of all possible moments. He had been a true knight in shining armor, and somehow there was a radiance coming off him still, a strength, a manly power, but a tenderness too.

He had been what she had needed most out there in the night. He had been a magic man.

And she needed that magic still.

"Sit down," she said, patting the cot beside her. "Please."

He squatted down on the cot, and sat there saying nothing, just being there for her. They sat there looking into each other's eyes for a long, long moment, hardly breathing.

"Touch me," Karen finally said.

He reached out and placed a hand on her thigh. She cringed at his touch, waiting for it to turn hard and cruel and insistent. It never happened.

"Hold me," she said after a long while. "Gently. I need to be held by a gentle man."

"Yo se . . ." he crooned, and hugged her to him, softly stroking her hair.

She put her arms around him and clung to him for a long, long while, feeling his chest pulsing against her, syncing her breathing with his.

"Can I kiss you . . . ?" she finally whispered into his ear, and pressed her lips against his, spreading them slowly and hesitantly with her mouth, then opening it, and tasting his breath as it poured sighing into her.

"Make love to me," she asked. "Show me how to forget."

Once again, it was like an oft-remembered dream, and yet not like a dream. For when Mucho Muchacho finally found himself naked in the velvet chamber on the bed of gold satin with the blond chocharica of his longings, there was no ice in her blue eyes as she drew him into her, nor was there resistance between her satiny thighs as she spread them wide for him, nor was there a sense of vengeful triumph in his heart, nor was his cock a mighty battle ram prizing open the tight white cunt of look-but-don't-touch as it slid effortlessly home into snug harbor.

Verdad, he was Mucho Muchacho, the very cock of the world, and oh yes, his machismo was great, and he went on and on and on tirelessly forever as he had always known he would, and for sure she moaned, and cried, and screamed in endless ecstasy.

But there was nothing grudging in her warm and willing surrender, and he did not find himself watching his own perfect body in masterly performance from the ceiling.

And when, as she lay panting and sighing into sleep beneath him, he finally allowed himself release, it was no triumphant explosion of flashing glass shards, but a mighty wave of sweet soft fulfillment that swept up him and through him from his toes to his brain, to pour through his cock and into her, leaving behind only a long slow slide into mellow velvet blackness.

But just before he lapsed entirely into untrammeled sleep, he had the strangest little dream.

He was lying on a cramped and lumpy little cot in a tiny tent of musty-smelling old burlap. Beyond the wall of rags, he heard ragged gurgling snoring. Somewhere a leaky faucet was dripping. Somewhere someone farted.

There was a girl crammed against him in the little cot, sleeping on her stomach with one arm draped over his waist. She had a well-tousled mop of short, wet, honey-blond hair.

He had just enough time to wonder what color her eyes were before the dream faded into blackness.

THE GHOST IN THE MACHINE

Goin' up, this thing isn't like acid at all, Glorianna O'Toole thought as she dropped her hand from her head, turned, leaned on the railing of her deck, and looked out over the familiar glory of home. There was no clenched-jawed waiting for it to hit, and there was no rush or somatic distortion when it did, which was immediately.

It had been an unreal Santa Ana night divorced from season and time anyway, with the atmosphere charged with ions and incensed with eucalyptus and incoming desert essences, and the temperature that of an eternal Southern California summer night. The wind whipped the trees around the house and whistled down through the shaggy canyons and out across the endless electric nightscape of Los Angeles below, scouring the smog from the air so that you could see clear out across the hard-edged blackness of the channel to the sprinkling lights of Catalina.

South toward San Diego, Baja, the Third World, Los Angeles glittered and sparkled to the horizon along the edge of the Pacific, and to the north, the electric amoeba oozed into every nook and cranny between the Santa Monica Mountains and the sea, before the coastline bent west, and the mountains advanced to meet it, and the city of man gave way to the long glorious wilderness of the coastline road between.

This was not the first time she had stood here stoned and wondered whether the city was rising and spreading in triumphant glory from the dark landscape of nature, or slowly sinking back into the black tarpits of terminal decay.

In the Sixties, when everything was young, and times were flush, and the Beach Boys were high on the charts with "Good Vibrations," and you hitched up that road to San Francisco with flowers in your hair, and you just had some kind of mushroom, and your mind was movin', oh, the electric towers of power could be clearly seen to be ascending to the starry skies, even as the crystal ship of Rock seemed destined to become the crown of creation.

'Long about the Seventies with a bad moon a-rising and nothing for a poor girl to do but sing in a rock and roll band, the issue already seemed in doubt, and by the full fascist flower of the Eighties, Glorianna was already half-wishing that the Great Quake would finally arrive and drop lowland Los Angeles into the drink, leaving nothing south of Sunset but a Southern California version of San Francisco Bay.

Now, with her pipes gone and her body held together by metabolic enhancers, and the economy on its ass, and Muzik, Inc., long since having lobotomized rock and roll, and the fuckin' town full of people with nowhere to turn and no place to go, and jail a distinct possibility, and the end of her life a lot closer than the memory of glory days, Glorianna felt herself too personally close to the darkness herself to afford the luxury of welcoming the dying of any more lights.

And so now, as she looked out over the electric frenzy of the city nightscape from on high, with this thing on her head doing who the fuck knew what to her brain, and more things riding on this trip than she could quite yet put her finger on, she saw neither a celestial city arising to a rock beat from the virgin coast of the past, nor the fading lights of the future's slaughtered dream sinking inevitably back into the pitiless ocean of night.

Instead, she seemed to be standing center stage before a vast audience of unseen eyes out there in the ballpark grandstands on the hills of the natural amphitheater beyond the lights, waiting for the band to finish its endless tuning up, and knowing that when the music began to play, the outcome would at least in some measure be the result of what moved through her heart on this night.

You sure were naked up here singing lead; if you didn't have it tonight and you bombed, as Glorianna had certainly done from time to time even in her heyday, you might as well be standing there blowing off enormous loud farts. Nothing felt worse than the amplified vibes of your own bummer bouncing back at you off a huge pissed-off crowd.

But of course nothing felt more glorious than hitting the groove and knowing it, when your voice was riding the curl of the music's wave up you and through you, when those good vibrations came roaring back from the perfect audience, and you laughed, and danced, and belted out anything you fucking well pleased, knowing that on this magic night you could do nothing but right.

Glorianna shrugged and held up her hands, as if telling the audience, that was a long time ago, I'm an old lady now, don't expect miracles, what do you want from me, I was never really up there with Pearl or Slick or Tina Turner even then.

But they were all sitting out there in the darkness. The lights of a quarter of a million joints lit up the night in Woodstock and they were toking up at Altamonte too. Mama Cass was there, and Hendrix, that grab-ass son of a bitch Jim Morrison, and Janis, already half-plowed. Bob Marley passed a huge spliff to John Lennon, and Elvis winked at her knowingly from on high.

Don't hand *us* that shit-kicking bullshit, Glorianna, they told her. It's time for *your* set now, and if you fuck this one up, none of us will ever work in this town again. You're all that's left now, kiddo, said Billy Beldock. Now go out and win one for the Big Bopper.

With great reluctance she finally turned her back on the audience of ghosts, and faced the real-time music.

Sally Genaro sat on a deck chair, drumming her fingers on the arm, a pudgy little kid with a bad complexion and an itch that no one wanted to scratch. Bobby Rubin stood beside her, wrinkling his nose, a nerdy little cyberwizard who knew he was far too good for her, and wondered why all the hot young numbers he leched for thought the same of him.

Fuck a duck! Glorianna thought. Is *this* how far we've come from Woodstock? Are these poor kids really the last best hope of Rock and Roll?

Yeah, and who are you to talk, Glorianna O'Toole? A broken-down old has-been, or to be honest about it, a never-quite-was, peddling wire in a schoolyard to try and save your own ass!

But the kids had the technical talent, she told herself, and while she may have never had quite the voice of Mama Cass or quite the fuck-it-all energy of Janis or quite the lysergic charisma of Grace Slick, and while she had never known what it was like to headline a grand tour or hit the top of the charts or be for a shining hour the voice of her generation, she had always been true to the spirit in her fashion, and it in its turn had never really let her down.

And if it all had to sink into the tarpits sometime, as long as there was still some life left in these old bones, it would go out rockin', or she wasn't the Crazy Old Lady of Rock and Roll!

Sally Genaro had chipped a little wire back in her horrid high school days, and the Razor Dogs had always had a dubious assortment of ups and down floating around, and of course she had done plenty of dust since signing her Muzik Factory contract, but the closest she had come to anything remotely like a psychedelic, anything that tripped her through her blighted inner landscape, was grass, and she never much enjoyed smoking dope.

Wire just like turned a piece of your brain on and made you indiscriminantly horny or had you staring mindlessly blissful into space; downs were an escape from bummers into a gork-off; ups gave you energy and made you a little paranoid; and dust made you feel good.

But while grass sometimes made her feel like the rock and roll queen her face and her body would never let her be, and while it sometimes really made the music flow, she never knew when it would turn on her in the next breath, and torture her with the heightened perception of what a pathetic fat little creep she was.

She felt poised on that razor edge now, as she sat there staring out over Los Angeles from on electronic high.

She felt music moving through her; the millions of lights below seemed to shimmer and dance in flashing and interpenetrating rhythms like the magic dance of the electrons in a VoxBox and she was catching it in her fingers and rapping it out on the arm of the chair. Random bars of tunes emerged and receded and recombined in her head, and she was ready to sit down and commune with her rock and roll machineries.

But she was not alone out here with her VoxBox. Glorianna O'Toole turned away from whatever it was she had been staring at down there in the dance of the cybersphere, and looked at her with huge green eyes, around which her face began to go through like these weird time-lapse *changes*.

She was like this gray-haired little old lady old enough to be Sally's grandmother, and then she was this incredibly sexy redheaded young fox who was everything Sally could never be, and she was someone else, someone who had always been a million years old and who had never been anything but young and beautiful, solarized and computer-enhanced into eternal unreal perfection like one of Bobby's synthesized rock goddesses. Back and forth and back and forth these faces pulsed in a heavy driving beat, one, two, THREE, one, two, THREE, THREE, two, one, THREE, two, one, one, two, THREE. . . .

Sally *hated* Glorianna in that moment with a queasy puke-green envy; she saw something still singing in this faded old lady that it had never been given to her to know, and yet somehow she felt the same rhythm beating inside of her, and tapped it out on the deck chair arm, and the lyric her longing put to it threatened to make her pop out of her skin like pus from an angry little pimple.

Why not ME, why not ME, WHY not me, WHY not me, why not ME!

Bobby Rubin's worst opinions of wirehead garbage seemed quite confirmed as he stood there regarding Sally from the Valley from within the flash of the piece Glorianna O'Toole had seduced him into wearing. What he saw was a poor little fat girl who realized all too well what a toad-lady she was, but who nevertheless presumed to allow herself to run pornographic pictures of *him* slavering to possess her unwholesome body on the video screen of her mind.

This much he needed no Silicon City wire to see; Project Superstar forced him to allow his nose to be rubbed in it for hours every day. But what this thing was making him *feel* as he saw the Pimple mooning at him now was a psychedelic vision he could well do without.

For he was seeing *himself* in a kinestatic flicker of perspectives and he didn't like what he saw at all. He saw himself in high school watching the jocks and the hunks make off with the foxes who wouldn't look at him twice and feeling like a pallid little nerd. He saw himself screwing the leavings of the bands he did visual tracks for and trying to convince himself they were hot stuff.

Worse still, he saw himself from a foxy lady's perspective as he gave her the eye, and what he saw was a male version of *Sally Genaro,* a wimpy little creep with some nerve to presume such fantasies.

Most horrid of all was the sense of *kinship* this piece of evil wirehead shit was making him feel for the Pimple. She lusted after him just as he lusted after all the prime Hollywood pussy, and when they looked at him, they saw what he saw when he looked at Sally, namely a complete turn-off they wouldn't be caught dead in bed with.

He caught himself remembering the drunken scene at that party with more clarity than he had experienced it with in realtime. Oh yes, they had both been bemoaning the same eternal wallflower invisibility in the eyes of the Beautiful People, the same seemingly genetic inability to score with the objects of their dreams, the same mean-spirited envy of those who were born to be what they could never become.

But the final turn of the wirehead screw was that Sally had tried to comfort him at the end with a genuine caring that he absolutely could not tolerate, an understanding of that which he most emphatically did not want understood, and certainly not by the likes of her.

And that, judging by how he felt now, was precisely what had made him puke.

"Come on kiddies, time to boot up and boogie!" Glorianna O'Toole declared, fracturing the vision, and when Bobby turned at the sound of her voice beside him, he beheld something that might have, that should have, that must have come from his own image organ.

Glorianna O'Toole stood out against the backdrop of the brilliant pixels of the shimmering cityscape, outlined in their kirilian aura, her hair blowing in the wind. Her eyes shone with electronic luminescence. Her lips grinned a smirky smile. She was like an album cover treatment of the rock and roll queen she had once been. Somehow the young child of the Sixties who still lived behind that mask of old flesh had found the power to shine on through.

This was *Glorianna's* Glorianna, this was Glorianna as his own AP version of what must once have been, this was the Crazy Lady of Rock and Roll with the years shaved back with a wizard algorithm, this was his time-warped vision of the ultimate dream lover the likes of him would never know. This was every woman who would never even look at him.

But Glorianna O'Toole did.

She looked right at him, and she winked, and a rock and roll goddess out of the fabulous Sixties was giving little Bobby Rubin the eye. She winked again, and a dirty old lady was giving him a sarcastic perverted parody of same, and that was all right too.

He wondered if she was seeing what he hoped she was seeing,

for no woman whom he had ever really admired had ever looked at him and showed him the Bobby he wanted to see reflected in her eyes, the Bobby he dreamed of being in his heart of hearts.

And something clicked.

Why not?

If her, why not me?

"Pleased to meet you, hope you guess my name," Glorianna sang at him.

But Bobby was already walking across the deck toward the living room, toward his image organ, toward the bits and bytes, toward the cybersphere where, he had suddenly realized, he had the power to make her see the Bobby he wanted her to see, Bobby Rubin, the Prince of Rock and Roll, Bobby Rubin as Bobby Rubin deserved to be.

"What are you *doing,* Bobby?" Sally Genaro moaned, the music leaving her head, the wirehead magic suddenly shattered by the truly ludicrous sight on the screen. "Jeez, that's a picture of *you!*"

"So?" Bobby said. "I've got to start somewhere."

He had made a beeline for his image organ rig and started popping this silly picture of himself up on the monitors without even saying a word like he was in some kind of *trance,* and what peered out at her from her own monitor was a grainy old photo of a hunch-shouldered figure in baggy jeans and a funky old red lumberjack shirt squinting in bright sunlight and posing with wimpish pride beside his car.

The VoxBox and the image organ were set up facing each other, with a monitor beside Sally's VoxBox slaved to Bobby's output, so that they could look each other in the eye while they played and both view the visual track at the same time, Glorianna's inspiration for a set-up that might "intensify the creative vibes."

But the Bobby who smiled foolishly from her screen was the same Bobby who looked at her from above their consoles, a little younger maybe, but still not even *her* idea of any rock star snaky enough to ship gold!

"So he's not really your idea of perfection?" Bobby said, grinning strangely at her. He did something with his controllers. The car and the background disappeared, leaving Bobby Rubin standing in blue matte space. He did something else and the picture snapped into crystal-clear color-corrected focus.

"What kind of body turns you on?"

"Huh?"

"What kind of body turns you on?" Bobby repeated blandly. "Is your dream lay a bodybuilder or a ballet dancer or a baseball player?"

"Bobby Rubin, if you think I'm—"

"Do it!" Glorianna O'Toole hissed peremptorily from behind Bobby, where she stood staring at his monitor with the most *intense* expression.

"Come on, Glorianna," Sally whined, "this is like *dumb*!"

Glorianna glanced at her narrowly. "Do it, Sally!" she repeated. "And do it like . . . *this,*" she said, giving Sally's touchpoint a sudden tap.

"Surfer," Sally found herself blurting.

Bobby Rubin's head squinted at her owlishly from a tall, naked, bronzed beach boy's body, downed with sun-bleached fuzz, his huge rosy cock crowned by a golden shock of pubic hair.

Sally's ears burned scarlet. "At least give him like a *jockstrap*!" she moaned. Bobby laughed and dressed his surfer self in a red bikini bottom.

Sally grinned at him. This silly game suddenly began to seem like *fun*. "Do something with his hair," she said. "I like it long and blond. . . ."

Bobby's head grew a sun-bleached mane of thick straight blond hair flowing to within about two inches of his shoulders.

More than fun, it seemed as if Bobby, in the only way the shy little guy knew how, was at long last trying to turn her on.

"Make your nose a little smaller, Bobby. . . ."

Surfer Bobby's nose lost its slight bend, shrank, grew long, wide, expressive nostrils.

"Bitchin'!" Sally exclaimed. "Now like give yourself neater eyebrows, black ones, and you know, dark sexy lashes!"

She practically drenched her panties at the sight of what now appeared on her screen. There was Bobby Rubin, undeniably Bobby's recognizable face, but haloed by flowing blond hair, atop a surfer's fuck-me body, with a thin flaring nose like some picture of a Russian prince, and with his eyes set off by hot black brows and long dark lashes so sexy they were just *this much away* from being gay.

"The eyes . . ." she said. "Make them . . ."

"Leave the eyes alone!" Glorianna O'Toole snapped. "Fucking hell, *I know that face*!"

* * *

"Shit . . ." Glorianna muttered in frustration as she found herself popping out of the flash, staring at the face on the screen, trying to recall who or what had been looking back at her out of the dreamtime the magic moment before, who had seemed to say, remember me, babes. . . .

"The hair's wrong," she found herself saying. "Paint it black, black as night, black as coal. . . ."

His hair turned black. Goddammit, who are you? I know you, you smart-ass motherfucker! Come back to me, you son of a bitch! she demanded. Fuck it, she thought, I'm coming in after you! And she gave her touchpoint another tap.

The face on the screen seemed to nod at her, beckoning her onward.

"Your hair's curlier, isn't it?" she said. "Falls to your shoulders in wild windblown waves."

His hair curled and tumbled in the flowing breeze.

He was beginning to come back to her, this creature from her dreamtime, this lover who had never been.

Glorianna laughed. At this late date, was she quite literally about to meet the man of her dreams?

For that, of course, was who this was shaping up to be, someone who had never been, but someone who had never been very far away, someone who she had found in every man she had ever loved, someone whose spirit she had long feared had vanished from the world—Mr. Tambourine Man, the Mighty Quinn, Jumpin' Jack Flash himself, the Lizard King of Rock and Roll.

Glorianna stared at the face of the man on the screen, she looked at the face of Bobby Rubin, hunched over his console and creating it. The same, and yet not the same. As if the long-lost rocker inside this poor little thwarted kid, inside this whole fucking dead-ass sold-out generation of poor little kids, was somehow struggling up out of dreamtime to be reborn.

This wire was the wizard McCoy all right, something wonderful and weird was for sure beginning to happen.

"What would you like to wear, Jack?" she asked the figure on the screen. "Blue jeans or sequins or bell bottoms or black leather?"

"This is the Electronic Age, not the Age of Aquarius, Glorianna," he said with a wicked little grin. Glorianna was just barely surprised enough when he began to speak to realize out of a dim mundane corner of her mind's eye that Bobby Rubin had jacked a mike into his console and booted up a lip-sync program. He was talking to her through his transmogrified image.

Or was he?

Or was someone beginning to break on through to the other side *through him*?

What the fuck was I talking about? Bobby Rubin found himself wondering as he popped out of someplace wonderful into this dimmer realm, where Sally Genaro sat staring at her screen most strangely, where Glorianna O'Toole, her eyes glowing, regarded what he had wrought with rapt wonder. Who the fuck *was* I? What *is* this piece of wire doing to me?

He shrugged, he hit his touchpoint. For sure, he wanted it to do it to him again!

"In the Electronic Age, I wear everything, or I wear nothing at all," he found himself saying through his alter ego on the screen. He sketched out tight pants tucked into high flaring boots, a form-fitting shirt open halfway down the chest with a high collar and flowing balloon sleeves that ended in bell bottoms just below the elbow. He laid it in over his body, and then matted it all to blue.

He keyed in three separate interface programs for the boots, the pants, and the shirt, so that he could moving matte them independently.

And zap, he was wearing tight black leather pants, gunmetal boots, and the stars and stripes for a shirt. He grinned sexily, wriggling his ass in narcissistic delight, preening like a peacock.

"Play me some rock and roll, Sally," he said, "and let me dance for you."

Sally Genaro couldn't take her eyes off the creature on the screen; the living room with its eucalyptus, Glorianna, even the figure hunched over the facing console, faded away into unreality. All that was real was herself and her dream lover.

It was Bobby, but it was Bobby as she had always wished him to be; perfect Bobby, a Bobby who didn't put her down, who wouldn't call her Sally from the Valley, who was opening up his secret inner beauty just for her, as it was always meant to be.

She stored a beat-loop in her sequencer, the same beat that had been going through her head since she had seen Glorianna O'Toole's face pulsing through its changes out there on the deck.

"One, two, THREE, one, two, THREE, THREE, two, one, THREE, two, one, one, two, THREE. . . ."

She ran it through a muzzy bass drum, added a heavy conga, put a funky electric bass to it, saved the result, and slaved the visual track to the multiplexed rhythm sequence.

Smiling at her, he began to do a crude and jerky bump and grind. And his clothes began to change in time with the rhythm, in a kinestatic flicker of chromakeyed overlaid images, a flash of ever-changing shapes and colors too fast for the eye to follow, a mirrored strobe-suit that burned an infinite regression of overlapping afterimages onto her retinas.

She laid a trumpet across her keyboard, dropped it an octave, funked it up with filter programs, square-enveloped the vibrato, overlaid a guitar twang with feedback loops, and when she started diddling fragments of random melody with her fingers, out came something that sounded like Gabriel doing Jimi Hendrix on his horn spaced-out on wire.

Bobby was dancing, dancing as he only could in his dreams, letting the beat move his bones, and the notes nuance the flesh of his body, and the laughter inside come rockin' right on through. It made him feel like singing.

"I'm the me I always told me that I could never be . . ." he chanted in a ragged croak.

Sally ran the voice through her vocoder, syncing it to her lead-line, squeezed it through filters, ran it through reverb, tinkered with envelope parameters. Out came a male lead singer directly on the beat, rough-crooning the words with a fluid liquid rasp that phrased itself insinuatingly around the melody like the snake in the garden singing the blues.

I'm the me I always told me
That I could never be. . . .

"Put some feedback in it, make it sound a little electronic," Glorianna O'Toole said behind her. "Let's hear the old bits and bytes sizzle and spark. . . ."

Sally adjusted some parameters and filters. She did things to the overtone mix. The figure dancing on the screen for her to the music coming out of her fingertips sang now in a voice that surprised even her; male, and powerful, yet with a female fluidity, rough around the edges when it wanted to bite, yet sticky-tongued sensuous when it was in a mood to purr like a smart-ass cat, and omnisexual in a way the world had not yet heard, the line between male and female blurred not by bisexual androgyny, but somehow encompassed by the vocal range of a third sex, the forthrightly artificial yet entirely human, indeed hyperhuman, voice of a rock and roll machine.

Sally's fingers danced across the keyboard. The Rock and Roll Machine danced before her, giving her the eye, strobing in a kaleidoscope of flashing patterns and colors, warping her into its cyberspace, inviting her to sing along. . . .

Glorianna popped out of the flash, but this time the dreamtime magic did not entirely go away. What the fuck were these kids *doing*?

Out of the corner of her eye, she could verify that Bobby Rubin and Sally Genaro were completely spaced into their controllers, microphones, and screens, like video-game junkies on amphetamine, their fingers flying, their mouths muttering into their mikes, zapped together into their cybersphere. She knew that Sally was making the music and Bobby was creating the visual track, and they were both inputting vocals, but who was the singer, and from whence came the song?

I'm the you they always told me
That I could never be
I'm the crown of your creation
In your wizard dreams
Let me dance into your dreamtime
I'm your Rock and Roll Machine!

He sang in that unreal yet magically human voice, a singer with a range from shining crystalline clarity that could shatter glass on the high notes to subsonic bass that you heard only in your bones, and he had the tones and phrasing of every rock singer who had ever lived at his command in between, and oh did he let you know it, tying it all together with electronic swoops and glides and lightnings that never came from a set of human pipes.

He danced like Mick Jagger and he danced like Michael Jackson and he danced like Pearl on Southern Comfort and whites, and he danced like all of them together; he danced like

Rock and Roll itself. She wouldn't have been the Crazy Old Lady of Rock and Roll if she didn't hit her touchpoint and dance along with him back into the dreamtime.

His strobe-suit vibrated her retinas, burning the vision on the screen into her brain in a cascade of afterimages, flashing him out of the raster-universe of bits and pixels, and then perspective reversed polarity, and as he came bursting *out,* she was sucked right *in*.

They met somewhere between, in the timeless onstage realm where they had always been performing their eternal set together, a long, long set that had begun when she and the world were young and that would never end while the music lived.

And what a band was backing them, the infinite grand touring road show of Rock and Roll Valhalla! Everyone was there for a few bars, living and dead, Grateful and otherwise, Hendrix and Lennon, Clapton and Ginger Baker, Charlie Watts, and Larry Ellis, Billy Preston, and Frank Fox, and every anonymous sessions musician who ever lived got to play too, even poor old Billy Beldock, hot and handsome as the night she met him, on his old acoustic drum kit.

Out beyond the stage lights, the audience clapped its hands to the beat and danced in the aisles, an audience that spread out to the far horizons in space and in time, rocks in black leather jackets and greasy pompadours, hippies in paisley and bell bottoms, bikers in their painted denim colors, skinheads, punks with pins through their cheeks and electric sparky hair, and clean-cut yuppies just droppin' in to boogie.

And wonder of all rock and roll wonders, Bobby Rubin and Sally Genaro and their whole fucked-over generation of nose-to-the-grindstone balls-to-the-wall hackers and computer wimps were there too, learning to boogie at last via the grace of everyone's fave raves of the dreamtime, the Queen of Crazy Ladies and their own electronic resurrection of the Jack of Rock and Roll.

Boot me up and boogie
Sez this ghost in your machine
I've been sealed up in your circuits
I've been nowhere to be seen
But now I'm here to tell ya
Raise up your voice and scream
You and me together
We're a Rock and Roll Machine!

"Ya done good, babes," he whispered into her ear during a long wild instrumental break.

"You're all right too, Jack," Glorianna said, and she knew to her surprise that they were both telling the truth.

For out of the most evil notion the Muzik Factory had ever had, out of two nerdy little kids and a broken-down old second-rate singer desperately trying to save her own ass, out of the very bits and bytes that had all but automated real rockers out of existence, and a piece of wizard wire, that which had been assassinated by circuitry had contrived to be reborn in this new electronic avatar, as if he had been there all along waiting for this moment to arrive.

The break ended, and she found herself singing a solo riff whose words, as she sang them, she seemed to have always known.

You're standing here beside me
Just where you've always been
You've been hiding right inside me
You're the ghost in the machine
You're just bits and bytes and programs
But baby, you ain't Mr. Clean. . . .

The music thickened, grew ominous, more bassy, guitars wailed insinuatingly, drums sneered, somewhere in the distance the forlorn foredoomed sirens of the riot squad began to wail. Jack's long, curly, raven-black hair turned a brilliant punk American-flag red, frosted with a thin white webwork that mimicked the Shunt as he pranced and swaggered to the lip of the stage, and chanted gutturally with the voice of the endless audience itself, the voices of all the boys and girls out there on the unarmed road of flight, and yet transmogrified by his circuitries into the mighty electronic voice of pure unpersonified Rock and Roll itself.

I make more of you
You make more of me
You make more of me
I make more of you. . . .

And over it, in the high hard voice of her youth, in the voice of her dreamtime, in the voice of her generation that she had not quite ever been, Glorianna O'Toole sang out her wicked triumph over Carlo Manning and all the other pinheads upstairs.

Red ripe anarchy
For all the world to see
What will the Fat Men do?

Red Jack swaggered over to her microphone, and they belted it out together, eyes linked, lips close enough to kiss.

You make more of me
I make more of you....

Red Jack laughed, she laughed, the guitars and basses and synthesizers and saxes and drums all laughed after their fashion, the audience laughed, the whole wide world seemed to laugh a dirty Rock and Roll laugh, the one the world is always waiting for, the one that always laughs last.

After that, who wanted to stick around for an encore? "See ya later," Glorianna said, reaching up to hit the touchpoint of the Shunt.

"Sooner than you think," said Red Jack.

And she was standing in her own living room with a microphone in her hand and the fragrant Santa Ana wind blowing in from the open doors to the deck, rustling the leaves of her bonsai eucalyptus.

She blinked. She had no concept of the passage of time. Bobby and Sally were still zoned into their screens and controllers, their fingers flying, their eyes glazed in a cybersphere trance.

Through the speaker system came the last bars of the very duet she and Red Jack had been singing, and if Sally Genaro's VoxBox wizardry was not quite up to the ultimate rock and roll band of the dreamtime, what she had laid out across her keyboard with layer upon layer upon layer of interlocked emulation programs was pretty fuckin' close to the next best thing—lead guitar with rhythm and bass slaved to it, doubled and tripled on horn and sax, backed by at least three different synth voices, a whole rock and roll symphony orchestra at her command in realtime as her fingers danced across the keys.

And if there was no transmogrified Glorianna O'Toole singing along, the voice of Red Jack was *everything* it had been in the dreamtime, the collective electronically enhanced voice of Rock and Roll itself.

And there he was on the monitors, big as life and twice as nasty, his strobe-suit Jumpin' Jack Flashing, his long bright-red hair webbed with the white traceries of the Shunt and blowin' in the wind, and that paragon of male charisma he wore for a face lookin' right at her with Bobby Rubin's eyes.

Tell me *this* little man who isn't there isn't the mayor of Solid Gold City! Tell me *Red Jack* isn't for real!

Clearly this séance had done its work and then some; all that remained was to whip these raw tracks together into a demo.

She started to reach out for Bobby's touchpoint.

But something held her back. Maybe it was Red Jack himself, peering into her eyes from out of the screen. Even without the Shunt, she seemed to hear someone or something tell her that there was more to resurrecting real rock and roll than conjuring up out of nothingness a superstar who was a lock to ship gold.

Red ripe anarchy
For all the world to see . . .

That was *her* line, now wasn't it? Hadn't it always been? She laughed wickedly. Oh yeah, there was more to rock than the fuckin' bottom line! She'd give Carlo Manning his gold, she'd give all the pinheads upstairs so much fuckin' *platinum* that they'd expire from heavy metal poisoning, and she'd give them the great big kick in the ass they so richly deserved in the bargain!

She moved closer to Bobby Rubin's ear. "Run it through from the top," she whispered. "Once more, with feeling . . ."

Bobby Rubin danced through his dreamtime, through the halls of high school, through endless Long Island parties, through the corridors of the Muzik Factory, through a thousand and one horny Hollywood nights, and into Eddie Friedkin's mansion, where he had baptized his ultimate nerdhood in vomit on the lawn.

But this time around, he was another Bobby, the heavy metal hero of his dreams, Jumpin' Jack Flash, the Mighty Quinn, the Electric Red Jack of Rock and Roll, his long wild lightning-streaked red hair sparking and flowing in the breeze, the object of every woman's dreams, the me they always told him that he could never be, the rockin' cyberwizard, the Rock and Roll Machine.

"Hey Jack, let's you and me raise some hell together for old times' sake," said the Queen of Rock and Roll, with a wicked wink and leer.

She stood there in the dreamtime with him against a backdrop of pixels shimmering like a nighttime cityscape, haloed and solarized in their kirilian aura, her green eyes flashing with electronic luminescence, the dream lover the likes of him would never know, every woman who would never look at him with the very look this Crazy Lady was giving him now.

"What did you have in mind, moma, as if I didn't know," Red Jack said, laughing.

"You know the words, Bobby, you can hear the music now, so let's boogie, let's kick out all the jams and knock down all the walls, let's bring back the Revolution, and kick all the pinheads in their balls!"

"Red ripe anarchy for all the world to see? What *will* the Fat Men do?"

Sally Genaro played her heart out, she sang into her microphone from someplace deep inside, and Bobby winked and wriggled his pelvis just for her, and at long last, at long pimply fat lonely last, she knew what it was like to be part of him, to be smiled upon by a Prince of Rock and Roll, to feel the music trapped inside of her bursting forth in full unashamed and unafraid flower, to be onstage in the spotlight at last, to be released, to be the me every man's eyes told her that she could never be.

I make more of you
You make more of me . . .

Bobby took her hand and took her away, away from the San Fernando Valley, away from sucking the cocks of the Razor Dogs of the world, away from being the ugly duckling at Hollywood parties, away into the cybersphere, a brand new *rockin'* cybersphere, where the fat and the meek inherited the earth, where all the nerdy little wimps and pimply little fat girls could be Queens of the starry pixels and Jacks of Rock and Roll.

We've been sealed inside our circuits
We've been nowhere to be seen
But you and me together
We're a Rock and Roll Machine.

"All right my little rock and roll wizards, rise and shine!" Glorianna O'Toole burbled happily as she popped the touchpoints of their Shunts in rapid sequence and stood there grinning. Bobby looked at Glorianna, then back at Sally. Glorianna stared into his eyes for a long long time before trying to make eye contact with Sally. Sally had eyes only for Bobby. No one said anything for quite a while.

"What . . . what the fuck happened?" Bobby finally said. "Was I . . . ? Did you . . . ?" He didn't even have the words to form the concepts in his head as he stared at this gray-haired old lady looking straight back at him with the eyes of the queen of his dreamtime. *His* dreamtime? *Her* dreamtime?

"How much of it was real?" he finally managed to articulate.

"Quién sabé?" Glorianna said gaily. "Does a bear shit in the woods? Do we all live in the same yellow submarine?"

She brought Sally over to his console and punched up a replay of the rough master mix.

"You were synthesizing and editing all these tracks, kiddies, that's for sure," she said, "and I think we all had a hand in the vocals, but whoever or whatever did which to whom, meet the crown of our creation, Red Jack, the Superstar who isn't there, doin' 'Your Rock and Roll Machine,' and if our boy doesn't crack number one with his debut disc, I don't know shit about rock and roll!"

Red Jack, the AP star on the screen, looked nothing like him, with his tall, well-muscled body, his long, flaming, white-frosted red hair, and yet the eyes that looked out at him were definitely his, and somehow that made Bobby feel that some essential and wonderful part of him was up there singing like the greatest rock star who had never lived.

I make more of you
You make more of me
You make more of me
I make more of you. . . .

And oh, was that set of clothing matte programs a wizard piece of software! As he danced and sang against a blue matte background, Red Jack's pants and shirt went through endless strobing changes, as bits of old movies, starscape still shots, crowd scenes, faces, endless data-bank footage and images even Bobby couldn't pick out, flickering across them continuously, proclaiming his discorporate existence, and waving it in the face of the world triumphantly like an electronic battle flag.

Red Jack dissolved into pixels for a long moment, colored confetti filling the screen, then reformed slowly out of a dissolving montage of ordinary homely little faces, including Bobby's own, as if tentatively coalescing out of electric dreams and secret desires.

I'm the you they always told me
That I could never be
I'm the crown of your creation
In your wizard dreams . . .

Bobby found himself marveling at the visual tracks he himself had wrought, at the secret story of himself dancing to the music across the screen.

Audience footage from old concerts matted itself grainily behind Red Jack, conventional stuff everyone used from Woodstock and Live Aid and Beatles tours and Springsteen at the L.A. Coliseum, but segueing into a weird montage of nerd city, bits and pieces of computer training films and documentaries on the cyberkind generation, an endless dreary expanse of drudges and hackers beavering away at their consoles.

Red Jack danced through the endless aisles of computer consoles, tossing discs that appeared magically in his hands to all the hacking drudges like a crazy electronic Johnny Appleseed.

And all the little computer nerds began inserting the discs into their computers, which magically blossomed into glowing jukeboxes painted in fantastic neon swirls and paisley patterns.

And the montage of wimpy little faces melded into the face of Red Jack, a multiplexed multitude kicking out the jams. All the hackers danced in a crazy chorus line behind the figure in the strobe-suit, out of the computer room, and off down Hollywood Boulevard, Fifth Avenue, Bourbon Street, Telegraph, and Market.

More of them poured out of buildings, like cockroaches fleeing in a tide from their tenements, like huddled wimpy masses yearning to breathe free, their faces transforming into the face of Red Jack as they hit the streets and joined the parade, then flickering back and forth between the nerd masks of the cybermasses and the rockin' face of Red Jack in time to the beat and the colored strobing of his shirt and pants.

Then Red Jack was all by himself in close-up on the screen, looking right into Bobby's eyes *with* Bobby's eyes, annihilating thereby the psychic space between, and warping him into his own song.

You're standing here beside me
Just where I've always been
You've been hiding right inside me . . .

Bobby actually found himself singing along to the cut, something he had never done before in his life, and wondering *why the fuck* he had never sung along with himself before.

We're the ghost in the machine
We may be bits and bytes and programs
But baby, we ain't Mr. Clean. . . .

Red Jack sang on a stage before tiered grandstands that were also row after row of computer consoles. Behind them a vast audience of hackers played their keyboards like pianos, fingers flying, heads rolling to the beat, stomping their feet, and rolling their eyes. For a brief moment, Red Jack flashed in his multiplexed multitude across their features.

I make more of you. . . .

A reverse perspective over the shoulders of row after row of rockin' hackers behind blank monitors, their keyboards replaced by synthesizers, guitars, pianos, drum kits. And as they swayed to the music, the face of Red Jack appeared on each and every screen out of a cloud of pixels.

You make more of me. . . .

Back and forth between the figure of Red Jack performing on stage and his face arising out of the bits and bytes on every hacker's screen, four reversals to a bar.

You make more of me....
I make more of you....

A manic, rapidly cut Keystone Kops routine. Banks, missile control centers, tv control rooms, department store check-out counters, stock brokerages, offices of government and industry, monitors and industrious old farts everywhere, reacting in gross comic horror as the facts and figures and news features vanish before their eyes, to be replaced anywhere and everywhere by the leeringly triumphant Red Jack.

Red ripe anarchy
For all the world to see
What will the Fat Men do?
You make more of me
I make more of you!

When it was over, Bobby sat there staring numbly at the blank pearly screen. He looked back at Glorianna, who was fairly cackling and rubbing her hands in glee.

"I didn't know I had it in me . . ." he croaked weakly. "That thing's . . ."

"*Subversive?*" Glorianna suggested archly. "No fuckin' shit!"

"You don't understand, I mean . . . something tells me that he's going to . . . to *get out* . . ." Bobby stammered, without quite knowing what that might really mean.

Glorianna O'Toole winked at him, and for a moment, even without the Shunt, he wasn't looking into the eyes of any gray-haired old lady, oh no, in that moment she was the consort of Red Jack himself again, the ageless Queen of Rock and Roll he had met in the dreamtime.

"Why what *will* the Fat Men do?" she said, and laughed uproariously.

"I don't know about the Fat Men, but the pinheads upstairs will never release a thing like that!"

Glorianna flashed him a slow sly grin. "Oh yes they will," she said with utter certainty. "Their beady little eyes will light up with dollar signs, and they'll go for the sure thing solid gold, and they won't even *see* anything beyond the bottom line."

She shrugged. She winked at him again. "That, after all, is *why* they're pinheads in the first place!"

* * *

Sally Genaro sat behind the barricade of her VoxBox, watching Bobby make like *goo-goo eyes* at Glorianna O'Toole, watching the horrid old lady giving him the eye back as if they had, yech, *made it* or something, and not knowing whether she wanted to shout for joy or cry.

She knew full well that she had laid down the best tracks of her life, that she was really the one who made Red Jack sing, who gave him voice, who made him rock and roll, for without her it would all be just a bunch of words and pictures. And even the body and the face were the child of her longing and his fantasies of how he wanted to look for her.

He was the proof for all the world to see of the intimacy they had shared in their heart of hearts. He was the Bobby of her dreams, and the Bobby who had revealed his secret spirit to her and her alone.

It had been as good as balling him.

In some ways, maybe better.

For sure, this was going to ship platinum, for sure, this was going to make her career, and for sure, she had for a shining moment been the me they always told her that she could never be.

But it was *Bobby* who had somehow been transformed into an AP rock star, not Sally from the Valley, and it was Glorianna O'Toole who he had turned his snaky eyes on in the aftermath of what *they* had shared.

The bassline with which she had *started* the whole thing beat like a mocking aural afterimage in her wounded heart.

Why not ME, why not ME, WHY not me, WHY not me, why not ME!

DO ME LIKE YOU DID THE NIGHT BEFORE

Karen Gold awoke to the clanging and pounding cacophony of the morning's charge of steam rising into the loft's pipes and radiators, to the stirrings and gruntings and flushings of people abluting and relieving themselves beyond the maze of burlap curtains, to the pressure and smell of a hard, unwashed male body crammed into the narrow cot beside her, to an alert pair of dark brown eyes watching her own open.

Memories of the night before swam up disjointedly into consciousness as her eyes brought his face into focus. The Temple of Doom, $1600 in bedbug sales. Hard brown eyes, under dark bushy brows, framed by almost feminine dark lashes. Footsteps behind her. Those animals, tearing at her clothing, pulling down her panties. Olive brown skin, smooth and soft, a young face, younger than her, maybe. Her savior, appearing out of the darkness. A short kinky afro of black hair strangely and subtly shot with unlikely filaments of silver. A tender creature, and then a demon lover, without a doubt the best she had ever had.

A Puerto Rican!

The night before and this morning after coalesced into a more or less coherent skein of events, one leading to the other, but as they did, Karen shut her eyes again, not yet quite ready to deal with today's reality, which presently found her curled up in bed with some Puerto Rican *streetie*.

Like most educated white New Yorkers of her generation, Karen would never admit to racial prejudice—Malcolm was black, after all, Tommy was Vietnamese, Teddy Ribero himself was Puerto Rican, they were her friends, she was living in the loft with them, wasn't she—so, like most of her compeers, she felt quite mortified when such feelings nevertheless arose in extremis, as they did now.

Particularly since . . . what was his name, Paco . . . had gallantly rescued her from two vile rapists at considerable risk to himself, and been such a perfect gentleman in the aftermath that *she* had actually asked *him* to make love to her to wipe the memory away.

If this guy was your *white* knight in shining armor, you'd be giving him a tender thankful blow-job right now instead of trying to pretend you're still asleep so you don't have to deal with him! she told herself angrily

Then again, maybe this wasn't racial prejudice at all, which certainly was reprehensible, but prejudice against *streeties*, which, being a matter of self-preservation, was entirely rational and forgivable. . . .

Jeez, there was *$1600* in my purse! she suddenly realized in a hot flash of paranoia. Did this guy . . . ?

This was more than enough to snap her eyes wide open without further thought, as she shot a hurried glance past Paco into the corner, where her clothes, his crummy rags, her purse, and his unmistakable street bag lay piled in a hurried heap. Once having done this, there was nothing for it but to meet his gaze, smile, and say, "Uh . . . hello."

"Hello . . ." he said quite guardedly. He looked quickly around the little tent of burlap hangings in some confusion. "Chingada," he said uncertainly, "where the fuck is this, muchacha . . . ?"

"You don't remember?"

A very strange look indeed passed across his swarthy face. He started to say something, obviously thought better of it, said something else. "It was dark . . . it looked . . . different. . . ."

Karen was suddenly quite conscious of his hard, thin, naked body entwined around hers, and despite the situation, despite the fact that something about his attitude was beginning to piss her off, indeed perhaps because *he* was acting so paranoid and distant, she found herself becoming aroused.

"And what about me?" she demanded. "Did I look better in the dark too?"

His eyes widened. It almost seemed as if he were about to laugh. This was about all Karen could take. She grabbed his limp cock, squeezed it rhythmically. "What about *this*?" she said. "You *do* remember at least *that* much, don't you?"

His sudden soft moan and the quick stiffening against her palm told her that he wasn't quite *that* far out of it. Clumsily, crudely, he started to roll himself over onto her, pumping into her hand and moaning. She resisted, slid him inside of her as they lay side by side, put her free hand over his mouth.

"Be quiet about it," she whispered. "There's a lot of people out there who don't even know you're here. . . ."

She slung one leg over him and began rolling her pelvis as best she was able in tight, smoky little circles. He groaned softly, kneaded her breast with one hand, and came in about two minutes, leaving her more confused than hot and bothered, though there certainly was that too.

Nor did he even plant a perfunctory kiss on her lips when it was over. Instead, he lay there regarding her with narrow-eyed suspicion. "People?" he hissed. "This ain't your apartment? *What kind of people?* Qué pasa? What kind of place is this, muchacha?"

"This is the Reality Liberation Front. . . ."

"*Qué?*"

"That will take some explaining," Karen sighed, rolling away from him off the cot and onto her feet. "I'm sure Markowitz will fill your ears with more than you want to hear over breakfast," she said, rummaging in the pile of his and her clothing and dressing quickly before he got up to cover her covert search of her purse.

"Breakfast?" he said sharply behind her. "Kibble . . . or real food?"

"We've got some cornflakes and milk, some coffee, and I think some bread," Karen said, stepping into her shoes of the night before and turning slowly to face him.

He was climbing off the bed now with an eager but still guarded look on his dark, dangerously attractive face, and she saw how thin his body was, well-muscled in a wiry sort of way, yes, but with ribs clearly showing through the tight skin of his flanks, and the knobby line of his breastbone not quite fleshed into invisibility.

He eyed her narrowly. "I got no dinero . . ." he said uncertainly. "I mean . . ."

Karen felt like a perfect shit.

The $1600 was still in her purse, this poor half-starved kid was a hero who had saved her life, the first thing she had done fresh from his arms had been to check whether or not he had ripped her off, and here he was with his ribs sticking out, shuffling his feet and trying to work himself up to panhandling a bowl of cornflakes!

She smiled at him. She went to him. She put her hands on his shoulders and gave him a great big tender kiss. "Paco," she said, "you can eat as much as you want of whatever we've got."

"Verdad?" he said wide-eyed, as if not quite ready to believe in such an incredible bonanza.

"For sure," she said softly, taking his hand. It was pathetic, it was touching, but she could hardly afford to feel superior or patronizing about it. For after all, not so long ago she had been looking forward to an existence of eating kibble and crashing in the subway herself, now hadn't she? And from the look of him, this poor sweet guy had probably never known much of anything else.

There but for fortune . . . she thought. If I hadn't gotten caught in the rain, if I hadn't ducked into that bar, if I hadn't met Leslie . . .

If Paco hadn't come along when he did . . . if he had really been the savage monster she had always assumed such starveling streeties to be . . .

She shuddered. It didn't bear even thinking about. She felt quite ashamed before him and not because of his nakedness.

"Come on," she said with real warmth in her heart, "put on your clothes, and let me introduce my friends to a real hero."

As he pulled on his pants, Paco considered a tap of the Zap, but immediately decided that until he at least knew where the fuck he really was and qué pasa, it had better be no way, Jose.

Verdad, the Zap gave him *powers,* he sure had handled himself a whole lot better with this muchacha last night than he was doing so far este mañana. But then, last night this place had seemed like a palace and she had been a chocharica princess of the city with mucho dinero. Better play it cool and straight, muchacho, at least till you figure out who and what you're playing *with*!

Karen, sí, that was her name, Karen Gold, led him out of the tent of old potato bags and into a corridor made of more burlap, bedsheets, tarps, and smelly blankets, sewn together and hanging on ropes from a high unfinished ceiling.

"Fuckin' weird," he muttered, looking up, around, and down. "What is all this shit?"

"Just the living part of the loft," Karen told him. "We've all got curtains around our beds for privacy." She blushed. "But everyone can hear just about everything."

Paco put on his best Mucho Muchacho swagger as she lifted the corner of a big curtain that ran across the whole width of the place, admitting him to a huge room cluttered with all kinds of dingy, mismatched furniture and incomprehensible junk, where eight people sat at a long table made out of sawhorses and boards at the far end.

Three muchachas and five men, all clocking him as Karen led him by the hand through the clutter as if they had for sure heard every moan and scream of last night's performance.

Two of the girls, one thin and brown-haired, the other a little pudgy with spiked black hair, whispered dumb shit to each other like they hadn't gotten laid in years. The third one wasn't that bad at all; short blond hair, a tough little mouth, blue eyes that looked him up and down and then glanced knowingly at Karen.

Two of the men were gordos, one was some kind of chink, and another was a tall, thin, vaguely faggotty-looking nigger with thick glasses that made him look pop-eyed. The fifth was a light-skinned Borinqueno a little older than Paco, a *Blankriqueno* by the look of him, who Paco would have bet had never really spent time out on the streets.

In the light of day leaking in through tall grimy windows, this joint looked like anything but a plushie-tushie palace, and they were all wearing old jeans, faded workshirts, T-shirts, and shit that did not exactly mark them as rich gordos, but they obviously weren't a bunch of kibble-eaters like him, either.

There was a refrigerator and a sink and a stove close by the table. On the stove was a big urn of coffee sending a delicious steam into his nostrils that went straight to the back of his throat. On the table were a king-sized box of cornflakes, a liter container of milk, almost a whole loaf of sliced whole wheat bread, a box of sugar, bowls, cups, and plates, and what looked to be a fuckin' half pound of soft golden butter!

"This is Paco," Karen Gold announced, "Paco . . ." She shot him an embarrassed sideways glance.

"Monaco," Paco said distractedly, pulling up a chair and filling a bowl almost to the rim with cornflakes.

"Hey. . . ."

"What the . . ."

"I told Paco he could have breakfast," Karen said sharply, picking up two cups and filling them from the spigot of the coffee urn. Paco glared around the table, daring anyone to try to stop him, snatched the milk container, poured so much milk on his bowl of cornflakes that it dribbled over the rim, and began rapidly spooning the wonderful, wet, milk-sweetened golden flakes into his mouth, gulping them down and shoveling in more as fast as he was able.

"Jeez . . ."

"Who told you you could . . ."

"Paco saved my life," Karen said, handing him a cup of coffee and seating herself beside him. "Or anyway, kept me from being raped . . ."

"Yeah, well that's not what it sounded like last night," the pink-skinned, beefy blond gordo said with a leer.

Paco glared at him and slurped in a big swallow of coffee that burned his tongue and went straight to his head like a flash of wire.

"Just because he's a good lay doesn't give you the right to give him *our* food!" the pudgy chocha with spiky black hair whined.

Paco smacked his lips loudly at her, grabbed a slice of bread, and slathered it with about an inch of soft greasy butter.

"It's *communal* food, Karen," the nigger said mildly. "Paid for with *RLF* money . . ."

Karen reached into her purse as Paco bit off a big chunk of well-buttered bread. "Like this?" she said, slapping a huge wad of bills down on the table.

Paco's jaw dropped so far open he almost lost his mouthful.

"Last night's take at The Temple of Doom," Karen Gold said. "Sixteen hundred dollars. I sold *a lot* of bedbugs. Paco saved that too. Think it's maybe worth a bowl of cornflakes and a piece of bread to the Reality Liberation Front?"

There was a long moment of dead silence. They all looked at Paco quite differently now. Paco began chewing again, but he had lost the ravenous edge off his appetite.

Sixteen hundred dollars! Chingada, hijo de puta, you asshole, this chocha had *$1600* in her bag, and you let it slip right through your fuckin' fingers playing hero! Sixteen hundred! He had never even *seen* a quarter of that much money at one time in his life! It was literally inconceivable to him. Some fuckin' crash and grab artist you are, muchacho! Sixteen hundred dollars yours for the taking, and all you end up with is a bowl of cornflakes, a piece of bread, a cup of coffee, and a piece of ass!

A toilet flushed loudly behind him, and a big, burly, strong-looking putamadre with long wavy black hair and a full black beard came out of the crapper.

"Who's this?" he said, measuring Paco with piercing blue eyes.

"Name's Paco Monaco," the little chink said.

"Saved Karen from some muggers last night."

"Saved the RLF *sixteen hundred bucks,* Larry," said the light-skinned Blankriqueno.

"Is that so?" the big man said evenly, drawing himself a cup of coffee, taking a seat across the table from Paco, and studying him carefully with those no-bullshit eyes. He took a slow sip of coffee. He smiled a wary smile. "You don't look like a rich man to me," he said, "so you must be an asshole."

"*Markowitz!*" the short-haired blond girl groaned, rolling her eyes.

Paco stopped eating and started thinking as he locked gazes with the jefe, for that was obviously who this putamadre was, and stupid he was not. "Why you have to say a thing like that, man?" he said, as if he really had to ask.

" 'Cause sixteen hundred dollars is a lot of money."

"And if I ain't rich, why didn't I grab it?"

The jefe just shrugged.

"Maybe I'm an honest man. . . ."

Nada.

"Maybe I didn't know she had it. . . ."

"Which is it?"

Paco smiled thinly at him. "Maybe I'm not asshole enough to tell you."

The black-bearded jefe continued to stare at him for a long moment. Then he suddenly burst out laughing. "You're okay, Paco Monaco!" he said, holding out a beefy hand. "I'm Larry Coopersmith," he said.

Paco shook his hand. Unlike a lot of big men, this Larry didn't bother to turn a handshake into a macho squeezing contest. Paco found himself liking this gordo; in a funny way the putamadre reminded him a little of Dojo.

Paco took another big bite of buttered bread and washed it down with coffee, his mind racing. The $1600 on the table was gone money, but just maybe there was more where that came from. These people had this loft, didn't they, and all this real food. That meant dinero. . . .

Chingada! What was it Karen had said, the $1600 was last night's take at The Temple of Doom, she had sold a lot of, what did she call it . . . bedbugs. . . .

Well he didn't know what the fuck *that* was, but The Temple of Doom was a fancy meatrack, and Karen must have been *dealing* something. . . .

He took a good long careful look around the loft for the first time. A videodisc deck and a wall screen, more fuckin' telephones scattered around than he had ever seen, dozens of what looked like the screen parts of old tv sets. That much he recognized. But there were endless heaps of all kinds of old electronic junk, cables and wiring all over the place, soldering irons, bits and pieces of stuff sloppily connected to each other. He had no idea what most of this stuff was or what it really did, but it seemed obvious that they were taking it all apart and putting it back together, and that added up to only one thing.

"Wire," he said. "You're making wire."

A chorus of groans went up, and then all of them were giving him hard nasty looks like they thought he was *wire heat* or something. All except Karen, who was smiling a thin little smile, and Larry Coopersmith, who seemed to be studying him very carefully.

"Hey . . ." Paco said uneasily. "No sweat. I'm no fuckin' cop! No problem! Maybe we can do some business."

"Oh . . . ?" Coopersmith said slowly.

"Yeah . . . I mean, I *know some people*. . . ."

"Do you?"

"For sure," Paco said. "I've got some good connections, man. Hey, I'm the *doorman* at Slimy Mary's! I could move a lot of pieces for you there!"

Well, why not? Hadn't Dojo said he could deal whatever he wanted at the door? If Dojo gave him any shit about competing with the stuff he had his zombies turning out upstairs, he could always cut him in for a piece of the action . . . a *small* piece. . . .

"*Slimy Mary's?*" Coopersmith said.

"Yeah!" Paco said. "Everyone knows Slimy Mary's. The fuckin' place is full of wireheads! We could really clean up, man! What you got? The Prong? Uncle Charlie? The Blue Max?"

"Not exactly," said Larry Coopersmith. "What we're making here is bedbugs, Paco."

"The Bedbug . . . ? That's a new one on me, man! What's the flash?"

"That's a little hard to explain . . ." Coopersmith said slowly.

Paco laughed a secret laugh inside. *Sure man,* he thought. As hard to explain as the flash from the piece I'm wearing under your nose right now, huh? Somehow he doubted it.

"It's not exactly wire, Paco . . ." Karen said.

"But I suppose you could say it's not exactly *not* wire, either," the blond girl said.

"Qué?"

The black guy's eyes kind of lit up behind his thick glasses as if he had just flashed a piece of something himself. "You could think of it as wire for *computers,* Paco," he said brightly.

"Huh?"

"How do you feel about computers?" Coopersmith said.

"Quién sabé?" Paco said. "I don't know shit about no computers. . . ."

"But they know everything about you," the chink said.

"So? Who gives a shit? What's there to know?"

"Well think about this," the black guy said. "Most of the money in the country is *inside computers*. Credit card balances. Stock market accounts. Savings accounts. Corporate cash flows. Just bits and bytes zipping around inside computers."

"So what? I ain't got no plastico, I ain't got no savings account, and I sure as shit don't play the fuckin' stock market!"

"But the gordos who own the whole fuckin' world sure do, now don't they, man?" said the Borinqueno. "That's how Ciudad Trabajo runs, no? The big money is all stashed inside computers, man, where the likes of *you* can't get at it."

"Chingada . . ." Paco muttered.

How many times had he done a crash and grab and netted only a few bucks in cash and a wallet full of plastico he couldn't do anything with? Even those cash machine cards couldn't get you any money unless you managed to beat the secret number out of someone. . . .

The banks, the fancy department stores, the cash machines, verdad, that was where most of the money was, any asshole knew that. But somehow he had always thought of it as great big piles of high denomination bills, jewels, furs, appliances, tvs, furniture. . . .

That most of it was really just floating around inside computers, that it wasn't exactly real, that there was no way you could get your hands on it no matter how good a thief you were, that was a revelation of the obvious, of something he had always known but had never considered before, the sudden contemplation of which somehow managed to piss him off at someone or something he couldn't even name. . . .

"How do you feel about that, Paco?" Coopersmith said. He smiled a crooked little smile and stared at him with those hard blue eyes. "Does it seem like the world is being run by people and things you can't even get back at . . . ?"

"Verdad . . ." Paco said softly. "Fuckin'-A!" Was this putamadre reading his mind? "But what the fuck does all this have to do with *wire*?"

"Everything," Coopersmith said. "Most of the money there is is just bits and bytes moving inside computers. They keep track of who owes who what. They send out bills. They cash checks and collect taxes. They keep track of parking tickets. They're the brain of the whole system. . . ."

"So?"

He smiled evilly at Paco. "So what happens when you plug a brain into all different kinds of wire all at once?" he said.

"It turns into the fuckin' Count!" Paco exclaimed.

"What?"

"Who?"

"This burnt-out combo wirehead I know," Paco told them. "A fuckin' zombie . . ."

The black guy got up from the table, went over across the room to a big pile of what looked like videodiscs, came back with a big heap of them, and spread them across the table like a hand of cards.

"Bedbugs," he said proudly. "*Wire* for *computers*." He began picking them up at random and displaying them like a street dealer. "*This* one makes your electric bill disappear. *This* one convinces the IRS computers that you never existed. *This* one lets you transfer funds into your bank account. *This* one scrambles a whole data bank. *This* one wipes out traffic tickets. *This* one makes voice synthesis software speak in tongues. . . ."

Paco stared speculatively at the goods. He eyed Karen Gold. "*This stuff* is what you were dealing before those putamadres jumped you?" he said.

She nodded.

"And you turned sixteen hundred dollars in one night?"

She shrugged, then smiled. "Business isn't always *that* good," she admitted.

"What do these pieces go for?"

"Depends on how complex the program is and how hot people are to have it. I guess three hundred is about average."

"And how much is your cut?"

"It doesn't work that—"

"You got something in mind?" Coopersmith interrupted sharply.

"For sure, man," Paco said, and for sure he had more things in his mind right now than had ever been there at one time before.

In just a few hours he had stolen an Uzi from a zonie, scored a Zap, gotten hired as relief doorman at Slimy Mary's, saved this gorda Karen, met all these weird people, and let $1600 slip through his fingers!

And now he was looking at a way to make more money than he had ever conceived of laying right out there on the table just beyond his fingertips. Chingada, a *chocha* had sold $1600 worth in one night! And he was *Paco Monaco,* he was a fuckin' *meatrack doorman,* wasn't he . . .?

He knew that he had to make his move right now, or he'd be kicking his own ass for blowing his only chance at a lot more than the $1600 he had already let get away. . . .

"Look, I told you, I'm the doorman at Slimy Mary's," he said.

"So?"

"*So?* Don't you know what that means? A doorman don't get paid shit. What I make, I make from *dealing*. . . ."

"You want to deal *bedbugs* for us?" Coopersmith said.

"At a *streetie meatrack*?"

Paco nodded. "I'll give you back three hundred dollars on each piece I move," he said. "That's what you're making now, right? I'll take my chances on jacking the price. You got nothing to lose."

The nigger laughed. "These things aren't *really* wire," he said. "You need a computer with a modem to drop a bedbug in someone else's system."

"What's a modem?"

The nigger groaned, rolled his eyes behind his thick glasses, and threw up his hands. Paco half rose out of his chair, fists clenched to punch out the motherfucker, and held himself back only by grabbing hard onto the lip of the table and thinking only of the money.

But the others had caught the aborted move. He could see it in the way their eyes flinched back. Karen inched away from him to the other side of her chair. Only the jefe kept his cool. He shot the rest of them lidded glances, then gave Paco a thin little smile and an almost imperceptible shrug.

"What Malcolm means is that bedbugs are as useless without a computer attached to a phone as wire would be without juice," he said. "No offense, Paco, but we just don't see how you'd find any customers."

Paco looked down at the bedbug discs scattered across the table, let his hand crawl toward them. "Let me worry about that," he said. "Just let me have a couple and see what I can do. . . ."

Coopersmith cocked his head to one side thoughtfully. He shrugged. "Well, if you've got the front money. . . ."

"Front money?"

"Three hundred bucks apiece, like you said."

"Three hundred bucks! Shit man, I don't have three hundred fuckin' cents!"

"You expect us to *trust you* for the money?" the chink exclaimed.

Paco's first impulse was to punch the putamadre out, but he found himself thinking with unaccustomed cunning and unfamiliar self-control. "Give me two of them for three days," he said. "If I don't bring back six hundred dollars, I'll bring back the pieces."

"*Trust you,* man?" the Blankriqueno sneered.

"You calling me a liar, motherfucker?" Paco shouted. He was on his feet with his fist cocked before he caught himself this time.

But his mind was really moving now. "Sorry," he said, sitting back down again. He looked at Karen Gold sweetly, with a wounded expression. "But it's kind of hard to listen to you people afraid to trust me with a lousy six hundred dollars' worth of pieces, seeing as how I've already proved what kind of man I am."

"How so?" said Coopersmith.

Paco never took his eyes off Karen Gold. "I've already saved you sixteen hundred, haven't I?" he said.

There was a long moment of frozen silence. Gotcha! Paco

thought. He put on his best hangdog expression and played it for all it was worth, which was plenty, muchacho.

"You all think I'm just some dirty spick off the street would rip you off in a minute if you gave me the chance, right? But *I'm* the guy that risked his life to save Karen's ass, and *I'm* the guy that got her back here with your money instead of grabbing it myself. Wasn't for me, you'd be out sixteen hundred already, verdad? Way I see it, you're a thou ahead even if I *do* rip you off."

"He's got a point . . ." the blond-haired girl said.

"We *do* owe him something. . . ."

"Give him a couple of cheap ones, Larry," Malcolm said. "The ones that bedbug Con Ed. . . ."

"Hey, wait, you're not gonna—"

"Besides," Paco said, "either I can sell the fuckers, or I can't. If I can sell 'em, I do better coming back with your money so you'll let me sell more than I would ripping you off for two lousy pieces. And if I can't get money for 'em, why the fuck would I steal 'em?"

He locked eyes with Larry Coopersmith. The big man glared at him expressionlessly for a long moment, as if he knew everything that was going through Paco's head, as if he knew fuckin' well that if Paco had known about the $1600 in the first place, he and it wouldn't be here now, as if he knew full well that Paco was running a number, but as if he also knew that, number or not, Paco really did have more reason to play straight than to disappear with two bedbugs.

Coopersmith finally cracked a smile. He laughed. "You *sure* you never studied symbolic logic?" he said.

Well Paco might not know what the words meant, but he understood the music, especially since Coopersmith started sorting through the discs.

So, however, did the others, and not all of them were liking it. Malcolm, the blond girl, Coopersmith, and of course Karen, were on his side, and the Blankriqueno sat there quietly giving him a funny look, but the rest of them took to bitching and moaning.

"Hey, wait a minute, Larry—"

"We should vote—"

"Yeah, this is a communal decision—"

Coopersmith had picked out two discs, but now he was rubbing them together, hesitating. Chingada! What would Mucho Muchacho do?

Then Paco smiled to himself, for he suddenly knew what Mucho Muchacho would do.

What he had done already.

Grinning shyly, he took Karen's hand. She didn't attempt to break free. He pulled their locked hands up in clear sight and placed them right out on the table.

"Anyway," he said softly, looking into her eyes, "I've got an even better reason for coming back here, don't I?"

Karen looked back at him uncertainly. Hidden from sight by the table, he reached out and placed the palm of his free hand on the inside of her thigh. Her lower lip trembled. Her eyes softened. She blushed. She giggled. She snugged her chocha right into his hand and wiggled it around.

Coopersmith handed over the bedbug discs. "Now *that's* what I call class self-interest!" he said, breaking up at his own joke, whatever the fuck it meant.

The mood broke up into raucous laughter.

Paco found himself laughing too. And even though he didn't quite know what he was laughing about, even though he had a feeling the laugh was somehow on him, he laughed from the heart, feeling that he had somehow crossed over some invisible frontera between the sombre and the sol, between the only world he had ever known and an unknown new world that was opening up before him, a world between Chocharica City and the sombre side of the streets that he had never even known was there.

And somehow he found himself promising, to his own surprise, that he would return, that he wouldn't fuck these people over, that he would try to show these newfound friends that he could be the man he pretended to be.

Chingada, he thought as he rose from the table with their cornflakes and milk and bread and butter and coffee warm in his belly, maybe I've run a number on myself.

For while honor may have been a word he had never heard, there was a warm aching tenderness behind his breastbone where such a feeling had never been, a feeling that made him want to throw open his arms, and declare to all the world, yo soy Paco Monaco, Mucho Muchacho, and hey, I won't let you down.

Leslie, Markowitz, Tommy Don, and Teddy Ribero were still sitting at the table when Karen came back from walking Paco

Monaco to the door, and, after the fact and behind his back, the second thoughts were getting a bit heated.

"You *really* think we can trust a streetie?" Tommy was saying.

"You really think we can trust a *spick,* isn't that it?" Teddy Ribero shot back.

"Come off the racism bullshit, Teddy, you really detect people around here not trusting *you*?" Leslie said with a disparaging wave of her hand.

"No, but—"

"Yeah, Teddy," Larry Coopersmith broke in, "if Paco *wasn't* Puerto Rican, *you'd* probably be bitching and moaning about how naive it is to trust some hard-core street punk with anything. . . ."

"Well, okay, now that you put it that way, why *should* we trust him. Larry, seems to me you're talking against what you've just done. . . ."

"Yeah, well, consistency is the hobgoblin of small minds," Larry said with a shrug.

"You're the one with the most, ah, intimate knowledge of the subject at hand, Karen . . ." Leslie said as Karen drew herself another cup of coffee from the communal urn. "What's he really like? Do *you* trust him?"

"That's a good question . . ." Karen muttered, sitting down and pondering it over a long slow sip of coffee.

Paco Monaco had certainly been a prince the night before; not merely a rough and ready rescuer, but a tender and understanding gentleman of the streets, a perfect paragon of the manly virtues.

But on the other hand, he had certainly turned into a bit of a frog the morning after; crude, foul-mouthed, paranoid, confused, and an entirely inept lover who had let her do all the work, came in a couple of minutes without even a perfunctory attempt at reciprocation, and hadn't even bothered to thank her afterward.

Still, he had even had a certain charm as a frog, so thin and half-starved, so disbelieving in the possibility of anything like gratitude that he had assumed he would have to pay for a bowl of cornflakes and a cup of coffee, so pathetically wide-eyed and grateful when she had told him he could eat breakfast for nothing.

You could forgive a certain lack of savoir-faire in a man to whom a free bowl of cornflakes was so clearly an event of cosmic significance.

"*Well?*" Leslie persisted.

Karen shrugged. "All I can really tell you is that there's more to Paco Monaco than what you saw this morning. . . ."

"Really?" Leslie said. "I don't suppose you'd like to fill us in on the juicy details . . . ?"

Karen gave her a good-natured drop-dead look.

"Well, at least you can tell us whether you think he'll come back. . . ."

Karen thought about it. The prince of the night before, she had a feeling, would feel honor-bound to come back with the money or return the bedbugs. The frog of the morning after was a creature she could not really trust or fathom.

"To tell you the truth, your guess is probably as good as mine," she finally said.

"Well, what about *you,* Markowitz?" Leslie said. "Do you *really* think a streetie meatrack doorman is going to be able to sell bedbugs?"

Coopersmith shrugged. "Seems unlikely on the face of it," he admitted. "But on the other hand, I agree with Karen, there's more to Paco Monaco than meets the casual eye. . . ."

"*Oh?*" Tommy said dubiously.

"The kid may be completely uneducated, but he's fuckin' *smart,* he's fast on his feet, he's streetwise, he ran some nice numbers on us. . . ." Coopersmith laughed appreciatively. "Shit, he even backed *me* into a moral and logical corner, now didn't he?"

"So he's a cunning little streetie with a sharp eye for the main chance," Tommy said. "Is that really a good reason to trust him with our merchandise?"

"Yeah, Tommy, I think it is," Coopersmith said. "It's a long shot for sure, but the stakes are real attractive. I mean, what are we really risking? We can copy those programs onto blank discs for about five cents' worth of electricity, so if he rips them off, all we're really out is the cost of the blanks, which is what, maybe forty bucks. But if he somehow manages to sell them and brings back the money . . ."

"We're six hundred ahead. . . ."

Larry Coopersmith leaned back in his chair and seemed to stare off into space, into some vision inside his own head. "Much more than that, maybe. . . ." he said dreamily. "Much more. . . . It'd be a breakthrough. . . ."

"To *what*?"

"Let's face it, in a certain sense we're bullshit revolutionaries. I mean, we sell bedbugs to people who already have money, who are already wired into the system, so they can use them to fuck over the system and steal a little more, but while we're playing our little games, there are millions and millions of Paco Monacos running around out there on the streets with nothing to lose. A whole other street-reality that might as well be another planet. So if by some chance Paco Monaco can serve as our vector into all that . . ."

"What, Larry?" Teddy Ribero said. "What would happen then?"

Larry Coopersmith laughed. He positively beamed with anticipated pleasure. "Pure fuckin' Chaos!" he exclaimed. "So I'm sure as shit willing to lay down forty bucks at any odds in the hope of seeing that! Take it from me, it beats playing the ponies any day of the week!"

"And what about you, Karen?" Leslie said. "If the guy does come back, are you willing to play the Mata Hari of the Reality Liberation Front?"

"Yeah, Karen," Coopersmith said, pinning her with those hard blue eyes. "How committed are you to the cause? Will you give your ah . . . all for the RLF if our boy Paco does come back for more?"

Karen thought about it.

She thought about haunting the meatracks in the forlorn hope of connecting up with a dream prince of the city who would rescue her from poverty and restore her to her rightful station. She thought about the real prince of the streets who really *had* saved her, who had so gently pulled up her panties, and wrapped her up in her parka against the cold and the dark, who had tenderly embraced her in his hard strong arms and kept her safe from harm, who had made such wonderful love to her in the aftermath of his knightly rescue.

She thought about the skinny little kid who had come in two minutes, who had been so touchingly grateful for the pitiful boon of a simple little meal. She thought shamefully about what she had felt upon waking up in bed with a *Puerto Rican streetie*.

"It's a test, isn't it?" she said softly. But of whom? Of whose dedication to what?

Larry Coopersmith nodded. "Yeah, you could say that," he said.

Karen sighed. Somehow, in that moment her heart was far

closer to that skinny little kid, to that prince of the streets, than to these friends who had given her shelter, or to any abstract cause.

"Well, if he passes," she said, "if he does come back, I'll sure take him." If he passes, she thought, then maybe so do I. But I won't be doing it for any cause. I'll be doing it for myself.

WORKING CLASS HERO

"Paco, my, man, you *know* we've got a jumper on the meter here," Dojo said. "So why should I pay you six hundred dollars for something I gotta find a computer to use when I'm getting my juice free already?"

"You're greasing the Con Ed cops, no?" Paco said, stamping his feet against the cold as he huddled in the doorway. "So you buy one of *these* mothers, tell them to fuck off, get your money back in a few months, and after that, it's free juice forever."

Dojo shook his head ruefully. "Even if I pull the jumper and use your wizard software, I *still* gotta keep greasing the Con Ed boys or they are going to see to it that I get shit from *somewhere,*" he said. "This building is supposed to be vacant, remember? And then there's the matter of what goes on upstairs in Florida . . ."

Paco had no quick answer to that. Trying to move a piece to Dojo had been a desperation move anyway. Everyone he had tried to sell one of the bedbugs to had either stared at him in brainburned incomprehension or just laughed.

"Where'd you boost shit like that anyway?" Dojo demanded, eyeing Paco narrowly. "How many did you steal? Come to think of it, how the fuck do you even know what they're supposed to do?"

"Didn't boost 'em, and I can score as many as I can move and mucho mas también," Paco boasted truthfully. "I made me a real heavyweight connection. . . ."

"Yeah . . . ?" Dojo said dubiously. "With what?"

"The *Reality Liberation Front*, man!" Paco said, as if anyone who wasn't a fuckin' zombie had to know what that was.

"The which?"

"The Reality Liberation Front, nigger," Paco said haughtily. "Don't tell me you never heard of the RLF!" He put on a look of smug arrogance. "Well, maybe not, man," he drawled. "It's a heavy duty *gordo* gang. Makes all kinds of these bedbugs in fuckin' truckloads and deals 'em to the gordos and the plushie-tushies. Mucho dinero aquí, Dojo!"

"Sure," Dojo said sarcastically. "Horseshit, Paco. Why would this so-called heavy duty gang cut in the likes of *you*?"

Paco winked. "You *know* how all the white pussy likes that dark meat, don't you, Dojo?" he said.

The big black man laughed. His eyes lit up in lubricious comprehension. "You got yourself a *moma* in this Reality Liberation Front?" he said.

Paco nodded. "Big-time bedbug dealer."

"How the fuck you manage that?"

"If you gotta ask how to do it, man, nobody's gonna be able to tell you. . . ."

Dojo laughed. "Ain't it the truth!" He studied Paco's face most seriously now. "This is really on the level, isn't it?"

"No, man," Paco said dryly, "I'm bullshitting you all the way."

"Hmmm . . ." The big man rubbed his heavy jaw thoughtfully. "You wait here while I get someone to take the door for a few minutes," he said. "You and me oughta have a little talk in private, my man." And he disappeared down the stairs into the cellar meatrack.

After Dojo had gone, Paco stood there, shivering in the cold and vibrating inside with anticipation. He had really laid on the manteca, and Dojo had bought it, so whatever Dojo had in mind, it figured to be serious business. He had to be at his best, he had to *really be on top of it,* man!

He reached up toward the breadbox snugged against the back of his head. He paused. Dojo would not be pleased if he knew he was dealing with someone who was flashing. On the other hand, Paco had taken to wearing his Zap all the time now and the big man hadn't seemed to notice.

Do I dare . . . ?

Chingada, how's he to know?

He heard Dojo's heavy footfalls coming up the metal staircase.

Do I dare *not*?

And before Dojo could see him doing it, he reached up and gave himself a tap of the Zap.

The flickering bulbs above the dance floor formed a clearing of light in the musty rank darkness as he followed Dojo down the stairs. Dancers twitched and jerked to a max metal beat like spaced-out jungle bunnies, wireheads lay back in the shadows like old piles of human refuse. All that was missing were a few starving cur dogs to complete a picture weirdly like those faded old Polaroids of the rural slums of Puerto Rico he suddenly remembered his abuelos showing him when he was muy pequeño.

Dojo led him to his jefe's hut, unlocked the door to his secret lair, and flicked on an overhead fixture which illumined it in pale yellow moonlight. Cardboard cartons piled up to the ceiling along three walls transformed the room into a great warehouse crammed with loot.

Dojo, his black skin shining in the moonlight, seated himself cross-legged on the rumpled bed, a pirate king on his treasure-house throne.

"There have been some unforeseen developments," he said. "The manufacturers, whoever the fuck they are, have dropped the wholesale price of the Zap to one hundred dollars, and in a few weeks, a huge supply of the fucking things is going to hit the street—"

"Chingada! You talked me into trading an *Uzi* even up for—"

"Don't *you* bitch and moan at *me*!" Dojo snapped. He nodded sourly at the endless piles of cartons that surrounded him. "I bought all *these* at the old price! In a couple months, the street price will be so low that I'll have to unload each one at a dead loss. I'll really be screwed. Unless . . ."

"Unless . . . ?"

Paco found himself sitting down on the bed, folding his legs under him without taking his eyes off Dojo's. The big man seemed to be getting smaller. Or was *he* getting larger?

"Unless maybe you and me can turn this mess into a golden opportunity to rip off the fat cats for big, big money."

"What you got in mind, Dojo?"

"Your bedbug dealer girlfriend. Your uptown connection with this Reality Liberation Front. They deal their shit at the fancy meatracks, don't they?"

"So?"

"So you know what uptown wirechippers end up paying for a

piece like the Prong or Uncle Charlie that goes for about two hundred dollars down here by the time it moves through the whole chain of connections between us and them? Four hundred fuckin' dollars, at least!"

"Chingada!"

Dojo frowned. "And the difference all goes to the middlemen, what I see is the same fuckin' two hundred bucks I'd get from selling it to you. . . ."

Mucho Muchacho squatted on the beaten earth before the Brujo's hut in the jungle moonlight. Somewhere muffled drums beat softly as the black-skinned Brujo imparted his knowledge of the secret magics beneath the thin skin of the world of illusion to the favored son of the tribe.

"But if you and your old lady and her compadres dealt these fuckin' Zaps *direct* from me to the uptown suckers, we could unload them at four hundred apiece no matter what the street price drops to! The Zaps I've already bought cost me two hundred a pop, so we clear two hundred if we can cut out all the middlemen. One fifty for me and fifty for you on each and every one, my son."

The Brujo smiled at him somewhat patronizingly. Mucho Muchacho knew that this was a test of his spirit. He straightened his back, hardened his warrior's heart, and stared fearlessly into the black magician's eyes.

"Down the middle," he said.

"One forty, sixty," the Brujo chanted hypnotically. But now a certain secret approval leaked into his cold hard eyes.

"One twenty, eighty," chanted the candidate warrior.

"You trying to bust my balls, my son?" the Brujo said. But his eyes sparkled with unconcealed pride.

Paco Monaco, Mucho Muchacho, at last allowed himself to reveal his true warrior's smile, the newborn smile of a boy passing through his midnight rite into adulthood and finding himself acknowledged at last as an equal, as a man among men.

"Cojones de elefante . . ." he sang.

"I'll give you seventy-five," the Brujo said. "Know when you've reached the bottom line, my man."

Solemnly, the warrior offered the hand of an equal. The drums pounded to a crescendo and then suddenly fell away to silence as the Brujo clasped it. The rite was over. The bargain was sealed.

"I'll give you five now," the Brujo said, rising to his feet, crossing the moonlit clearing, and rummaging in a cardboard carton. "How long you think it'll take you to move 'em?"

"Give me three—"

Give me three days, and if I don't bring back the money, I'll bring back the pieces, Paco caught himself about to say as he popped out of the dreamtime squatting on the rumpled bed in Dojo's room at Slimy Mary's in the dim light of the overhead bulb.

"What?"

Dojo stood there with five plastic-wrapped Zaps in his hand, eyeing him peculiarly. "You got a problem, Paco?" he said.

Chingada, do I have a problem! Paco thought. He could only move these Zaps for fancy prices in the gordo meatracks through Karen and the Reality Liberation Front. But if he didn't show up at the loft by tomorrow night with $600, then all he'd be to them would be a streetie spick who was all mouth and no action.

And he sure as shit couldn't tell Dojo *that,* not after the line of bullshit he had fed him!

Or could he . . . ?

"What about my bedbugs, Dojo . . . ?" he said slowly.

"What about 'em?"

"Look man, the RLF is a heavyweight outfit, why should they help me deal these Zaps at fancy prices to their fancy customers if—"

"For a piece of the action, what else?"

"A piece of *whose* action?"

Dojo dropped the Zaps in Paco's lap with a frosty little sneer. "Don't be ridiculous," he said.

"You expect me to take care of them out of *my* end?"

"Fuckin'-A I do!"

Paco thought fast. He thought like Mucho Muchacho. "Seems to me I'm doin' you a lot more good than you're doin' me," he said harshly, in a tone of voice he had never used to the big doorman before. He gestured toward the cartons of Zaps piled to the ceiling. "I mean, I connect you up with the RLF, you make one twenty-five on each one, I gotta split my seventy-five with them, they're gonna want at least fifty, which don't leave me with shit! And without this deal, you're gonna lose mucho dinero. . . ."

"'So?" Dojo said, scowling. No one ever talked to Dojo like this, and the big man clearly didn't like it. But then, he had never dealt with Mucho Muchacho before, now had he?

"So if the RLF is going to save your ass, nigger, then you gotta help us out too . . ." Paco told him. "If you won't *buy* bedbugs from us, then *deal* 'em for us . . ."

"*Deal 'em . . . ?*" Dojo scoffed. "There's not much of a market down here for something that gets you free electricity. . . ."

"That ain't half of it, my man," Paco said. "The RLF makes *all kinds* of bedbugs. . . ."

"They do? Like what?"

Paco racked his brains, trying to remember Malcolm's rap. "Don't you get around, Dojo?" he said. "I mean, you gonna tell me you don't have no yak connections?"

"You accusing me of consorting with un-American criminal elements?" Dojo said. But he was smiling as he said it.

"You think the yaks you don't know might be interested in something that fixes traffic tickets? Something that lets you get money out of cash machines with stolen plastico? Something that fucks over the tax computers? Something that moves money into bank accounts?"

"Your girlfriend can really get me shit like that?" Dojo said, sitting down on the bed beside Paco and eyeing him narrowly.

Paco smiled. "*I* can get you shit like that," he said. "My compadres are like a little paranoid. You deal through me."

Dojo squinted at him. "Why didn't you tell me this before?" he said.

"You never let me in on *your* action before, amigo," Paco told him. "I had to be sure I could trust you."

"What's your cut of all this?"

"That's between me and the Reality Liberation Front."

"What's the price to me?"

"I told you. Six hundred a bedbug."

"Four."

"*Four!*" Paco whined. "Hey, man, I don't even make a dime at that price!"

"The fuck you don't!"

"The fuck I do!"

Dojo leaned back against his own bedstead. "Shall we stop bullshitting each other, my man?" he said. "What's the cost to you?"

Paco locked eyes with the big doorman. He realized he had reached the bottom line. Besides, Dojo was as close as anyone had ever come to being his friend. And what he needed to keep this whole deal going was $600 in his pocket right now.

"Three-fifty," he said.

"I'll give you four-fifty."

"Fuck you!"

"Fuck you too. . . ."

"Okay," Paco said, "I'll take your cheap shit four-fifty. But you've gotta give me nine hundred in cash for what I've got here now."

Dojo laughed. "Why do I get the feeling that that's what all this bullshit has been about all along?"

Paco glared at him silently.

"Okay, I'll front you the yen," Dojo said. "Just because I like your style, my man."

Paco sighed. "Deal," he said, holding out his hand.

Dojo took it. "I like a man who knows when he's reached the bottom line," he said.

"What do you *mean* the Reality Liberation Front won't deal no wire?" Paco Monaco snapped at Malcolm McGee.

Malcolm and Larry Coopersmith sat together on the couch opposite Karen's at one end of the loft while everyone else except Leslie, who was out dealing, beavered away at their computers turning out more bedbugs. Paco paced in tight paranoid circles between the two couches, waving his arms angrily at all the manufacturing activity.

"Chingada, what about all *this* shit?" he demanded. "*You're* the putamadre who called it wire for computers!"

"That was just a metaphor," Malcolm said owlishly, shrinking back from Paco's fury.

"A *which*?"

"It was just a way of explaining what bedbugs do," Karen said gently. "It wasn't meant to be taken literally. . . ."

"Taken how?"

Karen sighed. Paco was far from stupid. Indeed, she found herself wondering if *she* had half the smarts he had shown! Not only had he sold the two Con Ed bedbugs, he had orders for a dozen more assorted discs: bedbugs to null traffic and parking tickets, bedbugs for cash machines, bedbugs for bank account transfers, even stock account bedbugs, of all things!

And what was even more impressive was that he had grasped and remembered more or less what they all did well enough to convince someone to buy them.

Quite a demonstration of native intelligence by anyone's standard! But how could you explain "metaphor" or "figure of speech" to a poor kid who was so uneducated that he didn't even know the words you were trying to use to explain the concept?

"You know, like when I called you my knight in shining armor," she said. "You weren't really a knight and you weren't really wearing armor, but—"

"Yeah, yeah, yo se, like the words in a song," Paco said irritably, perching on the edge of the couch beside her. "But the music *sucks,* man," he told Malcolm. "It don't explain why you guys won't deal Zaps for me! I get 'em for you for three hundred, you sell 'em for five. It's a good deal!"

"But it's bad karma," Larry Coopersmith told him.

"Bad *what*?"

"Bad shit, Paco," Coopersmith said not unkindly. "Wire is bad shit, you've seen enough burnt-out wireheads to know that."

Paco snorted contemptuously. "You guys are the ones talking about turning *computers* into burnt-out combo wireheads," he said.

"That's different," Coopersmith said. "Computers aren't *people*."

"No shit?" Paco snapped sarcastically. "But what about the people you're ripping off?"

Larry and Malcolm regarded him with blank looks of innocence. Karen smiled possessively. Oh no, not stupid at all!

"You're so fuckin' high and mighty about dealing a little wire for me to a bunch of gordo wirechippers who are only out to get a little flash, but what am I dealing for you? Fuckin' fancy *burglar tools*! For people to rob banks with, no? To fuck the city with, right? To rip off cash machines and the tax man!"

"*Now* who's bullshitting who?" Coopersmith said. "You're telling me it offends your morality to help people steal from the system that's fucked you over all your life?"

Paco smiled at him triumphantly. "Shit no," he said sweetly. "I'm selling your bedbugs for you, ain't I? *You're* the one telling *me* it's wrong to peddle wire to the same fuckin' assholes your own goods are being used to rip off, verdad? Pick their pockets, fry their brains, maybe I'm just a dumb spick, but I just don't see how the fuckin' . . . *karma's* any different. . . ."

"Touché!" Karen exclaimed. "He's got you there!"

Larry Coopersmith shot her a dirtier look than she had ever seen on his face before. "*You* dealt wire when you were in college, didn't you, Karen?" he snapped.

"So what?" Karen shot back.

"Wire is an instrument of reality control!" Coopersmith said shrilly. "You plug in and you flash into whatever headspace the piece is programmed to warp you into. It fuckin' circuits your brain into *its* trip, not yours! It . . . it . . ."

"You ever chip wire, Larry?" Karen said softly. It didn't really seem to be a question that needed answering.

"*Enough,*" Coopersmith snapped. He shrugged, he smiled wanly. "*More* than enough, if truth be told. . . ."

Paco studied him carefully. "The Prong? Uncle Charlie? The Blue Max?"

Larry Coopersmith grimaced. "I may have done a lot of brainburning shit in my day," he said softly. "But I was never far gone enough to screw with the Blue Max. . . ."

Paco, poor little streetie-in-the-raw Paco, smiled at Larry Coopersmith sympathetically, and all at once he did what no one in the Reality Liberation Front had ever done before; he managed to completely seize control of a conversation from old motor-mouth Markowitz himself.

"Me neither man," he said. "That's really bad shit. And between you and me, Uncle Charlie ain't much better. But the Prong, now . . ." He smiled. He shrugged. "Wire's like . . . like . . . like *sex,* man! I mean, bein' fucked up the culo by some slimy faggot, that's *sex,* right, and the Blue Max is *wire,* verdad. . . ."

He paused, placed a gentle hand on Karen's thigh. "But like between me and Karen, *that's* sex too, no, just like the Prong or the Zap is *wire,* I mean you're not gonna tell me that all *sex* is bad for you because *bad* sex can fuck you up, right, so . . ."

"I've heard this wirehead bullshit before," Coopersmith said bitterly. "Even from myself . . ."

"Yeah, well," Paco said, reaching into his street bag and pulling out something wrapped in clear plastic, "believe me, my man, you've never flashed on a piece like the Zap before."

"I've heard *that* shit before too," Coopersmith said sourly.

Paco tore open the plastic, pulled out a crumpled wad of thin wirework, shook it out, and then held up a hairnet of very thin flexible wire with a flattened ovoid breadbox at the back, a piece unlike anything Karen had ever seen.

Paco stuck the Zap under Larry Coopersmith's nose. "Never seen a wizard piece like this before, now have you, man?" he said. "Runs on a little battery."

He reached up to the back of his head with thumb and forefinger and lifted a breadbox and a section of wire mesh out of his bushy hair, then let it fall back. "Wear it on the street, wear it to Ciudad Trabajo if you got a fuckin' job, and no one even notices unless they're lookin' for it."

He glanced sideways at Karen without really taking his attention off Coopersmith. "You can even wear it in bed," he said.

Karen's stomach dropped and her head turned inside out. Paco was a *wirehead*? It certainly explained the difference between his masterful lovemaking that night before and his pathetic performance of the morning after. . . .

"You . . . you were *flashing* when you . . . when we . . . that night . . ." she stammered.

"I didn't hear no complaints."

But . . . but it was all wrong! He had been wonderful *on wire* and lousy when he had been straight, and not the other way around!

"I was flashing on the Zap when I saved Karen and your money," Paco told Coopersmith. "So you could say this piece has *already* put you ahead of the game, Larry."

"Je-sus . . ." Karen whispered.

She had heard that the Prong let a man keep it up indefinitely. She had never heard of any wire that made you a better street fighter, but she could barely credit the possibility that some wizard piece might amplify reflexes and increase physical strength.

But Paco Monaco had been *more* than a better fighter and a better lover on the Zap. He had been more sure of himself, gentler, more tender, more understanding, a true knight of the streets. There was no way around what only she really knew—in every sense of the word, Paco was a better *man* on the Zap.

How was that possible?

What did this piece really do?

She stared at Paco in wonder. Larry and Malcolm stared at the piece in his hand.

"What's the flash . . .?" Larry Coopersmith finally said.

Paco grimaced. He squirmed. He shrugged. "No se . . . I mean you can't . . . Shit man, it's something like bein' in a dream, you know, but . . ."

He finally threw up his hands in inarticulate frustration. "Only one way you can ever know," he said, offering the Zap to Coopersmith. "*Try it.* First flash is on the house."

"It always is. . . ." Coopersmith muttered, shrinking back.

But Malcolm McGee reached out and took the piece from Paco's hand. He stared at it, shook it out, held it up at arm's length, began lifting it toward his head.

"Malcolm!" Coopersmith shouted, snatching the thing out of his grasp. "Are you out of your fucking mind? You want to burn out your brain with some piece of street garbage? You don't even have any idea what the flash is! And *he* can't even tell you!"

Malcolm and Coopersmith glared at each other defiantly for a long moment. "Aw, Larry . . ." Malcolm finally whined petulantly, looking down at the floor and squirming.

When he looked up again, his eyes were wary and thoughtful behind his thick glasses. "Well at least let's buy one, Larry," he pleaded. "Let me take it apart, figure out what the circuits do. . . ."

"Three hundred dollars just to satisfy your curiosity!"

"Aw, Larry. . . ."

"Come on, Larry, do it!" Karen finally broke in. "I think it's important we at least find out what it does."

"Why?" Coopersmith demanded.

"Because maybe we *should* deal the things for Paco."

"Deal fucking wire! It's an instrument of reality control!"

"You don't *know* that, Larry Coopersmith! You don't know a damn thing about it!"

"And *you* do?"

Karen hesitated. She blushed. She wanted very much to say *something,* but she didn't know what it was, and she didn't know how to say it. She glanced at Paco, who sat there beside her shaking his head ruefully, as if he were listening to an argument among fools. And maybe he is, she thought.

"You weren't there, Larry," she finally said.

Coopersmith snorted.

"I don't mean in bed, I mean out there on the street! Paco . . . Paco had . . . powers . . . I mean . . . he didn't just . . . he was like . . ."

She threw up her hands in exasperation. "You're always blathering about *random factors,*" she said. "Well, you don't know what this thing does. I was saved by whatever it does and *I* can't tell you, and even Paco can't explain it! How much more of a random factor can you find than *that*?"

Larry Coopersmith glared at her with those hard blue eyes.

But Karen thought she could detect a slight softening in them. "*Please*, Larry," she said softly.

"Come on, Larry, it's not like you to not at least want to know. . . ."

"Just because *you* had some bad experiences on wire . . ."

"Aw . . ." Coopersmith muttered, but his determination had melted. "Aw, shit . . ." he said, reaching into his pocket, "give the fucking thing here!"

He took the Zap from Malcolm, fingered it dubiously as he pulled out his wallet. He counted out the money, flipped the Zap back to Malcolm, and handed the bills to Paco.

Paco took the money and stuffed it into his pocket without even looking at it, shaking his head disdainfully at Malcolm and Coopersmith all the while.

"Maricónes sin cojones . . ." he muttered under his breath.

"What?"

"What pussies you guys are!" he exclaimed scornfully. "Man, I show you the best fuckin' piece of wire there is, and all you want to do is take the fuckin' thing apart to see how the mother works! *The Reality Liberation Front, mi culo!* None of you even have the balls to find out what fuckin *reality* really is!"

"Maybe I do!" Karen found herself blurting out.

Paco turned his head slowly to face her with a look of surprise. A look that turned to an expression of *pleased* surprise with a possessive pride beneath it that sent a surge of warmth to Karen's loins.

He reached into his street bag, pulled out another Zap, and began unwrapping it for her. "You wanna flash with me, muchacha?" he said.

Karen nodded silently. "Maybe I wouldn't be here at all if *you* hadn't flashed with me," she said.

"Karen, you're not—"

"Oh yes I am! I owe him that much!"

Paco handed her the Zap. Karen shook it out, put it on, and glared at Larry Coopersmith defiantly.

"The lady's got more balls than you do, man," Paco said, rising from the couch and taking her hand.

She let him pull her to her feet. With a brave little smile she raised her hand to the touchpoint of the breadbox snugged against the back of her head.

Gently, Paco pulled it away. "Hey, not here, not with these guys standing around watching," he said, nodding toward the door. "Just you and me, girl. I flashed on *your* turf, no, how's about you flash on *mine*?"

"*On the street?*" Karen exclaimed in horror.

Paco laughed. "Chingada, even I ain't that loco," he said. "I just want to take you to Slimy Mary's, where I'm, you know, *somebody*. . . ."

"*A streetie meatrack?*"

"Chingada," he said in a wounded tone that touched her heart, "we're fuckin' people too!"

"I don't know. . . ."

"You afraid, Karen?"

Karen looked him squarely in the eye. She shrugged. She forced a little smile. She even laughed. "Fuckin'-A I am, Paco," she admitted.

As once he had before, Paco Monaco put a gentle hand under her chin. "Hey, girl," he said, "you're gonna be with *Mucho Muchacho*. Nothing can hurt you now."

Her heart melted. "I may be crazy, but I believe you," she said. And she planted a tremulous closed-mouth kiss on his lips. And found the courage to let him lead her off into his unknown world of night.

YOUR ROCK AND ROLL MACHINE

"Who's the lady, Paco?" the big ominous-looking black doorman said with a slow leer that made Karen feel he was undressing her with his eyes.

She was finding the situation paranoid, to say the least. She had never even dreamed she would ever venture into a hard-core streetie district like this before tonight, and now here she was, about to flash wire in some terminal streetie meatrack.

"This is Karen Gold, Dojo, the lady I told you about," Paco told him proudly, squeezing her hand with conspicuous possessiveness. Amazingly enough, the doorman's manner changed abruptly, and he became almost deferential.

"Ah, the big-time bedbug dealer from the Reality Liberation Front," he said expansively, breaking into a rather winning smile.

"*You've heard of the RLF?*" Karen exclaimed in no little surprise.

The big doorman frowned at her haughtily. "Think I don't get around?" he said. "Where do you think my man here gets his Zaps from, Bloomingdale's?" He eyed her speculatively. "And speaking of business, you got those bedbugs I ordered?"

"I'll bring 'em over Tuesday," Paco told the doorman quickly. "Karen here wants to check you out first."

The doorman shook his head somewhat belligerently. "Do I really look like a cop?" he demanded.

"Can't be too careful . . ." Karen said. "A lot of agencies would love to bust us." She forced a conspiratorial smile over her shoulder as Paco led her inside past him. "So if anyone comes sniffing around, you never heard of me, right?'' She was beginning to almost enjoy this.

But as she descended a flight of metal stairs into a musty infernal pit of a cellar, it was quite another matter.

A primitive light show of naked colored bulbs set in a tinfoil-covered ceiling flickered spastically over a central dance floor, where about a dozen ragged spaced-out creatures of various sexes twitched and stomped to the cloddy max metal beat coming from speakers flanking a sleazy wall screen. On the screen, a heavily muscled diesel dyke in black leather motorcycle pants and blue denim biker's colors howled from the seat of an antique Harley as the Manhattan skyline went up in flames behind her.

Sweat hog mothers
Ape hanger brothers
Burn down your bridges
In the bloodred night!

More grungy streeties, sprawling on the piles of filthy pillows and junk furniture ringing the dance floor on three sides, were dimly visible in the fringes of the strobing light. Like the dancers, they wore raggy jeans, cracked old black leather, giveaway promo T-shirts, and hair tinted, shaped, and lacquered into helmets, crests, rude animal heads or even more obscure personal totems.

What Karen couldn't see was somehow worse than what she could, for the cellar extended out from this tackily lit area into increasingly impenetrable darkness, where shadowy figures were doing even more shadowy things, and where, judging by the rank miasma of mildew that hung in the air, whole armies of rats and cockroaches were no doubt lurking.

''I can see why they call it Slimy Mary's . . .'' she muttered sarcastically in an attempt to keep her courage up. ''What's a girl like me doing in a place like this?''

Fortunately, perhaps, this bon mot entirely blew by Paco. ''Wanna dance?'' he said, dragging her forward without waiting for an answer.

Karen dug in her heels. Paco paused, turned, looked into her eyes, finally saw what was there, grimaced. ''Yeah,'' he said with a hangdog expression, ''it ain't exactly The Temple of Doom.''

But with a visible effort he made his expression brighten. He winked at her. "But it'll look a lot better with a little tap of the Zap," he said, and without further ado, he reached up and hit the touchpoint of her breadbox.

"Hey—"

Before she could do much more than utter a single syllable of protest, he had hit his own touchpoint and pulled her out of the shadows and into the strobing curtain of flickering light. And through it into—

Someplace else.

Cruel laser beams of red, white, and blue light lanced down, flickering on and off, sizzling in entirely unpredictable patterns around her to a burning leaden beat, BOMP ba-ba-ba-ba, BA ba ba BOMP BOMP! blocking her, turning her, making her twitch and jerk this way and that, like some unseen max metal gunfighter laughing as he fired his rayguns at her feet for the evil pleasure of making her dance.

Shafts of varicolored light strobe-danced about an infinite stage like celestial spotlights wielded by spaced-out gods, arbitrarily and capriciously picking out her fellow dancers in a kaleidoscopic flicker of freeze-frame tableaus, BOMP ba-ba-ba-ba, BA ba ba BOMP BOMP!

A gaunt pale specter of a girl with deep black hollows under her eyes and hair conked up into an orange mushroom-pillar cloud, moving only from the waist down as she stared into nothingness.

BOMP ba-ba-ba-ba, BA ba ba BOMP BOMP!

A black couple in matching white dreadlocks standing on end like porcupine quills, dancing back to back.

BOMP ba-ba-ba-ba, BA ba ba BOMP BOMP!

A pimply-faced young boy in a torn Dow Chemical T-shirt with rusty razor blades glued to it and a steel-blue buzzsaw hairdo.

BOMP ba-ba-ba-ba, BA ba ba BOMP BOMP!

A fat girl, her face shadowed by an overhanging helmet of purple hair, pendulous breasts flopping beneath a Gucci T-shirt, suety bare belly-flesh wadding out over the belt of her jeans.

BOMP ba-ba-ba-ba, BA ba ba BOMP BOMP!

An evil-looking male creature in black leather and recurved green demon-horns leering vacantly with a mouthful of broken brown teeth.

BOMP ba-ba-ba-ba, BA ba ba BOMP BOMP!

Isolated from each other by the strobing spotlights, the human flotsam and jetsam danced their figures of spastic determinism like pathetic marionettes moving to the random will of some mindless electronic puppeteer, BOMP ba-ba-ba-ba, BA ba ba BOMP BOMP!

Yet as her body danced its own jerky pattern through the strobing lights of the laser maze, as the denizens and the spotlights danced with her and around her, BOMP ba-ba-ba-ba, BA ba ba BOMP BOMP, as the rhythm took her away, Karen found herself experiencing an unexpected empathetic unity with these poor lost creatures of the street, a pathetic tenderness toward all her fellow victims she had never known before, BOMP ba-ba-ba-ba, BA ba ba BOMP BOMP, as she, too, found herself capering and dancing like a fleshy cog in fate's indifferent clockwork machine, BOMP ba-ba-ba-ba, BA ba ba BOMP BOMP, as a ragged female voice from somewhere shouted out what was pounding in her heart.

Sweat hog mothers
Ape hanger brothers
Burn down your bridges
In the bloodred night!
Spaced out sweeties
Aced out streeties
Don't go gently
To the dying of the light!

A blue neon spot flash-froze Paco for a moment as he danced before her, his lean body arched backward, his pelvis thrust forward, his dark brown eyes gleaming at her with a cold blue shimmer of reflected light, BOMP ba-ba-ba-ba, BA ba ba BOMP BOMP!

He flickered back into the darkness as she stepped suddenly into a hot white beam, BOMP ba-ba-ba-ba, BA ba ba BOMP BOMP! As if their separate realities were strobing out of sync, as if unseen sadistic gods were conspiring to tease each of them with glimpses of the other's forbidden world and then with an electric laugh and a negligent flick of their electronic wrists, to flip them back into the lonely dark.

Then for a random magic moment, their eyes met in a blood-red shaft of shared spacetime, and Paco's face was transformed into an unyieldingly angular Aztec mask; proud eagle's nose, cruel knowing lips curled around perfect white teeth, sensuous liquid bedroom eyes, a face she had never seen but knew full well, mockingly tender and deliciously terrifying, the face of a mighty warrior lover burning out at her from inside this grubby child of the streets.

Bad-ass momas
Hog-hard popas
Damn the torpedoes
And let right make might!

BOMP ba-ba-ba-ba, BA ba ba BOMP BOMP!

"Chingada, you like *that* shit?" Mucho Muchacho said in some small amazement as the dead-ass cut ended.

Karen Gold smiled at him radiantly, her ice-blue eyes shining, her long blond hair tumbling wildly over her bare shoulders, her hard, upthrust nipples all but piercing the shiny white satin of her gown.

A breathy voice-over oozed hype on the MUZIK feed over a still shot of some weird gordo maricón, his long white-veined red hair making him look like he was wearing a fuckin' Zap himself.

"Live tonight from The American Dream, well almost, the sneak preview of the first disc by a new star who's gonna light up the rock and roll sky like no one's ever done before—"

"Let's have some *real* music, momacita!" Mucho Muchacho said, taking the hand of the Queen of Chocharica City, and gliding over to el Lizardo with his prize in tow. He reached into a pocket of his tight white cut-off jeans, fished out ten dollars, and slapped them down on the table before the disc deck.

"Let me guess . . ." el Lizardo said dryly, already rummaging in his pile of videodiscs.

" 'Tu Madre También. . . .' "

"And you're another," the dj said, popping the disc into his deck.

Tu ma-dre TAMBIÉN
Tu ma-dre TAMBIÉN
Tu ma-dre TAMBIÉN

A rhythmic blare of air horns, a heavy beat of drums, and he was dancing a chingada stompada to the pounding of his own blood in a penthouse disco under a brilliant starry night high above the jeweled towers of Ciudad Trabajo.

The cool blond chocharicas all sighed and moaned and blew kisses as they grabbed their crotches in hot wet lust, but he ignored these lesser creatures, bestowing the favor of his lordly gaze only upon the queen of them all, dancing just for him—her blue eyes never leaving his, her blond mane flaring and flowing above her alabaster shoulders with the pounding rhythm, her pink tongue licking the inside of her lips, her tight hard ass moving in fuck-me circles, as it was always meant to be in the timeless realm of his perfect wet dream.

Ah but it was something else again now, muchacho, for a part of him knew that behind this vision was a *real woman* sharing the flash with him, a woman who had been saved by the real power of Mucho Muchacho from real danger, who had really known the glories of his mighty cock, who had fed him real food, who had made him real money, who had opened a door and led him by the hand into a wider world.

His cock was hard and proud and enormous against his tight white pants, and yet it felt light as air, free as a bird. His huge balls glowed with manly power, and yet they felt soft, and warm, and tender, as if they were cupped in willing vulnerability in the palms of her hands.

His ears burned. His heart thumped in his hollow chest. He felt his finely chiseled cheeks blush with a strangely delicious embarrassment.

Chingada, thought Paco Monaco, Mucho Muchacho, as the word intruded itself entirely unbidden into his mind, is this what it feels like to fall in love?

Karen Gold couldn't take her eyes off his face, for while there was something terrifying in those hot dark eyes staring so hungrily into hers, in that cruel predatory beak of a nose, in that gleaming white smile, in his prancing jungle rhythm, it was an intoxicatingly sensual terror, whereas what she sensed rustling and stomping beyond the clearing that they shared in the fetid jungle of burnt-out buildings inspired a terror of a simpler and far less ambiguous kind.

She *knew* what was out there, the dark filth-smeared faces, the rotten teeth, the open flies, the clutching hands; she could hear the heavy panting, smell the foul garlicky breath and sour sweat of the creatures of the street waiting to pull her down. The harsh, heavy rhythm mocked her and the jagged max metal guitar clawed at her all-too-pallid skin, and a horrible voice leered its lip-smacking Puerto Rican lust to work its will on her helpless white meat.

Get it while you can
(Tu ma-dre TAMBIÉN)
From a red hot macho man . . .

Mucho Muchacho leaned forward, gathered the slim blond queen of Chocharica City up into his arms, felt her soft white breasts pressed up against his hard-muscled chest, his mighty cock against her chocha, and, dancing cheek to cheek and belly to belly now, crooned his love song into her ear, easing her back into the waiting darkness.

Oh God, he was dragging her into the darkness, into a foul alleyway in the cold rain, spread-eagling her backward across the garbage cans, she could feel his insistent prick fumbling against her, smell the stale piss and the rotten refuse, hear the chittering of the cockroaches and the rustling of the rats in the awful voice grunting in her ear. . . .

We all remember when
Y TU MADRE TAMBIÉN!

And yet . . . and yet this was *Paco,* a part of her knew, her prince of the street, her knight in shining armor, the man who had saved her, and this wasn't really that dark alley, that terrible night in the rain, this was . . . this was . . .

With an enormous effort she remembered; she remembered, and reached up to hit the touchpoint of the breadbox at the back of her head. . . .

"Not here," she whispered throatily, snaking from his grasp, but gently, teasingly, taking both his hands in hers, and leading Mucho Muchacho now, smiling at him, promising him worlds with her ice-blue eyes. "Let me take you someplace you've never been."

"Where?"

"Let's go . . . let's go to The American Dream!"

"*The American Dream?* You can get us in *there,* muchacha?" Paco exclaimed, popping out of the flash into what seemed like yet another dreamtime.

He had seen The American Dream often enough on the screen; MUZIK broadcast live from there all the time, it was just about the numero uno meatrack in todo el mundo. But never had he imagined, even as Mucho Muchacho, that he could ever actually get *inside* a place like that!

"The pit, anyway, I deal bedbugs there all the time, the doorman knows me," Karen said. "Come on, let's go get a cab!"

"A cab?"

Chingada, never in his life had he been in a fuckin' *taxi*! Even if he had had the dinero and felt like blowing it, no fuckin' cabbie would ever stop for anyone that looked like *him*.

"A taxi ride? Hey, momacita, I'll flash on *that*!" he exclaimed, and gave himself a tap.

Sí, this was la noche magica, and verdad the queen of Chocharica City was his lady tonight, for she led him by the hand out into the streets, and when a taxi finally appeared, and she waved a bejeweled hand, chingada, the putamadre pulled up right in front of them.

And Mucho Muchacho and his lady snuggled together on velvet-upholstered seats, while their uniformed chauffeur, screaming and cursing at the traffic in fuckin' Chinese or some such shit, drove them across Houston, and then south down West Broadway like a great white yacht sailing on a river of golden light right up between the soft smooth thighs of Chocharica City, just as he had always dreamed, just as he had always known it was meant to be, Mucho Muchacho, Prince of the City, borne through the streets behind the black mirror glass of her limousine by the blond, blue-eyed queen of his night.

"Let me do the talking," Karen Gold said as she climbed out of the grungy yellow gypsy cab and paid off the crazed Thai driver. Jesus, what a ride! Didn't these things even *have* springs to be broken anymore?

The American Dream didn't look like much from the outside, just one more looming gray loft building on a Soho side street without even a sign to tell the day-trippers from Jersey that this was the famous Muzik, Inc., meatrack.

But none was really needed, for the street outside the entrance was clogged with cabs and the sidewalk was the usual mob scene of decently dressed people waiting to pay their forty bucks to get in and streeties hoping to gain Fritz's favor and a freebie to the pit.

With Paco in tow and looking ready for trouble, Karen was able to elbow her way to the door with less hassle than usual. Fritz the doorman, a big hulk with pasty white skin and a military-looking blond crew cut, stood diffidently in the plain doorway in a sharp black trench coat, scanning the crowd, and occasionally summoning a streetie forth with a mere crook of his leather-gloved forefinger.

Karen caught his eye, he nodded, motioned her inside, but then frowned and moved to block them with his body when he saw Paco, holding his street bag with one hand and hers with the other, attempting to enter beside her.

"Whozzat?" he muttered disdainfully.

"He's with me."

Fritz shook his head firmly and dismissively. "Uh-uh," he said.

"I'm paying for him."

"*I* say what streeties get in. Don't like his looks. Money don't buy no streeties past me."

Oh shit! Paco came up beside her, glaring at the doorman, then pushed in front of her—

"Come on, Fritz—"

Paco came swimming up out of the golden flash into a hassle starting to happen, into the sort of shit he knew all too well from the other side, into someone giving a meatrack doorman a hard time. Karen was doing this all wrong; no one would be about to get past *him* by pissing and moaning like this.

"Man's just doin' his job," he told Karen smoothly, staring right into the big blond doorman's eyes. "Ain't that right, my man? Tell the lady you're just doin' your job, Fritz."

The doorman stared back in complete puzzlement.

"I work door too," Paco told him. He smiled a Dojo smile. "We don't want no shit from bad-asses like us, do we, my son?"

The gordo doorman laughed. He reached into a coat pocket, pulled out two cards color-printed with the American flag and the name "Fritz" in gold script, handed them to Paco. "Sorry," he said. "Where'd you say?"

"Slimy Mary's. Ain't got no passes with me, so just ask for Paco."

"He gave you freebies!" Karen said as they passed inside, her eyes wide with admiration. "How did you . . . ?"

He squeezed her hand. He beamed at her. "Hey, girl, this may be your turf," he said, "but that putamadre comes from mine."

Paco slipped Fritz's freebie cards to the cashier, Karen checked her coat, and then she led Paco down the dark narrow passageway which did a sudden ninety-degree bend as it opened out into the enormous chaos of the pit.

Three walls of the immense atrium were video screens whose giant tripled moving images destroyed interior perspective and any sense of containment. MUZIK was playing a Space Cowboy cut called "Three Ring Blues" as they entered. A four-story-high space-suited and Stetsoned singing cowboy strummed an acoustic guitar as he rode his jet-powered robot hobby horse around the merry-go-round of NASA footage of great ringed Saturn. Spotlights picked out groups of dancers or single individuals in bright pools of light, then moved on. Multicolored strobe beams mounted just below the invisible ceiling fragmented the dance floor into flickering zones of syncopated freeze-frame color.

"Chingada . . ." Paco muttered beside her in a daze of wide-eyed goggle.

Yes indeed, Karen thought, even without a tap of the Zap, you sure knew you were no longer in Kansas.

The whole huge space vibrated evenly like a single great speaker enclosure with you inside it, yet the overpowering wall of music escaped being deafening by some magic of multiplexed speaker placement and acoustic design, allowing conversation at an almost normal decibel level.

A circular stage, now vacant, arose from the center of the pit on a smooth recurved black glass pedestal, attained from below by a staircase within, from which vantage live performances could be safely staged secure from the incursions of the groundlings ten feet below.

"I seen it plenty on MUZIK," Paco said, doing a slow, upward-staring circular dance of wonder, "but the fuckin' *size* of it, the sound . . ."

"Welcome to The American Dream, Paco, take a look at how the other half lives," Karen said, turning to stare up herself, with no little envy, at the fourth wall of the immense room, from beneath which they had entered.

A series of balconies ascended to the heights from ten feet above the pit of The American Dream, an image of the hierarchy of meatrack society, and the architectural arrangements for the preservation of same as well.

The lowest level, rimmed by a waist-high brass railing, was the main saloon, with a bar and cafe tables, attainable by staircases from the pit. That is by everyone but the streeties, who were confined to the nether reaches by armed zonies guarding them. This was as high up from ground zero as Karen had ever been.

Immediately above was the broadcast booth from which MUZIK sent its live feed from The American Dream into its national satellite network.

Above that, festooned with red and white striped bunting, was an elegant and monstrously expensive French restaurant behind clear plate glass, admission by well-screened prior arrangement only.

And above the restaurant, framed by blue and white starfield bunting so that the two levels together bore a vague resemblance to the American flag, was the VIP lounge for the princes and princesses of show biz behind great panes of black limousine glass.

At the very pinnacle, framed by the outstretched wings of an enormous golden eagle, was what in another age might have been the emperor's box, but reserved here for the faceless corporate gods—a small closed pavilion way up there in the darkness near the ceiling surveying the scene from the enigmatic top of the heap.

Paco, she saw when she looked back, had drifted out onto the dance floor, drawing angry glances from the people he kept bumping into as he staggered around blindly to the beat with his eyes toward the ceiling like a tourist from the jungle gazing up at the Empire State Building for the first time as he sleepwalked out into the traffic of Herald Square.

"Come on," she said, taking him by the hand, "let's sit down by the bar and take care of some business."

The video screens did not quite descend to floor level, beginning about eight feet above the dance floor to leave room for long bars on three sides of the pit, recessed under an overhang to provide both an illusion of intimacy and a measure of sound-baffling.

It was Scuz City in here. The long dimly lit mirrored bar and the plastic covered barstools could have been in any crummy joint on Avenue A. From under here, all that was visible of the rest of The American Dream was a ground level view of the dance floor itself, a tableau of spastically twitching humanity hung like a cheap tapestry across the mouth of a cave.

It was as if a sleazy ominous dive had been chiseled into the foot of a mountain of glitz, as in a certain sense it had. Indeed the sleaze was part of the decor, for this was where day-trippers from the upper levels came to ogle the streeties in a Disneyland version of their natural environment and score flesh, wire, and cheap thrills from same. This was where the streeties who were favored with admission for that very purpose were permitted to peddle their wares and their asses without interference by the management as long as they didn't get violent or barf on the fixtures.

It was also where Karen was constrained to deal her bedbugs, for Muzik, Inc., took a dim view of dealing of any kind beyond the confines of the pit.

"Just sit down here, have a drink, and don't get pissed off when I talk to other guys," Karen told Paco, ensconcing herself at the bar. "It's all just business."

He gave her the strangest leering smile, as if, far from being pissed off at this prospect, it somehow made him quite arrogantly proud of himself. "Bueno, muchacha," he said in an almost silky voice. "Bring home the manteca."

"Got something for long distance?" the gray-haired man in the tuxedo said.

Karen nodded, reached into her purse, pulled out a disc, slapped it on the bar, keeping her hand over it. "Cost you four hundred."

The gray-haired man reached into a pocket, came out with a fuckin' $400 bill, slid it across the bar, picked up the goods, smiled at Karen, eyeing Paco nervously. Paco scowled at him and he melted back into the crush of the dance floor.

Paco grinned happily to himself. He had come home to a place he had never been before. Here he sat in a bar in the Numero Uno meatrack in the fuckin' country, The American Dream, man, where all the rock stars and movie stars hung out, and who was the Cocko de la Calle here in the secret mercado where the deals were made?

He was.

There he sat, sipping his rum and Coke while he watched his momacita bringin' home the manteca.

A reedy guy in a tailored blue denim suit and silver shades whispered something into Karen's ear. She nodded, reached into her purse, pulled out another bedbug, handed it over, snatched up a wad of bills. Blue Denim gave Paco a little salute and faded away.

Ah yes, all these gordos in their fancy suits who oozed up to Karen to score bedbugs kept one eye on him while they did their business with her, and they were very careful to avoid giving him any idea that they might be coming on to his lady.

So he could just sit here on his barstool, sip his drink, sneer at the plushie-tushie putamadres like the prince of the street he was, count what was coming in, and clock the action.

Which was not unlike the action at Slimy Mary's.

Verdad, this bar seemed to go on forever, and verdad there were fancy chochas to watch out there on the dance floor instead of wirehead witches and raggy puercas, and for sure there was mucho mas dinero going down, muchacho.

But what was being dealt was pretty much the same, and most of the people doing the dealing would just as easily fade into the rat- and roach-infested shadows in the nether regions of Slimy Mary's.

Wirehead streetie hookers peddled their chochas to old men in two-thousand-dollar suits. Teenage streeties wiggled their culos for rico maricónes. Porn producers found streeties willing to fuck chickens for five bucks an hour. Fancy chocharicas who could afford to stuff designer dust up their noses with a shovel scored crude shit like the Prong or Uncle Charlie from burnt-out zombies like Monkey Girl and the Count for outrageous prices. And Karen, safe beside him, dealt her bedbugs to the owners of Ciudad Trabajo.

Verdad, he had at last slid himself straight up the cunt of Chocharica City!

For he had penetrated to the very heart of the Soho Zone, to the meatrack that MUZIK itself proclaimed the promised land, and what he had found in here under the fancy silk skirt of The American Dream was a fuckin' streetie mercado where at long last the gordos and the plushie-tushies found *themselves* fearfully slinking around the shadows of *his* turf.

And while he might not be the only prince of the streets in this bar, he had what none of these lesser chicos possessed, a trunkline connection to the Reality Liberation Front, to a level of the city above the street, to something too big for him to understand that he had managed to win as an ally.

Verdad, and while it might have been Karen who was now dealing bedbugs for money that would go straight to them, he had his own goods to peddle once he figured out how, Dojo's Zaps. And that, he realized, didn't have to have anything to do with the fuckin' RLF. Screw them. They were giving him such a hard time about dealing the Zaps for him, and now he didn't have to cut them in at all.

As long as Karen could get him in here, he could deal the Zaps direct and keep the cut that Dojo thought was going to the RLF for himself.

All he had to do was watch his momacita work and pick up on how it was done.

A long-haired blond guy in a red silk suit oozed up to Karen, muttered something in her ear. She nodded, palmed a bedbug disc, handed it over. He slipped it into an inside jacket pocket as Karen tucked the bills into her purse, smiled at her, glanced uneasily at Paco, then slithered back out of the bar and across the dance floor.

"Ain't I seen that guy before?" Paco said.

Karen shrugged. "Tv actor, I think," she said.

"You *know* him?" Paco said. "They all seem to know you."

"Jealous?" she said, licking her lips.

"Of those putamadre maricónes?" Paco said with hard-eyed scorn. "Shit, no. I'm just tryin' to figure out how everyone knows you're dealing bedbugs."

"They don't," she said, nodding toward the dance floor. "There must be thousands of people in here, and most of 'em don't know anything about it. A few of them have bought bedbugs from me before. Those who are looking to score know someone who has. It's all word of mouth." She laughed. "When you're dealing, it doesn't exactly pay to advertise."

Paco frowned. "Then how the fuck do I get started?" he demanded.

She cocked her head quizzically at him. "Get started?"

He reached into his street bag, pulled out a plastic-wrapped

Zap, palmed it, laid it on the bar, hid it under both hands. "Dealing these," he said.

"You want to deal Zaps in here? But Larry said—"

"Fuck what Larry said! This has nothin' to do with the fuckin' Reality Liberation Front."

"But you're here with me!"

"Hey, momacita, *you're* with *me*!" Paco snapped.

"Who got you in?"

"Who got the fuckin' freebies?"

She glared at him, her arms folded on the bar in a gesture of gordo arrogance. He glared back at her, putting out angry macho vibes. They sat there in a silent staring match like that for long moments, locked into a frozen posture of clashing wills.

Then the music suddenly died.

The abrupt silence was like a slap across the face. Reflexively, Paco whirled around on his stool. An even, pale, rosy light bathed the dance floor, where hundreds of people now stood staring up at something hidden from his field of vision by the overhang of the bar ceiling.

"Live from The American Dream!" a mighty male voice boomed out. All along the bar, people turned, slid off their stools, and rushed out onto the dance floor.

"Chingada!" Paco exclaimed, slipping off his own stool and reaching for Karen's hand. "Come on! They're doing a MUZIK broadcast!"

Karen was already on her feet. She grabbed his hand as they joined the crowd looking up expectantly at the black glass pedestal in the center of the dance floor.

A single bright white spot cast a hard-edged pool of light on the elevated stage. In it stood a black man in a tight white tuxedo embroidered with thousands of tiny mirrors sheathing him in a rainbow aura of refracted light.

"Ali Babble . . ." Karen muttered into his ear.

Paco nodded, not taking his eyes off the man on the stage. Ali Babble was one of the regular MUZIK vjs, and Paco had always thought of him as an asshole. But still, there was something magically mesmerizing about seeing such a *famous* asshole alive in the flesh for the very first time. He had never seen a famous *anyone* live before.

"Chingada, Karen, *this* we *gotta* flash on!" he cried, reaching out to give her Zap a tap before hitting his own.

"Yes, this is the Master Motor Mouth himself, coming to you

live from The American Dream, and tonight you're gonna be there as musical history is being made! Tonight the old Master Motor Mouth is just about as speechless as he's ever gonna be, because you ain't seen and heard nothin' yet, I mean MUZIK *is* music, the state of the art, but wait till you hear the state the art has reached now, right here, right now, live and not live, you won't even know what I'm babbling about until you see the impossible, not just a new star, but a new *kind* of star, hold on to your heads and dig *this,* he's here, he's not here, he's live, he's not live, he's somethin' else again, *Red Jack, your brand new Rock and Roll Machine*!"

The spotlight died and the entire world exploded into blinding white-out and The American Dream trembled to a bone-shattering nuclear roar. Out of the boom and flash came a pounding beat loaded with gut-thrumming subsonics and three huge video walls of colored snow that seemed to pulse with it as if he had suddenly been transported *inside* a video screen turned to an empty channel.

Empty?

Chingada!

A voice sang out of the walls of static, a voice unlike anything he had ever heard; male and powerful, female and insinuating, machinelike, but not mechanical, a solo singer, but also a chorus, something that sure as shit wasn't human.

I make more of you....

A huge face, tripled on the screens, four stories high, coalesced suddenly out of the random electronic confetti right on the beat.

You make more of me....

Flashing brown eyes set off by thick black brows and long dark lashes and a full-lipped smirking mouth made him seem like Mucho Muchacho's soul brother, but that thin flaring nose sniffed gordo arrogance, and the bright red shoulder-length hair made him seem like neither and both, a rock and roll monster.

The hair . . . the hair . . . a webwork of fine silver wire seemed flung over his red hair as if . . . as if he were wearing a Zap!

You make more of me
I make more of you . . .

The chorus repeated twice, and on the end of every other bar the face dissolved back into colored static for a beat, then snapped back into existence for the next. There, and not there, live, and not live, strobing in and out of reality to the beat.

I make more of you
You make more of me
You make more of me
I make more of you. . . .

Karen found her feet moving to the beat, found herself dancing in a frenzied multitude, staring up, up, up at the huge figure of this creature called Red Jack as he pranced and stomped across an empty blue matte background, as the pounding percussion and the throbbing bass, the scratchy guitar line, the eerie insinuating voice with the impossible range, teased her consciousness toward the edge of an elusive revelation.

Then his pants and shirt began to go through endless strobing changes, as bits of old movies, starscape still shots, crowd scenes, faces, endless data-bank footage and images, flickered across them kaleidoscopically.

I'm the you they always told me
That I could never be . . .
I'm the crown of your creation
In your wizard dreams . . .

Red Jack dissolved into pixels for a long moment, then reformed slowly out of a dissolving montage of ordinary faces, clearly proclaiming himself a pure creature of the cybersphere.

Of course! He isn't there! He isn't real! He's a *program,* not a live singer, and he's rubbing our faces in it!

Shots of a multitude of audiences melting into each other behind him now, as he danced and sang before them, arising wraithlike out of them like an electronic incubus, the software manifestation of their collective rock and roll dream.

Let me dance into your dreamtime
I'm your Rock and Roll Machine!

Then Karen was back in Rutgers, in an endless computer classroom cut together out of bits and pieces of computer training films and bullshit documentaries painting a glowing picture of the future of the cyberkind generation, beavering away with all the other drudges and hackers at their dreary line of consoles. And she, along with all the rest of them, joined in on the chorus.

I make more of you
You make more of me
You make more of me
I make more of you. . . .

She danced with Red Jack through endless aisles of computer consoles in the crummy shirt factory as they tossed bedbug discs to all the hacking drudges wage-slaving away in the service of Official Reality.

Boot me up and boogie
Sez this ghost in your machine. . . .

And all the little computer nerds began inserting the discs into their consoles, which magically blossomed into glowing jukebox consoles painted in fantastic neon swirls and paisley patterns.

I've been sealed up in your circuits
I've been nowhere to be seen
But now I'm here to tell ya
Raise up your voice and scream. . . .

And all the poor wimpy creatures became her comrades now, lithe and sexy and powerful in their Reality Liberation Front T-shirts, grinning at the world they never made with the face of Red Jack, singing together with the newfound, nonexistent voice of their generation.

You and me together
We're a Rock and Roll Machine!

Gordos poured out of some weird factory full of computers to join Mucho Muchacho's army of streeties as they danced their stompada of freedom up the main drag of Ciudad Trabajo, and Red Jack danced beside him leading the chorus line, and it was okay, it was all right, for gordos and streeties alike were wearing silvery wire hairnets, united at last in the brotherhood of the Zap.

> *I make more of you*
> *You make more of me*
> *You make more of me*
> *I make more of you. . . .*

More gordos poured out of tall glass towers, streeties surged from alleys and subways like an avenging horde of cockroaches, and as they hit the street and joined the parade behind Mucho Muchacho and Red Jack, Zaps grew in their hair, and their faces all became the face of Red Jack, then of Mucho himself, Jack, Mucho, Jack, Mucho, until they strobe-merged into a single face, and he *was* that face, singing with the voice of the underbelly of the city itself.

> *You're standing here beside me*
> *Just where I've always been*
> *You've been hiding right inside me. . . .*

Singing on a stage before tiered grandstands that were row after row of garbage cans with computer consoles sitting on top of them. Zap-wearing streeties played their keyboards like pianos, fingers flying, heads rolling to the beat, stomping their feet, and rolling their eyes, becoming Mucho Muchacho, Red Jack, Mucho, Jack, Mucho, Jack, in time to the max metal beat.

> *We're the ghost in the machine . . .*
> *We may be bits and bytes and programs*
> *But baby, we ain't Mr. Clean. . . .*

And he was out there in the audience with the rest of them, playing synthesizers, guitars, pianos, drum kits, conjuring up the face of Red Jack on every computer screen, back up on the stage doin' his Mucho Muchacho stompada. . . .

> *I make more of you*
> *You make more of me. . . .*

Back and forth, back and forth, back and forth to the beat of the music in a stroboscopic flicker, four reversals to every bar.

You make more of me. . . .
I make more of you. . . .

And suddenly it was riot time in Ciudad Trabajo as he led his army of flashing streeties, his horde of fuckin' Zapped-out gordos, through banks, missile control centers, tv control rooms, department store check-out counters, stock brokerages, offices of government and industry.

Generals and plushie-tushies, zonies and chocharicas, old farts in tuxedos, ran around in circles, freaking and screaming, rolling their eyes, waving their arms, and pissing in their fuckin' pants, as rats in suits and sheepskin coats and streams of cockroaches poured out of every nook and cranny, as Mucho Muchacho laughed and laughed and laughed, as all the tv monitors and computer screens lit up with the leering, howling face of Red Jack.

Red ripe anarchy
For all the world to see
What will the Fat Men do?
You make more of me
I make more of you!

"*The Zap?*" Karen said, staring at Paco in no little amazement. "You saw everyone wearing the Zap?"

"For sure, momacita," Paco told her, taking another long drink of rum and Coke. "Didn't you? It's what the whole fuckin' song is about!"

"*It is?* I thought it was about bedbugs."

"*Bedbugs?* Chingada! What the fuck does it have to do with bedbugs?"

Karen laughed and rubbed her thumb against the first two fingers of her right hand. "It's sure been working like a *commercial* for 'em, now isn't it, Paco?" she said.

The end of the song had left everyone standing on the dance floor like a collective of sleepers suddenly awoken from the same dream, too bonged to even start babbling about it till later. Certainly bonged enough without flashing further on the Zap. Karen had hit her touchpoint to come out of it as she wandered in something of a daze back to the bar, and even Paco seemed to have had enough flashing to last him for a while.

A good thing, too, for business had gotten hot and heavy

almost before she had time to pull up a stool and order a drink, and she had needed her wits about her just to keep the prices and change-making straight.

For whatever Paco had seen on his flash, enough people had seen what *she* had seen on *her* flash to cause a run on her merchandise that now left her with only one ATM bedbug disc left in her purse.

"You didn't see Red Jack wearin' the Zap just like us?" Paco persisted incredulously.

Karen thought about it. The frosting of thin silvery lines in the phantom rock star's red hair . . .

"Come to think of it . . ." she muttered. "You didn't see him handing out bedbug discs? You didn't see all those bedbugged computer systems going crazy at the end?"

Paco stared at her narrowly in slow comprehension. "Is *that* what all that shit was?"

Karen shrugged. "A lot of my customers seemed to think so," she said.

Karen shook her head.

Paco took another drink. "Fuckin' weird," he said. "First a fuckin' singer who isn't like really there, and now you—"

"You saw that too?" Karen said sharply.

"I may not know shit about computers, but I know old Red Jack there is . . . is . . ."

"An Artificial Personality . . ."

"A *what*?"

"An Artificial Personality, like the ones they use in tv commercials. You know, like Captain Coke and Ronald McDonald, only *this* program's good enough to seem like a real live human. . . ."

"Only it's like he don't *want* to fool you even if he can. . . . Chingada, what the fuck's it all about?"

"Random factors," Karen blurted. "And lots of 'em!"

"Qué?"

"You got bedbugs? I hear ya got bedbugs."

A short, rather squat middle-aged woman with an elaborately sculptured hairdo now in some disarray, and wearing an expensive-looking black silk sheath dress with sweat stains under the arms, had lurched, red-eyed and woozy, up to her stool, and was tugging insistently at her arm.

"Come on, come on, you're dealing the things, everybody knows you are. . . ."

"Well, I do have one left," Karen said, reaching into her purse and pulling her head to one side out of the wind of boozy breath.

"How much?" the stoned-out woman demanded.

"Four hundred," Karen said, laying her last disc down on the bar top.

"Whazzit do?" the woman woozed, already reaching for the bedbug.

"It's an ATM bedbug."

"A which?"

"Lets you use a cash machine with a phony card. Gets you into the data banks, and—"

"What do I want with shit like that!" the drunken woman demanded belligerently. "Ain't you got anything better?"

"I ain't even got anything *else,*" Karen snapped back. The woman scowled, started to turn away.

"I do!" Paco said.

Both of them stared at Paco, Karen in some surprise, the chocharica boracha with sudden interest. Paco gave her a sexy little smile.

"Una otra cosita," he said seductively, leaning closer to her, reaching up into his hair, and pulling the Zap net free for a moment before letting it snap back.

"Whazzat?"

"Se llamo the Zap, momacita," Paco purred. "What Red Jack was wearing in the video, you know . . ."

"Yeah . . ." the chocharica muttered, looking at him dubiously. "Whazzit, piece of street wire? Shee . . . I'm burned on dust and booze already, don't need no wirehead shit. . . ."

Paco smiled. He nodded sympathetically. "No street shit, momacita," he said in confidential tones. "Brand new, can't tell you where it comes from, but . . . it's what like gives *him* his powers, you know. . . ."

"Powers . . . ?"

Paco nodded. He reached into his street bag, pulled out a plastic-wrapped Zap, held it under her nose. "Put it on, hit the touchpoint, and you be who you want to be. . . ."

The chocharica leaned over to study the package. "Be who I want to be . . . ?"

"Be what you dream to be, momacita," Paco told her. "Young. Sexy. A bedroom queen and a rock and roll machine. Like the song says, the you they always told you that you could never be. Just give yourself a little tap of the Zap. . . ."

She cocked her head at him inquisitively. Her expression grew guarded, but she ran a thoughtful tongue sloppily over her lips. "How much?" she said.

"Usual price is six hundred," Paco said. He winked at her. "But for you, five hundred, momacita, just because I think you're so fuckin' sexy."

She stared blearily and hungrily into his eyes for a long moment. Paco gave her as sexy a look back as he could manage under the circumstances.

"Well fuckit," she finally said, reaching into her purse. "I've already blown that much on dust tonight already!"

Paco snatched up the money and handed her the Zap. "Hey momacita," he said as she started to turn away, "you tell your gordo friends, sí? You tell 'em Paco's got the Zap, you tell 'em they can find Red Jack's main man right here in The American Dream."

"Pretty slick," Karen told Paco with a little smile when she had gone.

"You're not pissed off?"

He looked so proud of himself sitting there on the barstool. Hell, hadn't she dealt worse wire than the Zap in college? She shook her head. She laughed. "At least I've taught you a trade," she said. "And one you can't get fired from too!"

"Just between you and me?" he said. "We don't have to tell Larry Coopersmith nothin' that ain't his business?"

Karen glanced out onto the dance floor, where hundreds of people were now dancing to the usual stuff in the flickering strobe light as if nothing had happened at all.

But something had. She didn't know quite what, she had a feeling she didn't know the half; Red Jack, bedbugs, something new was loose in the world, factors so random that even old Markowitz himself might find his cozy little view of reality threatened. Nothing was ever going to be quite the same again. Oh yes, red ripe anarchy for all the world to see! And something inside her gut insisted that Paco was somehow right, the Zap was part of it too.

She looked back at Paco. She smiled. She took his hand. She nodded her agreement. "I'm with Mucho Muchacho now, right?" she said.

He laughed. He beamed at her. "Let's dance to it, momacita," he said, pulling her to her feet.

She kissed him lightly on the lips as they glided out onto the floor. "You make more of me, I make more of you," she sang at him.

"I make more of you, you make more of me!"

They held hands for a beat, then whirled each other out into the fleshy maelstrom, into the strobing lights, and for a moment they found themselves caught in a brilliant white spot, as they giggled, and threw back their heads, and gave themselves over to the rhythm, and howled it out in ragged unison.

"You and me together, we're a Rock and Roll Machine!"

THE SACRED BOTTOM LINE

"What do you want from my life, goddammit?'' Glorianna O'Toole demanded with entirely unconvincing innocence, for what Carlo Manning wanted, as she well knew, could be neatly summed up in two four-letter words of one syllable each: *more gold.*

Manning did not insult her intelligence by bothering to answer. He just sat there behind the big gunmetal desk smiling at her like a traffic cop enduring the usual useless bullshit as he wrote out a speeding ticket.

Glorianna planted her ass gingerly in one of the four antique barber's chairs in front of the desk. ''There are personal problems . . .'' she said vaguely.

''Personal problems?'' Manning said evenly. ''What sort of problems?''

What was she supposed to tell this tight little asshole? That ''Your Rock and Roll Machine'' had been created on a magic wire flash whose chemistry she had been unable to summon forth since?

''My VoxBox wizard has the hots for my image organ genius and he's just not having any,'' Glorianna finally said. ''Those vibes worked on 'Your Rock and Roll Machine,' but they've gotten real old, and they've soured every session since.'' This much, at least, even Manning should be able to understand.

''*This* is what's holding up production on your second Red Jack disc?'' Manning exclaimed with more show of emotion than she had ever seen him display before.

He folded his hands on the desktop and lectured at her with the contained exasperation of a schoolteacher for a dimwitted but well-meaning student. ''Have you been paying attention to the numbers, Ms. O'Toole? We have shipped nine million copies of 'Your Rock and Roll Machine'! Red Jack has been at the top of the charts for three months! Don't you know what that means?"

"It means you've got what you wanted, so stop giving me such a hard time!"

Manning moaned in exasperation. "It means we need another Red Jack disc in the stores in four months!" he said. "Which means we need a master within ten weeks if we're to market it properly. Hits have a finite lifespan; this one's volume has started to decline, and the optimum time to release the next Red Jack disc is about two months after the first one is off the charts. Not when some horny little Valley Girl stops thinking with her vagina long enough to get some work done!"

"What do you expect me to do, order Bobby to screw her?" Glorianna snapped.

"Not a bad idea . . ." Manning said quite earnestly. "Yeah, if you explained the numbers to him, the need to get something out to hit the optimum market timing, if we offered him a point in the next album for services rendered . . ."

Now it was Glorianna's turn to moan in exasperation.

"If you've been at this impasse all along, Ms. O'Toole, then why on earth haven't you come to me for professional assistance?" Manning said petulantly.

"I guess I just never thought of you as a romantic, Manning," Glorianna drawled. "Or have I got you all wrong, Carlo baby, are you offering your own tender young bod in place of Bobby's? Just what *profession* you say you're in, anyway?"

"You don't have to like me, but it would be to your benefit to stop regarding me as an asshole, Ms. O'Toole," Manning purred at her almost diffidently. "I have, after all, managed to get where I am. And I got here through my successful career in the *research* department, Ms. O'Toole."

"So?"

"So Muzik, Inc., has *experts* who are paid large salaries to deal with these problems," Manning said. "If Sally Genaro has an unrequited fixation on Bobby Rubin, then the motivation boys should have been factoring it into the psychic specs they've been feeding the songhacks all along. How do you expect the research department to motivate the talent for you if you don't supply the relevant data?"

"Motivate the talent? Relevant data . . . ?" Glorianna muttered, feeling every one of her six decades. "What planet is this? What the fuck are you *talking* about?"

"If there's unresolved sexual tension in the studio, then the songhacks should be working *with* it, not against it; it should be factored into the lyrics they send down, so that it can be used to motivate the artists to get their act in gear. Grab them by the . . . ah . . ." Manning leered at her like Willy the Wolverine.

"You sure are a cold motherfucker, aren't you?" Glorianna said in a weird sort of genuine admiration for such a perfect little prick.

"It's a cold world out there and it's filled with motherfuckers like me taking care of business," Manning said evenly. "Perhaps you've noticed?"

"The sort of bastards who would threaten to put a poor old lady in the joint to *motivate* her?" Glorianna shot back.

"Precisely," Manning said sweetly. "So maybe you'd better tell me what else you're holding back right now."

Glorianna locked eyes with the current president of the Muzik Factory, with the man who had threatened to have her busted for the universal practice of buying dust with company money and feeding it to the talent.

Right, she thought, tell you all about the *wire* I bought with company money and plugged your little cyberwizards into! Give you another fuckin' felony charge to hang over my head!

"It wouldn't have something to do with *this,* would it?" Manning said, pulling something out of a drawer and flinging it negligently onto his desk.

"Oh, fuck!" Glorianna could not keep herself from admitting aloud, nor did it really matter, for now she was certainly screwed.

For sitting on Manning's desk like the fabled smoking pistol was the wire mesh helmet and sleek oval breadbox of a Shunt.

"Really, Ms. O'Toole," Manning said in his snottiest tone of all, "how unprofessional do you think we are? You think we don't know these things are flooding the black market? You think demographics doesn't notice when sales break out of the projected market to cross over into a wire cult hit, something we've never really had before? At least you can credit us with enough intelligence to see the stylized Zap Red Jack is wearing once the sales figures slap us in the face with it."

Oh shit, Glorianna thought, another ten years to my stretch, right. If there's no law against promoting wire on a videodisc and pumping it out on MUZIK, they'll invent one real quick.

"So may we come directly to the bottom line?" Manning went on relentlessly. "Bobby Rubin and Sally Genaro were plugged into this piece when they made the breakthrough on 'Your Rock and Roll Machine,' weren't they? And you were the one who gave it to them, weren't you?"

"How the fuck did you figure all that out!" Glorianna blurted in poleaxed amazement.

Manning got up from his desk and started pacing around the office, something Glorianna had never seen him do before, dancing around the furniture he had installed, and patting its solidity like a security blanket as he spoke.

The heavy antique chromed barber chairs were screwed to the floor. A big black marble monstrosity of a conference table that must have weighed at least a ton was surrounded on three sides by massive sectional sofas. The walls had been papered with peach-colored velvet flock that must have been almost as expensive as it was hideous.

Glorianna noticed what a statement all this was for the first time as Manning circled her barber chair like a predator.

Manning was proclaiming the substantiality of his determination to keep this office on a permanent basis. Whether he would succeed any better than all the others she had seen go through the revolving door was not her problem. The fact that he had already proven to be the most ruthless son of a bitch she had yet seen in this office emphatically was. He certainly had her wherever it was he wanted her! But where the fuck was that? What was he going to blackmail her into doing now?

But instead of twirling his black moustache and twisting her arm, Carlo Manning grew expansive, admiring his own work, patting his furniture barricades possessively, and giving her a chalk talk on the business.

"How did we figure it out, you ask? First we see that twenty percent of the sales of 'Your Rock and Roll Machine' are crossing over into a new demographic slice we've got no specs on. When we get them, they correlate to a trendy new piece of wire. Which in retrospect we see Red Jack is symbolically displaying. When our engineers take one of the things apart, we discover that it interfaces the dream centers with the waking intellect. And psych says that this brain state correlates to periods of creativity as well as to brain states induced by certain psychedelics. And Project Superstar was going nowhere for months and months before this sudden breakthrough. And everybody in the business knows about your garbage-head proclivities. . . ."

"Okay, fuck it, I admit it, you're a genius, so at least spare me the gloating." Glorianna sighed. "You already have enough to retire me to the joint for the rest of my life and then some anyway. So I might as well admit it. I bought wire with Muzik, Inc., funds and used it on the talent."

She levered herself off the barber chair and confronted Manning nose to nose.

"That's another one you got on me, sonny," she said, "but maybe it's one I got on you too. Prosecute me, and I'll tell the world that 'Your Rock and Roll Machine' is indeed a commercial for the Shunt and that *you* made us do it. Think anyone will believe the truth, that *none* of us knew what the fuck we were doing? That Muzik, Inc., wasn't involved? Have me busted for this, and it's the slam for you too, Carlo baby. They'll just love your tight little buns."

Manning stared at her in some bemusement, then sat down on the edge of his desk, assuming a slouchy posture that almost made him seem human. "Prosecute you? Arrest you? Why on earth would I do that?" he asked innocently.

"You threatened to have me prosecuted for buying *dope and dust* for the talent with company funds, didn't you?" Glorianna said, glaring down at him.

Carlo Manning actually laughed. "That was nothing personal, Glorianna," he said. "That was just *business*. Something to motivate you. You think I would've caviled at the drug bill you ran up if it had *worked*? You think I'm *angry* at you for resorting to wire to produce a disc that's already sold nine million copies with an even bigger megahit in sight?"

Manning smiled at her with some semblance of human warmth. "Relax," he said, "sit down." The guy was serious!

"I think I'd better . . ." Glorianna said, resting her weary bones and her weak knees in the barber chair.

"The depth studies paint a tasty bottom-line figure," Manning told her happily. "Red Jack's favorite piece of wire is not only the fave rave of the usual wireheads, it's the first piece of wire to compete with dust for the favor of the middle class, the people who usually buy both dust and *our discs*. Marketing predicts that the Shunt, or the Zap as they're calling it on the street, could be what Hula-Hoops were to the fifties or LSD to the sixties or coke to the eighties. Whichever is selling what or whether it's synergetic feedback, we're ideally positioned to piggyback our product on an emerging national fad."

"You mean you *want* Red Jack identified with the Shunt?"

"Are you kidding me?" Manning said. "Any marketer would sell his soul for a free ride like that! What else did you think this meeting is all about? You've given us a star image in a position to piggyback our product on a powerful and sustained emerging fad. If I thought you knew what you were doing, I'd make you a vice-president in marketing. But you lucked into it, didn't you? It was a happy, half-assed accident. Research, psych, and marketing didn't even know what was going on."

He slid off the desk and resumed his seat of authority behind it. "But now you will have the full resources of Muzik, Inc., behind you, and my assurance that as long as you succeed in fulfilling the specs, no one will question your methods."

He reached into a drawer and pulled out a sheaf of printouts. "Psych has already done these preliminary specs for the new disc, and now that we know what the creative problem is, we can refine them into guidelines for the songhacks. And we've already got a working title."

He ran a finger around the top of his head, tracing out a phantom circle of wire. " 'The Crown Prince of Rock and Roll,' get it? What do you think?"

"What do I think . . . ?" Glorianna stammered. "Does it matter . . . ?"

"Does it matter!" exclaimed Manning. "Marketing projects *twelve million sales or better* if we hit this right! The biggest thing . . . since . . . since . . ."

"Elvis or the Beatles?"

Manning nodded enthusiastically. "And without paying out any royalties to prima donnas and troublemakers like Presley or Lennon. Not just volume, but great profit margin on every unit."

"Wonderful," Glorianna moaned. "Far fuckin' out!" Fuck a duck, didn't this slimepit have any bottom?

"I'm glad you approve," Manning said humorlessly.

"And if I didn't . . . ?"

Manning gave her a negligent shrug and a sad little moue of regret which told her all she needed to know.

"Ten weeks," Manning told her. "We're all expecting great things from you, Glorianna."

"And if you don't get them?"

Manning began fiddling with some papers, and let her sweat awhile before he deigned to look up. "Think positively," he advised. "If 'The Crown Prince of Rock and Roll' ships gold too, we do your comeback; that should be sufficient motivation. Surely neither of us cares to contemplate the consequences of failure."

"For sure . . ." Glorianna agreed wanly.

There was no point in kidding herself, no point in fantasizing false heroics; if she refused to go ahead with the project now, Manning would see to it that her ass languished in the joint for the rest of her life.

As he would if she tried and failed; she had no illusions about that either, for it was pretty clear that his own precious ass was riding on it too.

"I'm glad we've reached this meeting of the minds," Manning said, and he buried his nose in his papers to indicate that the meeting was over.

"It's always nice to know the bottom line," Glorianna said dryly over her shoulder on the way out the door.

"Muzik *is* music!" proclaimed the logo on the wall opposite the elevators. "Yeah, well it sure as shit ain't rock and roll," Glorianna muttered. "They oughta change that thing to 'Muzik *is* the bottom line!' They wouldn't know the real thing if it bit 'em in the ass!"

But as the elevator door slid open, so did some sliding panel in her brain.

No indeed, they literally *wouldn't* know the real thing if it bit them in the ass as long as the numbers made their little pin heads happy!

So why not let it? she thought as she stepped inside.

If all they cared about was how many copies they shipped, then she could raise as much hell as she could summon as long as she did it at a profit.

The stupid bastards were bending over and asking for it! They had no concept of the power they were just begging to have reborn!

"The Crown Prince of Rock and Roll," huh?

It had been a long time since Rock had even had a contender for the title. A long time since Crown Princes of Rock and Roll like Elvis and Dylan and Jagger and Lennon had loosened a generation's pelvis and blown its collective mind and raised a rebel flag of revolution. A long time since there had even been a Springsteen crying out in the long dark night.

What do you say, Jack, are you up to it? Glorianna asked God knew what as the elevator descended to the garage. You got the electronic balls to openly claim the wirehead crown? What are they gonna do, Jack, bust you? How can they stop someone who isn't even there?

Glorianna O'Toole rubbed her hands together as the elevator reached the garage. "You want more gold, motherfuckers, I'll give you more gold, I'll give it to you up the ass while you gladly pay for the Vaseline," she promised all the pin heads upstairs.

"Red ripe anarchy for all the world to see, what will the Fat Men do?" she warbled on the way to her Rolls.

As long as they're making money on it, not a fucking thing.

It certainly had been a fair bargain as far as Bobby Rubin was concerned, even though he was still on the old work-for-hire contract, even though he didn't see dime one worth of royalties on all those millions of discs out there. The Factory had gladly raised his salary to just about as much money as he knew how to spend, a lot cheaper than paying out royalties to rock stars, as far as they were concerned.

He had bought himself the inevitable expensive new car, a four-seater Honda-Ferrari convertible in neon red that turned the girls' heads as it tooled down the street even in Beverly Hills.

He rented himself a two-bedroom house in Beverly Glen for half of his monthly salary. It had a big tree-shrouded redwood patio with a small swimming pool, a large hot tub, and a minimal sauna that never really worked.

The living room had a huge rose velvet conversation pit, a big wall screen, a state of the art disc deck, a lavishly stocked wet bar, an antique Wurlitzer jukebox, and a hand-tooled rosewood cabinet lined with silk and stocked with an abundance of assorted designer dusts. The bedroom looked down a ravine vaguely done up like a Japanese garden through a big picture window that faced the circular water bed. Instead of a mirror on the ceiling, there was a video screen that could display either disc or live coverage of the action below according to the whim of the moment.

And while he still might be a glamorless nobody at the A parties beside the likes of actors and rock stars, as a pampered favorite of the Factory, he was on all the A lists, at least. Which meant that if he wanted to impress some college student or club musician or groupie in order to melt her out of her panties, he could lay on a tour of Valhalla on his arm.

As for meeting prime pussy, from the perspective of his new lair in Beverly Glen, that proved far easier than he had ever imagined it could be.

All he had to do was throw parties.

Certainly not A parties dressed with movie stars and rock and roll queens, but rather good solid B parties, where the guest list ran to below-the-line movie people, rock journalists, minions of the Factory, and whole shoals of good-looking waitresses, lady dealers, amateur hookers, and professional social climbers who aspired to what they fancied to be such august levels of Tinseltown society.

If you were willing to lay on generous amounts of free dust and booze, you had about as much trouble attracting such freebie hounds to your feast as fresh horseshit had attracting flies. After the first few parties, Bobby actually had *girls* scheming and angling for invitations.

In these tight little circles, as the lord of the manor with the key to the dust cabinet in his pocket, Bobby Rubin could be something of a star. He had a credit line for visual synthesis on the number one hit in the country. Those in the know envied what weight that carried in the Factory and schemed for his favor. Innocents of the feminine gender dreaming of stardom themselves who ignorantly fantasized him as a trunk line to same gave enthusiastic head.

Bobby was awash in pussy for the first time in his life. After most every party, he found himself on the water bed with a tasty sex object plucked from the smorgasbord. In the beginning of this run, when about all he could do was stay dusted and marvel at how often he was getting his rocks off, it never occurred to him that said tasty sex objects, *being* in fact tasty sex objects, regularly enjoyed the performances of cocksmen far more experienced than he was even at the impressive rate with which he was catching up.

A bit later on, when he began to notice that most of these faceless beauties did not come back for more unless they were after something, Bobby, to his limp dismay, found that Pussy Paradise could be a hollow-ground sword.

For he was now in the company of women who really knew

how to fuck, beautiful women who could pick and choose at least their one-night stands, who rated the meat in the health club locker room, who might suck a cock or screw a nerd now and again for pragmatic advantage or the promise of same, but who expected any guy they took seriously to know his chops well enough to reliably make them come.

Alas, this sexual satori put Bobby's dick in a bit of a sling. He became embarrassed to take his clothes off before naked women he was slavering to fuck. He held at arm's length the advances of women he thought were too hot to handle. He couldn't get it up, or he couldn't keep it up, or he came too quickly, or he couldn't come at all, and of course, thinking about it all the time just made things worse.

Yes, in the real world, even Pussy Paradise had its treacherous serpent. As long as he threw his parties, he could get himself laid, he could in fact get laid beyond his station, by sexy ladies drifting through. But as long as he felt they were sneering at him to their girlfriends afterward, as long as he felt like a lousy lay, he *was* a lousy lay, and no doubt the object of no little ladies' room ribaldry, and the fact that the cyberwizard recognized the nature of the negative feedback loop did not mean that horny little Bobby knew how to untie his pecker from the Gordian knot.

It was just too much for him to handle alone.

And then one night, in desperation, it dawned on him that maybe he didn't have to.

It was the wee hours of Saturday night, and the party was winding down, and now that the geometry had become obvious, the last few guests dragged themselves to their cars, leaving him alone in the living room with the fearful and achingly tantalizing woman of the night's desire.

Her name was Fara Fay Marley, or anyway that was the name she used in the club band she fronted. She sat there on the sofa with her legs crossed under her and a belligerent little smile as he shooed the stragglers out the door.

Fara Fay wore skin-tight powder blue leather pants that broke into a long beadwork skirt three inches north of the knees, a curtain of thongs and brass doodads that served only to emphasize her long lithe legs. A chrome chain-mail halter, a double layer of fine links, squeezed her breasts into erect little mountains, the nipples dimpling the silver glaciers of metal. Her deep brown eyes seemed to look right through him, her full pregnant lips promised unspeakable delights, her nostrils flared and relaxed like a high-spirited thoroughbred, and there was something about her that seemed like spring steel.

She terrified him. Just looking at her made him afraid he would come in his pants.

He tried to convince himself it had nothing to do with her being black as he confronted her in the sudden solitude. But he knew very well what bullshit that was. It was not just that he had never come close to making it with a black girl before, it was not just that Fara Fay called up fantasies out of the woodhouse wet dreams of an aboriginal redneck, it was that she knew it, and was amused by it, and played to it with such style. Her hair was all done up in fine dreadlocks beaded with chrome to match her skirt, and she wore a little chrome dagger through her left nostril.

The reality behind the image, as Bobby's intellect knew, was a young girl singer going nowhere, performing in bars for pass the hat, and fantasizing against her own wiser wisdom that the dude that did the visuals on "Your Rock and Roll Machine" had to have connections that could rescue her from her unjust obscurity. He was therefore in the catbirdseat.

But go tell that to his sweaty little pecker.

"So you finally got rid of all those assholes," Fara Fay said as Bobby gingerly placed himself on the same section of sofa. "Now maybe you and me can finally get down to serious business."

"What do you have in mind?" Bobby stammered.

"Some serious fucking, white boy," Fara Fay said, lookin' right at him. "Later, when I've got you in my power, I'll show you some performance discs and persuade you to make me a star."

"I'll bet you tell that to all the boys . . ." Bobby managed manfully.

It had been like this since she walked in the door and forthrightly announced that she intended to be the last guest to leave, and since she had to get up by ten next morning to do some business, he should make sure the party ended early.

"Only the ones I intend to have eat me for breakfast," Fara Fay said, breaking herself up, but then running her tongue slowly around her lips to show she was serious.

Bobby just about lost it. He had never been more turned on in his life and he had never been more afraid of doing anything about it. But he couldn't bungle his way out of this one, no matter how much blood was drained south from his brain. Fara Fay was totally in charge, he didn't have to be able to do *anything* right.

And from somewhere at last came the courage to be pissed off about it. "You really think you're hot shit, don't you?"

In reply, Fara Fay flowed across the couch and all over him, flipping him on his back before he could even think about it, rippling her athletic body against him as she kissed him with a long slow tongue, and squeezed his balls with practiced gentleness. In about thirty seconds she had his cock out, and was running the back of a fingernail slowly up it from base to tip.

With a fingertip resting lightly on the throbbing head of his cock, Fara Fay broke the kiss wetly, and breathed perfume into his nostrils as she grinned at him like a leopard.

"My little man, I *am* hot shit," she said.

Bobby, who had been within a hairbreadth of coming in her hand like a fool, found himself in no position to argue with that.

"Where's the john, I already know where the bedroom is," Fara Fay said, springing off of him and pulling him to his feet. "Just give me a minute to take care of pussy business, and I'll see you there."

Bobby staggered into his bedroom in a state of no little psychic disarray, slapping his deliciously aching cock in hope of desensitizing it, for he was terrified that he would come the moment he got it inside her, and if she gave him head first . . .

At the same time, he was furious at himself for being such a wimp, for being afraid of this wonderful creature, for lacking the manhood to be on top of a situation that he had fantasized all his pubescent life. If this ultimate porn disc didn't come out the way nature intended, he certainly would have no one to blame but himself.

As he had done more than once before in more or less analogous circumstances, he popped "Your Rock and Roll Machine" into his disc deck with the sound off, plastering the dancing image of Red Jack across the screen above the big round water bed.

There he was in his hour of triumph, the Bobby Rubin of his dreamtime, not only his ticket to his present comparatively lofty status, but a piece of him, and not just the eyes, up there before the world burning bright as he was meant to be.

Red Jack would know what to do, he thought as he shed his

clothing. He looked up at the confident handsome face staring down at him with his own eyes. But you're me! he realized. Who else could you be? How can you be more than I made you to be? Why can't I be you now when I need you?

A tremor of recognition tingled through him as he realized that maybe he could.

He had a Shunt in his night table drawer, the one he had worn at Glorianna's house that magical night, and had seldom worn since. For the one Glorianna O'Toole insisted he chip at in the studio had become crown of thorns enough.

Sally from the Valley stayed plugged in through most of the sessions; she was turning into a hard-core wirehead, or anyway Shunthead, and it was all too obvious what she was flashing on. She warped the lyrics the songhacks sent down in a single-minded direction, and the music she turned out was relentlessly gonadal, and she paid no attention at all to syncing any of it with what he was trying to do with the visual track. All she produced was sweaty-thighed lust songs to Red Jack, or worse still, lyrics she put into the mouth of Bobby's electronic alter ego which were *his* love songs to *her*. It was to puke.

And because of it, he had become quite reluctant to Shunt himself, to let her music insinuate itself into his dreamtime as he was flashing, to become the figure dancing on her obscene screen, to participate on any but the most superficial level in this loathsome collaboration.

But this, he realized, as he found himself fumbling in his night table drawer, was his own bedroom, not the studio, and Fara Fay Marley was about as far away from being the Pimple as a woman could get.

He smoothed the wirework web into his hair, snugged the breadbox against the back of his skull, lay down naked on the bed with his hands behind his head and a raging hard-on, and tried to smile confidently like a jaded pasha. Should I really do this? he wondered nervously.

Fara Fay entered the bedroom mother-naked, or almost. She still had the little dagger through her nose, and a heavy chrome chain clung in a snug loop over her hips, dipping down into the upper edge of her pubic hair. Her chocolate-brown breasts were high conical little mountains, the nipples hard dark little rose-buds at the pinnacles.

"Not so badly hung for a white boy," she said around her tongue as she glided to the bed, and so much for playing Mr.

Cool. Bobby had just enough time to tap his touchpoint before she was on him.

As Fara Fay moved over him like a warm brown tide, he felt a wave of energy pouring down his spine from his brain to meet her, a long cool roll of something sure and smiling and rhythmic, like a great snake uncoiling, and as she pulled his head down into a deep open-mouthed kiss, her tongue moving in a pulsing rhythm in and out of his throat, it reached his cock as she did, and he moved it into her hand in sure counterpoint on the afterbeat, confident that the spirit now moving through him would not permit betrayal by the tremulous weakness of the flesh.

He rolled her over and stretched his long lithe body out atop her, fiber by fiber, grabbed her cunt hot and hard, forced her tongue gently back into some intermediate region with his own, then broke off the kiss and, still stroking the quick of her with one hand, propped his head up on the other, and looked down right at her with a smirky little smile.

Fara Fay regarded him with new eyes, mirrors of the new man he saw reflected in them. ''Well, well,'' she said in rather bemused appreciation, her hand stroking him more tentatively now, ''the worm takes a turn.''

''I may be bits and bytes and programs, but baby, I ain't Mr. Clean,'' he told her, tweaking her clitoris playfully.

''Say what?'' Fara Fay's eyes looked past him for a moment at something on the ceiling, rolled in a little flash of ecstasy as he played with her, refocused on his.

''You and me together, we're a rock and roll machine!'' he declared, and thrust himself deep inside her in one long hard stroke, just pinning her there to the water bed with his cock and smiling down at her without moving.

''This is starting to get a little kinky . . .'' Fara Fay observed uncertainly but not without enthusiasm, as if she couldn't decide whether she was intrigued or a little scared and had decided to be both.

He began rolling his hips in short slow strokes, forward on the downbeat, back on the uptake, confidently playing her with his torso propped up on his arms above her, and his eyes staring directly into hers until she just closed her eyes and went with it, answering him with her pelvis, then wrapping her legs around his waist and drawing him in deeper.

He eased down onto her body, slid his hands under her ass,

kneading her into him, buried his face in the nape of her neck, then thrust his tongue into her ear, and began teasing the channel to her brain with it as she moaned, and shrieked, and clawed gently at his back.

For the first time in his life he felt himself really letting go—of fears and expectations, of high school fumblings and Hollywood visions, of memories of fleshy treasons—moving surely and confidently, slipping into a kind of fuck-space, where vision and hearing, smell and touch, him and her, cock and cunt, flesh and awareness, melted together in a synesthetic song.

He had never been here before, and yet it was like coming home to what he knew he always should have been. He could feel her body clinging to the root of him and trembling, and he could feel the waves of pleasure building toward crescendo in his cock, and yet from where he was now, he knew he could fuck like this forever; as long as he kept the beat, he was the maestro, the male soloist and the lead guitar, he was Red Jack, the ghost cocksman in his own wet-dream machine.

She shrieked and moaned and the muscles of her pelvis began to jerk and spasm as she climbed up the wave of an orgasm, but rather than pour himself out into her rhythm, he lagged back tantalizingly on the afterbeat, and let her rise into the curl heartbeats ahead of him, and then, as she crested, he moved into it, a slow, even, long beat that held her there right at the top, coming, and coming, and coming, again and again, thrashing and screaming and clawing.

It finally ended, not with his own exhausted release, but with Fara Fay, panting raggedly, moaning with dessicating soreness, prying him off her, and staring up at him in sated wide-eyed amazement.

And then, when he rolled off her and propped himself up against the headboard with his hands behind his head, a smirky smile, and his dick proudly in the air, she had gobbled him up and given him the most satisfying blow-job of his life, not so much because she was so expert, which she was, nor because it went on for such a long time, which it did, but because it was his first truly *appreciative* blow-job; heartfelt, and admiring, and more than justly earned.

So too the blow-job Cindy What's-Her-Name was giving him now, with his negligent hand wrapped in her long blond hair, and his lidded eyes gazing not at this latest manly conquest, but at his own electronic reflection up on the ceiling video screen.

Red Jack looked down on him approvingly with his own eyes. Since that night with Fara Fay Marley, he hadn't fucked without the Shunt, and he hadn't cut his hair either, and if some part of him knew that he would look quite ludicrous if he dyed it red when it reached his shoulders, another part of him was toying with the notion.

For as he lay there staring up at this electronic amplification of himself and getting abundant head from an actual starlet, it seemed that some circuit of cosmic justice had at last come full circle.

If Red Jack had not come from within him, then from whence had he come? Had he himself not written this software?

Now, flashing on the very same piece of wire by whose power his cyberwizard prowess had brought his dreamtime self into the realtime world, it seemed to him that the dualism between creator and creature, Bobby Rubin and Red Jack, had been annihilated.

Ah yes, he exulted as warm lips oozed up and down his prick, if only those assholes could see me now! All the jocks and hunks and musicians from high school. All the rock stars and actors and beachbum studs who preened at the A parties. If it had been his absorption into the world of bits and bytes and programs which had made him a horny little wimp in the first place, now he had transmogrified himself via those selfsame instrumentalities into an electronically amplified cyberstud.

You and me together, Jack, we're a fuckin' sex machine!

The chirping of the bedside phone brought him tumbling down out of the flash as Cindy paused in her ministrations. Bobby pressed her head gently downward. ''Don't stop now . . .'' he sighed.

The phone kept chirping away. It wouldn't stop. Shit! Who the hell can this be? Cindy let him slip from her lips, looked up with a little moue of annoyance.

Bobby shrugged at her. He reached for the phone. He paused. He gave her a little wink and a leer.

''I'll take care of my business,'' he said, ''you just keep taking care of my business too, okay?''

The blond girl laughed. ''Bet I can make you come while you're still talking,'' she said, and gobbled him up again.

"You're faded," Bobby said, picking up the phone and holding it to his ear.

"*Bobby . . . ?*" said the breathy voice of Sally Genaro on the other end of the line.

"What the hell do you want at this time of night, Sally?" Bobby's voice on the other end of the phone was angry and curt, but there was a sultry undertone to it that purred through the circuits into Sally Genaro's ear.

What do I want, Bobby? she said woozily to herself. I want to *ball* you, you asshole! I want to invite you to come over to my apartment right now so I can lick you all over and give you head till you scream! I want you to be in love with me, or at least like me well enough to once invite me to one of those parties.

But of course she wasn't really drunk enough to say any of that, he knew it all already, and wouldn't even like admit that he knew it, let alone take her up on it.

"Sally . . . ? Are you still there? *You* called *me,* remember?"

Like *do it* already, before he hangs up! Sally told herself angrily.

Sally lay on her bed in her fancy new Studio City condo gazing absently out the sliding balcony windows at the nightscape of the San Fernando Valley glittering and gleaming below her. She wore a gauzy lavender hip-length low-cut nightie that she had bought in an expensive Melrose sleaze shop which pretended to cater to hookers, and the usual wire-mesh hairnet of the Shunt. One hand held the telephone to her ear, and the other was creeping up her own thigh.

She *knew* that she and Bobby had touched for one long magic moment during that session in Glorianna O'Toole's house, for what was "Your Rock and Roll Machine" but their secret love song to each other, and who or what could Red Jack be but the Bobby of their shared dream?

But when it was over, his eyes had turned to that horrid old lady as if he had somehow shared the whole thing with *her,* and he had become even colder to her afterward, he wouldn't even shunt with her in the studio anymore, as if he were *afraid* to share that dream again.

She had tried *everything*. She had spent a *fortune* on dermatology. She had deliberately bought a sexy new wardrobe a size too small and practically *fasted* for ten days till she could squeeze herself into it. He *still* looked right through her as if she didn't exist.

Finally, she even tried to make herself forget about him. Screw you, Bobby Rubin, she had told herself when "Your Rock and Roll Machine" became a big hit. I'm a star now, who needs a nerdy little wimp like you! And she rented herself this bitchin' apartment in the Garden of Babylon, *sure* that living here would change her life.

The condo complex was terraced down a high hillside looking directly across the Hollywood Freeway at the combined studio, amusement park, and resort development that was Universal City. Every apartment had big balconies with a view off both the living room and bedroom. Escalators running up the center of the apartment complex led directly to the fabulous Glitter Dome at the crest.

Everybody knew about the Garden of Babylon. A hundred choice apartments and not a married couple in them. Universal owned half of them and used them to house transients working in films and tv or doing live gigs in Universal City—actors, actresses, directors, singers, dancers, musicians. The other half was occupied by people with the money and desire to cruise this show biz scene, and what they got for the fortune these badly constructed glitz palaces fetched was guaranteed access, along with the show biz crowd, to the exclusive pleasure-palace above.

And while Sally didn't work for Universal, she did work for the Muzik Factory, and she had like *good credits;* she had a number one hit on the charts, so surely she would be a member of the in crowd at the Glitter Dome and meet all kinds of movie stars and rockers.

And if she couldn't quite convince herself even in her fantasies that some movie star or lead singer would fall for the likes of her, then surely, at least, she would attract her fair share of the rich kids, apartment-sharing pretty boys, and back-up talent who were there for the very purpose of screwing important show biz people like herself.

At least she would get laid regularly, at least she wouldn't always be so *horny,* at least she could stop all this *playing with herself* while thinking about Bobby. And maybe she would even meet some bitchin' guy who could make her forget all about the snaky little son of a bitch.

Alas, it had all turned out wrong. Sure, she was a big wheel at the Factory now, but like she hadn't *fronted* anything, nobody outside the inner workings of the Factory knew who she was at all, she wasn't *famous,* and those at the Glitter Dome who were, or thought they were, or wanted to pretend they were, treated her like she didn't exist. And so did the guys who were there to score with the beautiful and famous, for even if they couldn't score with the famous, there were plenty of desperately overextended beautiful women there playing the same game to shove poor pudgy pimply little Sally deep into the woodwork.

So tonight, like so many other nights, she had found herself alone on her bed, thinking of Bobby, and about to plug in and masturbate.

It had become something of a regular ritual. She would curl up with a big box of chocolates, put on her Shunt, as often as not pop "Your Rock and Roll Machine" into her disc deck, hit the touchpoint, and be transported to the only realm where she and Bobby had ever made love, where she tripped the lights fantastic with Red Jack, with the better Bobby she and the Shunt had made, with the dream lover who looked right into her eyes and shared the secrets of her soul.

But tonight something had made her pause between the thought and the act. Perhaps it was because she had heard Bobby was throwing another of those parties to which she was never invited and had drowned her dismay in two long lonely dumb movies, and then gotten more than a little loaded drinking all by herself up in the Glitter Dome before slinking home.

At least if she were going to flash and fuck her finger again, she could try doing it to the real thing.

The only time she ever shunted in Bobby's presence was in the studio, where he did his best to ignore her, where he could see her flabby body and the makeup covering her latest outbreak of pimples and be blinded to the beauty within.

But maybe now, connected only by the telephone audio link, in the wee hours of the night, with the Shunt on her head and her hand on her snatch and him not knowing, the electronic magic could emerge again, could give her the courage to speak from the heart, could make him see and cherish the sweetness of her soul, could recreate the timeless moment they had touched in all her jerk-off dreams.

Sally slid her hand all the way up and clamped it tightly in place between her meaty thighs. With the phone still in her hand, she reached up to hit her touchpoint, then brought it back into position and spoke.

* * *

"I'm still here . . ." Sally Genaro's voice said over the phone.

"Terrific . . ." Bobby drawled as Cindy started toying with his balls and moving her mouth up and down his cock with increasing vigor as he lay there luxuriating in it while listening to the Pimple. Too bad videophones never really got off the ground so you could see this, Sally, he thought. But then, on the other hand, that would mean I would be forced to see *you*.

"So Sally, did you wake me up just to say hello?"

"Were you really asleep?"

"Sure," he drawled in sultry facetiousness, "and I was having a wet dream about you. We were just about to come when you woke me up."

Cindy choked with laughter in mid-stroke. Bobby pushed her head down and thrust deep into her throat. Cindy gave his balls a little tweak.

"*Really* Bobby . . . ?" Sally's voice sighed in breathy excitement. "I like dream about *you* all the time, and not when I'm asleep . . . I mean . . ."

There was a pause, and then the voice came back in a purr. "You know what I'm doing right now . . . ?"

"Why don't you tell me?"

"I've got my hand on my *pussy,* I mean I'm *beating off* while I'm talking to you; we're on my bed looking out the window at the city and we're shunting together, and I can feel your big prick deep inside me. . . ."

"You're *masturbating*?"

Bobby's cock gave a huge involuntary throb. A bolt of lightning seemed to course directly down into it along his spine from his brain even as his stomach rolled over.

Cindy paused at the top of her stroke with just the head of his dick in her mouth, looked up wide-eyed, then snaked a hand between her own legs and went back to work with a redoubled frenzy, bringing herself off as she went down on him.

Too fucking much! Disgusting beyond belief, but what an ego trip! He moaned softly into the phone, hit his touchpoint, and surrendered to the pornographic moment.

"Oooh . . ." moaned the voice on the phone, strangely distant now, syncopated, talking to itself. "Ooh, Bobby, Bobby, it feels so good, don't stop, don't hang up, ooh, ooh, ooh. . . ."

He lay there spread-eagled on a rack of ecstasy by the down

and dirty triad of libido, disgust, and ego. The beautiful Cindy was sucking him toward a roaring explosion, while the voice of Sally from the Valley jerked off over him in his ear, and all the while Red Jack's rock star smile burned in his brain.

"Oh yeah, oh wow, harder! harder!"

Oh yes, this was what it meant to be a star, to be a lead singer up there on the stage in front of ten thousand horny pimply little Sallys, to preen and prance and have the queen of the groupies suck your cock in the dressing room, and lucky to be doing it, too, for out there beyond the footlights twenty thousand fat little thighs rubbed together in a sweaty hot longing for your bod that you could feel, that you could smell, that you could play to, that you could roll yourself around in like a pig in hog heaven, and the more of a swine you made of yourself, the more they loved it, running their hot little hands up their dresses, creaming in their panties with your face in their eyes.

And if there was something loathsome about being the jerk-off fantasy of ten thousand little Pimples you wouldn't touch with a fork, about a moaning voice in your ear like a forest of fat wet little tongues, there was also something vilely wonderful about being a fantasy sex-object for these unwholesome masses, while a favored beauty was permitted to laugh at them and give you head, and be turned on by it all too.

"Ah yes, tell me about it, Sally," Red Jack whispered throatily. "Tell me what it's like to have my great big wonderful dick inside you. . . ."

"Oh Bobby, Bobby . . ." Sally Genaro moaned, wrapping her big strong legs around him as he thrust himself deep, deep inside her, clutching her to him with his long strong arms, smiling down at her with his sultry dark eyes, his long, wild red hair billowing and flashing around his face like this flaming aura as he fucked her.

"Oh God, oh yes, fuck me, fuck me, fuck me," she grunted as he hugged her to him, planting tender little kisses on her nipples, nibbling her earlobes with frenzied little love bites, thrusting deeper and deeper, harder and harder, aching to pour himself into her flesh, into her heart, into the twitching, throbbing void at the core of her being. "I love you, I love you, you're so beautiful, oh Bobby, Bobby, Bobby. . . ."

* * *

"Oh yes, yes, yes . . ." cried the voice in his ear. "I'm coming Bobby, I'm coming, oh, oh, oh, you're wonderful, oh Bobby Bobby Bobby Bobby. . . ."

His cock was a throbbing pillar of fire, it was the fucking Empire State Building, tall and proud and towering above the landscape, a gigantic edifice of power, an enormous rocket poised on the launch pad, twitching and jerking as orgasm screamed electronically in his ear, as Cindy suddenly wedged a hand under his buttocks, thrust a finger into his ass, and his balls exploded, arching his body backward as he came and came and came into her pulsing throat.

His eyes rolled upward in ecstasy and then he came deep within her as she went screaming over the top, oh, she could feel him pouring into her as he planted frantic little kisses on the nape of her neck. "Oh Sally, Sally, Sally, I love you love you love you . . ." he cried as they expired deliciously in each other's arms.

Sweating, panting, Bobby Rubin came out of the flash with his ears ringing and little sparkles of light flickering in his eyes.

Cindy, sated, exhausted, and looking at him most peculiarly, knelt at his feet on the bed while the Pimple's ragged voice babbled on in his ear. "Oh Bobby that was lovely, it was everything I ever imagined it would be. . . ."

Bobby writhed in self-loathing as he looked down at his treacherous dick, pretending limp innocence now, and felt like strangling it. He shuddered. He grimaced as if he were coated in slime.

"You're flashing, aren't you, Sally?" he shouted into the phone. "You fucking sick bitch!" He wanted to choke her, to slug her, to chop her up and shove her down a garbage disposal for making him feel the way he felt now, revealed to himself as a disgusting pervert in the aftermath of a sexual act too loathsome to contemplate.

"Unplug from that goddamn thing, you fucking Pimple!" he screamed in white hot fury, a fury further fueled by the unavoidable knowledge that he had enjoyed it more than anything else in his life.

Cindy had climbed off the bed and was gathering up her clothes.

"What are you doing?" Bobby shouted at her.

Cindy gave him a moue of disgust as she started climbing into them. "Hey, I've been around," she said, "but this shit is getting too weird for me."

"Wait, don't go, I'll get rid of her. . . ."

"Oh no, you just finish your conversation with your crank call, maybe the two of you can jerk off together. . . ."

"Bobby . . . ? Bobby . . . ?" Sally Genaro shouted into the phone. "Have you got *someone there* with you?"

The distant filtered voices at the other end of the phone went on arguing with each other, getting angrier and angrier as she lay there on her bed holding the phone with one hand and wiping the other unthinkingly on her delicate nightgown.

"You enjoyed it too! Admit it!"

"I made it with a dyke once, too, but that doesn't mean I'm bragging about it!"

She had hit her touchpoint when Bobby, snugged in her arms, had asked her to, only to find herself, when she came out of the flash, alone in her room with her hand on her snatch, listening to him talking to some bitch over the phone.

"I'll bet you do this all the time . . ." the angry female voice snapped.

"No, I don't, Cindy," Bobby whined, "this never happened before, and I promise it'll never happen again. Don't go. . . ."

"Caio. Don't call me, and when I'm home and horny, I won't call you. You just don't give very good telephone, Bobby Rubin."

"Cindy—"

The sound of a door slamming.

"Now look what you've done, goddamn you!" Bobby's voice snarled in her ear.

"You had someone there all the time!" Sally snapped back. Oh, it was gross beyond belief. And yet . . .

And yet it really wasn't his fault, was it? He could have just hung up on me. He was being *nice* to you, Sally, she told herself. It was almost kinda sweet. . . .

"It's all right, I'm sorry I yelled at you, Bobby," she said placatingly, "it's not your—"

"All right! *What's* all right, you sick little pimple! What fucking right do you have to call me up and make me listen to you jerking off over me, you fat little creep! It makes me puke just to know you bring yourself off over me!"

Tears of rage and mortification filled Sally's eyes. "You

enjoyed it too, Bobby Rubin, I heard you come!" she whined. "If you didn't, why didn't you just hang up!"

There was a long silence at the other end of the phone. Bobby's voice, when he spoke again, was cold, and hard, and insinuating.

"You *really* want to know why I didn't hang up, Sally?"

Sally somehow knew that this was going to be the last thing in the world she wanted to hear, but found herself unable to say anything to stop it.

"Because I had a girl here the whole time sucking my prick," Bobby hissed viciously. "And it turned her on. Thanks a lot for getting me a better blow-job. Sweet dreams, Sally."

And he hung up.

"Fuck you, you wimpy little bastard!" Sally shouted into the dead phone.

She dropped it on the bed and lay there crying, looking out at the lights of the Valley through a mist of tears, until she finally dropped off into tormented fitful sleep.

MÉNAGES
À TROIS

Glorianna O'Toole glared at Bobby Rubin. She glared at Sally Genaro. They glared back at her individually. But the two of them refused to look at each other.

It had been like this since they had both turned up late for work at the studio. Bobby showed up first and announced that he would no longer work with Sally. Before Glorianna could ask why, Sally arrived, saw Bobby, looked away, and told her she would no longer work with Bobby.

"There's enough shit coming down on my poor old head without this," Glorianna told them. "I don't want to hear it. The pinheads upstairs have given us a deadline, a title, a set of specs, and some lyrics from the songhacks. We've got ten weeks to finish a master, and that's the bottom line."

She handed sheaves of printout to both of them. "So read this garbage and let's get our asses in gear."

Sally leaned against her VoxBox with the printout hanging limply in her hand. Bobby stood before his image organ rig holding the fucking thing with his arms folded across his chest.

"You want to tell me what this is all about?" Glorianna finally said.

Bobby and Sally stole nasty sidelong glances at each other, but refused to open their mouths.

Glorianna sighed. She seated herself on her high stool of producer authority. "Okay, so don't tell me," she said. "But *I'm* telling *you* Carlo fucking Manning will show no mercy to me or to you two. You're under long-term contracts for fat salaries, remember? And Muzik, Inc., has big bucks riding on this. If you refuse to work together on 'The Crown Prince of Rock and

Roll,' he'll not only can you, he'll sue you for breach of contract, and win, lose, or draw, like the old song says, you'll never work in this town again."

Sally simply pouted. Some dim comprehension began to come into Bobby's eyes, and his expression softened somewhat. "And what'll happen to you, Glorianna?" he said.

"At least I won't starve," Glorianna said dryly. "I'm guaranteed free room and board for the rest of my life. In the joint."

Bobby goggled. Sally collapsed onto the seat before her VoxBox. "How—?"

"Don't ask," Glorianna said. "Just get it through your heads that we're all in this leaky boat together and anyone who thinks they can swim away from it gets eaten by the sharks. We have no choice, believe me, that *is* the bottom line, kiddies!"

Bobby locked eyes with her, then shrugged resignedly. "I guess you're right," he mumbled. "I really can't let them throw you in jail, so I'm willing to hold my nose and get the job done for your sake, Glorianna. . . ."

"You're just concerned with saving your *own* ass, Bobby Rubin!" Sally cried angrily.

"Yeah, well you can *kiss* my ass, Sally from the Valley, you'd love to anyway, wouldn't you?"

Sally's face flushed red under her heavy makeup, and her hands balled into fists. What the fuck is this? Glorianna wondered.

"Stop this shit!" she roared, deciding she really didn't give much of a damn. "What about it, Sally, you want to be a pro about this, or you want to end up in the great army of the permanently unemployed? It's no crime to save your own ass, considering the alternative."

"Well . . . when you like put it *that* way . . ." Sally muttered unhappily. "But you tell *him* I'm not even gonna talk to him."

"And you tell *her* that I'm holding her to her promise."

"Consider each other told," Glorianna moaned. "Now, will you please read over these specs and lyrics so we can finally get down to work?"

Chairs turned back to back, their consoles barricaded between them, Bobby Rubin and Sally Genaro buried their snotty little noses in the printouts.

Marvelous, just fucking marvelous, Glorianna thought as she waited for them to finish. And they haven't even read this crap yet.

But she had.

Not only had the songhacks provided lyrics, the research department had sent down a script that reminded her of the singing commercials she had done when she was really down on her luck. Of course on a less diabolical level, that's what most of the Factory material was—commercials to play on MUZIK designed to sell the disc of themselves.

But "The Crown Prince of Rock and Roll," as conceived by research and marketing, was a new perversion. The idea was to take a product that was already becoming a fad and use *it* to sell *the song*.

Red Jack was not to mention the product in question by name, nor could he venture to clearly advocate the use of a piece of wire; the FCC or the FBI or the DEA or the IRS or the KGB or some other three-letter agency would be sure to display the government's extreme displeasure with anything as overt as that.

Instead, the cut was to be a wirehead cocktease, like a movie flirting with the very outer edge of its R rating. Research had worked out a whole image-system revolving around the Zap without quite mentioning it, and marketing had hit on a real cute device. Throughout the song, the audience identification figures would all have Red Jack's shoulder-length flag-red hair, frosted, of course, with the white pinstriping emblematic of the Shunt.

And the lyrics all danced around the central subject leeringly, the way fifties rock smirked and pranced around fucking, the way early sixties rock minced around dope, the way eighties heavy metal cashed in on the trendiness of the devil.

Bobby Rubin dropped his printout on the floor with a gingerly gesture like someone dropping a rotting fish into the garbage can by the tail. "This sucks," he observed. "Where do these assholes come off telling me how to lay down a visual track? What do they know about putting images to music?"

"Jack shit," Glorianna admitted.

"These lyrics are like *dumb*," Sally Genaro whined. "How do they expect me to turn this dead-ass crud into a song?"

"For money."

The two of them sat there regarding Glorianna with newborn sour wisdom. Bobby slowly, resignedly, picked up his printouts from the floor, shaking his head. "I never thought I'd hear *you* say that, Glorianna," he muttered.

"Well then let's just like *get it over with*," Sally said. "The sooner I never have to see this wimpy little shit again, the better!"

And she plunked the lyrics down on her easel, put on a pair of cans, plugged them in, starting doodling with her keyboard, and disappeared into the private world of her own music, listening to what she was doing only on the earphones, filling the studio with the sounds of silence.

"I've got a fucking *script,* haven't I?" Bobby snarled. "No reason I can't slap some shit together fast enough to get out of here before that fat little Pimple unplugs herself from her dream machine." And he began booting up his equipment.

And there Glorianna's two little darlings sat, zoned into their equipment, totally ignoring each other, and apparently determined to hack out something as quickly as possible just to get out of each other's sight.

No doubt they could give the pinheads upstairs what they wanted well under deadline running on this putrid energy. But Glorianna was now even more determined to give the bastards what they *deserved.*

It reminded her of a mess she herself had once created long, long ago, when she was fronting a quite forgettable band called Hard Candy. She had been having a thing with the lead guitarist which cooled, and she had then been cunt enough to immediately take up with the keyboard player. The first night they had to perform together under this new configuration, she had to break up a fistfight between the two of them backstage just before they went on. And the vibes onstage had been so poisonous that spiders dropped dead in their tracks all the way to the back of the balcony.

Glorianna smiled to herself wolfishly, remembering. For Hard Candy had been *great* that night, better than they had any right to be, touching a crazed peak of energy they had never hit before and never hit again.

Oh no, this was not going to be fun, but that didn't mean that what she squeezed out the other end of *this* sleazy little psychodrama couldn't also be real rock and roll.

But after two weeks of tense boredom in the studio, Glorianna was starting to wonder. For this was a horror show quite unlike anything she had been prepared for, and she had sung studio back-up with plenty of bands whose members hated each other.

Hatred, after all, had its creative uses; more than once she had seen a good producer extract stunning tracks by pitting enemies against each other musically. But here even that seemed impossible, for Bobby Rubin and Sally Genaro could hardly even be said to be on the same planet.

Day after day, Sally sat there playing into her own earphones, unwilling to even look at Bobby's visual tracks on her monitor, while Bobby, for his part, laid down his stuff without even asking to hear any music. Only Glorianna knew what both of them were doing, only she had a binocular vision of how dreadful it all was, and all she could do, at least at this stage, was sit back on her stool, fend off inquiries by the pinheads upstairs, and become more and more paranoid.

Got you by the nose and you wanna fight back
Tap yourself a hit of old Red Jack
Don't know what to do when you're out there all alone
Your dreamtime daddy gonna take you back home. . . .

On and on the lyrics from the songhacks went like this; verse after verse, chorus after chorus, of the same beat pattern, the same rhyme structure, so you could cut it to order like so much yard goods.

On and on and on went the instrumental tracks that Sally laid down; the monotonous, relentless, ancient Bo Diddley riff implied by the lyrics rolling along through percussion, and bassline, and even lead, like a speedfreak rock and roll robot.

It was tv commercial music all right; nostalgic, repetitive, and hypnotic, the kind of stuff that could keep you mesmerized for just about the required one hundred twenty seconds before it drove you crazy.

The vocal track wasn't any better. It was Red Jack's infinitely flexible hyperhuman voice all right—as long as Sally sang through the voiceprint parameters already in memory there was no way of blowing that—but it sounded like a demo for the wizard equipment, not rock and roll, aggressively dead-ass and defiantly mechanical.

Bobby Rubin, meanwhile, was following the specs sent down by research and marketing to the letter and not a creative centimeter beyond, as if he were deliberately coming as close as he could to parodying the script by being scrupulously faithful to the spirit of the pinheads who had written it.

The specs decreed that Red Jack be seen performing in locales identifiable with the top ten major markets, so Bobby dutifully danced him across cliché footage of the Golden Gate Bridge, the

Hollywood sign, the New York skyline, Bourbon Street, dredged up from old tv commercials.

The demographics called for chorus lines and background audiences composed of seventy percent clean-cut young middle class trendies and thirty percent obvious wireheads, so Bobby laid in animated figures from fashion magazines and news footage of grimy New York streeties, and while Glorianna was not about to do a head count, she was willing to bet her ass that the proportion would come out right on the numbers plus or minus five percent.

The pinheads upstairs wanted visual emphasis put on key words alluding to the Zap, so every time a word like "flashing," "dancing," "tap," or "dream" appeared in the lyric sequence, the webwork frosting in Red Jack's hair flashed like neon pinstriping.

As for the choreography, Red Jack and his window dressing made their moves like something out of an old Busby Berkley musical, which is to say with the same smooth musical comedy precision used to sell toilet paper or greaseburgers. And of course since Bobby hadn't even listened to Sally's music, it had about the same relation to same as Ronald McDonald had to Meatloaf.

By the Monday of the third week, there was more than enough of this Muzik to make half an hour of cuts, at least in terms of the amount of disc space that had been desecrated, and Glorianna finally decided that it was time to rub their faces in the awfulness of what they had wrought.

She had Bobby slave his visual track to Sally's sequencer, so that when she played back her rough mix, Red Jack more or less mouthed Sally's vocal track and his dance movements were mechanically synced to the monotonous rhythm line.

Since the music and the visuals had been laid down without any reference to each other, the result was like some jerky Fred Astaire robot off a Bavarian cuckoo-clock badly lip-syncing James Brown while dancing spastic show-tune breaks to Twisted Sister.

"Bites the Big One, doesn't it?" Glorianna said when the ordeal was over.

Bobby stared thoughtfully at his main monitor. "No problem," he said dully. "Easy enough to refine the animation. And of course the lip-sync program is just running off basic phoneme parameters at this point."

"I can lay in some weird electronic chord overlays where Red Jack does those stupid Shunt flashes," Sally snapped back. "Real loud and thick, and with super- and sub-sonics that'll make anyone's head ring like it was just plugged in."

"Great," Glorianna sighed. "Then we'll have *slick* dead-ass horseshit instead of *crude* dead-ass horseshit."

Bobby Rubin and Sally Genaro, while still doggedly refusing to look each other in the eye, gave her identical sullen stares from behind their equipment that under other circumstances might have seemed telepathic.

"I can clean up the visuals tracks fast enough to get my ass out of here by Friday . . ." Bobby said belligerently.

"Yeah, well *I'll* finish the music by like *Wednesday,* and that still won't be soon enough for me. . . ."

Glorianna slid off her stool and confronted them for this one on her feet. "You *really* think I'm going to even *show* this crap to the pinheads upstairs?" she demanded.

"They can't complain," Bobby said with insolent mock innocence. "I've followed their specs right down the line, now haven't I?"

"And my music's better than *his* stupid visuals or their dumb lyrics even deserve," Sally whined. "They can't come down on us for giving them just what they asked for, and six weeks under deadline too."

"Fucking hell!" Glorianna roared. "You think this is some high school homework assignment? What Manning wants is something that will ship ten million copies! This shit would be lucky to ship ten *thousand*! We are going to work on this thing until *I* say it's right! And from here on in, we are going to work on it together, whether you two little prima donnas feel like talking to each other or not!"

The two of them cringed under this assault, Sally withdrawing into herself, Bobby looking rather wounded.

Glorianna shook her head as she walked over to the filing cabinet where the Shunts were secreted under "W." "Let's lighten up, shall we?" she said in a much more conciliatory tone as she got out two of them and held them up invitingly. "Maybe a little dose of Red Jack's own electronic medicine will get you two over the hump."

Bobby started backward as if she had offered him a horse needle full of heroin. "No way!" he cried. Sally just stared woodenly at the Shunts and shook her head almost sadly. Were those *tears* in her eyes?

Bobby's reluctance to Shunt in the studio with Sally was no news to Glorianna, but until this new level of mutual loathing had been achieved, Sally had been plugging in in the studio all the time.

"Come on, Sally," Glorianna cooed, approaching her console and dropping a Shunt in her lap, "won't *you* at least give it a try?"

"Not with *him* here!" Sally snapped. For some weird reason, she seemed to be blushing.

"It would seem we have reached an impasse," Glorianna said.

"That's right!"

"For sure!"

Glorianna sighed. She fingered the breadbox of the remaining Shunt in her hand, rubbing it like a worry stone. What now? she thought. Maybe they were right. Maybe the only thing to do was to clean this thing up as much as possible and present it to Carlo Manning as the best he was going to get under the circumstances. . . .

After all, it *did* fulfill the specs sent down by research and marketing, and there sure as shit wasn't anyone left upstairs with any real musical judgment, so they'd gear up their marketing campaign, pump out a few million copies, and when the returns came pouring back, she could just point an innocent finger at the assholes in marketing. . . .

Glorianna frowned. *Sure* she could. And Mount Everest was covered with designer dust! Pumping marketing dollars into a disc on a megahit budget and getting back a disaster would be more than enough to get Manning canned, and the wormy little bastard had made it quite clear that in such an eventuality, he would get her ass thrown in the joint on the way out.

Besides, she had her own asses to kick with this thing, and if she had to go out defeated, she was not about to go gently, just because two little cyberwizards refused to talk to each other.

She shrugged, put on the Shunt, and smoothed the breadbox into place at the back of her skull. "If little children no longer have the guts to lead us," she said, "then I guess it's up to Crazy Old Ladies."

"What are you going to do?" Bobby asked slowly.

"Commune with the spirits and see if I can persuade them to

help me spin this straw into gold,'' she told him. ''And what you two are going to do is run these tracks and make every change I tell you to.'' She sneered at them contemptuously. ''*That* shouldn't be beyond your powers, should it?'' she drawled. ''You've had plenty of practice taking orders from bigger assholes than me already.''

And, drawing her stool up to a monitor where she wouldn't have to see either of them, she sat down and hit her touchpoint.

Ain't got no body
Ain't got no soul. . . .

''No shit, Jack?'' Glorianna muttered as Red Jack's face appeared before her, singing through badly synced lips in an echoing sci-fi film voice to an incongruous Bo Diddley beat.

But I'm your Prince of Rock and Roll!

''Not yet you ain't, love, but you and me, Jack, we're gonna get there,'' she promised him.

''Stop the disc and take notes,'' she ordered her unseen elves. ''I want a wee sad baby voice on the first two bars whispering it to a heavy metal beat, not this razzmatazz, and on the third I want to blow their ears off with your best multiplexed effects kickin' out the jams, and *that's* where you give 'em a happy little Bo Diddley bounce. And right where the music changes, I want out of this close-up and into Red Jack dropping down from a helicopter onto the stage in some giant rock festival footage with lots of little girls creamin' in their pants.''

The playback continued. Soon enough, Glorianna no longer saw whatever it was that Bobby had thrown together except as blocks of time, and she no longer followed Sally Genaro's music except for the lyrics and the beat.

''Awful! Horseshit! I want to see the scum of the earth shuffling around like zombies and plugged into the Blue Max; I want headache music.''

She picked up a mike and began inputting through the voice-print parameters, phrasing Red Jack's voice with her own pipes, and ringing her own changes on the lyrics from the pinheads upstairs.

Been down so long that you're ready to scream
Took my music then they took my dream
But I'm inside you when you're ready to fight
Flash your freedom in the broad daylight. . . .

It was passingly strange hearing herself singing through Red Jack's hyper-real voice. The carrot they had held out all along was her own cyborged comeback, and now here it was!

Bobby had personalized the lip-sync program to her input, the phrasing coming out of Red Jack's mouth, the very motions of his lips and throat were hers, so what difference did it make whether the cartoon avatar on the screen was the Crown Prince or the Crazy Lady, the spirit was hers, and it was beginning to really sound like Rock and Roll.

"Try following me with the changes in realtime," Glorianna said, picking up the mike again. "Two instrumental leads, synthetic shit for the cyberkids, max metal guitar for the wireheads. A street with computers and cyberkiddies on one side, wireheads on the other, Jack dancing down the middle, then he leads 'em up the street toward give-me-something-real-good. . . ."

She found herself really cookin', really getting into it, as she began to sing Red Jack's voice again; the spirit she was seeking to summon singing through her even as she sang through him, the world they danced through transformed by her commands like a lucid dream.

See, Jack, just like I promised, here we are!

Be my body
And I'll be your soul
Crown yourself the Prince of Rock and Roll. . . .

A curtain dissolved, an interface shattered like a soap-bubble film of space-time, and there they were indeed, dancing together hand in hand down the schizoid street, the Crazy Lady and the Crown Prince of Rock and Roll, leading the electronic incarnation of its timeless Children's Crusade.

Nose to the grindstone or balls to the wall!
Gotcha either way before you learn to crawl!

Right, you want market-bridging demographics, we'll give ya market-bridging demographics! Miserable computer nerds wage-slaving away at their bits and bytes in black and white, burnt-out wireheads and starving streeties crawling through the ruins in cockroach brown!

Whether she was thinking this or saying it, where the changes on the songhack lyrics were coming from, didn't matter at all.

For this was the dreamtime, and she was young and strong within it with Red Jack dancing at her side and tossing his own discs as they sang their time-and-program-warped duet to the wirehead zombies and rag-bag streeties, and the words and music emerged from that mysterious yet familiar place within them both where the heart of rock and roll had never stopped beating.

Boot me up and boogie when you wanna fight back
Tap yourself a hit of old Red Jack. . . .

Yeah, pop this song into your computers, kiddies, and on *Tap* you all flash red hair and the computers go off like Las Vegas slot machines, flashing, and ringing, and spitting out discs and money and sparks and fuckin' flying saucers!

Now streeties flash Red Jack hair in the ruins, yeah, that's right, eyes on fire, long hair flowin', and we dance through the ruins with them toward the glitzy downtown on the horizon. . . .

Yeah, department stores and fancy shops, glass towers and marble banks and let's have the cyberkiddies pouring out of them with their Red Jack hair too, throwing discs to the crowd like Frisbees. . . .

All together now, boys and girls, in the fuckin' voice of the pissed-off people!

Crown yourself on the garbage heap
Wake your soul from its starving sleep
Up against the wall with the money machine
You got the power but we tap the Dream. . . .

Just Red Jack, full-figure, with the mob scene matted in on his clothing, and fuck it, why not, a great big American flag waving in the background with the white stripes flashing, and let's have a little fife and drum in the instrumental mix, whose fuckin' country is it, anyway!

Flashin' dancin' like liberty
In the home of the brave and the land of the free
Tap your fingers, let me zap your soul
We're all the Crown Prince of Rock and Roll!

"Damn it, Glorianna, that's the best I'm gonna be able to do," Bobby Rubin snapped irritably after the playback of, what was it, the *fifteenth* remix and re-edit of "The Crown Prince of Rock and Roll." "Any more screwing around is just going to make it go downhill. I can't even stand to *watch* the fucking thing anymore!"

Of course while it was certainly true that five weeks of endless tinkering with the fine detail of the visual track *was* getting on his nerves, and while he really *did* honestly believe that he had long since reached the point where he was incapable of improving anything, it was more true, as he could hardly deny to himself, that being closeted in the same studio with the Pimple for eight hours a day and more was what he *really* couldn't stand anymore.

Not that the *first* three weeks on this thing hadn't been agony enough! But then, at least, he had been able to zone himself into his image organ and ignore Sally from the Valley; she wasn't talking to him, he wasn't talking to her, he could almost avoid even seeing her, and Glorianna had let it be.

But after that weird session when Glorianna had plugged in, started singing and barking orders like a drill sergeant, and manifested the rough-cut, things had gotten much, much worse.

For once the rough-cut had been disced, these last weeks had been a matter of adding verses and bits of footage, tinkering with the music, altering the instrumentation, playing with Jack's animation and voiceprint parameters, fooling with the imagery, and coordinating it all bar by bar, sometimes even note by note, over, and over, and over again.

And that, unavoidably, meant working *with* the Pimple, arguing points of musical and visual synergy almost frame by frame with the fat little cunt, while the best that Glorianna even tried to do, like a wrestling match referee, was keep them from using obvious chokeholds.

To turn the screw that much tighter, Bobby's love life had turned into a nightmare, and it was all the Pimple's fault. When he plugged into the Shunt in bed with a tasty lady, there was fat little Sally looking over his shoulder and bringing herself off in sweaty grunts, and when he tried it au natural, he couldn't get it up, or he couldn't keep it up, or he came too fast, or he couldn't come at all.

By now he had convinced himself that either way he could not untie the knot in his pecker as long as he was constrained to spend eight hours a day in the vile presence of Sally from the Valley. He hadn't thrown one of his parties in two weeks. He hadn't even *tried* to get laid in ten days.

He had resigned himself to the necessity of remaining celibate until he was released from this durance vile.

And he was determined that that was going to happen *now*.

"I mean it, Glorianna," he said. "Enough is enough! This is driving me crazy! And if I'm crazy, I can't improve my tracks any further, now, can I?"

"Come on, Bobby, it's almost right," Glorianna cooed at him, "give me another week tops, and it'll be perfect."

"Another *day* tops, and I'll be a basket case," Bobby snapped, rising from his seat and glaring at Glorianna, who sat on her stool confronting him at eye-level now. "It's good enough! The pinheads upstairs will love it! What do you want, blood?"

"I'll settle for some professionalism," Glorianna told him evenly.

"Yeah, Bobby," the Pimple chimed in, "don't be such a—"

"No one's talking to *you,* you fucking pimple, so shut your fat face!" Bobby screamed in white-hot rage, losing all control. "It's all your goddam fault anyway!"

"*My* fault, like what did *I* do, you wimpy little creep!" Sally Genaro whined in her horrid nasal voice, bolting to her feet, placing her pudgy little hands on her fat sloppy hips, and glowering at him nose to nose. "*You're* the one who's been such a picky little prick!"

"Oh yeah?" Bobby shouted at her, grabbing at his crotch. "You'd just love to *suck* my picky little prick, wouldn't you?"

"Jesus Christ, stop this stupid shit!" Glorianna cried, sliding off her stool and standing between them. "What the hell's gotten into you two?"

"It's what's *not* gotten into this sick little bitch!" Bobby snapped. "Like my *dick,* isn't that right, Sally from the Valley?"

A great bubble of nausea blossomed in Sally Genaro's stomach, and all the fight went out of her as Bobby's face grew cruel and hard.

"You *really* want to know what this is all about, Glorianna?" he oozed vindictively.

"Now that you—"

"*Please*, Bobby!" Sally pleaded, writhing and sweating.

But Bobby Rubin was merciless now, she saw. The little bastard was like *enjoying* this.

"Couple months ago, late at night, this sick little bitch gets wired up and calls me, and you know what she tells me. . . ."

"Don't, Bobby, oh please, please don't!" Tears welled up in Sally's eyes, her hands balled into fists, and her bowels spasmed. How can you be such a monster, Bobby Rubin? How could you *do* such a thing?

"She tells me that she's got her pudgy little hand up her fat cunt and she's *beating off* over me! I had to listen to her grunting and coming over the telephone!"

Glorianna's eyes bugged. Her jaw fell. She looked from Bobby to Sally, and her mouth twisted with loathing. Sally stared down at her feet, unable to face either of them, and began sobbing uncontrollably.

"*Now* do you understand why I can't stand to be in the same room with this fucking fat pimple? *Now* do you understand why I won't work with the bitch for another moment? *Now* do you understand why I'm going fucking nuts? *Now* do you understand why I'm not about to set foot in this studio with her again?"

"Jesus—"

"You're an animal, Bobby Rubin!" Sally screamed through her sobs. "I hate you, I hate you, I hate you!"

"Yeah, well, you're a *vegetable,* Sally from the Valley, you're a fat purple *eggplant*!" Bobby shouted back. "Go fuck yourself! Nobody else will!"

And, throwing up his hands, he stormed out the door.

EL TIEMPO RICO

Paco Monaco scanned the black couple for a long moment, making them sweat a little for appearance sake before he let them in. Chingada, blacks sure looked weird with long red hair, especially this guy, who had it done up in wild-looking dreadlocks.

In the end, he nodded them inside, of course. He had never seen them at Slimy Mary's before, but he had never bounced no Rojos either, even ones who only showed el Pelo.

Not that it was always so easy to tell who was really jacked and who was just wearing the hair. The guy with the dreads was jacked for sure; no way you could really frost dreadlocks to camouflage the wire hairnet right. But the muchacha with him, on her it was hard to tell. Her red hair was thick and straight, and the spiderweb frosting was silvery white just like the Jack wires and real finely defined, and there was enough of it to hide *two* Jacks in there.

But maybe she *wasn't* jacked, maybe the guy was taking her inside to score, she was sorta dressed like a streetie, but her clothes looked a little wrong, as if she had lots of 'em and had put on her worst to blend in down here.

Quién sabé? Even in the fancy meatracks, the going price had dropped to $200 but there were always some cheap-ass gordos and chocharicas willing to come to shitholes like Slimy Mary's or even score from street dealers just to save a few bucks.

Dojo was selling Jack inside for $175, less than what the things had cost *him* when he bought all those cartons of 'em way back when, and the stuff he still had was moving so slow he was starting to mutter about dropping it to $150, the bottom street price, just to unload the rest of 'em.

Paco sighed wistfully. One thing for sure, El Tiempo Rico was gone, no way for him to make money dealing the Jack anymore, not with street dealers selling it for less than Dojo's price to him, which was why he was standing here in the fuckin' melting March slush instead of flashing in The American Dream with Karen.

El Tiempo Rico, verdad, sitting there at the bar sipping rum and Coke, listening to the music, flashing on the action, and dealing Jack for Dojo while his momacita dealt her bedbug discs. And when they were through for the night, they'd go to a fuckin' *restaurant* somewhere before they went back to the loft and crawled into bed.

Paco had never even dreamed of making hundreds of dollars a week before and never did understand how much and how little it could buy before El Tiempo Rico evaporated.

It could buy as much real food in restaurants as he could stuff himself with, many changes of real clothes, as much liquor as he could hold, as much designer dust as he could manage to shove up his nose. But it was nowhere near enough to buy him a share in a co-op.

So while it was enough to make him a rich *streetie,* it wasn't enough to turn him into a Blankriqueno, to get him a room in a Zone somewhere, to have the fuckin' zonies working for him, not against him, to cross the line between the sombre and the sol.

And so, thinking El Tiempo Rico would never end, he managed to piss most of his dinero away more or less as fast as it came in, so that when the bottom fell out, all that he had left to show for it was about $2000 and a lot of fancy clothes stashed in Karen's room at the loft.

Still, he told himself, things could be a lot worse, chingada; they had *been* a lot worse, not so long ago, before he ever even heard of the Zap.

At least when the bottom fell out Dojo had given him this job back and continued to buy bedbug discs from him, so he was still making more money than when he was eating fuckin' kibble full-time. The RLF hadn't thrown him out of the loft, and Karen hadn't thrown him out of her bed, so if this was no longer El Tiempo Rico, at least he wasn't back to sleeping in the ruins and doing cheap crash and grabs either.

Better to remember El Tiempo Rico as just a primo flash, a golden dream that had just been passing through.

It had built slowly at first, starting with his very first sale in The American Dream, one Zap to one bombed-out old chocharica. Two days before he sold his second. Five more days before he sold two on the same night.

But then . . .

One night, Fritz, the big blond doorman, took him aside as he and Karen were entering The American Dream. "Hey, Paco," he said confidentially, "I hear you got the Zap. . . ."

"Quién? Qué?"

"The Zap," Fritz said, tugging at his own short blond hair. "You know . . . I hear you're dealing the Zap. . . ."

Paco studied the big doorman's face narrowly. Fritz wasn't exactly his amigo, but he *had* put him on the permanent freebie list. "What if I am?" he said carefully.

"How much?"

"What's it to you?"

"Shit, I gotta draw ya a picture?" Fritz said, rolling his eyes skyward. "I'm lookin' to *score*."

"Oh," Paco said, mightily relieved. "They go for four hundred." No use trying to bullshit Fritz, he'd know if he got burned muy pronto. In fact, he thought as he reached inside his street bag and palmed a Zap, best to make him a special deal.

"Tell you what, though, amigo," he said as he slipped it to the doorman, "I'll let *you* have this one for three hundred; that's my cost, I ain't making a dime."

Fritz stuffed the Zap into a trench-coat pocket, pulled out a fat roll of bills, started peeling off twenties, and eyed Paco suspiciously. "Why you being so generous?" he demanded.

" 'Cause maybe we can do each other some good, Fritz."

Fritz handed over the money, cocked an eyebrow.

"You get people sniffing after the Zap?"

Fritz nodded. "Dust's starting to go out of style."

"Send 'em my way, and I'll give you twenty off every one I sell," Paco told him.

Fritz eyed him dubiously. "How do I know you'll give me an honest count?"

"If I wasn't being straight with you, I coulda asked you for four hundred and you woulda given it to me, no?" Paco pointed out. "Besides, what you got to lose? Everytime you say 'go see Paco' you make twenty bucks for ten seconds' work, verdad? And *I* gotta trust *you* to do it, don't I?"

"Well, yeah, I guess so . . ." Fritz said slowly. He smiled.

"Yeah!" he exclaimed, and slapped Paco's palm to seal the deal.

And with that brotherly slap, El Tiempo Rico truly began.

Before then, Karen had been getting most of the action with her bedbug discs, and Paco just lay back at the bar, sipping drinks, plugged in, dealing an occasional Zap, and amusing himself by running ominous Mucho Muchacho on her gordo customers.

MUZIK was running the shit out of "Your Rock and Roll Machine," and as it zoomed up the charts, so did Karen's merchandise. By the time it hit number one, they were asking her for *Red Jack* discs instead of "bedbugs."

By the time Paco made his deal with Fritz, Karen was sometimes moving a dozen a night, taking in *thousands,* though who really gave a shit, seeing as how all the dinero went straight to the Reality Liberation Front, whatever the fuck Larry Coopersmith ended up doing with it, and neither of them ever got to enjoy spending any of it.

But then, about ten days after he made his little deal with the doorman, they started playing a *new* Red Jack song over and over and over again on MUZIK, and the lousy $100 he had invested in greasing Fritz began to pay off bigger than he could have ever expected.

Paco had been in Slimy Mary's the first time they played "Crown Prince," in Dojo's room delivering Red Jack discs, so all he saw was the end of the song as he was making tracks to the exit.

For a moment it was hard to tell where the other side of the video screen began and Slimy Mary's ended.

On the dance floor, the usual collection of streeties was twitching to a bouncier than usual max metal beat, and on the screen, a larger collection of streeties, and even more burned out by the looks of them, danced to the same music in the ruins of a burnt-out building that might have been the one outside across the street.

But their hair was long and bright red, just like Red Jack's, complete with silvery Zap nets flashing like spiderwebs of white lightnings, and their eyes were lit up like they had stuck their noses in light sockets, and sparks shot out of their fingertips.

Not many of the wireheads in Slimy Mary's could afford their own Zap at $400 a pop, but most of them had chipped at it for $40 a half hour, and even those who continued to dance without missing a beat stared in amazement at what MUZIK was putting up there on the screen—a fuckin' commercial for their favorite piece of wire, starring streeties who looked just like their own grungy selves.

From the twilight zone around the dance floor, from the deepest shadowy back regions of Slimy Mary's, burnt-out wireheads were shambling into the strobing light to join in the dance, staring into the screen as they twitched and jerked shakily to the beat like spaced-out zombies.

When it was over, most of the people in Slimy Mary's stood on the dance floor staring up at the screen. A strange low growl seemed to echo in the long moment of silence, a growl that Paco felt in his bones and his guts. Then MUZIK started running another cut, and the wireheads shuffled back into the darkness.

Paco hadn't even paid any attention to the words then, but he had left Slimy Mary's popping his fingers to the music with the certainty that something important had happened.

And over the next few days something started to happen in The American Dream, too, something that began to take on the golden dinero glow of El Tiempo Rico.

Gordos and chocharicas and plushie-tushies started oozing up to Paco and asking for "Jack" in slimy whispers; two, three, four, sometimes five a night, and they'd pay him just about any price he cared to name.

At first, he didn't connect it up with the song at all, even though they were playing "Crown Prince" over and over and over again. With the action so hot and heavy, he stayed rooted on his barstool next to Karen to keep himself conspicuously available and gave his deal with Fritz all the credit for his change in fortune. Down here in the bar, all you saw of the dance floor was a long, low slice framed by the low overhang. You heard the music, but it faded into the background of your attention.

"Will you look at that!" Karen exclaimed, tugging at his elbow. "Just like in the song!"

Paco put his rum and Coke down on the bar and turned on his stool. Karen was staring out onto the dance floor.

Ain't got no body
Ain't got no soul . . .
But I'm your Prince of Rock and Roll

They were playing "Crown Prince" yet again. Spotlights from on high were moving around the crowded dance floor like prison searchlights sniffing after escaping convicts. And everyone upon whom the spotlight lingered had bright red shoulder-length hair veined with a silver spiderweb tracery.

Some of them seemed to have frosted this emblem of the Zap onto their hair. But others were people Paco recognized, people who had scored from him, people whose heads openly displayed the real thing.

Paco's feet were already moving to the beat as he slid off his stool, and popping into the forefront of his mind as the spotlights picked it out of the shadows for him was the revelation of what he now realized he should have seen all along—that "Crown Prince," the song that he had been hearing over and over again as background music, was what was making his pieces move.

He grinned at Karen. He laughed. "Fuckin' MUZIK's been playing a free tv commercial for my wire!" he exclaimed in delight.

Ain't got no body
Ain't got no soul . . .
But I'm your Prince of Rock and Roll

"I'll fuckin' dance to *that*!" Paco said, dragging Karen toward the dance floor with one hand, and reaching for his touchpoint with the other. "Let's dance to the music of mucho mas dinero!"

And with a hit of the Jack, he danced into the maelstrom of some gigantic old-fashioned rock festival, for the pit of The American Dream was wall-to-wall dancers, and the three huge screens tiered up grandstands of screaming audience, and he couldn't tell where the dance floor ended and the video dream began.

With a whirl of rotors and a mighty helicopter roar, Red Jack danced out of the sky and onto the stage, his long red hair tossing and flashing, his dark eyes sharing secret communal knowledge.

"Saludo amigo," Mucho Muchacho told Red Jack as they danced their bad-ass stompada, "you and me, compadre, we're dealing the same shit!"

And then, as if to say, we *come* from the same shit, muchacho, he was back in Slimy Mary's, or some other roach-infested rathole in the ruins, where brain-burned wireheads staggered around in the rank darkness, where a screaming max metal guitar burned like a hot wire in his brain.

Been down so long that you're ready to scream
Took my music then they took your dream. . . .

Like the dance floor of Slimy Mary's seen from the perspective of the ratones lurking way in the dark back reaches of the cellar, a distant vision of the American Dream beckoned cockteasingly, where gordos and plushie-tushies, the rich and the famous, danced to the same music, their long red hair frosted with flashing white lightnings.

Then Red Jack exploded out of the instrumental break in a flash of pixels and flipped him through a twist of the dreamtime into a place where Mucho Muchacho and the rock star who wasn't exactly there looked out from behind the same eyes.

But I'm inside you when you're ready to fight
Flash your freedom in the broad daylight!

And he was leading the wireheads, their long red hair flashing, out of the nether regions of Slimy Mary's and into the burning sol of The American Dream, waving fistfuls of Jacks and hawking his wares in the multiplexed voice of Red Jack, the electronically enhanced song of the sombre itself.

Be my body
And I'll be your soul
Crown yourself the Prince of Rock and Roll. . . .

Red Jack danced his Mucho Muchacho stompada through Ciudad Trabajo, past ranks of pale gray gordos hunkered over pale gray keyboards, squinting listlessly into pale gray monitors—a grainy grim black and white world out of ancient video tape.

Tap all the pinheads
Down the willy-hole
Crown yourself the Prince of Rock and Roll!

Dancing down the middle of the street, right on the divide between the sombre and the sol, his brain aching and trembling on the edge of some enormous revelation—

Nose to the grindstone or balls to the wall!
Gotcha either way before you learn to crawl!

—Chingada, we're all in the same shit!

We've all been fucked over by the same damn putamadres, by the real owners of the world, whoever the fuck *they* are!

We're both on the same side, ain't we, Jack?

Hey, there's only one side, Mucho, and we're all on it. 'Cause all we want is *out* of the shit, and back into our own dreamtime, amigo.

Which is what we're both dealin', ain't it, compadre?

Boot me up and boogie when you wanna fight back
Tap yourself a hit of old Red Jack . . .

Red Jack tossed bedbug discs to the wage slaves of Ciudad Trabajo, Mucho Muchacho tossed Jacks, and their hair flashed Red-Jack red as they crowned themselves, and the black and white office reality bloomed into glorious color.

Crown yourself on the garbage heap
Wake your soul from its starving sleep. . . .
Up against the wall with the money machine
You got the power but we tap the Dream . . .

Mucho Muchacho and Red Jack led their avenging army of red-haired streeties straight up the skirt of Chocharica City. And the red-haired wage slaves of Ciudad Trabajo danced out of the glass towers to join them, and the sombre and the sol marched together in the dreamtime.

Flashin' dancin' like liberty
In the home of the brave and the land of the free.
Tap your fingers, let me zap your soul
We're all the Crown Prince of Rock and Roll!

He popped out of the flash-dancing before a giant American flag to a patriotic maxmetal marching band, and in that moment of transition, he was all of them—Red Jack, Mucho Muchacho, Paco Monaco—he was their body, and they were his soul, the electronically reborn Prince of Rock and Roll.

So did El Tiempo Rico flash into full flower to the anthem of the Jack, the first piece of wire to spark across the gap between the sombre and the sol.

Within a week, long red hair was the fave rave with the former designer-dust devotees, long red hair frosted with silver-white spiderwebs both to proclaim identity and to camouflage the fact, for by then Paco was moving half a dozen or more a night, and the hairdo, as often as not, concealed the real thing.

El Tiempo Rico, verdad, the best time of Paco's life. Restaurants and clothes and dust and cabs. And more.

For Jack was moving so well at The American Dream that Dojo had taken to calling him "my main man" even though he was no longer working the door, and his yak connections were gobbling up Paco's bedbug discs like there was no tomorrow.

And because Paco *was* moving all these bedbug discs for them through Dojo, he had gained a measure of respect from the Reality Liberation Front. Without anyone saying anything, he had become a *member* of the RLF, not just Karen Gold's streetie lover. An important member too—their mainline connection to heavy money.

El Tiempo Rico, muchacho! A million fuckin' miles from doin' crash and grabs for nickels and dimes! He had a girl, a free place to crash, a steady source of mucho dinero, and some respect, four things he had never had before in his life.

He could hardly imagine a better life than this, he saw no reason why it couldn't go on forever, and he certainly never thought the bottom was about to fall out and leave him here on the door at Slimy Mary's again and lucky to have that, my son.

But like all primo wire flashes, El Tiempo Rico zoomed up to a peak where it seemed like perfect bliss would never end, and then the unseen forces who owned the juice pulled the plug.

He should have seen it coming when he started seeing long red hair at Slimy Mary's, when streeties and burnt-out wireheads started saving up the money to buy the dye to color it themselves and the silver paint to do crude webwork frostings. He should have seen it when Rojos became a common sight on both the sol and the sombre sides of the street, fancy salon jobs on one side, and crude homemade imitations on the other.

It finally began to dawn on him that something beyond his

control was coming down when he noticed that some of the Rojos frequenting Slimy Mary's weren't just showing el Pelo. They were *wearing* the Jack just like the rico Rojos in The American Dream.

But *he* sure as shit wasn't dealing no Jack to streeties! The price at The American Dream had stabilized at $400, and no *streetie* ever had that kind of money in one piece, as he knew all too well from still-recent memory.

They were buying it elsewhere.

And they were buying it cheap.

Was Dojo somehow screwing him?

"Hey, my son, I *told* you this was going to happen up front, now, didn't I?" Dojo told him the night Paco finally confronted him at the door. "Or have you burned out so many brain cells you forgot why I made a deal with you in the first place?"

Paco looked at him blankly.

Dojo shook his head paternally. "You got to lay off that wirehead shit, Paco," he said. "I *told* you the bottom was gonna drop out of the price pretty quick. Why do you think I was willing to give you such a nice piece of the action? So we could unload as much of the shit I knew I was gonna be stuck with to the uptown suckers as fast as possible before the mountain of Jacks I'm sitting on became worth less than I paid for them!"

He clapped Paco across the shoulders. "You did a good job, my son," he said. "You moved enough of 'em at fancy prices while you could so I still at least come out ahead on my investment even though I'm still goin' to have to eat about a dozen cartons. You're still my main man, Paco, we made beautiful music together. And those Red Jack discs you're getting me from the RLF are still hot. But as far as the Jack goes, the sweet song is over."

"What the fuck is *happening,* man?" Paco demanded.

Dojo shrugged. "What I *told* you was going to happen," he said. "American enterprise has been japped again. The yaks shipped some samples of the Silicon City wire back home, copied the chip, and now they're churning the things out for peanuts in their robot factories and fucking us out of our own domestic market."

And sure enough, El Tiempo Rico, like the auto industry and the tv industry and fuck all knew what else, faded fast once the Japs set their robots to pulling the plug on the American competition.

Within a few more weeks they were just laughing at him at The American Dream when he tried to get even $225, the streets of Chocharica City were swarming with Rojos, and half the people in Slimy Mary's were wearing the Jack, just like the song said they would.

The price kept dropping like a stone, until by now you could score on the street for $150 if you looked hard enough, and here he was, standing on the slushy street as relief doorman at Slimy Mary's again, and lucky to have that, muchacho.

For sure he pined wistfully for the vanished days of El Tiempo Rico, but except when a chill wind blew and made him feel sorry for himself, he had to admit that it hadn't exactly left him with nothing to show for it.

He had this doorman's job, he was making some money off the RLF's Red Jack discs, he had a girl, he still had free access to The American Dream from Fritz, who he had made easy money for, and he had a place to crash where people still respected him as more than a piece of shit streetie.

And he had something more, something he couldn't quite put his finger on.

Like all those Rojos on both sides of the street out there, he had *Jack.* He had a piece of wire that could plug him into a place inside of himself, where he was an elusive something that he had never quite been before, not even when he was flashing on Mucho Muchacho.

You make more of me, I make more of you, like the song said, and if the words didn't really make much sense, the music somehow told him it was a fair bargain.

Weirdest of all, even though the flood of cheap Jacks had put him out of the business, he found himself smiling in satisfaction at all the Rojos on both sides of the streets, even when they were gordos and chocharicas. He knew for sure that it was *right* that anyone could now score the Jack for $150 on the street. Even though it had lost him a fuckin' fortune, he was *glad* that the price of the Jack had dropped down to streetie level.

Once, in bed, he had tried to explain this to Karen.

"It's drivin' me fuckin' crazy, momacita! I mean, I should really be pissed off, verdad, but when I see all those streeties flashin' on hundred-fifty-dollar Jacks, I feel like laughing. I feel like we all just did a great big crash and grab on Ciudad Trabajo together. I feel happy even though I've been fucked over on the dinero. Chingada, is Dojo right, is all this wire really frying my brain? Do you think I'm goin' crazy?"

She had hugged him to her and kissed him with a little squealing giggle. "No, Paco, you're not going crazy," she said, "don't worry about it, you're just developing a social conscience. A pain in the ass sometimes, but usually not fatal."

"Qué?"

She laughed and kissed him again. "Don't worry about the words, love," she said. "You already know the music."

"It's the perfect piece of wire, Larry," Malcolm McGee was saying when Karen Gold came back to the loft. "Higher cerebral functions are not impaired. The current's too low to burn out brain cells. Sensory input's still getting through and it's still being processed, people aren't jumping out of windows or trying to walk through walls. There's nothing physically dangerous about it."

It was after three A.M.; most of the loft was shrouded in darkness, but Malcolm, Larry Coopersmith, Leslie Savanah, Teddy Ribero, and Tommy Don were sitting around the kitchen table in the pool of light cast by the only burning overhead fixture, drinking red wine from a gallon jug and arguing about the Jack again from the sound of it.

"Even the *Time* cover story admitted that," Tommy chimed in. "All they could say to put down the Jack was that it was a recipe for psychic and social chaos."

"And we've been trying to bake that pie all along, now haven't we?"

Malcolm, Tommy, and Teddy all wore Red Jack hairdos, though Tommy's hadn't yet grown much past his ears, and Malcolm's bushed up into an untidy flaming afro aura. Leslie had been whispering to Karen lately about how maybe they should wear the Red to mark them as Red Jack disc dealers, but she still wore her hair short and blond so as not to get into it with Coopersmith, with whom she was still making it. Larry, of course, would cut his head off before he dyed his hair red.

"Don't you guys talk about anything else anymore?" Karen said, pulling up a chair and pouring herself a glass of wine from the jug.

This was all getting pretty old. After Malcolm had traced out the circuits, he had insisted on trying the Zap himself, and Larry had been unable to dissuade him. After he tried it the first time, he pronounced it a profound experience, and chipped at it regularly to Larry's increasing disgust.

Then Tommy and Teddy began chipping at it now and again openly, too, and Leslie was flashing on the sly, and it began to look like the Reality Liberation Front was heading for a schism.

But then one night Malcolm sat down at his computer and started chain-tapping like a maniac, hitting his touchpoint again and again and again every time he popped out of the flash for four solid hours, and when he finally came out of it with no apparent ill effects, he had Red Jack's voice and visual parameters extracted from a disc he bought of "Your Rock and Roll Machine" and interfaced to his own lip-sync and animation programs.

He duped the programs for everyone, and now, instead of on-screen print instructions and menus to lead the customers through the bedbug programs, Red Jack himself, manifested in sound and pixels, walked them through it.

Voilà, Red Jack had become the Ronald McDonald of their product, and sales soared, even more so now that "Crown Prince" had climbed to the top of the charts.

Even Larry Coopersmith had to agree that far from turning Malcolm's brain to lime Jell-O, the Jack had inspired him to a conceptual breakthrough that was performing yeoman service to the cause.

After that there was no way he could stop anyone from plugging in, nor could he find any coherent argument against it when Malcolm, and then Teddy and Tommy, and now Iva and Bill as well, took to wearing the Red.

But that sure didn't stop him from bitching about it.

"Yeah, okay, so it doesn't grow hair on your palms, but the way you guys are startin' to chain-tap the fucking thing, the pie you're gonna end up baking is your own brains à la mode! I mean, if you look around, you see a lot of people wearing the Red who look pretty fried already."

"Hey momacita, qué pasa?"

Paco was walking across the darkened loft toward them, peeling off his coat. He dropped it and his street bag into a corner, gave Karen a short sharp kiss, filled a milk glass to the brim with wine, slugged half of it down, and pulled up a chair beside her.

"The same old shit," Karen told him.

Paco shook his head. No red dye-job for him, but the wirenet and breadbox showed plain enough when he tossed his dark bushy hair. "What's the matter, my son," he jibed at Coopersmith, "afraid you'll end up chain-tapping yourself if you ever start plugging in?"

Paco had just flipped the words out with no apparent intent, but a dead silence fell like a lead curtain as Larry Coopersmith's hands balled into fists on the tabletop and his jaws gritted behind his black beard, and he glared across the table at Paco.

Paco flinched back, more in befuddlement than fear, and then, of course, had to glare righteously back into the face of this challenge to his machismo, whether he knew why Larry was pissed off or not.

There was still that much of the streetie in Paco Monaco, but her lost little boy of the streets had grown into the man she saw confronting Larry as an equal now, reading Larry while he was staring him down, his expression softening as he reached some interior comprehension.

"Hey, chingada, man, I was just running my mouth, it was only like a little bullshit . . ." he said, breaking off the staring contest, leaning back in his chair and taking another drink of wine.

"No, it wasn't," Leslie said softly, covering Coopersmith's right fist with her hand. "Was it, Larry?"

Larry Coopersmith's fists uncurled. He held Leslie's hand. He smiled a sheepish little smile. He managed a tiny laugh. "Guess the lady is right, Paco," he said, "seeing as how it did such a good job of freaking me out."

"Chingada, come on, I didn't mean to—"

"No, Paco, never back away from the truth!" Coopersmith insisted, holding up his free hand, and then he spoke from a private place inside him that Karen had never seen him reveal before.

"There were years when I plugged in more in a week than all of you put together have since you fell in love with the fuckin' Jack! Except for the really terminal shit like the Blue Max, there ain't a piece of wire I haven't fried my brains with until smoke came out of my ears, and you can see what a crazy motherfucker it's made out of me."

"Yeah, Larry, you're a human vegetable all right," Malcolm said dryly, "we can hardly even get a word out of you."

"You didn't know me then," Coopersmith went on earnestly. "Not that there was all that much of me there to know. Ever see those rats they plugged into primitive pleasure-center pieces?

They won't eat, they won't drink, they won't even fuck, they just chain-tap their touchpoints and flash and flash until they fuckin' croak, and no doubt they're sure they've achieved mickey mouse nirvana."

"Come on, Larry, the Jack's not like that at all!"

"Hey man, you see any of us staring at the ceiling?" Paco said. "We havin' any trouble taking care of business? Do I look like I'm ready to go to Florida to you?"

"Tell you what I *do* see, Paco," Larry Coopersmith said much less stridently. "I see the streets full of people all wearing red hair, flashing on the same piece, and listening to the same music. If that ain't textbook reality control, what is?"

Paco studied him narrowly, concentrating, considering it, rolling it around in his mind. "Yeah, well then who's doing the controlling and what for?" he demanded. "Ciudad Trabajo? The government? The cops? The plushie-tushies?"

Larry leered wolfishly at him. "The bottom line itself," he said. "For money. That's what really scares me."

"Qué?"

"It's these Red Jack songs that MUZIK is playing all the time that's doing all this, isn't it, Paco?" Coopersmith said, leaning forward. "That's why everyone's doing the Jack and painting their hair red, you with me so far?"

"For sure, man," Paco said, furrowing his brow in concentration and locking eyes with Coopersmith quite differently now. "It's been great for business!"

To a certain extent, Larry and Paco had come to represent opposite poles of the RLF; Larry Coopersmith, the founding father, the intellectual main man, and Paco Monaco, the son of the streets. Coopersmith, who hated wire, and Paco, who had introduced the RLF to the Jack.

When Malcolm and Teddy and Tommy and Leslie started flashing on the Jack, a certain distance had been created between them and Coopersmith, and Paco had threatened to become the factional focus of the Reds.

But it never really happened.

Because Paco and Larry *liked* each other. Paco carefully considered everything Larry said, but just as carefully told him what parts of it he considered bullshit, soaking it up not like a sponge, but through the fine filter of his own street-level perceptions. And Larry plainly enjoyed this in Paco. When he wasn't arguing with him, and half the time when he was, he treated Paco like an obdurate prize pupil. And nothing pleased him more than when Paco was able to turn the tables.

"Great for *Muzik's* business!" Larry said. "We put Red Jack on disc to sell our bedbug programs, and Muzik, Inc., puts a Jack on his head to sell their videodiscs!"

"Chingada . . ." Paco said, his eyes widening slowly in hard-won comprehension. He frowned. "But it's the *songs* that are like commercials for the *Jack,* no?"

"Works both ways, Paco," Coopersmith said. "The songs sell the Jack, and the Jack sells the songs. Quite a marketing scam! Making the product a commercial for the fad that's promoting it is definitely an advance in the state of the art."

"You're saying that *Muzik* invented the Jack?" cried Teddy Ribero.

"Pure paranoia!"

"I got inside information that it's the yaks who are flooding the market with cheap Jacks, Larry," Paco said.

Larry Coopersmith shrugged. "Could even be Muzik's got a deal with the yaks," he said. "I mean, here's a piece that sold for over four hundred before it became popular, and now that it's a major national fad, you can score it on street corners for one fifty! Does that follow any dealer's logic you ever heard of? The price *drops* and the supply goes *up* when demand goes through the ceiling?"

"Chingada!" Paco exclaimed. "Yeah, you're right! It looks like whoever's making the Jack is fucking up a chance to make millions. . . ."

"Unless the corporation that's *raking in* millions off the videodiscs that all that cheap wire is selling for it is paying off the manufacturers to keep the price down . . ."

Karen, absorbed with watching Paco and filtering her own reactions to the paranoid fantasy Larry had been building through her perception of his perception, had kept silent till now, but this was just too much.

"You've really gone off the deep end, Larry!" she declared. "Thousands of people are nibbling mouseholes in corporate and government data banks with our bedbugs, everyone who's plugged into the Jack is cheering them on, and you expect us to believe that a *corporation* is behind it? Why would a *corporation* loose such chaos on *the corporate structure itself*?"

"Like I told you," Coopersmith said. He laughed. "For money! That's all a corporate balance sheet cares jack shit about, after all. It doesn't care what happens to other corporations or the government or the sale of red hair dye or your fucking brain cells. It just runs along the bottom line on automatic."

He turned to Malcolm. "You expect me to plug into *that*?" he demanded. "The marketing device of a reality-control mechanism that doesn't even care to know what it's doing except in terms of dollars and cents?"

Could it be? Karen thought with a sinking sensation in her stomach. Try though she did, she could find no way to refute Larry Coopersmith's logic. But neither could she deny that something deeper inside insisted that he had missed the point.

"You don't understand, Larry!" she said with a passion that surprised her. "You're so busy trying to figure out *how* it happened that you don't see what *has* happened! The Jack hasn't been destroying lives, it's making them better! Red Jack isn't persuading people to turn themselves into zombies, he's bringing them together, he's giving them hope, he's . . . he's . . ."

She threw up her hands in frustration. She *knew* that the Jack made her more at home inside her own skin, yes, less of a snob, more at peace with the life that her karma had dealt her, but less willing to be a pawn in someone else's game too.

She knew what it was like late at night in her grimy little tent of a room in bed with Paco. Huddling in the narrow cot in each other's arms and listening to steam banging in the pipes and the snores and farts of nearby sleepers. And then they'd plug into the Jack together and make love in magic places, pleasing each other and themselves as never they could when they tried it straight.

Could what they felt really be nothing more than the deluded ecstasy of rats addicted to pleasure-center stimulation?

And what about Paco? Hadn't he been plugged in when he saved her from those two rapists and treated her tenderly and made beautiful love to her? Could Larry really contend that *Paco* had devolved into a lower creature on the Jack?

Of course not! He had watched Paco grow from a feral creature of the streets to a thinking feeling man and he had been part of the process himself.

"What about *Paco*, Larry?" she said. "He's been flashing on the Jack longer than any of us. And what's Jack done to him? Gotten him off the streets, made him your favorite verbal sparring partner, turned him into a real caring man, as good a man as you are, Larry Coopersmith!"

"Hey . . ." Paco cooed disparagingly, writhing into himself

with an entirely charming embarrassment, and regarding her from the warm center of it with soft, smiling eyes.

Larry Coopersmith looked at Karen, he looked at Paco, he looked at what hovered palpably in the air between them. He sighed manfully; he grimaced. "Okay," he said quietly, "so maybe you got a point."

Leslie immediately hugged him and planted a fat kiss on his hairy black cheek. "That's your saving grace, Markowitz," she said. "Just when you've proven yourself to be a complete egotistical asshole, you actually admit you don't know it all."

"I don't remember exactly admitting *that,*" Larry shot back to mask his own embarrassment.

"You ever think that maybe you're just chicken?" Paco said in quite another voice, as if forced to drop back out of such an unmanly public display of tender emotion into a more comfortable masculine posture.

On a little-boy level, there really wasn't that much difference between Larry and Paco.

"Okay, so I'm chicken . . ." Larry Coopersmith said.

"You *admit* you're chicken to try the Jack?" Paco exclaimed as if such an open admission were beyond his experience, as indeed perhaps it was.

"Sometimes it takes more courage to admit you're scared of something than to keep bullshitting yourself, Paco," Larry said gently.

Paco visibly mulled over this novel notion, then nodded his head in agreement. "Sí . . . verdad . . . I never really thought of it like that . . ." he muttered. "But whether that makes you like a pussy or not depends on what you do about it, tu sabés . . . ?"

Now it was Larry Coopersmith's turn to knot his brows in glimmering comprehension.

"I had to like . . . do me a deed, tu sabés, to get me my first Jack," Paco told him. "The only way I could get one was to trade a fuckin' Uzi for it, and the only way to get an Uzi is to do a crash and grab on a fuckin' *zonie*, man, and the only way to get an Uzi away from a zonie . . ."

Paco shuddered, paused, blinked, dropped his gaze to the table-top for a moment before he went on.

"Anyway, if you think tryin' the Jack's somethin' to make you piss in your pants, try *that* one, amigo!" he said. "Chingada, talk about miedo, man, I knew I had a good chance of getting myself blown away! But I fuckin' *did it anyway,* man! I mean, to do something like that because you're too fuckin' stupid to be afraid, that ain't so mucho macho, that's just fuckin' nuts, but to be afraid and do it anyway, that's the real cojones, tu sabés ahora, amigo. . . .''

Larry Coopersmith sat there for a long moment locking eyes with Paco. Slowly, he began to nod his head up and down.

''You're the jefe here, man,'' Paco said. ''This is like a deed you gotta do, comprende?'' He laughed. ''It ain't like you have to snatch an Uzi to prove yourself! All you gotta do is plug in to the Jack and take a walk around inside. I'll go with you, Larry. I won't even flash myself, so if I see you're starting to freak, I'll tap you right out of it.''

''I'll go too, Larry, I'll flash with you,'' Leslie said, clutching at Coopersmith's arm.

''Me too!'' Karen blurted. ''I'll take you to The American Dream!''

''Come on, man, what can happen?'' Paco coaxed. ''Karen and me promise one of us will always be straight to bring you out of any bad flash.''

Larry Coopersmith looked from Leslie to Paco to Karen and back to Leslie again, shaking his head ruefully. ''You guys are making me feel like some little baby askin' everyone to hold his hand in the horror house,'' he said sheepishly.

''Hey man, what are friends for?'' Paco snapped airily from the heart.

Larry Coopersmith actually blushed behind his thick black beard. He rose from the table. ''Well come on, aunties and uncles,'' he said, ''let's get our asses in gear before poor little chickenshit Larry changes his mind.''

AMERICAN DREAMERS

Larry Coopersmith had slouched along, nibbling at his lower lip and maintaining an entirely uncharacteristic silence, during the whole walk over to The American Dream, working up his courage, or so it seemed to Karen.

Paco talked Fritz into granting them all freebies, Karen got them past the zonies and up into the main saloon, they secured a table at the railing overlooking the pit and ordered drinks to nurse, and Leslie hit her touchpoint.

Only then, with a shrug and graveyard grin, did Larry finally reach up gingerly and tap the touchpoint of the Jack they had given him.

At first, he just sat there, staring out across the pit over the rim of a tumbler of tequila, sipping at it and soaking things up. ''So this is the famous American Dream,'' he finally said in a tone of less than overwhelment.

Then a strangely disdainful faraway look stole slowly upon his face as he turned from the scene below to gaze around the balcony bar, all brass, and smoked mirror-glass, and nobodies in particular, half of them wearing the Red, and all of them dressed up to try and look important.

''It reminds me of the first time I went on a run to Mardi Gras; we didn't know anyone in New Orleans, so I spent the first half of the week getting blitzed and partying at street level, and I remember standing stoned in a mob scene on Bourbon Street fighting for cheap plastic beads being tossed from fancy balcony parties by southern belles in taffeta, and rich fruits in white suits . . .''

''Mardi Gras?'' Leslie said languidly. ''I've always wanted to go to Mardi Gras and ride on a float in a long white dress, throwing doubloons to the crowds!''

But Karen could almost see what Larry Coopersmith saw, even though all she had ever seen of Mardi Gras in New Orleans was tv footage. For here she indeed sat at a balcony railing looking down from on high on the peasants below.

And if they weren't leaping for plastic beads like puppies for dog biscuits, they certainly were strutting their stuff and flashing their tits and asses in hopes of emerging for a golden moment into one of the limelight beams picking their way across the dance floor in search of tasty spectacles to display for the delectation of the balcony crowd.

Larry Coopersmith smiled a good-naturedly feral smile, a biker's partying smile, and his ageless bearded face, with its weathered cheeks and bright blue eyes, its mane of long black hair and beard, seemed indeed the face of the biker that rumor had it he had long ago been.

''For sure, that's what I thought, too, before I lucked myself into it,'' he said. ''I met me a fancy lady slumming in this Charles Street bar, and we got to talking, and I had these peyote buttons we picked on the way across Texas, and that was enough to pick her up with, and we ate 'em together, and after we got through puking, she took me around to a whole shitload of these balcony parties, and there I was up there doin' it myself, sipping champagne and snorting up lines and nibbling canapes and tossing plastic throws to the masses. . . .''

''That must have been *fabulous,* Larry,'' Leslie sighed in faded magnolia tones, leaning back in her chair, sticking her nose in the air, swirling a phantom cigarette holder, and becoming the lady in question, at least inside her own flash.

''*Fabulous,* Scarlett?'' Larry mimicked. ''It sucked! There I was with the queen of the hop, her friends done up like peacocks, and me in my leather pants and colors, and bored out of my mind. When I saw one of my brothers actually catch a fuckin' string of beads *I* had thrown, I finally knew it was time to goose the ladies, puke in the punchbowl, start a fight, and get my ass thrown back in the street where it belonged.''

''Oh Larry, how gross!'' Leslie declared, turning up her nose.

''Which?'' Larry said. ''Playing pissant prince on a balcony like this, or knowing when to puke and punch?''

''Chingada, you really do that, Larry?'' Paco said admiringly.

"Stick your hand up Chocharica City and barf in their punchbowl and all?"

"I'm a mean hog-riding motherfucker, citizen, and don't you forget it!" Larry exclaimed, becoming the perfect loud-mouth biker, up on his feet, red-eyed and long-haired and challenging the whole bar.

"Jesus, cool it, Larry, sit down, you're gonna get us eighty-sixed!" Karen hissed at him.

"You still think the Jack is a brain-burning piece of shit, Larry?" Paco said slyly.

Coopersmith paused, froze, glanced around the bar at the faces glaring at him, sat down, and regarded Paco with the strangest look in his eye.

"I guess I forgot why I became a wirehead in the first place," he owned. "I got to admit this is one wizard piece. Not like any wire I've ever flashed before. No body-image distortion, no energy drain, no paranoia, not even hallucinations exactly, but it's like space and time is . . . like reality multiplexes into . . . like . . ."

"It's the perfect piece, Larry," Karen enthused. "Look around this bar. All these people wearing the Red aren't burnt-out zombies, or they wouldn't let them up here. People like this are buying our Red Jack discs too; they've got bank accounts and stock portfolios and corporate scams, they're not gorked in the ruins like vegetables!"

"What about down *there*?" Coopersmith said, waving his arm and turning in his chair to look out over the dance floor below. A Tiger Lady cut was playing, something called "Back to Basics," and Tiger Lady herself, tripled into enormity on the huge video screens, loomed in her tight tigerskin leotards out of walls of urban jungle, burnt-out buildings, industrial wasteland, mean and angry streets, hissing the lyrics through full red lips over needle-pointed teeth and dancing like a cat in heat to an insinuating rhythm and a hot-wired lead guitar.

Bend your backs to the basics
Bend you back to the jungle
Where the natives are restless
And stone walls crumble. . . .

Karen wondered what Larry Coopersmith was seeing down there in the flux of dancing bodies, in the fragmenting realities of the overlapping multicolored strobes, in the moving spotlight beams showing him whomever the operators on levels above chose to favor, in all that red hair waving on the sea of humanity like the star-spangled banner.

"Come on, sweathog, let's boogie!" he exclaimed, bounding to his feet again, snatching Leslie up by the hand, and dragging her off without even bothering to ask any question for which no could be an answer.

So it went at The American Dream. Larry, flashing, danced Leslie, also flashing, around the pit through three numbers while Karen and Paco danced along with them half-heartedly playing watchful nursemaids.

When Larry Coopersmith dragged this retinue off the dance floor and under the overhang into the dim smoky twilight zone of the bar, Leslie was already hitting her touchpoint. She looked a good deal less ebullient than he did.

"What's the matter, Leslie?" Karen said soothingly. "You okay . . . ?"

Leslie blinked. "Yeah, yeah, I'm okay . . ." she muttered, as if confirming it to herself. "But out there . . . in there . . . dancing with this maniac . . . I dunno, like I was being pulled apart down the middle . . . like I was born in another time . . ."

"Like something old and something new, something wired, and something true, its hour come round at last, come a-rockin' toward dis here Babylon to be reborn!" Larry Coopersmith proclaimed, waving his arms extravagantly, but with a look of the most piercing seriousness in his glowing blue eyes.

"Chingada, man, are you fuckin' *wired*!" Paco exclaimed admiringly.

"Ain't I ever told you, Paco, I'm the wirehead king, wire was my thing, and all my plugged-in life, I was always waiting for this moment to arrive."

"Qué?"

"The right side of my brain is out there boogying but the left side is still booted up and running smooth, and that's the perfect flash all righteous wireheads have been looking for since Eohippus started chipping jimson weed!"

"Fuckin' *fried*!" Paco cried in delight.

"Motherfucker, this thing is to the street shit of my wasted wirehead youth as white port and lemon juice is to Courvoisier VSOP!"

I make more of you
You make more of me
You make more of me
I make more of you. . . .

Out across the dance floor, Red Jack's voice chanted the multiplexed opening chorus of "Your Rock and Roll Machine." Larry Coopersmith froze, turned, looked back out onto the dance floor.

"I'll fuckin' dance to that!" Larry said, and before anyone else could move or say a word, he was back out in the pit, disappearing into the fragmented realities of the multicolored strobes, into the red-haired masses, into his first plugged-in encounter with Red Jack.

Karen stood there under the overhang just off the dance floor, holding Paco's hand until the song was over, and wondered just what it was like now for Larry Coopersmith, remembering how it had been for her, meeting someone who wasn't there, and told you so.

Larry seemed to have popped out of the flash when the song ended, for he was shaking his head as he returned to the bar, and his eyes seemed narrower, and the grin that had been all but plastered across his face since he had first plugged in was softer and more thoughtful.

"Like meeting an old friend you've forgotten and remembering it's you . . ." he muttered. "The ghost in your machine . . ."

He turned to gaze back at the dance floor, where the streeties and stockbrokers, the trendies and hookers, the dealers and day-trippers, were now dancing to a different tune.

But even now the bright white spotlight beams were picking out the Red; here, there, everywhere, as if Red Jack himself were in the control room, revealing the communicants of the Jack to themselves in the chaos of the pit.

"Red ripe anarchy for all the world to see," he said. "Talk about your random factors!"

"Qué?"

"All those people jacked in to their own private dreams but dancing together, Paco," Larry Coopersmith told him. "Boy, was I ever wrong about this piece of wire! There's never been anything like it before. Every other piece zones everyone into the same somewhere the circuits are chipped to take you, overrides your software with brute hard-wired juice. But this fucking thing just plugs you in to another part of *your own head* and lets you literally dream up your own flash from there! The fuckin' song is true, it really *does* make more of you, it's a random factor flash, it's the first real piece of democratic wire!"

"I guess that means you like it . . . ?" Karen asked dryly.

"You sure changed your mind!" Paco said in smug delight. "How'd you figure it out so fast?"

Larry Coopersmith shrugged, smiled, nodded toward the dance floor. "Someone who ain't exactly there told me, muchacho," he said.

"Why don't we sit down at the bar and cool ourselves out?" Leslie said, finally breaking her silence, but still looking a bit bonged.

Larry Coopersmith took one long look up and down the bar, at the studied grunge of the decor, at the raggy streeties hanging back in the smoky shadows or offering up their asses and goods, at the tourists from the upper levels of The American Dream cruising for same, and wrinkled his nose.

"It's the fuckin' Disney version!" he said scornfully. "Fantasyland for bicycle-seat sniffers and gringo turistas!"

"Verdad!" Paco agreed.

"Yeah, well I still sell a lot of Red Jack discs here, you guys," Karen pointed out. "It's a great place to do business." The truth of it was that she *liked* this bar. True the streeties were admitted by the management to provide color; true too that they were there to peddle their flesh to devos and day-trippers slumming among the quaintly dangerous natives.

But where else did both sides of the street mix without zonies between them and on what other possible terms? Where else could Karen Gold and Paco Monaco sit easy together in public?

Larry Coopersmith, however, wanted nothing so much as to be gone. "A scene like this may be a great place to do business, but I don't wanna *boogie* in the plastic PG version, and especially not flashing on *this* piece, 'cause somehow, Toto, I think this *is* Kansas," he said.

He took Leslie's hand and patted it reassuringly. "I've got a better idea," he said. "How about the real thing? What about this place where you work as doorman, Paco? You can get us in for nothing, can't you?"

"*Slimy Mary's?*" Paco said. He grinned. "*For sure,* man, hey no problem!"

"Jesus, Larry, you don't want to go to Slimy Mary's!" Karen groaned. "It's—"

"What's fuckin' wrong with Slimy Mary's?" Paco demanded, giving her a wide-eyed look of surprise and a frown of impending wounded outrage.

"Well . . . ah . . . couldn't it be a little dangerous at this time of night . . . ?" Karen hedged weakly. How could she tell Leslie and Larry the truth in front of Paco, that Slimy Mary's was all too well-named, that it was a filthy roach- and rat-infested cellar full of burnt-out wirehead zombies and desperate streeties?

"Dangerous?" Paco scoffed. "Hey, I'm relief doorman, remember, and I'm Dojo's main man! *We* do the fuckin' with in Slimy Mary's, none of those putamadres is gonna do any fuckin' with *us*!"

"Fuckin'-A, brother!" Coopersmith declared, slapping palms with Paco. "On to Slimy Mary's!"

And there was nothing that Leslie or Karen could do to stop them.

"Relax, muchachas, you can stop pissing in your panties now, here we are," Paco Monaco said in high good humor as they rounded the corner of Third Street, with Karen grabbing tight onto his hand, and Leslie Savanah hanging on hard to Larry Coopersmith.

Way he felt, he almost wished they *had* run into some asshole putamadres on the way over. Mighta been fun to kick some ass with fuckin' Larry and give the muchachas a little thrill! But as it was, they had crossed paths only with solitary streeties, or couples, or at worst two guys together, and none of them had the cojones to shoot no mouth at their chochas.

Dojo was on the door, and Paco insisted on giving him an unaccustomed high-five handshake. "Hey, Dojo, want you to meet some real heavyweight people!"

Dojo frowned at him dubiously. "The lady I'm never supposed to have seen before I recognize . . ." he said.

"Yeah, well this is the honcho of the same gang you never heard of, Larry Coopersmith, and that's his old lady," Paco told him, shoving them forward proudly.

"We don't have no honcho in the Reality Liberation Front," Larry corrected. He shrugged. He laughed. "It's just that I can't seem to keep from doing most of the talking."

Dojo's eyes widened, then narrowed speculatively. "Then maybe you and me oughta do some talking, my man," he said.

"Could be," Larry said, sizing the big black putamadre up. "About what?"

"About this dumb idea I got could make us all some significant change," Dojo said. "A trade that could help both ball clubs."

He turned to Paco. "Take the door for a couple minutes while I get your friends a table, my man. I'll send someone right out to take it from you," he said like some fuckin' plushie-tushie headwaiter bossing around a flunky.

"Hey, nigger—" Paco began angrily as Dojo ushered Karen, Larry, and Leslie past him.

But Dojo cooled his anger instantly as he went past him, slipping him five, smiling at him, winking, and saying, "Paco, my son, you are truly my main man, if this works out, I really owe you!"

"Jesus, Karen . . ." Leslie whispered into her ear as they planted themselves in a nest of dusty cushions surrounding an unpainted cable spool table.

"It's not exactly The American Dream," Karen agreed.

Slimy Mary's was more or less as she remembered it.

A low parody of the dance floor of The American Dream done up with blinking bare colored bulbs and a tinfoil ceiling. A single video screen and slightly tinny-sounding speakers. Cable spools and old sprung sofas and nests of musty pillows around the dance floor, and the sense of an endless dark cave full of rats and roaches and worse creatures as a pressure at her back into which she dared not gaze.

The clientele was composed of all those savage streeties you tried to ignore when you saw them lurking at the edges of some Zone. Yet here, on their own home turf, they now seemed less like *dangerous dirty streeties* and more like people.

Maybe it was the long red hair more of them than not were wearing now. Even without a hit of the Jack, it flashed her back into that transitory sense of comradeship she had felt for these poor streeties the night she had flashed here and danced among them. I dream, therefore I am human, she thought.

How ironic that it took the ensign of someone who *wasn't* human to remind her of that.

"It's not as bad as it looks," she told Leslie softly as Larry

Coopersmith and the big ominous black doorman sat down facing each other like poker players across the cable spool table.

"It don't look so bad at all," Coopersmith said. "At least it isn't a fuckin' Muzik franchise like the last joint we were in."

"Yeah, well on the other hand, my man," the doorman said, "something like a franchise operation is what I got in mind. . . ."

Larry laughed. "Somehow I don't see a chain of Slimy Mary's in every shopping mall in America," he said.

Paco came prancing in across the edge of the dance floor, nodding to dancers, flipping some remark to the vj behind his disc decks, strutting his stuff to the beat of some African metal MUZIK was playing. Karen smiled warmly at him and squeezed his hand as he sat down beside her. It was good to see him in a place where he felt like the cock of the walk.

"I was just telling your friends about a little business deal, my son," Dojo said. The big black doorman made Karen nervous, but despite that she found herself rather liking the man for the genuine affection he seemed to display toward Paco.

He reached into a pocket, pulled out what Karen recognized as a Red Jack disc, and slid it across the table toward Larry. "One of yours?"

"Fifth Amendment," Larry said with a wide grin.

"Look here, my man," Dojo said, frowning intently at Larry Coopersmith, "let's can the bullshit, we're gonna have to be up front about our criminal activities if we're going to get anywhere. I'll tell you mine and then you'll tell me yours."

"Fair enough," Larry said evenly, smiling back at him.

"One of my best was this nice little wire workshop coining me significant change upstairs," Dojo said. "But now the only piece of wire anyone wants is the Jack and it's selling on the street for a hundred so I couldn't make a profit even if I had the chips to produce the things. So what I'm left with is a lot of expensive gear and a bunch of terminal wireheads I've retired to Florida at my expense who ain't making me nothing."

"Excess productive capacity . . ." Larry said. "You need a new product to soak up the unemployment. . . ."

Dojo beamed at him. "I had a feeling we were gonna be on the same wavelength," he said. "Now, I could convert my operation to copy discs myself and cut you out and nothing you could do about it. There are people out there doin' it already, and you're not exactly in a legal position to sue anyone. But I'm having a hard time doin' real well with the ones I'm already getting from you; I mean I can sell a certain quantity to the kind of people we don't want to talk about, but most of my trade isn't exactly into computers and bank accounts. . . ."

"You want to become a *subcontractor* to the Reality Liberation Front?"

"You got it, my man, I mean, we both know I could deliver 'em to you at a hundred a pop and still make out, and you can sell them to your uptown customers for three hundred and make out like a champ. . . ."

Larry shrugged. "We can already make more than we can move ourselves," he said. "Now, if *you* could figure out a way to make the discs move in the downscale market like *the Jack* does, why then, Dojo, we could have ourselves a sweet little deal. . . ."

Dojo grimaced. "How the fuck am I supposed to do that?"

Larry Coopersmith threw up his hands, shrugging.

Ain't got no body
Ain't got no soul . . .
But I'm your Prince of Rock and Roll. . . .

MUZIK began playing "The Crown Prince of Rock and Roll," and as the opening chorus played through the cheap speakers blasting at full volume and Red Jack appeared on the sleazy little video screen, more streeties materialized from the grungy black depths to join the dancers already on the floor, like moths called forth from a stale moldy closet by a sudden white light.

And all of them wearing the Red.

Larry Coopersmith, his hands still frozen in their gesture of frustration, stared past Dojo's head at the screen; seemingly of its own volition, his right hand reached up to hit his touchpoint. The doorman, perplexed at this, swiveled his head around to follow Larry's line of sight. But then, *he* wasn't flashing.

Some elusive revelation teased at Karen's consciousness.

What was Larry perceiving now that Dojo wasn't? That *she* wasn't?

Karen stole a look at Paco. Paco stole the same look at Karen. She nodded at him. He nodded back at her. In almost perfect synchrony, they both reached up and hit their touchpoints.

All during the jefe bullshit between Dojo and Larry, a tight unpleasant feeling had been building behind Paco's breastbone.

Chingada, *he* had put the two of them together, and now they were treating him as if he didn't exist, trying to work out some kind of deal that would eliminate the connection's cut in the Red Jack disc trade between them, and never mind that the guy they were contriving to fuck over was *him*.

At first, all he had allowed himself to feel was outrage, but then the most bizarre realization slowly began to force itself upon his awareness. For sure he was pissed off, but he was also *jealous*. Here were two heavyweight honchos, the only two men in the world that he had come to think of as friends, and somehow he was *jealous* of what was going on between them, as if each were a chocha that the other was trying to steal away from him.

It was too strong to deny, but too fuckin' weird to really think about, but now, with a tap of the Jack, the polarity of the human equation flipped through the flash into something Mucho Muchacho could deal with.

Slimy Mary's seemed infinite now. The shadowy back reaches extended out into the street, into the roach-infested ruins, into the sombre, into his own past scrabbling for existence on the garbage heap. But like a promise of escape at the end of a long dark tunnel, beyond the streeties dancing under the flickering bulbs, the dance floor of The American Dream shone brilliantly on the video screen, calling him forth to claim his rightful place in the sol.

And there he sat facing the jefes of the two halves of his dreamtime—Dojo, the jefe of the sombre side of the street that he had come from and knew all too well, and Larry, the jefe of the Reality Liberation Front loft, a little corner of the wider unknown world in which he had so recently gained a toehold.

But Karen, seated here beside him, was proof that between the sombre and the sol, there could be a place where what was divided might be made whole, where a muy macho muchacho could stand with his legs spread wide and one foot on each side of the street.

And there was Red Jack up there on the screen, over his shoulder, whispering into his ear, singing inside him with his own voice: "Crown yourself on the garbage heap, wake your soul from its starving sleep!"

He glanced around at the video screen, where the song was reaching its climax, where he danced at the head of his army of red-haired streeties up the perfect center of the main drag of

Ciudad Trabajo, where red-haired gordos poured out of the glass towers and onto the dance floor of Slimy Mary's, where the bright red bars and flashing white stripes of the American flag were flashin' dancin' like liberty in the home of the brave and the land of the free. . . .

Tap your fingers, let me zap your soul
We're all the Crown Prince of Rock and Roll!

He turned with a Mucho Muchacho smile, a Red Jack smile, a Paco Monaco smile. Larry Coopersmith had hardly moved during the whole song, sitting there plugged in and staring into the screen with his hands resting limply on the table, while Dojo shook his head, glowered, and frowned at this wirehead spaceout. He looked at Dojo, he looked at Larry, feeling in that moment every inch their equal.

"Red Jack knows what to do," he said.

"You finally burn your brain all the way out?" Dojo said with a disapproving sneer.

But Larry's eyes were locked on his, nodding his understanding, smiling the same smile, and for a long, strange, endless moment, he seemed to be looking at himself looking at himself, or rather, perhaps, there was a third presence, someone standing there inside him just where he'd always been.

"Boot me up and boogie when you wanna fight back?" Larry said.

"Tap yourself a hit of old Red Jack!"

"Nose to the grindstone!"

"Balls to the wall!"

Someone else was speaking through Paco and Larry, or so to Karen it seemed, as their voices interpenetrated and multiplexed, and, like the electronically augmented voice off a Red Jack cut itself, became a singularity arising out of a multitude, a one speaking with the voice of a many.

Dojo, though, was simply pissed off, his smooth powerful black face the loftily disdainful mask of an angry Buddha of the street, his hands gripping the lip of the table, his arms thrusting downward, as if he were poised to push himself up from the table and throw it over in a gesture of outraged contempt.

"I have to sit here and listen to a couple of burnt-out zombies babble in my own fuckin' place?'' he snarled. ''I thought we were supposed to be talking *business*!''

''Y yo también,'' that strange and familiar voice said through Paco.

''And Red Jack is the business we're talking about,'' it continued through Larry. ''You make more of me and I'll make more for you.''

Dojo squinted at him. ''Now you're telling me we got a deal?'' he said.

Paco nodded. ''Nose to the grindstone or balls to the wall, we get 'em either way if we tap the dream. . . .''

''Say what?'' Dojo exclaimed. ''Listen, you wirehead assholes, you wanna talk business with *me,* you unplug yourself from that shit right now so's at least I can talk with what's left of a human being instead of . . . instead of . . .''

Larry shrugged, reached up, and hit his touchpoint. Instantly something crystalline seemed to shatter. Larry blinked, glanced at Paco, cocked his head. Paco slowly reached up, hit his own touchpoint, looked at Larry, then at Karen, with a look of sad bewilderment, once more her little lost boy of the streets.

''We sell the Jack and the Red Jack discs together, that's what he's telling us,'' Larry said in a quite normal voice. And someone who hadn't been there was gone with the flash. Gone but still hiding right inside him just where he'd always been.

''Together?''

Karen reached up and hit her touchpoint. And there she was in Slimy Mary's with the cold musty pressure of the moldy darkness at her back and the streeties in their red hair now dancing to something else on the tacky floor, and Paco, Larry, and Dojo leaning forward toward each other and talking ordinary turkey as if the whole flash had been a discontinuity and nothing had changed.

But somehow, she knew, something quite important *had* changed, some connection made, some compact struck with that ghost in their machine.

''The Jack ain't worth shit anymore!'' Dojo said. ''I told you, it's going for a hundred, a hundred fifty bucks tops, on the street!''

''Meaning you could score it in quantity for, say, eighty, couldn't you?'' Larry said.

"Maybe, but ain't worth my while to make twenty bucks a pop like some starving street dealer!"

"What if you could sell it for two hundred, and in quantity?"

"You tell me how the fuck I'm supposed to do that, and you've got yourself a deal, my man!"

"Red Jack told us how. We supply you with master discs. Each one is a different bedbug program and on each one Red Jack does a little spiel. Buy your discs and your Jack from the Reality Liberation Front! And you sell 'em both in a package for two hundred."

"No way, man. At that price I wouldn't have enough of an edge unless you were just about giving the discs away!"

"That *is* the deal, Dojo," Larry Coopersmith said.

"Huh?"

"Chingada, man, what the fuck are you saying?" Paco exclaimed. He was still trying to digest what was left of the fading memory of what had happened inside the flash. Now it evaporated completely. "Why the fuck should the RLF give away its goods for nothing?"

"My main man here has a good point," Dojo said.

"Because of what Red Jack is going to tell the customers on 'em," Larry Coopersmith said.

"Which is?" Leslie Savanah said, looking at him as if he were fuckin' nuts, which, at least as far as Paco was concerned, he sure as shit seemed to be.

Larry laughed, and his eyes lit up, and he gave his long black hair a wild toss, and for a moment, in his mind's eye, Paco saw it flash flaming red.

"Hi, I'm Red Jack," he said. "I'm not here, as we all know, but I'm the leader of the Reality Liberation Front who's bringing you this cut-rate bedbug program and my own special brand of wire too, and now I'm making *you* a member of the Reality Liberation Front, so go out, copy this disc, and start your own local chapter!"

"Where's the fuckin' dinero in that?" Paco demanded.

"Huh?" Karen said. "You want to *encourage* every hacker with his own computer to *pirate* our discs, Red Jack and all?"

Fuckin' Coopersmith grinned from ear to ear. "For sure," he said. "Think of it! Hundreds of little independent Reality Liberation Front chapters from coast to coast; bust one, and two more spring up, and the only connection the cops can make between any of them is our national leader, Red Jack, a leader who's *impossible* to bust because there are thousands of copies of him floating around and he doesn't even exist! Mr. Random Factor personified! Red ripe anarchy for all the world to see, and not jack-shit the Fat Men can do!"

"Where's the dinero in that?" Paco repeated.

"There isn't any, Paco," Larry Coopersmith said. "That's our strength. That's the idiot thing we remember that everyone else seems to have forgotten."

"Qué?"

"Money is not everything."

"You're not shitting me?" Dojo said. "You'll just *give* me your master discs?"

"Exactly," Coopersmith said. "Since we've already liberated Red Jack from Muzik, Inc.'s, copyright, why not release him all the way into the public domain!"

He held out his hand. "Deal?" he said.

Dojo shrugged. "If you want to be crazy, I don't see where I've got anything to lose," he said, slapping Larry's palm.

Then he stood up and saluted Paco. "You got some crazy friends, my son," he said, "but I owe you. Every one of these packages I sell I give you twenty-five bucks."

Karen felt a surge of affection for him, a wave of comradeship. This Dojo might seem like a a cynical brute, but there was something soft and tender inside, something roughly just and grudgingly honorable; if nothing else, she could see quite plainly that in his way, he loved her Paco.

"Hey Dojo . . ." Paco crooned. "You don't have to do that, man. . . ."

"Don't go telling me what I don't gotta do in my own fuckin' joint!" the big man said gruffly, and then strode off across the dance floor.

Paco looked at Karen with a bemused plaintive softness about his eyes. "Hey, he really doesn't have to do that . . ." he said.

Karen squeezed his hand. "I know, Paco," she said.

"And what do you think *you're* doing, Markowitz?" Leslie demanded. "Maybe you were right in the first place, maybe the Jack *has* burned out your brain."

Larry Coopersmith took her hand in his, squeezed it, even as Karen was squeezing Paco's. He kissed her on the cheek.

"Hey sweathog!" he said, pointing to the breadbox at the back of his head, "this thing hasn't fried my brains. It's taken me to our leader." He laughed. He thumped the cable spool table with a meaty biker's hand.

"It's taken me to our leader, and he is us!"

RANDOM FACTORS

"You look like shit, Manning," Glorianna O'Toole said genially, giving Carlo Manning her number one obvious plastic smile to show him just how sympathetic she wasn't.

Manning's formerly perfectly groomed black hair was now in need of a trim, and for that matter, a going-over with a comb. The knot of his tie was awry, the top button of his white shirt was undone, and his eyes were a wee bit bloodshot and more than a little blackly hollowed. His desk was messily awash in printouts, unopened mail, folders, and video discs.

Fuck a duck, was that a sniffing straw and a vial of *dust* on the mirror between those two half-full mugs of cold coffee?

It didn't make any sense at all. "The Crown Prince of Rock and Roll" had been at the top of the charts for three months now, and "Your Rock and Roll Machine" had even climbed back into the top twenty as a backlist disc, something previously unheard of. This little corporate piggy should be in hog heaven.

Instead, Manning peered up at her with the disbelieving horror of a prisoner being slowly dragged to the electric chair, or a president of the Muzik Factory facing the inevitability of his impending flush down the corporate tubes. "I can't believe this is happening," he moaned.

"Can't believe what is happening?"

"You better sit down for this, Ms. O'Toole . . . Glorianna . . ."

Glorianna perched on the edge of one of the suddenly pathetic barber chairs Manning had once had screwed to the floor in a declaration of his determination to make his seat behind the big gunmetal desk equally permanent.

"I have to shitcan Red Jack," he said.

"What?" Glorianna grunted, and collapsed against the leather-upholstered back of the chair.

"Can you believe it?" Manning babbled distractedly to himself. "We've shipped over twenty million copies of his first two discs and now they say we can't do a third, ever. We can't even ship any more copies of 'The Crown Prince of Rock and Roll' or 'Your Rock and Roll Machine' and we have to destroy all copies of his visual algorithms and voiceprint parameters."

"That's the craziest fucking thing I've ever heard in forty years in this crazy fucking business," Glorianna observed rather neutrally.

For while this was indeed both shocking and totally incomprehensible, there was a bright side to it from where she found herself sitting. If they really *were* serious about axing Red Jack, she would never have to tell Manning or his impending successor that Red Jack was already dead at other hands, that Sally Genaro and Bobby Rubin could never be made to work on another disc together.

"Tell me something I don't know . . ." Carlo Manning groaned, pouring out about half a gram of dust onto his mirror and cutting it up into sloppy lines with the point of a pencil.

"But *why*?" Glorianna said as she watched him snort one up with a shudder. "And where is this assholery coming from?"

"From the board . . . from the legal department . . . from places I don't want to think about . . . to save my own ass . . ." Manning babbled shakily, and did up his other nostril.

"Get hold of yourself, Manning," Glorianna snapped, sliding off the chair and pulling the mirror with the rest of the dust across the desktop away from him. "What possible reason can anyone have for flushing a fortune down the toilet bowl?"

"To keep the *company* from going down the toilet bowl and me with it!" Manning snapped, completely losing it, and then, realizing he had lost it in front of her, making a visible effort to pull himself together.

"It's *these,*" he said, picking up a disc and sliding it across the desk at her. Glorianna assumed it was Factory product, but when she took a good look at it, she saw that it was a standard computer read-write disc with no label on it.

She cocked her head at Manning inquisitively.

"It's a piece of black market software. These things are all over the East Coast already, and spreading west fast. They're bugger programs, and they come in many loathsome flavors. Pop one into your home computer and the damn thing will get you into the mainframe at the bank or the utility company or your stockbroker or your school or the corporate records or God knows what all else and guide you through all sorts of computer-fraud scams. Change your grades, erase unpaid balances, credit yourself with nonexistent deposits, move stocks into your account from nowhere, get the picture?"

"Neato," Glorianna said with some enthusiasm. "Can you score me some?"

"Not funny, Ms. O'Toole!" Manning snarled with a ghost of his former hard-edged arrogance, chemically reincarnated, no doubt by the dust he had snorted. "This class of crime has increased three hundred percent in the last six months, and Muzik, Inc., is already the defendant in about two dozen lawsuits."

"Lawsuits?"

"*Lawsuits,* Ms. O'Toole," Manning said, patting a large tottery pile of manila folders. "So far we've avoided any criminal prosecution at least. . . ."

"You're *still* not making sense," Glorianna said. "Why are these . . . these bugger discs getting the Factory sued?"

"Because our number one AP rock star is fronting them and advocating theft, fraud, and outright revolution!" Manning said shrilly.

"Huh?"

"The sons of bitches who are making these things have pirated Red Jack's visual algorithms and voiceprint parameters," Manning told her. He arose somewhat shakily from behind his desk, snatched up the disc, and crossed the room to the disc deck. "They've laid an audiovisual track onto their bugger program discs." He popped the disc into the deck. "*This* is what the customer sees on his computer screen when he boots one of these up!"

Red Jack's face appeared on the screen. It was unmistakably him, down to Bobby Rubin's eyes and the smirky smile. Only the hair was different. It was long, and flaming American-flag red, but the stylized white webwork frosting had been replaced by the real thing, complete with breadbox worn in plain sight on the top of his head just in case anyone should miss the point.

"Boot me up and boogie when you wanna fight back, tap yourself a hit of old Red Jack!" he sang, dancing across the screen now, and hitting his touchpoint. It was Red Jack's voice right off "Crown Prince," shorn of the instrumental track, but his motion was jerky and spastic and the lip-sync not very convincing, like an old hand-animated cartoon.

"Greetings from the Reality Liberation Front," Red Jack said, standing in the middle of a blue matte background wearing a red T-shirt lettered with the initials "RLF" in lightning-bolt white, with his hands on his hips, and a shit-eating grin on his face. "They make more of me . . ."

His image multiplied. Dozens of identical little Red Jacks filled the screen.

"I'll make more for you!"

Just one Red Jack standing in the center of the screen as a crudely animated rain of money drifted down behind him.

"This is a Reality Liberation Front bedbug disc for increasing your bank balance, a, ahem, *Red Jack* disc, brothers and sisters," he said. "Just follow the leader through the program step by step and I'll show you how to insert phantom credits into your bank account and make those nasty old debits disappear right into the system itself, where no one will ever find them. . . ."

Red Jack sat down at a crudely drawn computer console, popped a disc into it, plugged in a modem. "Step one you've already done if you see me on your screen now. Step two, boot up your modem and dial your bank's electronic fund transfer access number. . . ."

Manning shuddered and hit the fast forward button. "How to defraud the banking system in ten easy steps that a moron could follow," he muttered as the screen blurred into multicolored smears and swirls. "And *this* at the end of every one of these damn things!" he said, hitting the play button.

Red Jack's face in close-up flickered and then popped into focus on the screen. "There, now wasn't that easy?" he said. "You are now a member of the Reality Liberation Front, the only organization in the history of the world that gives *you* money when you join up."

He stood before a huge American flag in his RLF T-shirt, staring intently out of the screen and pointing his finger in perfect parody of the classic Uncle Sam army recruiting poster. "The Reality Liberation Front wants *you*!" he proclaimed righteously. "Up against the wall with the Money Machine!"

Back to the close-up. "Ask not what you can do for the Reality Liberation Front, ask what the Reality Liberation Front can do for you! Which is plenty, brothers and sisters! We've got Red Jack discs for cash machines, for improving your grades, for making those nasty old phone and utility bills evaporate into the bits and bytes, for playing the stock market with phantom capital, for making you invisible to the IRS, for nulling parking tickets, and much, much more, and we're writing more every day."

Red Jack stood in an alleyway, handing discs to a series of stick figures, all of them wearing the Zap. "Ask for them in sleazy bars and meatracks everywhere!"

He tapped the breadbox on his head, and grinned. "And when you're in the market for the Jack, look for our extra-special offer, this wizard piece of wire and a Red Jack disc of your choice for only two hundred dollars. You'll make it back and more the very first time you boot me up, or I ain't the Crown Prince of Rock and Roll and the Peerless Leader of the Reality Liberation Front!"

A close-up on Red Jack as he hit his touchpoint and his hair flashed lightnings. "These Red Jack discs are *not* protected by federal copyright law!" he declared. "Permission to copy them by the zillions and zillions is expressly encouraged by the Reality Liberation Front! Down with Official Reality! Bits and bytes to the People! I make more of you, now you go make more of me!"

"Far fuckin' out!" Glorianna exclaimed as the screen went blank. You've gotten out, Jack, just like Bobby said you would, and they'll never stuff you back in again!

"Red ripe anarchy for all the world to see!" she sang out gaily as Carlo Manning slouched across the room and collapsed back behind his desk. She burst out laughing. "I'll snort to that!" she declared, and honked a big charge of dust.

"You find this *funny*?" Manning shrieked. "We're being sued for hundreds of millions by half the Fortune Five Hundred and that's a *joke* to you?"

"Seems to me it's the *Factory* who should be suing for trademark infringement," Glorianna said, and broke up again.

Manning didn't even seem to notice that she was laughing again at his expense. "Sue who? Sue what?" he said, yanking the mirror away from her suddenly. "Until they manage to arrest some perpetrators, there's no one to point a finger at except us! The pressure's on the feds to launch a criminal investigation of Muzik, Inc.! We've been able to hold it off so far, but it's already cost us two million dollars in grease!"

"Waste of money, Carlo baby," Glorianna said. "They'll never pin nothin' on ya!"

"Of course not!" Manning said earnestly, but with less than total conviction. "We're innocent! These lawsuits are pure bullshit!"

"I believe you, Carlo," Glorianna said as Manning stuck the straw in his nose and messily vacuumed up the remaining grains of dust on the mirror like a pig rooting out truffles. "You're pure as the uncut snow."

Manning peered at her narrowly. "But are *you*?" he said. "You produced 'Your Rock and Roll Machine' and 'Crown Prince,' and those discs are the basis of these lawsuits. They all allege that our songs have been *advocating* the use of these Red Jack discs. That's why legal says we have to ax Red Jack and destroy all copies of his software under fair witness and lose tens of millions in potential revenue."

He rubbed his lower lip reflectively. "If I have to, maybe I can pin it all on you and Rubin and Genaro . . ." he said slowly, his expression brightening somewhat.

Glorianna climbed back up on her barber chair throne and regarded him from on high. "I wouldn't try that if I were you, sonny," she said. " 'Cause I could testify truthfully under oath that we made 'Crown Prince,' at least, only under protest at your direct order and to specs sent down from research and marketing. And Bobby and Sally would back me up. Three against one if it ever came to court."

Manning underwent a complete transformation. He leaned back in his chair, uttering a hideous mechanical laugh, and then flashed her a grotesquely false smile.

"Now who's losing her sense of humor?" he said in a hollow tone of fellowship over a jagged edge of hysteria. "I didn't ask you here to threaten you. I may be in some temporary difficulties now, but my bad luck is going to be your good news."

"It is?"

"Can I be honest with you, Glorianna?" Manning said, pouring more dust out of his vial onto the mirror, and cutting it up into lumpy lines with the ivory snorting straw itself.

"You mean you haven't been true blue all along?" she drawled. "You coulda fooled me."

It blew right by him. "I *am* in some difficulty," he admitted inanely. "But we *can* recoup. The board will forget about this fiasco if we can come up with another AP rock star who will ship even more copies than marketing projected for a third Red Jack hit."

He rummaged around in the clutter of his desk and recovered a sheaf of printouts. "I put research and marketing onto it, and they came up with *this,*" he said, patting the papers paternally.

"What is it?"

"Specs for the next AP rock star," Manning told her, pushing the printout toward her with one hand and the dust-laden mirror with the other. "For your cyborged comeback, as promised, Glorianna. Read it, you'll love it, they've done a brilliant job."

Something told Glorianna she had better take a hit of dust before she read this thing, and when she had finished scanning the ten-page summary, she had to do another before she could contain herself well enough to deliver a succinct opinion.

"This sucks," she said.

"You don't like it?"

"It bites the Big One," she said, tossing the thing contemptuously across the desk at him. "I wouldn't have anything to do with sick shit like this if you pointed a fuckin' .45 at my head!"

Even that was an understatement as far as the Crazy Old Lady of Rock and Roll was concerned.

The specs called for her to become a creature called Electric Angel.

Her voice would be passed through enhancement programs designed to "optimize its depth penetration of aural centers of sexual stimulation (see Appendix II, *Voiceprint Parameters and Sexual Charisma in 17 Female Rock Stars*)."

Lyrics would be "tailored to maximize male libidinal response while creating role model identification fantasy appeal for the female target market (see Appendixes IV and V, *Key Words and Sexual Arousal in the Urban American Male* and *Female Sexual Frustration and Narcissistic Image Systems*)."

The instrumental tracks would "emphasize frequencies keyed directly into physiological central and peripheral nervous system response patterns in order to generate full excitation response," and "adopt percussion and bassline patterns modeled on coital rhythms."

Electric Angel's facial features would be "modeled on an idealized human female analog and have the flexion characteristics of muscle and skin," but "must be given the surface texture and tonal signature of burnished metal so as to emphasize the cyborged nature of the construct." Eyebrows and lashes should "maintain full human expressive subtleties," but the eyeballs themselves "should be crystalline ovoids from which rays, beams, image-trains, and other special effects may emanate at appropriate intervals."

The monstrosity's body would be "three-dimensionally modeled on ideal female nude form (see Appendix VII, *A Statistical Study of the Bioform Parameters of the Ideal Sex Object in a Demographic Cross Section of American Males*)" but rendered as "a metalized version of same, with pubes and nipples rendered in neon to the extent of realism permitted by relevant statutes (query legal re: legal status of stylized semi-human full frontal nudity under pornography law)."

"What's wrong with it?" Manning asked her in what seemed like true innocence. "It's brilliant! It has all the appeal to honest artificiality that made Red Jack such a hit, but it's got the max in sexual sell on top of it. It's a sure winner, it's a marketing manager's wet dream!"

"Is there a hole somewhere for me to get sick in?"

The fingers of Manning's left hand began drumming nervously on the desktop. "Look, these are only the preliminary specs," he said in a voice half an octave higher than usual, and then began to really gibber.

"If you see room for improvements, we'll be glad to factor in your input, nothing's written in stone, I know, I know, there's nothing in there about Electric Angel resembling you, but that's because these specs are general, we can give her your eyes and nasal structure, maybe do something with the lips, even change the name, Angel O'Toole, Electric Glorianna, whatever, I'll put research on it. . . ."

Glorianna stood up from the barber chair, rolling the sheaf of printout into a tight cylinder. It was too thick to fashion a proper point on, but it would have to do. She brought it down to waist level and thrust it toward the ceiling.

"Take it and stick it," she said, and then tossed it over her shoulder onto the floor.

"You can't do this to me!" Manning shouted in a fury, slamming both fists down on his desk as he bolted upright and upending a half-filled coffee cup.

"Oh yes I can, sonny," Glorianna said, turning toward the door. "I can even do it with a smile."

"Don't you realize I won't *survive* unless I can make the board forget about this Red Jack fiasco?" Manning whined, turning plaintive now. "I'm being held responsible for the legal costs and the grease and the loss of revenue. . . . My job is in your hands!"

"Is it now?" Glorianna purred. She made a pistol with her right hand, pointed it at Manning, smiled, then snapped her thumb forward.

"Bang!" she said.

Manning collapsed back into his chair. "Why?" he moaned. "What have I ever done to you?"

Glorianna stared at him in amused amazement. "What have you ever done to me?" she said. "Well, I suppose aside from threatening to get me thrown in the joint for the rest of my life and asking me to prostitute myself to make an evil sexist piece of shit to save your own worthless ass, I got to admit you've been a prince!"

"I'll take you with me!" Manning snarled, abruptly reverting to form. "There's still those drug charges. . . ."

"You can shove those up your ass too, Carlo baby," Glorianna told him calmly. "Once they can you, the last thing the next president of the Factory will want is me in court testifying as a witness against Muzik, Inc., in all those lawsuits, which anyone with the brains of a turkey will know I'll do if you get me busted. The next ass to warm that chair will be only too happy to let me alone and lay off as much of the bad corporate karma as possible on *you,* sonny. But look on the bright side—if you take my advice, allow yourself to be quietly fired, and keep me out of it, maybe, just maybe, at least you won't be doing any time."

"Wait, can't we—"

"Ciao," Glorianna said with a little wave bye-bye, and, turning on her heel, waltzed out, popping her fingers and singing.

Flashin' dancin' like liberty
In the home of the brave and the land of the free
Good Golly Miss Molly and up your hole!
Doncha fuck with no Crazy Lady of Rock and Roll!

Karen Gold trudged up the long dark flight of stairs to the loft with a dozen unsold Jacks, eighteen unsold discs, and a lousy $200 in her purse to show for a whole night's dealing in The American Dream.

The Revolution might be in full red ripe flower, but what was good for the Reality Liberation Front's cause had turned out, in the end, to be a complete disaster for its main source of income.

When Larry made his deal with Dojo and recruited Red Jack as the nonexistent front man of the Reality Liberation Front, sales of the new Red Jack discs had boomed, and why not, since she was peddling discs and Jacks together at $200 a pop, as well as being the beneficiary of endless commercials for her goods on MUZIK. Everyone who wanted to be *anyone* just *had* to plug in to the Jack and boot up one of his brand-name bedbug discs.

Tommy Don had even been inspired on the Jack to take a hint from Muzik, Inc., and distribute RLF T-shirts, not to indigent streeties as promo items, but for $30 apiece through a network of street dealers. He bought manufacturer's seconds in big lots for $8 a shirt on Canal Street, silk-screened the logo, and wholesaled them to the dealers for $20.

The Reality Liberation Front became a trendy fad. You could see people wearing the T-shirts all over town. Fancy boutiques put the logo on warm-up suits and rayon jackets. Hairdressers did a hot business in white-frosted red dye-jobs. The *Post, New York,* and *The Village Voice* did features on the phenomenon, and there was even a piece in *Rolling Stone*. Red Jack discs sold like crazy.

The banks, and the phone companies, and the utilities, and the credit card companies, and the IRS began to scream bloody murder as billions of dollars hemorrhaged out of the electronic economy into the bits and bytes.

Weaker banks folded. The SEC was constrained to tighten margin requirements and mandate that paper certificates be exchanged before any transaction became final. Utility companies demanded payment in actual paper.

The chronically anemic official economy slowed down and grew even paler as the electronic entrepreneurs of the underground economy fattened themselves up on its fiscal life's blood. The value of the currency surged and gyrated wildly, but the overall curve of inflation went up and up. It was a democratic inflation; the government wasn't running the presses, the people were printing out their own funny money on their home computers.

It was a high old time that seemed almost too good to last.

It was.

Even as Larry Coopersmith had predicted, even as he intended to have happen all along, pirated versions of the RLF's Red Jack discs began to appear, indistinguishable from the real thing. The

Maf or the yaks or whoever was really making the things flooded the country with cheap Jacks so that any enterprising hacker with a computer could run off his own Red Jack discs, buy a load of Jacks, call himself a chapter of the RLF, and sell the combo for $200 or even less.

What with all these independent sources, it didn't take long for the market to become saturated. Every hacker in the country had a collection of Red Jack discs and a Jack.

So while Official Reality was groaning under the economic strain, so was the RLF. While the electronic economy unraveled, their Red Jack disc business went south even faster. And whenever Karen or Leslie would complain about this to Markowitz, he'd just give himself a tap, laugh, and declare airily that true revolutionaries had to be willing to scramble some of their own eggs.

Inevitably, the Empire did its best to strike back.

The media coverage changed. The RLF was no longer a joke but a dire threat to the already depressed economy. ''Electronic inflation'' became an editorial page buzzword. Companies took to firing employees wearing the Red. A few so-called RLF chapters in Cleveland, San Francisco, Chicago, and Boston were busted. Muzik, Inc., up to its eyeballs in lawsuits, pulled ''Crown Prince'' and ''Your Rock and Roll Machine'' off MUZIK, stopped distributing the discs, and loudly announced that they had destroyed the masters and Red Jack's algorithms, though you could still score bootleg copies if you knew where.

Nothing, or so it seemed, not even the disappearance of Red Jack from MUZIK and the Muzik stores, could stop the fad now.

But the Revolution had gotten too successful for its own economic good, at least as far as Karen was concerned. Business sucked, and she could see no way for it to get any better.

Nevertheless, even at this late hour, the loft was a beehive of energy. Iva and Bill were modeming new bedbug programs to RLF chapters in Portland and New Orleans. Tommy and Eddie were still silk-screening T-shirts even though that enterprise, what with all the spontaneous competition, was also in the shits. Mary and Teddy were hunched over their computers writing God knows what. Malcolm sat on the floor in a corner cackling to himself as he wired together some pile of assorted electronic junk, while Larry Coopersmith looked on with a big shit-eating grin.

And while fingers flew over the keyboards, while Tommy and

Eddie passed T-shirts through their silk screen, while Malcolm soldered bits of electronic bric-a-brac together, every now and then, hands reached up to hit the touchpoints of the Jacks snugged into everyone's hair, for when economic reality intruded, and spirits flagged, renewed inspiration was just a tap away.

In fact, Karen thought somewhat sourly as she crossed the big room to where Larry stood over Malcolm, everyone was maybe spending a little too much time plugged in; here, as in The American Dream, and the streets too, come to think of it, there was a little too much chain-tapping going on for her taste, a little too much avoiding of the hard facts of cold economic reality.

"How'd it go tonight?" Coopersmith asked.

"How do you think, Larry?" Karen told him. She fished two hundreds out of her purse and handed them over.

"That's it?" Coopersmith said, eyeing the thin sheaf of bills dubiously.

"I've been telling you all along that business stinks!" Karen snapped. "If you weren't chain-tapping all the time, maybe you'd listen to what I'm saying. The market's saturated. There's just no one left to sell Red Jack discs to."

Markowitz beamed at her beatifically. "You're wrong, Karen," he said. "Malcolm has just figured out how to . . . ah . . . tap a whole new market for Red Jack discs that we haven't even touched yet."

"Yeah? Who?"

"Streeties!" Markowitz exclaimed.

"You guys are flashing right now!" Karen said angrily.

Markowitz grinned right through her. "Millions of new customers for our Red Jack discs!" he declared grandly. "Millions and millions of new random factors! It's time to *really* put the power of the bits and bytes in the hands of the people!"

"Yeah, sure. And where are they gonna get the money to buy them from?"

"Beg, borrow, sell their asses, but mostly steal, I suppose," Markowitz said blithely. "Every streetie in the city will be scraping together a hundred bucks bit by bit to buy their own Red Jack disc 'cause they'll know they'll get it back ten times over the first time they use it on a cash machine or the Social Security system or whatever! We'll soak the fat cats and spread it around thin!"

"You're out of your mind!" Karen told him. "You've fried

your brain! Come off it, Larry, unplug and listen to what you're saying. Why should streeties buy Red Jack discs? What are they gonna do with them? Pop them into their computers?''

Markowitz laughed. He reached up and hit his touchpoint. ''Not flashing now, Karen,'' Larry said more soberly. ''And I'm still telling you this is going to work.'' He pointed to the mess of stuff surrounding Malcolm. Karen took a second look, saw an old tv set, a keyboard, a cheap modem, a crummy old disc deck.

''What *is* all this junk, anyway?'' she said.

Malcolm McGee looked up at her with an enormous grin creasing his lips and a faraway flash glazing his eyes behind their thick glasses.

''The crown of my creation in my wizard dreams,'' he sang up at her in a truly demented cackle. ''It's the People's Cash Machine!''

''Computer?'' Dojo said, frowning at the cardboard box Paco and Malcolm McGee had lugged down the stairs and into his room. ''What do I want with a fuckin' computer?''

Malcolm unpacked the junk in the box onto Dojo's unmade bed: an old portable tv, a keyboard, a cheap videodisc deck, and a small steel box, and began wiring the stuff together. ''What do you want with a money machine?'' he said with a shit-eating grin.

''Money machine, my black ass!'' Dojo told him. He squinted at the mess. ''That doesn't even look like a computer,'' he said. ''Looks like a bunch of old junk from Canal Street.''

''Well that's about what it is,'' Malcolm said. ''Old tv set, used keyboard, Malaysian disc deck, sleazy 1200 baud modem I breadboarded myself, and an old 512K chip out of a junked game machine to run it. Put it together for under four hundred. Not exactly state of the art, maybe, but it does the job.''

''What job?''

''We're all having trouble moving Red Jack discs, right?'' Malcolm said. ''Everyone with the money to afford a home computer's already got a whole library of bedbug programs. . . .''

''Yeah, and for that matter, the Jack ain't exactly selling like hotcakes anymore either,'' Dojo said sourly. ''So tell me something I don't know, nigger.''

''Just getting to that,'' Malcolm said. '' 'Cause what you don't know is that you can plug this little piece of wizardry into any phone jack, pop in one of our discs, access some bank or whatever, and bedbug their computers just as easy as you can with the latest bells and whistles from IBM. And this one won't cost you anything."

"Say what?" Dojo muttered, and flopped down on the bed.

"Set it up here. Charge your customers, say, fifty bucks for ten minutes. *Sell* them the discs to use in it for a hundred. If the People's Cash Machine works out, the RLF will supply you with as many as you can move for four hundred bucks a pop, and you can sell 'em for whatever the traffic will bear to other meatracks like this, or rent 'em out for a piece of the action like pay phones."

Dojo's eyes lit up in greedy comprehension. He shook his head in slow admiration. "For so-called revolutionaries, you folks *do* have a head for business . . ." he said. He frowned. "Only one little problem . . ."

"The streeties who hang out in joints like this are complete computer illiterates?" Malcolm drawled.

Dojo cocked his head and eyed Malcolm narrowly. Malcolm laughed.

"Ah, but remember we have Red Jack on our discs to lead the naive masses through the software by their hot little hands!" he said. "Set up phony Social Security or military pension or disability or trust fund accounts and have the computers mail out a nice little check every month to a post office box. Or have the bank send you a cash machine card to draw off a nice big fat balance. And you know what the best part is?"

"The best part . . . ?"

"Now we'll be selling the discs to a whole class of people who don't have computers! They won't be able to copy 'em and swap 'em around! They'll all have to buy them from us! Have I made you an offer you can't refuse?"

Dojo stood up, shaking his head in puzzlement. "Shit man," he said, "you've made me an offer I can't even *understand*! I mean why is the Reality Liberation Front being so good to me? What's in all this for you?"

Malcolm McGee peered at him owlishly from behind his thick glasses. "We're democratizing the economy down to the streetie level!" he said. "We've liberated the cybersphere from Official Reality, and now we're gonna give a share of the electronic pie to the downtrodden masses!"

"Never mind all that wirehead bullshit, nigger, even if I was crazy enough to understand it, I still wouldn't see how you're gonna make any money off of it."

"We're not in it for the money!"

Dojo flared his wide nostrils contemptuously. "What else is there?" he said.

Paco had been standing there like a piece of furniture during all this, trying to make some sense of it himself. Chingada, way things were now, the only money he was making was what Dojo was paying him to work the door here, and what with what Larry called the "electronic inflation," that didn't buy dick anymore.

So why did Larry keep grinning like a fuckin' ape and saying it was all goin' according to Markowitz, whoever the fuck he was, and what good was the People's Cash Machine gonna do for them while it was fillin' the bags of all those streeties?

Now, looking at Dojo, he thought he knew the answer.

"Hey, Dojo," he said, "remember what you said the night I brought Larry Coopersmith here? About how with the usual wire not selling, all the terminal wireheads you had upstairs in Florida were costing you dinero and not making you nothing?"

"So?"

"So why didn't you throw them all out on the street?"

Dojo scowled at him incredulously. "Are you for real, my man?" he said. "You know as well as I do that those fuckin' zombies are so burned out they'd fuckin' *starve to death* unless I made them shove some kibble down their throats every day or so. They'd shit in their fuckin' pants and stew in it unless someone told them to drag their asses to the crapper!"

Paco smiled at him. "Chingada, so I guess even a big tough nigger like you ain't *always* just in it for the money," he said.

"Arrrr . . ." A soft throaty growl emerged from Dojo's mouth, and he looked away for a moment. Paco was sure that if the big man were white, he would have seen the putamadre blush.

Sally Genaro had never even *met* a president of Muzik, Inc., before, let alone been asked to take a meeting with one in his office, and she felt especially privileged to be summoned here *now*, by this mystery man, only a week after he had taken over, with the Factory buzzing with all these weird stories about Nicholas West.

West had been brought in from back east, he had never worked for Muzik, Inc., before, and nobody in the music business, at least in L.A., had even *heard* of the guy. Some said he had been the head of an advertising agency, some said he was a banker, some said he was a shrink, some even said he had come from the government. But it was all just gossip; nobody in the business even seemed to know somebody who knew somebody who knew West before he took over the Factory from Carlo Manning.

So Sally entered the president's office riding the keen edge of mystery, anticipation, and the feeling that something very special and important was about to happen to her, else why would *Nicholas West* make the time to give a meeting to a mere VoxBox artist in the midst of organizing his takeover.

The presidential office was not quite the luxury palace she had expected. In fact, there was something bleak and cold and somehow *nasty* about it that made her shudder momentarily as the total effect hit her.

It was huge, all right, and of course it was a corner office with two big walls of window looking out on the brown smog bank hovering low over the flatlands, and there was a state of the art disc deck and screen, and a whole brag-wall of little gold discs, and a big freeform desk of burnished gunmetal.

But the ceiling was painted flat white, with a pinstriped pattern of squares in black. And the floor was its reversed image, some kind of phony black marble etched with a white checkerboard. The conference table was a big gleaming white slab on a polished chrome base, and the chairs around it were of black leather slung on more chrome. Four similar chairs were arranged in front of the desk, these white on chrome. No color inside the room at all.

It reminded Sally of some kind of 1980s-style Japanese modern sushi bar, or a clean-room for mainframe computers, or worse, a gigantic institutional *toilet* some *pervert* had furnished as an office.

But unsettling as the decor of the office was, it was nothing compared to the shock of seeing Glorianna O'Toole and *Bobby Rubin* sitting there in front of the desk!

"No one told me *they* were going to be here!" she whined at the man behind the desk as she stood there with a sinking stomach halfway across the room.

"Sit down please, Sally," Nicholas West said in a bland, calm, quite polite tone of voice that seemed to entirely ignore her outburst, and favored her with an equally neutral corporate smile.

He had thick, straight, silvery hair combed neatly down just past his ears, a strong cleft chin, even green eyes behind clear, swept-back, gold-framed glasses, slightly ruddy complexion, and he wore a powder-blue suit, matching tie, and pale yellow shirt. He might be fifty-five, or just as easily forty. He reminded Sally of the kind of actor you saw on half the tv shows on the air but whose name you never remembered.

Not exactly *sexy,* but for some reason she could not at all fathom, Sally found herself *liking* him.

Hesitantly, Sally crossed the room and took a seat as far away from Bobby as she could get, with Glorianna and an empty chair between them. Glorianna nodded an indifferent greeting. Bobby made a point of staring out the window into the smog.

"Read these specs, please," West said, fanning three folders out across his desk before them. "Just the summary will do for now."

Sally picked up her copy and saw that it was a set of specifications for a female AP rock star called Electric Angel. Bobby snatched up his copy and buried his nose in it. Glorianna picked up her folder, glanced at it, then dropped it back on the desk with a curl of her lip and a wrinkle of her nose as if it were a dead fish.

"I've already read this piece of shit," she said.

Nicholas West's only reaction was the slightest raising of his thin gray eyebrows. Cool! Sally thought admiringly. Like . . . *presidential* . . .

Dutifully, Sally read through the ten-page summary. It was full of a lot of the usual fancy jargon from marketing and research, but what it called for seemed quite simple—a kind of sexy-lady cyborg and music totally designed to make guys want to ball her.

Sally smiled to herself. It was kind of funny the way they used all these hundred-dollar words and scientific mumbo jumbo to tell her they wanted tracks that would make women wish they were this Electric Angel and give all the guys great big hard-ons. As if whoever wrote this thing had never even *heard* any down and dirty rock and roll!

"Well, Sally?" Nicholas West said when she laid the folder in her lap and looked up at him.

"Well what, Mr. West?"

"Can you give us the kind of instrumental tracks these specs call for? Do you understand what's called for in the way of voiceprint parameters?"

Sally smiled at him, shrugging. "For sure," she said. "No big deal. This kind of stuff is *easy.*"

"Bobby?"

Bobby looked up from this folder at West with a thin little sneer. "You mean can I synthesize the crap this script calls for?"

"Crap?" West said mildly.

Bobby laughed. "This reads like specs for porn targeted at *robots,*" he said. "I didn't think they were much of a market for discs."

"It doesn't . . . arouse your prurient interest?"

"It's *prurient,* all right, Mr. West . . ." Bobby said. He gave West a snaky little smile. "May I be frank with you?"

Nicholas West nodded.

Bobby shot a long poisonous glance at Sally, smiled broadly, looked back at the president of Muzik, Inc. "I wouldn't be *interested* in fucking this thing with *your* dick, Mr. West," he said.

Glorianna O'Toole laughed uproariously. Nicholas West's only reaction was the gentlest of frowns. "What's wrong with these specs?" he asked mildly.

"Too mechanical," Bobby said. "I mean, what you got here is sick, but it's not *twisted* enough to be a sick *turn-on,* know what I mean, it needs more *kink,* more crazy energy." He grinned at West slyly. "Nothing that a genius like me couldn't fix, though," he said dryly.

Nicholas West smiled. "Good," he said. "Then it's settled. The songhacks have already done some lyrics. You'll go into the studio with it on Monday. You'll do the visuals, Sally will do the instrumentals tracks and the voiceprint parameters, and Glorianna, you'll sing Angel's vocals through them, just like you did for Red Jack on the last disc."

He broke into a modest grin. "We know all too well how big a hit *that* was," he said. "This will be even bigger!" The grin suddenly evaporated. "It had better be."

"No fucking way!" Glorianna and Bobby shouted in unison, and then looked at each other in some surprise.

"I'm not going to do sick shit like this," Glorianna declared. "I only showed up for this meeting out of curiosity anyway."

"I'm not going to work with *her* again," Bobby said, snarling, and giving his head a contemptuous toss in the direction of Sally.

Same to you too, Bobby Rubin! Sally had been about to say, but some vibe that suddenly came off Nicholas West held her back. He didn't shout, he didn't frown. His face didn't change at all, but somehow the air around him got ten degrees colder.

"I must ask you to put aside any creative or personal differences you may have with Sally for the good of the company, Bobby," he said evenly.

"No."

"Perhaps I have not made myself entirely clear," West said just as calmly. "*No* is not an answer I'm prepared to accept." He nodded at Glorianna O'Toole. "That goes for you too," he said.

Glorianna folded her arms across her chest and sneered openly at the president of Muzik, Inc. "Screw you, Charlie," she said.

Now West's eyes *did* harden. But he *still* kept his cool. "You two don't seem to understand the situation, either the company's, the nation's, or your own," he said.

Jeez, Sally thought in somewhat queasy admiration, this guy's carved out of steel! They're like *crazy* to be pissing him off! She immediately resolved that, come what may, she would not make the same mistake.

"Muzik, Inc., now has over two billion dollars in lawsuits pending against it," West said. "These Red Jack discs have become a national menace. Total corporate losses are already estimated at some fifty billion dollars, and that's only the computer theft that has already been discovered, of course. The integrity of the data bases of the IRS, state and local tax authorities, universities, public school systems, and other governmental agencies is being nibbled to death by millions of anonymous electronic mice. What's worse, much worse from a certain point of view, is that the Social Security system and the military pension system, *the Treasury itself,* is being looted in dribs and drabs by millions of phony fund transfers into nowhere. Do you begin to realize what's at stake here?"

"Fuckin'-A!" Glorianna O'Toole said. "Red ripe anarchy for all the world to see!"

"Well put," Nicholas West said. "The economy is in bad enough shape as it is without Red Jack and his damned Reality Liberation Front!"

"He really *has* gotten out . . ." Bobby muttered. "All the way out and no way to put him back in, either . . ."

"*What?*" Nicholas West snapped sharply, his cool cracking a bit for the first time.

Bobby shrugged. "Any one of forty million out of work or underemployed hackers can easily enough pirate his voiceprint parameters and visual algorithms off copies of 'Crown Prince' or 'Your Rock and Roll Machine.' In fact, by now there must be pirates pirating him off pirate discs!"

He gave a snaky little laugh that sent a quick thrill through Sally despite herself. "Maybe there isn't any Reality Liberation Front either," he said. "Maybe some wirehead cyberwizard somewhere just made it up, copied Red Jack onto a few bedbug discs he made, and now the whole thing's just being spread by copycat pirates. How can anyone stop a revolutionary conspiracy that exists only as millions of easily duplicated copies of the same software?"

"What will the Fat Men do?" Glorianna said, and they both broke up into raucous laughter.

Nicholas West grimaced, frowned, then smiled. "Use what we have learned from this fiasco in a scientific manner," he said, patting a copy of the Electric Angel specs. "Use every resource at our command to replace a dangerous national fad for economic anarchy with a new AP cult figure keyed into the only human drive stronger than greed."

"Sex . . . ?" said Sally.

Bobby snickered, but the new president of the Factory beamed at her. "Very good, Sally," he said. "We will make Electric Angel the wet dream of every American male and the role-identification model of every female. We will give her discs maximum exposure on MUZIK. We will do makeup and clothing marketing tie-ins. We will create the biggest and brightest star the world has ever known. We will use all our professional resources to do scientifically what these RLF terrorists have done by the seat of their pants. We will create the ultimate AP rock star, one that will make everyone forget there ever even was a Red Jack."

He looked at Bobby, Glorianna, and Sally in turn. "This is war," he said, "all-out media war, my major area of expertise, and I am not calling for volunteers. The three of you have just been drafted."

Glorianna O'Toole stood up, turned on her heel, began walking toward the door.

"Where do you think you're going?"

Glorianna paused, looked back over her shoulder. "Canada," she told West. "Hanoi. Fuckin' Moscow! 'Cause I'm a conscientious objector. Pixels to the people! Long live the Reality Liberation Front! Viva Red Jack!"

"You don't quite understand your situation," West said. "If you refuse to do the vocals, life can be made very unpleasant for you. . . ."

"Don't tell me. . . . I'll never work in this town again!"

"Permanent unemployment will be the least of your problems . . ." West told her ominously.

"Right, you'll sue me, you'll shove flaming toothpicks under my fingernails, you'll have me thrown in the joint!" Glorianna snarled at him. "Well go ahead, I dare you, you little pissant asshole!" she said, giving the president of the Factory the finger. "You just try it, sonny, and see how you like reading all about this little corporate plot as a cover story in *Rolling Stone*!" And she stormed out of the room, slamming the door behind her.

Nicholas West bolted to his feet, his hands gripping the edge of the desk, his face contorted, a deep red flush spreading across his fair complexion.

"Forget about that old has-been," Sally blurted. "We don't need her. Anything she can do, I can do better! *I'll* be Electric Angel!"

West slowly subsided back into his chair. The blood drained from his face. He regarded Sally quizzically. "You?" he said. "There's nothing in your personnel file about you ever having been a singer. . . ."

"But I'm the best VoxBox artist the Factory has!" Sally declared, and it all came bursting out of her on a wave of long-frustrated energy, the final crest of a life long breaker of longing washing over her and through her, hiding in the background while the guys fronted the Razor Dogs, churning out tracks for dead-ass singers with nothing but a face and a body, watching Glorianna O'Toole sing the vocals on "Crown Prince" and crying inside, why not me? why not me? why not me?

"Just give me the lyrics, Mr. West, and I'll do the music, and I'll input the vocal line, and I'll run it through vocoders and voiceprint parameters, and filter it, and sync it to the instrumental lead, and out the other end will come something that will make all the boys cream in their jeans, I promise, I promise, just give me the chance, let me show you what I can do, I won't let you down. . . ."

"Cyborg Sally!" Bobby Rubin sneered, his lips curled in amused disgust.

"Cyborg Sally . . ." Nicholas West said slowly. His strong green eyes lit up. He smiled at her. "Cyborg Sally . . ." he said. "Yes . . . It scans! Cyborg Sally it is!"

He beamed at Sally. "I like a team player," he said. "I like your attitude."

He studied her face for a long moment, then ran his eyes slowly up and down her body, making her painfully aware of every individual pimple, every imperfection, every fold of flesh, every extra ounce.

"And it deserves to be rewarded . . ." he said slowly. "So I'm going to give you a real *personal* stake in the success of Cyborg Sally. . . . You give me what you've promised, and I'll give you something very special, Sally, something that will make you the envy of every woman in the world. You'll not only be the *voice* of Cyborg Sally, we'll model her face on *you*. Your eyes, your nose, your lips—perfected, augmented, enhanced, and placed atop the perfect body." Nicholas West smiled knowingly. "You'd like that, wouldn't you, Sally?"

Like it! It was the impossible dream of her whole life! And all she had to do to make it come true was the one thing she did best. . . .

"Oh yes, Mr. West!" she cried, hardly able to believe her good fortune. "You can for sure count on me!"

"I think I'm going to puke," Bobby said.

"Well, at least that's one thing we all know you're good at, Bobby Rubin," Sally snapped.

Bobby flushed, opened his mouth to snap something back, but Nicholas West cut him off with an upraised hand and a sharp, hard voice. "No more of this! *I* know what you're *really* good at, Rubin, and that's visual synthesis, and that *is* what you're going to do!"

"You expect me to take this . . . this . . . *fat little pimple* and rotoscope her into an algorithm for this goddamn sex machine?"

"I don't *expect* you to do it. I *know* you will."

"No I *won't*!"

"Oh yes you will," West said evenly. "Must you make me resort to crudities . . . ?"

Bobby just glared at him.

Nicholas West sighed. He shrugged. He smiled a horrible false smile at Bobby.

"You have already been good enough to provide me with the or else, Rubin . . ." he said. "We'll charge you with causing Red Jack to advocate computer theft on our discs and then pirating his copyrighted voiceprint parameters and algorithms and selling them to the so-called Reality Liberation Front. Multiple counts of theft and copyright infringement, Rubin. Even if you somehow manage to weasel your way out of them, no one in the industry will ever hire you again. Ms. O'Toole is in no position to arouse our ire as long as we keep her out of court in return for her silence, and Sally here will back us up, won't you, Sally? For the good of the company? For the good of the nation?"

Sally smiled sweet poison at Bobby. "All the way, Mr. West," she said, savoring this icing on her cake.

Bobby's hands balled into fists. He glared furiously at Sally. "So you've got me by the balls, you son of a bitch!" he said, turning his rage on Nicholas West.

"Why don't we just say that we're both willing to be reasonable . . . ?" West said smoothly. "A two hundred thousand dollar bonus to you when we ship the five millionth disc, just so there's no hard feelings."

Bobby's fists uncurled, he slumped forward, his face became petulant in defeat. "But I *won't* go into the same studio with her," he whined. "Just give me the finished audio tracks, and I'll put the visuals to them, and that's as far as I'll go." He turned to glare his disgust at Sally. "As you may have noticed," he said, "this bitch and I do not get along."

Nicholas West shrugged. "All I'm concerned with is *product,*" he said. "I'm willing to leave *process* in the hands of the talent as long as I get it."

Bobby stood up to leave, grimacing, slump-shouldered, defeated. Sally certainly should have been enjoying this moment, and on a certain level she was, but somehow she found herself feeling *sorry* for him, somehow she found herself rising from her chair and moving toward him, somehow she found herself wanting to touch his shoulder, and comfort him, and tell him . . .

"Bobby . . ."

For a moment he glared at her, and then he seemed to read what was written on her face, and his expression softened.

But only for a moment.

Then, as if he had caught himself feeling something he was

determined not to let himself feel, he hardened his face and his heart, turned his back, and walked away.

Sally Genaro leaned back in her chair, pondering the lyric sheet propped on the music stand above her keyboard, fingering the breadbox pressed slick and cool against the back of her skull, knowing that sooner or later she was going to have to Jack. . . .

She dreaded plugging in, for ever since that horrid flash over the phone with Bobby, the Jack had taken her back to the same dreadful dreamspace every time she hit the touchpoint. . . .

Bobby in her bedroom, smoky-eyed, smiling down at her, slowly peeling off his clothing, bumping and grinding his tall, lithely muscled, smooth-skinned, bronzed body, in a private striptease just for her . . .

Bobby, with his long, flowing red hair, stretching himself out atop her, his eyes glazed with passion, his breath slow and heavy, moaning in delight as he entered her, then masterfully easing her up, up, up to the very edge, holding her there for an eternity as she wrapped her legs around his waist, then flashing her through orgasm after orgasm after orgasm, taking her higher, and higher, and higher, to places no other woman had ever been . . .

Bobby, standing in the corner of her bedroom, leaning back luxuriantly with his hands clasped behind his head, leering at her, sneering at her as she came painfully and messily into her own grubby hand, while a faceless blond with a perfect athlete's body knelt worshipfully before him giving him head . . .

She dreaded this flash, and yet she craved it, plugging in again and again, hoping the next time it would be different, that it would end with him coming deep inside her, collapsing sweetly into her arms, kissing her tenderly on the lips, cuddling to sleep against her.

But it was always the same. . . .

And now . . .

And now she knew that she would soon have to go there again. But this time . . . maybe this time it would be different . . . this time it *had* to be different. . . .

The lyrics the songhacks had sent down promised her it would be different, Nicholas West had promised her it would be different, she had to *make* it different. . . . So first . . .

She picked up her mike and inputted the chorus into memory,

just the words themselves chanted in her own flat nasal voice, not even trying to sing them yet. . . .

I'm Cyborg Sally
I'm your blood-hot wire
I'm the blazing bytes
Of your meat's desire . . .

She keyed in a rhythm line, a heavy bass drum smeared down with low gut-thrumming subsonics, and a brush of electronic flares across the brass cymbal above it, and an almost subliminal keening growl from rhythm guitar, and then a hissing, twisting, synthesizer lead.

She programmed these tracks onto an endlessly repeating sequencer loop keyed to the drum-line, and then sang the chorus onto it.

She multiplexed the back-up vocal through layer after layer of voiceprint parameters; a throaty electronic growl right on the lower edge of audibility, a wailing sexpot insinuation a little bit above that, a grunty dirty-moma chant in the middle ranges, and a forthrightly electronic static hiss of a cyborg voice up there at the top.

Yeah, right, that's getting to be Cyborg Sally, the me they always told me that I could never be!

She laid multiple instrumental voices across the keyboard—guitar, lyric electronic organ, a sound sampled off a sparking wire, her own voice moaning orgasmically and filtered and smeared into something immense and oceanic—and played the lead-line into memory.

Finally, she constructed a set of voiceprint parameters through which to sing the vocal lead—sultry, sexy, human on the lower notes, breaking into hissy electronics on the highs, multiplexed to a vanishing point with a subtle infinite lag-program in the middle, and then the whole thing underlaid with its own mirror image way down in the subsonic and overlaid with the burning wire of a supersonic ghost.

And then there was nothing for it but to pick up the mike, play the whole thing back from the top, plug in, and *become*—Cyborg Sally.

She picked up the mike with her right hand, hit the playback button and then her touchpoint in quick succession with her left, then dropped it into her lap and clamped her thighs tight around it. . . .

And she was standing triumphantly nude before her own bed, her smooth, tight, golden body glorified in a brilliant pool of white light. On the bed lay Bobby Rubin, the real Bobby, black-haired, pasty, and thin in his nudity, gazing up at her in wimpy shyness.

She grinned at him wickedly, running her hands over her perfect breasts, blue sparks arcing from her fingertips to her golden flesh, danced over to the bed, spread her arms wide, arched her back, and belted it out from her cyborged heart of hearts.

I'm Cyborg Sally
And I've never been
Plug into me
And I'll make you scream. . . .

Bobby slowly rose to a seated position, a hungry little boy with his tongue all but hanging out as his mouth reached upward for the sparkling chrome nipple of one perfect breast.

As his lips closed around it, she snaked one hand into his hair and pushed his head down, down, down, grabbing his shoulder with the other, dancing backward, pulling him off the bed with her superhuman strength and onto his knees, and there he knelt, eyes heavy-lidded, staring worshipfully and imploringly up at her, where he belonged.

Then she laughed, and let him thrust his face deep between her legs as she towered above him in her perfect flesh, disdainfully accepting his groveling homage.

Laser lips bring you to your knees
Darkling sparkling ecstasy
Lick my flashing circuitry . . .

Then she lifted him off his knees with her mighty arms, flung him backward onto the bed, impaled herself on him, arched her back, flung her arms wide, and sang out her triumph, dancing in the hot white spotlight to the vast unseen audience beyond the footlights—the Razor Dogs, high school jocks, Bobby Rubin, every grubby little Valley club, moaning and groaning, and singing along with her with their grubby little hands in their sweaty pants, rockin' and rolling in the endless aisles.

Comin' to dance
And I'm comin' tonight
Comin' in crystal and neon light
Comin', comin', you just can't hide
Comin', comin', comin' deep inside
Comin', comin,' comin' so free
Comin' right atcha
Come along . . . come along . . . come along . . .
Come along with me!

Sally Genaro emerged from the dreamtime slumped over before her VoxBox, her throat dry and raspy, her garments plastered to her body with thick oily sweat, her left hand thrust deep past the waistband of her jeans, cold and slimy with vaginal juices.

She writhed convulsively. She wiped her hand on the thighs of her pants. She shuddered. Her flesh crawled. Her spirit soared.

She grimaced. She smiled. She leaned back in her chair. "I'm Cyborg Sally . . ." she muttered. "And I've never been. I'm Cyborg Sally, I'm a sex machine. . . ."

Bobby Rubin sat there before his image organ with a bubble of cold nausea in the pit of his stomach, a dull rage smoldering in his brain, and a shameful and treacherous hard-on in his pants.

He could hardly believe what he had just played back. The instrumental tracks alone were enough to have a dead monk up out of his grave and slavering for pussy.

And the vocals, especially that lead voice, he had to admit, were a kind of loathsome genius.

Ultimately female but openly artificial, wrapping itself around the cynically sexual lyric like a perfect blow-job mouth, and sub and supersoniced to the max with subliminals that went straight to the back-brain and the balls, it was more than enough to have most any man reaching helplessly for his fly.

And there was more to it than mere cynical craft or even artistic inspiration. There was unmistakable, unavoidable, undeniable, passionate sexual *conviction.*

The voice of Cyborg Sally was the voice of female heat itself, wired and filtered and processed and multiplexed into a pure dick-throbbing abstraction of lust, somehow amplified, not diminished by the transhuman artificiality.

But it was precisely this final turn of the vocal screw, this ultimate level of the turn-on, that turned Bobby Rubin's stomach and aroused his ire.

For he could not listen to "Cyborg Sally" without seeing the Pimple in his mind's eye, sitting behind her VoxBox with the Jack on her head and a hand between her legs, dreaming of *him,* beating herself off, and singing this damn thing directly to him through her machineries.

Oh yes it was an ego trip, oh yes his mind could not keep his body from being turned on by it on a deep cellular level! That was what made it the ultimate violation.

For that voice told him all too well what *he* was in Sally Genaro's dreamtime. Like any man hearing this thing, he was the avidly willing sex slave of Cyborg Sally.

But of all the men who would fall into her power when the disc was released, only he would be tortured by the knowledge of who and what lay behind Cyborg Sally—a fat sweaty little Pimple bringing herself off behind a vision of Bobby Rubin groveling before her in total ecstatic submission.

"Yeah, well let's see how *you* like being in *my* power, bitch," Bobby snarled aloud to the head and shoulders still-shot of Sally Genaro that he punched up on his monitor.

He pondered the pudgy face, the hint of acne under heavy makeup, the dumb green eyes, the ratty, teased blond hair. Make *this* a turn-on . . . ? He fiddled with his keyboard, erased everything but the eyes, the high curving nose, the full fat lips—what else of this mess, after all, was the least bit salvageable?

He overlaid a few mods on a basic lip-sync program, opened the mouth to reveal his handiwork—gleaming stainless steel teeth, two rows of perfect little daggers framing a sinuous, somewhat tubular tongue of slick black leather with the slightest hint of a fork at the tip. He modified the nose into an angular stylization of itself, curves transformed into subtle planar approximations of themselves. Leaving the eyes protoplasmic and human and vulnerable, he trapped them in a smooth silver ovoid head, laid in sculptured ears, and crowned the Sally-monster with a billowing Medusa afro of writhing black neon snakes flickering and flashing from within just on the edge of the ultraviolet.

He smiled wickedly at the disembodied head of Cyborg Sally,

then sequenced a chorus off the sound track through lip-sync and animation programs.

I'm Cyborg Sally
I'm your blood-hot wire
I'm the blazing bytes
Of your meat's desire....

The black leather tongue licked and spit the lyric seductively through dagger rows of teeth, the ultraviolet neon hair crackled and sparked and writhed, the whole effect a sickening, enticing, entirely perverted turn-on that perfectly expressed what Bobby felt while technically fulfilling the specs sent down by the pinheads upstairs to the letter.

"How do you like yourself now, Sally?" Bobby asked the sex monster, blowing her an ironic kiss.

Then he accessed an image bank and tried a series of nude female bodies—starlets, nymphets, porno queens, magazine centerfolds—before hitting on a wiry black female bodybuilder with unreally perfect conical breasts and only slightly overdefined musculature. Sexy and intimidating to the max, but also a subtle caricature of itself.

Following the specs, he colorized this paragon of muscular feminine flesh to silver. Then he split the screen and built up its abstract simulacrum, mimicking the musculature with tight coils of braided steel cable.

He overlaid the silverized bodybuilder with the cyborg head on this coiled steel creature like a thin sheaf of flesh, then turned the skin slightly translucent.

When he synced this composite through an animation program to the audio track's sequencer line and danced it through a few bars of the chorus, the result was quite uncanny; sensual yet terrifying, blatantly artificial yet sinuously reptilian, a cyborg snakewoman bumping and grinding her soft silvery flesh over cruel serpentine wire, a vision that made his cock throb nervously against the fabric of his pants even as it made his flesh crawl.

"Down and dirty sick, sick, sick, Sally. . . ." he told the thing on the screen. "*Solid gold* perversion . . . All you need is a few finishing touches. . . ."

The pinheads upstairs were a bit nervous about the legality of naked human nipples and full frontal nudity, so . . .

At the tips of the muscular, silvery breasts, he put tiny flickering serpent's tongues, then solarized them into sparking blue flames.

But the cunt . . . Hmmmm . . . now, *that* would take some finessing. . . .

He fooled with flame effects, animal mouths, a traditional vagina indentata out of a psychology text, a steel-jawed bear trap, but everything was either way over the top into low humor or far too terrifying to get past the pinheads. . . .

He laughed aloud when he finally came up with the inspiration.

He dressed Cyborg Sally in a pair of skin-tight black leather panties, then laid in twin nebula-whorls of tiny sharp chrome spikes curving down from both hips to form counterrotating spirals enclosing a central void between the legs of the image where the blue matte background now showed through. And in that void . . .

He matted in a short animation loop from an astronomy text disc—a stylized black hole, a wound through the fabric of time and space, a vision between those perfect silvery thighs of endless downwardly spiraling terminal night.

He sequenced an animation program to the instrumental leadline and danced Cyborg Sally through the whole song, leaning back in his chair quite drained; marveling, shuddering, fascinated, repelled, and yes, queasily turned on by the beautiful and vile creature of flesh and wire, sex and vengeance, he had wrought.

At the end, he keyed in the final verse of the vocal track, and there she was on the screen before him, this reptilian cyborg, with her writhing Medusa crown of hair flashing ultraviolet fire, her perfect breasts tipped with electronic serpents' tongues, her muscular metal arms reaching out for him, her rolling hips offering up a terminal void, and the pathetically human eyes of Sally Genaro.

Cyborg Sally!
Flesh and wire!
Queen of Heat!
Electric fire!
Blazing bytes!
Meat's desire!
Rockin' rollin' sex machine!
Plug your self in
And scream, scream, SCREAM!

CYBORG SALLY

Paco Monaco strode into the smoky bar of The American Dream feelin' pretty good. The Red Jack discs that Dojo was turning out upstairs in Florida were really moving again now that there were People's Cash Machines in half the fuckin' streetie meatracks in town, and Dojo, true to his word, was giving him twenty-five dollars off every one sold. El Tiempo Rico might not have exactly returned, he might not be pulling down anything like the same dinero, but now he didn't even have to work for it, the bread came dribbling in just like he was some fuckin' Ciudad Trabajo capitalist.

The peanuts he got working the door at Slimy Mary's didn't really mean dick no more. For the first time in his life he was working just for the hell of it, just because it felt good to stand there and be important, to be Paco Monaco, Dojo's main man, well connected to the RLF, and the Cocko de la Calle, you better believe it, motherfucker!

"Hey momacita, how's it goin'?" he said airily, pulling up a stool beside Karen, who sat there hunched over her screwdriver at the bar lookin' not so hot.

"Lousy," she grunted, looking up at him with a hangdog expression. "Nothing moving . . . haven't sold a single disc . . ."

Paco frowned. "Hey, no problem," he said, fishing a couple of fifties out of his pocket and slipping them under her palm. "Come on, muchacha, cheer up, I'm doin' okay, and no one's blaming you. Like Larry says, the RLF ain't in it just for the money."

"Thanks," Karen said glumly, crumpling up the money and stuffing it into her purse.

"Hey, don't take it out on me, okay?" Paco said irritably, for he had a pretty good idea what was *really* sticking in her chocha behind all this bitchin' about how the disc business was dead in the fancy meatracks. She had liked it much better when she was the hot-shit gorda dealer lifting her little streetie out of the gutter. She just couldn't handle the way the sombre and the sol had changed places.

Now that she was makin' zip and *he* was bringin' in the manteca, now that he was a main man in the RLF and she was just along for the ride, he had the feeling that she was getting jealous, though she would never admit it, and he wasn't ready to pin her on it.

Karen sighed. "Sorry, Paco," she said in a little voice. "I just don't like feeling that I'm not pulling my own weight. I mean, the RLF's flying high on the Revolution, and you're making money, and everyone else is writing their wizard programs, and me, I'm sitting here all the time drinking and waiting for nothing to happen. . . ."

Paco patted her hand. "Hey, momacita, yo se, chingada, I know how you feel. . . ." Something softened inside. Just when he was starting to think she was just another fuckin' chocharica, she owned up to it and—

I'm Cyborg Sally
I'm your blood-hot wire
I'm the blazing bytes
Of your meat's desire!

"Hey, what the fuck is *that*?"

The music from the dance floor had suddenly doubled in volume, and this incredible fuckin' unreal chorus of female voices was belting it out to a heavy drumbeat and a wall of music that seemed to wrap itself right around his cock and squeeze.

"It's called 'Cyborg Sally,' " Karen muttered. "Some new AP rock star, they've been playing it a lot since yesterday. . . ."

I'm Cyborg Sally
And I've never been
Plug into me
And I'll make you scream!

A single voice was singing it out above the chorus now, chingada, a woman's voice for sure, but nothing like anything

Paco had ever heard before, hissing and spitting electric sparks like a live wire, purring between his legs like a great big cat licking at his balls with a hot wet tongue, chingada, it was givin' him a hard-on just to listen to it. . . .

"Come on, Karen, let's dance, it'll do you good!" he found himself saying, bounding off his barstool, grabbing her by the hand, and pulling her out onto the dance floor before he even thought about it.

Most of the men weren't even looking at who they were dancing with, if they were dancing with anyone at all. Instead, they were staring up at the huge screens with their fucking tongues hanging out and their hands slowly rising to their touchpoints like they were all reaching for their flies.

When Paco followed the collective turned-on stare upward, he saw why.

With my heart of ice
And my ring of fire
No living soul
Gonna take you higher
No mother's child
Turn you on so wild!

Huge sleek silver legs towered over him, rockin' and rolling this fuckin' sparking black hole of a *chocha* right above his face, a whirling vortex of an enormous cunt that seemed to be sucking him up off his feet into it!

He goggled, he blinked, he pulled his eyes out of the whirlpool, and looked slowly up a giant naked silver body, past great perfect tits with blue lightnings sparking from their nipples, and straight into horny eyes of . . .

A silver robot's face with teeth like daggers, with a sinuous tongue like a whip of black leather, with soft human lips that seemed ready to wrap themselves around his cock and bite it off and make him like it, dancing like a demon and singing straight to his cojones in a snarly electronic voice.

I'm Cyborg Sally
I'm your blood-hot wire
I'm the blazing bytes
Of your meat's desire!

"Fuckin'-A!" he could only agree, as he found himself swaying to the beat, to the bone-hard heat of his meat, reaching up almost languidly to stroke his touchpoint.

Yes I'm Cyborg Sally
I'm your sex machine
My crystal chips
Gonna make you cream. . . .

Mucho Muchacho danced his stompada up the gleaming silver thighs of Chocharica City, up the brightly lit avenue, shoving the gordo putamadres and the plushie-tushies out of his way with his elbows. "Out of my way, motherfuckers," he roared, "this silver chocha belongs to Mucho Muchacho, maricónes!"

And so she did as he stood before her in her penthouse bedroom beside a great round bed with gold satin sheets—eye to eye, nose to nose, chingada, almost belly to belly.

She challenged him with her eyes, she licked her silver dagger teeth with her wet black tongue. Mucho Muchacho stepped foward until the sparking tips of her nipples trailed electric fire down his bare bronzed chest, reached out to bend her back over the bed beneath him—

A steel hand whipped out, grabbed him by the hair, and her irresistible strength shoved him, down, down, down, no way to fight it, chingada, he didn't want to fight it, as his legs buckled deliciously under him, and this wonderful warm queasy feeling blossomed behind his breastbone. . . .

Laser lips bring you to your knees
Darkling sparkling ecstasy
Lick my flashing circuitry!

And he was where he had never thought to be before, down on his knees before the silver Cyborg Queen of Chocharica City, his mouth reaching out hungrily, tonguing oiled metal flesh, fused in surrender to the electrode of desire between her sleek hard metal thighs. He moaned in shameful pleasure as nails bit into the flesh of his back and her knowing, insinuating voice hissed and purred into his ear.

As I bite your flesh
As you taste my wire
No father's son
Ever flashed such fire!

He was hers to command, she was the master of his flesh, he was the slave of her wire.

I'm Cyborg Sally
I'm flesh and wire
I'm the Queen of Heat
I'm a funeral pyre!

She tore his mouth away from the quick of her, and threw Mucho Muchacho onto his back, onto the golden satin sheets, and he lay there in supine ecstasy as she wrapped her coiled cable steel legs around his waist and mounted him like a man.

I'm Cyborg Sally
I've got legs of steel
Wrap around you
Make a dead man squeal!

He reached up tentatively toward her breasts, but her steel robot hands pinned his wrists to the bed, and she leered down at him from beneath her crown of neon snakes, using Mucho Muchacho like a woman and making him love it.

Rock your roll
In my electric chair
It's looking for you
And it's loaded for bear!

And he surrendered to it, to this silver sex machine, he wrapped his legs behind her waist as she fucked him, transported into another realm, where figure reversed with ground and macho pride with pussy pleasure.

Comin' to dance
And I'm comin' tonight
Comin' in crystal and neon light

Comin', comin', you just can't hide
Comin', comin', comin' deep inside
Comin', comin', comin' so free
Comin' right atcha
Come along . . . come along . . . come along . . .
Come along with me!

Paco came popping out of it, panting and blinking and sweating, and when he saw where he was and what he was doing, flushing shamefully.

He was rocking back and forth on his feet on the dance floor of The American Dream, arched over backward with a raging hard-on, making a fuckin' fool out of himself, by the way Karen was lookin' at him.

Cyborg Sally!
Flesh and wire!
Queen of Heat!
Electric fire!
Blazing bytes!
Meat's desire!

High above him, the enormous figure of Cyborg Sally danced in triplicate on the big video screens, a vision of lust still calling to him, unlike any he had ever seen, chingada, unlike any fuckin' chocha *the world* had ever seen!

Rockin' rollin' sex machine!
Plug your self in
And scream, scream, SCREAM!

"Sick . . ." Karen muttered sourly as the cut ended.

"Hey, I thought it was pretty fuckin' good!" Paco snapped defensively.

"Tell me about it," Karen said dryly. "You should have seen yourself!"

Paco squirmed, for in his mind's eye, he did see himself. He saw himself down on his knees before a silver chocharica, he saw himself where he should have wanted Cyborg Sally to be, and he found himself longing with a still-raging hard-on to be there again.

"Okay, okay, so it turns me on, so fuckin' what?" he said

with shamefaced belligerence. "You jealous of some sexy robot momacita who ain't even there?"

"I guess boys will be boys. . . ."

"What's that supposed to mean?"

"It's *supposed* to turn you on, Paco!"

"What's wrong with that?"

"Something about it scares me. . . . It's a *perverted* turn-on, it's just not natural!"

"For sure it ain't natural! It's Cyborg Sally! It's a sex machine!"

Yeah, there were men and what they did with women, and women and what they did with men—and Cyborg Sally, your sex machine! What she did to him was only a wirehead wet dream. And because he was only surrendering his machismo to a sex fantasy in the dreamtime, he could get off behind it and there would be no one there to know.

"Question is, why is MUZIK pushing a thing like that so hard?" Karen muttered as she stared around the dance floor at all the guys, streeties and gordos alike, who stood there sharing Paco's secret knowledge with nervous grins on their faces and hard-ons in their pants.

"For the *dinero,* that's why!" Paco told her. "Cyborg Sally's gonna be their biggest star!"

Karen grimaced. "That's what scares me, Paco," she said. "Something tells me you're right."

I'm Cyborg Sally
I'm your blood-hot wire
I'm the blazing bytes
Of your meat's desire. . . .

"Oh, no, not *again*!" Karen Gold moaned as the opening chorus of "Cyborg Sally" boomed out one more time and Paco's hand reached reflexively for his touchpoint.

They had been playing the damned thing about once an hour for weeks here at The American Dream and the national MUZIK feed was giving it at least as much airplay.

Karen had never been one to follow the trajectories of hits up and down the charts or the means by which they were launched and sustained, but you had to be deaf and blind and living in Outer Mongolia not to notice the unprecedented extremes to which Muzik, Inc., was going to hype Cyborg Sally.

Posters and billboards featuring the silver sex machine were everywhere, five million Cyborg Sally promo T-shirts had already been given away, every Muzik store window featured piles of her disc and an endless playback of the song on its display screen, and the merchandising tie-ins touched bases no one had even heard of before.

From where she sat at the bar, she could look out through the haze of smoke and see scores of grotesque simulations of Cyborg Sally grinding and strutting their stuff out on the dance floor.

The basic silver body stocking you could buy in sleazy department stores for about $100 or in flea markets for maybe $60, and if you didn't have that, you could score a promo T-shirt, a silver job with chrome-plated studs on cartoon tits. Black leatherette briefs with lithographed black hole went for maybe $40. A ludicrous Sally wig with purple-black serpent hair made out of rubber cost about $50, and they were selling combo makeup and tooth-paint kits for $35. So you could turn yourself into a cut-rate imitation of a cyborg imitating a woman for under $200.

Of course here in The American Dream most of the Sallys, except for the sprinkling of streeties, went in for the high-budget versions. LED lightning-bolt nipples on the body stocking. Real black leather briefs with whorls of stainless steel or even silver studs and hologramed vortices at the vagina, even neon versions. Black plastic fiber-optic wigs, each strand glowing from within from a central ultraviolet light source.

And if money *really* was no object, you could go to a fancy boutique and have a foam-rubber undersuit custom cast to wear under a special translucent silver body stocking, a second flesh of coiled steel Sally muscles that could hardly be told from the real phony thing.

The unseen powers of The American Dream who controlled the moving spotlights from on high now highlighted the sexiest and most extravagant Cyborg Sally clones almost exclusively.

And when MUZIK broadcast the song live from the club using these Cyborg Sally clones as audience reaction shots, the circle was complete—the fad feeding the disc sales, the disc sales and airplay hyping the fad, which fed the sales of the tie-ins, which in turn fed back into the fad itself, selling yet more discs.

But of course few of the hordes of girls following the fad had anything like the money to go for deluxe versions, and so on these warm spring nights, the streets were full of girls in cut-rate Cyborg Sally costumes, fewer of whom had the perfect bodies to parade around in skin-tight body stockings without making fools of themselves.

One would have thought that such an unwholesome public display of skinny shanks, malproportioned asses, bony ribs, outsized and undersized boobs, and general blubber would have been more than ludicrously revolting enough to have killed off the fad before it reached the present epidemic proportions.

But even the cheapest rubber Cyborg Sally wigs were ideal camouflage for the breadbox and wire hairnet of the Jack—you could simply wear one over your piece—and once Jacked in to their own dreamtime, all these pathetic creatures easily enough lost all sense of the grotesque spectacle their imperfect flesh made dressed up to simulate the perfect nonexistent cyborg sex machine.

Particularly in the eyes of men who were themselves flashing—and conditioned to drool and throb in their jeans at silver flesh and Sally hair and black leather panties and steel teeth by the endless airplay of the "Cyborg Sally" song.

The plainest women, as long as they were Sallied, could be seen with relatively attractive men, no doubt only as long as *they* were flashing, and by the look in these men's eyes and the way they carried themselves, these cyborged femmes fatales seemed to have many of them thoroughly pussywhipped as well.

Oh yes, Karen could feel the appeal such a power reversal must have for downtrodden drabs all too accustomed to being used as sexual appliances! Once or twice, when she was really feeling down about the reversal of status and fortunes between herself and Paco, when she really got to feeling sorry for herself, she had even allowed herself the secret ignoble sleazoid vengeance of entertaining the fantasy herself.

Indeed, as Paco was sucked deeper and deeper into it, as their relationship deteriorated, she was perversely tempted to flash on it herself, if only to understand how a woman who wasn't there still had the power to come between them.

But Larry Coopersmith had convinced her that the forces behind the Cyborg Sally fad had designed their psychic mousetrap to snap shut around just such bait. Make the male audience fixate their libido on Cyborg Sally, make the female audience identify with the very image that was stealing them away into the dreamtime, and capture a 360-degree slice of the demographic pie.

"The Revolution is gonna be in deep shit," Markowitz had

insisted even before the Sally clones started appearing on the street.

"These boys really know their chops! They couldn't put Red Jack back in the bottle once he got out, so now they're fighting us with this libido snatcher designed to suck up all that energy into electronically twisted sex. Watch this thing rise to the top of the sales charts! See the Red start to fade! Watch women turn into animals and men turn into plants! Watch Official Reality grab at the gonads and squeeze!"

And sure enough, Red Jack discs became even harder to move in the saturated upscale market, and even the streeties became somewhat less diligent in the use of the People's Cash Machine to rip off the system once Cyborg Sally went platinum. Computer crime statistics started to slide as rape statistics inched upward.

"Go make a revolution with your hands in your pants!" Markowitz insisted when he caught Tommy and Mary and Eddie and Teddy all plugged in and watching Cyborg Sally on MUZIK. "Now they've warped even you guys back into their dumbshit Official Reality too!"

Everybody in the RLF, Karen emphatically included, had scoffed at this at first as paranoia; oh sure, maybe crude shit like Cyborg Sally might have some effect on the naive masses, but not on sophisticated aware revolutionaries such as ourselves!

"Just you wait and see," Markowitz predicted, "this is all-out down and dirty media warfare, and the guys on the other side got a fifth column between your legs!"

And alas, he had been right.

Case in point, what had happened to her and Paco.

There he sat on his barstool beside her, Jacked in and staring out past the lip of the overhang at all the Cyborg Sallies that the overhead spotlights were picking out for his delectation, his mouth hanging half open, and the bulge of a hard-on visible clearly against the fabric of his trousers.

She had long since given up trying to get through to him on the subject. She knew just what he'd say if she tried again now.

"Chingada, momacita, how can you be jealous of some electric chocha who ain't even there? It ain't like I'm steppin' out on you with a real muchacha! But maybe I will, if I have to hear too much more of this shit."

Since boys, whatever their age, race, religion, or national origin, will inevitably be boys, Karen just might have gritted her teeth and borne it, as a porn movie inside his head no worse than what he'd get off some tit magazine centerfold. Any girl over the age of twelve knew that men had been like that since they started scrawling their dirty pictures on the walls of caves. You had zero chance of ever reforming them, and besides, their jerk-off fantasies had nothing to do with your relationship.

Until, that is, they started crawling into bed with you.

Paco was such a wonderful lover when he was plugged in that it had never really bothered her that they seldom made love without flashing. They'd plug in, and Paco would become Mucho Muchacho, her white knight of the streets, her mighty cocksman, and she was all too pleased to be his chocharica queen, and let him completely overmaster her with his strength and endurance and prowess. Who could complain about a man whose style in bed was to get on top of you and master you with orgasm after orgasm after orgasm?

Even when he started to change, she put it down to a process of sexual maturation and found it rather endearing. She was quite touched the first time he stared longingly into her eyes, began licking his way between her breasts and down her belly, and avidly, if somewhat clumsily, went down on her. She put it down to an entirely admirable desire for variety the first time he rolled her over on top of him and let her take command.

It started seeming a little weird when she noticed that it was becoming a regular thing, and she found it rather disconcerting the first time he actually went down on his knees before her.

Still, Karen willfully avoided making the inevitable connection until the awful night that Paco came home to her bed in the loft with his loathsome little "present."

She was dozing there naked under the thin blanket. He took off his jacket, sat down on the bed beside her, smiled rather strangely, and handed her a paper bag.

"What's this?" Karen said groggily, not bothering to prop herself up into a seated position.

"Un regalo . . ." Paco said with his back to her as he kicked off his shoes. "Just a little present, momacita . . ." he said with unconvincing casualness, as he turned, unbuttoning his shirt, and smiling at her expectantly.

"Mmmm . . ." Karen muttered drowsily. "How sweet . . ." she said, smiling back up at him, rather touched. He had never given her a present before. . . .

''Well go ahead, muchacha, open it,'' he said rather more sharply, stripping off his shirt and undoing his belt.

Now Karen did prop herself up as she reached into the bag.

And pulled out a cheap rubber Cyborg Sally wig and a kit of silver makeup and tooth paint.

''Jesus Christ—''

''I thought we'd—''

They sat there on the bed, Karen glaring at him in a red rage, Paco smiling dreamily at her as he reached for his touchpoint.

''Well think again, goddammit!'' Karen shrieked, brushing the wig and makeup kit off the bed with one hand like a dead rat and slapping his hand angrily away from his touchpoint with the other.

''Hey . . . Come on . . . *Chingada* . . .''

''Chingada yourself, Paco Monaco!'' Karen raged at him. ''Larry was right, this sick shit is turning you into something I don't like at all, if you think I'm going to dress up like that . . . like that . . .''

Paco glared back at her, his hands balled into fists. She watched him choke back his rage, watched his angry expression fade into a sickly little false smile. ''Hey . . . come on, it was just a little joke, momacita. . . .''

Karen took a deep breath. She snaked across the bed toward him, laid a tender hand on his cheek. ''Paco, Paco . . .'' she cooed softly. ''What's happened to my Mucho Muchacho . . . ?''

Paco cupped her breast with one hand, fingered her nipple, reached for his touchpoint with the other. ''Still here lookin' at ya, muchacha,'' he said with a ghost of the old macho smile. ''Plug in, and I'll show you. . . .''

And she let him try. He gathered her up in his strong, sure arms, and rolled her over onto her back, and took command, thrusting himself deep inside her and riding atop her. Her white knight of the streets was back, her heroic cocksman, her Mucho Muchacho.

But when she stroked her own touchpoint to amplify her delight, she found herself moaning inside his skin, seeing herself through his eyes, and what she saw was Cyborg Sally riding in cold silver triumph in the dreamtime above him, and what she felt was his ecstatic surrender to the Other Woman who wasn't there.

And for a horrid moment before she hit her touchpoint to escape the flash, *becoming* that Other Woman, becoming Cyborg

Sally, getting off on it, luxuriating in her muscles of coiled steel, her heart of ice and her ring of fire. . . .

No living soul gonna take him higher
No mother's child
Turn him on so wild . . .

Out of the corner of her eye she stole a sidelong glance at Paco on his barstool, plugged-in, staring out at the Sally clones cavorting on the dance floor, wired into the song.

His body was close enough for her to smell the musky male heat of him, but his cocksman's heart had drifted far away from the woman of flesh who sat beside him.

She no longer dared flash with him in bed, she didn't dare meet the creature she became in his eyes, she had taken to faking it with him to keep the peace.

Oh, he gave her no need to fake orgasms, but when it came to flashing together in the loverly dreamtime, that once most intimate of communions was denied her, for in the dreamtime she knew she would find herself fucking him vengefully in the cold metal flesh of her nonexistent rival.

A TALE OF TWO CITIES

Sally Genaro closed the Velcro fasteners down either side of the crotchless foam rubber undersuit, pulled on the body stocking, zipped up the wrap-around fly, and regarded herself in her full-length bedroom mirror.

The padding at the shoulders and hips was cunningly exaggerated to make her waist look slim and sexy in proportion, her foam rubber flesh bulged taut and wiry against the translucent silver body stocking, the ass was absolutely perfect, and the breasts were really bitchin'; big, but high, outthrust, and precisely conical, with wonderful flickering blue neon nipples.

It was tight and itchy and sweaty inside the damned thing and the deluxe custom-cast undersuit had run her over two thousand dollars, but it was worth it. With the clever crotchless design, you could even pee or make love while you were wearing it!

She stepped into the tight black leather briefs, smoothed them down against her padded ass. They were just about the most expensive Cyborg Sally pants she had been able to find on Rodeo Drive—the double whorls of solid silver studs tipped with tiny black pearls, the crotch done up with red neon tubules for pubic hair, the vagina itself a hologram done from an actual photo of the great nebula in Andromeda.

Not so long ago she would have *died* before appearing in public in gear as extreme as this, but now you could see Sallys just like *everywhere*. In Los Angeles, of course, there were hordes of girls with perfect bods and no money who didn't wear the undersuit, but most anyone who could afford one *did* wear it because they *could* afford it, because the exaggerated steel cable muscles were part of the Look.

So for the first time in her life, Sally could wear the best version of the latest style without worrying about looking silly. It was like a *democratic* style—inside it, all bodies could be equal.

At first, Sally had *hated* the visuals Bobby had put to her tracks, this vicious caricature of the Cyborg Sally of her dreamtime.

But that was before the song had become such a hit, before the merchandising campaign, before all the Sallys started appearing on the streets and in the clubs, before she realized that what he had done, however evilly it had been intended, could let *her* have the last laugh.

Sally slipped on the wire mesh hairnet of the Jack, then put her wig on over it. Her Cyborg Sally wig was the max too—strands of black optic fibers lit by *two* internal sources, ordinary violet, and true ultraviolet for extra black light effect in the dark, sources with randomized flicker-programs chipped into them. It even had a perfectly placed little hole in the fabric under the hair through which to hit the touchpoint of your Jack without having to take it off or feel around conspicuously.

She sat down at her dressing table and began applying the silver makeup to her face and teeth, angularizing her cheekbones and nose with subtle shading, so that by the time she had finished and turned on the wig's light sources, Cyborg Sally had come triumphantly full circle.

Oh yes, there might be thousands of girls out there with better raw material to begin with, but *she* was the *perfect* Cyborg Sally. For Bobby Rubin had modeled the face of Cyborg Sally with *her* eyes and *her* nose and *her* lips. Cyborg Sally was a caricature of *her*.

Now, in her custom-cast undersuit, her silver body stocking, her bitchin' black leather pants, and her thousand-dollar Sally wig, with a makeup job stylizing her features into those of the nonexistent rock star that Bobby had stylized from *her* face, she was literally as close to the perfect image of Cyborg Sally as mortal woman could get.

She smiled at Cyborg Sally. Cyborg Sally smiled back at her from her own dressing table mirror. She stood up and twirled somewhat clumsily in front of the full-length mirror, singing the chorus of her hit song in her thin nasal voice, but hearing in her mind's ear the music she had crafted, the superhuman cyborg voice she had conjured up from the bits and the bytes and the longing of her own heart.

I'm Cyborg Sally
I'm your blood-hot wire
I'm the blazing bytes
Of your meat's desire!

"I *am*!" she told her reflected inner self. She laughed a Cyborg Sally laugh. If not *me,* then *who*? she told herself. I'm the only Cyborg Sally there is!

And Bobby Rubin had put himself completely out of the picture. He wasn't even *working* on the new disc. Nicholas West had given him the chance, and the jerk had turned it down!

Sally grinned at herself. West hadn't even bothered to twist Bobby's arm this time. He just shrugged, put Bobby on some other dumb project, and gave Sally to herself. The songhacks gave her some lyrics, and she was doing the voice and music, and when her tracks were finished, they'd just have some other nameless little contract nerd animate Sally from the Factory-copyrighted algorithms they already had in memory.

So screw you, Bobby Rubin, Sally told herself. You had your chance to be what all those millions of horny little nerds out there long to be, the true lover of the only real Sally, and you blew it!

She left her apartment, walked down the corridor to the escalator, boarded it, and let it carry her upward and onward, into the balmy Southern California night, up the landscaped hillside of the Garden of Babylon under the long protective awning, past the fragrant bougainvillea and rose bushes, through the aisle of palmettos.

She had had this Sally outfit for almost a week now, putting it on, taking it off, putting it on again, all in the secrecy of her own apartment, working up the courage to wear it in public.

But now, borne by the gliding machineries up toward the Glitter Dome at the summit, breathing the heavy floral air, glancing over her shoulder at the sparkling Valley lights, sweating beneath a layer of foam rubber, she was finally committed.

She took a deep breath, steeled herself, hesitated nervously. Then, at the last moment, just as the escalator desposited her on the marbled upper landing, she hit the touchpoint concealed by her wig, and made the connection that completed the circuit, that merged the dream of her flesh with the instrumentality of her desire.

* * *

Paco had hardly spent any time at all in Slimy Mary's lately. He'd do his time on the door, collect his pay and his cut of the dwindling Red Jack disc sales, then go meet Karen at The American Dream, where they'd hang out at the bar doing what little dealing they could.

But something he couldn't quite put his finger on made him linger in Slimy Mary's after Dojo paid him off tonight.

For one thing, the dealing scene at The American Dream was really in the toilet these days. He was hardly moving the Jack at all even at bottom prices, and Karen's Red Jack disc business was just about dead.

So mostly he'd just drink, and dig all the chocharicas in their fancy Sally suits, and listen to Karen bitch and moan about how lousy business was, and the only good thing about it was being able to plug into Cyborg Sally up there on the big screens.

But every time he got to flash on "Cyborg Sally," which was at least twice an hour in The American Dream, Karen would give him such shit afterward! Okay, so she was feeling down about feeling so useless and all, but why the fuck did she have to take it out on *him* just because he was still able to have a good time? What did she want him to do, just sit there and listen to her complain? He was starting to get really pissed off about bein' around a muchacha who was always pissed off at him.

She was even starting to turn off to him in bed. Oh yeah, she still wanted him to fuck her and she still got off on it all right, but she wouldn't flash with him, she'd fake hitting her touchpoint, and she thought he was too dumb to notice. Why the fuck *shouldn't* he make it with Cyborg Sally in the dreamtime when Karen refused to be there with him? And why *wouldn't* she flash with him in bed anymore?

Chingada, *he* needed the crash space in her bed, so he had good reason to stay there, but if she was so pissed off at him, why didn't she kick him out? Come to think of it, why didn't the RLF kick him out of the loft, why did they still let him eat their food, now that he wasn't bringing in any dinero for them anymore?

Did it have something to do with . . . *friendship*? Was that the other thing that kept him hanging around Slimy Mary's tonight?

Paco had never thought about friendship before that night when he and Malcolm had delivered the first People's Cash Machine to Dojo. Chingada, he had never even thought he had a friend. Karen was his momacita, the people at the loft were business partners, and Dojo was just a big tough nigger he wanted to be like. . . .

But when he had looked past that big tough nigger's scowl and seen something else inside, and let Dojo know he saw it, something had changed between them, or maybe, just maybe, he had seen something for the first time that had always been there.

There was more to Dojo than he let on. Some part of him was too soft to let a bunch of fuckin' wirehead zombies die to save himself some bucks. Shit, Dojo had made him doorman, had given him a piece of the disc action he didn't have to, called him "my main man," gave him back the doorman's job when the bottom fell out of the Jack market. No dinero in any of that for Dojo.

He must have done it all out of *friendship*.

Dojo was his friend.

He was Dojo's friend.

Was it possible that he had other friends?

Could his momacita also be his *friend*? Could the people at the loft be his friends? Now that he thought about it, didn't he feel the same sort of thing from Larry Coopersmith as he did from Dojo? Chingada, hadn't he been fuckin' *jealous* when the two of them got friendly with each other?

Did *that* explain why Karen hadn't kicked him out of her bed even though she was pissed off at him? Did it explain why they hadn't kicked him out of the loft? Chingada, could that be why they were all giving him such a hard time about his hard-on for Cyborg Sally? Was Larry *right*? Was it making him fuck up with his girl, with his . . . *friends*?

Was some gang of plushie-tushie putamadres in some glass tower in Ciudad Trabajo or Hollywood somewhere feeding him shit that was messing with his head and his cojones just to make money on Cyborg Sally, just to make him forget Red Jack, just to protect their own fuckin' turf somehow? Was *that* what his *friend* Larry was trying to tell him? Would the bastards really do such a thing?

Fuckin'-A they would!

So maybe that was why he was still here tonight. Maybe because he hadn't spent any time just hanging around in his *friend's* club for a long while. Maybe because he felt he needed to take a good long look at where he had come from to figure out where the fuck he was at now.

Maybe because The American Dream was Cyborg Sally's turf,

Ciudad Trabajo's turf, and just maybe his *other friend,* Larry, was right. Maybe it was turning him into the thing he hated just about more than anything else, a fuckin' Blankriqueno sucking up to the very putamadres who were keeping him down.

And maybe because there was something he had to find out by flashing on Cyborg Sally in the sombre—here in this crummy cellar, not in the fanciest meatrack in New York, here, with a bunch of grungy streeties and low-life puercas, not surrounded by plushie-tushies and chocharicas, here, where his long, strange trip from the garbage heap to The American Dream had begun.

Slimy Mary's had been going through some changes too.

From his vantage point at the door, Paco had watched the successive waves of changes sweeping by him into Slimy Mary's; the cheap-ass gordos sneaking in to score cheap wire back when the Jack was called the Zap and going for $400 at the fancy meatracks, the ominous heavies he had no intention of hassling who had brushed by him now and again to buy Red Jack discs when the RLF started moving them down here through Dojo, the fuckin' college kids in streetie drag who had passed through when the big thing was to score a disc and a Jack for $200.

Now, those waves of turistas had come and gone, leaving Slimy Mary's once more to the original natives. But what was left on the beach after the tide receded was something else again.

Just about all the muchachas were done up as half-assed Cyborg Sallys. Some had real silver body stockings, some just silver Sally T-shirts over ratty jeans. Some had sleazy black leatherette panties. Some had cheap rubber wigs, some had braided their hair into dreadlocks and dyed the mess electric purple. All of them had silver face makeup, though not all of them had painted their teeth. None of them had the dinero for fancy undersuits, and since few of them were primo pussy, the display of so much carne de puerca hanging out of and stuffed into revealing silver cloth did not quite set Paco's dick to throbbing.

A lot of the guys still wore el Rojo to conceal their Jacks, but even most of *them* wore the male version of the Sally T-shirt too—silver like the one with the tits that they passed out to the muchachas, but with a full-length picture of Cyborg Sally herself on it, hands on hips and lookin' right atcha.

Paco hunkered down on a pile of old cushions halfway back in the shadows of the twilight zone to clock the action. And found something about it pissing him off.

It had pleased him, when Red Jack was riding high, to see el

Rojo spread from the heads of his streetie compadres to the gordos of The American Dream; it had even made him hate the putamadres a little less to see Ciudad Trabajo picking up on the dreamtime of the streets.

But all these chochas wearing half-assed versions of Cyborg Sally gear and all these guys in their Sally T-shirts looked like they had all gone through the same garbage cans in Chocharica City. Like a picture he had once seen of jungle bunnies on some island wearin' a load of top hats that had fallen off a truck.

Paco frowned. It was fuckin' weird, there was something sad about it, it was . . . qué es la palabra . . . *pathetic*.

Yeah, pathetic. Chingada, it was one thing, somehow, to wear el Rojo and come here to plug in with your own people, but it was another to come to Slimy Mary's and see it turned into a fuckin' sleazoid *pathetic* cartoon version of The American Dream.

And when the opening chorus of "Cyborg Sally" sounded through the tinny speakers and she slithered across the washed-out video screen, and he caught himself rising and reaching automatically for his touchpoint with the usual automatic hard-on, Paco found himself wondering whether his *friends* were right, whether Cyborg Sally had turned *him* into something pathetic too.

"I'm Cyborg Sally and I've never been . . ." she sang, mocking him.

And he knew that that was what he had stayed here to find out.

The escalator deposited Cyborg Sally onto a long strip of marbled patio that ran along the northern crest of the hill. She paused for a moment to look out over the endless jeweled lowland of the San Fernando Valley, at the streams of red and white lights curving below her round the bend of the 101, at the darkened monoliths of Universal City looming just across the freeway, at the washed-out stars of the Valley night—remembering, like some dim daylight dream, the shopping malls, the endless ticky-tacky houses, the gas stations and 7-11s, the crummy clubs, the high school, her parents' home, the grotty reality hidden by the glorified nightscape from on high, the whole long adolescent bummer of some former life.

Smiling her steel-toothed smile, she turned her back on someone else's Valley Girl past, and strutted across the narrow width of the patio, through a hodge-podge show biz jungle—all overarching palms, winding flagstone paths, columns of tall thin cedars, fat fleshy succulents—toward the Glitter Dome, the huge Hollywood meatrack that towered above the landscaping on its squat concrete pillar like an immense and tasteless faceted rhinestone set on a pushpin thrust into the very nipple of the mounded hilltop.

Inside the pillar, another escalator carried her up into the club itself.

Under the transparent geodesic dome was a great round dance floor of polished redwood. At the axis of the dance floor four huge video screens formed a towering square kiosk about which the action rotated. The outer rim of the dance floor was a circular bar broken only by short staircases which led to the upper level, a circular overhang thick with cafe tables which jutted about ten feet out over the floor around the circumference.

The escalator debouched onto this upper level near the inner rim. On a warm night like this, there was no outer wall to the upper level; the glass panels which protected the interior during inclement weather had been removed, so that the interior space merged seamlessly with the wide circular porch that ran 360 degrees around the bottom of the dome like the flat brim of an enormous hat.

From this vantage Sally could view the Glitter Dome entire. The brass and black smoked glass cafe tables of the inner balcony. One of the central video screens upon which Mama Mia danced in her red velvet cape and golden tights. Below, across the dancers in the shallow pit, a curving slice of dance floor bar. Behind her, the open-air porch, with its rustic rough-hewn redwood chairs and tables and its potted palms.

And, looking outward in any direction, the vast electric nightscape of Los Angeles and the San Fernando Valley, a limitless vista of winking jewels on black velvet from horizon to horizon, a magic carpet spread out at the feet of this show biz Valhalla on the top of the world.

The scene here had always reminded her of that terrible and tantalizing party in that big mansion on Mulholland that Glorianna O'Toole had taken her to with Bobby; the same mixture of real rock and movie stars, bit players, producers, agents, and beautiful hangers-on and would-be hangers-on of both sexes angling for the Big Break, or even a few generous lines of dust, with their designer faces and perfect bods.

In the Glitter Dome as at that big time A party, she had always felt like an ugly little duckling who had somehow managed to crash the swan pond, invisible and ignored by these elegant, empty-headed, mean-spirited, and beautiful creatures. Whenever she had ventured up here, she usually spent the evening at a solitary barstool, slowly getting loaded and waiting for some magic moment that never came.

But now, ah, now through the electronic instrumentalities and her own talent, the ugly little duckling had become the Cyborg Queen of the swans, gliding along through the Glitter Dome with her head held high.

For sure, she could see a dozen phony Cyborg Sallys dancing below, for sure, impostors were to be seen lounging at barside down there, scattered around the tables of the upper level and the porch, and yes, most of them were beautiful, and a few were probably even tv actresses and singers. And indeed, there were bitchin' horny guys coming on to them.

But there was only one *real* Cyborg Sally in all the world, and she saw it mirrored in every man's eyes, in their amazed sidelong glances, their raised eyebrows, their shaking heads, their hot longing looks, as she wandered slowly and tantalizingly around the upper level, flashing a cruel little cock-teasing grin here, wriggling her perfect sprung-steel ass there, pausing, looking, sizing up one sleek stud after another, deeming them unworthy, and then turning haughtily away.

Yes, she told them all silently as she luxuriated in the liquid dance of her coiled-cable muscles tight against her shining steel skin, it really *is* me, with my heart of ice and my ring of fire, Cyborg Sally, flesh and wire, the Queen of Heat and your meat's desire, and don't you all wish I would take you higher!

Preening, prancing, lightnings sparking from the hard hot electrodes of her nipples, her proud head haloed by flashing electric fire, Cyborg Sally descended a short flight of stairs to the dance floor, past a tall muscular man with a red silk shirt open halfway to the navel on the arm of a pathetic imitation. He stared at her in no little amazement. Cyborg Sally favored him with a smile and a wink. The phony Sally tugged at his arm, shot her a poisonous stare with eyes that were nothing like the real thing. Cyborg Sally sneered at her, nodded toward her catch, gave a thumbs-down appraisal, and sashayed past them onto the dance floor.

And as she did, as if at her command, the music fell silent for a beat, and then—

—there she was, towering triumphantly above the dancing bodies of all the Beautiful People, with her hands on her hips, swaying like a great silver rock and roll machine, bumping, grinding, rocking her ring of fire, with her own true song pouring out in mightily amplified glory through her throat and her lips and her hot-wired circuitries from the blazing bytes of her soul.

I'm Cyborg Sally
And I've never been . . .

"Until now!" she cried, and then she did what she had never dared before. There, surrounded by the hordes of beautiful people beneath the black crystal ceiling of the Glitter Dome, with her cyborged voice singing out her triumph, there, towering in glory above all the swans of the show biz pond, there, at last, the one-time ugly little duckling whirled out onto stage center and began to dance.

"Plug into me, and I'll make you scream!" Cyborg Sally promised as Paco hit his touchpoint, and he found himself once more drawn onto a dance floor toward her.

But this was not The American Dream, and Cyborg Sally did not tower high above him. This was Slimy Mary's, and she was no larger than he was, and their eyes met on the same level, mano a mano, flesh and wire, and his bones seemed to beat to a different and half-forgotten rhythm, and his bare feet fell into an arrogant stompada, and there was a fanfare blare of airhorns deep inside him.

And it was Mucho Muchacho, his mighty right arm pumping in and out to the rhythm, his full sensuous lips sneering out his answer, who rose to accept the challenge of the Queen of Cyborg Heat.

Tu ma-dre TAMBIÉN, chocharica elegante!

Cyborg Sally licked her glistening dagger teeth with her black leather tongue, running her steel hands over her fire-tipped metal breasts, dancing closer, and closer, and closer in tight predatory circles around him.

Mucho Muchacho leered at her, arched his back, pumped his

right arm at her, cupped his bulging crotch with his left hand, and sang his defiance through smacking, puckered lips.

Besa me pica
(Tu ma-dre TAMBIÉN)
And ponga me your sister
(Tu ma-dre TAMBIÉN)
Better call me Mister
Y TU MADRE TAMBIÉN!

Circling each other closer and closer in tightening spirals, sneering and strutting and preening, dancing pelvis to pelvis, flesh to wire, her steel teeth biting off the words, the sparking tips of her nipples trailing tracks of fire down the naked flesh of his chest, his rock-hard meat brushing her cold metal pubes, their eyes locked in gonadal combat.

I'm Cyborg Sally
I'm your blood-hot wire
I'm the blazing bytes
Of your meat's desire. . . .

Enormous, triumphant, her perfect metal flesh vibrating to her own amplified voice, Cyborg Sally danced the lite fantastic on the floor of the Glitter Dome, arching her sprung-steel back, rolling her pelvis, whirling, twirling, flashing her fire, flicking her tongue, teasing this man and that from on high, then darting away with an electronic sneer and a bump of her tight silver ass.

And then she saw him, dancing in the crowd, shimmering in his rock star aura as if in his own perpetual personal spotlight, surrounded by the inevitable coterie of hot-eyed airheaded little groupies.

His skin-tight sequined black tuxedo was artfully ripped off at the knees above bloodred calf-length boots, and it was open across his bare chest to reveal golden curling hair. His great billowing blond afro haloed his perfectly sculptured and almost faggoty beautiful face in a nimbus of glory.

He was Lord Jimmy, the Golden Boy of Rock and Roll, the English singer whose latest disc, "At Your Command," had been riding the charts a distant second behind her for the last six weeks.

He was even more perfect in the flesh than he appeared on

MUZIK, as if he existed as some kind of cinematic cyborg himself, or anyway the next best thing, a mortal man of flesh and blood whose every move was choreographed by an unseen director, who somehow magically transformed every scene into his own stage center by the very act of walking into it.

He was every man she longed for and knew she could never have. He was the living star of rock and roll she had always known she could never be.

He was a beautiful dinosaur on his way to the La Brea tar pits, a mere *human* rock star, yes, but the tasty best of the dying breed.

And he had no eyes for the mob of sexy little groupies vying for the passing pleasure of his favor. The telltale wire mesh of the Jack glittered in his golden hair, and he was staring glassy-eyed at the huge screen, his thin nostrils flaring, his tongue absently licking his perfect white teeth as he looked up from far below into the vortex, into the beckoning black hole between her own perfect silvery thighs.

Cyborg Sally danced through the crowd toward him, slithering, sliding, elbowing past the silly little groupies until she stood sinuously rolling her hips before him, curving her pelvis into his body space, then back out again, as he danced his wide-eyed homage to her image on the great screen.

"You're Lord Jimmy!" she shouted at him over the music. "Can you guess my name?"

He frowned. His lips creased into an angry aristocratic sneer. Slowly he lowered his gaze, reluctantly deigning to notice this unseemly interruption from yet another adoring little bird.

His jaw fell open. His beautiful blue eyes widened. He looked up, down, up, back down again. "Fuckin' 'ell . . ." he whispered in a rich, melodious voice.

She smiled, oozed forward, touched the sparking tips of her nipples to his bare hairy chest, arched backward, brushing his bulge with her soft steel belly, leaned forward, and sung it with the voice of her multitude, just for him, into his perfect ear.

Oh yes I'm Cyborg Sally
I'm your sex machine
My crystal chips
Gonna make you cream!

Steel fingers curled themselves into Mucho Muchacho's hair, pulling his face forward and downward as Cyborg Sally ground her cold hard body against him, insinuating her song, wrapping her long leather tongue around it, and his knees folded as waves of cold electric fire poured down his spine, as coiled cable muscles pushed his face down, down, down. . . .

But somewhere a mighty chorus of streeties was roaring in his ears, and somewhere silver white-gowned women with long blond hair were dancing around him, legs aspraddle, just begging for it, longing for the mastery of his huge hard cock up their fuckin' chocharicas. . . .

He found himself rising to full erect posture, and he grabbed her by the cold hard quick, grinding and kneading, and then there he was, with her metal hand in his hair and his mighty hand of flesh gripping her by the cunt—face to face, eyeball to eyeball, proclaiming his machismo to Cyborg Sally.

Your sisters and your aunties
(Tu ma-dre TAMBIÉN)
Chocharicas elegantes
(Tu ma-dre TAMBIÉN)
Don't want no gay romantics
(Tu ma-dre TAMBIÉN)!

Cyborg Sally sank her steel dagger teeth into the tender lobe of Lord Jimmy's ear for a beat, felt him hard and hot against her, snaked her tongue into his ear as she sang into his very brain, feeling him shudder, hearing him moan, as they danced there under the Glitter Dome at the top of the world, thigh to thigh, and belly to belly.

As I bite your flesh
As you taste my wire
No father's son
Ever flashed such fire!

Yanking at his hair, grinding her hard unyielding breasts with their electrodes of fire into the muscles of his bronzed chest, her hair flashing, Cyborg Sally spat and snarled at him, her black leather tongue licking teasingly across her sharp steel teeth.

But Mucho Muchacho threw her down onto the golden satin sheets of the big round bed, tore off her gauzy white gown, pinned her steel wrists to the pillow, spread-eagling her beneath him, and rammed his manhood into the cold black vacuum again and again and again, howling at her in a fury.

You all want macho mucho
(Tu ma-dre TAMBIÉN)
Mucho Muchacho
(Tu ma-dre TAMBIÉN)
I know how to tussle
(Tu ma-dre TAMBIÉN
Feel my mojo muscle
(Tu ma-dre TAMBIÉN)

She pried herself out of Lord Jimmy's embrace, gripped his hands with fingers of steel, and held him out at tantalizing arm's length, writhing and grinding and prancing promisingly to the beat as he swayed hypnotically in her power, gorgeous mesmerized human prey for the coiled wire cobra.

''Fuckin' 'ell . . . fuckin' bleeding 'ell . . .'' he moaned in delight, shaking his head, his golden crown of hair billowing and foaming, as she whirled him through the press of dancers toward the balcony stairs.

She fought and snarled and bit at him with razor-sharp teeth, groaning and twitching, and singing out her defiance as he went on and on, mastering her metal with his flesh, forcing her up over the top into cold sparking angry ecstasy.

Cyborg Sally!
Flesh and wire!
Queen of Heat!
Electric fire!!

Mucho Muchacho sang his final triumph right back at her as they passed through the screaming cusp in mutual defiant loveless orgasm.

Get it while you can
(Tu ma-dre TAMBIÉN)
From a red hot macho man
(Tu ma-dre TAMBIÉN)
We all remember when!
Y TU MADRE TAMBIÉN!

"No, come on, really, who the bloody 'ell are you, this is *Lord Jimmy* you're talking to, girl, not some moony-eyed wanker!"

She had led him up to the balcony level and out onto the porch into the balmy and fragrant Southern California night, and now she had a steel arm snaked around his waist, and she was parading her prize in a long slow orbit around the outer rim of the circular porch, watching all the starlets and trendies, all the hunks and hangers-on, all the beautiful denizens of the endless party at the top of the Hollywood Hills, watching *them*.

They looked, and they chattered to each other, and they stepped aside, allowing Lord Jimmy and Cyborg Sally, the magic couple, the reigning king of rock that was and the ascendant star of the cyborged future, to glide through them regally undisturbed in their golden bubble of limelight.

Oh yes, this would be in all the fan mags, the mating of the ultimate flesh with the queen of wire. If anyone had a good camera, it would for sure be on the covers of *People* and *Rolling Stone*.

"I'm Cyborg Sally, I'm your sex machine . . ." she purred into his ear.

"But you don't exist," Lord Jimmy said in utter bemusement, "I mean . . ."

She reached across his body and grabbed his crotch in full view of a nearby table. "Don't I?" she said.

"But you're supposed to be, what do the bastards call it, a bloody *Artificial Personality,* filters and vocoders, and animation programs, and bugger all knows what else, like that bloody Red Jack thing. I mean I'm *wired* now, aren't I, and I'm talking to . . . to . . . I mean . . . Shit, what the fuck *do* I mean?"

She smiled a steel dagger grin at him. "I'm Cyborg Sally," she said, "flesh *and* wire."

"The blazing bytes of my meat's desire?" he said lightly.

"No living soul gonna take you higher."

Lord Jimmy frowned. "But bloody 'ell, *are* you a living soul, or *what*?" he said. "I mean, you on the discs, you right here, it's the same bloody *you,* but you *can't* be real, now, can you, that voice . . ."

"Haven't you ever used a vocoder? No special effects on *your* discs?"

"Yeah, but . . . luv a duck, it's really *me,* not just some bloody set of programs conjuring it all up from nothing!"

"You . . . *felt* me coming through up there on the screen, I saw you, was that coming from *nothing*?" She squeezed his hard hot cock again. "Is *this* nothing but a set of programs? You think you're talking to a set of programs right now?"

Lord Jimmy shook his beautiful head. "Damned if I know who or what I'm talking to now," he said. "I mean for all I know, I could be back home in London plugged in, wanking off, and talking to myself!"

He shrugged. He grinned at her. "Damned if I bloody care!" he admitted.

He frowned. "But if there really *is* a Cyborg Sally, and I really am talking to her, and she really does have her hand on me meat, then answer me this, Sally: why don't you bloody well *tour*? Why is it poor old Lord Jimmy booked into The American Dream in New York tomorrow and not *you*? I mean, real or not, ducks, Muzik's got you under contract, and they own the bloody joint! Why no live concerts?"

A cold sweaty chill blew through a fat girl from the Valley as she woke up inside a rubber suit trying to pick up a rock star. A meaty fear replaced the electric confidence of her clear clean circuitries. "Why . . . why bother?" she could only stammer.

"Why bother!" Lord Jimmy exclaimed, his blue eyes flaming with sudden passion. "Why bother eating? Why bother getting loaded? Why bother fucking? It's what it's all about, isn't it? It's better than stuffing your face at Maxim's or snorting up a million pounds' worth of dust or the best bleeding blow-job there ever was! To be up there on that stage with thousands of little girls and boys jumping up and down and soiling their knickers over you and the music pouring up through you like you were coming forever! It's the whole fuckin' raison d'être, isn't it? It's bloody rock and roll, isn't it, and the rest is just sitting around backstage with ants in your pants waiting for the next chance to go on!"

"Yes . . ." she whispered. "Someday . . ."

"*Someday?* Why in fuckin' bleedin' 'ell not *now*?"

They paused at the porch railing and she looked out over the shaggy shadowy shoulders of the Hollywood Hills at the blazing bits and bytes of the Los Angeles side spread out before them far below.

She reached up to reconnect herself to the current of power that had raised her to this pinnacle above it, and put her at the side of this bitchin' rock and roll star—

—and she was standing on the deck of Glorianna O'Toole's

house on another such balmy fragrant night, looking out over the very same cityscape. The night, in a certain sense, of her birth, plugged in for the first time, as Glorianna O'Toole stood there outlined by the jeweled lights with the years melting away and her spirit shining through; the solarized, glorified image of the true queen of rock and roll trapped inside her own pudgy flesh, taunting her with everything she longed to be and knew she could never become.

She blinked, she turned to look into the radiant blue eyes of Lord Jimmy gleaming like glowing sapphires in his finely chiseled face, the warm glow from the interior lights of the Glitter Dome backlighting his golden hair—another transcendent publicity photo vision of that selfsame shining spirit.

Why not me, why not me, why not ME?

"You're bleeding *Cyborg Sally,* aren't you?" he said. "And I'm Lord Jimmy, the fucking Golden Boy of Rock and Roll, at least for the next few weeks! We're number one and number two on the charts, now aren't we, luv? The last of the real live rock and roll princes and on me way out to hear the bastards tell it when we're trying to do a deal, and Muzik's nonexistent little cyborg queen! What do you say, Cyborg Sally, if you really are bloody real, why don't you pop on over to New York and do a surprise set or two with me at The American Dream?"

"I . . . I couldn't . . ." she stammered. "I'm in the middle of doing a new disc. . . . They'd never let me—"

"Never let you!" Lord Jimmy exclaimed. "What kind of way is that for a bleeding *rock star* to talk? You're number one on the charts, aren't you? You're the only thing between my own wonderful self and the top! Surely you know where and when a singer with a number one goes?"

She looked at him quizzically. He laughed.

"Where and when she fucking well wants to!" he exclaimed. "Fuck 'em! Show the bastards, oh blazing bits and bytes of my bloody meat's desire! Noblesse oblige, luv! We're *rock stars*! We're *obligated* to be unpredictable prima donnas and maniacs, my dear! From time to time we must give the bastards a good swift kick in the arse, or we're letting down the side, aren't we, ducks!"

She looked into his eyes, and perspective reversed as she saw the magic perfection of herself mirrored there, her flickering flashing nimbus of serpent hair glowing in the darkness, the silvery sheen of her face and flesh, and behind her, the immense multicolored pixel-field of the city lights, out of which, like an electronic goddess of his rock and roll dreamtime in more than metaphor, she emerged newborn and triumphant from the bits and bytes.

"Ah, what a set we could do!" Lord Jimmy exclaimed. "What a bloody Götterdämmerung! I'll back you on 'Cyborg Sally,' you back me on 'At Your Command,' and then we'll have it out with everyone else's moldy oldies! The Golden Boy of Rock and Roll and the Cyborg Queen who isn't fucking there! A battle to the death between the future and the past, and the devil take the hindmost! Be a sport, luv! I always said that when I go, I want to go out rockin'!"

He reached out, wrapped his arms around her, and kissed her, long, and deep, and passionately. Then Lord Jimmy held Cyborg Sally tenderly by the shoulders and smiled his perfect smile just for her.

Tears welled up in her eyes. A joy she had never believed she would ever know bloomed like an unfolding flower in her heart of hearts.

"Well, well, if it isn't Sally from the Valley!" said an all-too-familiar voice behind her.

Paco Monaco loped west on Houston like a frustrated and paranoid jungle cat sniffing pussy on the late night wind; moving at top speed in long restless strides, his head swiveling from side to side, his eyes darting from here to there, a painful hard-on chafing between his legs, his nervous system ringing with psychic overload, testosterone, and adrenaline.

Chingada, it had happened to him again!

On the last beat of "Cyborg Sally," Mucho Muchacho was coming deep inside the cunt of the silver blond-haired Cyborg Queen of Chocharica City, and then, all at once, he passed directly from a wet dream into nightmare.

There he was in the musty cockroach stink of the back reaches of Slimy Mary's grinding away at some chocha on a moldy mattress, listening to the shrill cackling laughter of giant rats in sheepskin coats and tuxedos standing in a circle around him, pointing bony rat-fingers, and stroking long thin gray rat-pricks.

What he was humping wasn't human. A featureless face like a silver department store dummy, with a cheap rubber wig, crudely painted eyes rendered in the frozen rolling moment of orgasm, and a mouth full of steel daggers clacking mechanically like a set of wind-up false teeth. He had an angry robot pinned by the wrists, a sex monster had its legs wrapped tight around his waist, and they were grinding away at each other like two fucking machines.

His dick ached cruelly against his tight white pants. Not only hadn't he come, he wasn't even fucking; he was dry-humping away at the thing like a horny dog beating itself off against someone's leg.

"Chingada!" he screamed, tearing away from the creature, bolting to his feet, and smashing his way through the circle of giant rats with a series of spinning karate kicks.

He dashed through the wan light of the twilight zone and across the edge of the dance floor, where faceless silvery dummies in cheap rubber wigs twitched and jerked spastically under the flickering bulbs, where burnt-out zombies in Cyborg Sally T-shirts and long red hair, with rotten green skin and dead fish-eyes, danced around them at the ends of marionette strings. . . .

Third Street had been dark and empty when he emerged onto it from the flash and the meatrack. Even now, under the dirty yellow streetlights of Houston, the only people to be seen were raggy figures asleep in garbage-strewn alleys between the looming gray buildings, and plushie-tushies and gordos gliding by in cars and taxis through the grim gray predawn hour.

Buena suerte for any putamadre who might have crossed my path! he thought as he hit his touchpoint. One way or another, this night was not going to end until Mucho Muchacho kicked some Chocharica City ass!

For his sleek bronzed flesh crawled with queasy self-revulsion, his treacherous cock throbbed in angry outrage at he knew not quite what, his mighty muscles were definitely cruising for a bruising, and his brain seemed to churn and itch inside the confines of his skull at the edge of some tormenting, illusive revelation.

If a fuckin' zonie with an Uzi had appeared to hassle him now, he probably couldn't have stopped himself from coming after the putamadre with fists and feet.

Like a dreamer awakening lucidly into his nightmare and seeking to bend it to his own happy ending, he had reentered this flash to ride it to its destined conclusion.

And that, he knew as he turned south on Mercer to avoid any confrontations with the zonies patrolling West Broadway, lay down here, in Soho, in Chocharica City, in The American Dream.

For that was where Mucho Muchacho must hunt down Cyborg Sally. That was her home turf, that was where she had given him this cold treacherous hard-on that had turned him into a fuckin' dog dry-humping something that wasn't even there, that was where he would find the bitch, and when he did . . . when he did . . .

Chingada! He didn't know what he would find! He didn't know what he would do! That was what was making his brain burn and itch, that was what was making him blindly follow the insistent arrow of this angry aching hard-on!

Cyborg Sally had betrayed him. The putamadres who owned the world had somehow made *his own fuckin' cock* betray him!

The only way to make himself the master of it once more was to find a way to ram the red-hot motherfucker up where it belonged!

When he turned the corner off Mercer, he saw that the usual nightly mob scene by the main entrance of The American Dream was long gone. There was no one at the door but Fritz, in his long black raincoat, and three big putamadres clustered around him and giving him some kind of hard time.

Chingada, what fuckin' ugly meat! They all had huge muscles bulging out of sleeveless leather vests studded with sharp chrome spikes and wore skin-tight black leather pants. Two of them wore heavy motorcycle boots and the other high-heeled black cowboy boots with motherfucking spurs. One had shaved his head bald, another wore a leather cap, and the third had a hard-greased black mohawk with a row of razor blades glued in a buzzsaw line along the crest.

"No man, no way . . ." Fritz was saying. He had the doorway blocked with his body, but he was inching backward away from them and there was an un-Fritzlike fear in his voice, and when Paco got there he saw why.

"We're not good enough for your fuckin' shithole, is that it, asshole?" the bald bastard said. He had half the length of a long chain wrapped around his right forearm. It snaked through his palm and he was twirling it in slow lazy dangling circles. The putamadre with the razor-blade mohawk was waving a long switchblade knife.

Mucho Muchacho's cock throbbed against his tight white

pants. Time seemed to slow to a crawl as he glided up to the doorway. His lips creased in a crooked smile.

"Hey, qué pasa, amigo?" he drawled easily. "These fuckin' maricónes givin' you a hard time?"

Fritz's eyes widened. He shook his head in warning. The putamadre with the chain turned to regard him with crazed bloodshot eyes. "Who the fuck are you, spick?" he said woozily.

"You don't really want to find out, cabrón," said Mucho Muchacho.

"You got ten seconds to get your spick ass out of here before I cut your fuckin' cock off, shitface," said the faggot with the knife, waving it under his nose.

"You got less than that to kiss my culo, maricón," said Mucho Muchacho.

"Hey Paco, fer chrissakes don't—"

The putamadre with the chain swung it at Mucho's head. It seemed to take all the time in the world. He ducked under it, stepped forward with his left foot, spun on it, and caught the motherfucker flatfooted with a kick to the balls. He screamed and folded and Mucho Muchacho chopped the back of his neck with the side of his hand as he brought his knee up into his jaw.

Mucho came whirling up and around out of his half crouch in plenty of time to catch the unarmed sucker with a straight-armed blow to the Adam's apple as he threw a ragged roundhouse punch past his ear, then kicked him in the guts, and he flopped over backward, gargling blood.

He heard a thin ululating scream, saw the third putamadre, the one with the knife, hunched down in front of Fritz, grinding the blade into him.

Dogmeat, Mucho had time to think, and then he kicked the motherfucker square in the base of the spine, felt something crunch, then punched the bastard in the back of the neck with all his weight behind it as he reared up and back, then hooked his foot behind the putamadre's knee and flipped him face forward onto the hard concrete sidewalk with a sickening thud.

There was the slow rhythmic sound of hands clapping. He whirled around, side to side to side.

The three leather faggots lay on the sidewalk, not moving.

Fritz stood on shaky knees in the doorway, hunched over and hugging his stomach. Thick bright blood oozed through his interlaced fingers.

Behind him stood a paunchy gray-haired man in a green velvet dinner jacket slapping his hands together in heavy meaty irony. Behind *him* stood two chunky men in black business suits.

"Bra-vo," said the man in the green dinner jacket. He nodded to the men in the business suits. "Call an ambulance for Mr. Fritz," he said. "But first make this garbage disappear."

He smiled thinly at Paco, crooked a finger. "You and I must have a talk."

"Who's this bloody little wanker?" Lord Jimmy demanded airily.

Cyborg Sally, turning at the sound of Bobby Rubin's voice, found herself looking into Bobby's eyes glaring back at her from the face of Red Jack. It was Bobby all right, his voice, his eyes, his sneer, but long red silver-webbed hair fell to the shoulders of his lean lithe body, and his shirt and pants were a pixel-field reflecting the scintillating city lights.

As she stared into those dark bedroom eyes, Red Jack's head dissolved into pixels around them, and Bobby Rubin's petulant, wimpy face and black hair appeared for a beat. Then it, too, dissolved back into the bits and bytes. Red Jack reformed. Bobby. Red Jack. Flick, flick, flick, flick to a steady simple beat of agony, and always the same sexy cruel eyes, the same sneer mocking her most magic moment, forcing her out of it, and into a real-life nightmare.

"Where'd you get the tacky rubber suit, Sally from the Valley," Bobby Rubin said, "Frederick's of Pacoima?"

"I never saw this little creep in my life," Sally Genaro insisted with a lead weight in her gut.

"You heard the lady, mate, so piss off!"

"Hey, that's *Lord Jimmy,* Bobby!" squealed a feminine voice. Sally turned again and noticed for the first time that a busty blond little airhead was clinging possessively to Bobby Rubin's arm.

"Why, so it is," Bobby drawled, "Lord Jimmy himself, reduced to picking up dogmeat!"

Lord Jimmy took a step toward Bobby, hesitantly cocking his fist. "Who the bloody 'ell do you think you are!"

"Just a fan of yours who thinks it's pretty pathetic to see a big rock star like you so brain-burned on wire that you're hustling some fat Pimple stuffed into a rubber suit!"

"Rubber suit . . . Wire . . . ?" Lord Jimmy stammered, popping, blinking, out of the magic flash.

"No!" Sally moaned. "Oh please, no!"

But it had already happened. Lord Jimmy stood there, frowning in confusion at Bobby Rubin. He shook his gorgeous head convulsively, as if trying to shake cobwebs out of his brain.

"Rubber suit . . . ?" Lord Jimmy muttered in a daze. Numbly he reached out a thumb and forefinger and pinched Sally's foam rubber breast. "Shit!" he exclaimed, his fair face flushing scarlet.

There was a scattering of giggles and then a general roar of laughter.

For the first time, Sally realized that a little crowd had gathered around this horrid scene. Tall elegant women, handsome actors in silk shirts and gold chains, middle-aged producer types, starlets with their tits bursting out of their bodices; the Glitter Dome elite stood in a semi-circle around them, laughing their beautiful empty heads off at her.

And Bobby Rubin laughed loudest of all.

"Fucking bloody 'ell!" Lord Jimmy shouted. "Out of my way, you wanking assholes!" And he shoved his way through the little audience, loping off around the curve of the porch at a near run. "Whole fucking country's turned into a *zoo*!"

Sally Genaro stood there glaring at Bobby with tears welling up in her eyes and her hands balled into fists.

"Why did you have to *do* that?" she screamed.

"Maybe I was jealous . . . ?" Bobby suggested archly. "After all, don't you usually beat your meat over *me*?"

"Really?" she said earnestly, feeling a sudden flush of warmth through her tears. "Really, Bobby?"

Bobby laughed and laughed and laughed.

"I hate you, I hate you, I hate you, I hate you all!" Sally shouted, and without pausing to think or hit her touchpoint, dashed off through the goggle-eyed onlookers after the disappearing figure of Lord Jimmy.

"You handled yourself real good out there, kid," said the man in the green velvet dinner jacket. "What's your name?"

"P-Paco . . . Paco Monaco, Mr. Steiner . . ." Paco said nervously.

He was sitting before a plain steel desk in a tiny office somewhere off a long dimly lit corridor in the basement of The American Dream. He had unplugged muy pronto when this putamadre had told him he was the security chief. He might have fuckin' *killed* somebody out there and he had to make real sure this old gordo didn't turn him over to the cops.

"You have a job, Paco . . . ?"

"No . . . yeah . . . well, sorta . . ."

"Sorta . . . ?" the gray-haired man said, steepling his fingers and regarding Paco closely over them.

"I'm relief doorman at a club called Slimy Mary's. . . ."

Steiner smiled at him. "You're an experienced doorman?" he said.

Paco studied the security chief of The American Dream as it began to dawn on him that this was no roust. What had this guy said, *Make this garbage disappear*? And Fritz had really gotten himself fucked up. . . .

"Oh yeah . . ." he said slowly. "I'm Dojo's main man, Mr. Steiner, I know how it goes. . . ."

"Can you guess what this little talk is all about?"

Paco risked a knowing little smile. "You're not gonna turn me over to the cops . . . ? And poor Fritz, looks like he's gonna be laid up for quite a while, I mean, he's my friend and all, I wouldn't want to . . . But . . ."

Henry Steiner frowned. "Don't worry about taking Fritz's job," he said very coldly. "He lost it the moment he couldn't control the situation. If those bozos had gotten inside . . . if you hadn't come along . . ."

He smiled just as coldly at Paco. "You get only one opportunity to fuck up on this job, Paco," he said. "After which, you are gone. Do we understand each other?"

"For sure, Mr.Steiner."

"We'll try you Tuesday through Saturday, ten to three, two thousand dollars, no dealing nothing on the door, no collecting bribes to get in, you pass through anyone who causes trouble inside, you're out," Steiner said. "Deal?"

"I'm your man, Mr. Steiner," Paco said, holding out his hand. The gordo didn't take it, and he didn't slap at it either.

"Turn up tomorrow night," he said distantly. "You can find your own way out. . . ."

"That's it? I'm hired?"

Steiner nodded. Paco stood up. He looked at Steiner for a long moment.

"What?" the gray-haired man said.

Paco shrugged shyly. "No se . . ."

"What do you want, a ceremony?"

Paco shrugged again.

"Okay, okay, so welcome to The American Dream, Paco Monaco. Now piss off kid, I got more important business to attend to."

Sally cornered Lord Jimmy on the escalator gliding down out of the Glitter Dome. "Wait!" she cried redundantly as she stepped onto the metal stair behind him.

"Leave me the fuck alone, will you, haven't you made a big enough ass of me already, whoever you are?"

"I'm Cyborg Sally, really I am!"

"Right! And I'm King bloody Charles, or haven't you noticed?"

She caught him by the arm. "Please," she said. "I didn't mean to . . . I . . ."

She was acutely aware of her own sweaty flab inside the foam rubber undersuit, of this ludicrous gear, of the fact that he was Lord Jimmy, a real rock star, and she was only . . . was only . . .

Lord Jimmy turned his regal blond head to regard her with a mixture of anger and pity. "All right, all right," he said tiredly. "I forgive you. Noblesse oblige, and all that."

He reached out and patted her on her rubber-padded arm as one might comfort a poor little puppy dog. "You're probably some poor sweaty little groupie who just wanted to tell her sweaty little friends that she actually got her hand on me magnificent joint. All right, all right luv, don't be sad. You've had your fun at my expense, and now you can treasure this moment for the rest of your life."

"No, it's not like that, I'm *her,* I'm her voice, I'm the music, I'm Cyborg Sally, really I am! Didn't you hear me? Didn't you feel me? Didn't you touch me?"

Lord Jimmy looked up slowly into her eyes. "Fucking 'ell, you know I almost believe you," he said. "I mean . . . that face . . . those eyes . . ."

"I am," she said. "I'm the VoxBox player on the disc, I wrote the music, I inputted the lyric, she's got my eyes. . . . Aren't the eyes the window of the soul?"

The escalator reached the landing. He could have escaped, but he didn't. Instead, he granted her a final moment, standing there, with the balmy wind tossing his golden curly hair.

"VoxBox player?" he said. "Inputted the lyric?" He sighed. "What the bloody fuck has happened to rock and roll? Oh yes, you poor pathetic little creature, it all makes a revolting sort of sense. Some creepy little nobody running some plastic words through her bloody little VoxBox. And more pathetic little bastards running it through their computers. And out the other end comes a bloody disc that wipes me off the charts. Rubber and greasepaint and fucking wizardware. Fucking 'ell, Cyborg Sally has to be something just like you, now doesn't she?''

Tears rolled down her cheeks, smearing silver paint. ''You're a beautiful man, you know that?''

''Of course I do,'' Lord Jimmy said. ''Me mum tells me so all the time.'' And he turned to go, with a gallant little wave.

''Wait! Don't go!''

''I've got a gig to do, luv.'' He gave her one last backward glance. ''But if you really are what you say you are, you can bloody well prove it to me, now can't you, ducks? If you really *are* Cyborg Sally, prove it to me in the only place that counts. Live! On stage! In The American Dream! Catch your act there . . . or not at all!'' He blew her an ironic little kiss, and then he was gone.

''See you in New York, you see if I don't!'' she called after him.

She stood there foolishly, confronting the emptiness of her promise for a long moment. Then she remembered Lord Jimmy's little joke.

Where and when does a singer with a number one hit go?

Where and when she fucking well wants to.

Sally Genaro might not be a rock star like Lord Jimmy, but Cyborg Sally was. Cyborg Sally could go anywhere she wanted to and any manager would cream in his jeans in gratitude if she showed up unannounced to do a free set in his club.

Lord Jimmy was right. It was time for Cyborg Sally to take her act on tour. Time for poor little Sally from the Valley to suit up, plug in, and show the Bobby Rubins of the world how to really rock and roll.

EAST SIDE, WEST SIDE

Sally Genaro had gotten a midnight first class flight out of LAX, gorked herself off with three quick stiff martinis, slept through the movie and the meal, and hadn't come out of it until the cabin lights came on, and the p.a. told her to fasten her seat belt, and the stewardesses started serving croissants stuffed with eggs and bacon, red grapefruit halves, and coffee.

By the time the plane passed over Manhattan on its way to the inevitable holding stack over Kennedy, she had wolfed down one breakfast, was started on the second, was working on her third cup of coffee, and was beginning to feel almost human.

Sally had never been to New York, she had never been east of *Las Vegas*, but of course she had seen just this locale-establishing shot in endless movies and tv shows: lower Manhattan through an airplane window on a clear early morning, the fabled clusters of skyscrapers at the tip and at midtown, the green rectangle of Central Park, the low sun flashing brilliantly on the mirrored bay, the webwork of bridges, the Empire State Building, the Chrysler Building, the World Trade Center, even the Statue of Liberty on its little island.

It was perfect, it was just as she had always imagined it, and a thrill of excitement burned away most of the lack of a good night's sleep, the time-zone displacement, the hangover, even the horror of the bummer scene at the end of last night's magic, if not the memory.

Here she was, gliding into the fabulous Big Apple, a star from Hollywood, the best-selling rock star in the country, on her way to her first live performance in the fabled American Dream. It was just like stepping into a romantic movie with like *script approval,* and herself as female lead, and *Lord Jimmy* cast as her heartthrob.

After circling JFK for forty-five minutes, waiting for a gate for another fifteen, and waiting in the shouting, cursing mob scene around the baggage carousel for her luggage to emerge from limbo for another twenty, however, she was tired, discombobulated, and starting to get paranoid. People here were so *pushy*. The baggage area was so *grimy* and *tacky* and there were mean and subhuman-looking *apes* tossing around suitcases like they were *garbage cans.*

They did not exactly inspire confidence in the reliability of the baggage handling system. What if they *lost* her suitcase? All her Cyborg Sally gear was in there, what would she do if—

Her big soft-sided canvas suitcase came bouncing and tumbling down the chute onto the conveyor belt. "That's mine, that's mine!" she squealed, and found herself kneeing and elbowing through the press of bodies with the best of them.

Disheveled, sweaty, and slightly bruised, she staggered out through the sliding glass doors onto a sidewalk fronting on some awful horn-blaring traffic jam, too dazed to even be very pissed off at the rip in the side of her suitcase.

"Wanna cab?" A grimy little oriental in jeans and a cracked brown leather jacket appeared at her side from nowhere. "Three hundred bucks off the meter anywhere in Manhattan, can't do any better than that, right?"

"Uh—"

He snatched up her suitcase, loped about seventy yards down the sidewalk to a filthy unmarked old green Toyota with Sally running after him, flipped open the trunk, threw the suitcase into a mess of jumper cables and oil cans, slapped the trunk shut, and opened the back door for her with an incongruous little bow. "Where to?"

"Uh . . ."

Sally's mind raced in neutral as she climbed into the cab. Maybe she was just being paranoid, but something told her that maybe this guy wasn't entirely to be trusted. He certainly didn't seem like someone she could ask to recommend a good hotel.

"Uh . . . the Waldorf-Astoria . . ." she said, trying to sound aristocratic and in control. That was the name of the fancy hotel in all those movies, wasn't it? Anyway, she didn't *know* the name of any other hotel in Manhattan.

During the hour and a half it took the cab to fight its way

through the rush-hour traffic into Manhattan and crosstown to the Waldorf-Astoria, Sally had more time than she wanted to observe the Big Apple from ground level.

The ride through Queens was not that much different from a bad morning on the Santa Monica Freeway, except that it seemed as if no one had paved *this* freeway for about four hundred years, the cab seemed to have no springs at all, and the suburban slums it passed through made Watts seem like downtown Beverly Hills.

The scene became more dramatic as they inched along an elevated portion through blocks of moldy gray tenements and industrial slums that reminded her of the approach to Long Beach on the Harbor Freeway, for towering in the distance before them she could once more see the famous Manhattan skyline, shimmering alluringly beyond this urban disaster area in the gray haze like the Hollywood Hills rearing up out of the smog as you drove east on the Santa Monica from the airport.

An endless crawl through a filthy tunnel full of choking exhaust fumes, and then they were bouncing and jolting in short fits and long stops through the narrow, traffic-clogged, teeming cross-town streets of mid-Manhattan.

Sally had never been in *this* movie before. The avenues they crossed were wide canyons of tall skyscrapers chockablock at ground level with the signs and facades and windows of restaurants and shops and stores, but the crosstown streets were narrow shadowy back canyons between endless gray stone and concrete cliffs where God knew what went on inside, and where everything—the street, the sidewalk, the buildings—seemed to be covered with mung and falling apart.

And the people . . .

They swarmed everywhere, they all seemed to be in a terrible hurry to get somewhere else, dodging across traffic in the middle of the streets, paying absolutely no attention to the lights, and while the majority of them wouldn't have looked that much out of place on Ventura or Hollywood or Wilshire, many of them looked really weird. Ominously weird.

There were filthy creatures of both sexes shouldering big burlap bags—girls wearing cheap rubber wigs, raggy jeans, and *her* T-shirt; guys wearing Cyborg Sally T-shirts, too, some of them, incongruously enough, also sporting badly done Red Jack hairdos. And there were all these mean-looking men everywhere carrying *machine guns*.

Nor was the Waldorf-Astoria quite what she had pictured from vague cinematic memories when the cab deposited her at the entrance and then drove away after the driver cursed her out in a mixture of English and Korean or something for not adding a *tip* to the three-hundred-dollar fare.

Oh yes, it fronted on Park Avenue—a broad boulevard with a central landscaped median through towering skyscrapers of steel and glass and a smattering of older, more ornate buildings—a famous street she recognized from film and tv. But the grass of the median was scraggly and brown and strewn with refuse, and half the trees looked like they were dying.

The facade of the hotel was grand enough, with an awning, and a uniformed doorman, and flags flying that she didn't recognize, and a bellman took her bag and led her up a dramatically broad staircase into a lushly carpeted and cavernous lobby.

But the carpeting was some phony Persian stuff already going to seed and all the dark woodwork looked like a Disneyland version of itself that was aging less than gracefuly and there were *guards* with *machine guns* standing around glowering, and the mirrored elevator was slightly grimy and smelled a bit of piss and garlic.

And what *$1500 a night* got her was a single room slightly smaller than her own bedroom, a bathroom with a mingy flow-control showerhead, and a single window looking out on a magnificent view of an airshaft.

"Gross . . ." Sally muttered as she flung her suitcase down on the bed and started to unpack. Well, maybe not quite gross, but not exactly a bungalow at the Beverly Hills either.

She had heard all the horror stories about New York, of course—that it was dirty and crowded, that over a million people lived on the streets, that people had to hire, what did they call them, zonies, to guard their apartments, that New Yorkers were rude and vicious and paranoid, that everything was incredibly expensive. But *seeing* it and *hearing it* and *smelling it* and paying $300 for a cab and $1500 a night for this tacky hotel room was something else again.

But, tired, sweaty, disoriented, and somehow disappointed as she was, her mood brightened when she started unpacking her silver body stocking and her wig and her bitchin' black leather pants.

Okay, so Sally Genaro was, what did they call it here, a hick from the sticks, a rube, a mark, and she was probably being ripped off. But I'll bet a rock star like *Lord Jimmy* isn't stuck in a crummy joint like this. I'll bet he's got a big suite somewhere and a limo with a chauffeur.

And Lord Jimmy is only *number two*. Cyborg Sally is number one! And once I connect up with him, we'll trip the lite fantastic on the sidewalks of New York!

"Please, Mr. Doorman, let me in, if you do, you can meet me after work, and I'll let you take me home and fuck me."

"Hey, I don't know, momacita, you look like trouble to me, and on this job I get offered more pussy than even I can handle."

Karen and Paco both broke up, and oh yes it felt good to be able to joke like this with her man again, but her laughter was a wee bit hollow. She could well imagine just how true that must be. Even now there was a great press of bodies squealing and squirming for his attention while they did their little number, at least half of them were female, and nothing less than foxes need apply.

Was *that* the worm in her apple, or was it something deeper that, despite her surface gaiety, was bringing her down?

"Hey, on this job they're *paying me* to pick out the primo chocha, Karen," he had told her in high good humor after his first night at the door of The American Dream. "They want a good-looking crowd for when MUZIK broadcasts from the club. Chingada, *everyone* wants to get in; they'll fire me if I let in a lot of dogmeat."

"You better let me in, Mr. Doorman," Karen whispered at him out of earshot of the sidewalk crowd of supplicants. "Otherwise, I'll tell your bosses you're a card-carrying member of the Reality Liberation Front."

"Hey, not funny!" Paco hissed, his eyes darting around furtively, and without further horseplay, he shooed her inside.

"Man, there's more to being doorman at The American Dream than keeping out drunks and bad-asses," Paco had expounded at the loft over breakfast yesterday morning.

"Yeah, I'll bet," said Eddie Polonski, "it must be a real drag sorting through all that pussy."

"Hey, you know, they got—*policies*, they call 'em, and I gotta enforce them. Chingada, sometimes I get to feeling like I'm some kind of fuckin' *zonie*!"

"Policies?" Larry Coopersmith asked sharply.

"Yeah, for instance, good-looking ladies is a policy. No junkies or drunks is a policy. No more than two hundred streeties a night, and I better keep count. Keep the crowd in the pit two thirds white. And nobody wearing the Red gets in."

"You mean you'd kick us out?" Malcolm McGee demanded indignantly. He, Tommy, Teddy, and Bill still defiantly wore the Red, even though it tended to attract unwelcome attention from the cops and zonies these days.

"He'd have to," Karen had told them. "They're really down on anyone they think might be a bedbug dealer. If Paco hadn't gotten the job, I think I would've been eighty-sixed by now even without the Red."

Karen made her way across the dance floor and took her usual stool at the bar. She ordered herself a screwdriver and surveyed the scene. There were the usual streetie hookers, most of them in tacky Cyborg Sally fetish outfits, and there were assorted male co-workers trying to sort out a similarly effective look, and there were guys dealing heavily stepped on dust and coke.

But all the pirate disc dealers who had been her competition were gone. Thanks to Paco, she was the only dealer who could still get into The American Dream.

She shook her head slowly as she sipped at her drink, trying to sort her feelings out, trying to understand why she felt so queasily ambivalent about this new turn of the wheel.

Okay, so the Red Jack disc trade was still near-moribund, but at least Paco's new job had given her a monopoly on what little was left. And, much closer to her heart, something he refused to talk about had completely turned him off his obsession with Cyborg Sally the night he lucked into it too.

Suddenly there was no one in the RLF who agreed more vehemently with Markowitz on the subject of Cyborg Sally than Paco.

"Chingada, Larry's fuckin' right, I mean, there isn't any Cyborg Sally, but that didn't stop her from making an asshole out of me, I mean I was being pussywhipped by fuckin' *nada,* by some tv commercial for a hard-on, had me thinking with my prick, had me right by the handle, had me sucking on the silver tit of Chocharica City, and that's all she is, chingada, a department store dummy puta turnin' tricks for her fuckin' pimps in Ciudad Trabajo!"

And it had been much more than just talk. He had been Mucho Muchacho in bed again these last few nights, if anything, even more so, as if determined to make up for what he now saw as his previous period of unmanly surrender by almost angry displays of domineering cocksmanship. He brought her little gifts. He held her hand in the street. He snuggled against her in the night. He kissed her awake in the morning. She had the feeling that someday soon he might even tell her he loved her in words of one syllable.

So what was this cloud in what should have been her clear blue sky?

She had gingerly confessed her incoherent misgivings to Leslie Savanah. "It's not your love life, Karen," Leslie had told her. "I mean, we all feel a little weird about the situation. Here we've got one of our members controlling the door of The American Dream, but instead of being able to flood the joint with random factors, poor Paco finds himself having to maintain Official Reality inside himself! This should be a big break for the RLF, but not even Larry can figure out what the hell we can do with it."

"Somehow I don't think I have quite that degree of political sophistication when it comes to what I feel about my man," Karen had answered dryly.

Now she peered out past the overhang at the dance floor, where scores of fancy Cyborg Sallys were strutting their arrogant cockteasing stuff, where the flashing women inside the gear were giving the mucho machos a good dose of what for.

Could *that* be it? she wondered. Am I really just like them inside? Did I really *get off* on having Cyborg Sally turn my macho man into my pussywhipped sex slave?

Or was there something even more dishonorable to her true feelings than that?

Energy was bleeding out of the RLF to the point where half the members were chain-tapping obsessively to escape the futility of the reality, she was spending her nights sitting here and accomplishing nothing, and while everything else was going downhill, her Paco's star was on the rise.

Was she *jealous* of Paco?

Was she jealous of the fact that it was now *Paco* who was *her* entree to The American Dream?

Was it one thing to watch with a superior sense of noblesse oblige as the uneducated Puerto Rican kid she had rescued from the streets flowered into independent manhood, but quite another to see him rising above *her* station?

Had her frustration really made her as mean-spirited as that? Or had she always been a secret snob, a closet chocharica bitch?

Sally Genaro slept till noon, ate a tepid room service breakfast, then pondered what to do until it was time to go to The American Dream.

Well this was *New York,* wasn't it, and she had never been here, so why not just go out and see some of the sights? She showered, dried herself, then went to the closet to peruse the meager wardrobe she had brought with her. The first thing that caught her eye was the silver body stocking and the foam rubber undersuit.

Well why not? She was going to be Cyborg Sally onstage tonight, so why not get used to it? Give all her fans on the street a little thrill.

She donned her Sally, applied her silver makeup, took the elevator down, caught a cab at the door, and told the driver to take her to Times Square. When that proved to be about as colorful as the Miracle Mile, just a complex of tall office buildings surrounded by the ever-present zonies, she had the cabby drive through Central Park. But she was not about to get out there after she saw all those cardboard shacks and crazed-looking streeties.

In fact she blew about $300 on a random cab tour of Manhattan before she found anywhere she cared to wander for a while on foot.

She saw endless blocks of burnt-out and boarded-up buildings infested by rats and roaches and streeties. She saw streets full of the most incredible sleazy hookers. She saw the glittering shops of Fifth Avenue. She saw fancy town houses and condo buildings on the Upper West Side. She saw museums with beggars and street scum on their wide steps. She saw a line of streeties around the block in front of something called a "Kibble Dispensary." She saw the bulls and bears of Wall Street.

She saw what looked like dead bodies four or five times, lying in the street, crumpled in doorways, sprawled on piles of rubble, with people swarming by and paying no attention. She saw the Empire State Building rising out of the surrounding flea market. She saw the "Berlin Wall" around Battery Park City. She saw a scrawny girl fleeing through the crowd at Union Square being chased by a zonie with a machine gun. She saw a wino blowing his nose in his fingers and wiping his hand on a Rolls limousine.

She saw some fancy politician pulling up in a motorcade outside the United Nations, and right around the corner she saw a fat lady taking a shit in an open phone booth.

She saw a lot of things they didn't show on tv. And the more she saw, the more courage it took to finally venture out on the sidewalks of New York on her own two feet. If there was anything like all this in Los Angeles, it was deep in the barrio, where no girl in her right mind would venture off the freeway even in her *car*.

Finally she had an inspiration.

"Take me to The American Dream," she told the silent black driver, who had ventured no stream of wisecracks like New York cabbies were supposed to do in all those movies.

" 'Eh's closed," said the cabby in some weird African accent.

"I know it's closed. Just drop me off in the neighborhood."

" 'Eh's nom *So-ho,*" the cabby told her pedantically, and then he dropped her on a street that seemed to be everything she had hoped an area where Muzik would put its New York club would have to be.

"West Broadway" and "Houston Street" the street-corner sign said, and she found herself looking down a long block of restaurants and bars and boutiques and art galleries quite unlike anything she had seen on La Cienega; fancy windows and signs lining both sides of the rather narrow street from the bottom floors of comparatively low warehousy-looking buildings, about half of which were dingy gray concrete, and half painted in bright pastel colors like buildings in Venice.

Even an Angelino like Sally could tell that this street, currently only scattered with occasional strollers, was a fancy midway that lived after dark. Now, in the waning afternoon light, it seemed just what she was looking for, a nice, funky but high class New York movie street upon which to venture for a quiet little dress rehearsal as Cyborg Sally.

Hitting her touchpoint, she strutted on down the avenue.

"We just *gotta* do something with this golden opportunity that's been tossed in our laps, Paco," Larry Coopersmith said. "For sure, nothing much else is happening!"

Paco and Larry were sitting on a couch at the far end of the loft eating ham and cheese sandwiches and passing a quart bottle of beer.

Up at the other end, Mary and Tommy and Teddy were still

playing with their fuckin' computers, and Malcolm McGee was even wiring together another People's Cash Machine, but Paco had to admit it was all pretty much of a jerk-off, since even Dojo was having a hard time moving anything now. The loft was turning into a bad scene; people chain-tapping all the time and just playing with their toys and bullshitting about some revolution that didn't exist. Wasn't for Karen and the fact that this was his only free crash space, he just might have finally said fuck it to the whole stupid thing.

"Hey, Karen is the only disc dealer I let into The American Dream, and my man Dojo is the only one really movin' any of your shit at all," Paco snapped. "What *else* you want from my poor streetie culo, Larry?"

"I don't know, Paco," Larry Coopersmith said glumly. "Shit, things were really starting to cook! The electronic economy leaking billions at both ends, money getting into the hands of the people, electronic inflation, banks forced to close their cash machines, goddammit, we had Official Reality on the ropes!"

"But all that's still goin' on! Only problem is everyone's already got a Jack and a couple discs already! Ciudad Trabajo's still taking it in the ass, ain't it?"

"Yeah, but what about the *people,* Paco? Hell, we had Red Jack waking 'em up, and then wham, he's off the air, and Cyborg Sally's got them asleep with their hands in their pants again! Just goes to show you . . ."

"Show you *what*?"

Larry Coopersmith pulled out a cigarette, stuck it into his mouth, and lit it automatically. Just as automatically, he reached up like he was scratching his head and hit his touchpoint. He had been doin' it a lot, lately.

"Whatever the people see on the tube *is* their reality," he said in his "Markowitz" voice. "And as long as the powers that be control *that,* they can impose their own official version on everyone, just like you control the reality in the pit at The American Dream."

"Why are all you guys always giving me this shit about the admission policies?" Paco snapped angrily. "You think I fuckin' *like* keeping it so white? You think I *like* letting in all those Cyborg Sallys and keeping out anyone who still wears the Red? They pay me to *enforce* their fuckin' admission policies; I don't make 'em!"

"But what if you did?"

"Qué?"

Larry took a long drink of beer, then rolled the bottle in his hands thoughtfully. "What if one night you followed *RLF* admission policies and let in a mob wearing the Red?" he said. "What if it was a night MUZIK was doing a live broadcast . . . ?"

"They'd fire my fuckin' ass!"

"Wouldn't it maybe be worth it?"

"Chingada, you're crazy, motherfucker! Worth it to do *what*? So everybody watching MUZIK sees a bunch of jacked-in wireheads bust up The American Dream for about two minutes before the fuckin' zonies blow us all away? Your fuckin' brains are fried!"

"It *would* be quite a media event . . ." Larry mused dreamily.

"Hey man, I ain't gonna lose myself a two-grand-a-week job for your stupid fuckin' media event!"

"Not even if we could shatter Official Reality in those two minutes? Not even if it could change millions of lives in one magic televised moment?"

Paco eyed Larry Coopersmith more narrowly. Larry stared right back at him. Okay, he thought, maybe this shit *is* getting to me. Maybe there is something fucked about a spick like me taking Ciudad Trabajo money to keep The American Dream white. Maybe it almost might be worth losing a two-grand-a-week job to . . . to . . . to give a shove and feel the whole world move.

He took a long thoughtful swig of beer. "Tell you what, amigo," he finally said, "you show me a way we can really do that, and I'll think about putting my ass on the line for it when you do."

"You really mean that, Paco? Or you just running your mouth?"

"Chingada, *you're* the one who's just running his mouth, man! You come up with something besides wirehead bullshit, and *then* we'll talk serious craziness!"

"Deal," Larry said real seriouslike. He took a swig of beer, handed the bottle to Paco. "Drink to it, amigo," he said just as solemnly.

Cyborg Sally promenaded down West Broadway, peeking into galleries, idly perusing boutique windows, flashing her ball-cutting smile at occasional passersby, shaking her ass, waving her tits, and feeling at last the steel mistress of the city, the rock star from Hollywood negligently cockteasing the masses on the lazy afternoon before her big live performance.

There were no mobs of people here and the bars hadn't yet started happy hour and there seemed to be a zonie every ten feet and even a number-one best-selling rock star like Cyborg Sally could walk down the street without being hassled.

This must be the famous New York *attitude* they talked about in L.A. Men looked her up and down, but they waited till she passed and did it over their shoulders. Everyone knew who she was, but no one would let themselves be caught admitting it or being so *crass* as to bug her for an autograph.

Maybe she would come here tomorrow with Lord Jimmy. By then her surprise appearance at The American Dream would be the talk of the town and this might be a good place to get away from all the reporters and news cameras for a romantic late brunch.

She decided to go have a peek at The American Dream before it opened up, just to sniff the vibes. When she approached a zonie to ask directions, he stiffened his hands on his machine gun like he wished he could stroke his *dork,* and gave her the strangest look, but even he was too cool to acknowledge the all too obvious fact that he knew he was talking to a real rock star.

He directed her two blocks down and one block east to a side street. There was nothing there but gray featureless loft buildings, a pasta shop, a wine store, and an Italian delicatessen. But the biggest of the loft buildings had a whole line of zonies in front of it with their machine guns at the ready as roadies unloaded gear from a van.

A surge of electricity flashed through Cyborg Sally's circuits as she stood across the street watching them preparing for tonight's triumphant performance, a flash that shot down the cable of her spine to her electric chair.

"I'm comin' to dance, and I'm comin' tonight," she sang to herself, squirming and snaking with the juice of the turn-on. Tonight seemed like *ages* away. She wanted to be the Queen of Heat and a funeral pyre and a rockin' rolling sex machine right *now*.

Aimlessly, restlessly, looking for you, and loaded for bear, she paced east for a few more blocks, dancing sinuously to her own music, and didn't pay any attention to where she was going until she got there.

And where she had got to was definitely someplace else.

Not three blocks farther east she could see tall luxury condo towers, but she was walking through quite another world in plain sight of them.

Rows of once renovated tenements, abandoned again during the devaluation crash, lined both sides of the narrow street. Two of them were half-crumbled masonry piles of burnt-out rubble. The rest were like skeletons of buildings; walls of decaying brickwork and cracked concrete with dank dark humors blowing out through scores of smashed-out windows, peering at her vacantly like empty eye sockets in a row of skulls.

And there were scavenger rats in the bonepile. Some of them were fat dirty gray rodents skittering from shadow to shadow, but most of them were of the human variety. There were people apparently *living* in these grotty ruins.

Through the open windows, she could see figures moving around inside. A skinny girl in a filthy torn silver body stocking arguing with a guy in a Sally T-shirt. A circle of ragged people eating something that looked like *dry dog food* out of paper cups. People fucking and grunting out loud. A gross guy *pissing* out a top floor window across the street onto the sidewalk, the naked wire mesh of a Jack gleaming defiantly on his shaved head.

He laughed when he spotted her and hosed his prick at her so that the stream arced out into the gutter in a wide messy spatter.

''Hey Cyborg Sally,'' he called out, ''how'd you like to lick my splashing circuitry!''

What kind of way was *that* to pay homage to the Queen of Heat and a funeral pyre?

''Rock your roll in my electric chair, asshole!'' she shouted, giving him the steel finger. She arched her back, grabbed her crotch, and offered it up mockingly. ''My laser lips bring you to your knees!''

''Oooh . . . don't go away, I'll be right down!''

And then she realized that there was rustling, shambling, scuttling motion in the buildings around her, and voices moving down level by level as a ratswarm of people came chittering out of the ruins and onto the street.

There were almost two dozen of them, rag-clad refugees crawling out of the bombed-out ruins of Berlin at the end of some World War II movie.

But these weren't Germans and this wasn't a celluloid Berlin. This was New York, and these were Americans, well New Yorkers anyway, and what was worse, all of these starving children of the streets looked as if they could have been her.

They were all more or less her age, and if her father had happened to be working *here* during the collapse, and if she hadn't had her music, and with the proof she already had that New York was every bit as expensive as the legends warned, it was hard to see what would have rescued her from a life like this. There might not be burnt-out ruins in the San Fernando Valley, but even in high school she had certainly seen lives like this with the hope burned out of them. And she had come awfully close herself.

"Hey, it really *is* Cyborg Sally!" a black boy cried. He was wearing fraying jeans, a Coca-Cola T-shirt, and a Jack.

"Bullshit man! Your brain is burned!"

"Plug in and see for yourself!"

All at once Sally Genaro realized that she had popped out of the flash into deep, deep trouble.

They were circling around her like a pack of feral dogs. Boys in torn dirty Sally T-shirts and filthy pants, their heads shaved and painted in garishly colored graffiti, or with their hair conked and dyed and lacquered into weird tribal crests, or long and red and frosted with white traceries. Girls wearing bits and pieces of Cyborg Sally gear, torn body stockings, T-shirts, crudely dyed black briefs, weird homemade wigs that looked like actual purple floormops.

And most of them were wearing Jacks.

Terror loosened Sally Genaro's bowels as they circled her slowly, inching inward. The pressure of eyes on the back of her neck kept her counterrotating in place in paranoid dread.

She knew with cold dead certainty that she was going to be robbed, and gang-banged, and maybe even killed, and she felt like such a *fool* for asking for it like this that she could hardly make herself feel indignant about it.

Come on, Cyborg Sally, you got me *into* this, she pleaded as she hit her touchpoint in perfect desperation; now you'd better like get me *out*!

Cyborg Sally danced in a slow circle, following the streeties with her eyes as they tentatively spiraled inward, as more and more hands went to their touchpoints, feeling not fleshly fear, but the mighty electric charge being generated within her by the choreography of this dynamo.

She smiled with her dagger teeth, she arched her back, she put her steel hands on her hips, and she transformed her wary rotating into a triumphant twirling display.

"Yes, I'm Cyborg Sally, flesh and wire . . ." she sang out in a ragged half chant.

The human rat-pack stopped circling.

"Queen of Heat and a funeral pyre . . ."

They were staring at her raptly, rapturously. They were no longer a human rat-pack working up its courage to tear her down. They recognized her. They knew her. They believed.

They were an audience.

"I really am," she said.

The girls in their pitiful imitations of her stood there regarding her with envy and longing and something else she could not quite fathom that was neither and both. The boys began to creep forward shyly, awestruck, a few of them reaching out tentatively in contemplation of touching her.

"Yeah . . ."

"Chingada . . ."

"Cyborg fuckin' Sally!"

Cyborg Sally was up on stage in the bright white light at last, and before her was the vast ragged sea of her audience, the great hitherto unseen army of the fans who had created her, whom she had created to dance with in the dreamtime.

She sang it out at them, riding the rhythm section, feeling the drums pounding up and down her steel spine, the bassline moving her hips and thighs.

I'm Cyborg Sally
And I've never been
Plug into me
And I'll make you scream!

"Oh Sally, make *me* scream!"

It was the bald-headed pisser from the top floor window. He shambled forward with his cock still hanging out of his fly and his hands reaching out to squeals and laughs and guttural moans.

He threw himself at her feet, wrapped his arms around her, and started licking at her black leather panties. Cyborg Sally clamped a steel hand hard on his bald head, leaning on it with negligent ease. Blue sparks shot out of her nipples. Cold electric lightning bolts shot up her spine.

Two boys, four, half a dozen, surged forward and crawled all over her in slow motion, feeling her breasts, stroking her thighs, lovingly massaging the coiled cable curves of her ass and sighing at the perfection, a wet mouth closed on her nipple, a hand found the tight steel crack of her buttocks—

The roar of an engine! A screechy skid of brakes locking!

"Motherfuckingsonofabitch!"

The crackle-pop of automatic weapons fire.

Her fans screamed and cursed and scattered in all directions. A hand grabbed the back of her head and began poking around with a finger.

Cyborg Sally turned to wrench her head away, and Sally Genaro found herself staring right into the florid scowling face of a cop. "You stupidfuckingasshole! Flashing on a street like this in a getup like that!"

There was another burst of automatic weapons fire.

Then a second cop, a black man holding a machinepistol, was right beside him. Sally could smell thin acrid fumes coming off his warm gun.

Only then did she have sense enough to be terrified. "I could have . . ."

"You coulda had your cunt and your asshole fucked bloody and then roasted on a spit, you idiot!" screamed the white cop.

But that wasn't true, was it? They were her fans, her groupies, her worshippers. . . .

"They wouldn't have—"

"They're fucking *streeties,* girlie, they would've fucked you till you were dead and then ground you up into kibble!"

"Hey, Sam, lighten up," the black cop said in a deep soothing voice. "This girl was just almost raped!"

"No fuckingshit!" the white cop screamed. He took a deep breath. "I'm getting tired of this motherfucking Cyborg Sally shit!" he said in a marginally calmer voice. "It ain't bad enough we got all these wirehead assholes plugged into this shit and running around with their dicks in their hands, now maybe we'll have a wave of wireheads like *this* flipped out and encouraging 'em!"

"You from out of town, girl?" the black cop said, gently pushing his partner backward.

Sally nodded. Only now did the memories flash back on her

like a piece of someone else's dream. They were slobbering all over her! They were feeling her up! They were going to tear off her clothes and gang-bang her!

"Well this is the *Big Apple,* lady," the black cop said. "And if you waltz around dressed like that and flashing on being Cyborg Sally, next time you space yourself out of a Zone, you ain't gonna be so lucky."

"We oughta bust her for the fucking wire she's wearing!" the white cop said. "Ain't they made that a misdemeanor yet?"

"Hey, Sam, if you want to fuck with all that paperwork for a two-hundred-dollar fine, you fuck with it yourself!"

Sally shuddered. She began to shake. She could have been killed! They were about to pull her down and rape her and she had been enjoying it. She had had no fear. She had been dreaming her way through it. If these cops hadn't come along . . .

"I'm sorry, officer . . . I didn't know . . . I won't . . . Are you going to arrest me?"

"No, we ain't gonna arrest you," the white cop said sourly. "But we ain't gonna give you no free ride home neither. We're gonna drop you on West Broadway and then you're on your own. Do I have to tell you to stay the fuck out of the subway?"

It was a heavy night on the door. There must've been a hundred fuckin' people in their fanciest clothes crowded around Paco and jumping up and down for his attention and fifty or more streeties hanging at the back trying to catch his eye. And cabs kept pulling up with more gordos.

Paco hated nights like this. He had already passed over a hundred streeties inside, and from here on in he had room for only whites, but of course almost all of the streeties trying to get in had to be blacks and latinos. They had passed out word from inside that he was to let in only twenty people an hour now, this fuckin' Lord Jimmy was packing 'em in, and the fire marshals could be expected to turn up for a booster shot of grease any moment now.

"Yeah, okay, muchacha, you," he said, crooking his finger at a bitchin' chic in a fur vest over her silver body stocking. A redhead in a bright blue jumpsuit oozed forward. "No, not *you. Her*!"

Some putamadre waved a $200 bill in his face. He felt tits brush against him. "Okay, okay, you three over there, yeah you, one, two, three!"

"Hey, he's with us too, how about it?"
"Chingada!"

Sally Genaro got out of her cab in front of The American Dream feeling awful enough already, being still shit-faced from all the whiskey she had drunk to work up her courage, and when she saw the mob scene in front of the door, her spirits sank even further.

She had gone back to her hotel and had a room service hamburger washed down with half the bottle of Canadian Club she had ordered with it without quite knowing why.

But as it became seven, and eight, and nine, and the level of the whiskey in the bottle dropped past the bottom of the label, the booze finally told her why she was drinking it.

She had been far too terrified before she started drinking to even venture out to a nearby restaurant. She couldn't face the streets of New York again.

But now the whiskey was telling her that she had known she would have to all along. That was why she was getting plastered. She had come three thousand miles to be at The American Dream tonight and she couldn't go back to L.A. without *doing it*.

By the time she had worked up her courage, she was so loaded that the best she could do was smear on a half-assed job of Cyborg Sally makeup, put on the body stocking, step shakily into her black briefs, put on her Jack, jam her Sally wig down crookedly over it, make it to the elevator and across the lobby, and get into a cab. She didn't remember that she had forgotten to put on the undersuit until she was giving the cabby directions, and she forgot it again as soon as he started jabbering at her in Thai.

And now here she was, stuck at the back of this *huge* crush of people, Cyborg Sally on her way to perform, trapped inside poor little Sally from the Valley, outside with her would-be audience trying to get in.

She tried to ooze through the crowd, but knees and elbows and an actual kick or two drove her back. She tried using knees and elbows herself, but it only moved her a few feet.

Jumping up and down, she caught sight of the doorman as he waved some blond inside, some greasy Puerto Rican with bushy black hair, and this sexy arrogant sneer, who leered at the bitch as she slid past him.

So that was how it was done.

She reached up and hit her touchpoint. Her laser lips would bring this little spick to his knees.

"Hey, watch it!"

"Fucking hell!"

"Who the fuck you think you are!"

Paco saw that some kind of shit was going on at the back of the crowd in front of the door. Some asshole was pushing through toward him in a way that was really pissing people off.

Then she managed to shove herself past the people in the front rank, prancing and grinding her chocha like a porno star, actually shoving people out of the way with her hands, and then grinning at him, shaking her tits, and rolling her pelvis like some fuckin' stripper with her hands on her hips, as if he were supposed to come in his fuckin' pants just from looking at her.

But chingada, what he was looking at was some dumpy little puerca with her blubber bulging in a silver Cyborg Sally body stocking. She had the silver Cyborg Sally makeup smeared all over about half of her fat little face, more tooth paint on her lips than her teeth, and the fuckin' wig on backward.

"I'm Cyborg Sally, flesh and wire, the blazing bytes of your meat's desire," she sang at him in a thin nasal voice.

"Hey, you're a fuckin' pain in my culo, get lost, chocha!" he shouted at her.

"I'm loaded for bear, and I'm coming tonight!"

"Not with *my* dick, you ain't, dogmeat!" Paco said to the laughter of the crowd.

"Lick my flashing circuitry!"

"Hey, suck my fucking prick, chocharica, and get the fuck out of here!"

She stared at him with eyes that . . . with eyes that . . . Chingada, where had he seen those eyes before? Why did they. . . ? Why did they . . . ?

"I'm Cyborg Sally! Flesh and wire! Queen of Heat! Electric fire!"

"Y yo soy gigante, cojones de elefante!" Paco shot back. "And I'm also the fuckin' doorman here, and you're not getting in!"

She pressed forward. He had to shove her back. Chingada, what a night! He glared at her angrily as the hands of the crowd started sucking her back out of his face. "And nobody gets in if

I have to take any more of this shit!'' he told the lot of them. ''This ain't a fuckin' zoo, this is The American Dream!''

Battered, reeling, Cyborg Sally found herself yanked, pummeled, and dragged backward by a forest of hands. Panting, bruised, with tears in her eyes, Sally Genaro found herself staggering at the back of the crowd of supplicants at the door of The American Dream.

Jumping up and down, she saw, in jagged cuts, the slimy spick doorman waving another blond inside.

''Screw you!'' she screamed impotently at him over the heads of the crowd. ''Next time I see you, I'll have you begging to kiss my stainless steel ass!''

Even though the traffic was crawling on the Long Island Expressway and the plane had been stacked up over JFK for over an hour, and he was zoned and pretty wasted from five hours' worth of free booze, this should have been a golden moment for Bobby Rubin.

He hadn't been back in New York for over two years, that had been for a rather deadly obligatory family Thanksgiving on Long Island, he had never exactly been Mr. Manhattan as a teenager, and before the Factory signed him up and whisked him away to Los Angeles he had certainly never imagined himself sailing into Manhattan in a big black limo after a first class flight from the Coast with a wallet full of credit cards, and a Muzik, Inc., expense account.

Yet here he was, returning as a Prince of Hollywood behind black limousine glass, with the brilliant nighttime skyline of Manhattan rearing up dramatically across the East River like something straight out of a movie, and a suite reserved at the Union Square Pavilion, and all of it being paid for by the Factory. It should have been his hour of triumph. He should have been on top of the world.

Instead, he was bummed to the max and in deep, deep shit.

Nicholas West hadn't even screamed at him. The son of a bitch hadn't even raised his voice. But his normally ruddy complexion had been flaming scarlet and the words emerged from his tight lips in a thick clipped voice that somehow made the corporate ire of the current Factory president more terrifying than any full-scale desk-pounding dingo act could have.

''I'm not even going to ask you how you could have done

such an imbecilic thing, Rubin," West said by way of greeting when Bobby arrived at his office. "It is a matter of no interest."

"Mr. West . . . ?" Bobby stammered innocently as he stood before the presidential desk. Something told him that it would not be a good idea to take a seat without an invitation.

"I am referring to the revolting spectacle you and Ms. Genaro staged for the benefit of numerous witnesses in the Glitter Dome two days ago. . . ."

Bobby flushed. "I don't see where that's any of the company's— "

"—business?" West finished for him. "Perhaps you have noticed that selling discs is a major part of the company's business, Rubin? Perhaps it has come to your attention that Cyborg Sally is our current best-selling artist? May I assume you are aware that a second Cyborg Sally disc is in the middle of production, since you so adamantly refused to work with Ms. Genaro on it?"

"What's all this—"

"Sally Genaro has not turned up for work for two days, Rubin," West told him. "She has not been in her apartment. Her parents do not know where she is."

"What's that got to do with me?" Bobby said with a sinking feeling blossoming in his stomach.

"It is your fault, Rubin," West hissed angrily, without quite fracturing his terrifying cool. "I am holding you directly responsible. Please do not waste my time with useless denials. There were many witnesses. You taunted her while she was in a vulnerable state. Her . . . lech for you is all too common knowledge within the company, as is the contempt in which you hold her. You humiliated her in front of this Lord Jimmy, causing her to run off to New York."

"Run off . . . ? New York . . . ?" Bobby collapsed unbidden into one of the white leather sling-chairs in front of the big gunmetal desk.

"Yes, she's gone to New York," West said. "It's taken all day and all night to find even that much out. It took . . . severe remonstration with his manager in London before Lord Jimmy would even agree to be interviewed by our representatives, but he was finally . . . induced to cooperate. Once we had the gist of their conversation, we checked with the airlines and learned that she had purchased a one-way ticket to JFK on her American

Express card. So we can reasonably assume she's in New York City."

"Where . . . ?" Bobby muttered weakly.

West shrugged and favored him with a perfectly horrid smile. "You'll have to find that out yourself when you get there," he said.

"Me . . . ? Get there . . . ?"

"You leave this afternoon," West said, flipping him a travel agency packet. "The travel arrangements have all been taken care of. You will find her and persuade her to return forthwith . . . by whatever means necessary."

"How the hell am I supposed to do that?"

"That's your problem, Rubin," West told him. "Need I elucidate just how much your problem it is?"

"Maybe you'd better!" Bobby snapped sullenly. "If you think I—"

West sighed. "I really do dislike crude threats," he said. "But if you insist on cheap melodrama . . . I have already had legal create quite a convincing case against you. It's all ready to be presented to the federal prosecutor. And if it is, I guarantee that you'll be indicted as the electronic mastermind behind the Reality Liberation Front, who pirated the Red Jack algorithms to hype the bedbug programs you sold to criminal elements. Every police agency in the country is under severe pressure to arrest *someone* in this Red Jack affair, and since he is nonexistent, they'll be delighted to make do with you."

Nicholas West steepled his fingers and frowned heavily at Bobby for the first time. "Not to put too fine a line on it," he said, "but Lord Jimmy was most uncooperative until we requested the assistance of the Immigration and Naturalization Service. The relevant point is not the nature of that assistance, but the fact that it was forthcoming. Have I adequately communicated the full gravity of your situation?"

Bobby nodded glumly. "But assuming I do find her, how do you expect me to bring her back?" he said miserably. "Conk her on the head and stuff her into a gunny sack?"

"Only as a last resort," Nicholas West said blandly. He was not smiling. "I suggest you appeal to her sense of company loyalty, to her artistic integrity, to . . ."

Bobby snorted derisively.

West shrugged. "Well, if that doesn't work, research believes that your best course is to fuck her."

"WHAT!" Bobby shouted, bolting from the chair.

"Fuck her," West said in the tone of voice of someone explaining an accounting procedure. "Fuck her very well. Fuck her when you find her. Fuck her several times a day. Then stop. Promise you will resume fucking her once she returns to Los Angeles." He studied Bobby critically. "You *do* know how to fuck, don't you, Rubin?"

"If you think I'm going to—"

"I hope you do, Rubin. Because you may rest assured that Muzik, Inc., knows how to fuck *you*. In the corporate legal metaphorical sense, of course. Which we will do quite royally if you fail. We *do* understand each other now, don't we?"

Bobby hadn't said another word. He had just acknowledged his utter defeat with a nod, and gone home to pack, and now, here he was, one first class dinner, one lousy movie, and many free drinks later, crossing under the East River into Manhattan via the grimy Queens Midtown Tunnel, still wondering what the hell he was going to do.

Finding the Pimple might not be as difficult as he had first assumed. Lord Jimmy was playing The American Dream this week and Sally would seem to have come to New York because she had the hots for the English rock star, so the chances were pretty good that all he had to do was hang out long enough at the Factory's flagship club and she'd show up sooner or later.

But *then* what?

If, for the sake of loathsome argument, his mind decided that it was willing to fuck the Pimple to save his ass, and if, for the sake of argument, she was still willing, which seemed only all too likely, what would his *dick* have to say about it?

The organ in question shriveled sweatily inside his shorts as the limo cruised down Second Avenue and then turned west on Sixteenth Street, as if it were already telling him, no way, Jose.

What would happen if he actually found himself *in bed* with the flabby body of Sally from the Valley? Could he maybe get it up if he turned out the lights? Could he plug in and flash on being elsewhere? Could he . . .

He shuddered groggily as the limousine pulled up in front of the Union Square Pavilion and a tall black doorman in a grotesque Uncle Sam suit opened the car door for him.

It was a warm humid night with a slight mist in the air, and the globes of the streetlamps cast a romantic muzzy golden glow over Union Square Park. The hotels and restaurants and fancy saloons surrounding the square were alive with lights and revelers even at this late hour. Elegantly dressed men and beautiful women drifted in and out of the fancy entrances to the tall co-op towers under the watchful eyes of an abundant supply of well-armed zonies.

The Union Square Pavilion was a twenty-story tower of gleaming glass and what might have been genuine white marble embellished with gilded fretwork. The doorman bowed slightly from the waist and let his hand dangle discreetly for a tip as he ushered Bobby under the colonnaded portico and into the lobby atrium, with its bars, and huge potted trees, and fancy boutiques, all redolent of glitz and money.

Good news and bad news, he thought as he glided through check-in as Mr. Hollywood. The good news was that here he was, in the poshest hotel in one of the most glamorous Zones of the Big Apple, all set up to play Prince of the City.

The bad news was that all he was able to think about was whether or not he could argue his own cock into getting it up for *Sally Genaro*.

The suite, when he got to it, was elegant indeed, though something less than gigantic. A little living room, with a plush blue velvet couch, two matching chairs, sleek tables, and a wet bar, done up in real oak in an overbaroque style that made them look plastic. A blue and white tiled bath with a Jacuzzi in the tub. A Mediterranean-style bedroom, all blue and white, with a huge bed looking out through sliding glass doors past a small balcony on the lights of the square below.

There was a bottle of decent California champagne in a silver ice bucket sitting on the bar with a card that read "Courtesy of the Manager."

He toyed for a moment with the notion of going out and picking up some wide-eyed and appreciative creature with which to share it or even seeing if he could obtain a high-class hooker from the bell captain at the Factory's expense.

But he was zoned, hung over, and exhausted already, and the contemplation of sex brought only unbearable images that quenched any desire.

He opened the champagne, and slugged down three quick glasses.

"Fuck it," he muttered, managing to peel off his clothes before he passed out on the bed. "Time enough to deal with tomorrow tomorrow."

DREAM DANCERS

Tonight it was going to be different, Sally promised herself as she tipped the doorman and climbed into the huge creamy white Rolls-Royce. Tonight it was going to be rock star flash all the way, no matter what it cost, which in the case of this magnificent limousine was *nine-hundred dollars* for a one-way ride from the Waldorf to The American Dream.

But it was going to be worth it when Cyborg Sally pulled up to the door in a white Rolls-Royce limo with a chauffeur in full evening dress at the wheel. She'd like to see some smart-ass spick doorman try to say no to that!

Upon the morning after's bleak hung-over reflection, she realized just how *stupid* she'd been yesterday, and that, peculiarly enough, gave her hope. She just hadn't been thinking very straight, is all.

She should have *known* that a rock star who was every streetie's wet dream should *never* wander around New York on foot! Three blocks in the wrong direction in this city, and suddenly there were no armed zonies to keep them away from you. You could find yourself on like *another planet* before you knew it, just by turning the wrong corner.

As for turning up at The American Dream half-dressed and completely plastered—just *gross*! No wonder the doorman hadn't recognized her! She hadn't looked like Cyborg Sally at all. She had looked just like poor dumb little Sally from the Valley in pathetic half-assed Cyborg Sally drag!

But it's all for the best, she told herself as she luxuriated on the soft tan glove-leather seat. What if she somehow *had* gotten in last night, without her undersuit, with her wig on backward, and fried out of her mind? Lord Jimmy wouldn't have even *recognized* her, and they would never have let her up on the stage!

If nothing else, yesterday's mortifying comedy of terrors had taught her what it took to really *be* Cyborg Sally.

Just as the Cyborg Sally she became on the Jack was nothing but her own true self set free by electronic circuitries, so was the image of Cyborg Sally that the world knew nothing but the face and form of Sally Genaro perfected and glorified by wizard software.

In her wig and her tights and her sculptured undersuit, she *was* the image of Cyborg Sally, for that image was just *her* done up like this electronically in the first place, and she must *never again* let that image slip in public.

When I hit my touchpoint and step out of this limousine, she told herself as the Rolls bulldozed its lordly way through the crush of cabs clogging the approach to The American Dream, I'll really *be* Cyborg Sally, won't I? That's all she really is—me, and my VoxBox, and the Jack, and these visuals. . . .

Yet something gnawed at her as the limousine finally rounded the corner and joined the cabs lining up to drop their passengers off in front of the door. For there had been a moment out there in the ruins just before the cops arrived, with the music moving through her, with her worshippers literally groveling and slobbering all over her perfect silver flesh, when she had indeed somehow felt like something more.

More, even, than she had been that magic night with Lord Jimmy in the Glitter Dome, more, even, than her perfect fantasy made real in the mirror of his eyes.

For a moment she had been more truly herself than she had ever been, for a moment the dreamer had awakened into a *shared* dream. For a moment Cyborg Sally had known that these poor ragged streeties were somehow dreaming *her* into existence.

Maybe the cops were right. Maybe they had saved her from being gang-banged and torn to pieces.

But maybe not. Maybe if they hadn't unplugged her against her will and shattered the collective dream with machine-gun fire, the dream could have gone on and on. Maybe she would have never had to wake up into a world where she was something less than the Queen of Heat.

Could it be that *this* was the dream, this mean-spirited unjust world, where she had been born into a sloppy body with the heart of a sex machine and the singing soul of a rock star?

Maybe the sad second-rate world she thought was reality was just a long stupid nightmare of Cyborg Sally's, and maybe, just maybe, for a moment the dreamer had truly awoken.

The Rolls finally made it to the curb in front of the door. There was at least as big a mob fighting to get in as there had been last night. The same sneery-mouthed Puerto Rican was teasing and torturing them with shakes of his head and crooks of his finger.

Maybe, she thought as her chauffeur held the car door open for her and she hit her touchpoint, maybe tonight Cyborg Sally can wake up for good.

"What's all this?" Bobby Rubin demanded of the cabby. The street was bumper to bumper with cabs, all trying to squeeze by each other at once in a blare of horns and a cacophony of curses.

"The American Dream, pal," the cabby grumbled. "That's where ya said ya wanned to go."

"Not *here*," Bobby told him. "The VIP entrance around the block. Go around and come down from the other side."

"*The VIP entrance!*" the cabby said sarcastically. "Well, why the fuck didn't you tell me so, yer Lordship? I coulda kept us out of this shit to begin with!"

As Bobby clutched tightly onto the door handle, the cab went whipping and jouncing around double-parked cars on the next side street, squealed around a corner, repeated the terrifying process, and dropped him in front of an unpresupposing steel door less than two minutes later.

Unpresupposing, that is, except for the two big gorillas sweating inside black business suits and holding their Uzis at port-arms.

"Where ya think you're going?" one of them grunted as Bobby approached the door.

"Inside," Bobby said confidently.

"Pass," said the other zonie, holding out a meaty hand.

Bobby reached into his inside jacket pocket, pulled out a white card with gilded edges with his name embossed under a full-color ID photo, and held it out in front of the zonie's face.

Instantly, the ape's demeanor changed. "Step this way, please, Mr. Rubin," he said obsequiously as his partner held open the door.

Bobby grinned to himself as he stepped inside. He had slept

late, eaten a huge room service brunch, then dressed and made his way to the New York office of Muzik, Inc., where West's office in Hollywood had already sent down the word. The VIP pass and a letter to the manager over West's signature ordering full and complete cooperation were already waiting for him.

Who knows, with any luck the Pimple might not show up tonight, might not show up for days, might not show up at all. He was glad he had decided to wear his Jack. Maybe, with his VIP pass and a little help from an old friend who had stood him in good stead in L.A., he might pick himself up an actress or a rock star, or at least a super groupie, and whisk her back to his palatial suite at the Union Square Pavilion to show her his rock and roll machine.

While this ride lasts, I might as well enjoy it, he told himself as the guard slammed the door shut behind him with a heavy metallic thud.

''Chingada, who the fuck is that?'' Paco muttered. What was a great big white Rolls-Royce that had to belong to a movie star or the fuckin' King of England doing pulling up *here*?

The heavies, the movie stars and the rock stars, the kings and queens of Chocharica City, MUZIK's tv people, the fuckin' mafs and yaks, always went around back to the VIP entrance, where they had zonies, where they could go directly upstairs without having to rub shoulders with what he let into the pit.

Something told Paco that this meant trouble. Something told him he might be about to get in over his head. Something told him that he was about to have to make a big decision fast.

He had never had to deal with no *celebrity* before; they just didn't use the front door. Steiner hadn't even laid down any *policies*. Did he keep out a famous star if he saw he was really fucked up? Were there stars who were in the shit with Muzik and might be trying to sneak in with the crowd? How the fuck was he supposed to know who they were? What if a bigshot turned up *wearing the Red*?

Why does this plushie-tushie putamadre have to hassle *me*?

And then the driver got out and opened the back door, and an electric shock went through him as he saw who or what got out.

Chingada, it was *Cyborg Sally*!

From this distance, it looked exactly like who he had seen so often on the screen. The wiry-muscled silver body with the perfect lightning-tipped tits, the black leather pants with some kind of hole for a chocha that seemed to peer through into a dark someplace else. The hair of flashing, glowing, neon snakes.

And she moved just like Cyborg Sally, snake-dancing through the crowd with a strutting roll of her hips that parted them with oohs and mutters, coming right at him, with her back arched, and her electric nipples flashing, and her pelvis offered up in front of her, just as she had in Slimy Mary's!

Paco blinked as the memory of that moment reminded him that he had ended up dry-humping a robot in the next, that that's what Cyborg Sally was, just an electronic robot in a wirehead flash, that there *was* no real Cyborg Sally, so this couldn't be her, driving right up to his face in a Rolls-Royce!

This must just be some crazy rich bitch dressed up like Cyborg Sally, flashing out of her mind and playing some dumb chocharica game!

Paco stepped more squarely in front of the door, folded his arms across his chest, and prepared a hard-eyed sneer. No way I gotta put up with *that* kind of shit! he decided. Dinero don't get no crazy chocharica thinks she's the Queen of Heat past *me*!

But a few moments later, when she had sailed to the front of the crowd like a hot blade through manteca, and he could see her face clearly, he forgot in a flash everything he had been thinking.

It was Cyborg Sally's face.

The eyes. The curve of the nose. The line of the full lips.

It was her! It was Cyborg Sally! But it couldn't be—

He started reaching up for his touchpoint to bring himself out of the flash, but then he remembered that *he wasn't plugged in*. There was Cyborg Sally staring right into his eyes, her steel hands on her silvery hips, her back arched, rolling her chocha slightly and wagging her tits to music he couldn't hear, just as she appeared in a flash. But *he wasn't flashing*! This was real! She . . . but . . .

"Well?" Cyborg Sally said haughtily. "Do I get in?"

"You're—"

"Flesh and wire," she said, flashing him a steel dagger grin.

"Hey, look, I—"

She reached out a hand and ran the back of a fingernail up the zipper of his fly. His cock reared like a charmed snake behind it.

"Any mother's child turn you on so wild?"

The murmuring babbling crowd was crushing closer. The streeties standing at the back were screaming "Cyborg Sally!" at passersby and things were beginning to deteriorate into a mob scene. Better cool it now and worry about figuring it out later!

"Okay, okay, inside!" he said, stepping aside, grabbing her by the hand, and sliding her past him. She didn't even look at him again as she slithered on by, just brushed his hip in passing with a flick of her tight hard silver ass, and strutted on through the doorway, disappearing like a wire flash into the darkness of the corridor.

"Hey, was that really Cyborg Sally?" some putamadre called out to him from the back of the crowd.

"For sure, man, she's my girlfriend, asshole!" Paco shouted back. "She just got back from havin' my car washed!"

The crowd laughed. Paco laughed with them. But it was nervous laughter. Who or what had he just let inside? Were Larry and Karen and all the rest of them wrong after all? Had that really been Cyborg Sally?

Chingada, had he just screwed up a chance to make time with the real thing?

There were a series of unmarked doors and a freight elevator door just inside the VIP entrance, and as Bobby Rubin stood there, the elevator itself came down, a big open-meshed wire cage that disgorged three stunning couples, two of the men looking very familiar, before admitting him.

He found himself alone in the big elevator with a beautiful redhead in a kind of tuxedo swimming suit, who was operating it, and yet another black-suited zonie with a machinepistol. It ascended past the rear of the saloon, a tv studio corridor where two guys were wheeling a camera, and a service pantry, before it came to a stop, and the operator opened the telescoping cage doors, and he stepped out into the VIP lounge.

This was more like what he would have imagined the living room of the biggest and fanciest loft in Soho to be like than any clubroom he had ever seen.

Scores of regularly spaced ceiling globes cast an even golden twilight glow. The forest-green carpeted floor rose and fell in many levels separated by low half-steps, forming a series of subtly self-contained areas.

There was a sunken leather-upholstered conversation pit around a big round brass table. There were areas where a few small cafe tables were clustered together, where blue and chromed art deco couches faced each other, where huge fan-backed peacock chairs of rainbow-painted rattan were arranged in semi-circles. There was a big brick fireplace at one end with a hologram of a log fire, and three couches ringing it in. There was a teakwood bar along one wall with no more than twenty matching stools and a black bartender in a tuxedo behind it.

The far wall was one big continuous picture window with a row of more cafe tables along it. From Bobby's perspective at the entrance, all that was visible through it was a slice of a huge video screen, about a quarter of some immense and incomprehensible moving image.

He saw that here and there there were small slave monitors—above the bar, in the corners—all very low-key and discreet. Nor were they piping in the music at a level that competed with conversation.

Okay, now what? he wondered, feeling like a fool already as he stood there and gawked.

The VIP lounge was thronged with, well, VIPs. He could tell that he had ascended to star country by the casually stunning beauty of the women and the dauntingly flamboyant elegance of the men, by the way people dressed like stars in a film of some fancy Hollywood party, by the amount of elbow room and body space they gave each other, by some indefinable aroma of gold jewelry and designer dust and black limousine glass.

There was nobody standing around like he was ogling all the incredible pussy. There was no one else to be seen with his eyes darting around nervously from focus to focus not knowing where to comfortably alight. Everybody here looked as if they knew everybody else, just as they had at that party on Mulholland that he had so fruitlessly and foolishly cozened Glorianna O'Toole into taking him to.

And maybe they did. For they were essentially the same people and this was essentially the same party. It had rooms in Beverly Hills and New York and London that these people flitted between in the first class sections of airplanes. This floating party was called *show business* and of course all the movers and shapers knew each other.

And of course, while he recognized many a familiar face, no one here knew him. Even having ascended to the loftiest level, he still found himself on the outside looking in.

But he couldn't stand here forever like an idiot! The bar seemed the most neutral corner. There were only half a dozen people seated at it. One of them was a woman in a low-cut black dress tight around her incredible ass, with long wild wavy carrot-red hair flowing down her bare back, who was enough to have him creaming in his jeans before he even saw her face.

There were two empty seats to the left of her, and what Bobby wanted to do was take the one right beside her and say something incredibly urbane. Instead, he put one empty stool between them, ordered a Wild Turkey, and tried not to be caught staring at her out of the corner of his eye.

But when he snuck a look, he blew all sense of cool.

The elfin freckled face. The big pouting lips. The cute little nose. Those incredible huge green eyes. The braless little breasts half popping out of her dress. The tiny tattooed rose on her left nostril.

It was *Mara Murphy*, no doubt about it! A real movie star was sitting right there all by herself next to him drinking vodka out of a tall frosted champagne glass and daintily sniffing dust off a long emerald-green fingernail that she kept dipping into an antique cameo snuffbox.

His cock bulged in his pants. His mouth went dry. His stomach went all queasy and hollow. Mara Murphy, getting loaded right in front of me! What can I say to her? How can I—

"Do I know you, sonny?"

Oh no! She had caught him staring at her! And now *she* was staring at *him*, her nose curled, her lips not smiling, those big green eyes making him feel he had forgotten to put his pants on.

"Uh . . . ah . . . I don't think so."

"Then why are you staring at me?"

"Uh . . . I wasn't staring at you."

"Oh yes you were," Mara Murphy said coldly. "You think I haven't been stared at enough to know when someone's feeling up my merchandise with his eyes?"

"Uh . . . uh . . . uh, bartender!" he stammered loudly, forced to look away from her piercing gaze.

"Another?" said the handsome black bartender.

"You ask me, he's had enough!" Mara Murphy said in a somewhat woozy voice.

"This fellow proving to be an annoyance to you, Miss Murphy?" the bartender asked in a silkily ominous tone.

"Summon the manager, my good man," Bobby said with as much lofty arrogance as he could muster before she could open her lethally luscious mouth again.

"What?" said the bartender, turning to regard him with an outrage lagging behind his sheer disbelief.

"I said, please summon the manager, will you?" Bobby said evenly. "Tell him I wish to speak to him at once."

"*Summon the manager?*" the bartender mimicked. "*Tell him I wish to speak to him at once?* I'm terribly sorry, your majesty, but the manager is occupied right now setting up for tonight's broadcast, but if you'll just wait right here, I'll be happy to summon some gentlemen from security who will throw you out on your ass."

Bobby had already reached into his inside jacket pocket and extracted Nicholas West's letter. He opened it out and negligently flipped it on the bar in front of the bartender.

"Oh, and do give him this," he said airily. "May I assume you know how to read?"

The bartender snatched up the letter with an angry gesture. When he scanned it, his whole demeanor changed. He smiled weakly. He folded the letter carefully. He pressed a button behind the bar.

"I hope there's nothing the matter, Mr. Rubin," he said obsequiously. He plunked a fresh glass down in front of Bobby and poured it full to the brim from a bottle of Wild Turkey. "I apologize for any misunderstanding, I'm having some problems with my girlfriend, and I'm afraid I'm a little tense tonight, you understand; here, do please have this one on me."

Bobby smiled at him patronizingly. "No problem," he said. "Just tell him Nick West asked me to look him up for a little chat while I'm in town from the Coast."

A man in a black suit appeared from an access door behind the other end of the bar and came up alongside the bartender, looking Bobby up and down speculatively.

The bartender handed him the letter. "Take this to Mr. Pham at once, Rollo."

"Hey, you know that Pham is tied up with—"

"*At once!*" the bartender hissed. "Tell him that a friend of Mr. Nicholas West is waiting at the bar to speak with him!"

He turned back to Bobby. "Will that be all, Mr. Rubin?" he said smoothly.

Bobby nodded and the bartender moved discreetly down the bar. He turned, and saw that Mara Murphy had sidled over onto the stool beside him. She had an elbow on the bar, her head cocked over resting on her palm, and she was leaning close and studying him quite differently.

"You *sure* I don't know you . . . ?" she said. "Those eyes . . . I never forget the eyes. Haven't I seen your eyes before?"

She was close enough to him now for him to reel drunkenly in her sweet clover perfume. He could see her soft freckled breasts panting and swaying and hanging free under the taut edge of her bodice.

He reached up as if to scratch his head in thought and let his finger hit the touchpoint of his Jack.

He smiled a brilliant Red Jack smile. He tossed his long red hair. He leaned forward into her body space.

"Could be," he said, "though lately I've been nowhere to be seen."

"Hey, aren't you . . . those eyes . . . that face . . . Naw, the hair's all wrong, I'm just stoned, you can't be . . ."

"Couldn't I be wearing a wig . . . ?"

Mara Murphy eyed him narrowly. "But like the song says, you're just bits and bytes and programs, so how can you be sitting here beside me—"

"Just where I've always been?"

She laughed, her smile made all the more brilliant by those huge green eyes, by the fact that she was laughing *with* him. He leaned even closer into the sweet clover aura of her perfume, an enormous surge of confidence and well-being coursing up his spine from his loins to explode in bright pixels of power in his flashing brain.

"Ain't got no body, ain't got no soul, but I'm your Prince of Rock and Roll," he said, courageously venturing to lay a light hand on her arm.

"And I suppose you wanna be beside me in the middle of the night . . . ?" Mara Murphy drawled sarcastically. But she didn't pull away and she didn't take those gleaming eyes off him either.

"Mr. Rubin? I'm Alan Pham."

He turned at the crisp, authoritative, perfect announcer's voice behind him. A wiry Vietnamese in a trimly tailored lime-green suit was standing beside his stool offering his hand. He had long curled black hair and lightly tinted wraparound glasses behind which his eyes were cold and black.

Mechanically, he shook Pham's hand. "Yes . . . ?" he said vaguely.

Pham frowned. "*You* asked to talk to me, remember?" he

snapped. He glanced at Mara Murphy. He forced a false smile. "Oh," he said, "I see. . . ."

Pham placed a firm hand on Bobby's shoulder. "Lord Jimmy is about to go on and I'm a very busy man right now, but I *did* have the courtesy to see you," he said irritably. "So if you'll excuse us for a moment, Mara, this business won't take any longer than Mr. Rubin thinks it has to."

"Take all the time you want, Alan," she told him. "I'm just passing the time till Ted gets it together to get his ass over here."

And Pham shooed him, gazing backward longingly over his shoulder, toward an empty cafe table by the wall of window overlooking the dance floor. "Bye . . ." Mara Murphy said with a negligent little wave, and then turned back to her vodka and dust.

Cyborg Sally spiraled lazily around the crowded dance floor, craning her neck upward to gaze in self-satisfied awe at the three immense video screens, at the wall of balconies ascending to the shadowy unseen ceiling high above, at the sheer scale of the place, which no tv coverage could ever hope to adequately convey. It was like the atrium lobby of the Bonaventure or some big Hyatt: so cavernous you didn't really believe you could be indoors, a whole little world, self-contained and complete.

Her world.

Right now, it was Debbie Nakamoto tripled and magnified to mythic proportions up there on the screens, but she knew that soon enough it would be *her* up there containing The American Dream within the walls of her triplexed electronic image.

And tonight she would make show business history. Tonight the electronic legend would reveal itself in her flesh. Tonight the goddess on the screens would be mirrored live onstage.

There were roadies up on the stage now running final checks on the amps and instruments. The stage itself was a circular platform sitting on top of a ten-foot-high glassy black pedestal, like a giant flat toadstool growing out of the center of the dance floor. How were you supposed to get up there . . . ?

Then two of the roadies suddenly began sinking out of sight as if they were walking down into the substance of the stage. Of course! There must be a stairway down to a green room beneath the floor. She had better get down there and find Lord Jimmy. More roadies were leaving the stage.

She whirled around looking for some access, but all she could see were stairways leading up to the open saloon of the first balcony. She had better go up there and find someone who could direct her to the green room.

She began dancing her way across the floor through the crowd, barely noticing all the long-lingering looks she was getting from the men she snaked her way past, the envious sneers from all the women in their fancy Sally outfits. She hardly paused for more than a moment to bask in the hot white circle of limelight from on high that snapped her into stage center for a brief turn and then moved on.

Then the music stopped and a sudden rustling hush descended like a great curtain. She turned, and saw that the stage was now bathed in interlocking pools of red and yellow light from above, into which Lord Jimmy's back-up band was emerging one by one from beneath the stage—a VoxBox player, a lead guitarist, and a horn player, all of them slim men with long black hair, bare-chested in tight black pants, calf-length kidskin boots, and long, elaborately embroidered and brocaded sequined frock coats.

The people on the floor shuffled expectantly in place, watching the stage. A hard white cone of light lanced out from the second balcony behind her, flashing the tableau of musicians readying their instruments into brilliant bold relief, and the three great screens, which had been running some disc promo silently, became realtime mirrors of the scene on the stage.

"Hey, take the door for a while, will you, just don't let anyone in till I get back," Paco called out to the security zonie who finally appeared behind him on his rounds of the entrance corridor.

"What am I, your flunky?"

"Come on, man, do me a favor, will you, I gotta . . . I gotta take a shit!"

The gordo zonie laughed.

"Hey man, it's not fuckin' funny," Paco said off the top of his head. "I had me a fuckin' greaseburger on the way over here musta been made out of rats and I'm gonna shit in my pants if I don't get to the crapper."

"Go ahead. I'm waiting. This I gotta see!"

"Chingada, man, don't be such a prick! Tell you what, you can let in one lady while I'm gone, make sure it's a tasty one who knows how to be grateful, comprende amigo. . . ."

The zonie scanned the crowd with a slowly growing leer. "You talked me into it," he said.

"Be back in five . . . I hope. . . ."

"Take your time!"

Paco ducked inside and hit his touchpoint as soon as he was out of sight in the corridor leading to the pit. He didn't have to take a shit at all, what he had to do was find . . . Cyborg Sally or whoever the fuck it was, and flash on her.

Standing out there on the door and wondering whether there really *was* a Cyborg Sally, whether she really had had her hand for a brief moment on his fly, whether he had let the woman or creature or dream he had so recently most wanted to fuck in all the world slither on right by him, gave him more ants in his pants than any ratburger dose of the trots could have.

But now Mucho Muchacho was strutting out confidently onto the dance floor, his hard dark eyes searching for the silver chocharica he had fought his guerra chingada with in the dreamtime, his balls remembered when, and if she was really here, Cyborg Sally también.

Chingada, there were plenty of tasty Cyborg Sallys inside The American Dream tonight, but they were all just fuckin' phonies no matter how perfect their gear was, standing around staring at the empty stage, where a bunch of maricón musicians in fruity sequined jackets were sitting down to their instruments in a cone of bright white light.

None of them had those eyes, that nose, that twist of mouth, and none of them had the look or the moves as they gaped like the fuckin' fancy groupies they were, creamin' in their fuckin' hundred-dollar silver tights at the faggots tuning up on the stage.

Alan Pham squinted at the ID photograph of Sally Genaro. "May I keep this?" he said. "I'll have copies run off and handed out to every man on the security force."

Bobby Rubin nodded his assent absently. He was having a certain difficulty attending to this mundane business, for he was still flashing, and finding Sally from the Valley was merely an annoying background hum to the music surging through him as he sat at the cafe table gazing out at the brightly lit stage far below, at the audience packed shoulder to shoulder on its feet waiting for the impending moment of magic.

I'm the me they always told me
That I could never be....

Oh yes, the me that he had seen in Mara Murphy's eyes, the Red Jack that was tapping his feet to his own music, wanted to tap this corporate pinhead down the willy hole, and go out there and crown himself the Prince of Rock and Roll.

"Probably won't do any good . . ." he muttered.

"What?"

He forced himself to turn to the manager of The American Dream. Pham was staring at him in perplexed annoyance.

"She'll probably be all done up as Cyborg Sally. . . ."

"There are a hundred women done up as Cyborg Sally passing through here every night," Pham snapped. "How is security to tell which one is Sally Genaro?"

"Look for Cyborg Sally, the same one as on the disc."

"Are you feeling all right, Mr. Rubin? You're not making much sense."

A sudden fanfare of guitar feedback and drum roll and bright clear horn split the hushed air of the VIP lounge, attention-getting even through the subdued level of its speaker system, and directing that attention outward and downward to the stage, where all the lights had been killed except for a bright golden spot.

Into which emerged Lord Jimmy, resplendent in golden hose, silver-buckled shoes, skin-tight royal blue breeches, and an ermine-fringed matching silk cloak flung over his bare shoulders. His blond afro glowed like a crown in the limelight. He carried a microphone in the form of a yard-long golden scepter with a jewel in the hilt the size of a goose egg that flashed rainbow kaleidoscope fragments from a light source within.

"Your Majesties, Princes and Princesses, Dukes and Duchesses, Lords and Ladies, and all you rockin' proletarian masses out there," an oily phony upperclass English accent intoned from somewhere. "MUZIK is royally overwhelmed to present Lord Jimmy, the Earl of Pearl, and the Crown Prince of Soul, the heir to the throne of Rock and Roll!"

Lord Jimmy paraded around the stage, waving his scepter at the groundlings with his magnificent aristocratic nose sniffing the stratosphere as if it were a line of the finest connoisseur dust.

The band played a max metal version of "God Save the King."

Despite all appearances
I am but a man
Hold yourselves together, girls
Try to understand . . .

Up on the stage, Lord Jimmy pranced and preened and whirled his cloak as he belted out "At Your Command" in a clear, ringing, infectiously self-amused voice, the bouncy, sassy beat and the sarcastic wavering horn playing nicely against his egomania.

He had the audience right where he wanted them, swaying and tapping their feet, rocking and rolling absently in place, but without taking their eyes off him, without turning his performance into background music for a disco dance.

Even Cyborg Sally found herself moving to it as she snake-danced her way toward the stage, rolling her hips and counter-swaying her arms to the beat, tossing her blackly luminescent flashing hair, as she parted the human sea on a bow wave of rocking energy.

Although I walk on water, girls
And really am quite grand
I can be the slave of love
At . . . your . . . command!

Lord Jimmy strutted in mock-stately circles around the stage, fairly glowing in a hot golden spotlight, dancing up to the lip of the stage during the instrumental break, teasing the front row with one hand on his hip and the other holding out his scepter like a great jeweled phallus, haughtily pointing it at this woman and that.

As Cyborg Sally danced toward him, it seemed that she was up there on the stage with him already, moving beside him in that bright circle of light up there on a pedestal high above the crowd.

And indeed she saw that she *was* dancing in the limelight high above the crowd, for up there on the huge video screens, she saw herself, a twirling silver figure tracked by a hard white beam from far on high as she danced through the darkness to the front of the crowd.

I'm Cyborg Sally
I'm your blood-hot wire
I'm the blazing bytes
Of your meat's desire!

She sang it out at the top of her lungs, only to have it blown away by the amplification of the band. But Lord Jimmy must have heard it, for he pointed his jeweled scepter right at her as she danced and sang her heart out, living her moment in the spotlight at last.

Gazing out the window from inside the flash, Red Jack was also the blue and golden little figure down there on the stage waving his magic wand and watching all those women rub their thighs together and moan, sneaking a peak at his glorified self towering up there on the screen, feeling his flesh gloriously explode into a cloud of burning pixels as he threw himself back into the song.

Mercy on me, birdies
Me bush is in your hand
Unconsumed but burning
At . . . your . . . command!

"Chingada . . ." Mucho Muchacho moaned, "es verdad!"

For there, dancing in the circle of light cast by a beam descending from the ceiling into the crowd not twenty yards away, and mirrored on the video screens too, was the very prey he had been tracking—Cyborg Sally herself.

Verdad, they were *both* her! Up there on the screens where he had seen her a thousand times, but dancing down here, too, for now the screens showed a close-up of the figure on the floor and it was *her* face—the eyes, the nose, the lips—the face that had challenged his machismo in the dreamtime, but the face of the Cyborg Sally who had touched his cock as he passed her through the door too!

Brushing away pissed-off gordos with arrogant sweeps of his arms, Mucho Muchacho strode across the pit of The American Dream, following the pillar of fire toward his destined nexus with Cyborg Sally.

* * *

''Who dropped that damned clip in there?'' Allan Pham snapped angrily as the face of Cyborg Sally flashed onto the triplexed video screens.

''It's her! What's the fastest way to the floor?''

He was up out of his chair as soon as he saw the camera zoom in for the close-up picking Sally's spotlighted face out of the crowd.

''What are you talking about? Some fool just got himself fired by hitting a replay button by mistake.''

''It's *her,* goddammit, I told you, the same one as on the disc, it's Sally!''

''Of course it's—''

''It's Sally Genaro, you asshole, quick, the fastest way to the floor!''

Alan Pham blanched. ''Take the elevator down to the second floor, through the service area, out the bar, down the stairs . . .'' he stammered. ''I'm sorry, Mr. Rubin, I could have sworn that—''

''She's flesh *and* wire, haven't you ever heard the song?'' Red Jack told him as he ran across the lounge. ''And I ain't Mr. Clean!''

Cyborg Sally belted out her duet with Lord Jimmy in the blazing circle of white light, feeling the pulsing heat of the audience coming up at her in wave after wave of—

—abruptly, her world went dark.

Ten feet away, a spotlight beam picked out a tall black girl in a silver suit and Sally wig moving her body in lubriciously sinuous spirals. Lord Jimmy had danced to the other side of the stage and was waving his blue silk cape over his head like a stripper as the band went into its instrumental finale.

''Wait! Wait!''

''Haven't you made a big enough ass of yourself already?'' shouted the voice of a man grabbing onto her arm.

She whirled in a fury and found herself nose to nose with Red Jack.

Bobby Rubin's disdainful dark eyes glowered at her from beneath his long red hair, images of L.A.—the Hollywood sign, Westwood street scenes, the Factory, the Glitter Dome, the Valley—rippling mockingly across his clothing.

''Lick my flashing circuitries, you has-been!'' Cyborg Sally snarled, pulling away from him. "You're just a wormy little wimp under the bits and bytes!"

Angry white webworks of lightning crackled in Bobby Rubin's black hair. "I'm the ghost in your machine, Cyborg Sally!" he said mercilessly, grabbing hold of her arm again. "You're trapped inside *my* circuits, remember? You're just bits and bytes and programs and I'm hitting the reset button now."

Sally Genaro's eyes gazed longingly at Red Jack even as Cyborg Sally's dagger teeth snarled their saurian defiance. Sally Genaro put her free hand on her hips and arched her back like an aroused cat. Cyborg Sally brushed the sparking nipples of Sally Genaro's flabby tits across his chest. He could feel the alternating currents of clashing energy spitting and hissing between them.

"Hey, momacita, this putamadre giving you a hard time?"

A magnificent bronzed warrior had appeared from nowhere to stand beside Cyborg Sally, poised on the balls of his bare feet in a karate stance, his muscles hard and wiry under his sleekly oiled skin, his deep brown eyes gleaming menacingly as they lased at Red Jack, accented by a nose as merciless and chiseled as an obsidian ax.

"Bet you I can show you a harder time than he can!" Mucho Muchacho said, glaring defiantly at the black-haired little maricón who dared to put his fuckin' paw on *his* silver chocharica queen.

"Mind your own goddam business!" he snapped back, and for a moment Mucho Muchacho found himself confronting a tall lithe figure in a mirror-suit with long red flashing hair. Chingada, no it can't be—

"Plug into me, and I'll make you scream," Cyborg Sally told him, crooking her free steel arm into his muscular bicep. "But you'll have to get me away from this asshole first!"

Mucho Muchacho smiled at Cyborg Sally possessively. "You heard her, she's with Mucho Muchacho now, the lady's coming with me!" he said, turning his gaze back on . . . back on . . . back on some skinny black-haired putamadre with Red Jack's face.

He blinked, saw Red Jack standing there before him, blinked again, saw a wimpy little black-haired maricón presuming to give Mucho Muchacho shit. But the face . . . the face never changed. . . . Chingada . . .

"I don't give a fuck *who* you are!" Mucho finally told him. "She's Mucho Muchacho's! She's coming with me!"

"The fuck she is! Piss off before I—"

"*You* piss off, motherfucker, before I kick your ass!" Cyborg Sally's champion snarled contemptuously at Bobby Rubin, pushing him away with the palm of his hand and breaking his grip on her arm.

Red Jack staggered backward, then reached for her again.

"He's trying to kidnap me!" Cyborg Sally screamed, rubbing up against her rescuer's leg like a stainless steel cat to egg him on, and grinning at Bobby Rubin in vengeful triumph. "He's a sex maniac who wants me all to himself!"

Red Jack snarled his disdain. Bobby Rubin snarled his disgust.

"Come on, momacita, and I'll pull down all your panties," said her Mucho Muchacho, and he turned his back contemptuously, and began leading her off.

"Come back here!" Bobby Rubin's voice shrieked behind her.

"Y TU MADRE TAMBIÉN!" shouted Mucho Muchacho, whirling on his heel, and catching Red Jack square in the breadbasket with a stiff-armed punch.

Bobby Rubin groaned, folded, clutched his stomach, then fell forward onto his hands and knees.

Mucho Muchacho swaggered and shoved his way through the swirling, yammering mob, out of the pit and down the entrance corridor, with Cyborg Sally, la vera Cyborg Sally, clinging to his bare waist, her cool metallic arm sending shivers of electricity straight to his throbbing cock.

"Get me out of here!" she told him. "Take me somewhere where they can't find me!"

"That's just what I was planning on doing, momacita!" he assured her. "Hey, don't worry, you're with Mucho Muchacho now!"

He brushed by the zonie he had left on the door.

"Hey, wait, where do you think you're going?"

"Some yaks or mafs or somethin' are trying to kidnap Cyborg Sally!" he snapped. "I'm gonna get her outa here, you don't let anyone in or out!" And he dragged his prize through the crowd around the entrance before the zonie could get out another word.

Buena suerte! A fat man was just getting out of a cab when they reached the curb. He shoved Cyborg Sally into it, crawled in behind her, and slammed the door. "Slimy Mary's, D and Third," he said without thinking, and the taxi took off just as Steiner and Alan Pham himself emerged, shouting and waving, from The American Dream.

Chingada, muchacho, you are gonna be in some deep shit, a voice from somewhere reminded him. But he paid it no mind. That was someone else talking from another time and place, as Mucho Muchacho and Cyborg Sally sailed through the nightstreets of Chocharica City in her big white limousine.

CASTLES IN THE AIR

Sally Genaro popped out of the flash into perfect terror, sealed in a cab with a crazy Puerto Rican street fighter who had so recently proven just how violent he could get, and he was taking her God knows where, and now the cab turned left off the reasonably well-lit main avenue, and onto a dark narrow side street past rows of ominous abandoned tenements, all too reminiscent of another side-street reality from which she had had to be rescued by cops with machine guns.

Or had she?

For sure, *Sally Genaro* would have been gang-banged and torn to pieces! She had known it, and she had called on Cyborg Sally to save her. And she was *doing it* when the cops arrived, wasn't she? *Cyborg Sally* had felt no fear, only the first full glorious blossoming of her stardom's power. Had the cops really rescued her from rape and death, or had they just stolen her away from her first live audience?

No way to be sure about *that* now, maybe, but Cyborg Sally had certainly been in control of this Mucho Muchacho well enough to make him save Sally Genaro from Bobby Rubin!

"Let *me* . . ." the electronic voice of herself seemed to whisper inside of her. "My laser lips bring him to his knees. . . ."

Shuddering at his touch, knowing she was irrevocably committed to she knew not what, she listened to it, and hit her touchpoint.

Cyborg Sally, in control, snaked an arm around his shoulders and touched a hand to his bulging fly, knowing she had Mr. Mucho Muchacho firmly by the handle in more ways than one.

"Hey, who was that maricón anyway?" he said, trying to

show her how cool he could be even with his cock throbbing in her hand. "Chingada, you know, for a moment there I almost thought he was Red—"

"He's *nobody*!" Cyborg Sally snapped. "Just some nerdy little has-been wimp the Factory sent to drag me back to L.A.!"

"The Factory? L.A.?"

"The Muzik Factory, Muzik, Inc. They want me locked back in the circuitry working to make them more money," she said. She nibbled his ear with her pointed teeth. "But you won't let them take me away from you, now will you?" she purred. "I want to stay out here with you and play!"

He flashed her a mouth full of perfect white teeth and pressed her hand deeper into the quick of him. "Hey, no problem, momacita, you can play with me as long as you want to!"

She flashed him a grin full of daggers and gave him a mockingly sweet little pat on the head.

"I know," she said.

It was dark and musty up here on the second floor above Slimy Mary's and he could feel phantom cucarachas scurrying across his bare skin and hear the rats rustling in the long-empty apartments as they felt their way down the hall past them. The ceiling creaked and groaned with the slower and heavier sounds of burnt-out wirehead zombies moving around on the floor above, and from time to time a gritty little cloud of plaster flaked off and chalked the air with dust.

Paco had come out of the flash as the cab pulled up in front of Slimy Mary's, and a good thing too, for Dojo did not feature dealing with anyone who was flashing, and it had taken some fancy bullshitting to get him to give him a room upstairs.

"Okay, okay, so take the honeymoon suite, my man," Dojo had told him dryly when he finally handed over a key, "it's the best in the house. But I'm afraid room service is gonna be a little slow tonight."

Paco's cojones shriveled in his scrotum up here in Florida. Dojo had told him that none of the zombies were stored below the third floor, but he seemed to see gaunt skeletal figures hunkered in raggy garbage piles behind every hinge-sprung door, slowly rotting away into People Kibble for rats.

Only one apartment, way down at the other end of the hallway, still had a door with a working lock. He fumbled the key into it, turned it, opened the door, felt for the light switch that Dojo had told him was still working, found it.

Now, only now, did he pause to take a good long look at the woman standing beside him in the darkness, her face a silver mask flickering in the neon strobe of her own hair, her sinewy metal body burnished by the ever-shifting violet highlights.

Verdad, there were ways to fake the body, padding and shit, he had seen enough chocharicas in The American Dream doin' it. But none of them had ever had this face. How *could* you fake the curl of those full lips, the curve of the nose, least of all those strangely soft eyes lookin' right at him out of that hard metal face?

Chingada, this was for sure the face of Cyborg Sally, no doubt about it! He had to blink a couple of times to remember that he *wasn't* flashing now.

It was fuckin' impossible, there *was* no real Cyborg Sally!

But here she was.

It was as if Cyborg Sally had somehow been able to pop herself out of the dreamtime to pull him back in with her. Could that really be? There's only one way to find out, muchacho!

He shrugged, hit his touchpoint, slipped her in past him, snapped the door shut behind them, took a deep breath, and flicked on the light.

And found himself once more inside the bedroom of the Queen of Chocharica City, with its smoked mirror-glass ceiling, its red velvet wallpaper, its crackling fireplace, its big round bed inviting the inevitable with its golden sheets of sleek satin.

But if this silver chocharica queen in her long white gown and jeweled leather panties *was* Cyborg Sally, then he was at last the mucho macho King of Chocharica City, for he had plundered Ciudad Trabajo of its ultimate prize, and now he had her willingly here in his power, under his protection, in the glass tower bedroom high above the streets which had now been transformed thereby into *his* turf.

Cyborg Sally danced around the grand hotel suite, which was everything her room at the Waldorf was not, a vision that fulfilled her cinematic expectations of what a rock star's accommodations in the Big Apple were supposed to be.

Besides the spacious bedroom, with its king-size bed draped in purple velvet, there was a large sitting room done up in peach and chrome art deco, a bathroom, and even a little dining room paneled in teak and outfitted with its own wet bar, stove, and refrigerator.

She whirled out of the sitting room, into the bedroom, into his strong brown arms, snaking a hand in his hair, and teasingly yanking his head backward by it when he tried to kiss her.

"Hey, qué pasa?"

"Heart of ice," she sang at him.

She leaned her pelvis into him, felt the vacuum of her blazing bits and bytes rub sparking up against his meat's desire, felt the sudden explosion into erogenous being of a mucous membrane interface between flesh and wire.

"Ring of fire."

"Better call me Mister!" Mucho Muchacho told her as he prodded Cyborg Sally backward toward the big round bed with his mighty manhood against her cockteasing slowly yielding resistance.

Then she suddenly let herself fall back on the bed, snaring him around the waist with her sprung-steel legs, and pulling him down on top of her.

"Lick my flashing circuitry!" she hissed, and, grabbing his head in both hands, she pushed his mouth down around her slick and sparking metal nipple.

He groaned as a wave of weak-kneed queasy surrender rolled down his stomach to his groin, and he sucked the electrode of pleasure deep into his mouth, trunklining it like a zombie flashing his perfect wire.

He quivered with delight as she cupped his soft cheeks in her metal hands, and laved her body with his tongue as she swept his head over the tangy silver surface of her machine-oiled skin in slow downward spirals.

"No mother's child turn you on so wild . . ." she crooned at him in a hissy voice full of faraway echoes and subsonic caresses as she guided him to the ultimate apex of power between the sleek silver thighs of Chocharica City.

Free at last, Cyborg Sally stood high above the crowded dance floor of The American Dream, live onstage in the hot white spotlight and singing her amplified glory to the whole wide world.

Kneeling between her feet, licking her laser lips into a darkling sparkling ecstasy, was every diffident musician whose cock she had ever had to suck, every perfect blond surfer who had never looked at her twice, Bobby Rubin, and Lord Jimmy, and Red Jack himself, all incarnated in the finely chiseled bronzed body of this street-hard superman on his knees before *her* where her worshippers belonged.

All her life she had waited for this moment to arrive. Now at last she knew what it felt like to be a star.

Mucho Muchacho found himself tasting the sweet secret truth hidden up the long white skirt of Chocharica City. The cool silvery Cyborg Queen of Ciudad Trabajo had a quivering little muchacha in her panties. For in the very act of turning *him* into *her* sex machine, she had reversed the polarity of the circuitry between them, and made *herself* helpless flesh to *his* blood-hot wire.

In the very act of seeming surrender, his was the power.

She was plugged into him, but he was making her *scream*.

When he was good and ready, he slid up her body like a great bronze snake, pulled down her black leather panties, pinned her hands to the satin sheets, and bridged himself tantalizingly above her body on his toes and arms.

"Get it while you can from a red-hot macho man!" he said sneeringly, teasingly brushing the tip of his mighty cock against her belly, expecting to see her buck and thrash her defiance.

Instead, soft eyes looked up at him out of Cyborg Sally's steely face, and tender lips around dagger teeth flashed him a radiant smile, and all the tension seemed to melt out of her sinewy steel cable body as she stretched her legs wide across the golden satin sheets and simply offered it to him for the taking.

Never had she known such a perfect body poised above her, never had she looked into hungry cocksman eyes gleaming down at her in avid expectation from the face of a proud warrior of the bedroom. Never before had she known what it was like to make love to someone who acknowledged her stardom, to be the shining object of blood-hot desire. Never before had she seen her true beauty mirrored in any man's eyes.

"Why don't you rock your roll in my electric chair?" she sang at him purringly. "I've been looking for you, 'cause you're the bear."

* * *

Mucho Muchacho eased himself slowly and wondrously down onto her soft silver skin. Never had he dreamed that he would ever see Cyborg Sally, the ultimate max metal chocharica, the rock star queen of Ciudad Trabajo, the cool blond adversary of la guerra chingada, looking into his eyes lovingly from a place beyond surrender. Never had Mucho Muchacho seen whatever that look meant in a woman's eyes, never had Mucho Muchacho felt this warm hollow space around the cavity containing his heart. Never had he known what it was to have captured the love of the queen of the world.

As he smiled dreamily and slid himself deep deep inside her, Cyborg Sally hugged her arms around his mighty shoulders, wrapped her legs around his slim hard waist, clinging to him with every possible purchase, and let him melt her heart of ice as she rocked her rosy ring of fire.

Oh, I'm comin' to dance
And I'm comin' tonight . . .

And she was. She was coming in long standing waves on purple velvet in a rock star's suite, riding the noble cock of a great bedroom warrior. And she was dancing somewhere in a great white light as an endless unseen audience swayed and stomped to her music. Hordes of bare-chested raggy street boys surged out of the ruins onto the stage to throw themselves at her feet, licking at her breasts, stroking her thighs, caressing the crack of her buttocks, whipped into a slavering frenzy by the touch of her cool steel flesh and blood-hot wire.

She was coming in crystal, and neon light—

Mucho Muchacho rode the mighty galloping steed of his own manhood higher and higher and tirelessly higher, into a place beyond Ciudad Trabajo, a place beyond Chocharica City, a place beyond even la guerra chingada—a place where pleasure, fucked free of anger and vengeance, and floating above the dance of power, had no him or her, no dimension save its own.

The voice of Cyborg Sally sang to him from out of the electronic whirlwind deep inside.

Comin', comin,' comin' so free
Comin' right atcha. . . .

"We all remember when . . ." he joined in as he felt a lifelong load of tension release itself soaring through him, carrying him away into a long helicopter ride above the darkling sparkling landscape of the earthbound streets.

Come along ... come along ... come along ...
Come along with me!

"Where the fuck you been, Monaco?" Henry Steiner demanded angrily. "You've been gone nearly three hours!" He and Pham stood over his hotseat in Steiner's office like two cops ready to send out for the rubber hoses.

Where have I been, putamadre? Paco thought sarcastically. It took a real effort to keep a straight hangdog expression on his face and not laugh out loud. Chingada, how am I supposed to tell you when I don't even know myself?

He had glided seamlessly down out of the flash, out of the long orgasmic helicopter ride, into perfect sated velvet blackness, from which he had emerged just as seamlessly into another darkness, with a warm body breathing heavily against him, not quite knowing whether he was awake or asleep, whether this was a shithole upstairs in Florida or a penthouse bedroom in the dreamtime, until the realization seized him that he was going to have to take care of this very business before he allowed himself to crash out again.

So he had prodded her awake for a moment, told her to cool it in the apartment till he got back, gotten up, put on his clothes, all without daring to turn on the light.

He opened the door and took one step out into the rat-shit and zombie stink of deepest Florida, into the hallway grayly illumined by the light oozing in through the window above the stairwell.

Chingada, what kind of disgusting puerca had he been humping on the Jack *this* time? he wondered shamefacedly as he stood there halfway out the door.

He had to look. He tiptoed over to the mattress on the floor. There, outlined in the dim light, curled up on the grimy sheets, was the unmistakable form of Cyborg Sally! The snaky hair, the cable-muscled body, the silver skin, the whole works. He leaned closer to study her face. The points of silvery dagger teeth were visible between Cyborg Sally's parted lips. Her eyes were closed, but that was for sure Cyborg Sally's nose.

Chingada, he wasn't jacked now, so somehow she was *real*, somehow, in some way, it had all been real! This might be a shithole upstairs in Florida and not a fancy bedroom in a penthouse condo, but he really had fucked *Cyborg Sally*, and she really *was* his prize if he could keep her!

But if Mucho Muchacho was to keep Cyborg Sally to himself, then Paco Monaco was going to have to cover his ass with Pham and Steiner.

And, it seemed, with the putamadre he had punched out, this maricón sin cojones Rubin, who had been sitting behind Steiner's desk in his own office when the security chief dragged him in here.

Chingada, it had seemed for a weird moment back there that this pasty-faced little creep was *Red Jack*! Talk about fuckin' *wired*! Talk about *fried*!

And yet . . .

And yet the eyes glaring at him out of Rubin's face still *did* look unsettlingly familiar, and even though he was slumped in Steiner's chair looking like shit, he *was* sitting there, and he *did* seem to be in charge somehow, almost as if Pham and Steiner saw the same fuckin' thing in those eyes too. . . .

"Well, Monaco, where the fuck *have* you been?" Steiner snapped, popping Paco's attention back into focus almost as if he had popped him out of a flash.

"We kept changing cabs, Mr. Steiner," he said. "We rode all around the fuckin' city for hours, making sure we lost them."

"Lost who?" snapped Alan Pham. "What are you talking about?"

"The kidnappers, Mr. Pham. The yaks or the maf or whoever it was who was trying to snatch Cyborg Sally."

"There weren't any kidnappers!" Pham said exasperatedly.

"Hey, how was I supposed to know that?" Paco moaned woefully. He nodded toward Rubin. "She told me *this guy* was trying to kidnap her, so I punched him out. Then she was sure some car was following us, and we had to keep hopping in and out of cabs until she thought she was safe. . . ."

He had carefully concocted this story on the way over from Slimy Mary's but now he improvised a little grace note. "And she didn't have any fuckin' cash either," he whined plaintively. "*I* had to front the fuckin' money!"

"You expect to be *reimbursed* for fucking up like this, Monaco?" Steiner shouted.

"I was only doin' my job. . . ."

"You really think you have a job here after this?" Steiner snapped. "I never want to—"

"Forget this shit!" Rubin snapped. "Argue about it among yourselves later!

And even though he seemed like some wimpy little nobody, Steiner, and even Alan Pham himself, shut right up and let him do the talking.

"Where is she?" Rubin demanded. "That's all that matters. You want to keep your job, you tell me where she is, and they won't fire you." He glanced at Pham. Pham nodded meekly.

"Hey man, I'm sorry I hit you, I hope you're okay. I was just doin' my job, you know, no hard feelings. . . ." Paco hunched his shoulders and lowered his eyes and did a fuckin' ass-kissing act.

The putamadre didn't even seem to notice. "*Where?*" he said.

"Chingada, I'd tell you if I knew, man, she fuckin' owes me money," the damned stupid spick doorman whined miserably. "As soon as she figured she didn't need me to protect her no more, she bullshitted me out of my last two hundred bucks, and then took off in a cab by herself without even telling me how I was supposed to get it back!"

"Oh shit!" Bobby groaned, dismayingly convinced that this son of a bitch was telling the truth, for it sounded just like the Pimple, using this poor dumb slob as a convenience and then leaving him in the shit without a thought for anyone but herself, just as she had gotten *him* into the shit he was in now, and punched in the guts in the bargain.

"Well what now, Mr. Rubin?" Pham said. "Do we bring in the police?"

"The police . . . ?" Bobby muttered distractedly.

The doorman, the same son of a bitch who had socked him in the stomach and sent him puking into the john, was looking at him imploringly, and despite the dull ache below his rib cage, he could empathize all too well with how the poor schmuck felt.

Because of Sally Genaro, they were both about to join the great army of the unemployed! The doorman was begging him with his eyes for brotherly mercy, a mercy it was momentarily in his power to grant. But Nicholas West would show *him* no such mercy. A word from him could save this poor fucker's job, but who could save *his* ass from being flushed down the toilet bowl?

"Should I call the police, Mr. Rubin?"

"What?" Bobby's attention jump-cut away from his contemplation of the doorman and his grubby little problems to matters of his own survival.

"Jesus Christ, don't call the cops!" he said. "She hasn't committed any crime except being a pain in my ass, but scores of witnesses heard her screaming that I was trying to kidnap her! I'm in deep enough shit already without getting myself arrested!"

"Well, then what are we supposed to do?" the security chief demanded.

"Fuck, I don't know . . ." Bobby moaned. "Just keep your eye out for her in case she comes back and keep your mouths shut about this. I've gotta have time to think of *something*. . . ."

He got up wearily from behind the desk. His stomach hurt, he still had the taste of puke in his mouth, he saw no way out of this mess, and, in the wake of his helplessness, he found himself washed over by an enormous wave of terminal exhaustion.

"I'm going back to my hotel to crash," he said, staggering across the little room and opening the door. "Call me at the Union Square Pavilion if you hear anything, but please, not before noon."

"What about the doorman?" Pham said. "Do we fire him or not?"

"Huh . . . ?" Bobby muttered, leaning on the doorknob. "What the fuck do I care. . . ."

The doorman was begging for mercy with his eyes again, hunched forward obsequiously, but there was also anger in those eyes, and contempt for the cowardly blow that they expected to fall.

This greasy spick had kicked his ass in public and no doubt now expected him to take the cheap wimpish vengeance of the paper-pushing boss. Little did he know that Bobby could feel the very same ax and worse falling toward the back of his own neck!

"Oh, for chrissakes, he was just doing his job, so let him keep it," Bobby said tiredly. He didn't even have the energy for sadistic cheap thrills, and besides, he somehow felt that inflicting bureaucratic vengeance on some poor little doorman was not exactly going to make him feel more manly when he was forced to face the morning.

"Hey thanks, man," the doorman said. "I mean, you didn't

have to . . ." He locked eyes with Bobby for a long moment, freezing him in place halfway out the door. "Hey, would you mind telling me something, I mean like I really got to know . . ."

Bobby shrugged his assent wearily.

"Is she . . . was she . . . you know, the real Cyborg Sally?"

"There *is* no real Cyborg Sally, everyone knows that," Bobby snapped.

The doorman studied him most strangely now. "Like there really ain't no Red Jack?" he said slowly.

"Bits and bytes and programs . . ." Bobby muttered.

"Then who the fuck is . . . was she?" the doorman demanded. "I mean, if she ain't Cyborg Sally, then what's the big deal? Why's it so important to you to get her back?"

Bobby groaned. " 'Cause she's the damn little Pimple behind the voiceprint parameters, that's why," he said, stepping out into the corridor. "Without her, there can't be any more Cyborg Sally songs."

"Huh? But you just said there ain't no—"

"That's show business!" Bobby said dryly, and slammed the door behind him.

"You're lucky he's such a nice guy," Steiner told Paco.

"Yes, he's a truly charming individual," Alan Pham said dryly. "You really shouldn't have punched him in the stomach, you know. . . ."

Paco's heart skipped a beat.

Pham laughed. "You should have given it to him right in the mouth!"

Steiner's attitude did a quick one-eighty. "Yeah, he sure is an arrogant little shit. Who the hell is he?"

"Nobody," Pham said. "Just an errand boy from the home office getting his rocks off by playing big man."

Paco smiled his sympathetic solidarity with the ire of his bosses, but somehow he doubted that Pham was telling the truth.

Somehow he had the feeling that Rubin had been trying to tell him something in a language he couldn't quite understand. There wasn't any Cyborg Sally up there in Florida, but if he didn't get her back, there would be no more Cyborg Sally songs. That didn't exactly add up.

Or maybe, somehow, it did.

He wasn't exactly Mucho Muchacho, but Mucho had sure as shit punched out Rubin, and just as surely hidden *someone* without whom there couldn't be a Cyborg Sally in Slimy Mary's. There wasn't any Red Jack either, but he had seen his eyes again in Rubin's face when the guy gave him back his job.

Whoever the little putamadre might be, he hadn't pulled the chain when he could have, even on someone who had whipped his ass.

Wasn't that what Red Jack would have done?

Wouldn't Mucho Muchacho have to respect that?

Didn't that make them compadres somehow?

Paco had a lot to think about. There was a lot going on here that just didn't make sense. But he had the feeling that it just might add up to the biggest thing that had ever happened to him in the dreamtime. To the chance of a lifetime.

Sally Genaro awoke suddenly to a heavy thump above her and a spattering of plaster on her face. She was lying on a musty, lumpy mattress somewhere in a rank-smelling darkness. She could hear the distant sounds of rat feet skittering across linoleum and the slower falls of much heavier feet shaking the thin ceiling.

She blinked, bolted upright, and, in the act of trying to step out of the bed onto the floor, discovered that the mattress was *on* the floor, bruising her heel in the process.

The clumsy moment of pain jolted her into full awareness. This certainly was not the lavish hotel suite she had fallen asleep in!

Remembering the hotel suite of her dreamtime, she remembered the purple velvet spread on its king-size bed, and remembering that, she remembered what delights had taken place there, delights whose reality was confirmed by the sated languor of her loins.

And then she remembered that Mucho Muchacho, or whatever his name was, had woken her up for a moment, left for somewhere, and told her to stay here until he got back.

But who really was he? And where in the world was *here*?

Hadn't he turned on a light when they came in . . . ?

She gathered herself to her feet and staggered toward a door whose form she could dimly perceive in the tendrils of wan light leaking in around the edges of something shaped like a window, tripping over something that clattered before she reached it.

She felt around near the doorframe for a light switch, found it, flicked it on, blinked her eyes into focus in the sudden cruel light of a naked overhead bulb, then flicked it off with a moan.

In the flash-frozen moment, she had seen more than enough.

Peeling plaster walls covered with graffiti. Three mattresses covered with mung-crusted raggy sheets on a green linoleum floor. Four or five big rotten pillows. Orange crates and cardboard cartons in lieu of dresser and tables. A window covered with tinfoil. Something she tried to tell herself was *not* a dead rat shriveled with its paws in the air in a corner.

"Oh *gross*!" Sally Genaro moaned. Someone grunted in a toilet on the floor above. Rat feet clattered in another room. She could feel an army of cockroaches closing in on her in the darkness.

Stay *here* until some crazy spick got back? No way, Jose, or whatever your name is, not one more minute!

She opened the door and crept out into a hallway. There was a broken window down at the other end by the stairwell and there was enough light coming in from an airshaft so she could see where she was going well enough to pick her way through the garbage past two rows of doorways toward it.

Some of the doorways were doorless, others had doors hanging open crazily from a single hinge, and as she walked nervously past them, they reminded her of the skeletal eyesocket windows of rows of abandoned buildings on a side street not far from West Broadway where she had wandered so innocently what seemed like half a lifetime ago. . . .

Terror gripped her intestines. That must be where she was—*inside* one of those abandoned buildings! But unfortunately not *really* abandoned. There were *people* clumping around on the floor above, and the sound of voices and music drifting up the stairwell.

She paused at the top of the stairs, peering down into dim flickering illumination, listening to the music, and the muzzy chattering of crossed conversations. There were *a lot of people* down there between her and the street.

Sally Genaro could well imagine what kind of people they were and what the street outside would be like in the unlikely event that she passed safely through the gauntlet. Sally Genaro froze. She *couldn't* go down there, but she couldn't stay here either.

She remembered mouths and hands at her body in the backwash of machine-gun fire—

—and was flashed back into *Cyborg Sally's* memory track of the moment before, up there on the stage in the bright white light, surrounded by a tremulous circle of the worshippers who had dreamed her into reality, feral streeties who *she* had dreamed into an audience.

Sally Genaro could never walk down these stairs.

But I can, said a voice deep inside her. "Come along . . . come along . . . come along with me!" sang Cyborg Sally.

Sally Genaro reached up, hit her touchpoint, and once more surrendered the fate of her clammy flesh to the bits and bytes of her blood-hot wire.

Cyborg Sally danced down the rickety stairs to the beat of the music below and emerged out of the ruins and into the deep dark back reaches of a secret tribal cave.

The walls of the cave receded into the blackness beyond her cone of vision. Before her, across a twilight zone of figures sprawled and hunkered around simple tribal furniture scattered on the floor, a score or more worshippers danced under flickering lights before their idol.

The current devotional object was the washed-out figure of Lady Leather dancing on a bedsheet-sized video screen. But Cyborg Sally smiled a dagger grin as she saw the rubber wigs, the face paint, the cheap leatherette panties, the tacky body stockings, the silver T-shirts on both men and women—the bits and fragments of her own promos and tie-ins worn as tribal totems.

Cyborg Sally stood in the wings, tapping her feet and popping her fingers as she waited for her fanfare, waited for her music, waited for her turn in the spotlight, waited for the magic moment that all her fans were waiting for—

And then it came.

The opening bars of "Cyborg Sally" drew even more dancers out onto the floor, and there she was, the full glory of her impending live performance palely mirrored on the cheap video screen as her own recorded voice sang the opening chorus of her song.

Cyborg Sally danced down the long backstage runway and out onstage in her own magic circle of white spotlight, out into the side street between rows of skeletal buildings, each tenement a grandstand packed with streeties, with girls in rubber wigs, with boys in tattered Cyborg Sally T-shirts, plugged into her, shrieking and cheering and pounding their feet, her army of fans, hot to boogie.

And then they did, pouring down out of the skeletons of long-dead buildings and out onto the street, out of the rat-infested darkness to dance in the aisles.

Cyborg Sally pranced across the stage beneath flickering strobes that fragmented each moment into a still-shot poster frame of her electronic glory. She twirled around slowly, displaying the reality of her perfection, and then stomped around with her hands on her hips and her hair crackling lightnings as she sang through a challenging sneer full of steel dagger teeth.

At her command, her avid groupies surged forward and mobbed up onto the stage, dancing into the hot silver limelight of her aura, bobbing and rearing to the music like puppets on the strings of her wire, circling her slowly at a hesitant distance, hands daring to caress only the invisible cone of her stardom's spotlight.

Round and round they danced, round and round she spun in the hot white spotlight, the strobe flashes slicing reality into a flicker-flash of faces frozen in ecstasy, of devotional figures carved on the walls of the electronic temple of Cyborg Sally.

Comin' to dance
And I'm comin' tonight
Comin' in crystal and neon light. . . .

She danced out of her spiral and into the sparking center of the whirlwind, with her arms spread wide over her head to embrace the skeletal hulks of the ruined buildings, the audience tiered up high around her, the swirling streeties she had summoned up into the limelight with her.

And it seemed to her that a power flashed back and forth between them, the power they all agreed to share in the dreamtime, the power of her wire over their poor fleshly reality, and a power which in that moment seemed as if it could sweep them all away into a place where this song need never end.

Comin', comin,' comin' so free. . . .
Come along . . . come along . . . come along . . .
Come along with me!

"You know, my man, I do believe I'm beginning to believe you," Dojo said, rubbing his hands together. "If that ain't

Cyborg Sally, it sure is someone got all these wirehead assholes convinced she's the real thing!"

Out on the dance floor, Cyborg Sally, the very same Cyborg Sally as the one up there in pale video on the screen behind her, was lip-syncing the track of the final multiplexed chorus, while nearly forty dancers circled her adoringly.

"Hey, I told you, nigger, would I shit you?" Paco said as they moved through the mostly empty seats and cushions of the twilight zone toward her.

Qué fuckin' pasa? There *was* no real Cyborg Sally, Rubin had said, yet here she was surrounded by a whole mob of people who sure as shit thought there was.

"You know what this means, my son?" Dojo said avidly.

Paco cocked an eyebrow at him. Chingada, had Dojo really figured this shit out?

"It means we got ourselves a money machine, Paco. Fifty-fifty, my man, you keep her here, and for that you get half of everything we take in!"

"Take in off *what*?"

Dojo shrugged unconcernedly. "Ransom money, cover charges, white slavery rights, who the fuck knows right now, we got plenty of options to consider . . . if Muzik really sent some guy all the way from Hollywood to bring back whoever the fuck this is. . . ." He held out his big meaty hand. "We got a deal?"

"For sure, man," Paco said absently, sealing it with a slap, for his attention was now entirely on Cyborg Sally herself as they reached the dance floor and pushed their way through the crush around her.

Cyborg Sally stood inside an inviolable sphere of body-space in the midst of the jostling streeties, smiling at them, nodding, occasionally reaching out to touch an outstretched hand. Paco broke through the circle and snatched her by the elbow. "Chingada," he snapped, "I told you to stay in the fuckin' room!"

Oohs of surprise and groans of sullen anger as she turned to face him, lips sneering over gleaming dagger teeth. "You're talking to *Cyborg Sally,*" she hissed, "and no one's gonna ever drag me out of the spotlight again!"

A really spaced-out creep in a Cyborg Sally T-shirt took two tentative steps toward Paco. Two more putamadres decided they wanted to get brave.

Paco hit his touchpoint and Mucho Muchacho came up whirling into a sweeping spin kick that drove them back.

"Hey cool it, my man!" Dojo said, stepping between him and the ugly crowd. "You cool it too, you wirehead assholes! You know the rules! Anyone who throws a punch in Slimy Mary's gets the shit beat out of him by me and eighty-sixed for what's left of his life!"

He turned to Cyborg Sally with a placating smile and spoke in quite another voice.

"No one wants to drag you out of the spotlight *here*," he cooed at her. "You're a star! You're good for business! In fact, I want to book you in as a headliner at Slimy Mary's for a good long run. So why don't we just do some dust in my office and talk about it?"

"Look," said the club owner, pacing in nervous circles around his small but lavishly furnished office, "I can't pay what a big star like you deserves, but just having you around is gonna let me charge a hundred-dollar cover, and I'm willing to give you half of the gross. See if any of the plushie-tushie meatracks will play that straight with you!"

"You'll be safe upstairs with me," Mucho Muchacho told her, "those putamadres who want to snatch you away to L.A. will never find you here, and if they do, Dojo and me will make them fuckin' disappear, won't we, my man?"

"Fuckin'-A!" the big black man promised. "Paco and me are mean motherfuckers, and nobody gets away with trying to crash the door here!"

She was seated side by side with Mucho Muchacho on a green velvet divan. He passed her a silver mirror and an elegantly carved matching straw, contriving to brush his arm across her breast in the process.

Cyborg Sally snorted up a line of dust for the sake of her rock star image, but of course any mere chemical flash meant nothing to the Queen of Wire.

"I don't care about the money," she said, "as long as you keep them from trapping me back in their software. As long as I can perform live for my fans."

"Perform? Live?" said the man called Dojo. He shot a glance at Mucho Muchacho. "Can she really do that?" he asked. "You think she can really *sing*?"

"I'm *Cyborg Sally*!" she snapped at him.

"Yeah, sure you are, but—"

"Cyborg Sally! Flesh and wire! Queen of Heat! Electric fire!" she sang out at him triumphantly.

The big black man looked at her strangely. "Uh . . . yeah, that's really terrific," he said. "But . . . ah . . . it don't exactly sound like the voice on the disc. . . ."

"I need my 'Box," said a small voice inside her.

"Your what?"

"Get me a VoxBox and I'll show you the crystal chips that'll make you cream," Sally said.

"You heard my momacita," said Mucho Muchacho, throwing a possessive arm around her shoulder. "You can score a VoxBox somewhere, can't you, Dojo?"

"Yeah, sure, no problem," the big man muttered. "Man, if she really *can* play the thing, we're in heavy bread city."

"No living soul gonna take you higher."

"All *right*!" Dojo exclaimed. "If you ain't full of shit, lady, we're gonna ring up some figures together!"

He slapped at her palms, clapped Mucho Muchacho on his naked bronzed shoulder, and loped toward the door. "I'll get the ball rolling, my man," he said. "You keep our little rock star happy!"

Mucho Muchacho led Cyborg Sally up a triumphant flight of oak and brass stairs and down a hall papered with red velvet to the penthouse bedroom and held her at arm's length before the great round bed with its sheets of golden satin.

Paco Monaco came out of the flash standing over a filthy mattress in a fuckin' shithole upstairs in Florida, holding in his arms . . . holding in his arms . . .

Someone with the face of Cyborg Sally. Someone who looked just like her. And yet . . . and yet . . .

Sally Genaro found herself in a foul-reeking hovel in some cockroach-infested ruin, face to face with some savage Puerto Rican streetie, smelling the sour unwashed stink of him, feeling his rough hands on her shoulders, looking into his hard dark eyes. . . . She shuddered in terror and loathing.

And yet . . . and yet . . .

"You know, whoever you are, we're like two of a kind . . ." she said. "I mean . . ." She shrugged. She reached out a tremulous hand, found the touchpoint hidden in his bushy hair, stroked it tenderly. "Flesh and wire," she said. "Promise me we never have to be anything less again. You and me in the dreamtime . . . For ever and ever . . ."

"In the dreamtime, momacita," said Mucho Muchacho as Cyborg Sally snaked a steel leg around his knee, and, arching over backward, pulled him down on top of her as she stretched herself out beneath him onto the warm golden sheets. "We all remember when . . ."

"Let's never leave here again."

FLESH AND WIRE

Bobby Rubin? The telephone call had been like a bad acid flashback from an old bummer Glorianna O'Toole would just as soon forget.

Yet here she was, sipping her third after-dinner Courvoisier and trying to nod off to a bad movie in the first class cabin of an airplane heading for New York.

She had stayed well away from anything having anything to do with Muzik, Inc., ever since she had given Nicholas West a ripe juicy finger and stormed out of his office, and she was pleased, if somewhat surprised, that the Factory had let her be too.

No indictments, no lawsuits, no bad-mouthing around town. They hadn't even cut her off their freebie list! Hell, they hadn't even demoted her to the B list. She still got all the pr sheets, party invitations, discs, and promo T-shirts that the Factory sent out.

She threw away the pr sheets without unsealing the envelopes, sold the discs at the usual sixty percent discount to Discomania, donated the T-shirts to the Salvation Army, stayed away from any event sponsored by the Factory, carefully avoided any contact with Bobby Rubin or Sally Genaro.

There was no sense pushing her luck. While they were working on "Cyborg Sally," she knew without having to be told that West would take a dim view of any hint of interference with the project by her after she had told him in words of one syllable what an evil piece of shit she thought it was.

And after the disc came out and soared to the top of the charts on a surge of promotion, tie-ins, bad vibes, and hype, she had no desire to have anything to do with any soulless mercenary who had collaborated with the enemy on such a piece of sinister mind-fucking schlock. The only promo T-shirt she had kept was the one for Cyborg Sally, and that she used to wipe out the inside of her kitchen garbage pail when she changed plastic bags.

Nor, for that matter, had either of the little ingrates ever thought to say hello to the producer of their first two hits. Sally Genaro she had never really gotten along with or cared to, but Bobby Rubin had shown flashes of being a human being, and their spirits had touched in some complex time-warped manner in the creation of Red Jack, so beneath the indifference, there was a small reservoir of hurt to be tapped by his voice on the telephone after all this time. Especially when it awoke her at seven A.M.

"Bobby Rubin . . . ? What the hell do you want from my life at this hour . . . ?"

"This hour . . . ? It's ten— Oh shit, I forgot! I'm sorry Glorianna, I'm calling from New York. I'm in deep deep shit, and I don't know who else to turn to. . . ."

"New York?" That was enough to rouse her to full wakefulness. "What're you doing in New York?" she asked without thinking, propping herself up against the bedboard, and then she was caught in his long, rambling tale of woe.

"So Sally Genaro has disappeared somewhere and you can't find her," Glorianna said peevishly when he finally let her get a word in edgewise. "What's that got to do with me?"

"I . . . I was hoping you'd come and help me find her . . ." blurted the voice at the other end of the phone.

"*Me?* What am I, the missing persons bureau? Leave me alone and call the cops."

"I can't call the cops, she hasn't done anything, and I . . . well, let's just say I'm not in too good a legal position to talk to the police. . . ."

"Well then hire private detectives!"

"I've already done that. She left all her stuff in her room at the Waldorf. She didn't even check out, they're still running a bill on her. That's all I could get for ten thousand dollars."

"Shit," Glorianna moaned. "You know that's a good little description of you, too, Bobby Rubin! You've been a perfect little shit to that girl, and now that she's probably just run off to have a little fun, here you are, trying to drag her back into the sweatshop you made a bummer for her in the first place! Don't you have any conscience at all?"

"You think I *want* to be doing this?" Bobby moaned. "I *have* to do it, I told you, Glorianna, if I don't bring her back to L.A. to finish the disc, West is going to get me *arrested* as the ringleader of the Reality Liberation Front! I had to grovel and plead to the son of a bitch to get him to give me two more weeks! So I've got my two more weeks, but I don't even know what to *try* next."

"Maybe what you should try next is a dose of what you deserve!"

"*What I deserve?*" Bobby whined. "Okay, so maybe I let Sally get under my skin, okay, so I treated her badly, okay, so I've been a shit—but are you gonna really tell me I deserve to be butt-fucked in the joint for it?"

"Assuming anyone in the joint would *want* your silly ass!"

"Glorianna! Come on! I seem to remember that West threatened to have *you* thrown in jail too!"

"That was Carlo Manning," Glorianna corrected.

"West, Manning, Beldock, what's the difference, they're all the fucking Factory, aren't they? Up against the wall with the money machine, remember? Well, the money machine's got *me* up against the wall! Come on, Glorianna, don't just throw me to the enemy!"

"Oh now it's the enemy, is it?" Glorianna said. But her voice had lost some of its edge now, he was starting to get to her. This, after all, was no cold-hearted polished lady-killer caught in his own devices; this was just a somewhat selfish nerdy kid who the Factory had now dragged in way over his head.

"What makes you think I can help you, anyway . . . ?" she asked somewhat relentingly. "After all, I'm just—"

"The Crazy Old Lady of Rock and Roll! You've been everywhere! You've done everything! You know everybody! You can cope with this crazy city!"

"*You're* the New Yorker," she reminded him.

"I'm from *Long Island*, Glorianna, that's like the *Valley*. I'm not connected to anything here but the Factory's expense account!"

Glorianna's ears pricked up. "Expense account? Did you say expense account?"

"Yeah, yeah, I've got an open Muzik, Inc., expense account, they don't care what I do as long as I get results. . . ."

"Do tell . . ." Glorianna purred. "Tell me, Bobby, just what is it that you'd have us do if I were to fly to New York . . . first class, of course. . . ."

A long silence. "I was hoping you'd tell *me* that . . ." a small voice finally said.

"What if I were to say that the best course is for me to check in at the best hotel in town, rent a limo, buy about a pound of dust, and take you on a grand tour of the restaurants, meatracks, clubs and saloons at the Factory's expense until either we find Sally or they pull the plug?"

Bobby managed a little laugh despite his dire straits, endearing himself to her for a bright little flash. "Hey Glorianna, you don't have to be coy with me. Pig out on the expense account all you like, buy yourself a whole new wardrobe, clean out Tiffany's, who cares, it's *their* money, isn't it, the motherfuckers? If you'll give me a hand, it's the least I can do."

"You're beginning to talk me into it for some reason," Glorianna said dryly. Finances had certainly been a little tight lately, and New York was quite a town to boogie in as long as you were pissing away someone else's money. . . . Particularly tasty when you were sticking a corporation who richly deserved such a shafting with the bill.

Now who has no conscience, Glorianna O'Toole? For a glorious freebie ride you're willing to collaborate with this kid in hauling some poor little fat girl with her first chance to boogie back to the Factory's salt mines.

"Just one thing, Bobby," she said. "If I agree to ride this gravy train with you, I ride it only until you find Sally, and then I get off. And if you want me to help you find her, you've got to promise you'll keep our bargain if we do."

"Bargain . . . ?" Bobby said nervously.

"Yeah. No rough stuff. No private detectives. No snatches. You don't try to drag her back to L.A. against her will. I don't want any part of the karma in collaborating with such shit. Any of that, and *I* call the cops. We find her, you've got to convince her to *want* to come back of her own free will."

"How am I supposed to do that?"

"Hey, kid, I think you got the wrong number, this is the missing persons bureau, not advice to the lovelorn. Get the message?"

"I already got it from West," Bobby Rubin's voice said sourly. "Will you come?"

"Do we have a deal?"

"Yeah, Glorianna, we have a deal."

"Where are you staying?"

"Union Square Pavilion."

"Hey, not too tacky! Book me a suite there. Rent a limo to meet me at Kennedy. Make it a Rolls. Have another one pick me up here. And I'll have a first class window seat on a major. A dinner flight."

"Anything else, madam?" said Bobby Rubin's relieved voice on the other end of the phone.

Glorianna laughed. "You might have a bottle of Dom Pérignon on ice in my room and a little caviar, the real Russian stuff, none of that Iranian shit," she said, hanging up the phone, rolling over, and going back to sleep.

Karen Gold put on her rattiest pair of jeans and a Cyborg Sally T-shirt and had the cab drop her off around the corner from Slimy Mary's, feeling a little foolish and more than a little trepidatious dressing up in streetie drag and arriving incognito, but determined to learn what was *really* going on here, and unwilling to give up her man to a phantom without a fight.

The first time Paco had disappeared after his shift on the door at The American Dream instead of joining her at the bar, Karen had blamed herself. She *had* been really down lately, and she couldn't deny that she had been letting herself take out her frustrations on him. She really *had* been acting like a little princess in exile, and she promised herself she would make it up to him in bed when he got back to the loft.

But when he didn't show up at the loft that night, she didn't quite know whether to be furious at him or herself.

"Hey, come on Karen, so I had some business to do, lighten up," Paco had cooed at her when she pinned him on it at the door the next night.

"What kind of business? *Monkey* business?"

"Hey, I'm a big boy, you ain't my moma, okay. . . ."

Paranoid on the one hand, but blaming herself for this new distance between them on the other, Karen held her temper, touched a hand to his cheek, and made herself speak softly.

"Yeah, you're a big boy, Paco, you're my Mucho Muchacho, and I don't want to be your moma, and I know I've been a bit of a bitch lately," she said. "But I *would* like you to tell me I'm still your momacita. . . ."

Paco looked at her strangely, almost regretfully, or so it seemed to her. "Yeah, sure momacita, you're my momacita," he finally said with less than overwhelming conviction, giving her a dry little peck on the lips, and then shooing her on in past him. "We'll talk about this shit later, okay, I don't want to get my ass fired, they don't like me holding long personal conversations on the door."

But he failed to show up in the bar again that night, and when he *did* turn up in her bedroom it was the wee hours of the morning, and though he insisted that all he had been doing was taking care of some business at Slimy Mary's, and though he *did* make love to her, his performance was inept and perfunctory and he gorked off immediately thereafter, or at least pretended to pass out.

He didn't show up in the bar or the loft again for two days, and when he did, he crawled into bed with her after three A.M. when she was stone asleep, without even the gallantry to try to wake her, and split right after a silent sullen breakfast.

Then, for this last week, he had hadn't shown up at all, and wouldn't even discuss it with her at the door of The American Dream, the only place she had seen him, pleading the pressure of the crowd.

Okay, a girl could take a not-so-subtle hint. The son of a bitch was seeing someone else; that, at least, if sad, and infuriating, was an oft-told tale, and one she could figure out for herself. But that he didn't have the nerve to come out and tell her, *that* just didn't add up, that just wasn't like Paco.

She finally *did* corner him at the door by emerging from The American Dream unexpectedly right at the end of his shift as the graveyard-shift doorman was taking over and he was about to leave for God knew where and God knew who.

"All right, Paco, who is it?" she demanded, grabbing him by the arm.

"Qué?" he said distractedly, with a faraway look in his eyes.

"Don't give me that wounded innocence stuff!"

"Hey momacita, qué pasa, don't give me no hard time, I got people to see and important business to—"

"*Who do you think you're talking to?*" Karen snapped angrily.

She looked deep into his eyes and didn't seem to see anyone she knew looking back.

"Who *do* you think you're talking to?" she said much more softly. "Jesus, Paco, you're flashing right now, aren't you? You starting to flash *on the door* now? You know they'll can you if they catch you!"

Paco blinked. "Hey, they can besan mi pica; Mucho Muchacho don't—"

"Inside!" Karen hissed, dragging him by the arm. "You and me are gonna talk right now, you owe me that much at least."

"Hey—" he started to shout at her, his eyes hard and furious, yanking his arm free from her grasp.

"—Chingada . . . okay . . ." he muttered in quite a weaker voice, looking down at his feet, taking her hand, and allowing her to lead him inside. At least she had succeeded in dragging *him* down out of the damned flash.

She didn't say another word until they were seated at the bar. Then she ordered two martinis straight up, not at all her usual brand of poison, choked down the first one in three quick stomach-souring gulps, and took a long sip of the second as well before she secured sufficient dutch courage to have it out.

"Well long time no see, macho man!" she finally snapped as the gin began to hit.

"Hey Karen . . ." Paco crooned unhappily, shoulders hunched over slightly, looking down at the bar top.

"*Karen* is it, huh?" she said. "May I therefore assume it's the real Paco Monaco I finally have the dubious honor of addressing?"

"Come on, momacita, what's got up your chocha?" he said guiltily, still not meeting her gaze.

"Not *you,* macho man, that's for goddamn sure!" she snapped. "Who's the lady, Paco?"

"Chingada," he said, glancing significantly at her martini glass, "tu eres boracho, why you drinking that shit?"

"I think I've got a right to get a little drunk under the circumstances, don't you? I mean seeing as how my man has left me for someone else without even having the balls to tell me!"

"It's not what you think . . ." Paco muttered.

"It's not what I think!" Karen snapped at him. She defiantly slugged down another big gulp of gin. "Then what the hell is it? *Who* the hell is it? And don't try to tell me I'm drunk out of my mind and imagining it!"

Paco sighed. He studied his fingers as he drummed them on the bar top. "You wouldn't believe me . . ." he said hesitantly.

"I don't believe you already, goddammit! Stop treating me like this!"

Paco finally met her gaze. Something in his eyes, the mixture of pain, confusion, regret, and defiance, told her that he was about to finally speak the truth.

"It's Cyborg Sally," he said. "Hey, I'm sorry, I really am . . . but she's . . . you know . . . I mean . . ."

So much for feminine intuition!

"You've finally fried your brain, Paco," Karen said more in sadness than in anger. "There isn't any Cyborg Sally, she's just a bunch of programs, remember, and you're not jacked now, so how can you sit there like a terminal wirehead zombie and tell me you're making it with someone who doesn't exist?"

"Yo no se . . . I mean, she does exist, I mean, sort of, you know, in the dreamtime . . . I mean . . ." He shrugged in frustration and looked away again.

A dim comprehension slowly began to burn its way through Karen's alcoholic haze.

"It's that bimbo in the fancy Sally outfit who almost got you canned, isn't it?" she said much more sympathetically. "She really didn't disappear, you've got her stashed somewhere, haven't you? Slimy Mary's, right? And you're chain-tapping with her all the time and never coming down, I'll bet. You're so brain-burned from the damned thing some silly bitch has got you convinced she's a rock star who doesn't exist!"

"Yeah . . . I mean no . . . Chingada . . ." He looked up at her again, and for a moment he was her Paco again. For a moment that lost-little-boy look in his big brown eyes went straight to her heart.

"Hey, you don't understand," he said plaintively. "I mean, it's like you and me and Mucho Muchacho. I mean, I ain't really him, but I make him real for you in the dreamtime, verdad, and the Jack makes him real inside me, tu sabes. Real enough to save your ass. Real enough to make me your red-hot macho man . . ."

"But that's just a flash, Paco," Karen said much more softly. "Just a harmless little dream we . . . we used to share. It's not real, it's not flesh, it's just wire. It can't . . . it can't . . ."

Maybe it was the gin, but Karen found her own words not quite entirely convincing. Guiltily, she found herself understanding a little more than she wanted to. Who, after all, had she really fallen in love with, a grungy streetie or Mucho Muchacho, her knight of the streets? Who was her masterful lover, the natural Paco, fumbling and inept, or who he became on the Jack?

And what about Red Jack? You make more of me, I make

more of you, his song promised, and hadn't it, at least for a while, come true? Did these phantoms of the dreamtime somehow have the power to inhabit men and women of flesh in the real world for good or ill?

Or am I just drunk out of my mind?

She blinked. She placed a tender arm around Paco's shoulder. "Paco, Paco," she crooned, "I don't know what's really going on, but I do know you can't be balling a video screen phantom! It's all just inside your head, it's *got* to be!"

"Oh yeah?" Paco said. "Well it ain't just me!"

"*What?* You mean she's balling—"

"I mean, we got Cyborg Sally *singing* at Slimy Mary's now, and we got plenty of people paying a hundred bucks a head to see her, so how the fuck can she not really be there?"

"That's impossible!"

"Verdad?" he said, fishing a fat wad of bills out of his pocket. "So *this* ain't really there either?"

Karen leaned closer to him. "Considering how you've treated me, I really shouldn't be saying this, but I do still care about you. . . . And you're in trouble, someone's really messing with your head. . . . Let me in, Paco! Please let me help."

He laid a tremulous hand on hers. "Hey Karen, you won't believe this either, but I still care for you too," he said miserably. "And you know, I mean, like this ain't like you and me, it ain't about . . . *love,* it ain't even really about sex exactly, tu sabes . . . it's something muy grande, Karen . . . I don't know what . . . something important . . . like the RLF, you know, like liberating something . . . like pushin' against all the shit of the world and feeling it move. . . . I gotta do it, Karen, I gotta play it through. . . ."

"Paco, Paco, what about *us,* what about you and me?"

He craned his neck over his shoulder and peered out through the smoky haze at the dance floor, as if willing himself to see something or someone that wasn't there. He rose from his barstool.

"Yo no se," he said. "I mean, I couldn't blame you for telling me to fuck off now, but I gotta go, she's gonna go on soon, and I gotta be there. . . ."

And then he had turned his back on her, and walked away into the crowd.

Pausing at the bottom of the dark piss-stinking flight of stairs and staring up into what he knew fuckin' well was the second floor of a shithole, Paco Monaco found himself wondering whether maybe Karen wasn't right, whether the Jack wasn't frying his brains, whether he wasn't halfway to Florida himself.

Cyborg Sally had made him promise that he would never climb these stairs without plugging in, that they would never meet outside the dreamtime. Not that she had really had to. For whenever he popped out up there, and found himself in that crummy apartment, with the filthy mattresses, and the roaches, and the orange crates, and the fuckin' graffiti, and a muchacha who fuckin' *couldn't be* who he knew she was, he would reach for his touchpoint, and he wouldn't stop chain-tapping until it was time to return to his other life standing outside The American Dream.

Chingada, which was real, and which was the dreamtime? For sure Karen was real, and the shit she had laid on him was real, and The American Dream was real, and the fuckin' pain he saw in her eyes was real, and his job there was real, and what he felt right now was real.

But the bulge of the fat wad of bills in his pocket, hey, that was real too, and so was what it felt like to be Mucho Muchacho fucking Cyborg Sally, or if it wasn't, it *should* be, muchacho!

And if it *should* be, and with a tap of his touchpoint *could* be, then why the fuck not? Besides, it was gonna be time for her to go on soon, he was late already, better worry about all this shit later.

So Paco hit his touchpoint, and Mucho Muchacho bounded up the stairs two at a time into the magical realm of the second floor.

A long white marble corridor led straight up the thighs of Chocharica City to their penthouse apartment. He unlocked the carved oaken door with the golden key to his kingdom, and strode into the throne room, where Cyborg Sally was holding court.

She reclined luxuriantly on a powder-blue velvet couch with her long white gown rucked high up her smooth steel legs to reveal the sparking vortex of her chocha.

Half a dozen regulars sprawled on huge paisley floor cushions before her, staring worshipfully up into it as if it were a long dark tunnel with the promise of a bright white light at the other end—plugged in and swaying and bobbing to the soundtrack of "Cyborg Sally," playing on the ornate tv console at the far end of the room behind them.

He had been righteously pissed off the first time he had walked in on a scene like this only two nights after he snatched her away from The American Dream.

"Hey, what do you putamadres think you're staring at?" he had demanded angrily. "What the fuck are these guys doing here?"

"They're my fans," Cyborg Sally snapped back.

"They're a bunch of fuckin' street meat lookin' up your cunt is what they are!"

Cyborg Sally arched her sparky nipples at him and glared her dagger smile. "And what does that make you?" she purred.

Mucho Muchacho loomed above her, grabbed her by the chin, and lifted her face to within inches of what throbbed in his tight white pants. "A red-hot macho man, chocharica!" he told her. "And the only man who's gonna get into your hot little rock star pants around here!"

He flipped her head away from him with a flick of his wrist and turned to confront her fuckin' fan club with his hands on his hips. "Any of you maricónes got the cojones to try and tell me any different?"

There had been four guys in the room at the time, Slimy Mary's regulars, and he knew all of the putamadres.

Rico had been on the Prong so long before Cyborg Sally hit the scene that he had been known to fuck perros. Uncle Ugly had been the direct wirehead descendant of Uncle Charlie. Ratfuck had been halfway to Florida on the Blue Max express. Billy had worn the Red and run numbers with the People's Cash Machine back when Red Jack had his moment in the spotlight.

Now they turned to gaze up at him with the strangest awestruck look in their eyes, with the weirdest slow twisting of their necks like flowers following the sun in stop motion, with the same rapturous expression with which they had regarded Cyborg Sally.

And Cyborg Sally herself had gotten up off the couch to stand beside him. "Come along, come along, come along with me!" she sang into his ear, and when she took his hand, they stepped into someplace else.

A television camera bathed them in hot white light as it dollied backward before them. Bouquets of microphones were thrust in their faces as they walked arm in arm down an endless street between tall glass towers and neon theater marquees. Flashbulbs lit up the darkness of a vast audience as they stepped up onto the stage.

Skeletal buildings tiered up around them like grandstands, streeties jamming the windows, pouring out through the doors onto the street—Mucho Muchacho's ragged army, waiting for the music to begin, waiting for their orders to march.

Cyborg Sally roared it out, and a mighty music played, and the audience began to dance in the aisles, marching out of the endless blocks of abandoned buildings and straight up the main drag of Chocharica City behind Mucho Muchacho and his silver Cyborg Queen.

Besa me pica!
And ponga me your sister!
Better call me Mister!
Y TU MADRE TAMBIÉN!

She smiled at him through dagger teeth as they danced their stompada up Fifth Avenue and down West Broadway and into The American Dream, as their fan club of the streets followed their doorman prince out of the sombre and into the sol of Cyborg Sally's bright white spotlight.

Come along with me
Come as what you are
Every man a king
Every girl a star!

Blinking, Paco Monaco suddenly found himself standing in a fuckin' shithole upstairs in Florida. Rico, Ratfuck, Uncle Ugly, and Billy were on their feet now, swaying back and forth to the rhythm of the disced music. He was holding hands with Cyborg Sally, or with someone who looked just like her. It was Cyborg Sally's face all right, but her body, it wasn't really metal, was it . . . ?

But . . . Chingada, it *had* to be Cyborg Sally, didn't it, 'cause she hadn't just been lip-syncing the disc as he popped out of the flash, she had been singing a *new* Cyborg Sally song!

"*Our* fan club," she purred into his ear, leaning closer, smelling not like shining silver metal, but like female flesh in need of a bath. What the—

Then she blinked at him, and though her face didn't change at all, somehow he got the feeling that someone else was looking at him out of Cyborg Sally's eyes.

"Don't spoil everything," Cyborg Sally said in an unfamiliar voice. "Stay with me here in the dreamtime!" And she reached up into her hair with one hand, hit his touchpoint with the other, and the weird moment passed.

That had been, what, a week and more ago in some other life, no time at all here and now, in the throne room of their kingdom. And the Cyborg Queen of Wire had told him true, this was *their* fan club sprawled on the floor of it before her.

And he was getting a charge off the guys, and chingada, even the muchachas, staring up look-but-don't-touch with their tongues hanging out. Cyborg Sally could and did cocktease these maricónes till they went blue in the balls, but none of them would dare the anger of Mucho Muchacho to grab for it. Chingada, none of them seemed to have the cojones to even be thinking about it.

All they wanted to do was sit here and flash on being in the presence of their Cyborg Sally, the Cyborg Sally *he* had snatched from under the noses of the putamadres who owned MUZIK and The American Dream, who *he* protected from the plushie-tushies and their zonies with his street warrior body, who *he* ruled with the power of his mucho macho cock.

And, by so ruling the Queen of their Wire, became the jefe of her tribe.

When he said go, they all went. When he went downstairs to clock the action, they all gathered round. Half of all the admission money went straight to him. A hard glance from him was enough to cool any hassle in the meatrack, even when it was jammed with bad-asses and brain-burned wireheads. Even Dojo gave him looks that called him Mister now.

At long last he knew what it felt like to have a power beyond the reach of his fists, power that made people obey him because they wanted to, because they believed in him and were ready to march to his music, a strange elusive power that he drew from the chocha of Cyborg Sally with the great machismo of his manhood that now rose triumphantly against his tight white pants.

"Hey, momacita, we got about fifteen minutes before it's time for the show, so get it while you can from a red-hot macho man," he told her now, striding to the couch, grabbing her by the hand, and taking his rightful seat on the blue velvet throne beside her.

He waved negligently at the half-dozen streeties who were even now rising in anticipation of Mucho Muchacho's command.

"Hey, everybody out and go downstairs," he told them, and out of the apartment they obediently went, four men and two women, still plugged in and dancing out the door to the music.

Oh yeah, Cyborg Sally might be their Queen of Heat and their blood-hot wire, but *he* was the blazing bytes of *her* meat's desire. He wrapped a mighty arm around her, bending her over backward against the sprung steel of her resistance, and pressed her to the couch with his body, pinning her arms, and grinding himself against her as she bucked and moaned and thrashed beneath him.

Cyborg Sally wrapped her legs around Mucho Muchacho's waist and clasped him to her with her legs of steel. Beyond the dressing room walls she could hear the murmurous rumbling of the great crowd filing into the auditorium echoing down the backstage runway, the roadies adjusting the p.a. system, smell the ozone tang of the electric charge building in the air.

Oh yes, no mother's child could turn her on so wild, no father's son could flash her through such fire, not without the blazing bytes of her fans' desire. Not till her stardom had sung its way free of the prison of a little fat girl's flesh had she known the darkling sparkling ecstasy of a heroic cocksman reduced to willing groupiedom.

But oh yes, she remembered from some dim distant nightmare what it had been like to be where she commanded him to be now, as she wrenched her arms free against his mere teasing resistance, rolled him over beneath her, rose into arching majesty, snaked a hand in his hair and pinned his face between her sleek silver thighs.

A pimply little VoxBox player knelt before the lead singer of the Razor Dogs, giving him head backstage before a performance in a grotty Valley dive, cementing her lowly position with the band, getting off the only way she could and hating both of them for it, and yet, at the same time, thrilled and transported at the throbbing quick of her to be sucking at the root of second-hand stardom.

"Dance along with me, don't you dare look back, not *ever,*" Cyborg Sally told that poor little ugly duckling, for she felt the darkling sparkling ecstasy of the other side of that transaction now, with *her* groupie giving her avidly abasing head backstage before *her* performance.

She was coming in crystal and neon light, she was rising up, up, up, dancing in a bright white spotlight before a vast ragged audience that poured out of the skeletal buildings up onto the stage to kneel, gurgling and slurping, at her feet.

"I'm ready now," she said, pushing him away from her, and standing above him with her hands on her hips. "I'm coming to dance, and I'm loaded for bear!"

Mucho Muchacho, her great bronzed warrior, rose from his secret posture of tremulous groupie abasement and became her mighty champion and manager once more, taking her possessively by the arm and leading her down the long backstage runway. He left her in the shadows of the wings and strode out for his moment in the spotlight of her stage.

A bone-chilling chant began to build in the darkness beyond the circle of light. Hands clapped in supplication. Feet beat in rhythmic anticipation.

Cyborg Sally
Flesh and wire
Queen of Meat
Funeral pyre!

Now, as Karen rounded the corner of Third Street, she saw immediately that Paco had at least been telling the truth about one thing—*something* had changed at Slimy Mary's.

Though the building still looked abandoned from the outside, there was a small crowd of streeties clustered around the door to the cellar meatrack, more than a dozen of them.

Some of the women wore complete Cyborg Sally outfits—cheap rubber wigs, leatherette panties, silver body stockings—the rest the all-too-familiar promo T-shirts, face and tooth makeup, and purple dreadlocks lacquered into cut-rate Cyborg Sally hair. A few of the men even attempted to affect Sally hair rather ludicrously, a few more still wore the Red, many had painted their teeth into silver daggers, and some seemed to have actually filed them to points. And all of them to a man sported the male version of the Cyborg Sally T-shirt.

It reminded her of a pathetic low-budget version of the current scene outside The American Dream in a curiously touching manner, though the skinny blond man at the door was passing one and all inside quickly and democratically, without playing any selective ego games.

And when she got to the door, she saw that he was indeed collecting admissions.

"You gotta *pay* to get in here now?" she asked him in dubious mock outrage.

The pimply, sallow youth wore an uncamouflaged Jack quite openly, and, from the faraway look in his eyes, appeared to be flashing right now. He looked her up and down just as dubiously, seemingly put off by her lack of Sally hair or Jack.

"Hundred dollars," he said, holding out his hand. "Ain't you ever been here before?"

"Not since this has been going on. What's suddenly so great about Slimy Mary's that makes it worth a hundred bucks to get in?"

"You ain't heard?" the doorman asked in some amazement.

"Heard what?"

He flashed her a vulpine smile with a mouthful of silvered pointed teeth. "*She* plays here every night," he said in a tone of breathless confidentiality. "The Queen of Heat . . . You don't think *that's* worth a hundred bucks, you try and see Cyborg Sally anyplace else at ten times the price! She's ours now, gonna take the whole world higher, brain-burn all the plushie-tushies on her funeral pyre!"

Karen shuddered, but she handed over the money and descended the dark staircase into the cellar.

At first the place seemed much the same, though a good deal more crowded. The flickering bulbs in the tinfoil ceiling above the little dance floor. Scores of people squatting, sitting, and sprawling on the makeshift furniture in the twilight zone enclosing it. A sense of musty darkness falling away to a rat- and roach-infested infinity around the edges.

Two guys were hunched over the keyboards of the People's Cash Machines set up in the shadows just beyond the zone of light. But no one was dancing, no music was playing, and the only sound was a low expectant susurrus of collective murmurs.

The video screen was dead, and there was a VoxBox and a stool set up before it. Karen grimaced as she found herself a cushion way back in the anonymous darkness. Something about the whole scene made her think of some primitive jungle tribe waiting for a dark ceremony to begin.

Then Paco appeared out of the darkness at the other side of the cellar, strutting slowly and haughtily through the twilight zone and into the center of the dance floor, Mucho Muchacho indeed, as a bone-chilling chant began to build, murmurous at first, then rhythmic, and accompanied by the drum-beat of handclaps.

Cyborg Sally
Flesh and wire
Queen of Meat
Funeral pyre!

"Who's the queen of your meat, who's your blood-hot fire?" he chanted.

"Cyborg Sally, flesh and wire!"

The answering chant was low, and slow, and somehow quite threatening, as Karen saw hand after hand reaching up to hit touchpoints. The video screen came to life with the opening visuals of "Cyborg Sally," but the sound was off as the familiar silver face lip-synced nothing on it to the chanted dialog between Paco and the audience.

Cyborg Sally! Flesh and wire!
Blazing bytes of the street's desire!

And out of the dark back reaches, through the audience, and out into the flickering reality of the makeshift strobes sauntered—

What the hell—

Cyborg Sally!

Or someone in a fancy foam rubber undersuit and perfect Sally gear who looked just like her, the identity amplified by the freeze-frame poster of the nonexistent rock star mirroring the flesh behind her. The same eyes. The same curve of the nose. The same full twisted lips.

Karen stared at this impossible apparition, entirely transfixed. It couldn't be, and yet it was. And she wasn't even flashing!

But everyone else in the meatrack was. And as . . . Cyborg Sally sat down at the VoxBox console, they poured out onto the dance floor.

Sally Genaro popped out of the flash for a horrid moment in a foul dark cellar crammed with terrifying streeties, zoned into her VoxBox just as if this were the studio in the Factory. She shuddered, she trembled, she felt the Queen of Heat reaching up for her touchpoint to regain command.

Hey, like let me do *this* by myself, okay? she whined with tremulous courage to herself. *I'm* the VoxBox wizard at least!

She put on a throat mike, programmed in a challenging pounding rhythmic sequence, keyed a whole orchestra of jungle drums to it, then laid a bad-ass rock and roll band—guitar, bass, trumpet, electric synth organ—across her keyboard, shadowing the bassline way down in the subsonic, edging the lead guitar with howling peaks way up in the supersonic.

Then, only then, did she willingly surrender her trembling flesh to Cyborg Sally's strong sure wire, hit her touchpoint, and play a random flaring fanfare.

Like the crackle of machine-gun fire fracturing another crystal moment, the first chords shattered the silence, and set the world into sudden swirling motion.

A tide of streeties poured out of the buildings and onto the dance floor. Music she had never heard before poured out of her sparking fingertips onto the keyboard; harsh, and hard, and rocking with the beat of the mean streets she had never known. Words sang themselves through her from the blood-hot wire of the war dancers circling round her, sparking along the flashing circuitries that united them in the burning bytes of their hearts' desire.

Flesh and wire!
Heart's desire!
Throw the world
On my funeral pyre!

Round and round they danced in an ever-widening gyre, round and round round the stage of The American Dream, where she stood in stardom's bright white spotlight, round and round the dance floor of the Glitter Dome, round and round the studio where once she had painfully pined after wimpy Bobby Rubin, round and round the circuit of the tacky little Valley bars, round and round the poor little fat girl, round and round the queen of the street's heat, a vortex of triumphant wire pulling them all through into the eternal dreamtime of Cyborg Sally.

Scream it from your rooftops
In the hard-hearted night!
Dance into the dreamtime
Of my broad daylight!

Oh, yes, she could feel the rage of the streets of lost dreams, of cockroaches scurrying for pitiful scraps at the feet of life's banquet table, of fat girls at the feet of third-rate musicians, of wallflowers at the endless Hollywood party getting slowly drunk at the bar and eyeing the movie stars longingly in secret sidelong glances.

Flesh and wire!
Heart's desire!
Throw their world
On my funeral pyre!

But so too could she feel an enormous power rising up her and through her with the music, the power of that very shared longing and frustration, captured by the stardom of Cyborg Sally and turned outward against the world that had cheated them, and transformed thereby into the instrument of her ultimate triumph. For a vertiginous moment it seemed as if she possessed the power to lead her fans into the dreamtime and never have to come back.

I'm Cyborg Sally
I'm the leader of your pack
Dance along with me
Don't you dare look back
Come along with me
Come as what you are
Every man a king
Every girl a star!

Mucho Muchacho stood proudly in the twilight zone at the edge of the dance floor watching his warriors stamping their feet to the rhythm, dancing faster and faster, sucked deeper and deeper into the frenzied tribal war dance by the battle song of Cyborg Sally.

It was time for the war chief to proclaim his rightful place in the center of the world once more, time for Mucho Muchacho to dance his lordly stompada across the churning dance floor to the silver singer sitting before the altar, time to throw a great protective arm around her and tower triumphantly above her.

The song ended in a final multiplex chorus that segued immediately into an endless raving instrumental break—a frenzied beating of mighty jungle drums, an angry demanding guitar that got under the skin and set the nerves afire, a shrieking trumpet call to battle, a rolling breaker of complex electronics that dissolved reality into the sparkling pixel-field of its bits and bytes.

But when the music finally ended, and he stood there with Cyborg Sally framed by the arch of his arm, his hard commanding eyes gazing in lordly surveillance of the throng of streeties still jamming the dance floor and circling them slowly and ominously to the sounds of unheard music, the warm itch of warrior pride glowing behind his breastbone flashed him back to a previous somatic memory.

Back to a barstool at The American Dream, intimidating the gordo putamadres with his lordly stare as he stood watch over his big time bedbug-dealing momacita.

And when Paco came blinking down out of the dreamtime, chingada, there she was, back in the edge of the twilight zone—Karen, her sad eyes capturing his for a long moment, her face a mask of terror that made him want to wrap his arm around her and be her knight of the streets again and take her home.

But when he started pushing his way through the crowd toward her, she turned and dashed up the cellar stairs, disappearing from view at a dead run.

He paused, hesitated, looked back at Cyborg Sally, now slumped over her VoxBox blinking peculiarly at him, and looking kinda ragged.

She reached up to hit her touchpoint, and her spine stiffened, and she sat up erect, her lips pouting ironically, her eyes pinning his. She crooked a steel finger at him and leered at him with her dagger teeth.

"Dance along with me, don't you dare look back!" she called to him over the heads of her fans, of his street meat army.

Paco hesitated again, turned, looked up the empty staircase, heaved a great sad sigh. Then he hit his touchpoint, and Mucho Muchacho marched back into the dreamtime, back to the head of his warriors, where the Cocko de la Calle belonged, back to the side of Cyborg Sally.

Karen Gold slugged down another gulp of the cheap red wine, still shuddering at the memory. "You had to see it," she said. "Everyone in the place must have been out there on the dance floor, plugged in all together and dancing like zombies to—"

"Cyborg Sally?" Leslie Savanah said. "Come on, Karen, so

maybe it's all over with you and Paco, but you're not really telling us that the Other Woman is *Cyborg Sally*!''

''I know what I saw!'' Karen snapped shrilly. ''I saw someone who looked exactly like the AP on the disc, and I saw hundreds of people who sure as shit thought they saw her too, and I saw them dancing round and round in a trance even after the song ended, and—''

She sat bolt upright at the big kitchen table as the realization hit her.

''And it was a different song!'' she exclaimed. ''It was the voice of Cyborg Sally singing something I had never heard before! And it was full of rage and hate and—''

''And you *still* insist you weren't flashing?'' Malcolm McGee scoffed.

''You really think I'd be stupid enough to flash in a place like that all by myself? It was *terrifying,* Malcolm, it was like some awful voodoo ceremony. I mean wherever those people all were, they were all there together, and she had them hypnotized, and I think if she had pointed her finger at me and told them to get me, they would've torn me apart! You think I was about to flash on that? And Paco . . . Jesus, Paco . . .''

''What about Paco, Karen?'' Larry Coopersmith said sharply in that ''Markowitz'' voice he seemed to be using now whenever he was flashing, which was starting to be most of the time.

When she had come bursting into the loft babbling perhaps not too coherently about what she had seen at Slimy Mary's, Malcolm and Tommy had tried to calm her down as if she had had a bad wire flash, and Leslie had been gossiply sympathetic about the inevitable discovery of Paco's Other Woman.

But Coopersmith, or Markowitz, or whoever he thought he was by now, had just sat there chain-smoking and chain-tapping, and nodding his head approvingly as she had tried to make them understand that she had seen and heard the impossible, that she had watched a cellarful of streeties merging into something whose objective reality was irrelevant, something angry and hungry coalescing out of the dreamtime darkness and into the world before her very eyes.

''Paco was the scariest thing, Larry,'' she said. ''You should have seen him! He had his arm around this goddamn robot monster, or whatever it was, like he owned her, like he was sucking current right from her wire. They were all so far gone they would've done anything he told them to, and he looked like he was ready to lead them out in the streets to take on the world!''

''Maybe he should,'' Markowitz said.

''What?''

''Do *what,* Larry?'' Leslie drawled.

''Just what Karen said, lead the masses out into the street to take on the world,'' Markowitz said. He laughed maniacally. ''Red ripe anarchy for all the world to see, what else can a good revolutionary do?''

''Are you out of your mind, Larry?'' Karen cried. ''You want Paco to lead a rat-pack of streeties into some Zone so the zonies can chop them to pieces with their Uzis?''

''I'm not talking about marching the masses into the street to be uselessly slaughtered,'' Markowitz said. ''I'm talking about marching them out onto *television,* where they really *can* take on Official Reality and win!''

''Say what?'' Malcolm said slowly. But he hunched forward, supporting his head in his hands and his elbows on the tabletop, hit his touchpoint, and he gave Markowitz his rapt attention.

''I've been going crazy ever since Paco got the doorman's job at The American Dream,'' Markowitz said. ''I even talked to Paco about it. I mean, here we had our man controlling the door to the meatrack where MUZIK does a live national broadcast every week, and I couldn't figure out how to do jack-shit with it.''

He swept a conspiratorial smile over Leslie and Malcolm and Tommy, over Eddie and Iva, who had been drawn away from their consoles by the beginning of this wirehead Markowitz rap.

All of them had hit their touchpoints and were sucking this babble up.

''But now . . .''

Markowitz let the words hang in the succeeding hush as Teddy Ribero also joined his revolutionary circle-jerk.

''But now what, Larry?'' Teddy finally said.

''But now we have our Che!'' Markowitz said. ''He's got a street army in the faevelas and he's also the captain of the guard at the presidential palace! He's Mr. Outside and Mr. Inside all rolled into one!''

''En inglés, por favor,'' Teddy said dryly.

''Look, Paco's supposed to let two hundred streeties a night into The American Dream, right, his choice, anyone he wants to.

So what's to stop him from packing the joint with his own people?"

"Are you really saying what I think you're saying, Larry?" Karen exclaimed in incredulous horror.

"How many zonies can they have in there? What can they do, fire into a crowd in front of their own television cameras?"

"This is insane!"

"We block the exit. We surround the stage. And we refuse to leave until they give us half an hour of airtime."

"They'll call in city riot troops and take the place by force first!"

"Everyone on the floor will be our hostages."

"They'll starve us out."

"We could tell them we have a bomb and they wouldn't dare call our bluff over a few mil worth of airtime."

"Jesus Christ, it sounds bugfuck, Larry," Malcolm said, "but it just might work. . . ."

"*Work?*" Karen cried. "We'd all end up in jail for sure unless you got us killed! And for *what*?"

"For what!" Markowitz exclaimed, bolting to his feet and into full arm-waving declamation. "To liberate MUZIK from Official Reality for half an hour and turn it against the system! To show the people themselves on the national network feed! To bring red-ripe anarchy a-rockin' back live on the tube! To push on the lever that moves the *world* and feel the motherfucker *move*!"

"Wonderful, Larry, we all get busted so you can make a speech on tv," Karen moaned.

"Who said anything about a speech?" Larry Coopersmith said, blinking, in quite another voice.

"Then what did you have in mind?"

"What did I have in mind . . . ?" Coopersmith muttered, frowning in concentration. He fished out a cigarette, lit it, and tapped his touchpoint in a choreographed sequence of automatic motions.

"What if Ronald McDonald suddenly announced he was becoming a vegetarian on the tube!" he fairly cackled in his Markowitz voice. "What if Smokey the Bear turned into a giggling pyromaniac before their very eyes? What if they saw the American Eagle devour the Easter Bunny? What if Uncle Sam did a dingo act on the evening news with his cock hanging out?"

He paused to let the laughter blow by him with a shit-eating grin, but when he spoke again, he was deadly serious.

"What if *Cyborg Sally,* their nonexistent sex machine, defected to *us* on the air? Think of it, their own creature joins the Reality Liberation Front before millions of viewers!"

"You are a crazy man, Markowitz," Malcolm said admiringly.

"Hey, we could play the audiovisual track off one of our Red Jack discs too, we could put Red Jack back on MUZIK!" Teddy exclaimed.

"We'd give you five minutes to make a speech too, if you can hold it down to that, wouldn't we, guys?" Leslie said magnanimously.

"Hey, maybe if we're good, they'll pick up our option!"

Karen just sat there listening to them chain-tapping every time they came back to reality and talking themselves into this insanity.

Even watching them hit their touchpoints compulsively like the rats in the pleasure center experiments Larry, ironically enough, had once warned them about, she could hardly believe that they were serious.

But then, flashing or straight, none of them had seen what she had seen. None of them had seen that obsidian gleam in Paco's eyes as his jungle warriors whipped themselves into a frenzy to words and music none of them had heard either. None of them had felt that angry energy burning its way out of the darkness.

"You can't do this, Larry," Karen finally insisted loudly. "You don't know what you're playing with!"

Everyone fell silent. Markowitz fixed her with his bright blue gaze as he slowly seated himself back at the table across from her. "Then tell us, Karen," he said. "Have I missed something? Where's the hole in the plan if you see one?"

Karen opened her mouth to speak. Nothing came out. Nothing came into her head either. She threw up her hands in frustration. "You have no idea of what's going on down there," she said, "and I don't know how to tell you. You just didn't see it, you didn't feel it, you didn't—"

"You're right!" Markowitz exclaimed. "Let's all go on down to Slimy Mary's tomorrow night and catch the show!"

"Yeah, what'd you say it cost, Karen, a hundred bucks to get in?"

"Maybe we can get ourselves freebies."

"No way!" Karen shouted.

"Come on Karen, what can happen?"

"Nothing I even want to think about . . ."

But she couldn't help thinking about it. She couldn't help remembering the last time she had looked into Paco's eyes, the last time she had seen him look into hers. For a moment there, she had seen her white knight of the streets, her lost little boy, still in there somewhere, looking back at her from within the angry mask of the streetie war chief.

"With you or without you," Markowitz said. "Your choice."

One by one, Karen looked into the wirehead eyes of the only friends she really had in the world. One by one they looked back and told her what she already knew.

She sighed. She shrugged. "With me," she said wanly. "When it comes down to it, I guess I can't just turn my back and walk away."

THE MAGICAL MYSTERY TOUR

"Shit, Glorianna, this has been a blast, but it's getting us nowhere!" Bobby Rubin said torpidly, lifting his snifter to his lips to mask a gross liquid belch, then taking another sip of his second after-dinner cognac, hoping it would help dissolve the immense rich meal that lay gurgling heavily in his belly.

"Nowhere?" Glorianna O'Toole said in mock righteous indignation. "Hell luv, we've been just about *everywhere* that is *anywhere*!"

Bobby couldn't help grinning weakly despite his dire circumstances, a psychic posture that had become almost a habit. Glorianna might have turned out to be a total bust as his savior, but the Crazy Old Lady of Rock and Roll had certainly given him a first class education in going out in style.

She had taken one disdainful look at the suite he had rented for her at the Union Square Pavilion—a clone of his own accommodations—and summoned the manager forthwith. "We want to see the top suite in this joint, sonny," she told that worthy. "These broom closets are for peasants."

"Perhaps you might find the Imperial Penthouse more suitable, madam," the manager said icily, curling his lip at her dubiously as he measured her bank balance with an experienced eye. "Of course you might find it a wee bit *pricy*, it *does* go for twelve thousand a—"

"We're on an unlimited expense account," Glorianna told him airily, and his attitude improved instantly. Nodding and smiling unctuously, he personally ushered them to the top floor of the hotel and into a penthouse suite bigger than Bobby's house in Beverly Glen.

There were two gigantic bedrooms, each with a big round water bed suitable for a major orgy and a private bath with Jacuzzi, Japanese-style wooden hot tub, and intimate little sauna. The monster living room between had a huge sunken conversation pit, antique Chinese divans and tables, two of the biggest Persian rugs Bobby had ever seen, a wall of leather-bound books, potted palms, rubber trees, and a big saltwater aquarium, all under a greenhouse dome. Sliding doors opened out onto a formal Japanese garden overlooking the city. There was a small heated swimming pool lined with blue Delft tiles.

Bobby wandered around the suite with his eyes bugged out and his mouth hanging open. Glorianna poked at this and that disdainfully as if she had been accustomed to such luxury from birth.

"Well, the pool isn't exactly Olympic class, is it?" she drawled at the manager. "But I guess it'll have to do. We'll take it."

No sooner had the bellmen moved them into their bedrooms than Glorianna was on the phone calling dealers. Within the hour a sleazy character had arrived with three ounces of designer dust. "Should hold us for a few days," Glorianna opined after she had snorted up half a dozen lines as an appetizer. "Time for supper!"

So it began, and so it continued.

Dinners and lunches in restaurants so expensive that the house wine went for $400 a bottle. Eggs Benedict and caviar omelets from room service for breakfast, washed down with a bottle of French champagne. Unreal shopping forays up and down Fifth Avenue by Rolls limousine, with Glorianna even persuading Bobby to spruce up his tacky wardrobe. "*Front,* kiddo, we need *front* if we're gonna make ourselves really conspicuous in *this* town!"

And so they did, making the grand tour of New York's plushest meatracks, fanciest nightclubs, most exclusive private casino clubs, swankest saloons; five or six of them a night, without ever hitting the same place twice.

Glorianna bought drink after drink for chance acquaintances, she sent bottles of Dom Pérignon to random tables, she laid out mountains of dust, so that if she really didn't know everybody in these joints, she certainly made everybody pretend that they knew *her,* to the point that after three nights of these rounds, their reputation for largesse, their names, and even their mission, preceded them.

At every stop they showed around pictures of Sally Genaro like sleazy private eyes in some silly novel, offering a pound of primo dust for information leading to, and generously spreading around gram-sized sample packets as bona fides of their seriousness.

No one had really seen Sally from the Valley, though plenty of dust hounds tried to pretend they had. There were some weird third- and fourth-hand rumors going around about some streetie Cyborg Sally imitator doing her act in the ruins, but of course none of the denizens of these environs would venture into streetie turf without an armored personnel carrier, and that bullshit, like all the rest of the false leads people tried to sell them, went nowhere.

Of course they *did* get themselves invited to dozens of private parties in town houses and fancy apartments. They met tv stars and dust dealers and music business executives and stockbrokers and gallery artists and musicians and yaks and mafs and club owners. They tripped the lite fantastic.

It was exhilarating but also weirdly frustrating for Bobby, and not just because time was running out without any real lead to the whereabouts of Sally Genaro.

In these circles, dauntingly beautiful women were as much part of the decor as they were at Hollywood A parties. But here, thanks to Glorianna's and Bobby's ever-spreading reputation for tossing freebie dust around as if it were going out of style, far from holding themselves unapproachable to the likes of Bobby Rubin, they eyed him greedily at bars, displayed themselves provocatively to him on the dance floor, swarmed all over him like ants around the honey pot.

Yet somehow Bobby never made a move on any of them. He couldn't quite understand why. True, Glorianna whipped them around from club to club, party to party, with dizzying speed, but surely he could have scored on the fly under these circumstances if he tried, or even if he just let it happen.

But he didn't. Somehow, the idea of taking one of these eminently available beauties back to the hotel suite he shared with Glorianna unmanned him.

Well, not exactly. He certainly found himself walking around with a permanent hard-on, and he didn't really believe that having Glorianna two closed doors away would really prevent him from doing anything with it. Nor did he imagine that

Glorianna herself would be *jealous* or do anything to spoil his fun; she was, after all, literally old enough to be his grandmother.

Yet somehow her presence *was* keeping him celibate. Glorianna O'Toole might indeed be old enough to be his grandmother, but he had never met a granny who could boogie like the Crazy Old Lady of Rock and Roll!

She might not retain anything Bobby could recognize as sex appeal, but, energized by dust and glorified by money, she certainly had a charisma that made the cookie cutter beauties seem pallid by comparison. She dressed flamboyantly, she carried herself like a rock star, she knew how to dominate a room just by walking into it, and old lady or not, she could easily dance, drink, and snort him under the table.

She was obviously the senior member of this duo in more than age. She was the one who knew who was who and where was in, she was the one who made grand entrances, she did most of the talking, and indeed, from the looks he got, Bobby could tell that many of the people they met assumed that he was her pet gigolo, that *he* was riding *her* gravy train in return for his sexual favors.

No one had ever taken him for a male hooker before; far from feeling put down by this assumption, he found himself getting a nice little down and dirty thrill off it.

If only Glorianna were forty years younger, if only Nicholas West weren't going to pull the plug on this glorious expense account cakewalk, if only he weren't facing the joint at the impending end of this fantasy, he would have been in hog heaven.

Bobby sighed and gulped down the rest of his cognac, grimacing as it sent a trail of sour fire down his throat and into his churning stomach.

Alas, Glorianna *was* an old lady, West *was* going to throw him in the joint, he *did* have less than a week to save his ass, and all this glorious partying *was* getting them nowhere.

"What's the matter, Bobby?" Glorianna said. "You look like shit."

"Aw Glorianna, it's been fun, but, I mean, how much fun am I going to have in jail? We've got to get *serious*."

Glorianna O'Toole held up her snifter, swirled the brown liquid in it reflectively, and studied him with quite a harder expression.

"What did you have in mind?" she asked.

Bobby shrugged miserably.

"How serious are you willing to get?" Glorianna said coldly.

"What do you mean, how serious am I willing to get?" Bobby snapped. "My life's on the line! How much more serious *can* it get?"

"Depends on how far you're willing to go," she said. "I mean, you could go up to the diamond center tomorrow, load yourself up with as many jewels as you can carry, and split for someplace where they can't extradite you. Brazil. Angola. Maybe even Switzerland."

"Jesus Christ!"

Glorianna grinned at him mirthlessly. "Okay, so we've established that you don't have what it takes to be an expatriate on the run. Question is, are you willing to try something just a little less drastic?"

"Which is?"

"The magical mystery tour."

"The what?"

Glorianna fortified herself with a sip of cognac. "Look," she said, "partly this has been just a great big freebie ride, but we *have* learned something in the process."

"We have? What?"

"No one who is anyone has seen Sally Genaro. She isn't anywhere that is *anywhere*. Meaning that she must be out there in nowhere with the nobodies who are everybody."

"Meaning what, Glorianna?"

"Meaning *this* is the only shot we've got left, kiddo, if you've got the balls to try it," Glorianna O'Toole said, laying her brand-new purse on the peach-colored tablecloth.

It was a big bag she had bought in Soho for $3000; solid silver clasp, black silk fabric covered with turquoise and amber beadwork in a stylized sunburst design.

She opened the clasp, held the bag open, and thrust it into Bobby's face.

Inside, amidst the cosmetics and compact and wallet and packets of dust, were two crumpled Jacks and a chrome-plated pistol.

"According to you, she was convinced she was Cyborg Sally when you lost her, right?" Glorianna said. "Meaning she had to have been jacked, right? Can you guess what I'm thinking?"

Bobby looked from the contents of the bag to Glorianna's eyes and back again. He shuddered. He snapped the thing shut and pushed it back at her. But he nodded his head just the same.

"She's still flashing . . ." he muttered miserably. "She's out there somewhere—"

"—in her own dreamtime. Maybe there *is* something behind that bullshit about a streetie Cyborg Sally imitator. Maybe it *is* our little Sally out there somewhere, spaced out of her mind and swimming like a wirehead Maofish in the sea of the street people. Where no Hollywood expense account hotshots like thee and me can hope to find her. We've had our fun finding that out, now haven't we? Time to give up, or get serious, Bobby. Time for the magical mystery tour of the down and dirty. Time to get crazy."

"You mean what I think you mean? Plug in and wander around *outside the Zones* in the middle of the night jacked out of our minds? That's why the gun?"

Glorianna nodded. "I said get crazy, not get stupid."

"And that *isn't* stupid?"

Glorianna smiled at him. "You got any better idea?" she said. "For that matter, you got any other idea at all?"

Bobby Rubin studied the wrinkled skin and the gray hair of the Crazy Old Lady of Rock and Roll.

She *was* old, and this sure as shit *was* crazy, but the bright green eyes that looked back at him with manic serenity seemed to belong to another face; younger and braver in that moment than he had ever imagined he himself could ever be. He loved those eyes in that moment, he envied them something he couldn't understand, even as they shamed him.

"You'd do this for me, Glorianna . . . ?" he said softly.

"Don't get sloppy on me kiddo," she said just as softly.

"Don't bullshit me, Glorianna, you've got nothing to gain, you're putting your ass on the line for me. . . ."

Glorianna shrugged. "Maybe you remind me of somebody I once knew and would like to meet again before I go out rockin' . . ." she mused. She put on a cynical smirk.

"Aw, that's bullshit too," she said in a much airier tone of voice. "Let's just say I'm doing it for fun. They don't call me the Crazy Old Lady of Rock and Roll for nothing, sonny!"

"You know, if you were forty years younger . . ."

Glorianna O'Toole curled her upper lip disdainfully. "Don't flatter yourself too far," she said. "If I were forty years younger, I wouldn't look at a kid like you twice!"

* * *

Karen Gold was rather pleasantly surprised when the RLF finally managed to arrive at Slimy Mary's without any untoward incident.

It was a clear balmy night, and so rather than pile into cabs, the entire Reality Liberation Front, all ten of them, had decided to walk from the loft to Slimy Mary's.

It had started innocently enough, with the RLF marching three and four abreast east on an empty side street, but when they turned the corner onto West Broadway and started scattering nervous solid citizens before them, one by one they started hitting their touchpoints, and by the time they reached Houston, they were all chain-tapping and having a high old time playing urban guerilla band, marching in exaggerated cadence, and causing more than one paranoid zonie to tighten his grip on his Uzi.

Unlike the rest of them, Karen found it anything but amusing when they sent streeties scattering into the shadows of the ruined buildings along Avenue D, nor was the unruly crowd of streeties outside the meatrack exactly pleased when Markowitz, who by this time probably thought he was Che, marched his troops straight through them to the head of the line.

She was mightily relieved to see that Dojo himself was on the door as the streeties flowed forward to surround them like an angry amoeba.

"Who you think you are, motherfuckers?"

"Back of the line, cocksuckers!"

"Fuckin' assholes!"

"Cool it, or nobody gets in!" Dojo roared, folding his arms commandingly across his chest before the ugliness could get beyond the verbal. "What the fuck is this, Larry?" he demanded righteously of Coopersmith for the benefit of what was on the edge of turning into a lynch mob.

"The Reality Liberation Front!" Markowitz announced grandly. "We're here to recruit Cyborg Sally."

The streeties crowded even closer, but the muttering assumed a more respectful speculative tone. Apparently the RLF still had something of a rep from the good old days of Red Jack, and, from the relatively prosperous look of many of them, there were streeties here who had lined their pockets with the RLF's bedbug discs and People's Cash Machines.

Dojo frowned ominously. "Cyborg Sally has an exclusive deal with me," he said. "She ain't going nowhere."

"All we want to do is borrow her for a tv commercial," Markowitz told him. "It'll be good for your business."

"Say what?"

"We'll talk about it later," Markowitz said. "Right now, we just want to catch her act. Are we on your freebie list?"

Dojo scanned the crowd nervously, and just snorted. Markowitz nodded his understanding, shrugged, fished out his wallet, handed him five two hundreds, and shooed his troops past the doorman and down the stairs.

The cellar was packed wall to wall with people. They were jammed together shoulder to shoulder on every available seat. They squatted in a solid mass all around the dance floor and into the twilight zone. They stood in solid ranks all the way back into the deep darkness beyond. The heat was horrific. The sweaty stench was overwhelming.

A low guttural murmuring surged and growled around the packed room like a heavy sea rolling against a rocky coast on the leading edge of an impending storm. Hungry eyes stared expectantly at the empty dance floor, the dead video screen, the silent VoxBox console waiting like an altar for the ceremony to begin.

"God, can you feel it?" Markowitz said dreamily as they all stood at the rear of the mob just inward of the staircase, unable to penetrate any farther. "Feel the power of the people, its hour come round at last, rising from the tar pits of history to be reborn!"

Jacks were displayed on every head, and hands reached up to chain-tap back into the flash the moment anyone popped out. Malcolm, Leslie, Tommy, Larry himself, all of them, stood there chain-tapping like the streeties too, staring at the empty makeshift stage, mesmerized by their wire, by the flickering lights, by the anticipation of what was to come.

Karen shuddered. Nothing in the world could have made her hit her touchpoint now, nothing could have made her willingly warp herself further into *this* collective dreamtime.

She could feel the power, all right. She could see it in all those fever-bright eyes fixed on a single focus. She could hear it with her stomach in the deep threatening collective mantric murmur. She could smell the heat and sour sweat and ozone expectancy rising miasmically off all that angry meat.

Then there was a stirring in the crowd and a sudden rise in the noise level emanating from somewhere in the rear way across the room. The murmuring grew louder, grew rhythmic, found words, became a foot-pounding, roaring chant—

Cyborg Sally!
Flesh and wire!
Queen of Meat!
Funeral pyre!

—as Paco and Cyborg Sally, hand in hand, slowly made their way through the chanting crowd to the strobing cube of light encompassing the dance floor.

Cyborg Sally's violet Medusa crown flashed and writhed in the darkness, casting flickering highlights over her sinewy silver flesh. Paco's face was a cruel Aztec mask glowing bronze in her reflected light, the wire webwork of his Jack glinting and glimmering, his eyes shimmering with purple phosphorescence like a cat out of the jungle night.

He let go of her hand and strode ahead into the rectangle of bright light, and stood there with his hands on his hips, basking in the awful chanting like some cannibal war god.

"Queen of our meat! Flesh of our wire!" he shouted.

"BURN DOWN THE WORLD ON HER FUNERAL PYRE!" howled the massed voice of the raging streets as Cyborg Sally, preening and prancing, snarling silver daggers, emerged from the darkness into the blood-hot light.

"Well, what do you say, kiddo, are you ready?" Glorianna O'Toole said as she and Bobby Rubin crossed Twelfth Street headed south on Broadway.

Bobby managed a weak little smile. "You're the tour guide, grandma," he said with shrug. "You've got the pistol. . . ."

"And I'll use it on the next motherfucker calls me *grandma*, you better believe it, sonny," Glorianna snapped back in mock anger.

"The name is *Bobby*, Glorianna, and the next person that calls me sonny or kiddo is a dirty old lady!"

Glorianna laughed. "Takes one to know one she smiled," she sang at him, and put her hands in her back pockets, Bette Davis style.

Fuck a duck, but she felt juicier and feistier than she had in a decade or two, and she wasn't even flashing yet!

She had insisted they go back to the hotel to change costumes, and now she was wearing a loose black blouse, matching running shoes, and antique bell-bottom jeans with a pistol in the right front pocket.

What was more, she also wore an ancient blue denim vest that had been given to her as a secret love gift decades ago—Hell's Angels colors, which she really had no right to possess by their old code, let alone presume to flaunt in public.

But the Angels were long gone now, busted and disbanded by the feds for dope-dealing years ago, no initiated Angel dared to put on the colors these days, and so she had a feeling that the shades of the tribe would only smile to see even a Crazy Old Lady carrying them into one final run in the dreamtime. And if Lou the Jew was still alive, she felt reasonably certain that the hard-hog mother would just give her a great big wink and goose if he could see her now.

What he would say if he saw the last colors-bearer of the Angels trooping into battle with the likes of Bobby, however, would probably melt the poor kid's ears.

Then again, just maybe not.

Against his moaning protests, she had given his hair a crude Red Jack dye-job. "I've got the piece, Tonto," she had insisted, "so the least we can do for you is give you the war paint."

She had dressed him in blue jeans, gunmetal boots, a Red Jack T-shirt, and an open black jacket with the collar turned up. If it wasn't exactly Red Jack's mirror suit, at least it was the right silhouette. If his hair wasn't quite long enough and she hadn't been up to giving it a white webwork frosting, he *was* wearing the piece of wire it was designed to simulate in the first place, and that *was* Red Jack's face looking out at the world from beneath the half-assed hairdo.

With a little bit of luck it just might fool a wirehead who wanted to be fooled if it came down to the nitty gritty. With a little bit more, and a little bit of help from his friends, he just might be able to fool himself.

Indeed, Bobby *was* starting to wear the persona a little now, walking up on the balls of his feet, popping his shoulders back out of his usual slouch, and feisty enough to come back at her when she gave him mouth.

Glorianna caught him by the arm as they reached the corner of Broadway and Eleventh. "Good a place as any to break on through to the other side," she told him as she hit her touchpoint.

They were smack in the middle of one of the biggest and

plushest Zones of Manhattan. It was all glitz and glitter and zonies and monstrously expensive condos and lofts north all the way to Twenty-third, south to the fringes of Chinatown, west to the river, and east to Tompkins Square Park. Indeed, they were just about in the geographic center of the territory they had been fruitlessly searching all along.

"Better than most, come to think of it," she said as she stood there flaunting her old Angels colors and peering back over her shoulder through space and time.

For she was seeing this pivot point as it had been in another era, when a young singer from California had first wandered wide-eyed down these streets stoned out of her mind. A pistol in your pocket would have been a good friend to have back then in this borderland between the West Village, where she was singing for pass-the-hat, and the roach-infested crash pads of the East Village hippie quarter.

A few blocks south and west along these dark and ominous warehouse streets was Washington Square Park and the Macdougal Street circus and the safety of crowd and light, but just as close was a Bowery full of bums and savage junkies, and the jagged jangly streets of the old East Village, where at any moment it could be hippie don't let the sun set on you here.

And if this was the high rent district these days, with gourmet cheese shops and fancy bars six to a block and a zonie on every corner, still some karmic ghost lingered, for there were blocks of ruined buildings in the Far East now that made the old East Village seem like Park Avenue, and there were ten times as many people living on the streets on ten times less money, and if the borderline had been pushed eastward, the rift between the two worlds was deeper and wider and sharper than ever it had been before.

And if a spaced-out young musician fresh from California and dressed as conspicuously as an archbishop in a whorehouse had succeeded in disappearing into the shadows of the city, there was only one direction she could have traveled from the place where they stood now.

"Come on," she told Bobby Rubin as he hit his touchpoint, tugging at his arm. "We're going east, young man!"

"East? But that's—"

"Back to the basics, back to the jungle," she sang at him, "where the natives are restless and the stone walls crumble."

Flesh and wire
Heart's desire
Give the world
To my funeral pyre!

Cyborg Sally screamed it out through multiplexed voiceprint parameters; a roaring martial chorus doubled an octave down into the subsonic, a shrieking of near supersonic pain like a thousand robot cats being fed through a tree chipper, her own mighty lead voice riding above it at tooth-rattling volume, her once mortal flesh singing, triumphant and transformed, through her blood-hot wire.

Rhythms looping within rhythms looping within rhythms, the drumlines she had programmed seemed to have taken on a life of their own, congas and booming basses, machine-gun snares and synthesized explosions, egging each other on in the hard-hearted night.

She had laid so many instrumental voices across her keyboard—howling guitars, keening synth voices, battle trumpets, contorted waveform envelopes, static serpent hisses—that as her fingers danced across the keys *they* seemed to be playing *her*, dissolving the interface between the music and the instrumentalities of the bits and the bytes.

Down from the rooftops!
Out of your holes!
Dance to the music
Of your motherfucking souls!

And they did.

Out into the dance floor they shambled, down from the ruined buildings they scrambled, out of a thousand tacky Valley bars and through the bright clean shopping malls they danced behind a pimply little fat girl down on her knees before third-rate musicians, up through the levels of the Muzik Factory to the president's office, out onto the dance floor of the Glitter Dome, up into the bright white light crowning the stage of The American Dream.

Puke at where we came from
But look at who we are!
Every man a king!
Every girl a star!

Glorianna led Bobby east along Eleventh Street, past blocks of condo high-rises, converted loft buildings, renovated tenements, down Second Avenue, with its bars and restaurants, its saloons and gourmet groceries, to St. Mark's Place, the main crosstown street leading eastward through the storefront aisle of low renovated apartment buildings to dead-end at the Avenue A border of Tompkins Square Park.

Second Avenue was crowded with the young princes and princesses of the city strolling from saloon to meatrack in their fancy finery, or rather, he began to perceive, with alter egos of the Bobby Rubin that would have been, were it not for rock and roll.

Software designers and junior executives, minor civil servants and ad copy writers, bank tellers and data pushers, beavering away at their nine-to-fivers, living three and four to a condo and worse, all for the illusion of being able to walk down this street on a warm summer's night and deem themselves true New Yorkers, Manhattanites, citizens of the center of Where It Was At.

"Nose to the grindstone, balls to the wall, gotcha either way before you learn to crawl," he sang out half under his breath, and only then, hearing himself, did he realize that he had already crossed over, that during this passage poor little Bobby Rubin had become the third person, that a soul had wakened from its starving sleep.

Glorianna O'Toole squeezed his hand and smiled at him as they crossed Second Avenue. "You've been standing here beside me, just where you've always been," she sang at him.

And he was, now wasn't he? he realized, seeing the two of them through the eyes of the Second Avenue trendies.

Not a nerdy little wimp and a gray-haired granny, but an intrusion from another rockin' reality; a dynamic duo, a pair of streetwise bad-asses, the Crazy Lady and the Crown Prince of Rock and Roll, flashing their freedom in the middle of the night.

Glorianna laughed and nodded as they walked ever eastward on St. Mark's, as strollers eyed them warily and stepped aside, as a zonie studied them narrowly and tightened his grip on his piece, as they moved together to the bopping rhythm of the streets.

Her long red hair whipped around her shoulders as she tossed her head and sung out a long whoo-ee just for the hell of it, and her sparkling green eyes were agelessly young in her solarized face, and somewhere an electric guitar burned down their bridges in the bloodred night.

"This may all be bits and bytes and programs, lady," Red Jack sang at her, "but baby, we ain't Mr. Clean!"

"Fuckin'-A!" shouted the Crazy Old Lady of Rock and Roll to the scandalization of the sidewalk audience.

Flashin' dancin' like liberty
In the home of the brave and the land of the free!

They sashayed east on St. Mark's, singing in unison, happily freaking out the citizens.

Scream it out from the rooftops
In the hard-hearted night!
We got the world by the balls
And it's time to bite!

Karen Gold, giddy with the sweaty stink of her own terror, had her back quite literally to the wall. She could no longer see the crazed creature pounding out the raving instrumentals on her VoxBox and shrieking out the demented lyrics through her vocoder circuitries with the multiplexed voice of a wirehead lynch mob over the dancing bodies of that selfsame human pack.

They crowded around Cyborg Sally hip to hip and shoulder to shoulder on the dance floor, swaying and circling with their heads thrown back, and their eyes rolling sightlessly, twitching and jerking like worshippers possessed by the voodoo gods. They danced in tight spastic patterns through the rude furniture of the twilight zone, kicking over crates, couches, cable spool tables, moaning, howling, stomping their feet.

I'm Cyborg Sally
I'm the leader of your pack
Dance along with me
Don't you dare look back!

Even as she had found herself inching backward step by step without conscious thought until her back was against the wall, Karen had watched Larry and Leslie, Malcolm and Tommy, Bill and Iva, all of them, oozing forward in a dancing, flashing daze, surrendering their selves to the raging group mind coalescing to the music, schooling with the rest of the piranhas in the feeding frenzy of these darkened depths.

She couldn't even pick any of them out anymore. Indeed, there seemed to be no sense of human individuality left anywhere in this terrible place. Even the song of Cyborg Sally, multiplexed, filtered, augmented, transmogrified through the arcane machineries, seemed sung in the collective voice of the multitude itself.

Come along with me
Come as what you are
Every man a king
Every girl a star!

Pressed against the wall by a solid crush of writhing bodies, never had she felt more alone in her life.

Flesh and wire!
Blood-hot fire!
Burn down your bridges
On my funeral pyre!

Trembling, she began to ooze her way along the wall toward the stairs, toward an exit that seemed a million miles away.

Bend your back, to the basics
Bend your back to the jungle
Where the natives are restless
And the stone walls crumble....

Or anyway a Disney-version jungle, Glorianna O'Toole thought, singing it out with a certain sardonic edge as she popped out of the time-warped dreamtime into the present of Tompkins Square Park.

The crumbling roach-infested tenements that had once surrounded the park had long since been renovated into plushie-tushie town houses or low-rise condos, or replaced by primo high-rise developers' money-machines for house-poor trendies. Golden glow-globes set high on lampposts at regular intervals illuminated the park in a seamless pool of security light where once feral junkies had lurked in every shadow. Armed zonies were everywhere where once any sane cop feared to tread.

Time was only dealers and street gangs and whacked-out junkies dared cross Tompkins Square after the sun was well down, but now the park was thronged with well-dressed strollers—young couples, singles on the make, even the occasional babe in arms—meat for the monsters in the good old days.

The Disney version, all right, Glorianna thought sourly, and yet . . . and yet . . .

And yet, as she reached up to tap back into it, some subliminal music told her that the old spirit lingered just below the sanitized surface, that the living ghosts of the East Village past still haunted Tompkins Square Park in plain sight of streetwise eyes.

A hooker in a tight Cyborg Sally T-shirt and lacquered purple hair making a quick deal with a middle-aged john in a fancy white safari suit. A skinny kid in another Sally T-shirt, his shaved head openly displaying the wire of the Jack, hunched over on a bench, staring off into another world, clenching and unclenching his hand over and over around a glassine envelope of dust. A girl in a Sally wig slipping a piece of wire to a guy in a radically tailored seersucker suit.

There were, in fact, when you put it all together, scores of streetie infiltrators all throughout the park, peddling dust, wire, speed, and their own asses right under the eyes of the zonies. Fuck a duck, there was one slipping a packet of dust *to* a zonie!

Glorianna smiled beatifically. About the only thing that had really changed was that the borders of tight white asshole had been pushed farther east, so that Tompkins Square Park, former urban jungle, had now become a border zone, where the inhabitants of the town houses and condos could chip at some street action and feel that they were hip under the watchful eyes of their own zonies.

Oh yeah, you could push it from North Beach to the Haight, from Washington Square Park to the garbage docks, from Selma to Franklin, from Coconut Grove to Katmandu, but the eternal floating flea market of the Street would always be out there somewhere, getting ready for the hanging, painting the passports brown, and dancin' and dealing to the stony rhythm of a bad-ass guitar.

But *this* street-dealing scene was dancin' with Mr. D. Far-off drums pounded black vibes out of the east. You could feel his current girlfriend pounding it out on her VoxBox in some cellar out there and you could see her dagger snarl everywhere.

A couple slouching down the path with hooded eyes. A dealer leaning against a lamppost. A rubber-wigged hooker slipping her hand inside the belt of a john.

Streeties with silver-painted teeth. Streeties with hungry glowing eyes, looking back to the basics, back to the jungle, restless natives waiting for the stone walls to crumble . . .

And leering out at the world from their cheap promo T-shirts, that angry thwarted face, that stainless steel sex machine with Sally Genaro's eyes, shrieking out the angry blood-hot rhythm of a vengeful marching song.

Cyborg Sally!
Flesh and wire!
Queen of Heat!
Electric fire!
Blazing bytes!
Meat's desire!

"I hear a bad moon a-risin'," Glorianna O'Toole sung softly.

"Huh?"

Bobby Rubin stood there squinting at her in owlish befuddlement from under Red Jack's long flowing hair.

"Don't you feel it, Jack, can't you hear that east wind howl?"

He glanced around nervously, moaned under his breath, eyed her narrowly.

Glorianna realized that Red Jack was not at home right now, that poor little Bobby had come down out of the dreamtime to find that he had followed a space cadet out into the deepest streetie barrio, or so at least the poor innocent thought.

"Stop lookin' at me like I was crazy!"

"*Aren't* you?"

"Fuckin'-A I am, sonny!" she told him, stabbing his touchpoint with an imperious finger. "And if we're gonna follow this scent where the trail leads us and not get eaten by the alligators in the process, kiddo, you'd better stay crazy too!"

She grabbed him by the hand and danced him toward the drums of Cyborg Sally, the down and dirty beat rising from the eastern jungle.

The natives are restless. . . .

Watch the stone walls crumble.

* * *

The song disintegrated into a final jagged instrumental shout of ear-killing white noise as Karen Gold finally reached the cellar stairs, dying away into a sudden sinisterly unresolved silence as she mounted them.

A low guttural murmuring quickly rising into a roar of rage made her look back over her shoulder, and what she saw froze her in place.

Cyborg Sally sat slumped behind her VoxBox hyperventilating in ragged gasps, her arms hanging limply from her shoulders. Beads of oily silver sweat rolled slowly down her face, leaving pinkish trails in their wake.

But no one else in Slimy Mary's was in any condition to notice her makeup slipping. Eerily, ominously, the denizens of the meatrack swayed and schooled in unison like a vast shoal of fish for a few more phantom bars—

Larry Coopersmith bulled his way through the crush toward Cyborg Sally at the point of an RLF flying wedge just as Paco arrived from the other direction. They were nose to nose before they saw each other, and were almost fist to fist before they recognized each other, with the outraged mob howling for the intruder's blood.

"Fuck you, asshole!"

"Chinga tu madre!"

"Up yours!"

"Who the fuck you think you are, cocksucker!"

"Kick his fuckin' ass!"

The streeties pressed in angrily, shouting, waving fists, pulling out knives.

But Larry said something to Paco, and Paco said something to Larry, and then Paco roared out his authority in words of one syllable.

"SHUT THE FUCK UP!"

They did.

Paco's shout froze them in place. He stood there haughtily with his hands on his hips and his hard commanding eyes just begging someone to give him shit.

Nobody did.

Larry and Paco had some conversation that Karen couldn't hear that seemed to go on for a million years before Paco draped a protective arm around Larry's shoulder.

"This putamadre is an amigo of mine," Paco said, "and any amigo of mine is a friend of Cyborg Sally también, motherfuckers!

He says he's gonna tell us how we can all be tv stars, ain't that right, Larry?"

"Fuckin'-A!" Markowitz shouted, striding forward to face the front wall of the crowd behind the dubious protection of the entire RLF save Karen herself.

"Why *shouldn't* we all be tv stars?" he demanded. "Ain't we as pretty as the shit they feed us on MUZIK? Why the fuck *shouldn't* everyone have their time in the spotlight? Every man a king! Every girl a star! That's what we're gonna do!"

"Who the fuck is *we,* white man?" someone shouted out to nasty laughter.

"We're the motherfucking revolutionary ass-kickin' *Reality Liberation Front,* that's who we are!" Markowitz shouted. "Remember us?"

Murmurs guttered into silence. Markowitz smiled slowly in satisfaction, nodding his head.

"That's right, suckers, the Reality Liberation Front," he said. "The people who brought you the Jack, and the People's Cash Machine, and the Red Jack discs put more bread in your fuckin' pockets than any of you motherfuckers ever seen!"

He paused, put on a disdainful expression, and raked it around the room like a laser beam. "So you guys wanna grab the world by the balls and take a great big bite, do you?" he said challengingly.

Growls, shouts, waving fists and knives, a chorus of angry wordless curses.

"Well then fuck just screaming it from the rooftops in the hard-hearted night! We gonna bite the bastards where it counts! We gonna do it on *national television*! We gonna kick ourselves some prime-time ass!"

Markowitz paused again, folded his arms across his chest in imitation of Paco, who stood behind him in the same pose, but with the attitude of an Aztec emperor watching his high priest whip up his warriors.

"We are gonna liberate *The American Dream,* motherfuckers, and turn it into our own fuckin' tv show on MUZIK!" Larry Coopersmith raved on in his Markowitz voice, fortifying himself with another tap of the touchpoint. "We're gonna take over their joint and make them show us doin' it on tv! We all gonna be *stars*!"

Cyborg Sally, or whoever she was, had hit her touchpoint too, while he was rapping, and now she was the rock star goddess again instead of the exhausted musician, on her feet and grinning steel daggers at Markowitz as she leered sideways at her fan club of wirehead warriors.

"You're going to put *me* on MUZIK, that's what you're going to do, you're gonna put me up there in the spotlight where I belong, and I'm gonna do a surprise premiere of the new song that I've been working on down here, and when I do . . . when I do . . ."

Cyborg Sally and Markowitz regarded each other like creatures from two different planets wondering whose this one was, while Karen wondered whether it wasn't getting way past time to leave.

Markowitz flashed her a maniacal grin. "We'll throw Official Reality on your funeral pyre!" he exclaimed.

"Come as who you like, come as who you are, every man a king, every girl a star!"

"Pixels to the People!"

They were babbling to each other as far as Karen was concerned, but it was plain enough to see that within that babble, two dreamtimes had touched sufficiently for a compact to be made.

Markowitz had succeeded in recruiting Cyborg Sally for the Reality Liberation Front.

And as Karen stood there on the stairs looking back, on Markowitz standing beside Cyborg Sally, on the Reality Liberation Front at last dissolving the interface and mingling with the street people, a part of her desperately yearned to be there with them, to hit her touchpoint, and share the dreams of the only friends she had in the world.

But then the chanting began, and it was Paco, her Paco, who led it, looming behind Cyborg Sally with a hand on her shoulder, his eyes as black and hard as obsidian, the merciless war chief greedily contemplating the righteous carnage to come.

"Cyborg Sally! Flesh and wire!"
"Burn down their world on her funeral pyre!"

And they were all chanting it, Leslie, Iva, Malcolm, all of them, even Markowitz, who stood there as the completion of the unholy triad singing to the tune of Cyborg Sally.

Who had recruited whom into what?

Whatever it was, she could hear it calling to her in the

mingled voices of the chanting, in Larry's voice, in Leslie's voice, and oh God in Paco's voice, telling her she really didn't want to be left behind here all alone.

She hesitated, found herself reaching for her touchpoint, found herself taking a step down the staircase, and then, realizing what she was doing, freaked completely, and with even less pause between the impulse and the act, found herself dashing up the stairs to the relative psychic safety of the feral night of the streets.

"Next Saturday night, Paco," Larry Coopersmith said. "They're set to do a broadcast at ten, primo prime time, amigo, we come in about eight, you start filtering your people in right after that. Five of ten, you seal the door, come inside, get everyone out on the floor and move them toward the stage, but wait till MUZIK goes on the air, then surround the stage, and—"

"Hey, hold on, I'm the jefe here, so despacio, *amigo,* stop doin' all the talking!" Mucho Muchacho snapped. Friends or not, the fuckin' gordos tried to do it to you every time!

Oh yeah, Mucho was up there on the blue velvet throne with Cyborg Sally, where he belonged, and Coopersmith and the rest of his Reality Liberation Front were squatting on the big paisley cushions at their feet where *they* fuckin' belonged.

And for sure, the warriors he had packed the penthouse apartment with made it clear who had the muscle, but the fuckin' motormouth was talkin' like this was all *his* idea, like *he* was running this war council.

Chingada, Larry had for sure worked most of this shit out, but if the putamadre thought he was gonna take over *Mucho Muchacho's* turf, he had another think comin'!

"You got a problem, Paco?"

"Yeah, *we* got some problems, man. Like what's to keep their zonies from blowing us away?"

"Live on MUZIK?" Coopersmith said archly.

"Yeah, well how do we get up on the fuckin' stage? You can't get inside from the floor."

"We got hostages. We hold the place till they let us in from below, maybe threaten to blow it up."

"You really gonna bring in *bombs*?"

"No, but *they* can't be sure of that, can they?"

"You really got it all figured out, don't you?"

Larry Coopersmith nodded smugly.

"Yeah, well what about Cyborg Sally? You know, Pham's got Steiner and his zonies lookin' to snatch her back! What's she supposed to do, walk right in like no one's gonna recognize her?"

Coopersmith looked up at him in some confusion. Mucho Muchacho smiled. At last he had brought the putamadre up short.

Cyborg Sally had not said word one during all of this bullshit, slumped on the couch beside him and really lookin' beat, lookin' a little scared, come to think of it.

But now she reached up, hit her touchpoint, stood up with her hands on her hips and a great big shit-eating grin, and suddenly took charge with a wicked metallic laugh.

"That's just what I'll do," she said. "I'll just make myself invisible and walk right in!"

Oh yes, Red Jack could hear that east wind howl now as they left the park, crossed Avenue B, and moved into the hot dry breath of it, redolent of ozone, and machine oil, and frustrated sex pheromones composting into rage, following the scent eastward along Seventh Street, following the psychic drumbeat deeper and deeper into the angry heart of the urban jungle, down the dark, empty street, through the aisle of crumbling buildings, where here and there a dim light flickered in a shattered upper-story window, where the shufflings and scramblings in the shadows were a muffled bassline to the unheard voice of Cyborg Sally blowing on the wind.

"The last time I smelled vibes like this it was at Altamonte," Glorianna said as they turned the corner onto Avenue D, "and that ain't exactly a good omen."

Two little gangs of streeties passed each other on opposite sides of the street a block or two north of them on the avenue, streeties in Sally gear, chanting something whose words he didn't need to hear to understand, chanting to the same beat they had followed eastward, the angry ass-kicking rhythm of Cyborg Sally. From even deeper in the ruins, he could hear shadows of it at the edge of audibility, like the far-off howls of scattered coyote packs summoning each other down out of the hilltops on a hot Santa Ana night in Beverly Glen.

"Real close now," Red Jack said. "Just a shot away."

Though the block they were walking down was empty, he felt the pressure of unseen angry eyes on the back of his neck peering out from between the slats of the boarded-up windows, the pressure of unheard blades snicking open in the darkness around him, the pressure of a blood moon rising over the home of the brave and the land of the free.

"Look!" Glorianna suddenly hissed into his ear, wrapping her arm around his waist and pressing against him.

Suddenly rounding the corner of the next side street and coming up the avenue toward them was another gang of streeties, swaggering and sauntering across the whole sidewalk and chanting the same horrid chorus over and over again.

Scream it out from the rooftops
In the hard-hearted night!
We got the world by the balls
And we're gonna bite!

Bobby Rubin was yanked back down to earth and into a surge of total adrenal terror that buckled his knees and sung in his ears.

There were nearly a dozen streeties leering right at him with mouths full of sharp silver teeth. Women with their hair lacquered up into purple Sally spines or wearing glowing phosphorescent wigs. Men with long red hair, or silvered skulls, or buzz-saw purple spikes crested with rusty razor blades. All of them plugged in to the Jack, all of them wearing the silver T-shirt of Cyborg Sally, all of them marching toward him in angry cadence to their wirehead war chant.

Scream it out from the rooftops
In the hard-hearted night!
We got the world by the balls
And we're gonna bite!

"Oh shit . . ." Glorianna moaned, and she pulled him toward the useless shelter of the nearest doorway, slipping her hand into her pocket, drawing the pistol half-free.

"No!" Bobby found himself shouting, boldly taking charge much to his own surprise.

Jamming her hand back into her pocket, he stepped right out into the center of the sidewalk, dragging Glorianna with him, suddenly possessed of a hopeless berserker courage he had never felt in his life before.

Yet a courage which, as he hit his touchpoint, he knew in that moment had been hiding right inside him just where it had always been.

A bad-ass band was playing a bouncy upbeat rhythm, a surging bassline pounded up him and through him. He stared into all those vengeful angry eyes and saw the poor wounded souls within. He smiled back into the silver dagger teeth, tossing his long red hair in the wind; he stared down the raging cyborg face challenging him from the T-shirts, letting them all know that another, brighter spirit of the bits and bytes had come a-rockin' back into the world.

A bright brave lead guitar lifted him up on its soaring vibes, and Red Jack began to sing.

I've been sealed inside my circuits
I've been nowhere to be seen
But now I'm here to tell you, babes
Raise up your voice and scream. . . .

The streeties stopped in their tracks, hunched over, spread out across the sidewalk in a two-deep skirmish line, chanting the war song of Cyborg Sally.

Cyborg Sally! Flesh and wire!
Throw your world on her funeral pyre!

"I'm standin' right beside you, Jack, just where I've always been," a mighty female lead sang out, and she stepped right up to the mike with him, a red-haired, red-hot rockin' moma, joining in face to face, breath to breath, on the chorus.

You and me together,
We're a Rock and Roll Machine!

"It's the perfect disguise," said Cyborg Sally. "I'll smear flesh-colored makeup on my face, put on an old raincoat and maybe even stuff it with a pillow."

She grinned at the fans gathered before her in her dressing room, at these stupid fools scheming to use the Queen of Heat for their own devices.

"Who would ever think it was me?" she crooned slyly. "All they'll see is a pathetic pimply little fat girl from the Valley trying to dress up like Cyborg Sally. . . . And then, when the music begins to play, and I step into the spotlight. . . ."

She flashed daggers, she laughed an electric laugh. These Reality Liberation Front assholes kneeling before her, the Razor Dogs, the audiences in a thousand tacky Valley bars, the denizens of the Glitter Dome, the fools who still thought they owned the world, all eyed her patronizingly, as if she were mad, as if she were some poor little Pimple with her fat little hand clasped between her sweaty thighs dreaming an impossible dream.

But her true fans, standing worshipfully around them, out there at the edge of the bright white spotlight, swaying to the music, listening to her song, oh yes, they understood, they knew, she was the leader of their pack, and they were dancing to her music and they never looked back.

Cyborg Sally! Flesh and wire!
Throw the world on her funeral pyre!

They screamed it from the rooftops in the hard-hearted night, they danced into her dreamtime in the broad daylight. And as they poured from the ruins of the abandoned buildings, as they marched out of the Valley clubs through the streets and shopping malls, the vision spread itself out before her.

High up on the great stage she danced, whirling and twirling in the bright white shooting lights, a million eyes upon her, the tv cameras displaying her glory for all the world to see, the music playing, and the whole world swaying, and the great vortex forming beyond the footlights. Hands caressing the tight silvery crack between her perfect thighs, tongues, lips, Bobby Rubin drooling and slavering, all the blond hard-limbed surfer studs, all the third-rate musicians on groveling knees, a whirlpool of their flesh at the feet of her wire, breaking on through, going higher, higher, higher!

And when this dreamtime vision burned on through into television reality, when Cyborg Sally stood there in the bright white national spotlight on MUZIK, free at last from the bits and bytes for all the world to see, she would be realer than any flesh could hope to be.

She would be all the way out. They would be all the way in.

And the song she would sing would be nothing all those who ever humiliated a poor little fat girl from the Valley ever wanted to hear.

Oh yes, she would make them all scream with her heart of ice and her ring of fire, she would burn down their world on her funeral pyre!

She would call all her sex slaves and worshippers up out of their hiding places in the ruins, and millions of them would dance out of the tacky Valley clubs and through the shopping malls behind Cyborg Sally, into the Glitter Dome, and The American Dream, and the Polo Lounge, into every show business party they had all never been invited to, and *she* would be the queen of MUZIK forever.

Once she really got to go on, millions of her fans would be out there in the dreamtime streets with her, making sure that her set would never end, that no silly little fat girl from the Valley could ever hit her touchpoint and snatch her back into the bits and bytes again.

Ain't got no body
Ain't got no soul
But I'm your Prince of Rock and Roll!

And he was as far as Glorianna O'Toole was concerned, he was what poor Mick had failed to be at Altamonte—a true Crown Prince of Rock and Roll singing a sweeter song to a more upbeat drummer into the dreamtime of the angry meat.

And here he was right beside her singing that very song! The song that had emerged rockin' from the dreamtime in her own voice singing through *his* voiceprint parameters, and here she was, singing back-up to her own creation, to her newfound son and long-lost spirit lover, and singing for her life.

I make more of you
You make more of me
You make more of me
I make more of you . . .

In her long and checkered career, Glorianna O'Toole had faced some pretty hostile audiences. She had sung in biker bars, before PCP-fried maniacs in the Haight, for antiwar rallies just before they turned into riots, before speed freaks, and drunks, and junkies, and even a turn backing up an opening act at Altamonte.

There had been times when she just hadn't had it and had

gotten out just before the bottles started to fly, and there had been times when the spirit of the music had moved through her so loud and clear and pure that she could have healed the sick, raised the dead, had the fuckin' pigs themselves talkin' out of their head.

But now she felt a power moving through her that she had never quite managed to tap into but had always known was there, all her long, rockin' life, it seemed to her now, she had always waited for this moment to arrive.

The dozen ragged streeties still stood there in a two-deep skirmish line blocking the sidewalk, but while some of their mouths were still working soundlessly, their chanting had stopped, and their jacked eyes glowed at her like burning joints in the upper balcony. They didn't move. They stood there and listened.

Rock and Roll had tamed the savage beast or at least captured the focus of its energy.

And turned it into an audience.

"Been down so long that you're ready to scream, took your music, now they took your dream . . ." sang Red Jack, dancing slowly toward the lip of the stage, toward the crowd poised on the razor's edge of explosion.

"Red ripe anarchy for all the world to see," sang Glorianna O'Toole as she strutted across the stage at Altamonte beside him, down Haight and through the biker bar.

I'm inside you when you're ready to fight. . . .
What will the Fat Men do?
Flash your freedom in the broad daylight . . .

Multiplied through time and space, the audience filled the dark night street, opened out into the bright avenues beyond, climbed the hillsides of the great natural amphitheater, a towering tsunami of angry meat, a huge threatening breaker of black vibes cresting to a baleful peak, its karma suspended in the balance between the dark and the light.

And then seemed to exhale the sweet perfume of an enormous collective toke, and began to sway ever so gently to the music of the Crown Prince and the oh-so-crazy lady of Rock and Roll.

I make more of you
You make more of me. . . .

You make more of me
I make more of you . . .

So she did and so did he as they sang it to each other, to the audience; his song, her song, and their song, too, the song of spirits waking from their starving sleep.

A Crazy Old Lady had given a nerdy kid named Bobby Rubin voice and music, had released the rockin' ghost in his machine, and that was the more she had made of him.

And the red-haired rock and roll queen singing beside him now, that was the more Red Jack had made of her, her ageless spirit liberated from the wrinkled gray prison of time and flesh by music, love, and wire.

Cyborg Sally's face, an icon of dagger-mouthed rage with sad tormented eyes, shrieked soundlessly at him from the T-shirts of the streeties, from the secret shadows of the ruined streets, from the deeper darkness in the hearts of the ruined lives of the underbelly of the world.

But the audience was swaying to his music now, to their own true song, to a rockin' rhythm deep inside, to something that still lived within even the meanest human heart, to the power of a dream.

Flashin' dancin' like liberty
In the home of the brave and the land of the free
Tap your fingers, let me zap your soul
We're all the Crown Prince of Rock and Roll!

Karen Gold found herself raging, despairing, as she fled aimlessly up Avenue D with no direction home. How could she fight back? What could she do to save Paco and the only friends she had in the whole world? Where could she even *go*?

Back to the loft to wait for the crazed conspirators to return? Back to Poughkeepsie for the rest of her life? Throw herself on the nonexistent mercy of these pitiless streets?

What have I ever done to deserve this? she demanded of she knew not who. What did I do wrong? Why are all my dreams destined to be shattered?

Four years of college to get a shit job, and then that gets automated out. Sweating and slaving for a down payment on a condo share, and then swindled out of it.

Rescued from poverty by the RLF, finding a man she loved

and something she believed in, and now all that had been stolen away from her too!

And by *whom*? By *what*? By a faceless enemy she couldn't even name, and a phantom conjured out of bits and bytes, and the very piece of wire which had once been the door to the better world she had now lost!

Then she heard the singing.

> *I make more of you.*
> *You make more of me....*
> *You make more of me*
> *I make more of you ...*

A quavery, out-of-tune, nasal male voice, unpleasant to the ears, but somehow strong and brave to the hearing of her heart. A woman's voice, frail and scratchy, but right on the melody, pure and clean, and somehow transcending the limits of the flesh. It was the weirdest damn duet she had ever heard.

When she turned uptown to face the music, what she saw was weirder still.

A small crowd of streeties, their backs to her, blocked the sidewalk halfway up the next block. Beyond them, she could make out a gray-haired old lady in some kind of blue denim vest, and a skinny young guy in a too-short Red Jack hairdo, standing together, singing into the face of what surely must be an impending beating.

Karen faded back into the shadow of the nearest building, prepared to turn and run. But something stopped her. Something kept her there against all caution and reason. Something about the insane bravery of the singers wouldn't let her leave.

> *Flashin' dancin' like liberty*
> *In the home of the brave and the land of the free....*

Off-key, quavery, they were singing Red Jack's song.

And the streeties weren't moving. They weren't surging forward. They just stood there swaying back and forth to the music.

Before her eyes a power she thought had been lost was being conjured back into the world. Somehow the former nonexistent leader of the Reality Liberation Front was out here in the night holding back the minions of Cyborg Sally.

The streeties standing there mesmerized by an off-key boy and a gray-haired old lady proved that that power was real, at least as real as Cyborg Sally's.

She found her hand reaching up slowly toward the touchpoint of the breadbox she still wore at the back of her head, the touchpoint she had thought she would never hit again.

If that power was real, maybe it could help her. Certainly, nothing else could. And there was only one place she could go to find out.

Where the battle between Red Jack and Cyborg Sally that she was witnessing was really taking place. The psychic arena of the dreamtime.

Tap your fingers, let me zap your soul. . . .

Right you are if I think you are . . . I hope, she thought wanly as she summoned up the courage to hit her touchpoint and step hesitantly forward into—

—the shadowy back reaches of Slimy Mary's, the sour reek of tightly packed sweating flesh, the bodies swaying together to the music, the dark heart of the collective beast growling and howling, Paco, and Coopersmith, and all her friends, calling to her to join them in the bloodred night.

But now it was Red Jack singing beneath the flickering strobe lights of the dance floor, and singing beside him, not Cyborg Sally, but an anti-Sally, a Rock and Roll Angel in jeans and a blue denim vest.

We're all the Crown Prince of Rock and Roll!

And they strode across the dance floor of Slimy Mary's inside a glowing nimbus of white light, a circle of safety pushing back the knot of streeties blocking the sidewalk, who melted into the shadowy back reaches of the cellar meatrack as Red Jack and his Rock and Roll Angel emerged through them toward her.

Karen dashed forward into that white aura of rescue, and threw herself into Red Jack's arms. "You've done it, Jack!" she cried. "You can stop it! You're stronger than she is, I saw it, you won't let it happen, will you! You'll save them!"

Bobby Rubin found himself hugging a hysterical blond girl who had appeared from nowhere and thrown herself raving into his arms, while a gang of streeties started inching closer to them, hunched over, swaying back and forth ominously on the balls of their feet. What the—

"Stop what? Save who from who?" he demanded, holding her out at arm's length and shaking her by the shoulders.

"Cyborg Sally! Can't you hear her out there in the darkness? She's got them all, Markowitz, and Leslie, and poor Paco—"

"Sally!" Bobby cried, shaking her more violently. "*You know where she is?* Take me there! Right now!"

"No! We can't go there! I won't go back!"

"You've got to! It's my ass if you don't!"

"No! No!"

Glorianna O'Toole came tumbling out of the dreamtime to find a dozen streeties closing in on them, thought she saw the gleam of a knife, certainly saw that this girl was jacked out of her mind, that the whiny face of Bobby Rubin had melted through the visage of her newfound Prince of Rock and Roll.

"Back off, motherfuckers!" she shouted at the top of her lungs, whipping out her pistol and waving it in wide arm's-length circles. "In fact, get your asses out of here right now!"

The streeties froze, then broke and ran down the block.

Glorianna stepped between Bobby and the blond girl, pried them apart, hit the girl's touchpoint.

Karen Gold came blinking out of the flash onto Avenue D. The gang of streeties had turned on their heels and were fleeing down the block into the shadows. A gray-haired old lady stood in front of her brandishing a pistol. Beside her stood . . . beside her stood . . .

Karen blinked again. She was not still flashing. But the apparition was still there!

A slightly built young man in his twenties wearing not a mirror suit but jeans, a Red Jack T-shirt, and a black jacket. His hair was bright red and he wore a Jack in it, but it barely came down below his jawline.

Yet the face beneath was unmistakably that of Red Jack.

"You're . . . you're still . . . *him*?"

"In a manner of speaking," the old lady said dryly.

"Pull yourself together, dammit," the boy with Red Jack's face said petulantly. "What's this about Sally? You know where she is? Where the hell is she?"

"Slimy Mary's," Karen told him. "They've got her there . . .

I mean *she's* got them all in her power, and something terrible's going to—''

''*Them? Who?* Make some sense, fer chrissakes, will you!''

''Paco! Markowitz! The whole Reality Liberation Front! They're out of their minds, they're gonna—''

''*The Reality Liberation Front!*'' he exclaimed with the strangest expression. ''So there really *is* a Reality Liberation Front after all?''

''You've heard of us . . . ?''

Red Jack, or whoever he was, gave the weirdest bitter laugh. ''*Heard of you?*'' he said. ''Hell, if I don't get my hands on Sally, I'm gonna get my ass thrown in the joint as your leader!''

He grabbed her by the arm. ''Come on,'' he said, ''we're going to this Slimy Mary's right now!''

''No! We can't! They'll tear us to pieces!'' Karen cried, pulling away from him.

''Look, you don't know how important this is to—''

''Oh yes I do!'' Karen told him. She studied him more calmly. He had Red Jack's face, all right, but he certainly wasn't acting like any Crown Prince of Rock and Roll. Still . . .

''You want to get Cyborg Sally away from them, right?'' she said. ''Well I want to get *them* away from *her*. So it's the same thing, really. You help me, and I'll help you, okay?'' And now *she* grabbed *his* arm and started dragging him down Avenue D.

''I thought you were afraid to go to this Slimy Mary's . . . ?''

''We're not going there,'' Karen told him. ''We're going to the loft. They'll come back there soon.'' She actually found herself managing a little grin. ''And when they do, they're gonna be taken to their leader!''

ALIVE AS YOU AND ME

Even without a tap of the Jack, the lair of the Reality Liberation Front was a blast from an ancient revolutionary past, a touchingly tacky attempt at the reincarnation of a sometimes gallant and always threadbare old spirit that Glorianna O'Toole would have sworn had long since vanished from the world.

The grimy windows that no one had bothered to wash since the assassination of JFK, the burlap curtain cordoning off the sleeping quarters, the old kitchen equipment complete with a restaurant sink overflowing with dirty pots and dishes, the Salvation Army furniture, the toilet door that didn't quite close properly . . .

Ah yes, when she was young and the Revolution was in flower, there had been about a thousand little communes like the RLF trying to live out their dreams of Liberation in crumbling old wooden houses off Shattuck, in faded Spanish colonial villas in Silver Lake, in Haight-Ashbury and Avenue C crash pads, in half-finished industrial lofts just like this. . . .

So despite Karen Gold's sad old story of the RLF's co-option by the dark side of the Revolutionary Force, despite the fact that this was definitely not the dreamtime now, Glorianna found herself bopping around this latter-day incarnation singing snatches of moldy revolutionary oldies.

She danced over to the musty old couch where Bobby Rubin was sitting with Karen Gold in a high old revolutionary humor.

"I dreamed I saw Joe Hill tonight, alive as you and me," she sang at him in a chortling cackle, "sez I but Joe you're forty years dead—"

"Who?"

"—I never died, sez he!"

"Who the hell is Joe Hill?" Bobby snapped petulantly. "And who cares? Will you get serious? Haven't you heard what she's been telling us? These people have Sally stashed with a streetie gang they're gonna use to take The American Dream by force! Can you imagine what West will do to me if she gets herself killed by a bunch of crazed terrorists?"

Alas, Bobby had never heard the chimes of freedom flashing or had romantic dreams of revolution in his head. All he could think about was getting his hands on poor Sally Genaro and saving his own ass.

Glorianna decided he was bringing her down.

"Joe Hill is *you,* kiddo, as far as the Reality Liberation Front is concerned!" she told him. "Haven't *you* been listening to what she's been telling you? Her revolutionary comrades have been co-opted by West's Cyborg Sally mindfuck and you're the only one who can save the day!"

"She's right!" Karen said. "That's *exactly* what I've been trying to tell you! You look just like Red Jack—"

"Just because I modeled an AP rock star on my own—"

"—so if they're wired enough to take this Sally Genaro for—"

"You're both out of your minds!" Bobby whined. "You expect me to stop these wirehead revolutionaries and crazed streeties from trying to stage a coup on MUZIK single-handed?"

"Stop the Revolution!" Glorianna exclaimed indignantly. "Shit no, you're gonna *lead* the Revolution, kiddo, you're gonna bring back red ripe anarchy for a national tv audience to see!"

"Huh?"

"The intrepid Reality Liberation Front uses the little heroes of the streets to liberate The American Dream from the pinheads upstairs and turn it over to the audience for one bright shining hour! MUZIK to the masses! Pixels to the people! Isn't it wonderful! Isn't it grand!"

"'Wonderful! Grand! Jesus Christ, Glorianna, even if they *do* take over The American Dream without getting killed, what the *people* are going to see is the Pimple, freaked out and howling for blood!"

"Shit no, they're gonna see *Red Jack* flashin' dancin' like liberty on live tv as the leader of the Revolution!" Glorianna declared triumphantly.

She put an arm on Karen's shoulder and gave her a sisterly

smile. "Jack here will do the right thing in the end," she said, "but sometimes, when he forgets who he is, he gets to being a dull boy."

"Huh?"

"That's why you brought him here, isn't it?" she purred. "To *lead* the Revolution, not to *stop* it! So Red Jack can lead it out of this Cyborg Sally bummer and flash our freedom in the broad daylight!"

Karen Gold stared at Glorianna, comprehension slowly dawning on her face. "Well, yeah, I guess . . ." she said.

She turned her attention to Bobby Rubin, laid an imploring hand on his shoulder. "You can do it . . . Jack . . . Bobby . . . whichever you are . . ." she cooed at him. "You can be Red Jack for just a little while. . . . And besides, it's the only way you can get near this Sally Genaro. . . ."

"Why *me*?" Bobby moaned, shrugging off her touch and bolting up from the couch as if someone had lit a firecracker under his ass.

Glorianna pointed her finger right in his face. "Who else, Bobby?" she told him. "There isn't anyone else, is there? There never was, was there?"

"You've done it already," Karen Gold crooned seductively. "You were able to do it out there tonight, or you wouldn't be here to talk about it!"

"I'm . . . I'm . . ."

The scared little eyes of Bobby Rubin stared imploringly into Glorianna's as if to say, please let this burden pass from me, and his shoulders slumped as if with the weight of the world.

But as Karen Gold spoke, Glorianna had hit her touchpoint, and from where she was now, she saw Red Jack there inside him just where he'd always been. And she saw that he was starting to see it too.

Glorianna saw a frightened boy reaching tremulously up toward his touchpoint, toward the courage to dare to become the hero of his own dreamtime that his whole poor little life had told him that he could never be.

"Yes you are if you think you are," she told him. She took his uncertain hand. "Do it for me, Jack," she said, kissing him lightly on the lips, and then touching his finger to his touchpoint against only token opposition. "Be what you've already been when it counted. Be my little hero in the night."

And there he stood before her, a frightened little boy's face beneath a crown of long flashing red hair, dissolving into pixels, reforming, dissolving again, poised on the interface of flesh and wire, the long-lost spirit from her dreamtime calling out to her from within this uncertain fleshly instrument to be his baby tonight, to carry him on all the way through, to sing him rockin' back into the world.

The song that came rolling up through her seemed to come from nowhere and everywhere. It was Jack's song and her song, and everyone else's too. It was the rock and roll of her dreamtime singing itself back into existence through her tired old pipes and his electronic circuitries in the perfect ageless voice her flesh had never had.

Little hero in the night
Little creature full of fright
Fear not the call to trust your heart to battle. . . .

Bobby Rubin stood there in the dusty deserted loft, with a crazy gray-haired old lady singing just for him in the voice of a courageous youth that he himself had never known, a love song to the daring of his own secret spirit that shamed him even as it set that spirit soaring.

Though you think you're far from home
And you're out here all alone
Never let your song sing surrender
Though the dark is deep and long
And you may never see the dawn
Never will your spirit be forgotten. . . .

Yes, he was out there far from home, out there on the desperate streets, out there searching for Sally Genaro in the ruins, out there in the deep dark night looking raw meat in its bloodshot eyes.

But not out there all alone. A pistol packin' moma in a Hell's Angels vest held his hand and sang beside him.

For every little life
Is a candle burning bright
And in the story of ourselves
We all are heroes . . .

And she was, and so had he been when he had had to, when they stood their ground together with nothing but a song.

Little hero in the night
Little beacon of the light
Stand beside me and unfurl your freedom's banner!

That was truly the moment when Red Jack had woken his soul from its starving sleep. Out there looking into those savage eyes and singing beyond the blood-hot wire to the fellow souls within, a deeper song that had tamed the beast of battle.

I am just the same as you
Only you to see me through
But together we are all there is that matters. . . .

At last he saw the truth in Karen Gold's eyes and accepted it.

Hadn't Nicholas West also proclaimed him the leader of the Reality Liberation Front? Hadn't he been set up to take the rap for it anyway? Wasn't West righter than he knew? Hadn't Bobby Rubin created Red Jack? Hadn't he really always known what he was doing? Who else was the Red Jack of his dreamtime but him?

Who else was the true and rightful leader of the Reality Liberation Front? The little hero who wasn't there?

The world is in our lovers' arms
We must keep us safe from harm
There is no one else to keep this song a-singing. . . .

If not him, who? If not now, when?

So let every little life
Stand together in the night
Let us all become our story's little heroes!

As Glorianna O'Toole finished her song, Bobby Rubin popped out of the dreamtime to the clicks and ratchets of locks being opened.

Then a big burly black-bearded man opened the door at the other end of the loft and strode inside followed by two, four, six, eight other people, jacked to the max and babbling.

They froze in their tracks when they saw the intruders and fell silent. Some of them frowned menacingly. Others blinked in amazement.

"What the fuck . . ." the black-bearded man finally shouted. "It can't be. . . . Can it?"

Bobby sighed, shrugged, took Glorianna's hand, hit his touchpoint, then took Karen's.

He was a scared little kid just trying to save his own ass. He was ten feet tall in the bright white spotlight. He was a little hero in the night. He was the crown of his creation, and he was stuck with it.

"Red Jack!"

"It can't be!"

"It is!"

"You're jacked!"

"Fuckin'-A I am!"

"Well I'm not!"

Hands reached up for touchpoints as they all crossed the loft toward Karen in a babble, some popping themselves out of the flash, some back in, some chain-tapping every few seconds to give themselves double vision, and goggling in even greater confusion.

Bobby Rubin, Red Jack, let go of Karen's and Glorianna's hands, walked across the room to the big kitchen table, and leaned back against it, folding his arms across his chest.

"If you schmucks are all convinced some little fat girl in a rubber suit is Cyborg Sally, then why can't I be standing right beside you just where I've always been?" he demanded. "You freed me from the Factory's bits and bytes and programs and made me your leader, didn't you?"

He shook his head disparagingly. "Oh yes, Karen's told me all about your asshole scheme," he said. "You call yourselves *revolutionaries*? Why do you think they created Cyborg Sally in the first place? So they could flush *me* down the tubes and the RLF with me! Even if your scheme works, all you'll end up doing is selling *her* bum trip and about twenty million of *their* discs for them!"

No one moved. They all stood there around the table staring at this skinny kid playing the Crown Prince of Rock and Roll while he stood there looking just magnificent.

"Hey Jack, you got it all wrong," Markowitz finally said, walking up to the table, and turning to declaim to the others.

"We're just using a preexisting revolutionary situation! Without Cyborg Sally's people, we'd still be here just talkin' to ourselves! We gotta use her to mobilize the people, we gotta let her go on the air to take over MUZIK, and when we do—"

"And when you do, *what*?" said Glorianna O'Toole, striding up to the table, turning, pointing a finger at Markowitz. "What are you gonna do when *you* have your ass in the catbirdseat, Charlie, you gonna burn down the world on her funeral pyre? Make some stupid speech?"

Markowitz stared at her. A strange faraway look came into his eyes. "I know you . . ." he said dreamily.

"Do you . . . ?"

"You're . . . fuckin' hell, you're Glorianna O'Toole!"

"No shit?"

A soft sensuous look suffused itself onto Larry Coopersmith's face, a tender worshipful longing Karen had never seen there before. "Don't you remember, Glorianna?" he said. "Jesus, you're wearing the colors! Nobody's had the balls to do that for ten years!"

Glorianna O'Toole squinted at him. "I know you . . . ?" she said slowly.

"Know me? Shit, moma, in the biblical sense! Altamonte, remember, we were all fried to the eyeballs on speed! And you came out there right into the middle of all that shit, it was the craziest bravest fuckin' thing I've ever seen, me and Lou the Jew, some hippie asshole had kicked over my fuckin' bike, and I was wasted man, shit, I was just a kid, me and Lou was gonna kill that asshole, and you smiled at me, and you took my hand, and you took me under the stage, and . . ."

"Hey, I was peaking on acid," Glorianna O'Toole said, "you know, things were gettin' pretty heavy, and it seemed the only thing to do. . . ."

"Hey people, this is Glorianna O'Toole!" Markowitz shouted, rounding on the others, "the greatest fuckin' rock and roller what ever lived! If she says this is motherfuckin' Red Jack in the ectoplasmic flesh, you better believe it! You wanna give her any bovver, you gotta come through me! If she says this motherfucker can walk on water, you better get your swimsuits out!"

"Nice to be remembered," said Glorianna O'Toole. She leaned back up against the table at Red Jack's side, green eyes flashing, and Karen could well believe that this fiery old lady she had never heard of was a secret queen of rock and roll.

"Now remember who's talking to you now, kiddies, remember who's come back from the electronic grave to lead you again at great cost and danger to himself, you better believe it!" Glorianna said.

She smiled, she waved her hand in an emcee's introductory gesture. "Ladies and gentlemen, Red Jack, the Crown Prince of Rock and Roll, and your Peerless Leader! Okay, Jack, let's hear your plan!"

My plan? Bobby Rubin thought as he popped out into a musty loft sitting in the catbird seat before his own little revolutionary cabal. What *is* my plan?

The only idea he had had in his head was that the Reality Liberation Front had their mitts on Sally Genaro, and that he must therefore figure out some way of using them to get to her. How he would manage this without getting either of them killed and what he would actually do when he confronted Sally were matters he had been content to let Red Jack worry about.

But the lesson Glorianna had taught him in the dreamtime lingered. Red Jack was only Bobby's Bobby. So if Bobby Rubin was to get Sally Genaro back to Los Angeles, Red Jack was going to have to dance her and these people out of Cyborg Sally's dreamtime and into his own—which was precisely what destiny demanded of the true leader of the Reality Liberation Front.

Glorianna was right. It was a kind of karmic justice. He had to lead the revolution to save his own ass.

So why not lead it to victory?

"Okay, so a strike force seizes The American Dream," he temporized without an idea in his head. "What's to keep them from just blowing us all away?"

"Our hostages. Everyone in the club. They won't just cut loose with automatic weapons into a crowd."

"Very good," Bobby said, starting to get into it. This was really just like some wizard strategy game. Hadn't he once spent a week playing with something called "Terrorist Commando"?

"So how do we force them to put us on MUZIK . . . ?"

"We tell them we have a bomb," Coopersmith, or Markowitz, or whatever his name was, said. "They've got too much capital invested in The American Dream to call our bluff for half an hour of airtime, that's their bottom line."

"Yeah!"

"Right on!"

"*A bomb!*" Bobby moaned. Jesus Christ, these people were chain-tapping like fiends and talking about bomb threats, not playing "Terrorist Commando" on their game machines!

"No bomb threats," he told them. "What kind of tv image is that for the Reality Liberation Front? Instead . . . instead we take over the broadcast booth, yeah, that's it! You got anyone who can run the board and the cameras and keep the satellite transponder captured?"

"I always wanted to be a video pirate!" declared a tall black man.

"But how do we get Cyborg Sally up on the stage without a bomb threat?" Markowitz demanded. "There's no way up there from the floor!"

"Yeah, and how do we get to the broadcast booth, come to think of it?"

"We get up onto the stage through the entrance on the level below the dance floor. We get to the broadcast booth by the elevator from the VIP entrance."

"Say what?"

"We just walk right in past all their zonies?"

Bobby paused. How much could he tell them? "I've got . . . this friend . . ." he said slowly. "Hiding right inside me, you might say, kind of a ghost in *my* machine. He's got some magic paper from Hollywood. He'll get us all VIP backstage passes."

"Oh yeah? Just who the hell is this little man who isn't there?"

Bobby sighed. He shrugged. It was going to have to come to this sooner or later. "He's standing right beside you, just where he's always been," he said. "Time for all of you to unplug and meet your *real* leader, suckers!"

He was right, Karen Gold realized. They had bought it, they had believed it, but this was about as far as the charade could go, it was time for a cold hard slap of reality.

"You'd really better," she said. "You've been chain-tapping all night, remember? There *isn't* any real Cyborg Sally, and there *isn't* any real Red Jack, so this *can't* be him. . . . Well, not exactly . . ."

Leslie peered owlishly at her, blinked, then hit her touchpoint. She stared at the figure standing by the table and gave Markowitz's touchpoint a tap.

"What the . . ." Larry muttered, shaking his head in confusion. "Hey, guys, I think you'd better . . ."

One by one they hit their touchpoints and stood there looking at who they had let do all of the talking.

A red-haired young man in jeans, an open black jacket, and a Red Jack T-shirt; an impostor, but one with Red Jack's face, with Red Jack's own eyes, still looking right at them. A real man of flesh and blood simulating his own electronic phantom. And yet within those eyes, those windows into the soul, Karen thought she saw a deeper truth behind the deception. And sensed that the others were struggling with that paradoxical perception too.

"Jesus . . . the face . . ."

"It *is* Red Jack!"

"The hell it is!"

"Okay man, just who the fuck are you?" Larry Coopersmith demanded.

"The me they always told me that I could never be . . ." said Bobby Rubin.

A great collective groan and a shuffling of feet.

"We're not flashing now, so don't give us that shit!"

"Just the same as you . . . one of our story's little heroes . . ."

Groans and angry mutters.

"Does it matter?" Bobby Rubin said. "I *can* be Red Jack when I have to, can't I? Didn't you just prove that to yourselves?"

"Yeah, how *did* he do that . . . ?"

"You know that face. . . ."

"*Still* looks like him . . ."

"Come on, man, how *can* you look just like Red Jack if he doesn't exist?"

Bobby Rubin shrugged. "*I* don't look like *him,* I made *him* look like *me*. I'm the guy who wrote his algorithms." He smiled a perfect little Red Jack smile. "He really *is* the ghost in my machine. Which kinda really makes *me* the ghost in yours, now, doesn't it? You make more of him, he makes more of me. . . . And whoever I am, my plan will work."

Larry Coopersmith shook his head slowly. "You can really get us the paper to get us past the zonies . . . ?" he said dubiously.

"For sure."

"You can get Cyborg Sally up onstage?"

"We're not gonna put Cyborg Sally on MUZIK!" said

Glorianna O'Toole. "It's going to be Red Jack up there flashin' and dancin' like liberty!"

"Him!" Larry snorted. "Okay, so he *looks* like Red Jack, but if we got a mob howling for Cyborg Sally, we're at least gonna have to give 'em someone who can *sing,* or the whole shitpile goes up. He can't do *that,* can he?"

Karen groaned aloud. Only she knew the full awfulness of the truth.

But Bobby Rubin grinned like the cat that ate the canary.

"*She* can," he said. "In your own words, my man, Glorianna O'Toole, the greatest fuckin' rock and roller what ever lived!"

"Me?" said Glorianna O'Toole in a frail old voice. "Shit, I haven't performed since—"

"About half an hour ago, babes," he said. "Remember when? And there's no one else to keep that song a-singing."

"But she's—"

"Just a Crazy Old Lady? A has-been?" Glorianna O'Toole snapped. Her whole demeanor changed. "You give me a mike and a vocoder, and I'll fuckin' move the world!"

"Show the suckers, Glorianna," Bobby Rubin said. "Sing for them just like you sang for me."

Glorianna O'Toole executed a little bow, and hit her touchpoint.

"Plug in and imagine *this* through a vocoder!" Bobby Rubin said, hitting his own touchpoint. "Multiplexed! Purified! Glorified! Me and this old lady together, we're your Rock and Roll Machine!"

Glorianna O'Toole held a phantom microphone up to her lips and waited as they all hit their touchpoints. All but Karen, who held back, anticipating a greater magic, a magic of the naked spirit, the magic she had already borne witness to on the street.

Nor was she disappointed.

For there in the dusty old loft, a gray-haired old lady shrugged, and grinned, and began to sing—a cappella, shakily, softly at first, but with the phrasing growing more and more certain, the volume growing louder and louder, tapping her feet, popping her fingers, rockin' her heart out, and rolling back the years to her time of glory.

Little hero in the night
Little creature full of fright
Fear not the call to trust your heart to battle

Though you think you're far from home
And you're out here all alone
Never let your song sing surrender....

And when her song was finished, Karen found herself joining in the wide-eyed clapping, needing no wire to make herself believe.

I make more of you
You make more of me....

Glorianna O'Toole and Red Jack came sailing and singing through the lobby of the Union Square Pavilion in the wee hours to the outraged consternation of the doorman, and the desk clerk, and the security guard who moved to intercept them at the elevator banks.

"Hey who do you think you—"

"This is Glorianna O'Toole, the greatest fuckin' rock and roller what ever lived, don't you recognize her, asshole!" Red Jack declared grandly.

"And who do you think *you* are?" the guard snapped back crossly, brandishing his Uzi.

Glorianna fished the fancy gold key to the Imperial Penthouse out of her pocket.

"If you gotta ask, no one's gonna be able to tell you, sonny!" she said, giggling. "Guess you don't get too many rock stars in this mausoleum." She dangled the oversize key in his face. "Now be a good boy and get the penthouse elevator for the Crown Prince of Rock and Roll."

The guard did a take, fidgeted nervously, then shook his head, went to the elevator bank, and unlocked the door to the penthouse express. Glorianna reached into her pocket, grabbed the first bill that came to hand, and slapped it into the goggle-eyed guard's palm as they stepped inside. It was a four hundred.

"Oh yeah, Jack, you and me together, we're a Rock and Roll Machine!" she exclaimed as the elevator zipped them upward and onward, hugging him to her, and planting a great big delighted kiss on his lips.

Whoo-ee! This was just like the good old days, the Summer of Love, the Swingin' Sixties, the Stoned-Out Seventies, the Golden Age of Rock and Roll!

Like what the Golden Age *should* have been! she corrected

herself as the private elevator deposited them in the big marble foyer that led into the immense living room.

This was how the Kings and Queens of Rock and Roll lived then, and Glorianna had been a duchess at best, an opening act, a backup, a sessions singer, and her only experience of life at the top had been parties in places like this, and an occasional night in the beds of various reigning Lizard Kings.

Ah, but here she was at last in the ultimate rock star penthouse suite with Red Jack himself, the electronic crown of rock and roll creation, the crown of *her* creation, that *her* song had conjured back a-rockin' into this dead-ass latter-day world.

And if she had made more of him, so had he made more of her this magical night, holding out his hand to her and bringing forth from her dreamtime into the world the Glorianna O'Toole that had lived only in her heart, Glorianna the Superstar, Glorianna in the Sky with Diamonds, Glorianna the Rockin' Queen of the Revolution, flashin' dancin' like liberty!

She grabbed a bottle of Dom Pérignon out of the refrigerator, hooked his arm, and dragged him across the living room toward the garden doors. "Come on, luv," she cried, "let's go look at the stars!"

He took another long sloppy slurp of champagne from the bottle and held it up to her full red lips, his free arm snaked around her waist and hugging her tightly to him, as they stood there looking down over the Big Apple of the dreamtime.

Zones of brilliant flash and glitter in the City That Never Sleeps. Islands of dark streets abandoned to the night of the urban jungle. The spires of the skyline towers illumined by colored spotlights. A squad of police helicopters in formation droning angrily toward Central Park. A rooftop garden from which to survey it all, and a rock goddess by his side.

Never had he known a moment so golden. Never had a wimpy little kid from Long Island dreamed he could ever aspire to stand where Red Jack stood now, looking out from his penthouse rooftop garden with Manhattan spread before his feet, swilling champagne from the bottle, with a song of freedom in his heart, and a woman like this beside him.

The backlighting of the city nightscape solarized silver highlights across her wild tousled red hair and illumined her visage into the poster-perfect image of a rock and roll queen. She made his cock ache with someone's teenage memories of every untouchable dream goddess to whose pulsing and unobtainable perfect image he had ever beat his frustrated meat—a rock star, a crazy lady of courage, a free spirit, an ally, the perfect paragon of every woman that Bobby Rubin always knew he could never have.

Oh how wrong you are, Jack! her eyes told him. You *are* the you they told you that you could never be, my little hero in the night! You have only to hold me in your arms and unfurl your freedom's banner.

Out there in the ruins the night was deep and long and there would be a battle come the dawn, but tonight was the only thing that mattered.

As if reading his thoughts, she smiled at him, nodded her head, pressed herself against him, snaked her hands in his hair, and pulled his open lips into a long, deep kiss.

The years rolled back, the decades, as Glorianna once more kneaded a smooth tight ass, felt a hot young cock inside her, let him send her through cusp after cusp after cusp, let the screams and moans of her pleasure caress him, let Bobby Rubin ride her like a little hero, reveling in the role of mighty cocksman on the billowing sea of the big water bed.

His eyes stared off into elsewhere, his heart thumped against her breast, as she let him know he was throwing her the fuck of her whole long life, or so at least he thought, and in that very gifting, gifted herself with the reality, with the mirror of her spirit, with Red Jack, the long-lost perfect lover of her dreamtime.

But holding him deliciously maliciously and lovingly on the edge until his breath was ragged and panting and his rhythm began to break and stumble into exhaustion—with unexpected back-beat counterpoints, startling little bites, teasing pinches, frozen hesitations, playing this strong young body like the master musician she was, using every fret and key, teasing a bright green pleasure machine out of his tremulous fleshy instrument, showing him the glory of his own unsuspected perfect manhood.

And then, when she felt him finally waning into tumescent but exhausted torpor, she wrapped her legs around him, rolled him over, pinned his arms to the pillow, and, arching her back proudly upward and looking down into his glowing eyes, turned the loverly tables, and began to ride *him*.

He bucked and thrashed and tiredly tried to regain command.

"Shussh, luv!" she whispered. "You just lean back and enjoy it, Jack, this one's for you. . . ."

Towering above him, pearls of sweat beading on her perfect breasts and pointing her hard pink nipples, her wild red hair tossing and rolling, her green eyes glowing tenderly, her tongue licking a loving smile just for him, the perfect lover of his dreamtime squeezed and teased his cock, milking him for every last drop of pleasure, drawing him up, up, up, to the edge of an endless plateau of delight, into a bright white all-enveloping brilliance, where phosphorescent flashes shimmered between them and a tidal wave of ecstasy came soaring up his legs from the soles of his feet, up his nerve trunks, exploding at the base of his spine—

And then, at the very crest, she suddenly rolled off him with the liquid grace of a jungle cat, seized him by the root, and met his screaming, throbbing, loving release with a long, slow lowering of warm wet lips—

Glorianna closed her eyes, found herself coming in sympathetic pleasure one surprising last final time as she took his warm slick flesh into her mouth, letting her lips glide slowly down the full length of him, cupping his balls in a gentle squeeze, meeting his orgasm with her nose tickling in his curly pubes.

He groaned, and screamed, and her willing mouth was filled with the transient savor of Bobby Rubin's sweet young life's juices, with the eternal time-defying essence of Red Jack, with both of them together, her newly awakened little hero and never-lost spirit lover, mingling, united, in this most precious moment in the lifeline of her dreamtime.

When she opened her eyes again, he lay there on the pillow with his eyes closed, fast asleep, smiling like a found little boy deep in a dreamtime of his own.

Bobby Rubin awoke out of the seamless dreamless darkness blinking into bright golden early morning light. A delicious torpid languor suffused his limbs and his spine lay loose and easy. He smiled to himself groggily, and began to roll over, snuggling down into the toasty fragrant bedding.

He started into full wakefulness as he came up against a warm naked body.

"Hello sleepyhead!" said Glorianna O'Toole.

"Oh shit!" Bobby moaned.

There he lay on his side, looking right into the green eyes and wrinkled parchment face of a sweetly smiling old lady. Her gray hair was a matted rat's nest fanned across her pillow. He could feel her slack breasts pressed up against his chest, her knee snugged into his shriveled crotch.

"Is that the best you have to say for yourself the morning after, kiddo?" Glorianna said not unkindly.

"I . . .? We . . . ? You. . . ?" Bobby stammered.

Glorianna nodded. "Uh-hum!" she purred contentedly. "Don't you remember?"

Bobby rolled back onto his back, then propped himself up into a seated position against the headboard. "We almost got ourselves killed!" he moaned. "That street gang . . . that girl Karen . . . the Reality Liberation Front . . ."

It all came flashing back. "Terrorist Commando." Glorianna's song. A crazy plot to seize The American Dream. Red Jack returning to lead the Reality Liberation Front.

"Oh my God, what have I talked us into!" Bobby cried.

"Red-ripe anarchy for all the world to see!" Glorianna cackled.

He looked down at her in utter dismay. "It all really happened, didn't it?" he groaned. "I'm really supposed to lead a bunch of wirehead revolutionaries and streetie terrorists into The American Dream? I really talked myself into it, didn't I? And we . . . and then . . ."

"And then a dirty old lady took shameless advantage of your hot young bod," Glorianna said, giving him a little goose. "And now you feel thoroughly terrified and thoroughly disgusted, right sonny?"

Bobby jerked away from her. "Don't call me sonny, grandma, I'm old enough to fuck your brains out!" he found himself saying to his complete befuddlement.

Glorianna laughed as she propped herself up to sit in the bed beside him. To his further amazement, he found himself laughing with her.

"This . . . this is crazy!" he muttered.

"Fuckin'-A! I'm the Crazy Old Lady of Rock and Roll, remember? And you're—"

"The Crown Prince of Rock and Roll . . . ? Jesus Christ . . ."

"Poor baby . . ." Glorianna crooned. "It must have been so awful for you, huh . . . ?"

"It was . . . it was . . ."

It was the best goddamn sexual experience of my whole life! he caught himself about to say. It was like the perfect wet dream, the ultimate jack-off fantasy. . . . Shit, it *had* been a dream, or something like a dream. . . .

But . . . but this old lady had been there with him, she had sung him a love song, she had woken something deep inside of him, she had been young, and perfect, and beautiful, and what he had felt. . . .

Though what he had felt with his cock was now far, far away, he found, when he looked for it in the green eyes set in that wrinkled old face, that what he had felt in his heart was somehow still there, that the little hero who had awoken at long last from his starving sleep was still there deep inside him just where he had always been, the me that this old . . . that this Crazy Lady had shown him that he could dare to be. . . .

Say it, asshole! he told himself. Say what you feel!

"It was the best goddamn sexual experience of my whole life," Bobby Rubin said. "And you . . . ?"

Glorianna O'Toole winked at him. "Hey, you were okay, y'know, but don't flatter yourself too far, kiddo!" she said.

"You *are* a dirty old lady, grandma!" Bobby shot back, punching her on the arm.

"You better believe it, luv!"

Bobby sighed. He felt wasted, and confused, and more than a little frightened. Yet at the same time, he felt wonderful. He felt strong and courageous. He felt at peace with himself for perhaps the first time in his life, sitting here in bed with a woman old enough to be his grandmother.

"We're gonna have to go through with it, aren't we?" he said softly. "It's the only way to get to Sally, and besides . . . besides . . . if we don't, the whole thing is going to turn into a horror show on MUZIK. . . ."

Glorianna nodded. "Welcome to the human race," she said.

"Isn't there some way we can—"

"Don't look so glum, Jack, you and me are gonna be stars! I don't know about you, but I wouldn't miss it for the world."

"But the place is full of zonies, if something goes wrong . . ."

"Then we get to go out rockin'!"

Bobby grimaced. He suddenly admitted to himself that the prospect of facing armed zonies, bad as it was, was not what was getting to him at all. "But what about Sally?" he said.

"Cyborg Sally?"

"Sally Genaro, Sally from the Valley, the Pimple. Have you forgotten? She's what it's all about in the first place. We've got to bring her back to L.A. or my ass is grass."

Glorianna eyed him narrowly. "What do you mean *we,* white man?" she said.

"All right then, *me,*" Bobby groaned. "What the fuck am I going to do about Sally?"

"You know what, sonny," Glorianna said softly. "You just said it. If it comes down to it, what that bastard West told you to do . . . Give her what you've known she wants all along, and she'll follow you anywhere. . . ."

"Oh, my God . . ." Bobby moaned forlornly. "How can I possibly . . . ?"

Glorianna O'Toole looked at him quite strangely. Her lower lip actually trembled as the fingers of her right hand reached tentatively for the bedclothes. "I really shouldn't do this, but for you . . ." she muttered.

And with a sudden flourish she tore aside the cover to reveal the full naked length of her poor old body, the flabby flesh, the pendulous breasts, the graybeard shock of pubic hair.

"You got it up for *this,* kiddo!" she said, looking at him with courageous, tremulous, fearful eyes.

Bobby, aghast, met them, unwilling to look down at . . . at . . .

But Glorianna was relentless; she seized his chin in her hand, yanked his head downward to gaze at the flaccid wrinkled breasts, the folds of graying skin, the spindly legs, the bluish ancient vaginal lips.

"But . . . but . . . that was . . ."

"Bobby, Bobby . . ." she crooned at him, "we all lose our shape in the end. But square-shaped or pear-shaped, our hearts don't lose their shape . . ." She winked at him. "Get what I mean, kiddo?" she said.

Bobby Rubin forced himself to gaze full face upon that fleshly vista of time's cruel landscape. He looked up into her brave green eyes burning bright in the evening of the unjust night.

Tears rolled down his cheeks. Slowly, tenderly he kissed her poor withered dugs.

Glorianna gathered him up into her embrace.

"Today," she said, "you are a man."

As Saturday night crept closer and closer, Karen Gold found herself watching with mounting unfocused trepidation, as, strategy session by strategy session, the plan she had catalyzed into motion mutated into something that seemed to have taken on a life of its own, something uncontrollable and unknown that seemed to approach on rails like a runaway train running unguided on its own momentum.

Larry, Malcolm, and Bobby Rubin did most of the talking, while the rest of the RLF sat around soaking it up, plugged in, as often as not, to the revolutionary fantasy.

Two hours were spent actually arguing about hairdos.

Larry wanted the Reality Liberation Front to flaunt its colors, to wear the Red into The American Dream, to ''flash their freedom in the television lights.''

But Bobby Rubin pointed out that management enforced an admissions policy against it, that not even his credentials from Hollywood could get them all in wearing the Red, at least not without arousing entirely counterproductive attention from security.

''We could all wear wigs and whip 'em off when the action starts . . .'' Malcolm finally suggested.

Bobby Rubin snorted derisively.

''Well, *you* gotta wear the Red, man,'' Larry pointed out. ''You gotta go on as Red Jack, remember?''

''All right, all right, so I'll wear some stupid hat that'll cover it,'' Rubin said, throwing up his hands. ''Now, can we get down to some *serious* business?''

And they did. They started arguing about bombs.

Larry insisted they needed a bomb threat. Rubin would have none of it.

''I *told you* no bomb threats! Forget it! I am *not* going to front a bunch of bomb-throwing terrorists! And neither would Red Jack, it would be poison to his image.''

''Then what's to keep them from using riot troops?''

''You told me yourself. We'll have two hundred streeties inside, we'll have the zonies outnumbered twenty to one, and they won't dare use their weapons in a mob scene like that!''

''But how do we get them to put us onstage?''

''Worst comes to worst, *I'll* make Pham do it. With the whole shitpile going up out of control, he'll be only too glad to let Nicholas West's errand boy take full responsibility,'' Rubin said. He smiled wanly. ''That's my insurance too. West will forgive a lot if I get Sally back to L.A. and can claim I saved The American Dream from being torn to pieces by my quick thinking.''

''But how do we get on MUZIK?'' Malcolm demanded.

"Jesus Christ, we've gone through all this! You take the broadcast booth and—"

"With *what?*" Malcolm said. "With our bare hands? You really want this whole thing depending on the outcome of a fistfight?"

"He's right," Larry insisted. "If they don't have at least a phony bomb, they're gonna have to have guns."

"*Guns?*" Malcolm shrieked in horror.

They had taken half a day to work out a compromise. Malcolm could carry a phony bomb into the broadcast booth to scare out the techs, but there could be absolutely no talk about bomb threats from the stage or on the air.

On and on and on it went. Who would go with whom where and who would do what when.

On Wednesday, Bobby Rubin had an endless technical discussion with Malcolm that Karen could barely follow but which had everyone rubbing their hands together and cackling. Glorianna O'Toole, so it seemed, had some nebulous connection with the even more shadowy video pirate underground. . . .

"They'll pick up the Northern California earthstation feed from the MUZIK satellite and capture the rebroadcast transponders of the major network satellites. Then it's just a bank shot—your feed to MUZIK up to the NBC, ABC, CBS, and CNN transponders—and our show will preempt prime time nationally on all five networks!"

"Just like a presidential speech!" Malcolm giggled.

"Better!" Rubin said. "MUZIK never gives the White House free airtime!"

"Can they really hold the transponders?"

"They've got some kind of black box that emulates the control commands. They can stay locked on for at least fifteen minutes before the FCC can get a fix on their transmitters. Question is, how long can *you* hold MUZIK?"

"With their own ground station?" Malcolm said haughtily. "Forever!" He smiled dreamily. "Hey, you know, we could broadcast a bunch of our bedbug software too; hell, we could send out Red Jack's algorithms and voiceprint parameters to every disc recorder and creaky old VCR in the country. . . ."

On and on and on.

On Thursday, Bobby Rubin showed up at the loft with Glorianna O'Toole and some equipment—a plug-in vocoder rig he had crammed with wizardware, and a directional vocoder mike programmed with Red Jack's voiceprint parameters—and they had spent the whole day laying out the program as if this were some kind of crazy tv production conference.

Malcolm and his crew would take the broadcast booth at ten P.M., while Paco's streeties were surrounding the stage and all hell was breaking loose in the pit, but they wouldn't put any of those visuals on MUZIK, they'd hold camera on the stage and broadcast generalized crowd noise so that when Markowitz appeared in the spotlight to make his little speech, the crowd reaction would appear to be for *him,* not the expected advent of Cyborg Sally.

It would have to be a *short* Markowitz rap for once, what with all the crazies down there howling for Cyborg Sally, just a triumphant introduction of Red Jack, reincarnated from the bits and bytes by the power of the people and the Reality Liberation Front.

Bobby Rubin would come onstage miked through Red Jack's voiceprint parameters. He couldn't sing, but he would look more or less like Red Jack, and he'd make a "Pixels to the People" speech in Red Jack's voice telling all the little cyberwizards out there to start recording, and Malcolm would broadcast the visual track of "Your Rock and Roll Machine" off a disc at condensed high speed while pumping out Red Jack's visual algorithms and voiceprint parameters as the digitized audio.

After which, Glorianna O'Toole would come out and do her star turn through the vocoder, while Red Jack danced around the stage miking the *audience* with the directional vocoder pick-up and letting them all truly be the Crown Prince of Rock and Roll themselves for one bright shining nationally televised moment.

Malcolm would then load an assortment of Red Jack discs into the deck in the broadcast booth for automatic playback while everyone tried to escape as best they could in the ensuing chaos.

"Pixels to the People!"

"Red-ripe anarchy for all the world to see!"

"We're gonna make television history!"

It would make history all right, if it all actually worked as planned.

Every garage band in the country would be able to have Red Jack himself as lead singer doing *their* material on pirate discs. Everyone with a computer would have an instant library of bedbug programs. The Reality Liberation Front would recruit twenty million self-proclaimed new members in one fell electronic swoop. The tv networks would have one hell of a time figuring out how to regain full-time control of their own broadcast satellites. What was left of the electronic economy would be beyond anyone's control. Official Reality would be riddled with so many random factors that it would cease to exist, and those who had once controlled it would be forced to start the game over, whatever *that* might turn out to mean.

Oh yes, it was a wonderful revolutionary fantasy! And somewhat to her own surprise, Karen found herself hoping against all logic and reason that the RLF could actually pull it off.

Even though she knew full well that there would be dire personal consequences. Larry Coopersmith, Bobby Rubin, and Glorianna O'Toole would certainly be arrested and charged with everything from terrorism to computer theft to copyright infringement. She and the others just might get out during the confusion, but even if they did, they'd be identified as video terrorists when witnesses were interrogated and face a life on the run underground.

That certainly was a terrifying prospect at first, but as the revolutionary fantasy took on the inevitability of inescapable destiny, she found herself slowly resigning herself to accepting it. After all, as a member of the RLF and a bedbug dealer, she realized in retrospect, she had put herself outside the law already. She even managed to convince herself that there would be a certain romance to being a political fugitive on the run, a criminal in the eyes of the powers that be, but a heroine to the millions who would have witnessed the RLF action on television.

She could see her mother's face smiling sadly. Her mother had known such people in her Berkeley days, had even claimed to have sheltered them once or twice. Perhaps she would understand.

Hey mom, she told herself, at least I won't be wasting the rest of my life in Poughkeepsie.

Besides, if you couldn't make a revolutionary omelet without breaking eggs, you were hardly in a moral position to complain when some of them turned out to be your own.

Less so still when you were the one who had brought the co-conspirators together. Come what may, she was morally committed to this thing. She could hardly back out now. This glorious lunacy was as much her creation as Coopersmith's, or Rubin's, or Malcolm's, and then some.

By the time Friday rolled around, she had agreed to join Malcolm's group in seizing the broadcast booth, had put her personal fears behind her in the name of adventure, and accepted her destiny. But still this elusive misgiving remained, and she couldn't put a name to it until Larry Coopersmith returned to the loft from Slimy Mary's and reported to Bobby Rubin that everything was set on that end too.

Then she realized that its name was Paco.

"What did you tell him about the change in plans, Larry?"

"What you told me to. That we had ourselves an inside man now, so we'd all be coming in the VIP entrance instead of past him out front."

"Nothing about me . . . ?" Rubin said nervously. "If he should find out . . ."

Bobby Rubin had been paranoid about Paco getting wind of his involvement all along. Paco knew him by sight. Paco knew that he had come to New York to snatch Cyborg Sally. If Paco found out that he was involved in this scheme, he'd know why, and he'd pull out, or worse, do something crazy himself to preempt. Every time Karen had ventured to suggest that Paco be told the truth, Rubin had shot her down in the same manner.

"Tell him what? That your inside man is the guy who he punched out and snatched Sally from and that he should therefore trust me?"

"You *sure* you didn't let anything slip . . . ?" Rubin persisted now, as he, Larry, Karen, and Leslie sat at the kitchen table over coffee. "He still thinks you're gonna go up there with your bomb threat and demand they put on Cyborg Sally? He doesn't have wind of—"

"Hey, wait a minute!" Karen cried.

It had finally clicked. All this time that she had been feeling queasy about hiding Rubin's involvement from Paco, she had been escaping from her knowledge of the larger and more outrageous betrayal, and now, unbidden, it had suddenly slapped her across the face.

"You're setting him up, aren't you?" she said. "You're selling him out! You're double-crossing him!"

"Aw come on, Karen . . ." Larry moaned deprecatingly, but his eyes refused to meet hers.

"Aw come on yourself, Larry Coopersmith! While the rest of us are safely onstage, or backstage, or in the broadcast booth, he's gonna be down there in the pit all by himself with a mob of streeties he's got whipped up into a rage howling for Cyborg Sally, waiting for you to force them to put her on. Which is not going to happen! What's going to happen to Paco when—"

"Hey come on, Karen, lighten up, will you?" Larry said soothingly. "When all those people see Red Jack come up onstage and hear him talkin', the whole mood will flip around, they'll be so—"

"And if it doesn't? If something goes wrong, if this whole crazy house of cards—"

"Aren't you forgetting whose idea this was in the first place, lady?" Bobby Rubin said sharply. Karen shut up in mid-sentence and stared at him with a dead weight in her stomach.

"*You* were the one who dragged me into this, remember?" Rubin said relentlessly. "*You* were the one who begged me to play Red Jack and save your friends from Cyborg Sally. So if there's anyone here double-crossing Paco Monaco . . ."

"I only meant to . . . I only wanted . . ." Karen heard her own voice stammering into silence.

"Karen, Karen, you did the right thing," Larry said gently. "All's well that ends well, like the man says. Or would you rather you'd never brought Bobby here? Would you rather we went ahead and gave Paco what he thinks he wants and risk all we're risking to put on Cyborg Sally?"

"No, but . . ."

"The guy left you flat for some damned video phantom, didn't he?" Leslie said not unkindly, reaching across the table to touch her hand.

"And he double-crossed *me,*" Rubin said. "The son of a bitch punched me out, but I took pity on him and saved his job anyway. And how did he repay me? He lied to me about Sally when it meant *my* ass. . . ."

"You don't understand. . . . It's not really his fault. . . . He never . . . Cyborg Sally . . ."

"Sure we understand," Larry told her. "Hey, Cyborg Sally had us all going, too, remember, until a real friend did what she had to and brought Bobby here to run a number on us and pop us out of it. . . . Sometimes too much honesty is not the best policy."

"What else can you do for him?" Leslie said. "If you tell him what's going to happen and he backs out, it'll only be right into the arms of Cyborg Sally, won't it?"

"And *you'd* be betraying *us* if you did that," Larry pointed out. "You'd be betraying the RLF. Jesus, Karen, you'd be betraying *your own plan* to save the whole damn situation."

"Of course you could always walk away," Leslie said. "Keep your mouth shut and just go back home to Poughkeepsie." She glanced at Larry. "Knowing how you feel, no one here could really blame you. . . ."

Larry nodded, grimaced, shrugged his reluctant agreement.

Karen sighed. "Only myself," she said in a small voice.

And Leslie smiled at her and squeezed her hand. Larry hugged her around the shoulder.

These people were her friends. They were the only friends she had. They had rescued her from the streets and she had rescued them from themselves. And if she had never quite believed in their revolution with wholehearted fervor, indeed if she could not even feel completely dedicated to it now, even though she knew she was committing herself to something that would change her life in ways she could not really presently comprehend, she knew in her heart that she would despise herself forever if she turned her back and walked away.

Was this what Markowitz meant by class self-interest? Could there be such a thing as class self-interest of the spirit? Was that what she felt?

Even Bobby Rubin nodded in sympathy, as if he understood, as if, somehow, he had once stood where she was standing now.

And Paco?

He, too, had saved her. And she had repaid him as best she knew how. She had given him what it was in her power to give. And yet he had abandoned her, he had left her for a phantom, he had betrayed her for a succubus of the bits and bytes.

So her conscience should be clear now, should it not? Logically, she was blameless, reason told her that she was doing the only honorable thing that she could, her mother's poor sad voice told her to congratulate herself for her bravery.

But she felt herself a traitor still. A traitor to she knew not what.

IT AIN'T OVER TILL THE FAT LADY SINGS

"Hey nigger, what are *you* doing here?" Paco Monaco said, more pleased than he would admit to see Dojo shoving his way forward through the huge Saturday night crowd around the door.

"Why I'm here to see the show just like everyone else, my man," Dojo said sardonically. "Word is it's gonna be quite a performance."

He scanned the back of the crowd for familiar faces, found them, gave Paco a funny little smile. "Besides, somehow I don't think Slimy Mary's is gonna draw much of a crowd tonight, what with our main draw . . . otherwise engaged."

"Chingada, man, cool it, will you," Paco hissed nervously, "things are dicey enough tonight as it is!"

He didn't dare plug into the power of Mucho Muchacho yet, not on the door, not till he had gotten everyone inside, and the longer he stood here slowly infiltrating his forces into The American Dream, the more time he had to think about what was going to come down from this unaccustomed ground-level perspective.

And the more time Paco had to think about what Mucho Muchacho had gotten him into, the more paranoid he became.

He had already passed about fifty of his people inside with no sweat about it and no real reason to think the rest of the infiltration was going to be any hassle.

Nor was there any reason to suppose anything would go wrong when he had Uncle Ugly and the Toad seal the door behind him when it was time for *him* to go inside. It would never occur to Steiner and his zonies to check why no one was getting in after the place was filled up. No sweat either to surround the stage with his warriors, all they had to do was dance themselves into position real naturallike just before Black Flame was supposed to go on.

But after that . . . Chingada, after that, it was all in the hands of Coopersmith and the RLF, and the mysterious change in the plan made him more nervous the longer he thought about it.

Originally they were supposed to come in past him so he could be fuckin' sure they'd all be inside with their bullhorn and phony bomb before he committed to anything. Now, with this bullshit about getting in through the VIP entrance, he had to *trust* them to show up, not to chicken out and leave him a big fat target with his dick in his hand when the action started.

And something else was starting to get to him too, something he was more and more losing the handle on the longer he stood here—what the fuck was he *really* putting his ass on the line for, what the fuck was *Paco Monaco* gonna get out of it except maybe thrown in the slammer or even blown away?

It all seemed so clear when he was chain-tapping with Cyborg Sally and a great big hard-on; they were gonna scream it from the rooftops in the hard-hearted night, and throw Ciudad Trabajo on her funeral pyre, whatever the fuck *that* meant. Liberate MUZIK from Official Reality and turn it over to the people, whoever the fuck Larry Coopersmith thought *they* were.

But now, as Paco Monaco stood there all alone nerving himself up for it without benefit of the Jack, it was all starting to dissolve into words and music and wire and fancy gordo manteca. . . .

Chingada, man, he told himself, it's natural, you're just gettin' itchy waiting for it to happen, it's too late to worry about it, *you* ain't gonna be the maricón that chickens out, are you, muchacho?

Still . . .

"Hey Dojo," he said, hooking the big man by the elbow as he was about to pass inside, "will you do something for me in there?"

Dojo scowled. "Hey look, my son," he said, "I'm not gonna get myself involved in this wirehead bullshit, I've done *time,* Paco, I get myself busted, they throw away the key. Like I told you, I'm just here for the show. . . ."

"Come on, all I'm asking you to do is keep an eye out for those putamadres from the Reality Liberation Front. If you see even one of them, everything's cool and you don't have to do nothin'. But if none of them show by say a quarter of ten, you come out here and tell me, I'll know they've fucked us, and the whole thing gets called off. Is that too much to ask, amigo?''

Dojo shrugged. ''You got it,'' he said. He smiled, he punched Paco lightly on the bicep. ''Good luck, my son,'' he said softly. ''Whatever that means under these asshole circumstances.'' Then he disappeared inside.

Cyborg Sally got out of the cab two blocks away on West Broadway when she saw that the jammed traffic was going nowhere, and made her way to the back of the crowd around The American Dream on foot.

No one seemed to recognize her as she made her way down the crowded main drag and no one paid any attention to her as she meekly waited her turn at the door with the rest of the crowd filing inside, just like some fat little tourist from the San Fernando Valley. So far, so good.

She had let Sally from the Valley out to put on this loose-fitting brown raincoat, turn off the wig's light sources, and mess up her makeup, leaving only a little smudgy silver greasepaint on her cheeks and chin and forehead, exposing great untidy areas of pale pink skin.

It had been strangely disorienting when she plugged herself back in and surveyed the result in the dressing room mirror before leaving for The American Dream.

The disguise was perfect. With the wig lights off, and the bulky raincoat on, and an amateurish makeup job, Cyborg Sally looked just like some pudgy, pimply, nobody pathetically trying to dress herself up as the Queen of Heat.

Almost *too* perfect . . .

For there staring back at her with those sad trapped eyes, with her *own* eyes, she saw a poor little Valley Girl stuffing herself into a foam-rubber undersuit, silver tights, and black leather panties, plugging herself in in her apartment, and nervously boarding the escalator to the Glitter Dome. . . .

No one could see the spirit of Cyborg Sally peering out from that false mask of pasty, blotchy skin; all they could see was the mask itself, all they could see was this sweaty fleshy creature trying to intrude herself into the perfect dreamtime of Cyborg Sally's blood-hot wire, whining why not *me,* why not *me,* why not ME. . . .

She shuddered, twitched convulsively, hit her touchpoint to bring her true self back into the present out of the fracturing flash, as the press of bodies around her surged forward again, and she saw Mucho Muchacho, standing tall and proud, ushering half a dozen people past him into The American Dream.

"You're *Cyborg Sally,* flesh and wire, Queen of Heat, electric fire!" she told herself under her breath. "You're *Cyborg Sally,* the leader of the pack, get your shit together, don't you *dare* look back!"

And strode like same up to the door.

The steel door of the VIP entrance swung open, and Alan Pham—natty in a black silk suit and red-ruffled shirt, but scowling angrily—emerged, trailed by the door zonie that Bobby had sent to fetch him. "What now?" he snapped pettishly. Then, seeing Bobby and his entourage, "I should have known it would be you."

"I need some passes," Bobby told him. "Backstage passes."

"For all of *this*?" Pham said unhappily. "Don't be ridiculous!"

Glorianna O'Toole stood beside him with her vocoder rig in her big purse. Bobby himself, his red hair and Jack hidden under a rather silly-looking panama hat, carried the disassembled shotgun mike in an outsized clarinet case. Behind them stood the entire Reality Liberation Front, all ten of them, shuffling their feet nervously and looking mighty scruffy for this side of the building.

"I shouldn't really tell you this, but . . ." Bobby muttered with mock uncertainty. He took Pham aside, spoke to him in low, confidential tones.

"I got word from sources you don't want to know about that Sally Genaro is gonna be here tonight. West is really getting on my case. . . . Has he called you yet?"

"N-no . . ." Pham said nervously.

"Phew!" Bobby sighed in relief. "I guess that means I still had the clout to talk him out of it!"

"Talk him out of what . . . ?"

Bobby grimaced. "Believe me, it's not my doing, I know it's not your fault and I told him so," he said. "But he's really pissed. He's convinced your security fucked up, doesn't trust Steiner and his boys at all anymore, and if Sally gets away tonight, it's Steiner's ass, and yours, as well as mine. . . ."

"Oh shit . . ."

"Not to worry," Bobby told him, "that's why I've hired these Pinkertons, in case your boys fuck up again. They're real pros, fooled *you,* didn't they? We'll fan them out through the whole club and with any luck we'll be able to handle this nice and quiet. That's why we need backstage passes. No telling where she might show."

"Jesus . . ." Pham moaned. "Why me . . . ?"

He turned to one of the security guards. "Go to Steiner's office and get me twelve gold badges!" he snapped. "Move your ass! I want you back here with them in five minutes!"

"Gold badges?"

Pham nodded. "Just pin them on and they'll get you in anywhere with no noise and no hassle," he said. He glanced at Bobby's clarinet case, really noticing it for the first time. "Jeez, I hope you've really got a clarinet in there!"

"As a matter of fact—"

"Please!" Pham cried, holding up his hand. "I don't really want to know!"

Chingada, where the fuck was Cyborg Sally? It was getting to be almost nine, he had already passed most of his people inside, and she still hadn't showed. And the longer he waited, the more muchachas in silver makeup and $3000 worth of fancy Sally gear he let through the door, the more unlikely it began to seem that the real thing could just slip inside without any of Steiner's boys copping to her.

Right, sure, she'd just wear that crummy raincoat he bought for her and dance right in, and no one would be able to tell her from the hordes of phonies!

Shit, what if she never showed up, what if they—

Oh fuck, here came another one, and what a puerca this one was! Wig light turned off, silver makeup half smeared over her pimply face, sleazy brown raincoat draped over her body like a goddamn tent . . .

Standing there with her fuckin' hands on her hips like she was Queen of Heat herself! Chingada, man, this dogmeat don't get in, no way, no how. . . .

But something about the eyes . . . something about her nose . . . something about the lips around that silver tooth-paint . . . something about the way she was giving him this cow-eyed stare . . .

He *knew* her, he was horribly sure he did, he knew her like he knew the cool blond chocharica out of all his wirehead wet dreams. . . .

Only this was something out of *Mucho Muchacho's* dream-time, not his, out of Mucho Muchacho's *nightmare,* where he fell asleep in a penthouse throne room with Cyborg Sally, and dreamed he was lying on a crummy mattress in a stinkin' shithole upstairs in Florida with . . . with . . . with what he was seeing now, with what Cyborg Sally made him promise never to see, with . . . with . . .

Chingada . . .

"Well?" she said.

She gave him this horrible wink. Motherfucker, that raincoat, those eyes, that stupid little grin . . . No, not this puerca, not that fat little face, not . . .

She touched a pudgy hand to his shoulder. She leaned forward, she whispered into his ear, he could feel her warm, wet breath, smell the sour chemical odor of a body sweating inside foam rubber.

"Come along with me, come as what you are, every man a king, every girl a star. . . ."

He jumped backward.

She smiled at him knowingly. She reached out, ran a teasing finger up the zipper of his fly. His cock wilted and cringed behind it. No, man, don't let it be—

"Oh yes, I'm Cyborg Sally, I'm your sex machine, my crystal chips gonna make you cream . . ." she purred, and, blowing him a slimy little kiss, slipped by him into The American Dream.

"Okay, group A, you get out here and stake yourselves out around the saloon," Bobby Rubin said officiously as the big VIP elevator reached the second floor.

Larry Coopersmith nodded. The girl in the black tuxedo swimsuit opened the gate, and he, Leslie Savanah, Eddie Polonski, Iva Cohen, and Tommy Don stepped off into a service area.

"Right through here and you come out behind the bar," said the now-helpful zonie. "They give you any trouble, you just flash those gold badges."

"Thanks," Larry said as the elevator operator closed the gate behind them. The elevator moved upward past the tv studio level, past the restaurant level, and then came to a stop on the VIP lounge floor, where Karen and the rest of them got off.

"Jeez . . ." Karen said softly. "It's like walking into a movie. . . ."

Even golden lighting from overhead fixtures cast a rich sunset glow over multiple levels—a sunken conversation pit area, some groups of small cafe tables, pairs of art deco couches facing each other, semi-circles of big rainbow-painted peacock chairs—each area cunningly set off in its own zone of privacy by the dips and rises of the free-form floor. The deep green wall-to-wall carpeting that ran seamlessly from level to level enhanced the ambience of an indoor garden of hills and dales.

It was the Hollywood version of a Hollywood mogul's party in a Broadway stage set of the ultimate Soho loft.

MUZIK was playing at low volume on the little monitors above the bar and on small screens tucked into corners, but nobody paid any attention. The stars of the VIP lounge were those who were there playing themselves in the flesh.

The place was filled with familiar faces from discs and films and tv, with unfamiliar faces that nevertheless looked like they belonged, with dresses and pants outfits from designer salons too exclusive to be famous, with ten-thousand-dollar suits, gold chains, and designer noses, with the heady perfume of wealth and power and show-business glory.

Karen Gold stood there at the entrance with Mary, Bill, Teddy, and Malcolm, feeling like a character that had wandered in from the wrong cartoon. What irony!

All her life she had worked and schemed to no avail to gain access to just this movie. And now that she was here at last, she knew at once there was no way she ever could have gotten herself a leading role in it. Here she was indeed, but not in her script as written, not as a true princess of the city, but as a terrorist about to stop the show.

This would never be her world and never could have been. In a sense it wasn't even real for people like her. It was just a television format for a dream that these very people had sold to her, a show-business fantasy that would always be on the other side of the screen.

But if she mourned the loss of that innocent lifelong fantasy, there was a strange exhilaration, a wild new kind of freedom, in perceiving the essential ignobility of her naive longings to become a citizen of the VIP lounge, of what Markowitz called Official Reality and Paco called Chocharica City, of the very world that had stolen whatever true dreams she might have had away, and left her, after having done everything she was told to, broke and desperate on the streets of New York, on the outside looking in.

What would I do even now if some Prince Charming magically emerged from the ranks of these beautiful people to lead me away into the Magic Kingdom? Would I be strong? Would I turn my back on my friends even now? Would I dance away from what's about to happen on the arm of some movie star if given half a chance?

But then that was the innocence she had just lost, and the freedom she had just been given.

She didn't have to worry about it.

It would never happen.

"Hey, spread out, don't cluster together, make yourselves as inconspicuous as you can, break up into pairs," Glorianna O'Toole hissed.

"Right," Bobby Rubin said. "And at exactly five of, no earlier, down to the broadcast studio, and not in a mob either, two in the elevator, three by the firestairs, rendezvous outside, go right in, got it? And for chrissakes, don't any of you wireheads plug yourselves in up here!"

Karen nodded, took Malcolm by the hand, and led him off toward the neutrality of the bar.

She found herself perversely pleased that she was here instead of in the saloon with the others, as she ordered a glass of champagne and savored it slowly, wondering whether she would ever get to taste the stuff again. She laughed a brave little, wan little laugh.

At least I can send a postcard to Poughkeepsie to show the folks I *got* here once, she told herself.

"What's so funny?" Malcolm said.

Karen shrugged. "You. Me. Sitting up here at the top of the world sipping champagne and waiting for the revolution to begin."

Malcolm nodded, sipped at his whiskey, smiled nervously. Something about his posture, something about his expression, something about his dark skin and his bushy hair, sent a flash of warmth, and then a chill of loss, through Karen, flashed her back to another bar, with another man sitting beside her, sipping his drink, and waiting for some action. She had to blink her way back into the current reality. Malcolm caught it.

"Something wrong?"

"What could be wrong?" Karen said with a bitterness that surprised her.

"Paco . . . ?" Malcolm said. "I guess you'd rather be sitting here with him . . . ?"

Karen smiled at him wanly. "Nothing personal, Malcolm . . ."

"Yeah, I know," Malcolm said. "You know, I had a white girlfriend once—"

"Spare me the—"

"Not what you think. I was a cyberwhiz, black middle class, and she was umpteenth generation white trash, my parents looked down their long black noses at her. But we did love each other. We were gonna maybe get married. And then I got this scholarship to MIT. Well, it was her or Boston. And class told, Karen, I took Boston. And I got my degree, and she ended up slinging hash in Jersey City, and after a couple years pounding the pavement, here I am in the Reality Liberation Front, sitting here with you, waiting for the revolution."

"The point of which being . . . ?"

Malcolm shrugged. "You tell me," he said. "Which side are you on?"

"Half an hour," Bobby said, checking his watch. "Should we kill it at the bar or drift backstage . . . ?"

Glorianna ran her gaze jaundicedly around the VIP lounge. This joint and the people in it held no charms for her. She had hung out in places like this with people like this all her life, and, in fact, had just spent a week and more doing little else. She studied the faces inside more closely from the relative cover of the entrance. Shit, that was Tommy Dupar over there by the fireplace! And Ella Carmody! And Jonny Janes! Damn, there must be a dozen people here likely to recognize her! This would never do!

"We'd better get our asses out of here before someone recognizes me!" she said, hooking Bobby's arm, dragging him toward the elevator, and hitting the call button.

"Where to . . . ?"

Glorianna fingered the gold badge pinned to her blouse as the elevator motor whined and the cables sang, glancing upward through the open cagework. . . . "I wonder . . ." she mused.

Yes, the stories must be true, the elevator shaft *did* extend one story higher. . . .

"Wonder what?"

"I've heard stories about this joint," she said. "Never talked to anyone who had really been there, but there's supposed to be a level above the VIP lounge, the Summit they call it, strictly for corporate presidents and certified royalty, or some such shit. . . .''

''What's up there?''

Glorianna shrugged. ''That's the thing of it,'' she said, ''never talked to anyone who knew . . .'' She stroked Bobby's gold badge playfully. She laughed. ''But maybe with these and a little bullshit, we can get to find out. . . .''

''Jeez, Glorianna, get serious, we didn't come here to—''

''All work and no play makes Jack a dull boy!'' she told him with a wink as the elevator came to a stop before them. ''We got some time to kill, and something tells me that after what's gonna come down tonight, we're not gonna get a chance at a peek at the top again!''

The elevator door opened, half a dozen people got out, Glorianna dragged Bobby inside, the operator closed the gate. This being the highest floor for mere mortals, there was no one inside but the girl in the tuxedo swimsuit and a zonie with an Uzi. The operator started to crank the control level toward the descent position.

''Uh-uh, honey!'' Glorianna said, grabbing her hand. ''We're going up!''

''*Up?* There isn't any up!''

''Oh yes there is! My friend and me are going to the Summit!'' She gave the girl a lubricious wink.

''Nobody goes there!'' the zonie snapped.

''Nobody who is *nobody* goes there, sonny,'' Glorianna told him, stroking her gold badge.

The zonie and the elevator operator exchanged nervous glances. ''I dunno . . .'' the zonie said uncertainly.

''Well I do!'' Bobby snapped, finally getting into the spirit of things. ''I'm here from the *home office,* my man, from Hollywood, and if I don't like what I see, Pham gets canned, and Steiner gets canned, does that tell you anything about what's going to happen to you two if this fucking thing isn't moving upward before I can count to three? One . . . two . . . two and a half . . .''

The zonie shrugged. He nodded to the elevator operator, who hit her lever. A moment later the elevator came to a stop at a small landing. There was nothing there but a short corridor capped at both ends by blank walls and a plain steel door.

''I'll have to unlock it for you,'' the zonie said as the operator opened the gate. He fished a ring of keys out of his pocket and started to lead them out of the elevator.

"Don't bother," Glorianna told him, "just give me the key; we may want to come back here later."

"Hey, I can't—"

"You heard the lady, fork it over!" Bobby snapped. "One . . . two . . ."

"Okay, okay," the zonie grunted unhappily. He handed Glorianna the key, they stepped out of the elevator, the operator closed the gate, and the elevator departed, leaving them alone in the dimly lit corridor.

Glorianna fitted the key into the lock, turned it, pulled the door open. A sudden radiance filled the corridor as an automatic switch turned on the interior lights.

"Holy shit!" Bobby exclaimed as he crossed the threshold and looked inside.

Cyborg Sally prowled restlessly around the periphery of the pit like a caged silver cat, peering into the crowded smoky bar, watching the dancers cramming the floor and moving to the dumb-ass max metal beat of some chrome and black leather group, checking her watch every thirty seconds, willing the digits to change as they marched with agonizing slowness toward ten o'clock.

She scarcely heard the music, she was hardly aware of the dancers or the denizens of the bar as anything but a faceless sweaty mass waiting for her advent, waiting for her to take them higher, waiting to throw their world on her funeral pyre.

As she circled round and round, her eyes stayed hypnotically focused on the great pedestal of black glass rising from the eye of the maelstrom—the stage, darkened now, but with a team of roadies setting up Black Flame's gear in the anonymous shadows.

Only when bright white beams from on high picked out her own groupie avatars, pale pathetic shadows with perfect movie-star faces and porn-queen bodies, was her fixation on the stage diverted.

Then, she would pause for a moment to watch, and smile her secret smile, so cunningly concealed behind the mask of the fat girl she wore.

Let them have their passing moment in the spotlight, she thought magnanimously. Let all the little nobodies in all the

Valley bars have their dream of being *me* while I hide here right in plain sight disguised as *them*!

And when the spotlight passed and the latest Cyborg Sally was yanked back into the darkness from whence she had come, she would peer intently into the maelstrom of bodies and seek out her fans, the people of the streets wearing *her* face on their chests, dancing with the secret knowledge of what was about to come glowing in their eyes, as one by one, in couples, in little groups, they spiraled slowly inward toward the stage.

Suddenly, unexpectedly, the opening bars of ''Cyborg Sally'' blared out from on high, her trumpet call to battle, and there she was, towering up there on the great video screens, triplexed, multiplexed, amplified, summoning her army of fans to burn down this world on her funeral pyre.

I'm Cyborg Sally
I'm your blood-hot wire
I'm the blazing bytes
Of your meat's desire!

''CYBORG SALLY! CYBORG SALLY!''

The chant erupted from all over the dance floor. The streeties who had already reached the stage tried to link their hands around it, while the others pushed and shoved through the dancers toward the gaps in the line.

''CYBORG SALLY! CYBORG SALLY!''

Then destiny reached out at last from on high as a bright white spotlight descended to bathe her in stardom's glory, and she tore off the raincoat, tossing it high above the heads of the crowd, and danced into the limelight, casting aside her disguise, and revealing herself at last to her worshippers.

Cyborg Sally!
Flesh and wire!
Throw the world
On my funeral pyre!

She shoved and snaked and danced her way toward the stage, sailing through the screaming audience in the spotlight of her stardom as the children of her night started stomping their feet and waving their fists as their simple chant coalesced into a hoarse and ragged version of her battle song.

Cyborg Sally!
Flesh and wire!
Throw the world
On my funeral pyre!

"*This* is how the big boys get their rocks off?" Bobby Rubin muttered to himself as he began poking and puttering around the Summit.

The chamber was much smaller than he would have expected, indeed it was hardly larger than his own Beverly Glen bedroom. But it was, in a sense, *all bed*.

A big picture window looked down from Olympus on the floor below. The ceiling, canted downward toward the window at a forty-five-degree angle, was an enormous video screen.

Every other surface—the walls, the entire floor—was softly upholstered in rolling curves reminiscent of breasts and thighs and buttocks and covered with an obscene synthetic the color and texture of rosy pink flesh. The stuff was heated from within to what Bobby would have bet was human blood temperature plus or minus a tenth of a degree.

The wall opposite the window was mounded into a kind of fleshy headboard; on the left hand was a small but well-stocked bar and a cabinet of drugs, above this a phone; on the right some kind of strange little control console with some conventional tv knobs, and, for some weird reason, two little joysticks.

It was like walking around on some huge pink tongue. It was opulent, it was obscene, and it was also, at least as far as Bobby was concerned, incredibly tacky. It belonged in Vegas, it called up images of fat men with gold rings receiving expert blow-jobs from $5000-a-night bleached-blond hookers.

"Welcome to the womb at the top," Glorianna drawled. Bobby looked up from the control console he had been examining, groaning.

Glorianna shrugged. "Sorry," she said with a silly grin, "I just couldn't resist."

"Wonder what all this is . . ." Bobby muttered, returning his attention to the controls. Seemed like a straightforward home video rig except for the joysticks . . . He flipped a power toggle.

The big ceiling screen came to life with a full shot of the dance floor far below, where tiny figures were crammed together in frenzied motion like a nest of angry army ants. A simple volume control bled audio in and out. Big fucking deal . . .

Bobby twiddled one of the joysticks experimentally.

The scene on the video screen moved jerkily around. A camera controller for morons! He twisted the joystick clockwise in its socket. The camera zoomed in. He twisted it counterclockwise. The camera pulled back.

"Cute . . ." he muttered. "Wonder what the other one does . . ."

He twisted the other joystick around. Nothing happened. Then he noticed the button on the end and pressed it down with his thumb.

Instantly a bright white spotlight beam lanced down from the top of the video screen frame and pinned a male dancer with a rainbow mohawk in a circle of light. Son of a bitch!

"Hey Glorianna, have a look at this!" He lay back against the softly mounded wall with the control console close to hand, a jaded videohead pasha playing with his controls.

The spotlight glided smoothly around the dance floor, picking out tiny figures. Bobby zoomed the camera as he moved the spotlight around, catching a tall girl in a flashing Sally wig in the spotlight circle. He centered the shot on her, moved in for a close-up.

"Not my type," he said, pulling the camera back, scanning the dance floor with it from left to right, picking and choosing among the dancers with his spotlight beam, moving in for close-ups, pulling back, passing on.

"Room service pussy!" he drawled dryly. "Just lay back here playing with yourself and video shopping, and when you see one you like, keep the spotlight on her, pick up the phone, and have a flunky fetch her for a command performance. . . ."

Glorianna scowled. "Far fucking out," she sneered. "Jerk-off styles of the rich and impotent!" She glanced at her watch. "Enough fun and games," she said, "we'd better—hey, wait a minute! Jesus Christ, Bobby, something must have fucked up, I think it's going down already! Bring the spotlight back! No, on the stage! By the *bottom* of the stage!"

Bobby fiddled with the controls and caught two streeties in the spotlight and a slice of a third, pumping their fists in the air, and screaming, red-eyed, at the top of their lungs.

"Pull the camera back!"

Bobby pulled back into a long shot on the base of the stage, but from this angle all he could see were bodies shoving each other in the darkness and tiny shouting figures in the spotlight circle as he swept it around the crowd trying to piece together the big picture.

"Hey, look!" Glorianna shouted. "Isn't that *her*?"

She pointed to a dim little figure just outside the circle of light in the bottom left of the video screen. "A little to the left . . . No, you've gone past . . . Yeah, now up a bit! Yeah! Yeah! That's it, you got her!"

Bobby held the spotlight control steady and zoomed in as close as the camera would go.

There, gyrating wildly in the circle of light, was Sally Genaro, lithe and sinewy thanks to her foam rubber undersuit, but definitely the Pimple, dancing her heart out, with her wig lights off, and a really crummy half-assed silver makeup job doing nothing to hide her face.

"Shit, what luck!" Bobby cried, bolting to his feet, grabbing Glorianna by the hand, dragging her toward the door. "Come on!"

"What are we gonna do?"

"*What are we gonna do?*" Bobby said as he opened the door. "We're gonna grab her and lock her in here until it's all over, that's what we're gonna do!"

"But the whole shitpile is going up! We've got to—"

"We've got to get her up here before something happens to her, before we lose her again," Bobby told her, yanking her out into the corridor and jabbing at the elevator call button. "Have you forgotten what we came here to do?"

"Have you? We've got to get backstage so—"

The elevator came whining up the shaft.

"No time to argue," Bobby moaned, his mind working frantically. "Give me the key! You take this!" he snapped, handing her the shotgun mike case. "You go backstage, I'll go get her, and get there as soon as I can."

The elevator came to a stop and the gate swung open.

"Don't you think—"

"No time to think now, move, move, move!" Bobby hissed as he shoved her inside.

Paco was in a freaked enough state already! He half-whirled around in a karate kick when Dojo came up on him from behind and tapped him on the shoulder.

"Dojo! Chingada, what's wrong—"

"You betta get your ass out of here or in there right now, my son! MUZIK's playing 'Cyborg Sally' and it set your street meat off! What's going down is *coming down*!"

"Motherfucker!" Paco moaned, making frantic get-your-asses-over-here gestures at Uncle Ugly and the Toad, who stood near the back of the crowd.

"My advice to you is to disappear, Paco, it's getting to be bugfuck city in there! Pretty soon the zonies are liable to go apeshit."

"Hey, man, I can't do that, I'm like the jefe. . . ."

Dojo shrugged. "It's your funeral, my son," he said.

Uncle Ugly and the Toad pushed their way to the door.

"Remember, nobody gets in, nobody gets out!" Paco told them as he slid past them into the dimly lit entrance corridor. He paused as Dojo reentered the club behind him.

"Hey nigger, if you're so afraid of the zonies, why you comin' back in here?"

Dojo scowled at him. " 'Cause someone has to watch your silly ass," he said.

"Yeah, nigger, well you're another," Paco said affectionately, hitting his touchpoint and dashing down the corridor.

"One, two, three, *go*!" Malcolm McGee shouted, and he, Teddy, and Bill slammed into the control room door with all their weight behind their shoulders. The door flew open so easily that they nearly tripped over their feet as they fell forward inside, followed by Karen and Mary Ferrari.

"What the fuck!"

"Jesus!"

There were only four people inside the compact studio: a cameraman pointing his camera down at the stage, a sound man hunched over his console, a female lighting technician behind her board, and a director sitting behind a bank of monitors and a video mixer. One monitor showed the MUZIK logo, another ran a Coke commercial, the middle one showed Ali Babble standing alone in the spotlight atop the stage waiting to begin his introductory rap.

"What the fuck is this, you assholes!" screamed the director. "We're about to—"

"This is the Revolution, motherfuckers!" Malcolm shouted, whipping a string-tied cluster of red-painted dowels with a short fuse out of one pocket and a cigarette lighter out of another. "Get your asses out of here before I blow us all up!"

"Hey you can't—"

"Watch me!" Malcolm said, and lit the fuse.

"Holy shit!"

"Out of my way!"

Pushing and shoving and cursing each other, the technicians and director tumbled out the door. Bill wedged the back of a chair under the doorknob.

Malcolm laughed as he pinched out the fuse, sat down in the director's chair, and tossed the phony bomb over his shoulder into a corner.

"Lessee," he said, scanning the controls, "satellite feed . . . camera feed . . . standby monitor . . . piece of cake! Mary, take the lights, Bill the camera, Teddy sound . . ."

For want of anything more useful to do, Karen went to the front of the booth and looked out the window at the living reality of the pit below.

"Oh my God . . ."

Ali Babble stood there on the stage waiting for his air cue as if nothing were happening. Maybe from where he stood inside the spotlight looking out into darkness, nothing was. But from where Karen was standing, she could see that a ragged line of streeties had already surrounded the base of the stage, shouting, stomping, waving their fists, and what looked to be knives. More streeties were fighting their way toward them through the rapidly panicking crowd, and being none too gentle about it.

It was happening already! It was happening early! And it was nothing like anyone's revolutionary fantasy; it was raw red meat, and a riot about to happen, out of anyone's control.

And Paco must be right down there in it! Helping to whip up that frenzy! Frenzy that would turn to murderous outrage when Markowitz went on instead of Cyborg Sally, when those maniacs finally realized that they had been sold out.

And he didn't even know.

He didn't know that he was going to be left there to face that thwarted anger all alone.

MUZIK had finished playing "Cyborg Sally" by the time Mucho Muchacho emerged into the pit, but the audience wasn't finished with it, oh no!

The huge space echoed with feet pounding out the rhythm, with the angry impatient clapping of hands. Voices sang out random snatches of the words, but they were shouted down by the white noise of the gordos and plushie-tushies, screaming and babbling in a panic, as little squads of his warriors, waving fists and knives and lead pipes, bulled their way through them toward the stage.

Ali Babble, resplendent in a gold sequined tuxedo, stood in the spotlight up there above it all, adjusted his tie, acknowledged what the asshole must have thought was applause for *him* with a little nod, and went into his rap.

Chingada, what a mess, this is all fucked up! How am I supposed to find Cyborg Sally in all this shit? Where the fuck is she? Chingada, she better show herself fast when Larry gets up there with his fuckin' bomb threat!

"Ladies and gentlemen, boys and girls, devils and demonesses, sons and daughters of the lords of darkness . . ."

And he had better get these assholes organized well enough to shout this stupid motherfucker down! He was going on as if nothing were happening and they were miking his voice at full volume.

". . . live as you'll ever be, from the nethermost pit of The American Dream . . ."

With knees, and elbows, and back-handed chops, Mucho Muchacho broke trail through the crowd toward the stage. "Out of my way, putamadre; move your ass, motherfucker!"

Wasting no time on niceties, he shoved his way through the gordos and plushie-tushies like a karate-freak tornado, and reached the base of the tall black pedestal.

Their hands locked in a human chain around it, streeties in Cyborg Sally T-shirts surrounded the stage two and three deep, leering at the terrified citizens, swaying back and forth, snarling, spitting, hacking clams, fucked-up out of their minds!

"Come on, you stupid motherfuckers, scream it out from the rooftops in the hard-hearted night!" Mucho roared, circling round them, sweeping the mob out of his way with spin kicks when they pressed too close. "Come on, assholes, sing!"

". . . MUZIK *is* music, boys and girls, and tonight . . ."

Circling round and round like a black-eyed demon, like some fuckin' bandleader, Mucho Muchacho chanted raggedly at the top of his lungs.

Cyborg Sally!
Flesh and wire!
Throw the world
On her funeral pyre!

By the time he had finished two circuits, two hundred voices were roaring it out to the pounding rhythm of their stomping feet, and by the time he had completed a fourth go-round, scores of crazies scattered throughout the pit had picked up on it spontaneously, too, and the whole fuckin' American Dream shook with the stomping of feet, rocked with the black vibrations, rolled with the chanting chorus.

CYBORG SALLY!
FLESH AND WIRE!
THROW THE WORLD
ON HER FUNERAL PYRE!

"Right, no sweat, gotcha!" Malcolm McGee said, and he hung up the phone. "They just ordered the director to release the satellite transponder," he cackled evilly. "They don't want this shit going out on MUZIK, and they're getting crazy calls from the other networks, can you imagine that, hee, hee, hee!"

The airfeed monitor showed a sanitized medium shot on the base of the stage. Bill had caught the line of chanting streeties with the camera and Mary was trying to widen the focus of the spotlight to encompass as many of them as possible, while avoiding the spitters, or the ones with weapons in their hands. Teddy had yanked Ali Babble's audio off MUZIK and replaced it on the air with the chanting voice of the people.

CYBORG SALLY!
FLESH AND WIRE!
THROW THE WORLD
ON HER FUNERAL PYRE!

Everyone laughed.

Everyone but Karen.

For while they all sat there chain-tapping and watching the reality they were broadcasting on the monitors, she had her nose pressed against the broadcast booth window, watching the full living catastrophe unfold.

It wasn't just the streeties chanting and stomping and clapping for Cyborg Sally now. Half the crowd in the pit seemed to have taken it up, and they were crowding toward the stage. Everyone else seemed to be trying to reach the exits. The counterflows mingled and swirled and frustrated each other in angry eddies. It seemed only a matter of time before the whole thing degenerated into a gigantic barroom brawl. Only the appearance of Cyborg Sally onstage could prevent it now.

And she knew that was not going to happen.

And Paco, down there far below her present vantage of safety, did not.

Karen moved away from the window and crossed to the back of the room. From here, all she could see was her chain-tapping friends playing their revolution on their consoles and monitors as if it were all some elaborate video game. From their perspective, those weren't people down there in the pit, they were crowd shots and cutaways.

But she knew that they weren't. She knew that real people were down there. She knew that Paco was one of them.

Despite her best efforts to save him. *Because* of her best efforts to save him.

She found herself backing toward the door, turning the knob, opening it. . . .

"Hey, where you going, Karen?"

Karen paused in the doorway for one last vision of her friends, her comrades, hunched over their camera and consoles. No blame, guys, she thought, but she knew that this, no less than the VIP lounge, was not where she belonged now.

"I've at least got to warn him," she told them. "I owe him that much, don't I?"

Malcolm McGee glanced over his shoulder at her distractedly for a moment, looked back at his monitors, turned again with an entirely altered expression, as if what she had said, and what he had seen, had popped him out of his chain-tapping flash.

"Malcolm! Look at this! I think Ali Babble has finally got the bad news. Should I do a shot on the stage?"

Malcolm blinked, he shrugged, he frowned, he nodded his agreement. "Yeah," he said, "I can see where maybe we do." Then he turned back to his equipment again, hit his touchpoint, and disappeared back into the bits and bytes.

Bobby Rubin dashed through the service area, out through the door behind the bar, across the saloon to the top of the stairs leading down into the pit. Only then, puffing and panting, did he pause for a moment to look out over the chaos below.

A solid wall of streeties surrounded the base of the stage, jacked completely out of their minds, spitting, shooting the bird, brandishing knives and lengths of pipes and bottles, stamping their feet rhythmically, chanting for Cyborg Sally in a great ragged roar.

CYBORG SALLY!
FLESH AND WIRE!
THROW THE WORLD
ON HER FUNERAL PYRE!

The part of the crowd that could see what was happening below the stage was in an angry terror. All they wanted was out, but they were going nowhere, for the rest of the crowd, the great mass of people crushing them back toward the monsters, had joined in the chanting and were trying to squeeze closer to the source.

Ali Babble stood trapped alone in his circle of light high up on the stage, glancing nervously this way and that at people who weren't there, shrugging his shoulders, waving his arms, as if searching for someone to get him off, or at least tell him what to do. His mouth was working frantically, but not even The American Dream's speaker system would have allowed him to make himself heard over this feral din, even if Malcolm McGee hadn't apparently killed his mike.

Bobby stood there, poleaxed, terrified, appalled. He had seen riots and revolutions in the act of progress often enough on television, far worse mob scenes than this. But he had never heard the voice of the beast with his own bones and eardrums, or felt its adrenaline-soaked body odor overwhelming his own air space.

This was not happening on television. This was no Red Jack fantasy of red-ripe anarchy. This was the real thing. People would get hurt. People might get killed. This was completely out of control. It probably always had been. He had let Karen Gold and Glorianna talk him into leading a video fantasy revolution that would rock the soul of the people awake on television, but what they had succeeded in awakening from its starving sleep was the raging soul of the streets, all the ire of thwarted spirits with more than plenty to be righteously and vengefully pissed off about.

When Larry Coopersmith got up there and they patched in his mike, when he told those freaking streeties who had been promised their wirehead vengeance that they were not going to get their Cyborg Sally, the bottles and pipes would start to fly, and when some poor schmuck in a red dye-job replaced her, this place was going to explode.

It all had to be called off. No way I'm gonna go up there and be target practice. It wouldn't do any good anyway.

Nothing can stop it now, he suddenly realized, that was the awful truth. It's over the top, all we can do is to try and get our asses out of here before—

—a spotlight circle passed across the crowd halfway to the stage, picked out a silvery figure, jerked away abruptly. But Bobby still saw the freeze-frame flash.

A bubble of space moving through the crowd like a whirlpool eddy moving across a stormy sea. Dancing within it, her head thrown back, her neon medusa crown rolling and flashing, oblivious to the tentatively seeking hands, the hot sweaty bodies crowding the border of her thus-far-inviolable body space, was Cyborg Sally.

Was Sally Genaro.

Bobby found himself dashing down the stairs to the pit on automatic, even as he had what seemed a lifetime ago when he had chased her down across this very dance floor only to have her escape thanks to the same Paco Monaco who was out there even now as the leader of her pack.

But what he saw at the foot of the stairs popped him back into the all-too-immediate present.

Two zonies stood at the foot of the stairs with their Uzis at port-arms, holding back, at least for the moment, a tide of panicked people trying to escape up into the safe sanity of the saloon, a wall of angry meat.

No way I can fight my way through that! Bobby told himself with considerable relief.

But as he felt that somatic sigh of relief pass through him, he also felt the shame of it. You're standing here because of her and pissed off about it, sonny, a voice inside him said, entirely unbidden. But she's out *there* because of you, deny it if you can. You gonna walk away from that one too, kiddo? Are you gonna be the me they told you that you can never be, or when it's time for little heroes will you be nowhere to be seen?

Bobby felt as if he were standing there with his soul naked for all to see. He felt that the questioning eyes of the world were upon him. And so, he saw, they were.

Somewhere along the line he had lost his hat, and now he

realized his hair was flowing freely around his ears, and he grew acutely aware of the Jack he wore, frosting his *red* hair with a silver webwork. In the frenzy of the moment there were eyes out there in the crowd beyond the zonies who saw what they wanted to see, who clearly took him for someone else.

And he found himself reaching for his touchpoint. Both honor and his own survival required that Bobby Rubin rescue Sally Genaro from where his own mean-spirited fuckups had landed Sally and himself. He knew he could never live with himself if he didn't do it, though he would have plenty of time to try in the joint.

He knew what he had to do.

And he couldn't do it.

But those eyes out there were telling him that maybe there was someone inside of him who could.

Cyborg Sally danced toward the stage to the pounding rhythm of her own song, following it inward, ever inward, laughing, snarling, rolling her hips, reaching out to brush the hands of her worshippers, letting the touch of her perfect silver flesh drive them higher, higher, higher, souls on fire in her funeral pyre—

—Sally Genaro popped out of the flash into stark staring terror. What had she been *doing*?

Hundreds of hands were trying to crawl all over her like tentacles, bodies were crowding all around her, streeties were waving pipes and knives, feet were pounding and people were screaming and maniacs were falling slobbering to their knees, and what she had been doing was egging them on!

Plug into me and I'll make them scream! an imperious electronic voice hissed inside of her.

Haven't you done *enough*? she found herself telling that other Sally. Look what you've gotten me into!

And only Cyborg Sally can get you out of it, that same electronic voice crackled at her knowingly as she found her circuits moving her hand toward her touchpoint. Better trust your fat sweaty flesh to my blood-hot wire.

"You crazy asshole! Where you think you're going?"

One of the zonies at the foot of the stairs whirled around as Bobby Rubin brushed his shoulder squeezing by. Bobby found himself staring down the barrel of an Uzi while the furious zonie found himself staring dumbfounded into the eyes of . . . of . . .

"To wake my soul from its starving sleep," said Red Jack.

A strange calm came over him as he stared into the zonie's eyes and watched the man's expression melt and reform into something more wide-eyed than angry or even terrified.

Time seemed to slow down. He felt an invisible invincible field of force forming around him. The chanting, the screaming, the panicked crowd, the madness of the moment, even the cold, unwinking eye of the gun barrel seemed to fuel it, seemed to reverse some polarity of destiny, and feed all that crazy energy into him. He was Red Jack, the Crown Prince of Rock and Roll, the ghost set free from his machine, booted up to boogie, and ready to fight back. . . .

"You . . . you really gotta go into all that shit?" the zonie said in quite a softer voice.

Red Jack stepped past him. "Gotta dance into her dreamtime, or I'll be nowhere to be seen," he told him as he snaked his way into the body of the crowd, against curses and resistance at first, but parting them for his passage with the aura of his sheer unexpected reborn presence as he picked up momentum, as he made his way toward his last sight of Sally.

Glorianna O'Toole emerged from the elevator into bugfuck city.

A long corridor led past dressing rooms, toilets, storerooms, and offices toward the stairway ascending to the stage. It was clogged with knots of people, all of whom seemed to be waving their arms, shouting at each other, and trying to push past each other in every direction at once.

Armed zonies were dashing in and out of one of the offices. Roadies were screaming at each other. Up at the other end by the stage stairs, Alan Pham, the manager, was engaged in some kind of argument with Black Flame; four male musicians in skin-tight black satin suits, long capes of hologrammed flame, leering devil makeup, and shaved heads with spikes of hair conked into silver horns. The ceiling shook with the rhythmic stomping of hundreds of feet. Dust motes, cigarette- and pot-smoke, flakes of plaster danced in the air.

Larry Coopersmith, Leslie Savanah, Tommy Don, Eddie Polonski, and Iva Cohen had apparently arrived on the previous elevator trip, and the place was such a zoo that the so-called "RLF Strike Force" was still standing around at the elevator end of the corridor in a daze unable or unwilling to bull their way through.

"Jesus Christ, why are you guys standing around like assholes?" she snapped at Coopersmith. "Move it, we've got to get through to the stage!"

"What's happening?" he babbled at her. "Where's our Red Jack?"

"We'll worry about that later, if there *is* a later," Glorianna told him. "Right now, we're carrying the ball, so get your asses in gear! Come on, form a flying wedge in front of me, and let's *do it*! Ain't any of you ever seen a football game?"

"Yeah, right, let's do it!" Coopersmith said, forming them up into a V-formation across the corridor with himself at the point. "Out of the way, motherfuckers! One side! Move it!" Shoving, elbowing, kicking, cursing, they pushed their way down the corridor like an offensive line through a subway rush hour, with Glorianna tucked into the pocket.

Karen Gold stood at the top of the stairs looking down from the saloon into the pit, where a sea of raw meat writhed and jerked and stomped and screamed. Eddies of the terrified tried to force their way to the periphery while riptides of chain-tappers tried to surge toward the base of the stage.

The streeties of the inner circle waved fists and knives, spat and snarled, and shot the world the finger. Bits of debris came flying above the crowd toward the stage, falling far short, and here and there where they fell into the crowd, shoving matches and fistfights were starting to break out.

The pieces of the plan—the RLF's piece, Rubin's piece, Cyborg Sally's, Paco's—she could now see all too plainly, were all fantasies out of entirely different dreamtimes, with no common vision to bind them, with no possible locus of intersection except the one confronting her now. Put them all together in flesh and blood reality, and the result was *this*!

And *she* was the one who had done it.

She had introduced a son of the streets to the machinations of the Reality Liberation Front. She had pulled in Bobby Rubin off those selfsame streets, she was the one who had brought Red Jack back from the bits and bytes to lead the RLF precisely to prevent exactly what was now happening.

This was her doing as much as Cyborg Sally's, or Markowitz's, or Paco's, or Rubin's, or anyone else's, and then some. And if she couldn't find the moment when she had consciously committed an evil act, she was now ready to believe that none of them could either.

But that wouldn't do anything for Paco when Markowitz went on and pushed it over the edge. He had been no more in control than anyone else, but he was going to be the only one facing the wrath of the outraged followers of Cyborg Sally down here in the flesh and blood of the pit.

No he isn't, Karen told herself as she descended the staircase. Not if I can get him out before this explodes.

And if I can't, she thought as she pushed by a strangely distracted zonie, then at least I'll be down here with him and my own consquences where I belong.

CYBORG SALLY!
FLESH AND WIRE!
THROW THE WORLD
ON HER FUNERAL PYRE!

"Hello Sally, remember me?"

A hand grabbed Cyborg Sally's arm, whirled her around snarling, to confront—

—Red Jack.

It was him, standing there holding her by the elbow, with his long red hair flashing silver lightnings and a face she knew all too well.

Images danced across his shirt—a homely girl sitting behind a VoxBox console in a recording studio, a solarized rock and roll queen and a nerdy little wimp outlined against the L.A. cityscape, a boy puking on the grass by a duckpond, his eyes looking into her as he lay atop her, Red Jack himself dancing with her across a tv screen. And his eyes, his sexy snaky little grin . . .

"No . . . no . . ." she cried. "Go away, go away, you're not real, you're—"

"Real as you'll ever be, Cyborg Sally."

"I'm Cyborg Sally, I'm the leader of the pack," she cried, but the reality of it was starting to fade against her resistance, as those eyes, that smirky smile, pulled a poor lost creature up out of her dreamtime.

She searched for an avenue of escape, but the crowd pressed

in even closer now, mesmerized, entranced, plugged into this ultimate drama of their dreamtimes.

"Look at them, Sally," Red Jack told her, "we're just ghosts in their machine. Bits and bytes and programs."

"I'm the Queen of Heat! I'm a funeral pyre!"

But Sally Genaro wasn't.

Sally Genaro found herself standing sweaty and trembling in the midst of pandemonium. Hundreds of voices were chanting. Feet were stomping like claps of thunder. A wall of bodies surrounded her, screaming, howling, reaching for her, pressing in. She could smell their sour stink. She could see their totally spaced-out eyes.

And in front of her, staring right at her with his dark bedroom eyes, skinny and frail, and smiling a sad, soft little snaky smile at her, was Bobby Rubin.

"You son of a bitch! Leave me alone!" Sally screamed at him, reaching for her touchpoint. Bobby slapped her hand away.

"Take a good look at the flesh before you hit the wire!" Bobby shouted in her face over the incredible din.

Sally did. She saw that they were entirely surrounded by wild-eyed creatures, people in fancy clothing as jacked out of their minds and freaking as the streeties wearing *her* . . . wearing Cyborg Sally's promos. Over toward the stage she could see a forest of hands waving clubs and fists and knives. Plastic glasses, wads of paper, even a bottle or two, sailed futilely toward the stage, falling short into the crowd.

CYBORG SALLY!
FLESH AND WIRE!
THROW THE WORLD
ON HER FUNERAL PYRE!

"Oh my God, we're gonna get killed!" she moaned.

"Not with me standing here beside you," Red Jack told her, tucking her protectively under his shoulder. Sally blinked, then looked up at his face, and had to blink again to convince herself she wasn't flashing.

It was Bobby's face looking back at her, but it was Red Jack's face too, and not just because of the silly red hair. For what she saw in that face was the Bobby of her own creation in the dreamtime, and the Red Jack who they had created together in the only magic moment in which their spirits had ever truly touched, and a bravely fearful little boy discovering himself to be a man.

And then she realized that there was a bubble of space around them like an invisible spotlight circle, not much larger than their outstretched arms, but as inviolable as stardom's aura.

Indeed, she saw, it *was* stardom's aura. The silver threadwork in his red hair was the real thing, and so, somehow, was Bobby. He was flashing his freedom in all this terror and fright, and Red Jack was shining through. He looked like Red Jack, in his dreamtime he *was* Red Jack, and the people who saw him believed it too.

Because at last it was true.

And he was with her here now.

"You came down into all this to save *me*?" Sally cried.

"Every little life, Sally," he said, and, cradling her in the crook of his arm, slowly began to part the crowd before them.

"Where . . . where are you taking me?" Sally Genaro shouted into his ear over the din of the chaos around them.

"'To a place I always told you that you could never be."

Ali Babble came charging down the stage stairs as Glorianna and the Reality Liberation Front finally reached them. Alan Pham blocked the bottom of the staircase with his body, shoving the black man in the gold-sequined tuxedo backward. "Are you out of your mind?" he shrieked. "Get your ass back up there!"

"You must be joking, it's an animal farm out there, I'm splitting, talk to my agent!" He shoved Pham aside, bulled his way down the corridor to his dressing room, and slammed the door behind him.

Pham whirled on Black Flame. "All right, you're on, get up there and knock 'em dead!" The four musicians, who had been staring up the steps at the rectangle of white light above in obvious terror, shrank back, inched their way down the corridor.

"No fucking way!"

"Sue us!"

"Get up there, you sons of bitches!" Pham screamed, grabbing the nearest musician by the lapel.

"Now's your chance!" Glorianna told Coopersmith. "They actually *need* someone to go on!"

"By myself? Without Rubin?"

"Wing it," Glorianna said, hitting his touchpoint, and shoving him past the band at Pham. "Do your dingo act and save their show!"

Pham let go of the musician's jacket as Larry Coopersmith staggered forward into his face, irrevocably committed.

"Hey, I gotta talk to you!" he began inanely.

"Piss off!" Pham snarled at him as Black Flame took the opportunity to escape en masse down the corridor.

But that got Larry Coopersmith's biker up.

"No, *you* piss off, motherfucker!" Coopersmith told him, grabbing him by the throat, lifting him bodily, tossing him aside, mounting the steps. "We're the Reality Liberation Front! This is *our* action!"

"You're *who*? This is *what*?" Pham shouted in a red rage.

Leslie Savanah, Tommy Don, Teddy Ribero, Eddie Polonski, and Iva Cohen surged forward as Coopersmith backed slowly up the stairs, forming a cordon of bodies across the landing.

"We're the Reality Liberation Front! We're comin' to dance and we're comin' tonight and you can't stop us!" Coopersmith shouted, and, turning, charged up the stairs into the hot white light.

Two men pushed past Glorianna, one gray-haired and paunchy, the other thinner and younger.

"Steiner!" Pham shouted at the older man. "Get these people out of here, get that asshole off the stage, get—"

He stopped short, goggled at the younger man. "Palacci! What the fuck are *you* doing here! Why aren't you in the broadcast booth?"

"Some terrorist group's taken over the broadcast booth, Mr. Pham," Steiner said unhappily.

"They're broadcasting the whole fiasco on MUZIK, and some damn video pirates are preempting it onto the major networks. We've got half of Washington screaming at us to kill it at our end!"

"We're doing it!" Tommy Don shouted triumphantly.

"The whole world is watching!"

"Pixels to the People!"

"Get your guys up there! Shoot your way in! Get them off that damned transponder!"

"They've got a bomb, Mr. Pham."

"A bomb!" Pham shouted. "A bomb . . ." he moaned softly, collapsing back against the wall, all the fight gone out of him.

"Sure, right, *of course* they have a bomb . . ." he babbled, shaking his head weakly.

"What do we do, Mr. Pham?"

"How the hell do I know . . . ?" Pham groaned. "What the hell do I care . . . ? What does it matter . . . ? I'm gone already. . . ."

"If I may make a suggestion?" Glorianna said.

"Who the hell are you?" Pham said, regarding her defeatedly. "Madame Nhu? The Dragon Lady?"

"Just a broken-down old singer," she said sweetly. "But I've been around, I was at Altamonte, I've seen plenty of shit like this, and believe me, the best thing to do right now is nothing. . . ."

"Nothing . . . ?" Pham muttered.

Glorianna shrugged. "You could storm the broadcast booth and have the top blown off this joint. You could send some zonies up there and drag him off the stage. But if the crowd sees that, they'll go apeshit, and when they do, there's gonna be shooting."

She nodded down the corridor. "Besides," she said, "your band and your emcee have split, and so you've got no one else down here to go on, do you?" She nodded up toward the stage. "At least this way you got an act up there doin' *something*."

"You got a point, lady . . ." Alan Pham admitted.

"Mr. Pham! You can't—"

"Yeah, well then let's hear your plan, Steiner!"

Mucho Muchacho turned his back on his warriors and shoved his way into the crowd away from the base of the stage, seeking an angle from which he could see what the fuck was going on up there.

He had done his part, he had gotten his warriors together well enough to get them chanting, and he had kept them whipped up into an ass-kicking rage just terrifying enough to make the zonies pretend they weren't seeing it, without yet freaking them out to the point where they were ready to wade in shooting.

But if Larry Coopersmith didn't go up there and give them their Cyborg Sally soon—

The sound level suddenly rose, a shower of debris flew out of the crowd at the stage, and the chanting changed to a simple four-beat rhythm, backed by the stomping of feet.

"CYBORG SALLY! CYBORG SALLY! CYBORG SALLY!"

Turning, he saw what he had feared. Coopersmith had come out onstage, and it had flipped his streetie army over the edge into total bugfuck.

Knots of them had shoved their way into the crowd, and turned to look up at the stage, shaking their fists and weapons, and screaming their red-eyed rage at the top of their lungs. Others were far gone enough to actually try climbing the slick glass pedestal, clawing and writhing in frustration.

And Ciudad Trabajo had joined the war chant of the sombre side of the street. Chocharicas in Sally gear from Bloomingdale's, gordos in fancy silk suits and gold chains, all the Ciudad Trabajo putamadres and daytrippers, were stomping their feet, waving their fists, and chanting for Cyborg Sally too.

And Larry Coopersmith stood up there in the spotlight holding a hand mike, waving his arms, and trying to give some stupid fuckin' speech that no one could hear even with the speakers at full blast! His giant mirror images towered high above him on the big video screens, but the RLF video pirates weren't showing how his act was going over with the live audience on MUZIK, you better believe it!

Chingada, you didn't need the street smarts of Mucho Muchacho to know that this whole shitpile was about to explode!

"Come on, motherfucker, get your ass out of there, and get Cyborg Sally up there!" he shouted futilely at Coopersmith. "CYBORG SALLY! CYBORG SALLY! CYBORG SALLY!" he found himself chanting along with the voice of his army of the streets.

Bruised, battered, her clothes ripped in several places, fighting her way through the mob scene with her knees and elbows with the best of them, Karen Gold finally reached Paco. He was screaming at the top of his lungs up at the stage and pumping his fist in the air.

"SHE'S NOT GOING TO GO ON!" Karen shouted at him. He didn't hear her.

She grabbed at his arm, and he came whirling around behind a fist that he was only able to pull back inches from her throat.

"Karen! Chingada!"

"They're not going to put Cyborg Sally on, Paco!" Karen shouted again. "They're not going to do it!"

"What?"

"We've sold you out! We've tricked you! We've used you!

No Cyborg Sally, Paco, it's not going to happen, we've got to get out of here before everyone realizes it!''

She grabbed his arm with both hands and tugged at him, and he staggered for a moment. When he caught his balance, his eyes were looking in a new direction, and all at once, *he* was dragging her toward it.

''It's her! It's Cyborg Sally! I see her! What the fuck's she doing *here*?''

Mucho Muchacho burst through a wall of bodies and emerged suddenly into the spotlight circle of the dreamtime.

Cyborg Sally was in there with him where she belonged, but this was not his Queen of Heat. Her cable steel muscles seemed all unwound. Her crown of hair glowed dully. Her jaw hung slack and her teeth seemed to have lost their fine steel points and her eyes had lost their fire. She looked as if she had just burned down *herself* on her funeral pyre.

And she was cowering beneath the protective arm of Red Jack.

Chingada, it really *was* him, tall and proud beneath his long flashing red hair, giving the crowd themselves on the magic mirror of his suit, striding through them fearlessly like the Crown Prince of Rock and Roll.

But whoever it was, Mucho Muchacho was in no position to be having any. Tu madre también, amigo, he thought, striding forward, and, grabbing Cyborg Sally's wrist, went nose to nose with Red Jack.

''Come on, man, she's gotta go on now, she's gotta come with me!''

Red Jack stared right back at him. He didn't make a move, but he didn't let go. ''Cyborg Sally can't go on,'' he said.

''The fuck she can't! She's got to!'' Mucho told him, cocking back his fist. ''*This* says so, compadre, yo soy Mucho Muchacho!''

Red Jack shrank back reflexively, but his eyes never moved. ''Go ahead, punch me out again, be my guest. But it won't do you any good this time. Cyborg Sally can't go on because there *is* no Cyborg Sally to go on. There never really was.''

Mucho Muchacho felt a slap at the back of his head, and Paco Monaco found himself eyeball to eyeball with . . . with fuckin' Bobby Rubin! With the asshole from Hollywood he had socked in the guts!

But that wasn't quite who was staring him down now. *This*

was the Bobby Rubin who had been man enough to save him his job instead of taking easy Ciudad Trabajo revenge. And it was also somehow the Bobby Rubin he had seen in a flash, Red Jack's fleeting image passing across these very same features, looking out from these very same eyes.

How could he bring himself to punch *that* putamadre out?

And who the fuck was this he was about to punch him out over?

Tucked trembling into Bobby Rubin's shoulder was someone with Cyborg Sally's unmistakable face. But most of the silver makeup was gone, and Cyborg Sally's eyes flicked from focus to random focus in reflexive animal terror.

"Look at her! That's the real Cyborg Sally, Paco! That's all there ever was!"

Karen was pressed beside him, pulling back on his fist. "He's right, you know," she said. "The Cyborg Sally that could go up there and give these animals their raw meat never existed!"

Paco let his fist arm go limp in her hand, and let go of the poor terrified little puerca. "Chingada, I seen you like this before, I remember, but you made me promise. . . . This is you? You're fuckin' Cyborg Sally?"

Her eyes met his for a moment, and then he knew for sure, for there was a sudden flicker of electric blue defiance in there, a last electronic laugh, a last dying ember of Cyborg Sally flashing at him from her funeral pyre on the way out.

Paco stepped back from Red Jack, from Bobby Rubin, from whoever the fuck he was. "Take her, amigo, if that's what you want," he said. "Looks like I gotta take care of my own ass as usual!"

For now he was aware that there had been a solid circle of wirehead assholes sucking all of this up, and they started to close in as the fuckin' free tv show ended, and a moment later Karen was shoved against him as the magic bubble burst, and they were crammed together in a writhing mass of bodies.

"Chingada, Karen, what are we gonna do!" he shouted into her ear.

"Get our asses out of here!"

But as Paco glanced up at the giant video screens and watched Larry Coopersmith trying to shout down the roaring rage of the streets, the camera angle widened for a moment to show him a freeze flash of the army thereof, brain-burned zombies out of their minds and howling for the ultimate flash that would never come, working themselves rapidly up to go mano a mano against Uzis with pipes and knives.

They were a bunch of brain-burned assholes, fuckin' street meat, cucarachas, verdad, but then, who the fuck was he to talk?

He was their jefe, that's who the fuck he was! Maybe he wasn't really no Mucho Muchacho, but they sure as shit were really his army of the streets, and he had led them into this rumble.

Even a tough nigger like Dojo hadn't been able to turn his back on his zombies in Florida when it came down to watchin' em die. A real macho man had like . . . responsibilities.

Only a pussy could cut his losses and run now. He had to try and stop this short of gunplay or all the people he had led in here would go down because of him, y mucho mas también.

"Hey momacita, you better get out of here," he told Karen. "Me, I gotta stay, this is like where I belong now no matter what happens, tu sabes . . . ?"

"More than you can possibly understand!" Karen shouted into his ear. And then she kissed him on the cheek. "Where you can't leave, neither can I."

"Hey, chingada, you can't—"

"Chingada yourself, Paco Monaco! I'm not some chocharica princess, I'm Mucho Muchacho's momacita, I had to kick plenty of ass to get here, including my own, and now that I have, you're stuck with me for the duration, so don't give me any more male chauvinist shit!"

And she kissed him again.

Red Jack opened the door to the Summit, took Sally Genaro inside, closed it behind them, glanced up at the ceiling screen, which displayed an off-center shot on the scene around the base of the stage.

The force of streeties surrounding the stage had unlocked hands and dissolved into a chaotic mass of individual crazies—chanting, screaming, waving their fists, brandishing knives, flipping the bird, hacking clams, some of them actually trying to climb the recurved stage pedestal. Here and there zonies had pushed their way to the front of the mob and stood there brandishing their weapons in impotent gestures that only further served to inflame the spaced-out street meat.

Without taking his eyes off the screen, Red Jack gently let

Sally slip out of his arm. There was something he must do. There was a place he must go.

He started backing toward the door.

Sally grabbed him by the arm. "Wait! Don't go! You promised! You can't leave me here like this!"

"I have to, or I'll be nowhere to be seen," he snapped at Sally from the Valley impatiently.

But what he saw when he looked back at her melted his heart.

A pale silver ghost of Cyborg Sally stood beneath the video image of her penultimate triumph. Sally Genaro, smears of silver greasepaint running pathetically down the blotchy skin of her cheeks, her full lips trembling, looked past him with red-rimmed weeping eyes at Cyborg Sally's funeral pyre.

Yet it seemed that she was crying for more than her forlorn farewell to Cyborg Sally's dreamtime. She was crying for what a poor lost little girl's unfulfilled longings had caused her to inflict in vengeance upon the world. She was crying for herself, but she was also crying openly for what she had done. There was a tender kind of bravery in weeping like that. Neither Red Jack nor Bobby Rubin had ever wept openly over any wrong they knew they had done.

Until now.

"Oh how you must hate me now!" she moaned. "Just look at what I've gone and done!"

"Hate you, Sally . . . ?" he said. "Oh no, I don't hate you. . . ."

He found that emotion reserved for the pathetic, wimpy, self-involved, tormenting little bastard he had once been, for the miserable horny little putz who had turned his own wormy despair on this poor little creature full of fright, and by so doing, in the end, brought her, and through her all those other poor souls in their starving wirehead sleep down there, to *this*.

And knew where the place was he had to go and what it was he had to do. If he didn't, Bobby Rubin would stay just bits and bytes and programs and Red Jack could be nowhere to be seen.

He gathered Sally Genaro up into his arms and hugged her to him, letting her huddle against him, letting her press her sobbing cheek into the hollow of his neck.

"I didn't know . . ." she sighed. "I couldn't know, could I? All I ever wanted was, you know, just to be wanted, just for a moment, even, by someone I wanted to want me. . . ."

"The me I always told you that you could never be . . ." Red

Jack said softly. "What a little shit I was to you!" said Bobby Rubin.

Sally Genaro turned slowly in the crook of his arm to face him. Silvery tears dripped down her cheeks, catching here and there on the points of a few tiny pustules. Flecks of spittle clung to the corners of her lips. Her eyes were watery and bloodshot. Never had Sally from the Valley looked more disgusting than this.

"You couldn't help it, Bobby," she said tenderly, laying a wet palm to his cheek. "I've had to look at me in the mirror every day of my life. . . ."

He sighed a great shuddery sigh as the truth escaped through him. "And I'm not exactly Mr. Wonderful, am I?" he said. "Just a horny little computer nerd wishing he were—"

Sally stopped his lips with a finger. "Oh no," she told him, "you were always snaky sexy Bobby to me."

Every little life is a candle burning bright, you stupid asshole, Red Jack told Bobby Rubin.

And he drew Sally Genaro to him, into a tender, soul-deep kiss.

Her thick tongue poured clumsily and hotly into his mouth, and her breath was sour with acetone, and yes, his flesh crawled at her sudden avid fumbling gropings.

But it was time to be her story's little hero.

He laid her gently down on the lust-pink padding, and slowly, hesitantly, made himself peel off the leather panties and the tight silver body stocking.

A cold sweat chilled his detumescent cock as he looked down at the body encased in a ludicrous gray rubber undersuit sprawled beneath him, at Sally Genaro's face, a smeary mess of caked and streaky silver greasepaint, at this poor forlorn creature staring back at him with lust and terror in her red-rimmed eyes.

But his soul went out to what he saw in those eyes, for his mind read the courage struggling against the shame behind them. And a sure hard-wired circuit between his heart and his prick opened up, a trunkline connection between spirit and flesh that he had never known before, and down it flowed the will of what could at last justly be called his manhood.

He bent over her, slipped his hand beneath her, found the zipper of the rubber undersuit, began to pull the tab downward—

* * *

Sally froze, rolled away from him, reached up toward her touchpoint, reached for the familiar magic of Cyborg Sally's wire, in which to hide, at least from herself, the nakedness of her own flabby flesh.

Bobby grabbed her hand, pulled it away, tore off her wig.

"No," he said, "Come along with me, but come as what you are."

Tears rolled down her cheeks as she looked into his dark, bedroom eyes, as she smiled bravely and shyly back at his sexy, snaky smile. "Let me . . ." she whispered, and, brushing his hand away, pulled down the tab of the undersuit zipper.

Red Jack gazed down at Sally Genaro's pale pasty body, at her heavy breasts, the erect tips of her nipples standing out from the centers of wide pink aureoles, at her thick thighs, at the jiggly rolls of flesh at her hips and belly.

He stood up, slowly peeled off his clothing, tossing the garments aside as he removed them like a stripper, forcing himself to smile down, holding his cock erect by an act of will as he finally stood naked before her.

Naked?

Not entirely.

Mirrored in her eyes he saw himself as the perfect crown of his own creation, Red Jack, the Crown Prince of Rock and Roll, deigning at long last to favor this poor groundling with his magic magnificence.

But that was just a ghost in someone else's machine, that was just the final veil. He was not truly naked yet.

Red Jack reached up and hit his touchpoint.

Bobby Rubin stood there, thin and trembling, above Sally Genaro, turned off by the vision before his eyes, maintaining his hard-on by the fleshly will of what he saw with his heart.

Now, only now, was the nakedness of his true manhood fully revealed.

Sally wrapped her legs around Bobby's waist as he entered her, clamping him to her, reveling in the eternal in and out between men and women that had existed since time began, in the sweaty, earthy slap-slap of flesh on flesh, the chafing of skin on skin, the gritty odor of her own juices.

No bells rang, no celestial choruses sang, and you couldn't really call his performance like *magnificent*. After a respectable while, she felt the pulsing of his cock slipping over the edge of impending orgasm inside of her, and she had to grind her pelvis against him and bring herself off a few beats after he had spent himself, and that was the grand high romance of it.

Yet it was something far better than any such moment had been in her dreamtime, for all the sweaty, hasty, fumbling ordinariness of it. It was real.

And just because it was real, it was grand, for what came soaring up in her long, sighing orgasm was an enormous, uplifting relief of lifelong tension, a soul-stirring moment of glorious release.

Release from the fat little body that had caged her spirit, release from the acne-marked face that mocked her in the morning mirror, release from the scorn of the hunks and the surfer kings, release from the years of sucking the pricks of indifferent musicians, release from the prison of her unloved flesh.

For the first time in her life, she had been released by a man who had gazed upon her nakedness, and reached out with a cock that had seen beyond it into her heart.

Was this love? How could she know? This was a place she had never been before. She really doubted it, but from here she could at least face herself with her head held high.

For while Bobby Rubin might not love her, he had kept his promise. He had truly made love to *her*, and she would have that forever. For he had taken her to the place that her whole life had always told her that she could never be.

LITTLE HEROES

The camera pans and zooms jerkily from shot to shot, as if whoever is behind it is not sure where to alight.

A full shot of a black-bearded man standing in a spotlight circle. A long shot on his giant image on the huge video screen behind him over an out-of-focus slice of crowd. Another angle including both the man and his video mirror, flesh and pixels moving in eerie unison. Back and forth between these same three shots in no particular order, and with no fades or cutaways for artful transition.

The man on center stage in the spotlight is pacing nervously, staring up at the camera and only occasionally flicking sidewise glances at things outside the frame that he'd obviously rather not see. He is declaiming like someone shouting into a whirlwind, like a game Shakespearean determined to finish a soliloquy over the boos and catcalls of the mob in the pit. And indeed, as he goes on, plastic cups, wads of paper, even an occasional bottle, come sailing up at him into the frame from below.

". . . the Reality Liberation Front! Hey, we're talking to *you* out there at the other side of the tube, how do you like seeing the flip side of Official Reality on national television for the first time? Pixels to the People! And that's just what we're gonna give you, the media power of the pixels, and the green power of the bits and bytes, free bedbugs to the whole American people, so boot up your disc decks, and get ready to download—"

"Jesus Christ, that's not what all that digitized confetti at the end of the broadcast was? It wasn't just a technical fuckup?"

" 'Fraid not. Research pulled about twenty bedbug programs

out of it and Red Jack's voiceprint parameters and algorithms too."

"And *how* many people recorded it all?"

"Those damn video pirates preempted themselves something like a ninety share. More people saw this on the tube than anything since Kennedy's funeral. How many of 'em recorded it? Marketing hasn't been able to get hard numbers, but they estimate thirty million as the rock bottom floor."

"And now they all have Red Jack's algorithms and parameters?"

"Believe me, that's the least of it, some of those bedbug programs are really cute. We'd better divest the company of all its securities and bank the money in francs in Switzerland. Or even convert it into bullion. We're going to have to put all disc distribution outside our own outlets on a nonreturnable basis or we'll eat more returns than we pressed. We'll have to demand all payments due us in certified paper checks. The upside is that the IRS is going to have its hands full collecting anything from anyone for a good long while."

"Oh my God, as bad as that . . . ?"

"Surely they can't pin *that* on Muzik, Inc.?"

"Maybe yes, maybe no, but we can sure count on being audited with a fine-tooth comb for the next thousand years."

"We're in big, big trouble!"

"We'd better not leave here till we've figured out how to cover our asses!"

"Believe me, gentlemen, that is what this meeting is all about!"

Glorianna O'Toole stood on the stairs just below the stage entrance, looking up into the bright white rectangle of light above her.

Below, Tommy Don, Leslie Savanah, Eddie Polonski, and Iva Cohen still blocked the bottom of the stairway, but the pandemonium in the corridor behind them had subsided into dull dazed tension.

Ali Babble and Black Flame had locked themselves in their dressing rooms, the zonies had cleared the backstage area of all extraneous people, and half a dozen of them stood by the elevator with weapons at the ready. Alan Pham slumped against a wall, gazing vacantly up the staircase with the security chief beside him.

From this perspective, all Glorianna could really see was the blinding white of the spotlight, and an occasional glimpse of Larry Coopersmith's legs as he moved around the stage. All she could hear was a continuous white noise of anger.

Coopersmith had been up there for what seemed like forever, or anyway a million years beyond his welcome, and for all she knew, Bobby might never show up. You didn't need to be a Weatherman to know you couldn't last too long feeding a crazed music-hungry mob Movement bullshit!

Someone had to do something right now. It wouldn't be the first time she had had to move her set up to fill in for an act that hadn't showed.

She laid down the shotgun mike case at the foot of the stairs, where Bobby would find it if he ever managed to show up, took the vocoder rig out of her purse, clipped the wizardware pack to her belt, and put on the throat mike.

"Hey you, Pham, come on over here, I wanna talk to you!" she called out. "I've decided I might be persuaded to save your ass."

Alan Pham, no doubt stirred from his defeated daze by the sight of this decrepit old fossil standing on the stage stairs girded for battle like a rock and roll Wonder Woman, dragged himself up the stairs and squinted at her in bemused disbelief.

"Yeah, I know, I look like a moldy oldie in her granddaughter's rock and roll gear, but this stuff is the max in wizardware, and I was at Altamonte sonny, I saw where Mick went wrong, and besides, I'm the only one here with the balls to go up onstage and give the monster its rock and roll!" Glorianna rapped at him.

"Or do I hear any volunteers?" she called out.

None were forthcoming.

"I can do it, Pham, I've played scenes like this before, what do you have to lose?"

"Nothing," Pham admitted glumly. "I've lost everything already."

Glorianna winked at him. "Maybe not," she said. "If nobody they can't grease into silence gets hurt, the Factory can pretend it was all staged as a record promo stunt, and make that a profitable self-fulfilling prophecy by discing the proceedings and selling millions. You know as well as I do that the pinheads upstairs will listen to you when you tell them that if they haven't thought of it themselves already. They'll be more than willing to keep you happy so you won't spill the beans, and who knows, with some luck, you could end up a little corporate hero."

Pham regarded her with real interest now. "Yes, it could work, it makes bottom-line sense . . ." he muttered speculatively. "No doubt you want something in return?" he said much more sharply.

"Only what's in everyone's best interest. When I've got things calmed down, you pull your zonies and grease away the cops long enough for everyone involved to get their asses out of here."

"Let *these* sons of bitches go!" Pham cried, nodding contemptuously at the revolutionaries of the Reality Liberation Front. "Let *him* go?" he said, nodding up at the entrance to the stage. "The whole country's seen them take over The American Dream on television! How can I let them go?"

"How can you not?" Glorianna told him. "If they don't get caught, they were paid actors, and you can blame unfortunate events on unknown terrorists and video pirates who crashed the show. If you bust anyone and try 'em, the truth will be in all the trades and you'll be out on your ass. Ain't I made you an offer you can't refuse?"

Pham nodded. "*If* there's no major violence we can't cover up," he said. "If there is, this little speech is enough to get *you* indicted as a co-conspirator! You have just made *yourself* an offer you can't refuse."

"I never intended to," Glorianna said. She turned to salute the people below, took a deep breath, and then stepped up through the white light onto the stage.

Larry Coopersmith stood there by Black Flame's equipment with a hand mike held limply in his hand, no longer speaking, shuffling back and forth in place, his shattered marble eyes darting this way and that, the fist of his free hand clenching and unclenching convulsively, his brows knotted in frustrated anger, his lips trembling.

Beyond Coopersmith, beyond the bright white spotlight bathing the center of the stage, she could see nothing, only a formless black void, a vortex of negative energy whirling blindingly about her focus.

But oh fuck, could she hear it, fuck a duck, could she feel it! Indeed, she could not tell where the roaring in her eardrums left off and the horrid vibrations thrumming her bones and crawling along her skin and socking her in the stomach began. It was like being in some tiny club overwhelmed by stadium amps turned up to full ear-killing volume way down in the evil max metal bass.

And oh could she smell it! The sweaty, sour, speed-freak, evil, raw-meat stink coming off the unseen screaming audience was the odor of the worst biker bar she had ever played as the beer bottles began to fly, the odor of Altamonte as poor Mick stood there on the stage suddenly faced with his unsympathetic devil.

She cringed under the sonic assault, she took a step backward toward the stairs. Fuck this! she thought. Mick had been terrified, and she wasn't even Jagger, just a tired old lady. . . .

But then she saw Larry Coopersmith staring at her. She saw the time-warped face of a crazed young biker ripped on speed and beer and acid down there in a crowd not unlike this. And something opened up inside her.

No, I ain't no Mick Jagger, she told herself, but I can't do much worse than he did. And I fucking well am the Crazy Old Lady of Rock and Roll, so if this is it, let it not be said in the back pages of *Rolling Stone* that Glorianna O'Toole didn't go out rockin'!

She pushed past Coopersmith, plugged her vocoder into an amp, keyed in a set of the voiceprint parameters Bobby Rubin had preprogrammed, hit her touchpoint, and shouted in his face above the din: "Introduce me!"

Coopersmith shouted something back that she couldn't make out.

"Introduce me!" she screamed at the top of her lungs, mimicking an emcee's bowing gesture. "I don't go on without no introduction."

Larry Coopersmith looked at her with dumbfounded admiration, lifted up his mike, and began to speak. She couldn't hear a word of it, but that didn't matter, she had seen that look before, and she knew just what he was saying.

"Ladies and gentlemen, Glorianna O'Toole, the greatest fuckin' rock and roller what ever lived!"

"Fuckin'-A I am, assholes!" she shouted into the angry black void, into the wall of noise. "You better believe it!"

And she took a long deep breath, spread her arms to the wide open spaces, and started singing.

Little hero in the night
Little creature full of fright
Fear not the call to trust your heart to battle!

"Oh my God," said Bobby Rubin, twisting the camera control to center the shot on the frail gray-haired figure on the stage, "that magnificent crazy old lady!"

On the screen, Glorianna O'Toole stood alone in the bright white spotlight, alone in the middle of what was rapidly turning into full-scale violent chaos. With her arms spread wide and her eyes coming right atcha, she was singing out above a sea of fistfights, screaming wild-eyed faces, jerking bodies, as a hail of garbage came hurtling from the crowd in her direction.

"Jesus Christ, what am I doing here?" Bobby muttered. "I'm supposed to be up there with her!"

Crawling on his hands and knees across the tongue-pink padding, not even bothering to scramble to his feet, he began gathering up his clothing.

"What are you doing, Bobby?" Sally muttered dreamily, turning over slowly to see him pulling on his pants.

"Bobby!" she shouted when she realized what was happening. "You're not going . . . out there!"

"That's where I'm supposed to be," Bobby told her, slipping his shirt on.

"You can't go down there!" Sally cried. "You'll only get yourself *hurt* Bobby, *killed*, maybe. . . ."

Bobby pulled on his shoes, stood up, looked down at Sally Genaro, who sat there, sweaty, pale, hunched over, naked, her heavy breasts dangling, her face a smeary mess, her eyes looking into his tenderly, fearfully. And despite the exigency of the moment, despite the unwholesome sight of her naked flesh, he paused, shrugged, smiled, and said softly, "We all gotta do what we gotta do, Sally. . . ."

"Don't go down there, Bobby, please, it won't do any good anyway, it's not *you* they want, it's . . ."

Sally stopped in mid-sentence. She locked eyes with him for a long long moment. She nodded.

Then she picked up her foam rubber undersuit and her silver body stocking, and slowly rose to her feet. She stood there, her breasts pendulous, the rolls of fat around her hips and belly all too apparent, her hair a tangled mat, her face a mess, looking so small, and helpless, and frightened.

"Time for me to go on now, Bobby," she said tremulously. "I wouldn't want to disappoint my fans."

"Sally!" He found himself reaching out for her.

She smiled at him. "Like you said, Bobby, we all gotta do what we gotta do," she said in a tiny voice. She started to step into the legs of the rubber undersuit. She paused. She looked down at the padded garment.

"Come along with me, but come as who you are," she said, then gave a frightened little smile, and threw the thing away.

She dressed quickly, and stood there with her hands on her hips before him, Sally from the Valley, the Pimple, a little fat girl with her flesh bulging against the tight silver fabric in all the wrong places.

She looked down at herself, shuddered, nibbled at her lower lip as she looked up to meet the image of herself in Bobby Rubin's eyes. "Well, how do you like Cyborg Sally now?" she said gamely.

"She never looked better," Bobby told her truthfully, taking her hand and leading her to the door.

"Where do you think *you're* going, Bobby Rubin?"

Bobby shrugged, he sighed, he smiled wanly. Well kiddo, he told himself in someone else's voice, at least you can't complain that there's no such thing as karmic justice.

"With you, Sally," he said. "Like it or not, you and I wrote this song, so it looks like what we gotta do is face our own music together."

Karen slipped through the gap as Paco straight-armed his way through and found herself emerging from the relative safety of the crowd into a border zone of clear space between the patrons of The American Dream and the rage of the streets.

Paco's street meat army had turned into a riot. Street people brandished their defiance and roared their outrage three and four deep around the stage. A dozen of them were driving themselves into a frustrated frenzy trying to scale a vertical pedestal of glass. Those at the periphery waved knives and pipes more tactically now, keeping the crowd and the zonies well clear of a double-arm's-length zone around them.

It was ripe-red anarchy, all right, a human amoeba sizzling on a frying pan, as, feet stomping, fists waving, bodies writhing, and neck veins bulging, the denizens of Slimy Mary's shouted at the top of their lungs for their Cyborg Queen.

"CYBORG SALLY! CYBORG SALLY! CYBORG SALLY!"

Paco paced clockwise around the clear zone, shouting inaudible ignored orders at what had been his street army, but he kept his back pressed up against the crowd, keeping well clear of his own people, several of whom waved their knives and pipes threateningly at *him*.

Karen kept his hand firmly in hers and her body pressed against his back as they circled round. "There's nothing you can do! We've got to get out of here!" she kept screaming into his ear. But if he heard, he didn't listen, as he desperately and hopelessly kept trying to gain control of a full-scale riot single-handedly.

Then there was a sudden rushing peak in the volume of the noise level that crested, incredibly enough, into a breaker of sound foaming with boos, and hoots, and yes, unmistakably *laughter*.

The background babble suddenly died to a murmur so that the chanting of the streeties emerged loud and clear from the vanished wall of noise.

"CYBORG SALLY! CYBORG SALLY! CYBORG SALLY!"

Paco ceased his pacing and stood there staring up at the stage. Karen looked up and she, too, stood there transfixed, her mouth hanging open, seeing it, but not quite believing it.

"CYBORG SALLY! CYBORG SALLY! CYBORG SALLY!"

Centered in the spotlight, standing behind the keyboard of a VoxBox console and fiddling with the controls was . . . was . . . was a grotesque caricature of Cyborg Sally, a cartoon version of the lithe, sinewy silver, nonexistent Queen of Heat, rendered, paradoxically enough, in living, ludicrous flesh.

"CYBORG SALLY! CYBORG SALLY! CYBORG SALLY!"

A pudgy girl stuffed into a silver Sally suit, pendulous sagging breasts, heavy thighs, belly roll, love-handle hips, all horrendously emphasized by the skin-tight fabric. In place of Cyborg Sally's flashing neon snake crown, an uncombed mop of mousy brown hair. Cyborg Sally's silver dagger teeth, the curve of Cyborg Sally's nose, Cyborg Sally's eyes, but set in a face of pasty-pink acne-dotted flesh.

"CYBORG SALLY! CYBORG SALLY! CYBORG SALLY!"

And then this pathetic apparition began to play the keyboard, and out came the opening bars of "Cyborg Sally," a perfect, fully orchestrated rendition of the version on the best-selling disc that commanded a moment of instant silence into which the multiplexed voice of Cyborg Sally herself sang it out, dripping with self-mocking irony.

Yes, I'm Cyborg Sally
I'm your blood-hot wire
I'm the blazing bytes.
Of your meat's desire!

And it was rolling out into the sudden hushed silence, washing out over the suddenly stilled crowd, all coming from the fat girl standing utterly alone in the spotlight on the stage.

I'm Cyborg Sally
And I've never been
Plug into me
And I'll make you scream. . . .

Paco Monaco stood there amazed, blinking against the double vision of sight and sound, at the puerca in the Sally suit singing with the voice of the Queen of Heat.

Chingada, it was Cyborg Sally's humanly impossible voice to perfection, soaring up beyond hearing into the supersonic on the peaks, doubled way below in a voice he could only feel with his guts and bones, wrapping its electronic hiss around the phrasing as no singer of mere flesh could, and as he listened with his ear's eye, he almost saw her standing there, her neon hair flashing, her sinewy silver body moving to the beat.

But no, it was all coming out of the girl he had handed over to Rubin, out of the fuckin' puerca who had made a wirehead fool out of him, out of a gross creature stuffed into a phony Sally suit two sizes too small for her flabby flesh.

And the song was somehow no longer Cyborg Sally's but *hers*. The music was the same, and the words were the same, but with tremulously ironic changes in the phrasing, she had made it her own.

With my heart of ice
And my ring of fire
No living soul
Gonna take you higher
No mother's child
Turn you on so wild. . . .

And she seemed to be singing it straight at him, saying, sí Mucho, sí Paco, I'm the wire of her flesh, she's the flesh of my wire, this *dumpy little puerca* was your funeral pyre!

I'm Cyborg Sally
I'm your blood-hot wire
I'm the blazing bytes
Of your meat's desire!

Yes I'm Cyborg Sally
I'm your sex machine
My crystal chips
Is what makes you cream. . . .

A tiny silver figure stands behind her VoxBox in a circle of white light high above the darkened floor of The American Dream. The hushed crowd stands shoulder to shoulder swaying to her music.

Cyborg Sally has turned them into her audience.

The camera zooms in slowly for a medium shot on the stage, then pans down the black pedestal into a shot of the street people crowding around its base.

They have given over their chanting now, given over their stomping, given over the waving of fists and knives. The mob of them has pressed the crowd backward away from the stage, and they are all standing there with their arms and their weapons hanging loosely at their sides, staring up at what they see in the spotlight.

The camera jump-cuts to a head-and-shoulders shot of the girl behind the VoxBox; the pinkish, slightly pimply face, the uncombed mop of hair, the eyes and nose and lips of Cyborg Sally.

The drums beat out an angry rhythm, the bassline booms a bad-ass sexy stompada, the lead guitar and the synth line scream sardonic defiance, but the face, vulnerable, ordinary, tremulous, belies all that, and the electronic voice of Cyborg Sally sings out its cyborged chops with tenderly mocking human irony.

My laser lips bring you to your knees
Darkling sparkling ecstasy
Lick my flashing circuitry
As I bite your flesh
As you taste my wire
No father's son
Ever flashed such fire. . . .

Paco Monaco stood there in the darkness holding Karen's hand, watching the puerca stuffed into the tight silver body stocking sing her fat little heart out up there on the stage. His cock shriveled in his pants with the horrid knowledge of where it had been, his palms were filmed with a sticky unwholesome sweat, and a brief spark of hatred flared within him for that puerca up there who had made such a wirehead mockery of his manhood.

But . . .

But there was something in the way that little fat girl stood up there singing worse than naked for all the world to see that touched his mucho macho heart.

Chingada, what . . . what cojones it must take for her to show them all that Cyborg Sally's voice came from her own ugly meat!

And much to his surprise, somewhere inside of him beyond the sombre and the sol, he found himself acknowledging a sister under the skin.

"Come on, momacita," he told Karen, "we gotta help her while we can!"

He dragged her across the border from the sol toward the sombre, toward the nearest streeties, staring up at the stage with their backs turned and their weapons hanging limply in their hands.

And began moving down the line hitting touchpoints. "Come on, come on, momacita, don't just stand there like some fuckin' chocharica princess," he barked at Karen over his shoulder, "we got to unplug all these zombies from the juice before the stupid putamadres come to life again!"

And smiled to himself as she got down to business with him.

And smiled even wider a minute later, when, circling clockwise, he came upon Dojo coming the other way, doing the very samething and then some.

"Move your ass out of here, you brain-burned asshole, before I lay one upside your ear," Dojo was saying, shoving one streetie in the direction of the crowd while he slapped the next one across the back of the head, being none too gentle about it.

"Dojo! I never thought I'd be so fuckin' glad to see a big ugly nigger like you!"

"Y tu madre también, my man," Dojo shot back, flipping another streetie away from the stage with one huge hand, and whacking yet another touchpoint with the other. "Come on, come on, my son, you're the *doorman* here, ain't you? You expect me to do *all* your work for you?"

* * *

"Do you believe this?"

"Solid platinum for sure!"

"More to the current point, if we do this as a saturation single, maybe it can smear some of the shit off our image. Our VoxBox player nerves herself to go on and saves the day!"

"Sally Genaro, our very own little hero!"

"Muzik tames the savage beast!"

"We *do* have her on a work-for-hire contract, don't we? It *does* cover her as singing talent?"

"Better query legal."

"You're not thinking about turning this plain little Jane into a rock star?"

"Asshole! You're looking at her first megahit right now!"

"That's right, fer chrissakes, we're gonna want plenty of her product around to ride on it real quick!"

Cyborg Sally!
Flesh and wire!
Queen of Heat!
Electric fire!
Blazing bytes!
Meat's desire!
Rockin' rollin' sex machine!
Plug your self in
And scream, scream, SCREAM!

The camera zooms in on the girl in the bright white spotlight as she finishes her song and stands there looking out into the darkness.

Then it pulls back into a wide shot on the vast audience standing there stunned and gaping in the awful backwash of the sudden silence. Then eyes begin to meet each other, see what is written there, are forced to look away.

Murmurs and whisperings begin, build into a guttural rumbling, the sullen growl of an audience that feels betrayed and cheated, and, entirely unwilling to admit that they did it to themselves, is poised to turn its outrage outward against the pathetic figure alone and naked in the spotlight.

"Watch this . . . blow up the lower left quadrant, yeah, there it is, you can clearly see that this Puerto Rican kid started hitting those street people's touchpoints *before* Rubin went on! Now him and this big black guy are actually shoving them toward the exits."

"We could have ourselves another little media hero! You think the kid can sing?"

"Wait a minute, that's *Paco Monaco*!"

"Who?"

"The American Dream's very own doorman!"

"Perfect! Footage of our guy out there doing his job! It'll look great in the papers, not to mention in court."

"God forbid! An ID was made on an RLF terrorist named Karen Gold, one of their big-time bedbug dealers too, who, it turns out, is Paco Monaco's girlfriend."

"*Our own doorman* was in the RLF? But if that ever gets out, Washington will never believe we had nothing to do with them. . . ."

"And if they stick the RLF to us, Jesus, who would believe we didn't put the *video pirates* up to it, seeing as how they got us such a wonderful free commercial for the discs we're gonna press off this footage. . . ."

"What do we do? Does the government have this?"

"*Forty million people* have it, remember?"

"Yeah, but the FBI doesn't have anything concrete to arrest Monaco on, nothing that will stand up in court. . . ."

"Who cares? The moment that guy starts *talking* in court, we get sucked into the video pirate case!"

"Therefore Monaco must never appear in court."

"*A hit?* Hey, I dunno, I mean we got enough image problems already. . . ."

"Christ no! We give Monaco a cover story. One that only we can back up. One that only we have the grease to make the authorities accept short of a grand jury. And we let him stay on his job where we can keep a close eye on him till all this is history. And we have Henry Steiner explain in words of one syllable our mutual self-interest in his silence."

"If he isn't as big an asshole as that putz and a half Nicholas West, he knows that already."

As a low tentatively building booing begins, rolls around The American Dream gathering up its shame-faced Dutch courage, a red-haired man suddenly emerges into the spotlight, holding a shotgun mike close by the business end and speaking into it.

The mighty and unmistakable voice of Red Jack booms out through the sound system.

"Come on, let's have a big hand for the little lady!"

The camera zooms in on him as he lifts the VoxBox player by the hand and leads her toward the lip of the stage, toward the sudden total silence. If she is a fleshy mockery of the electronic perfection of Cyborg Sally, he is the shade of Red Jack.

For he speaks with Red Jack's voice, and he has Red Jack's face, and he looks into the camera with Red Jack's eyes, and an elusive something more that mantles him in the cloak of Red Jack's true presence.

Slowly, dazedly, uncertainly, a few hands begin to clap, building into a smattering of stupefied applause. Red Jack stands there shaking his head with his hands on his hips while it limply dies.

"You don't really want to believe it, do you?" Red Jack's voice says sardonically. "That this little lady has been Cyborg Sally all along, and I've always been the Crown Prince of Rock and Roll!"

A sullen murmuring growl rolls around the crowd, rubes at the carnival reluctantly beginning to face the fact that they have been royally had.

"Hey, don't blame me, I told you up front I'm just the ghost in your machine. Ain't got no body, but *you're* my soul, *you're* all the Crown Prince of Rock and Roll! Don't you remember?"

Red Jack moves up to the very lip of the stage as guttural rumbling starts building again. "Listen to yourselves!" he shouts, and points his shotgun mike out into the crowd like a scepter. Out the other end of the circuit comes the whining of cranky babies.

"*You're* the you they told *you* that you could never be!" Red Jack proclaims into the microphone. "It's about time *you* took your turn at being me! So sing along with yourselves, raise up your voice and scream, 'cause you and me together, we're a Rock and Roll Machine!"

And he begins chanting into the microphone.

You make more of me
I make more of you
I make more of you
You make more of me. . . .

"Goddamn Rubin, he's a creative genius, but he's got no nose for the bottom line! What a concept he's inventing here! But what the hell product do we use it to market?"

"It's the ultimate singalong. We can use it in our clubs."

"Big fucking deal."

"You make more of me . . ." Red Jack chants into his microphone one more time, and then he pauses, and points it out into the crowd, where here and there a few lone voices have piped up to fill the silence.

And he picks one of those little voices out of anonymity, and he runs it through his shotgun mike, through his voiceprint parameters, and out the other side through the sound system it comes, Red Jack himself singing through a face in the crowd, singing with the voice of the people.

I make more of you . . .

The crowd begins to pick it up as Red Jack dances around the stage, chanting alternate lines into the mike himself, giving the audience themselves on the upbeat.

I make more of you
YOU MAKE MORE OF ME
You make more of me.
I MAKE MORE OF YOU. . . .

"Got it! Instead of marketing AP rock stars as *talent,* we market them as software!"

"Market them as *what*?"

"Market their *voiceprint parameters and algorithms* on disc! Sell the customers their very own selves as rock stars through the magic of Muzik! The biggest thing since Hula-Hoops! And at a much higher unit profit margin!"

"I love it!"

"Say four new sets of do-it-yourself rock stars a month to begin with until we get sales figures back for marketing . . ."

"They better be good enough to keep the customers from just rolling their own . . ."

"We'll put *Rubin* on it!"

"*Rubin?* Isn't he supposed to be the leader of the Reality Liberation Front or something?"

"It was a frame, or anyway we can claim it was if we have to, and the feds had better eat it. Because it's got West's fingerprints all over it, and if Washington screws with us again after the mess *that* putz made, we'll be entirely justified in blowing his cover. Right now, Rubin's worth a lot more to us in the studio than he is to them in prison."

"Let's make sure he understands that it's in our mutual interest to keep it that way."

"Nothing like truly motivated talent."

Red Jack zips his arm across his throat in a cut sign just as the chanting is beginning to become monotonous, reminiscent of a previous unfortunate performance. In the ensuing silence he looks around the stage nervously as if wondering what to do for an encore.

"Hey, Jack, come on!" a voice says. "Give us some rock and roll!"

"Yeah! Rock and roll!"

"We want some rock and roll!"

Red Jack seems to have found what he was looking for in the darkness outside the spotlight circle. He heaves a huge sigh of relief. He leads the girl in the Cyborg Sally suit back to the VoxBox.

"Hey, *I* can't sing no rock and roll, that's just bits and bytes and programs," quite another voice says through the microphone, an ordinary voice, just another voice from the crowd. "But hey, don't worry, here's someone who can, and this time it's the real live thing as it was meant to be, Glorianna O'Toole, the Crazy Old Lady of Rock and Roll!"

A frail-looking old lady leaps into the spotlight with a brave little bow.

Scattered laughter fractures the silence.

"The poor babies want their rock and roll, do they?" she chides them in a dotty old lady's voice, shaking a finger at them like a scolding granny.

She thumbs a control at her belt as the laughter gets louder and mocking.

"So you think I can't do it, do you, assholes?" Glorianna O'Toole says in a mighty amplified voice that cracks plaster from the ceiling. "You think this old lady don't know how to boogie? You think the time of my magic is past? Hey, kiddies, this old lady ain't even *begun* to kick out the jams! And if a relic like me can do it, what are you doin' there standing with your peckers in your pockets, huh?''

And she reaches into a pocket, pulls out a page of sheet music, hands it over to her VoxBox player with a flourish. ''Come on, sister, let's give 'em what they're paying for, let's play some rock and roll!''

''Fantastic!''

''Thirty million sales!''

''Something no makeup artist could ever duplicate happens here, watch this, and tell me this won't play with the over-sixty crowd who won't buy anything but reissues of Dylan and the Beatles!''

The camera tracks a frail gray-haired old lady into close-up as she dances to the center of the stage.

As she starts to sing, decades roll back without the benefit of makeup or electronic post-production processing, she does it with her eyes and the music alone. Grandma turns into a rock and roll queen stomping and strutting in full charge of the stage.

Little hero in the night
Little creature full of fright
Fear not the call to trust your heart to battle
Though you think you're far from home
And you're out here all alone
Never let your song sing surrender. . . .

''Listen to that voice!''

''Just a lot of vocoder wizardware . . .''

''Yeah? Show me software that phrases like that! That's charisma in its purest form!''

''That's the next president of Muzik, Inc., gentlemen.''

''Glorianna O'Toole?''

A murmur of surprise rises from the darkness. A spattering of disbelieving cheers. The fat girl in the silver suit fiddles with her VoxBox console and then, as her fingers begin to fly, a clarion bugle call rings out that sets the spirit soaring, mirrored in a martial rhythm of snares and stomping feet, an upbeat pounding bass, lead guitar and synth lines wrapping themselves around the vocal in a triumphant instrumental duet, taking them both higher and higher.

Though the dark is deep and long
And you may never see the dawn
Never will your spirit be forgotten!

The camera pulls back for a longer shot, a shot including the sea of people standing around the stage. Their bodies are swaying, their feet are moving, and here and there, people are actually beginning to dance.

For every little life
Is a candle burning bright
And in the story of ourselves
We all are heroes. . . .

"She's a hippie-dip relic from the sixties!"

"She's got an FBI dossier as long as your arm!"

"She had to be in on this thing!"

"She's a troublemaker!"

"Everyone in the business has heard her call us 'the pinheads upstairs'!"

"And that's just the image we need at the top under these circumstances. A real musician with a big hit on the charts and impeccable antiestablishment credentials!"

"Hey, it's crazy, but I like it!"

"Wizard piece of image judo, Muzik hires itself its own bad ass to clean up its own act!"

"But she doesn't know the first fucking thing about the bottom line!"

"So who cares, all she has to know about is getting the product made, we don't give her *anything* but creative control, we give her a comptroller with full power over finance and marketing who reports directly to us."

"How long do we intend to maintain this arrangement?"

"Six months. A year. The usual. Until President O'Toole's profit margin drops below ten percent."

Glorianna O'Toole dances to the lip of the stage, the spotlight tracking with her. Bobby Rubin moves around the edge of the limelight with her, pointing the shotgun mike out into the anonymous darkness, out into the audience.

"Come on kiddies, if a crazy old lady can be a rock and roll star, so can you," she challenges. "Lemme hear the voice of the people on the chorus!"

Little hero in the night
Little beacon of the light . . .

Slowly, hesitantly, a few lone voices begin to echo her, and the camera moves through a quick series of dissolving close-ups on streeties and citizens and even a zonie singing. The self-effacing figure of Red Jack circles slowly just at the edge of the white spotlight circle, picking up the singers with his shotgun mike and giving them back themselves—amplified and glorified through the vocoder circuitry.

Scores of voices find in this the courage to sing, and a mighty chorus builds, and in a few more beats, the whole audience is singing.

LITTLE HERO IN THE NIGHT
LITTLE BEACON OF THE LIGHT. . . .

After two good strong choruses, Glorianna O'Toole moves back into the center of the stage and tenderly takes back the song from her audience.

Little hero in the night
Little beacon of the light
Stand beside me and unfurl your freedom's banner!

"Hey, this sounds kind of subversive to me. . . ."

"So we'll matte in a great big American flag behind it if that will make you feel better."

"I don't like it! Put an American flag behind that kind of music, and we're asking for trouble!"

"Listen to Tom fuckin' Paine!"

"Yeah, lighten up."

"Look at her! She'll clean up our image like Lee Iacocca wiped the shit off Chrysler's bankrupt ass."

"If she doesn't kick it first."

"Hey, relax."

"She's not gonna really be *management*!"

"She's just talent."

"It's just product."

"Yeah, what are you worrying about—"

"We still control the bottom line—"

"It's just rock and roll."

"That's what I don't like about it. I can picture her listening to this and I know what she's saying."

"Which is?"

"This, assholes, is *why* you're the pinheads upstairs!"

I am just the same as you
Only you to see me through
But together we are all there is that matters
The world is in our lovers' arms
We must keep us safe from harm
There is no one else to keep this song a-singing!

The camera zooms in for a close-up on Glorianna O'Toole as she bows, and she winks right back into it, and tells the world what it already knows, that through the magic of MUZIK they are seeing a Crazy Old Lady becoming what a young back-up singer long ago had always known she was one day destined to be.

And if it was only for one brief shining moment in her December years, there she was at last—the voice of red-ripe anarchy for all the world to see, and the greatest fuckin' rock and roller whatever lived for as long as this song lasted.

So let every little life
Stand together in the night
Let us all become our story's little heroes!

END

ABOUT THE AUTHOR

Born in New York City in 1940, Norman Spinrad has traveled extensively throughout America and abroad to Europe and the Far East. He has been a sandal maker, a literary agent, a critic and columnist, and a radio talk show host. His novels and short stories, including *Bug Jack Barron, Child of Fortune,* and *The Void Captain's Tale,* have been translated into a dozen languages and nominated for many major awards, including the National Book Award. He is also the author of *Stayin' Alive: A Writer's Guide*. He currently lives in Los Angeles.